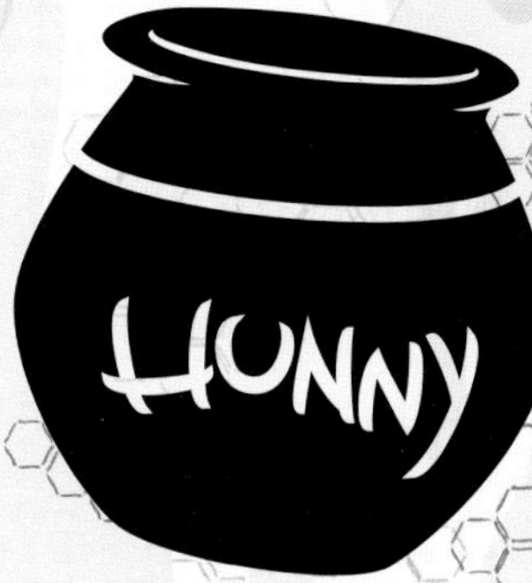
HUNNY

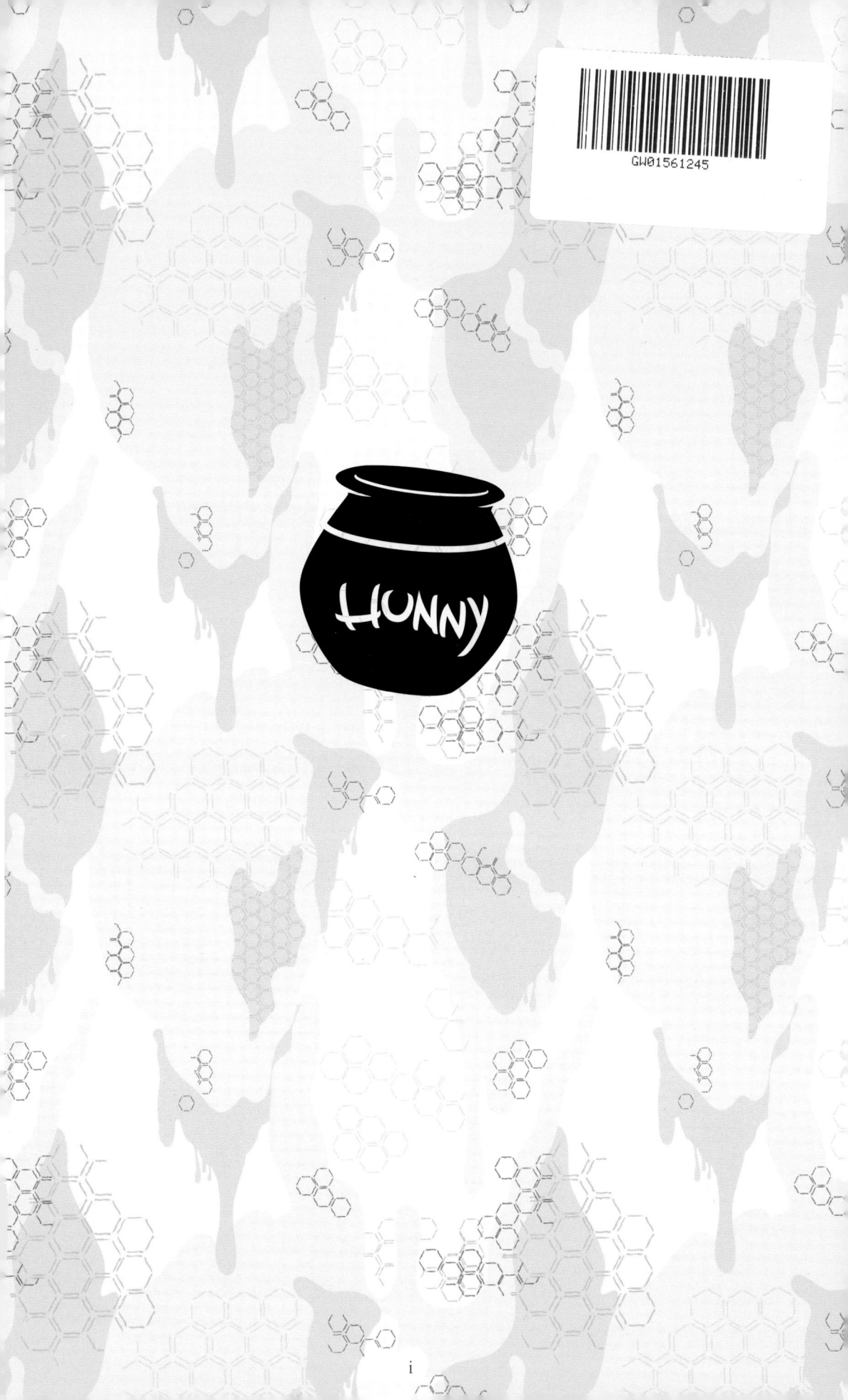

ALSO FROM JOE BOOKS

Disney Frozen Cinestory Comic

Disney Cinderella Cinestory Comic

Disney 101 Dalmatians Cinestory Comic

Disney Alice in Wonderland Cinestory Comic

Disney Princess Comics Treasury

Disney/Pixar Comics Treasury

Disney's Darkwing Duck:
The Definitively Dangerous Edition

Winnie the Pooh

Cinestory Comic

JOE BOOKS INC

Copyright© 2016 Disney Enterprises, Inc. Based on the "Winnie the Pooh" works by A.A. Milne and E.H. Shepard. All rights reserved.

"Winnie The Pooh Theme"; "The Wonderful Thing About Tiggers"
Music and Lyrics by Robert Sherman and Richard Sherman
© 1963 Wonderland Music Company, Inc. (BMI)
All Rights Reserved. Used By Permission.

"The Tummy Song"; "A Very Important Thing To Do"; "Winner Song"; "The Backson Song"; "It's Gonna Be Great"; "Everything is Honey"; "Winner Song (reprise)"; "Winner Song (Reprise)"
Music and Lyrics by Robert Lopez and Kristen Anderson-Lopez
© 2011 Wonderland Music Company, Inc. (BMI)
All Rights Reserved. Used By Permission.

No portion of this publication may be reproduced or transmitted, in any form or by any means, without the express written permission of the copyright holders.

Published in the United States and Canada by Joe Books, Inc.
567 Queen St W, Toronto, ON M5V 2B6
www.joebooks.com

Library and Archives Canada Cataloguing in Publication information is available upon request.
ISBN 978-1-98803-225-2 (Softcover edition)
ISBN 978-1-98803-226-9 (Hardcover edition)
ISBN 978-1-77275-250-2 (Ebook edition)

First Joe Books, Inc edition: January 2016

Names, characters, places, and incidents featured in this publication are either the product of the author's imagination or are used fictitiously. Any resemblance to actual persons (living or dead), events, institutions, or locales, without satiric intent, is coincidental.
Joe Books™ is a trademark of Joe Books, Inc. Joe Books® and the Joe Books Logo are trademarks of Joe Books, Inc., registered in various categories and countries.
All rights reserved.

Printed in the USA through Avenue4 Communications at Cenveo/Richmond, Virginia.

Winnie the Pooh
Cinestory Comic

ADAPTATION, DESIGN, LETTERING, LAYOUT AND EDITING
Robert Greenberger, Ester Salguero, Eduardo Alpuente, Alberto Garrido, Heidi Roux, Aaron Sparrow, Carolynn Prior, Robert Simpson, Amy Weingartner, and Stephanie Alouche

SPECIAL THANKS
Rachel Alor, Curt Baker, Julie Dorris, Behnoosh Khalili, Manny Mederos, and Beatrice Osman

To baby Gwendolyn.

Walt Disney
Pictures
Presents
Winnie the Pooh
story by
Stephen Anderson
Clio Chiang
Don Dougherty
Don Hall
story by
Kendelle Hoyer
Brian Kesinger
Nicole Mitchell
Jeremy Spears
based on the "Winnie the Pooh" works by
A.A. Milne and E.H. Shepard

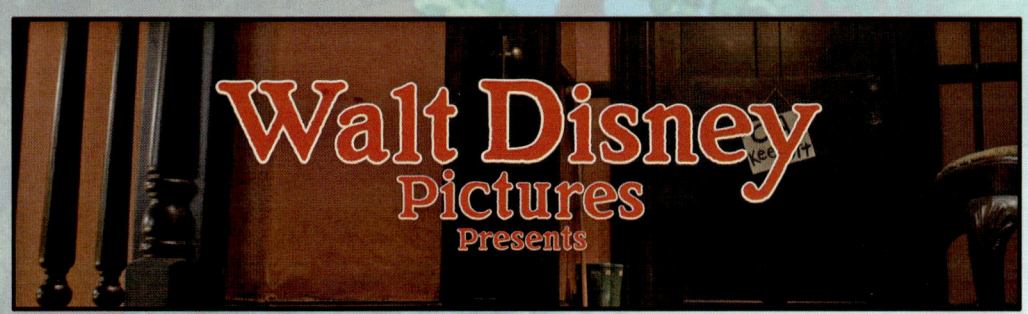

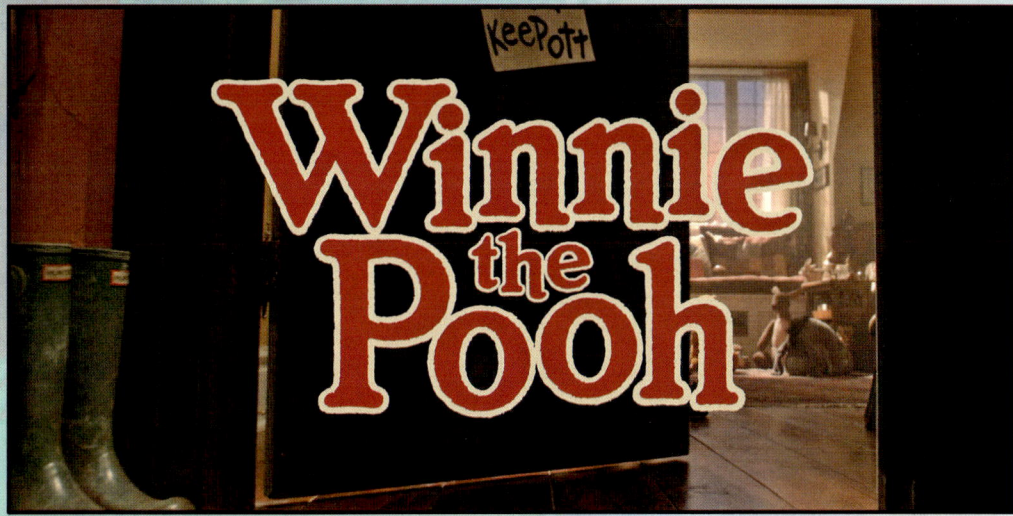

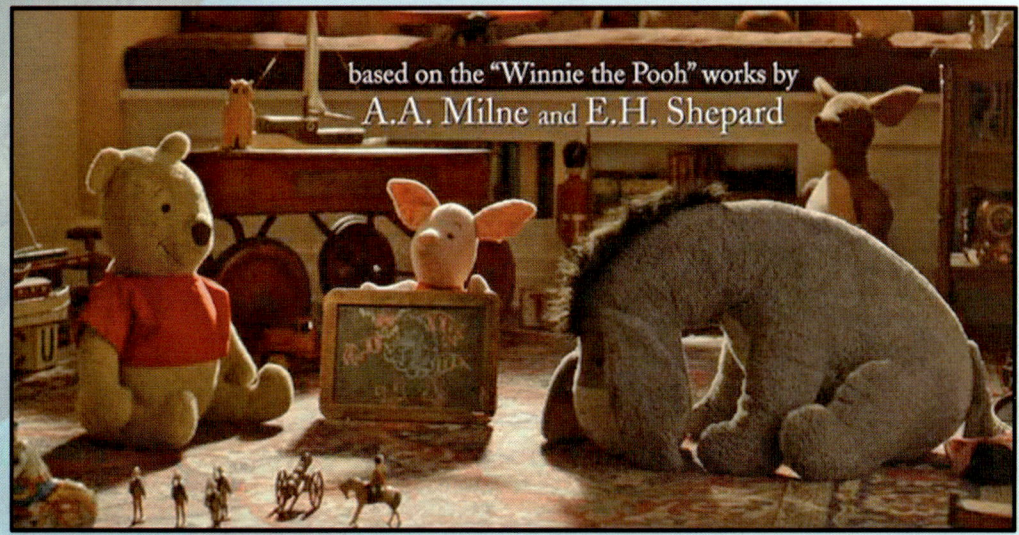

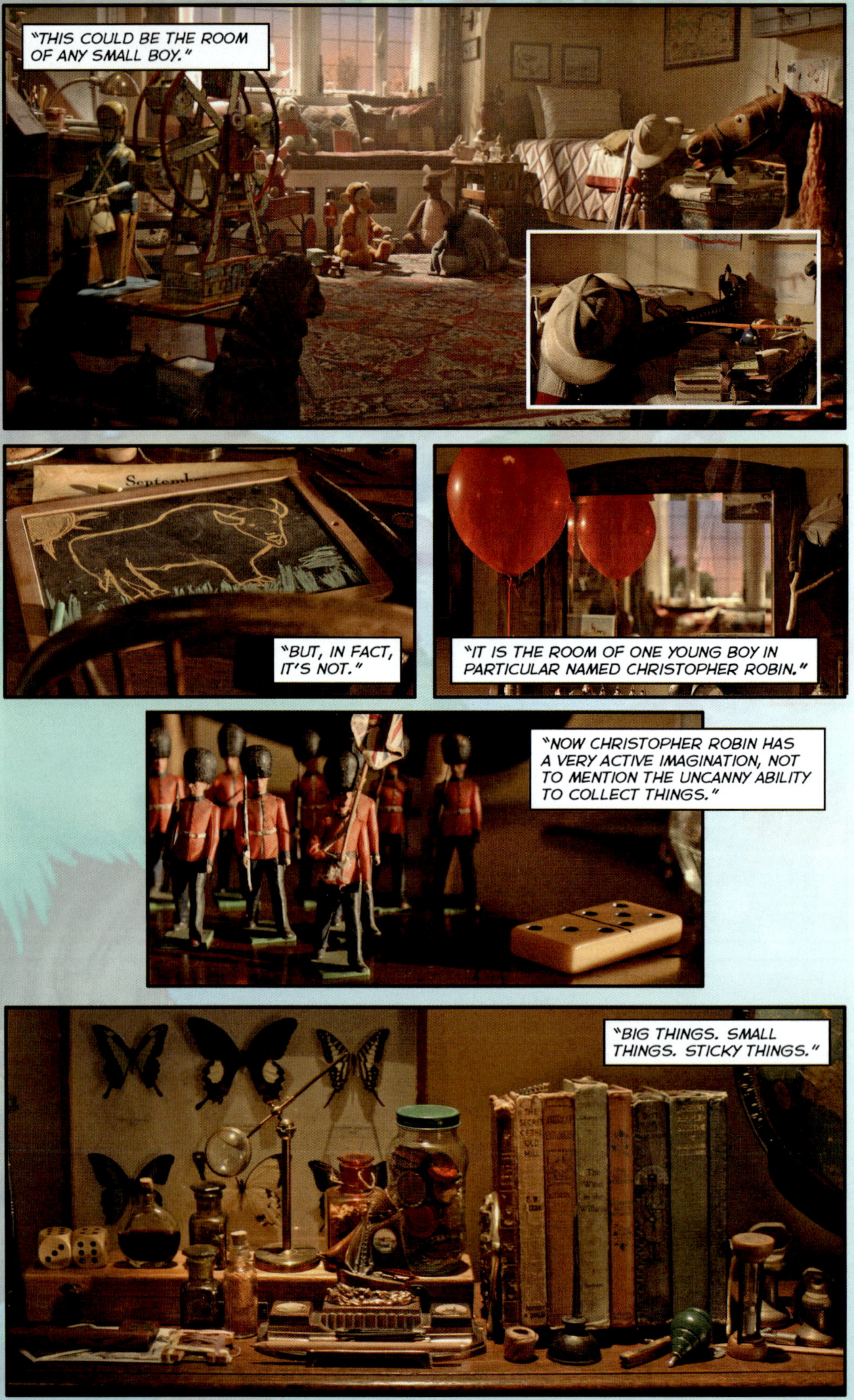
"THIS COULD BE THE ROOM OF ANY SMALL BOY."
"BUT, IN FACT, IT'S NOT."
"IT IS THE ROOM OF ONE YOUNG BOY IN PARTICULAR NAMED CHRISTOPHER ROBIN."
"NOW CHRISTOPHER ROBIN HAS A VERY ACTIVE IMAGINATION, NOT TO MENTION THE UNCANNY ABILITY TO COLLECT THINGS."
"BIG THINGS. SMALL THINGS. STICKY THINGS."

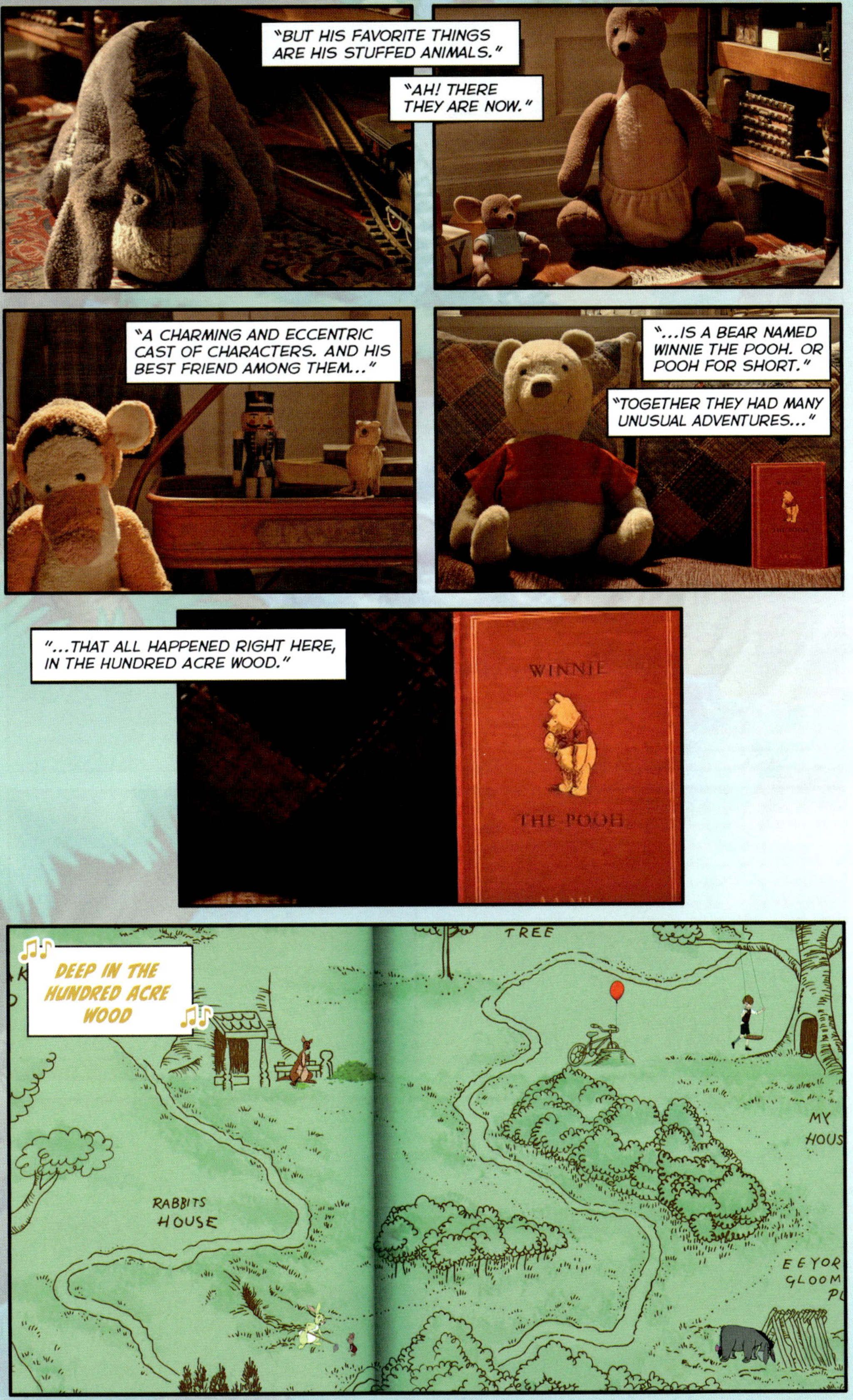
"BUT HIS FAVORITE THINGS ARE HIS STUFFED ANIMALS."
"AH! THERE THEY ARE NOW."
"A CHARMING AND ECCENTRIC CAST OF CHARACTERS. AND HIS BEST FRIEND AMONG THEM..."
"...IS A BEAR NAMED WINNIE THE POOH. OR POOH FOR SHORT."
"TOGETHER THEY HAD MANY UNUSUAL ADVENTURES..."
"...THAT ALL HAPPENED RIGHT HERE, IN THE HUNDRED ACRE WOOD."
WINNIE
THE POOH
DEEP IN THE HUNDRED ACRE WOOD
TREE
RABBITS HOUSE
MY
HOUS
EEYOR
GLOOM
PL

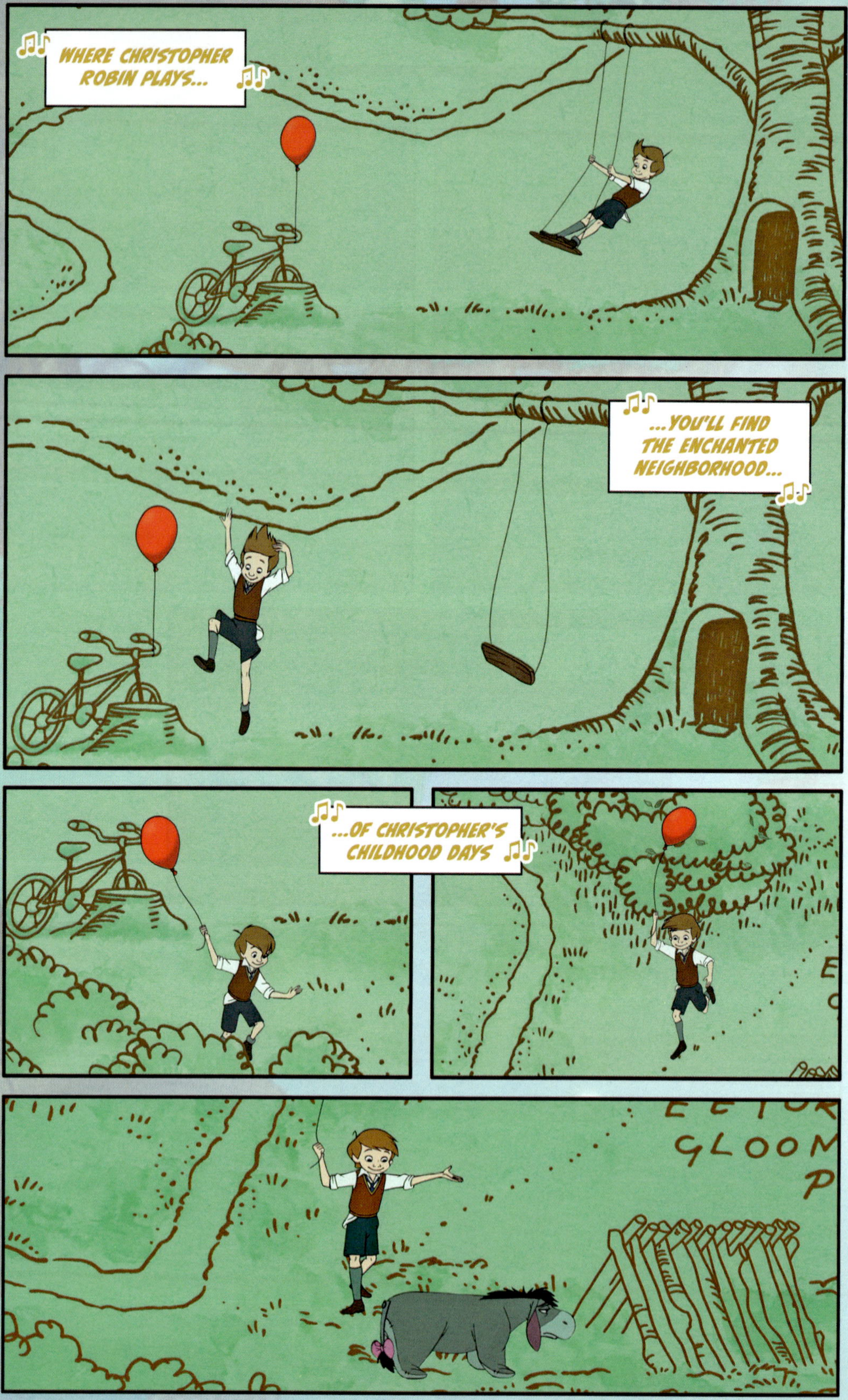
WHERE CHRISTOPHER ROBIN PLAYS...
...YOU'LL FIND THE ENCHANTED NEIGHBORHOOD...
...OF CHRISTOPHER'S CHILDHOOD DAYS

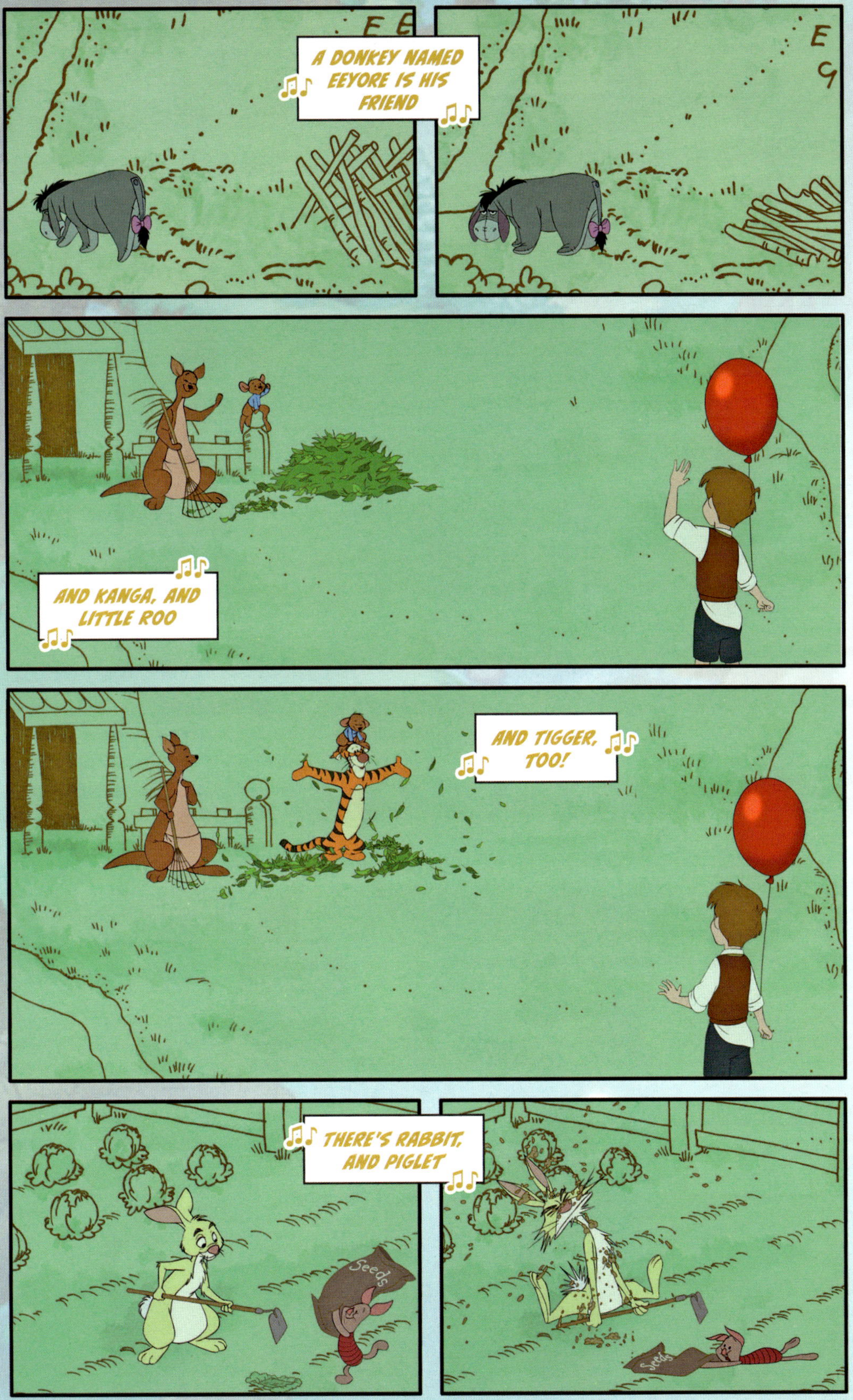
A DONKEY NAMED EEYORE IS HIS FRIEND
AND KANGA, AND LITTLE ROO
AND TIGGER, TOO!
THERE'S RABBIT, AND PIGLET
SEEDS
SEEDS

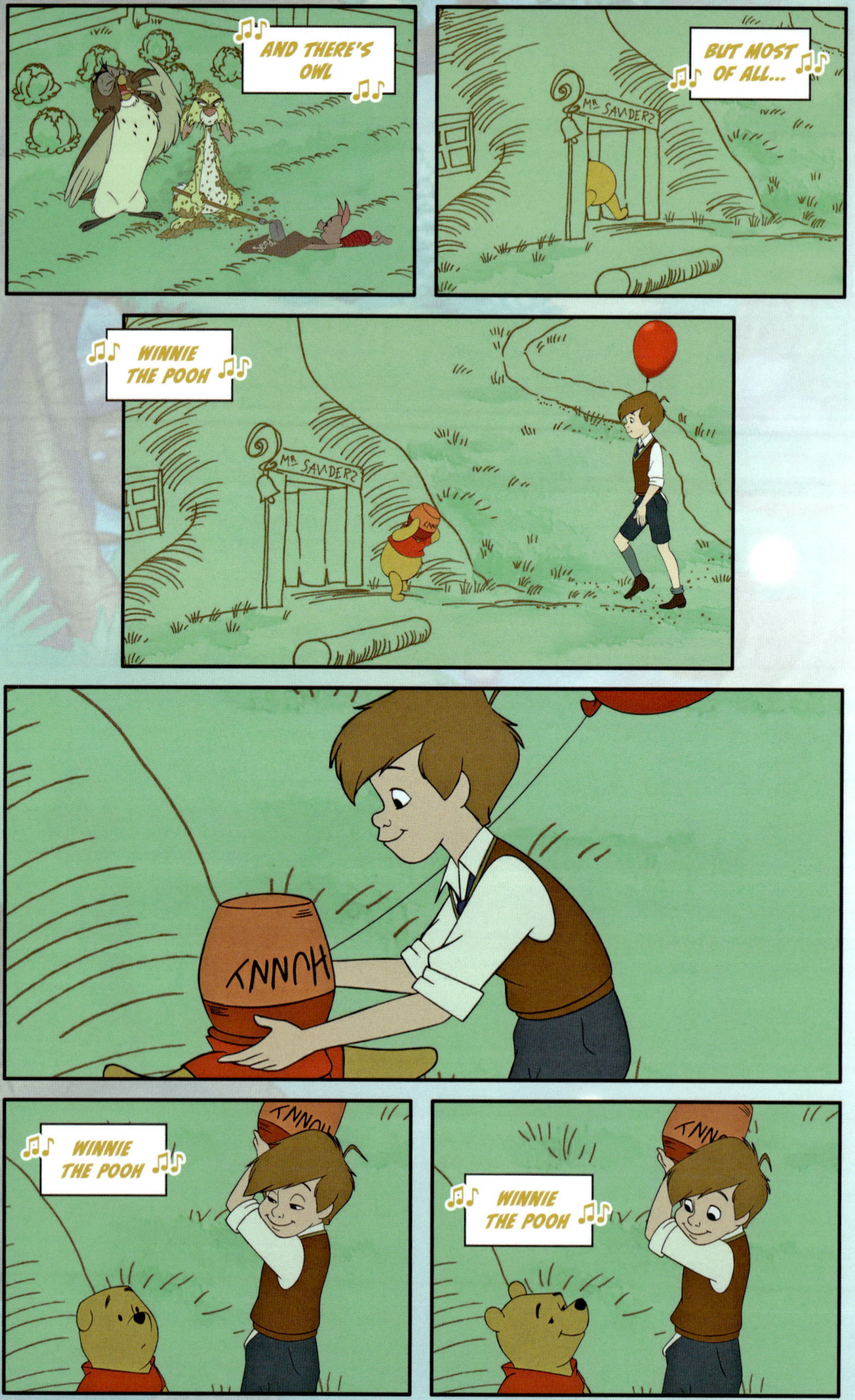
AND THERE'S OWL
BUT MOST OF ALL...
WINNIE THE POOH
HUNNY
WINNIE THE POOH
WINNIE THE POOH

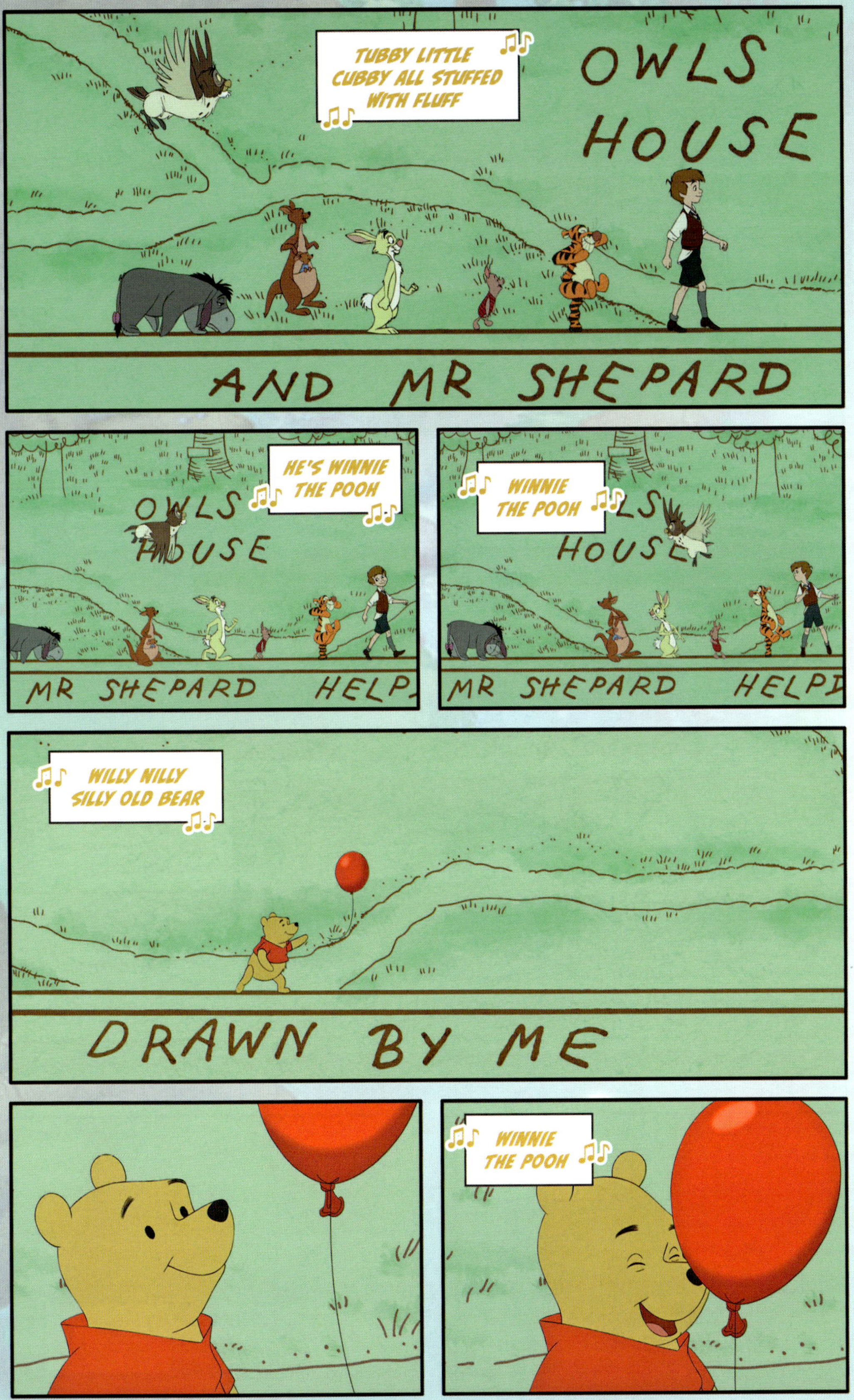

TUBBY LITTLE CUBBY ALL STUFFED WITH FLUFF
OWLS HOUSE
AND MR SHEPARD
HE'S WINNIE THE POOH
OWLS HOUSE
MR SHEPARD HELP
WINNIE THE POOH
HOUSE
MR SHEPARD HELP
WILLY NILLY SILLY OLD BEAR
DRAWN BY ME
WINNIE THE POOH

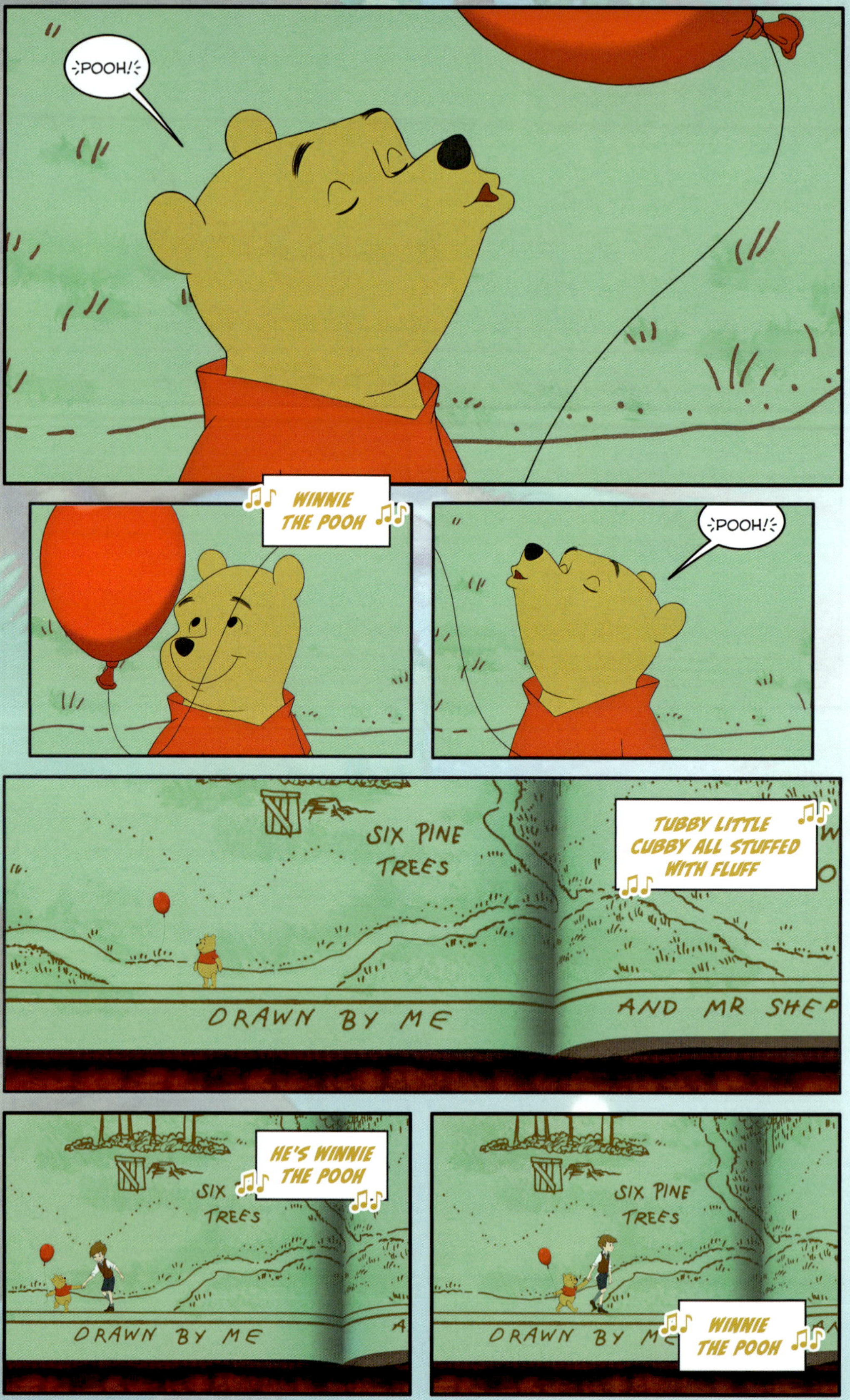
POOH!
WINNIE THE POOH
POOH!
SIX PINE TREES
TUBBY LITTLE CUBBY ALL STUFFED WITH FLUFF
DRAWN BY ME
AND MR SHEP
HE'S WINNIE THE POOH
SIX TREES
DRAWN BY ME
SIX PINE TREES
DRAWN BY ME
WINNIE THE POOH

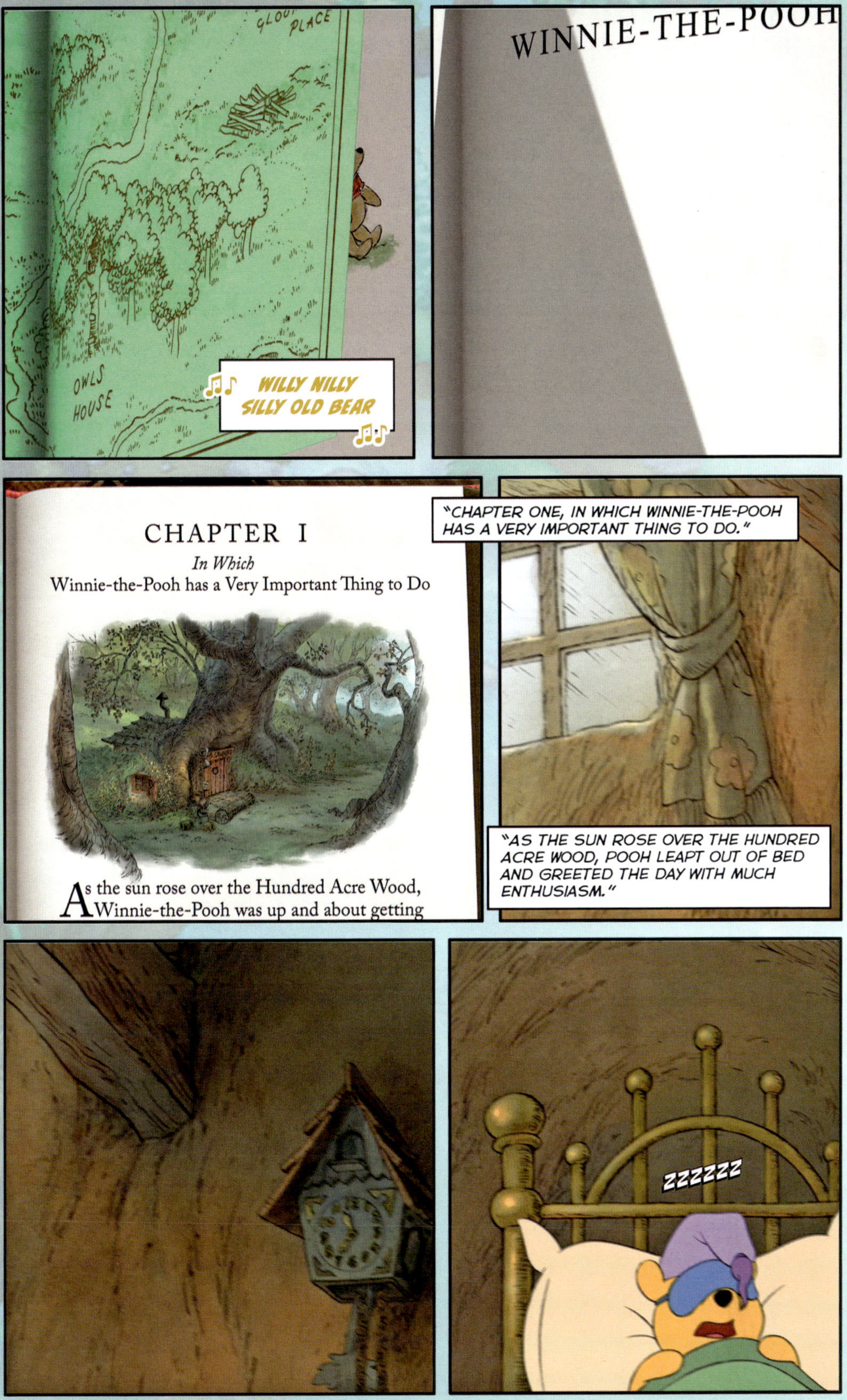

GLOOMY PLACE
OWLS HOUSE
WILLY NILLY SILLY OLD BEAR
WINNIE-THE-POOH
CHAPTER I
In Which
Winnie-the-Pooh has a Very Important Thing to Do
As the sun rose over the Hundred Acre Wood, Winnie-the-Pooh was up and about getting
"CHAPTER ONE, IN WHICH WINNIE-THE-POOH HAS A VERY IMPORTANT THING TO DO."
"AS THE SUN ROSE OVER THE HUNDRED ACRE WOOD, POOH LEAPT OUT OF BED AND GREETED THE DAY WITH MUCH ENTHUSIASM."
ZZZZZZ

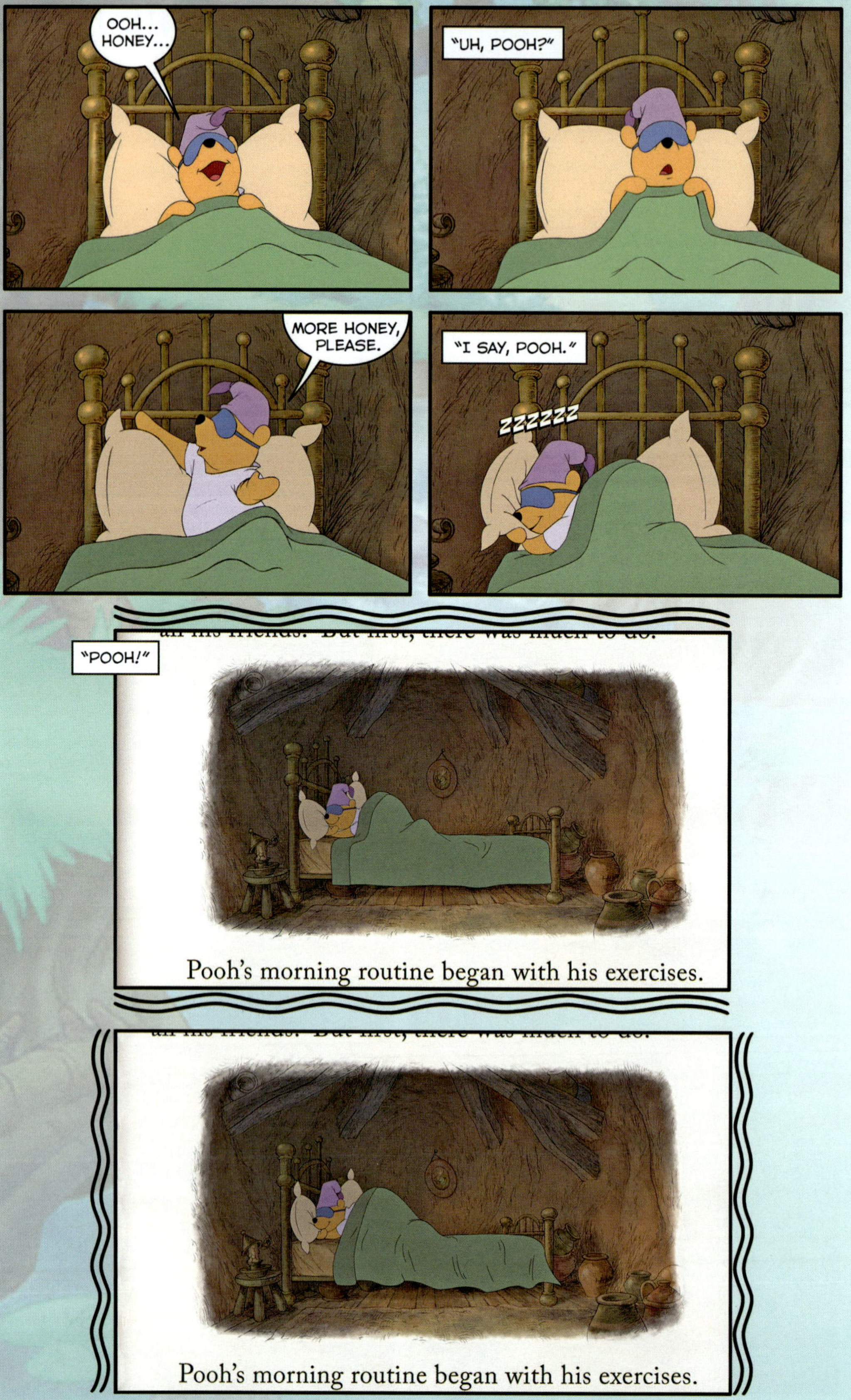
OOH... HONEY...
"UH, POOH?"
MORE HONEY, PLEASE.
"I SAY, POOH."
ZZZZZZ
"POOH!"
Pooh's morning routine began with his exercises.
Pooh's morning routine began with his exercises.

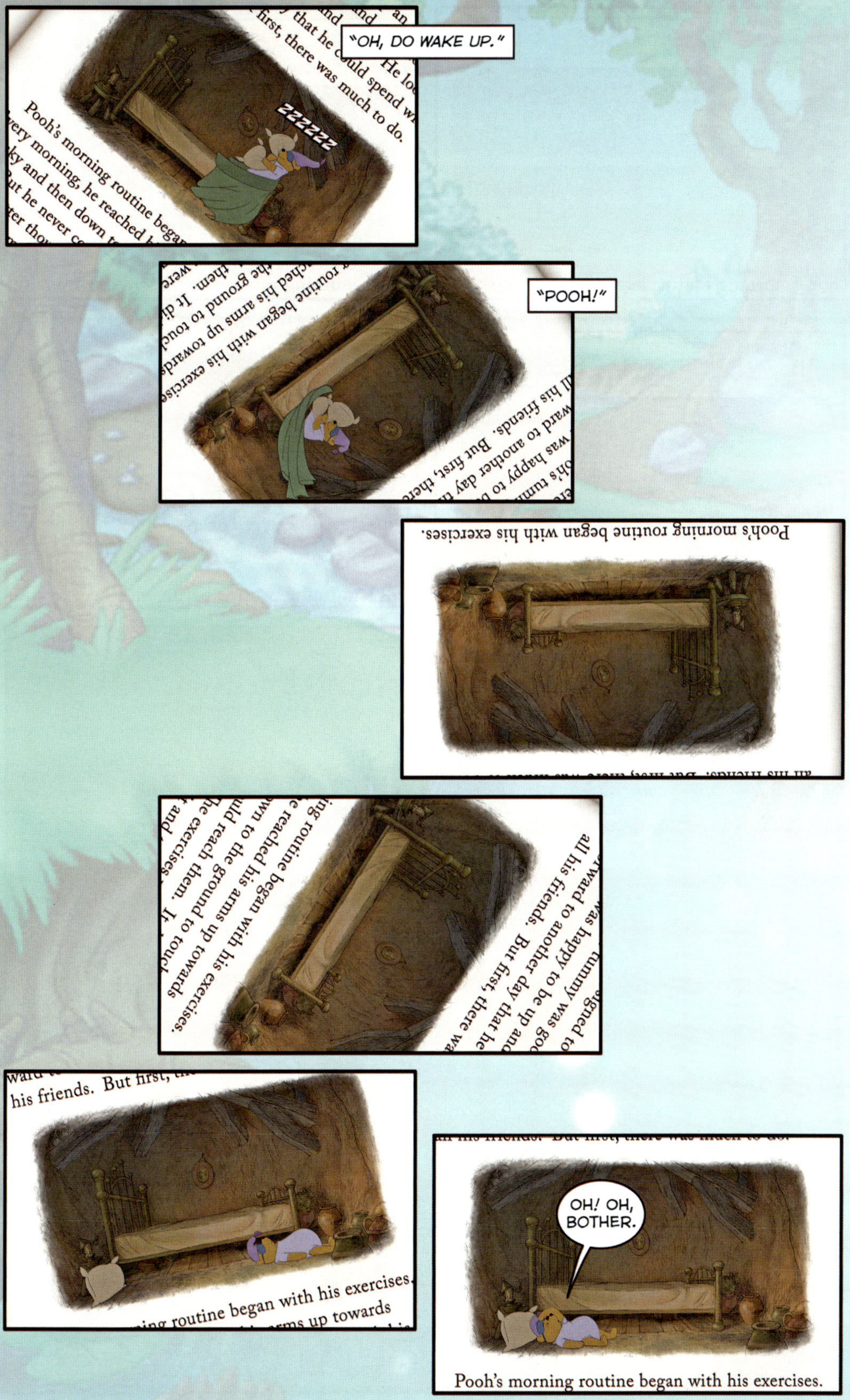
"OH, DO WAKE UP."
ZZZZZZ
"POOH!"
OH! OH, BOTHER.
Pooh's morning routine began with his exercises.

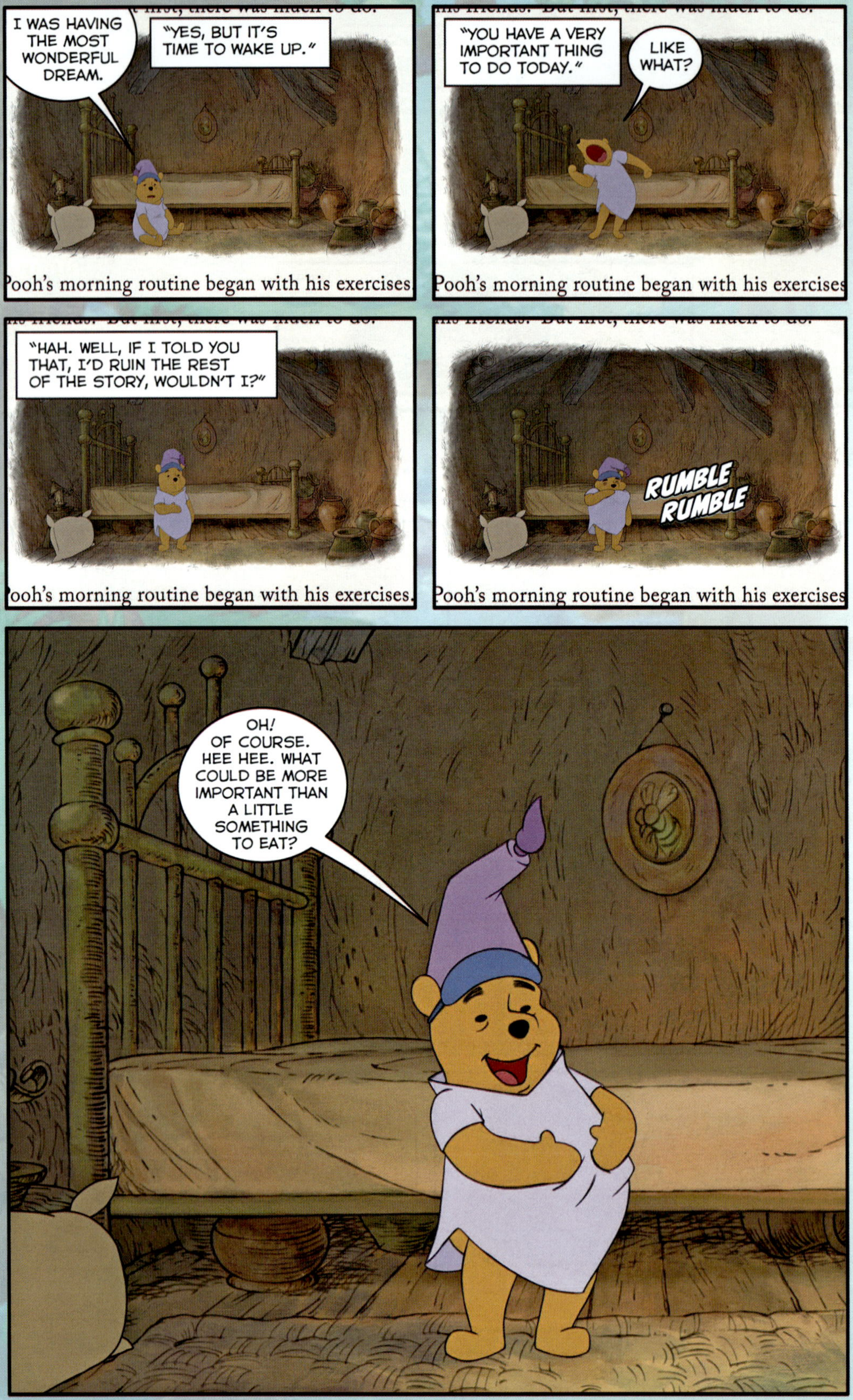

I WAS HAVING THE MOST WONDERFUL DREAM.
"YES, BUT IT'S TIME TO WAKE UP."
ooh's morning routine began with his exercises
"YOU HAVE A VERY IMPORTANT THING TO DO TODAY."
LIKE WHAT?
ooh's morning routine began with his exercises
"HAH. WELL, IF I TOLD YOU THAT, I'D RUIN THE REST OF THE STORY, WOULDN'T I?"
ooh's morning routine began with his exercises.
RUMBLE RUMBLE
ooh's morning routine began with his exercises
OH! OF COURSE. HEE HEE. WHAT COULD BE MORE IMPORTANT THAN A LITTLE SOMETHING TO EAT?

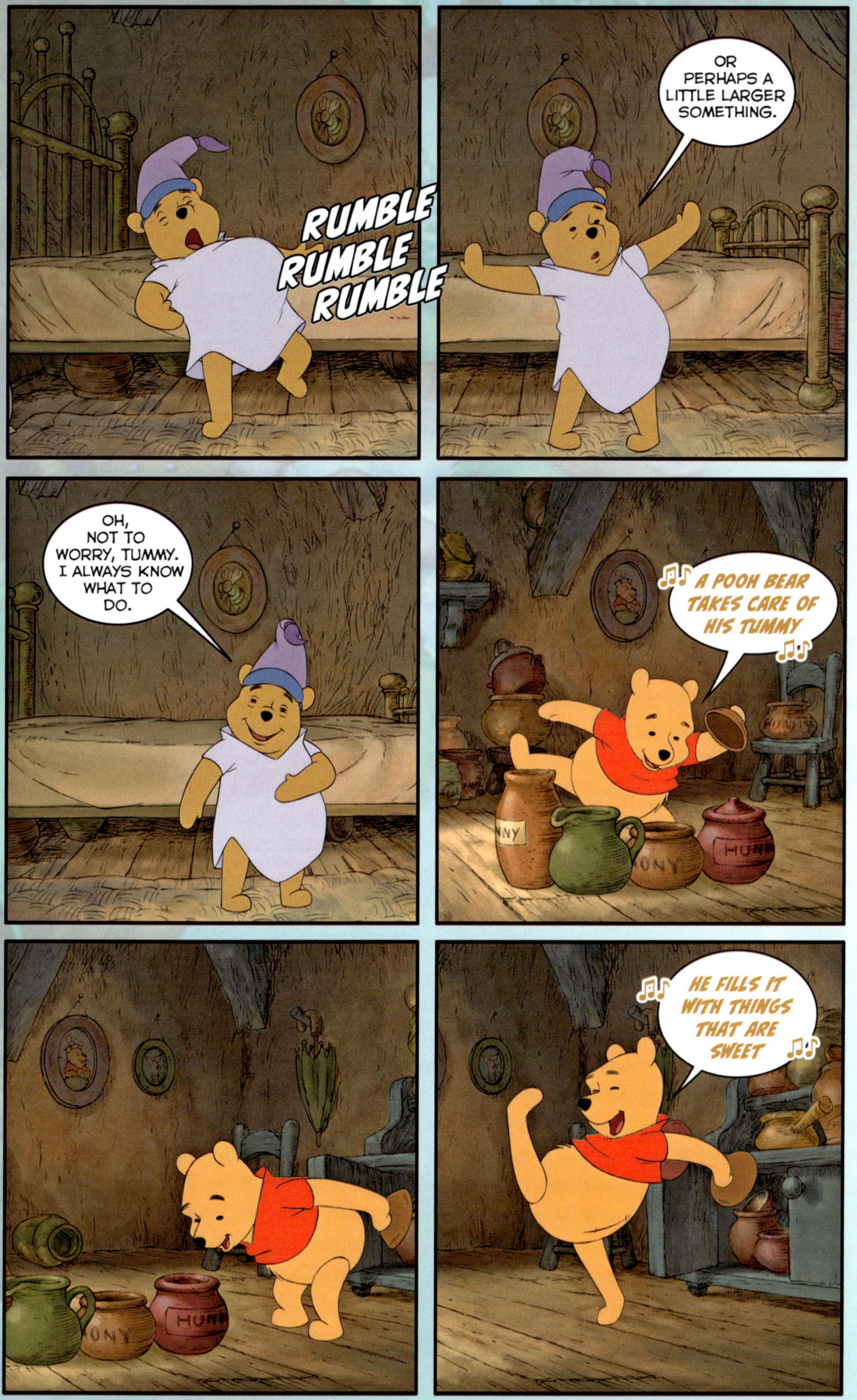
RUMBLE
RUMBLE
RUMBLE
OR PERHAPS A LITTLE LARGER SOMETHING.
OH, NOT TO WORRY, TUMMY. I ALWAYS KNOW WHAT TO DO.
A POOH BEAR TAKES CARE OF HIS TUMMY
HE FILLS IT WITH THINGS THAT ARE SWEET

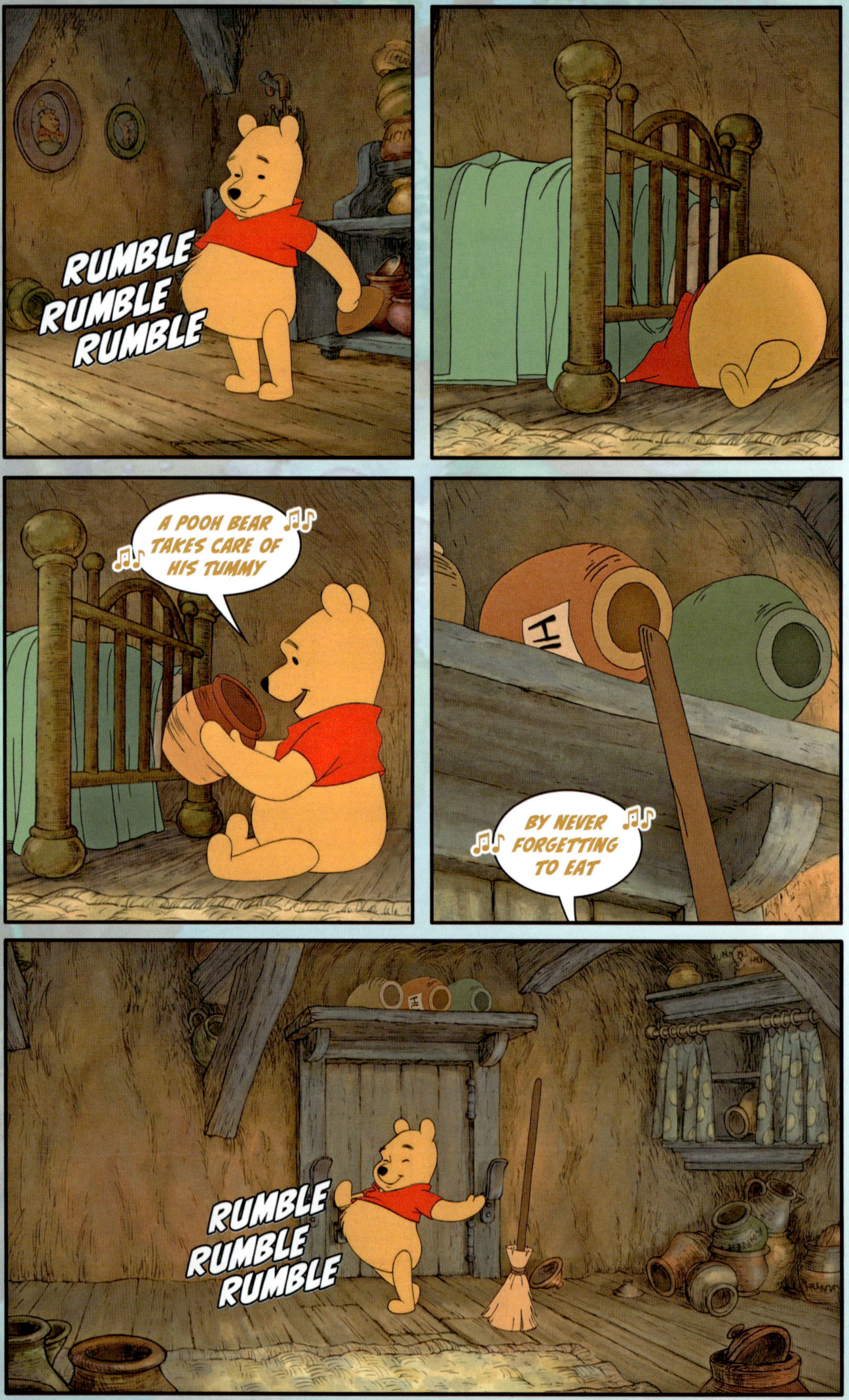
RUMBLE
RUMBLE
RUMBLE
A POOH BEAR TAKES CARE OF HIS TUMMY
BY NEVER FORGETTING TO EAT
RUMBLE
RUMBLE
RUMBLE

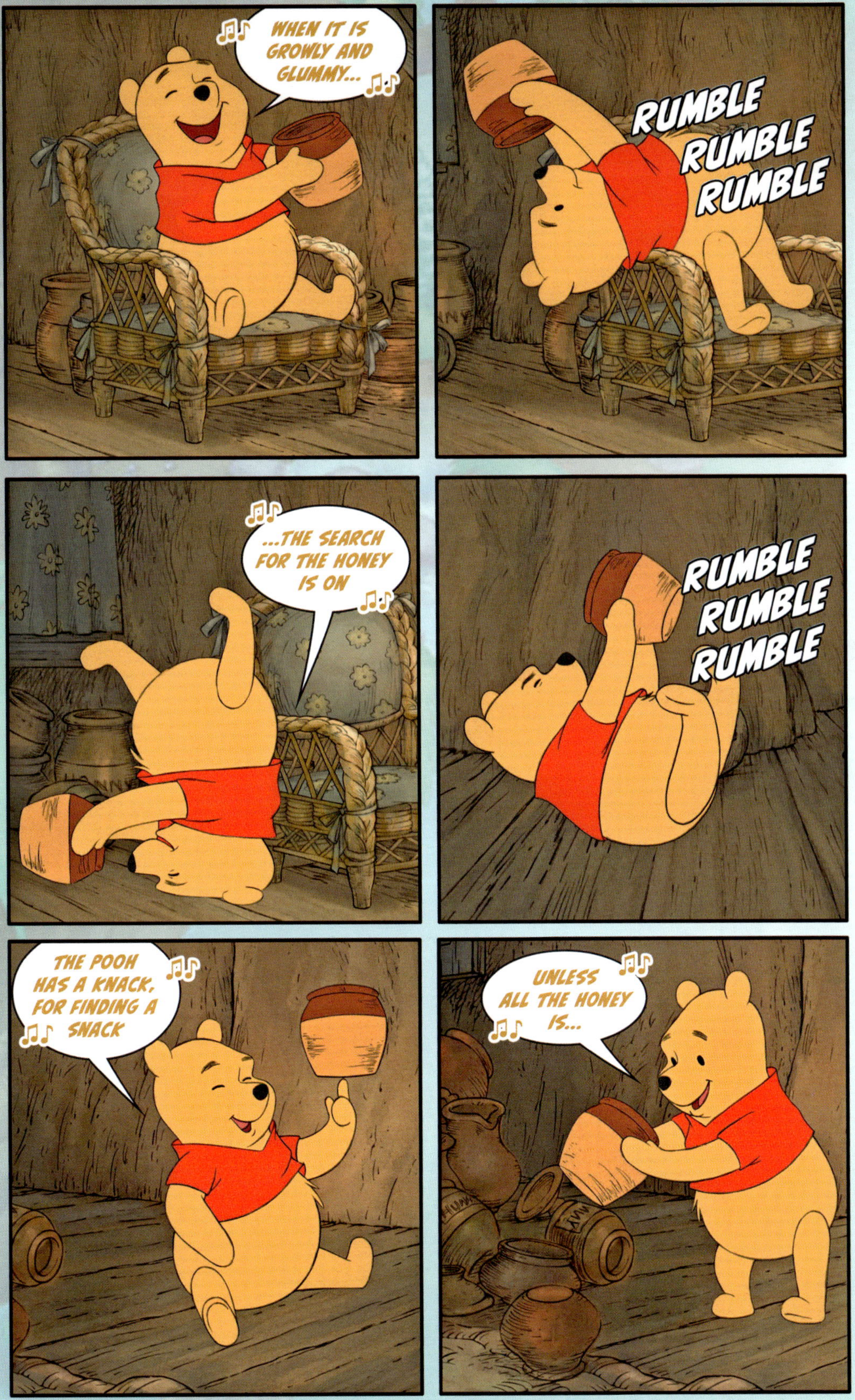
WHEN IT IS GROWLY AND GLUMMY...
RUMBLE RUMBLE RUMBLE
...THE SEARCH FOR THE HONEY IS ON
RUMBLE RUMBLE RUMBLE
THE POOH HAS A KNACK, FOR FINDING A SNACK
UNLESS ALL THE HONEY IS...

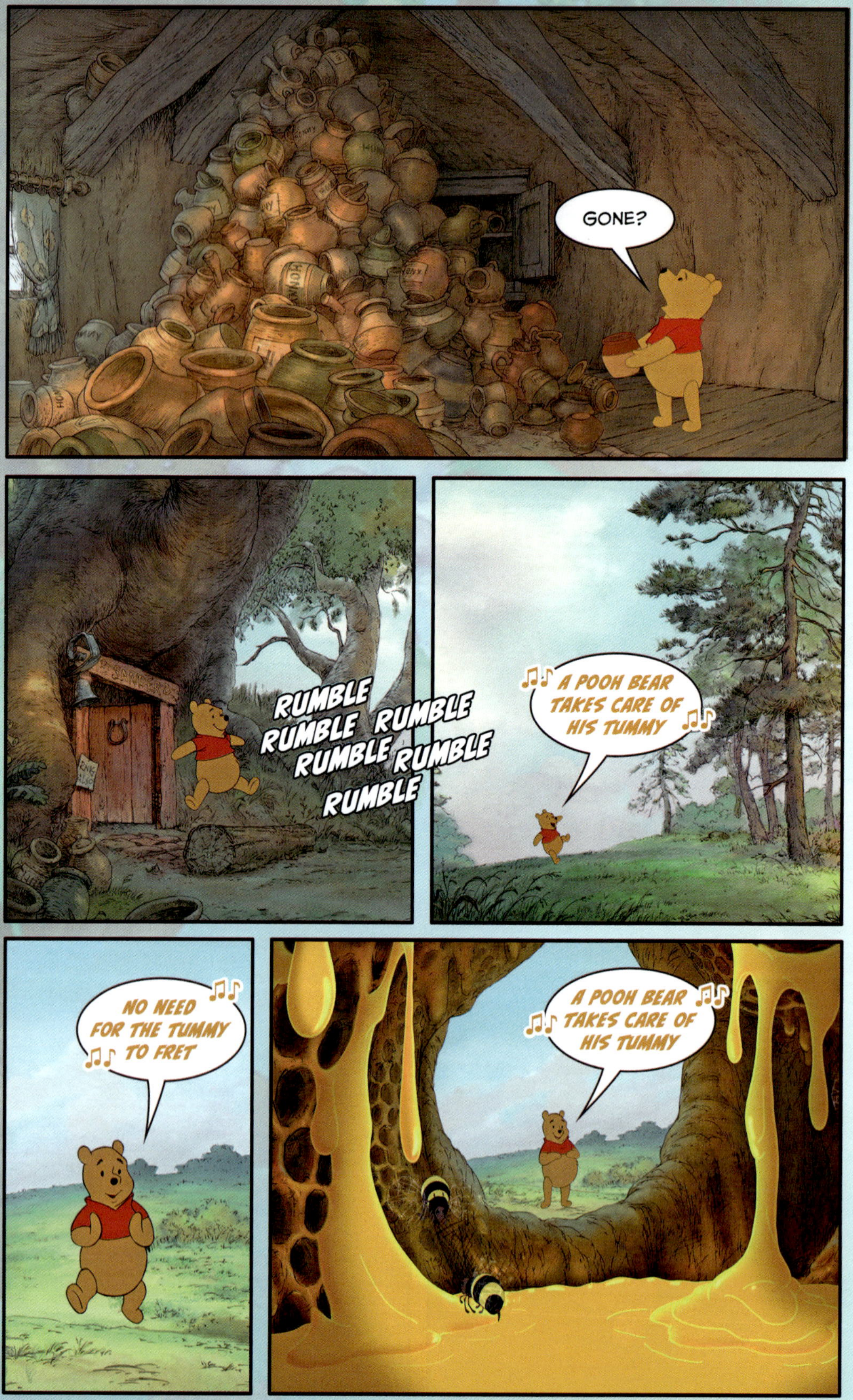
GONE?
RUMBLE RUMBLE RUMBLE RUMBLE RUMBLE RUMBLE
A POOH BEAR TAKES CARE OF HIS TUMMY
NO NEED FOR THE TUMMY TO FRET
A POOH BEAR TAKES CARE OF HIS TUMMY

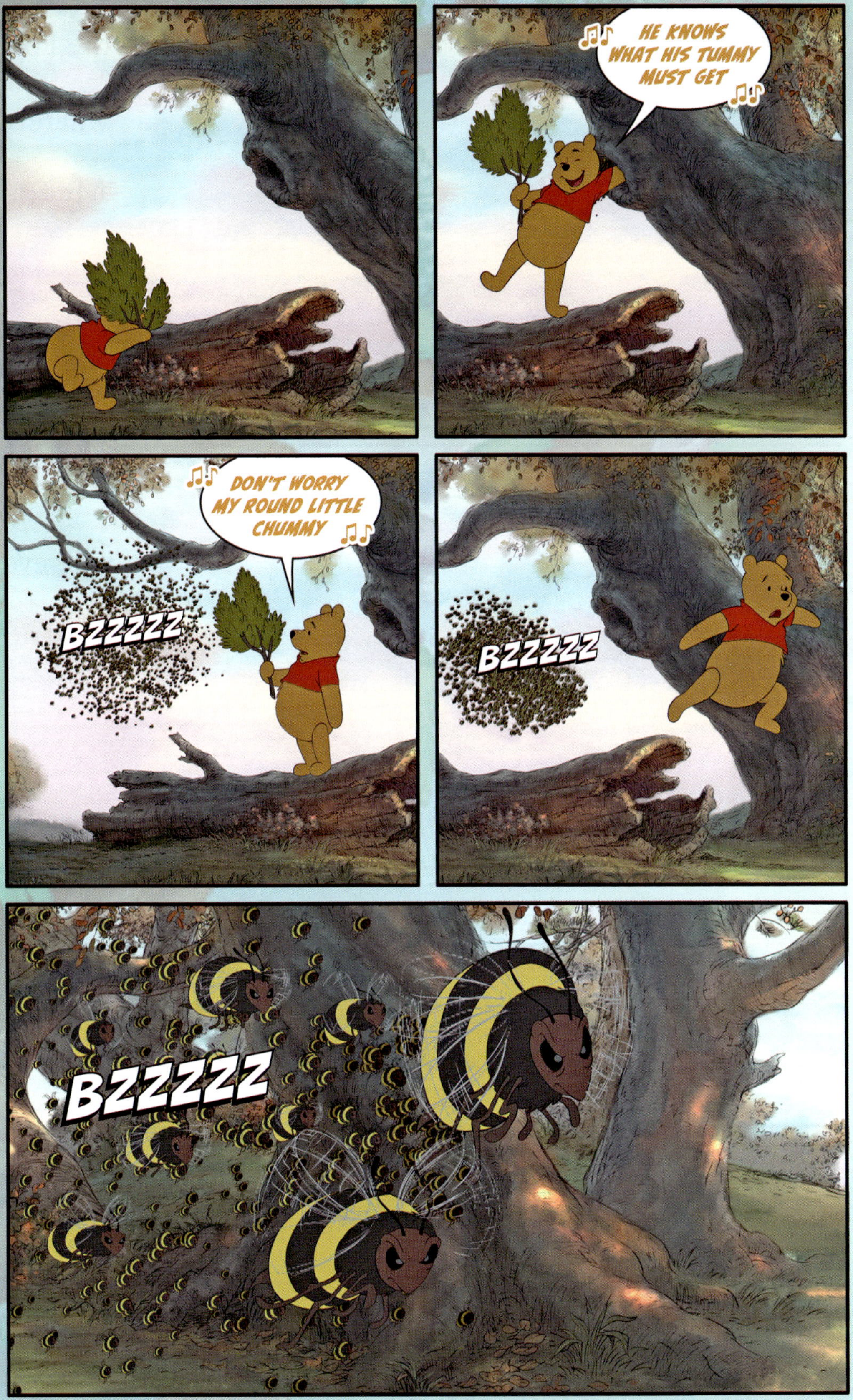
HE KNOWS WHAT HIS TUMMY MUST GET
DON'T WORRY MY ROUND LITTLE CHUMMY
BZZZZZ
BZZZZZ
BZZZZZ

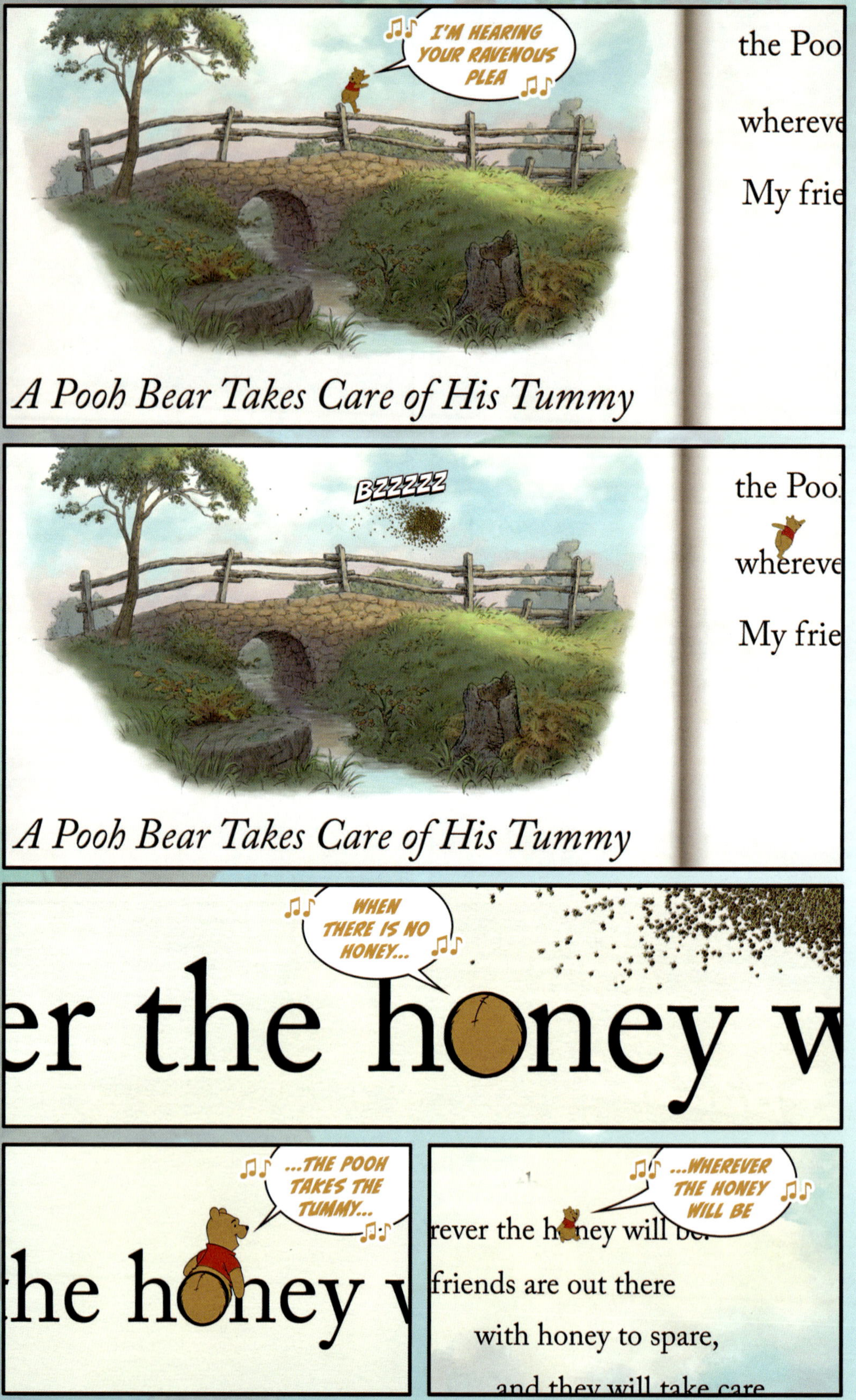
the Poo
wherev
My frie
I'M HEARING YOUR RAVENOUS PLEA
A Pooh Bear Takes Care of His Tummy
BZZZZZ
the Poo
whereve
My frie
A Pooh Bear Takes Care of His Tummy
WHEN THERE IS NO HONEY...
er the honey w
...THE POOH TAKES THE TUMMY...
he honey
...WHEREVER THE HONEY WILL BE
rever the h ney will be.
friends are out there
with honey to spare,
and they will take care

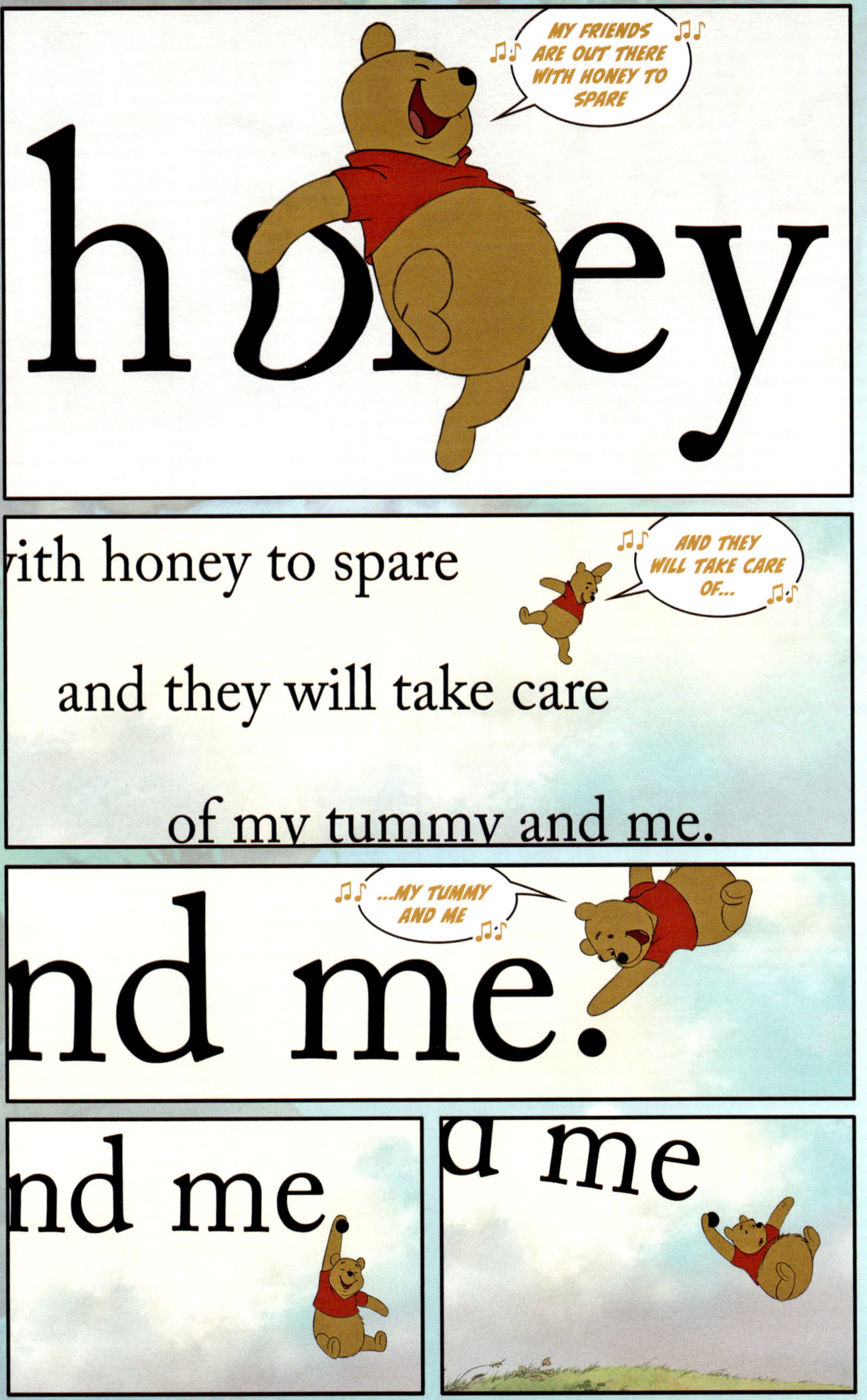
honey
MY FRIENDS ARE OUT THERE WITH HONEY TO SPARE
with honey to spare
AND THEY WILL TAKE CARE OF...
and they will take care
of my tummy and me.
...MY TUMMY AND ME
nd me.
nd me.
d me

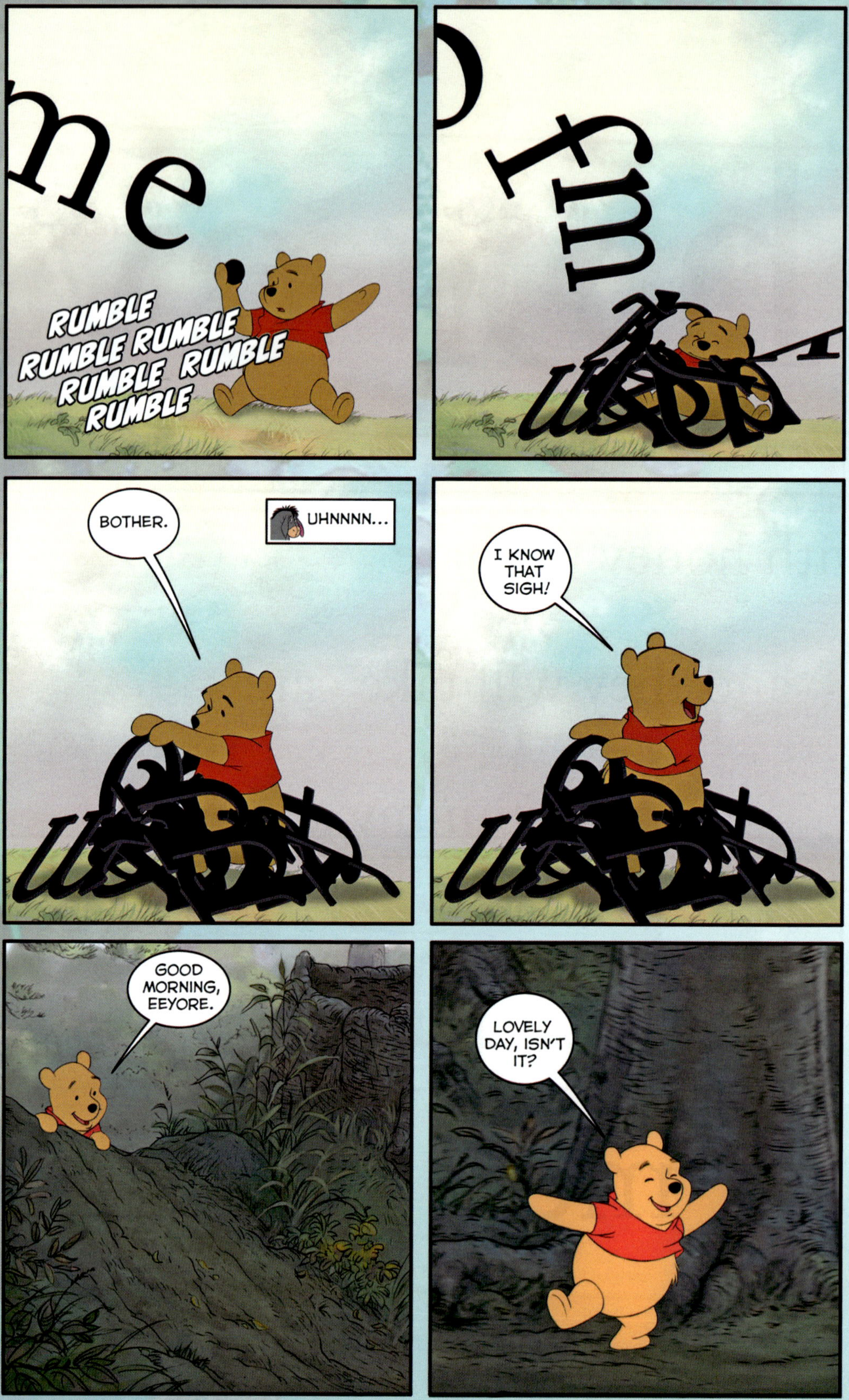
me
RUMBLE RUMBLE RUMBLE RUMBLE RUMBLE RUMBLE
BOTHER.
UHNNNN...
I KNOW THAT SIGH!
GOOD MORNING, EEYORE.
LOVELY DAY, ISN'T IT?

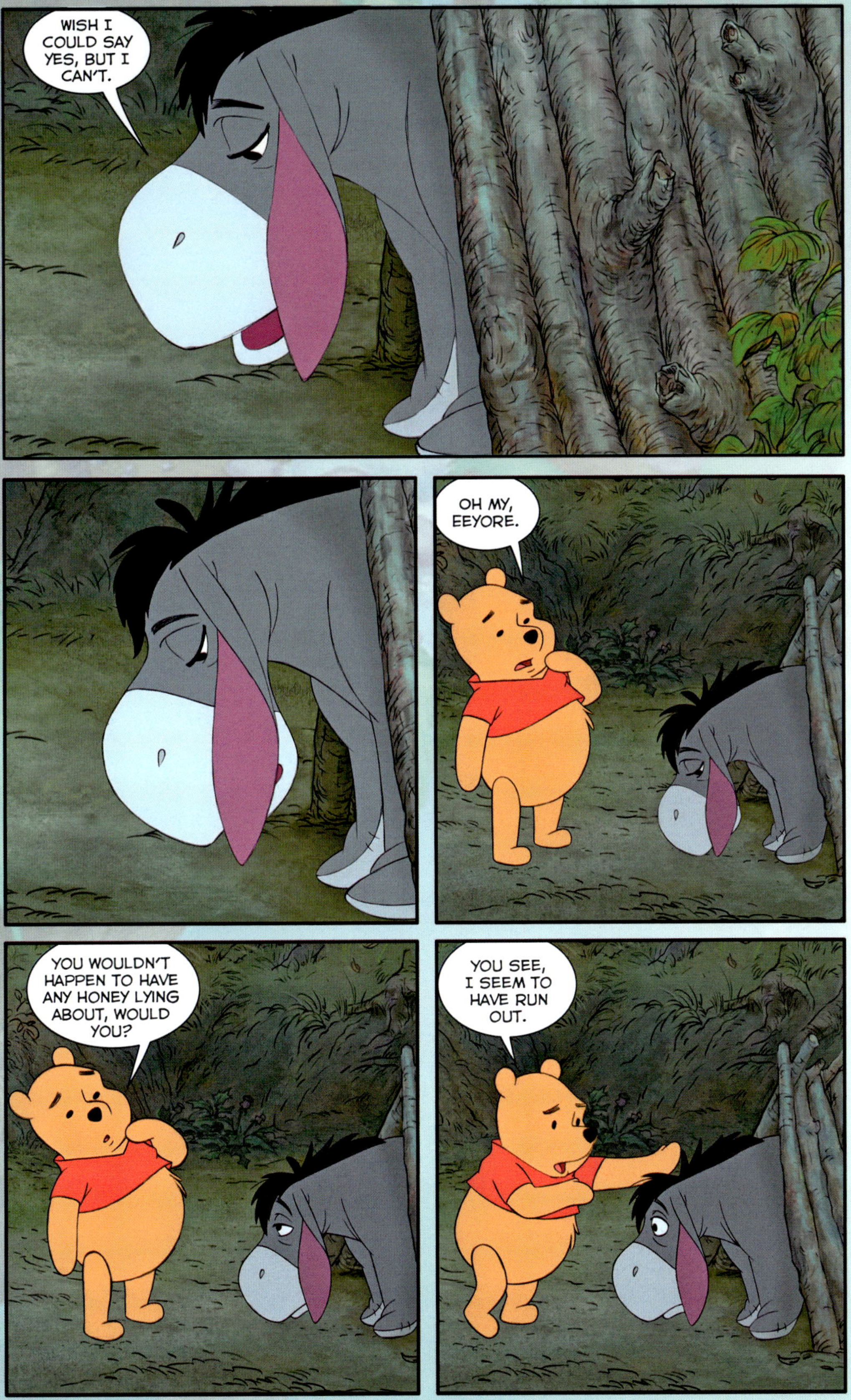
WISH I COULD SAY YES, BUT I CAN'T.
OH MY, EEYORE.
YOU WOULDN'T HAPPEN TO HAVE ANY HONEY LYING ABOUT, WOULD YOU?
YOU SEE, I SEEM TO HAVE RUN OUT.

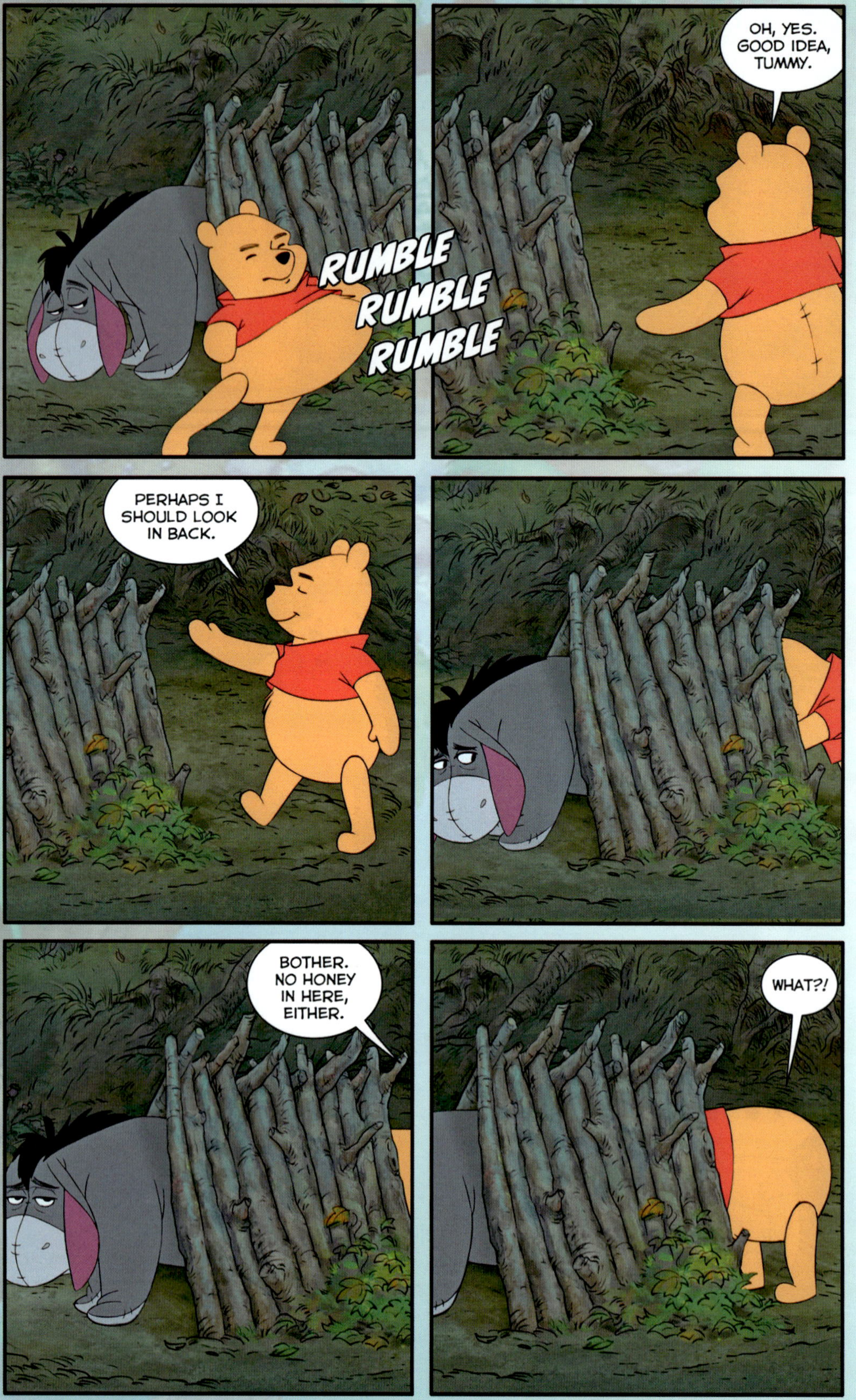
RUMBLE
RUMBLE
RUMBLE
OH, YES. GOOD IDEA, TUMMY.
PERHAPS I SHOULD LOOK IN BACK.
BOTHER. NO HONEY IN HERE, EITHER.
WHAT?!

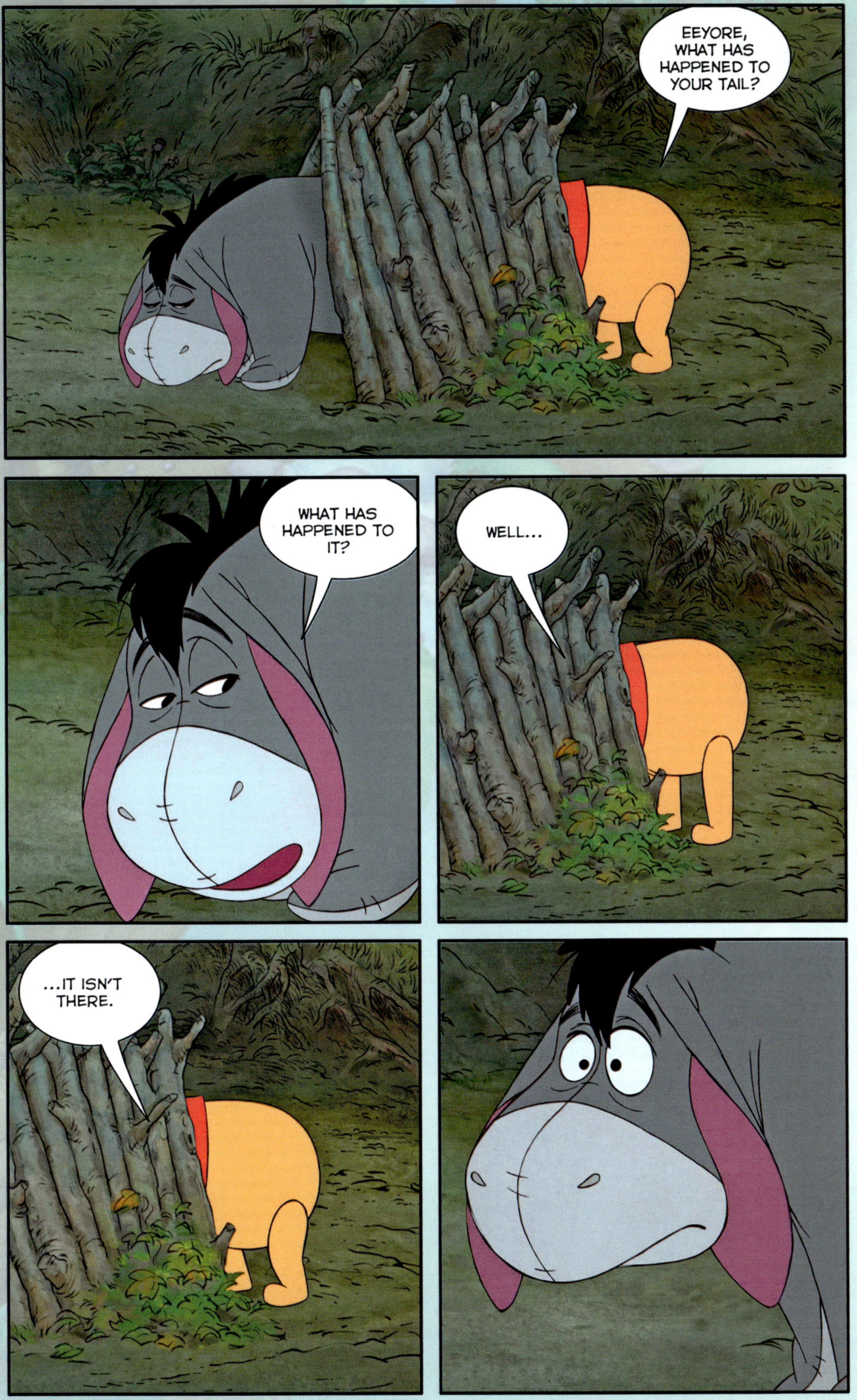
EEYORE, WHAT HAS HAPPENED TO YOUR TAIL?
WHAT HAS HAPPENED TO IT?
WELL...
...IT ISN'T THERE.

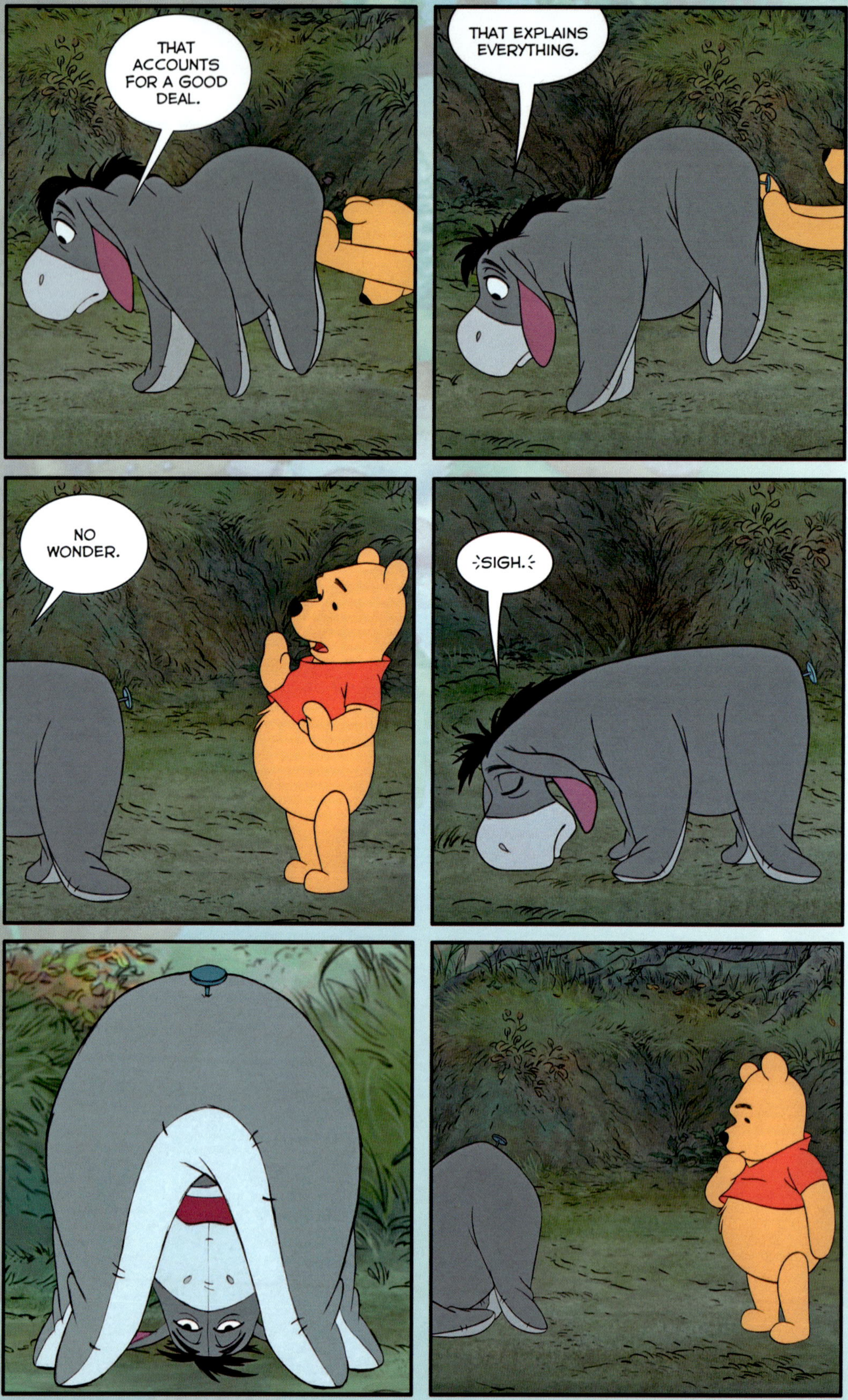
THAT ACCOUNTS FOR A GOOD DEAL.
THAT EXPLAINS EVERYTHING.
NO WONDER.
SIGH.

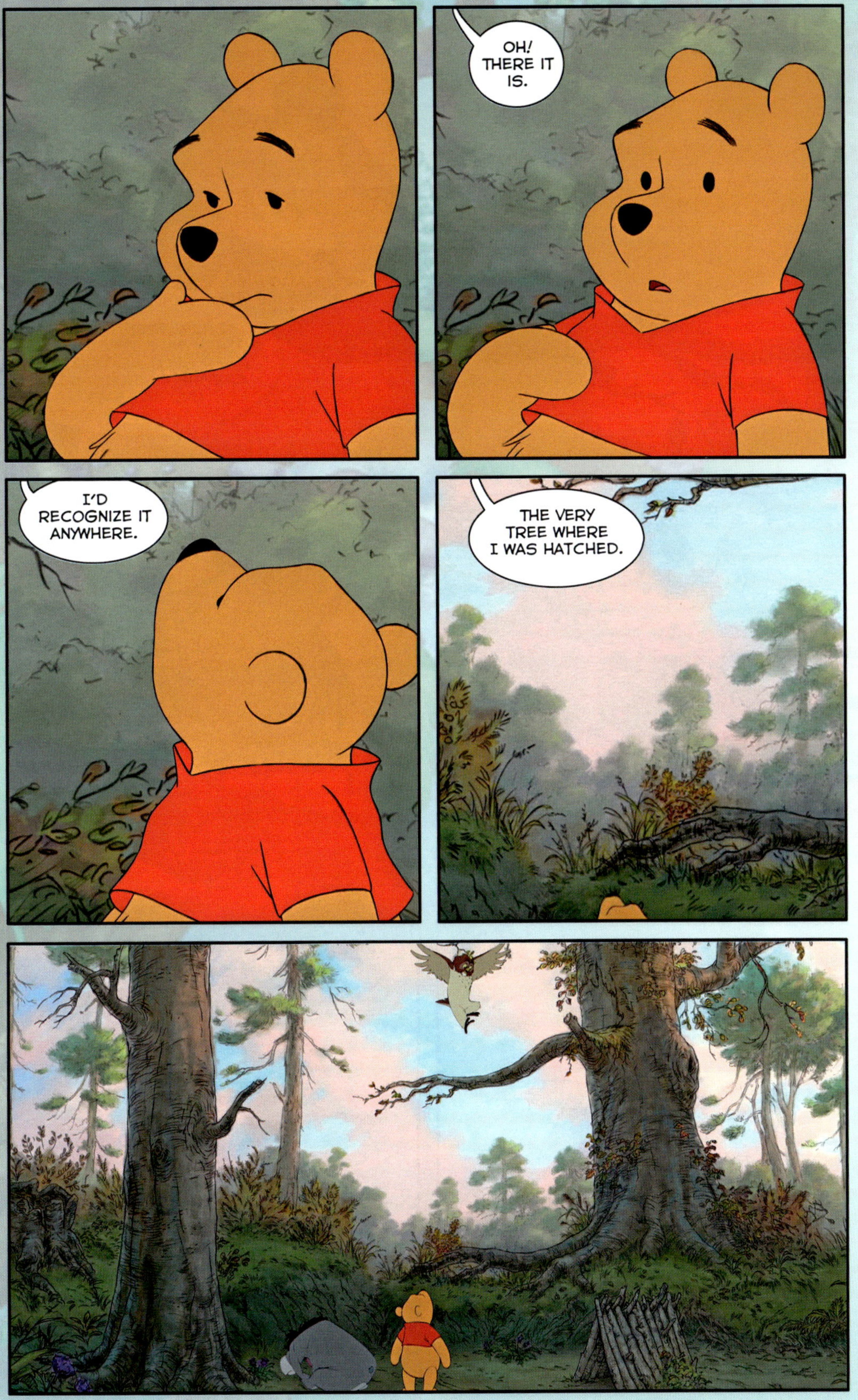
OH! THERE IT IS.
I'D RECOGNIZE IT ANYWHERE.
THE VERY TREE WHERE I WAS HATCHED.

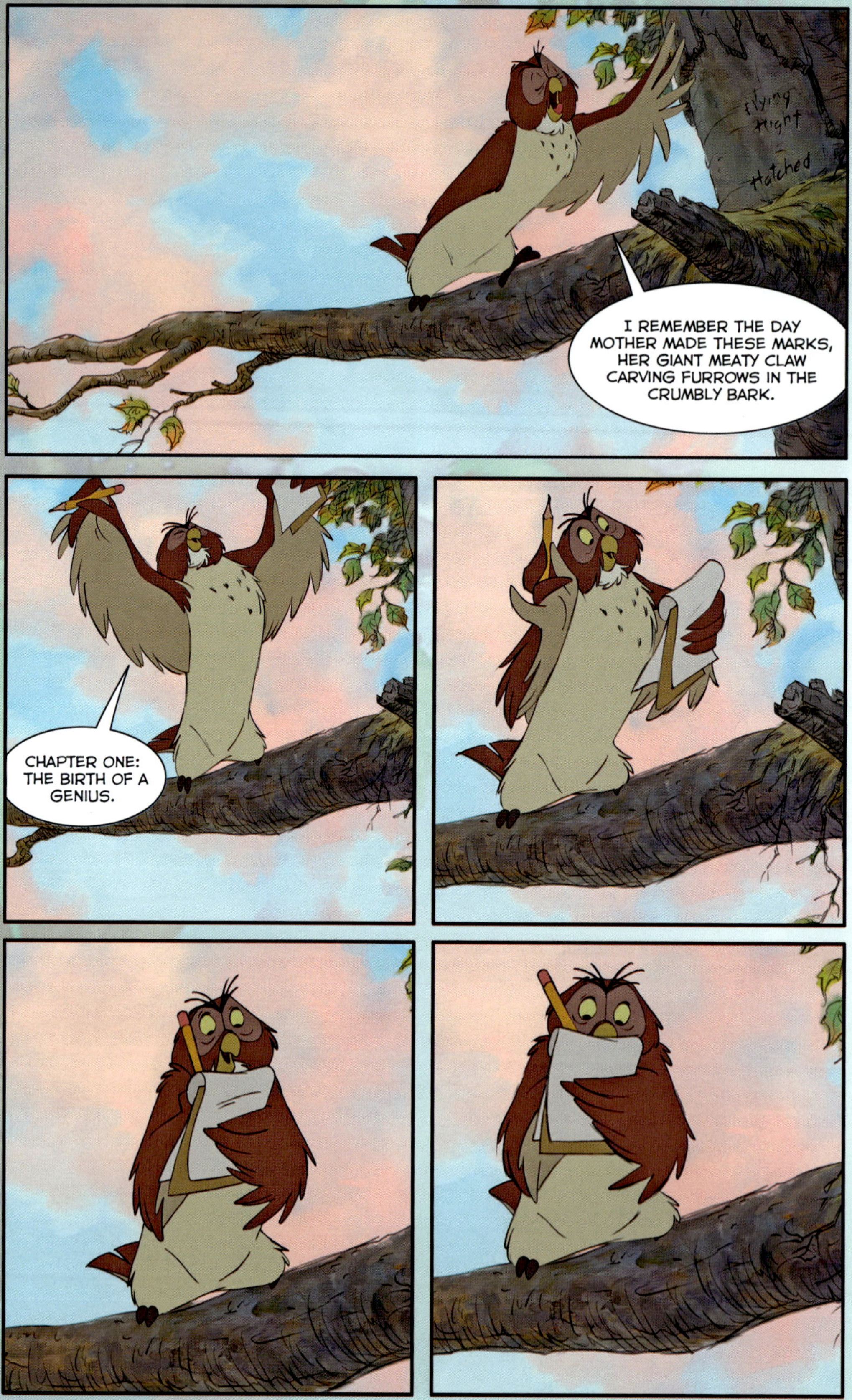
Flying
Flight
Hatched
I REMEMBER THE DAY MOTHER MADE THESE MARKS, HER GIANT MEATY CLAW CARVING FURROWS IN THE CRUMBLY BARK.
CHAPTER ONE: THE BIRTH OF A GENIUS.

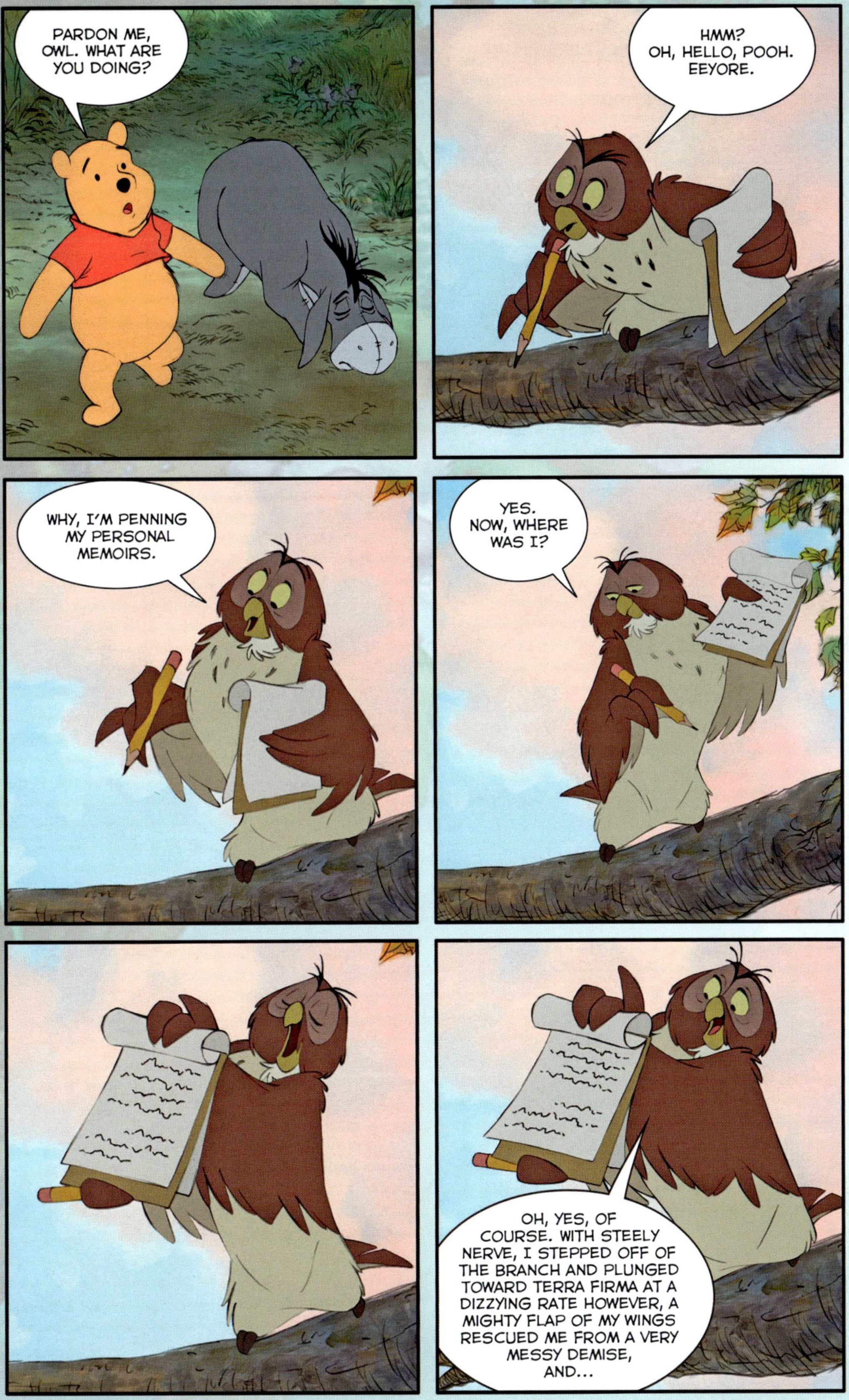
PARDON ME, OWL. WHAT ARE YOU DOING?
HMM? OH, HELLO, POOH. EEYORE.
WHY, I'M PENNING MY PERSONAL MEMOIRS.
YES. NOW, WHERE WAS I?
OH, YES, OF COURSE. WITH STEELY NERVE, I STEPPED OFF OF THE BRANCH AND PLUNGED TOWARD TERRA FIRMA AT A DIZZYING RATE HOWEVER, A MIGHTY FLAP OF MY WINGS RESCUED ME FROM A VERY MESSY DEMISE, AND...

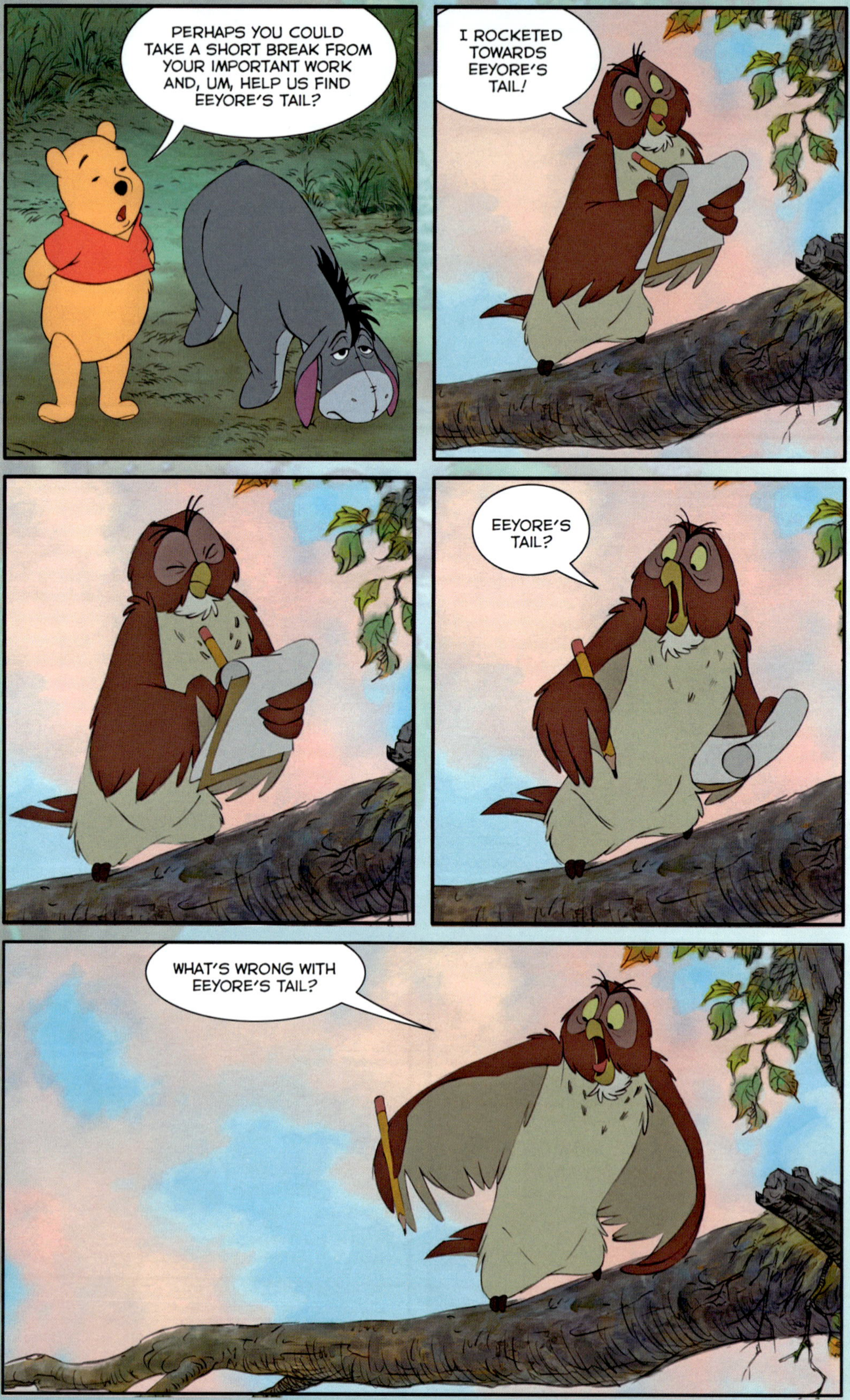
PERHAPS YOU COULD TAKE A SHORT BREAK FROM YOUR IMPORTANT WORK AND, UM, HELP US FIND EEYORE'S TAIL?
I ROCKETED TOWARDS EEYORE'S TAIL!
EEYORE'S TAIL?
WHAT'S WRONG WITH EEYORE'S TAIL?

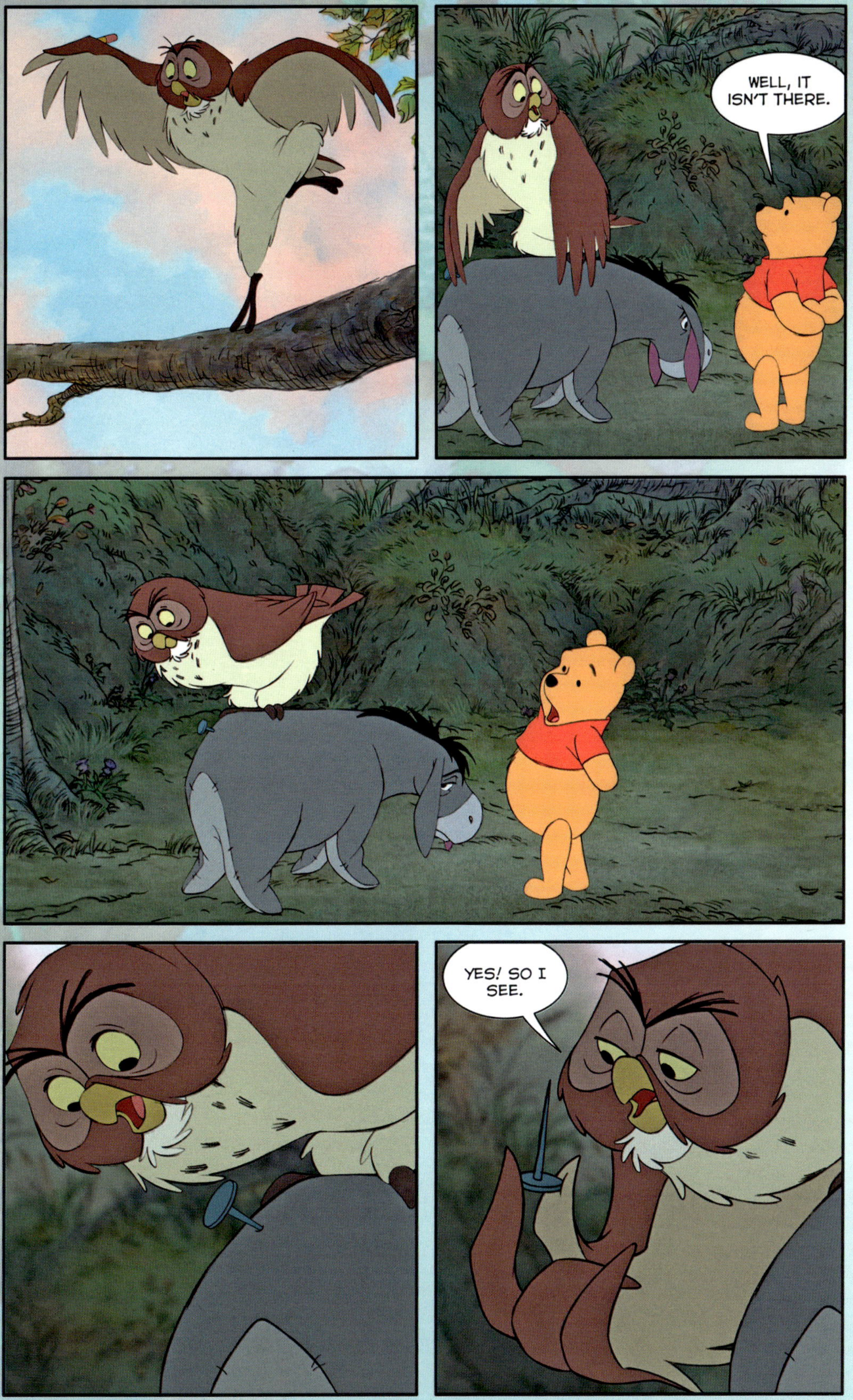
WELL, IT ISN'T THERE.
YES! SO I SEE.

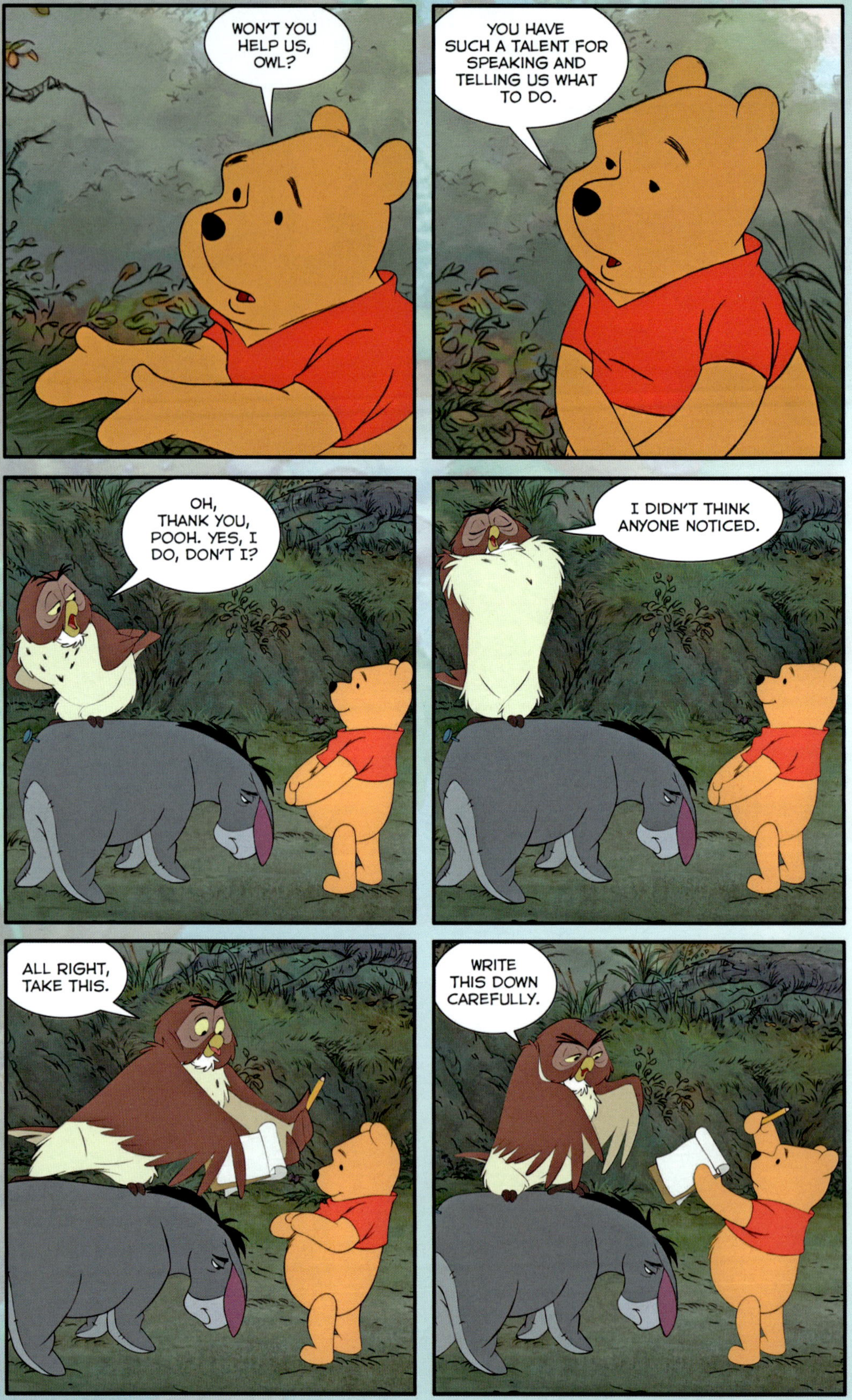
WON'T YOU HELP US, OWL?
YOU HAVE SUCH A TALENT FOR SPEAKING AND TELLING US WHAT TO DO.
OH, THANK YOU, POOH. YES, I DO, DON'T I?
I DIDN'T THINK ANYONE NOTICED.
ALL RIGHT, TAKE THIS.
WRITE THIS DOWN CAREFULLY.

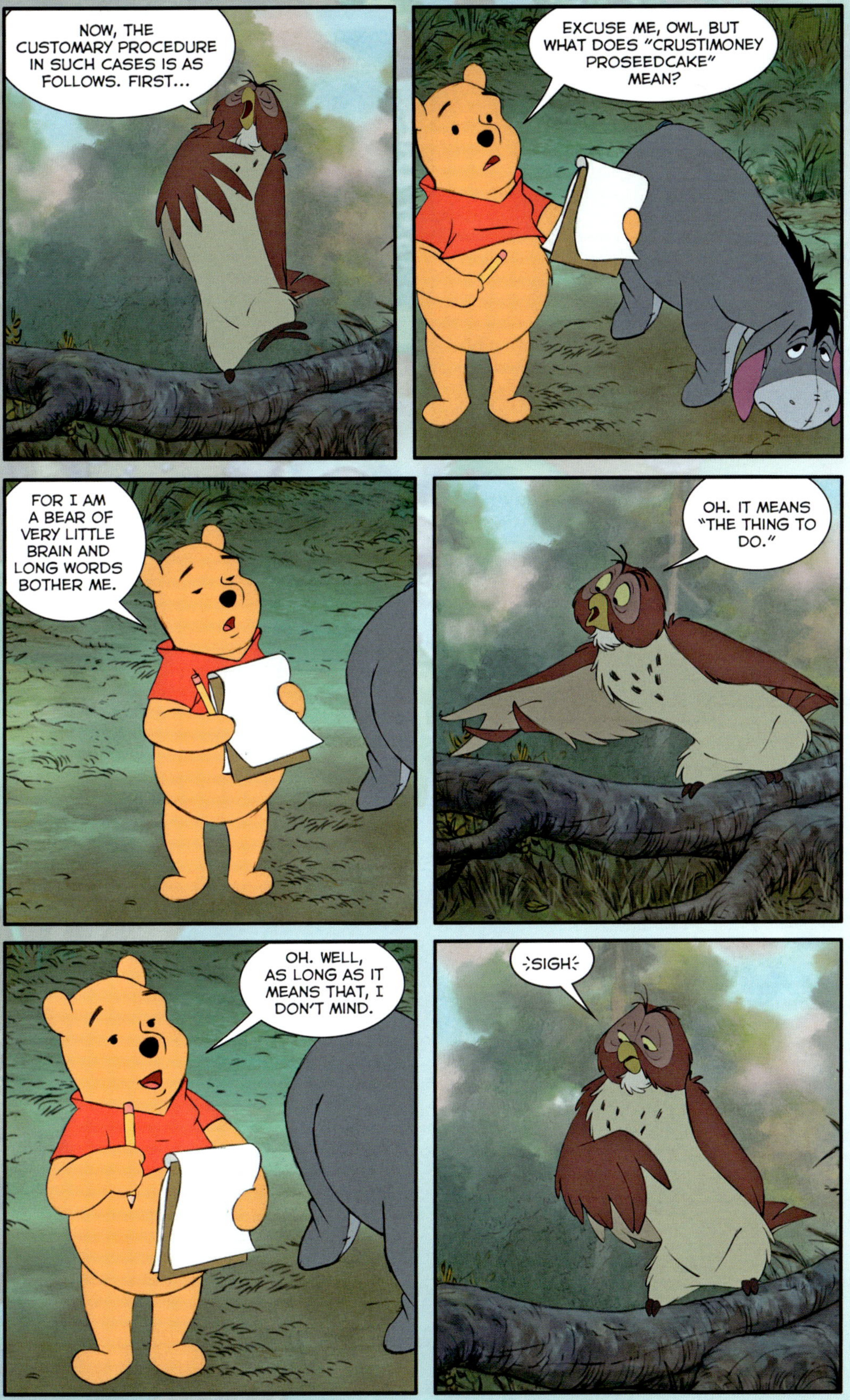
NOW, THE CUSTOMARY PROCEDURE IN SUCH CASES IS AS FOLLOWS. FIRST...
EXCUSE ME, OWL, BUT WHAT DOES "CRUSTIMONEY PROSEEDCAKE" MEAN?
FOR I AM A BEAR OF VERY LITTLE BRAIN AND LONG WORDS BOTHER ME.
OH. IT MEANS "THE THING TO DO."
OH. WELL, AS LONG AS IT MEANS THAT, I DON'T MIND.
SIGH

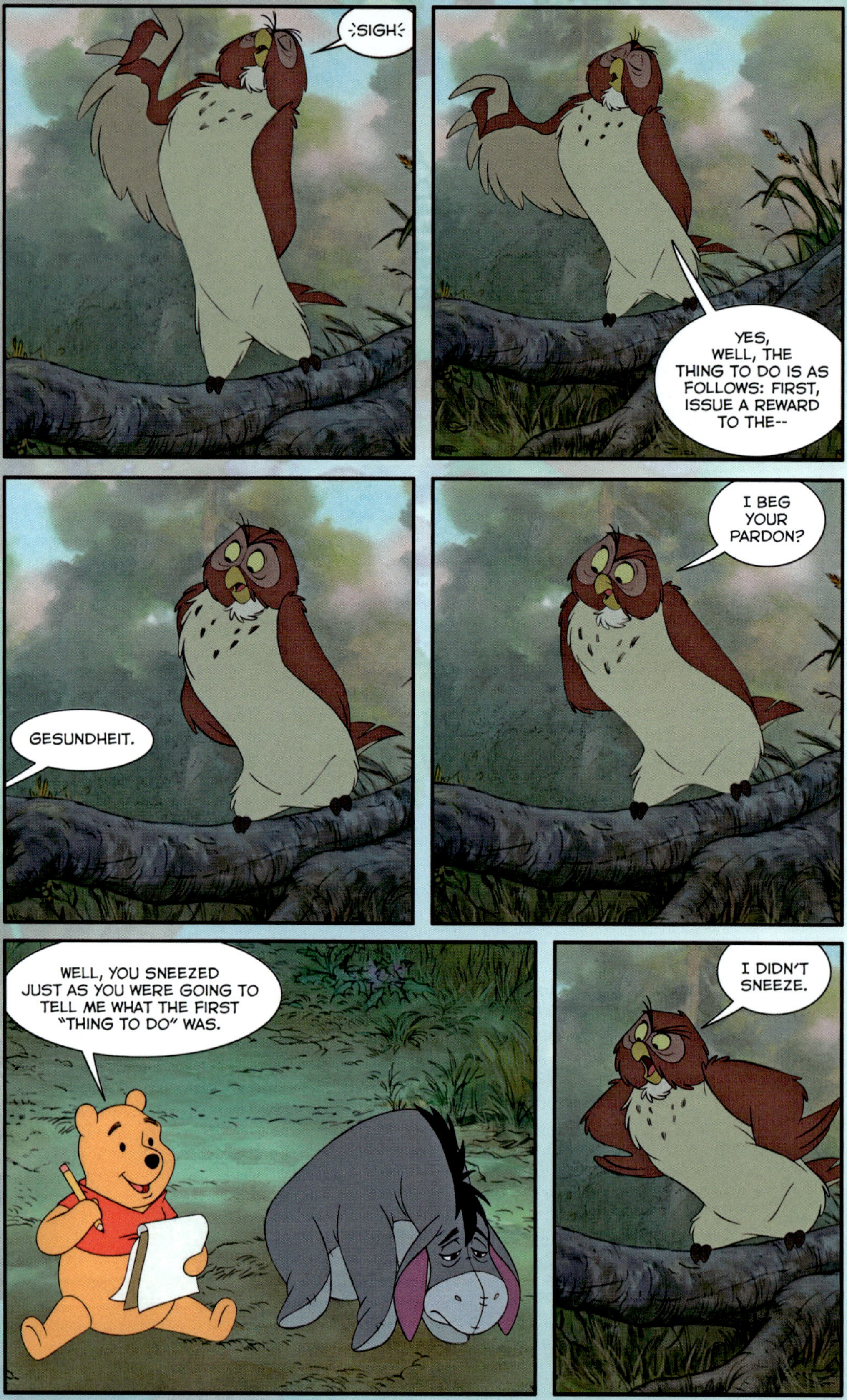

SIGH
YES, WELL, THE THING TO DO IS AS FOLLOWS: FIRST, ISSUE A REWARD TO THE--
GESUNDHEIT.
I BEG YOUR PARDON?
WELL, YOU SNEEZED JUST AS YOU WERE GOING TO TELL ME WHAT THE FIRST "THING TO DO" WAS.
I DIDN'T SNEEZE.

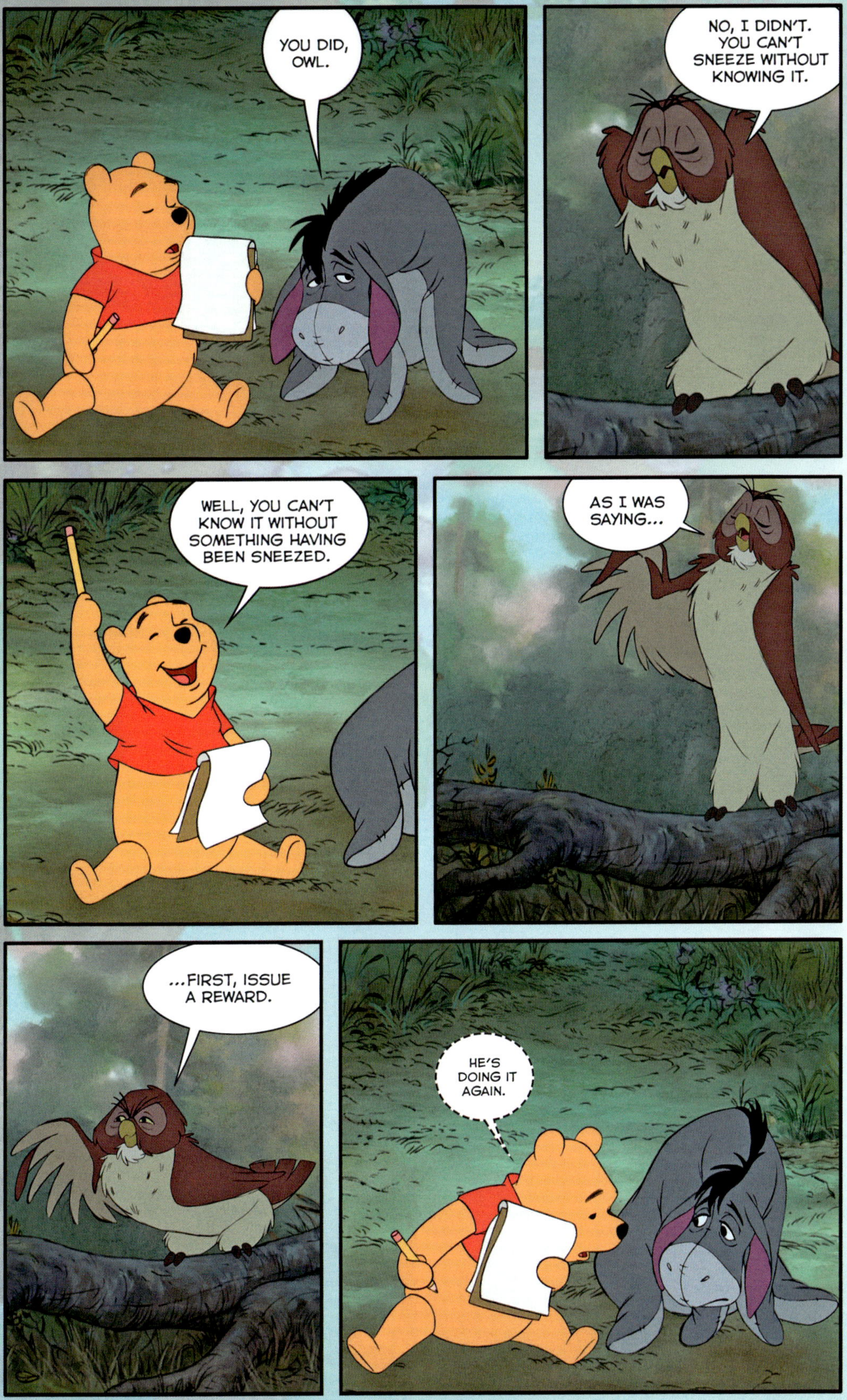
YOU DID, OWL.
NO, I DIDN'T. YOU CAN'T SNEEZE WITHOUT KNOWING IT.
WELL, YOU CAN'T KNOW IT WITHOUT SOMETHING HAVING BEEN SNEEZED.
AS I WAS SAYING...
...FIRST, ISSUE A REWARD.
HE'S DOING IT AGAIN.

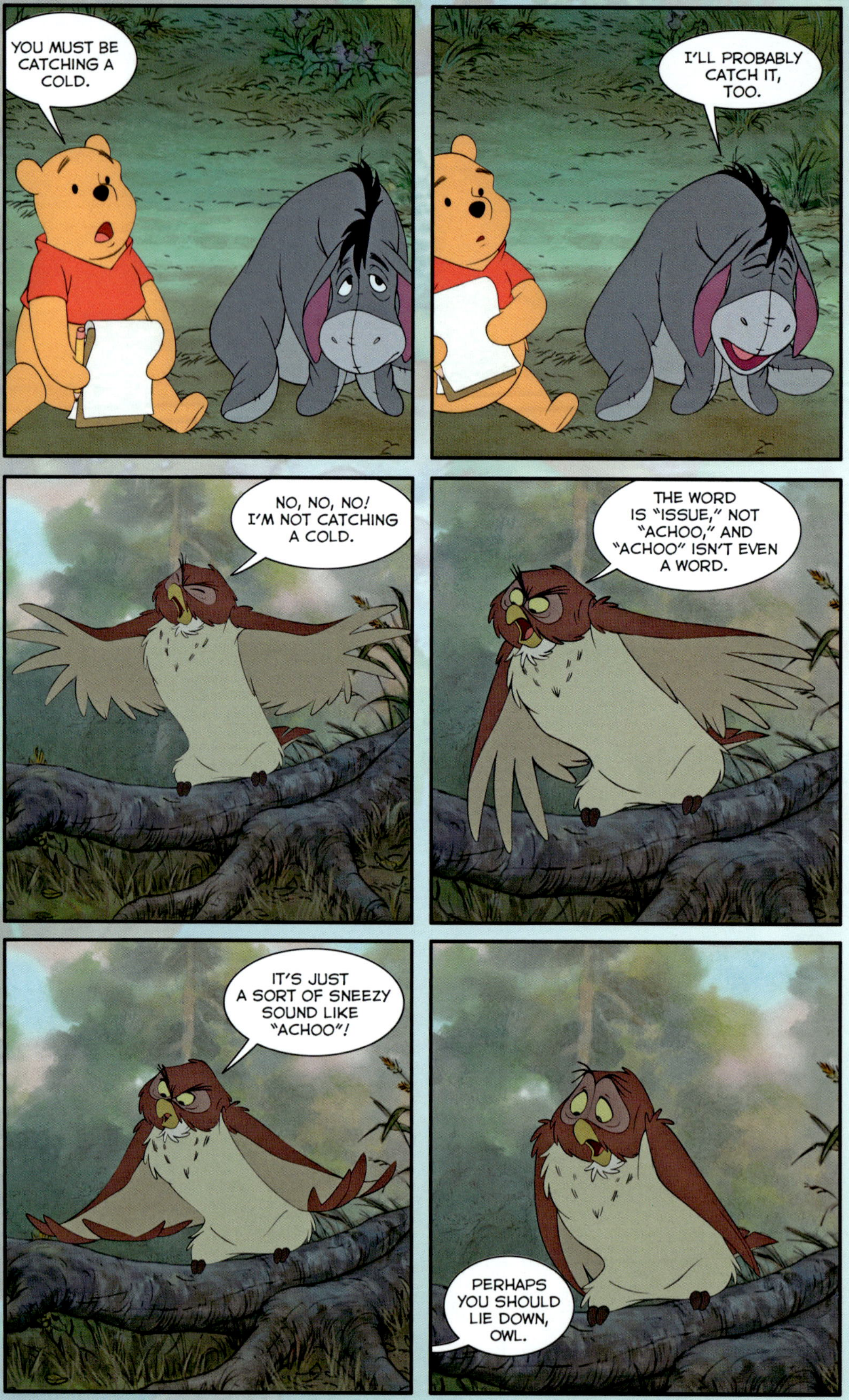
YOU MUST BE CATCHING A COLD.
I'LL PROBABLY CATCH IT, TOO.
NO, NO, NO! I'M NOT CATCHING A COLD.
THE WORD IS "ISSUE," NOT "ACHOO," AND "ACHOO" ISN'T EVEN A WORD.
IT'S JUST A SORT OF SNEEZY SOUND LIKE "ACHOO"!
PERHAPS YOU SHOULD LIE DOWN, OWL.

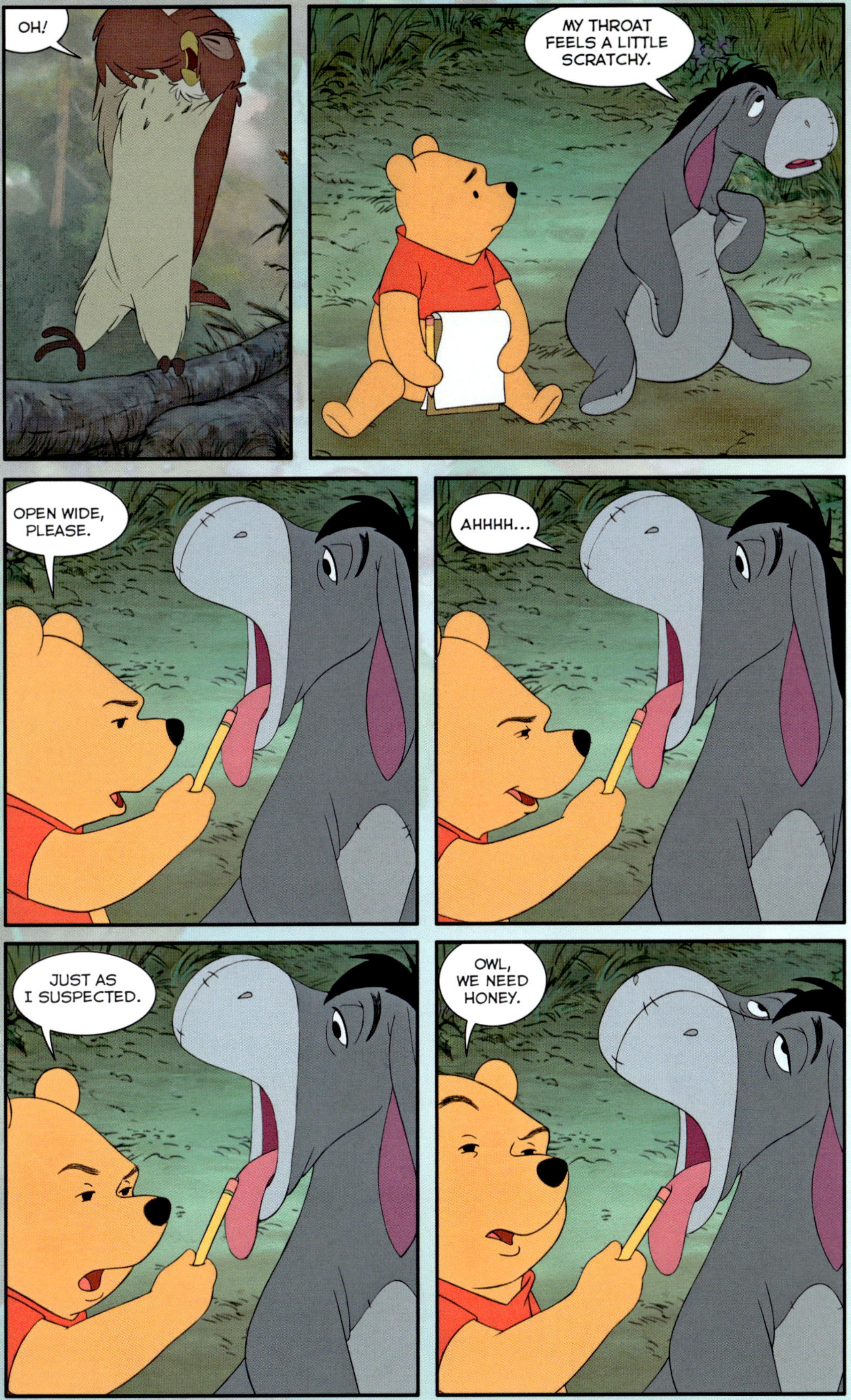
OH!
MY THROAT FEELS A LITTLE SCRATCHY.
OPEN WIDE, PLEASE.
AHHHH...
JUST AS I SUSPECTED.
OWL, WE NEED HONEY.

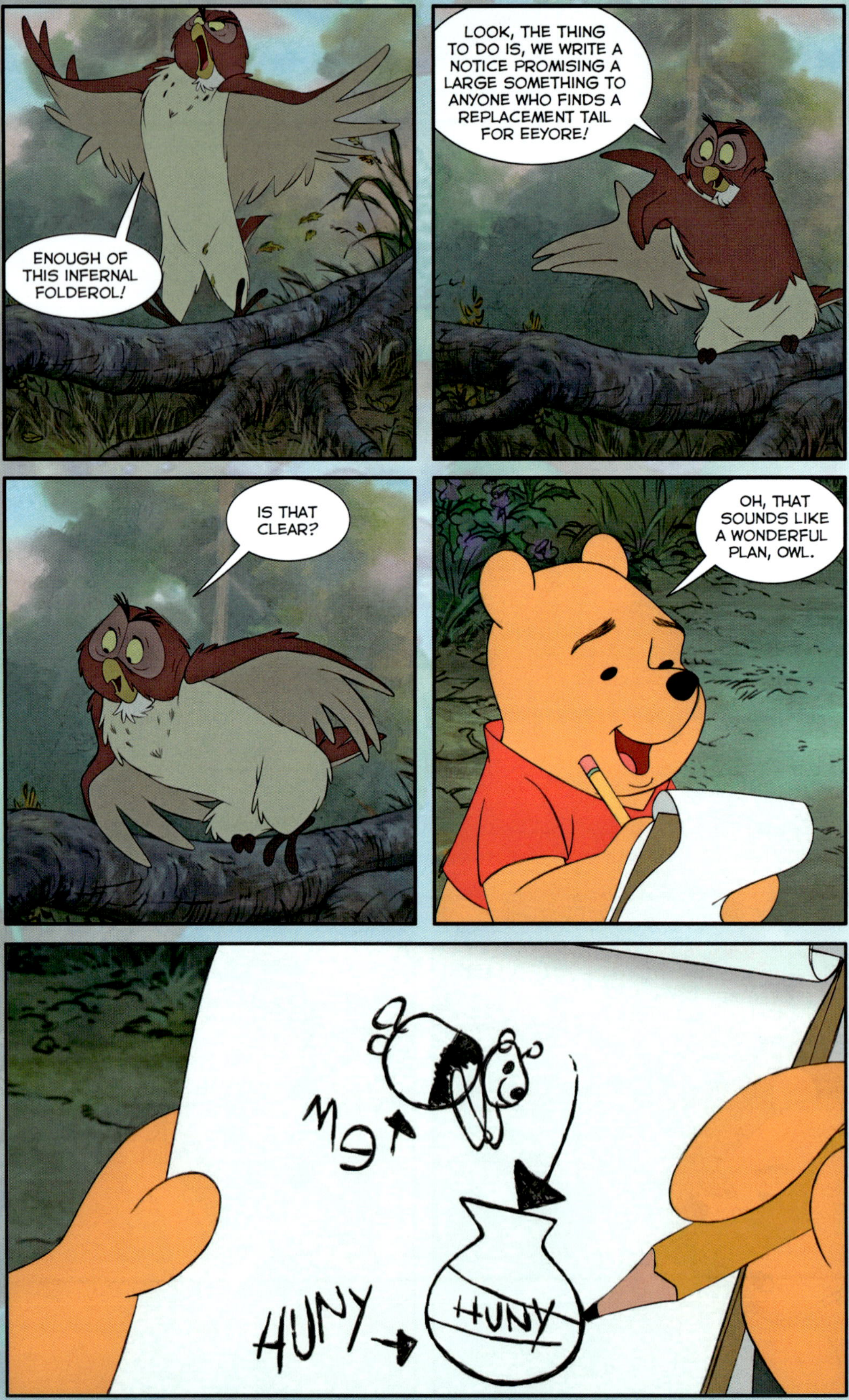
ENOUGH OF THIS INFERNAL FOLDEROL!
LOOK, THE THING TO DO IS, WE WRITE A NOTICE PROMISING A LARGE SOMETHING TO ANYONE WHO FINDS A REPLACEMENT TAIL FOR EEYORE!
IS THAT CLEAR?
OH, THAT SOUNDS LIKE A WONDERFUL PLAN, OWL.
HUNY
HUNY

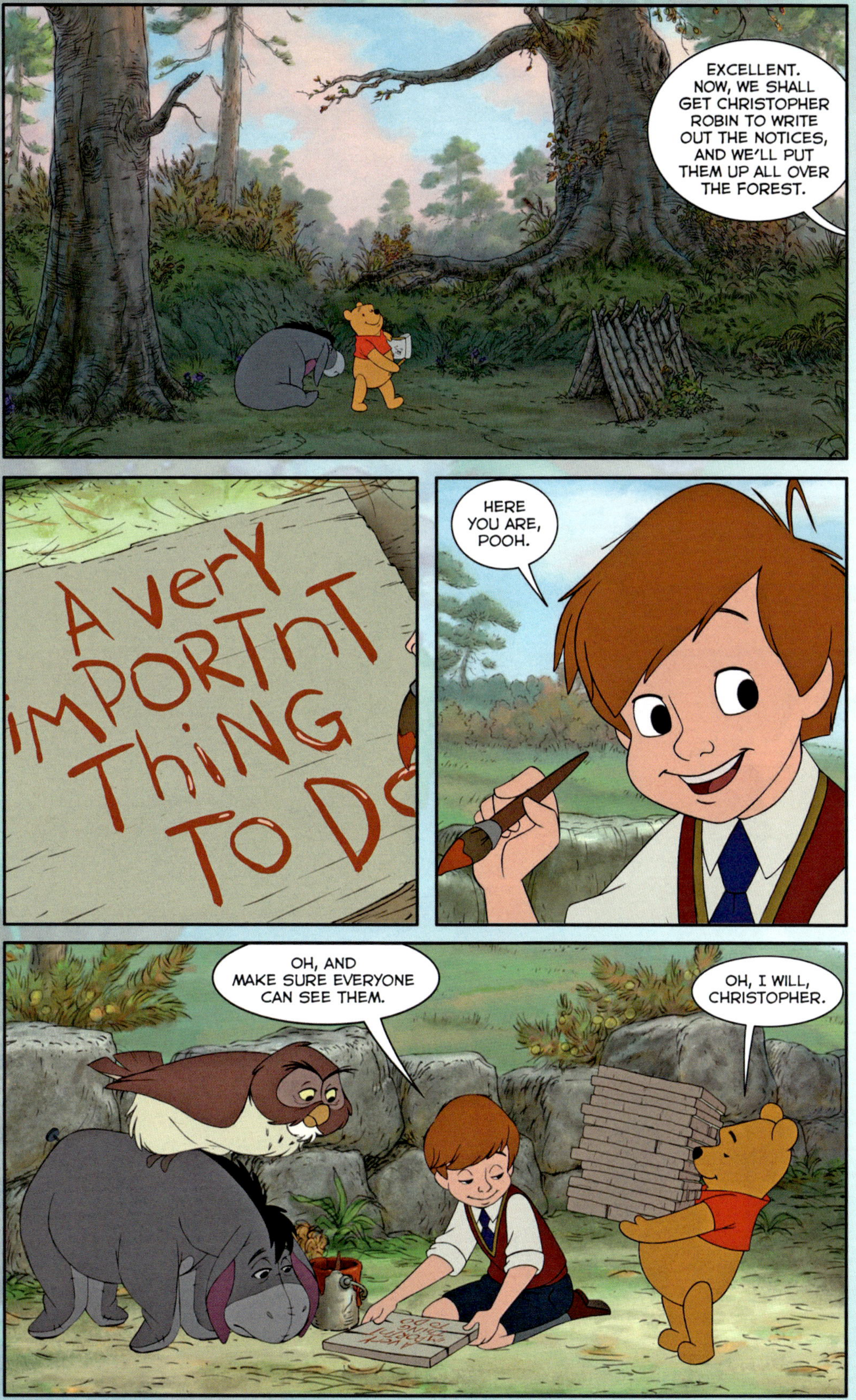

EXCELLENT. NOW, WE SHALL GET CHRISTOPHER ROBIN TO WRITE OUT THE NOTICES, AND WE'LL PUT THEM UP ALL OVER THE FOREST.
A very importnt thing To Do
HERE YOU ARE, POOH.
OH, AND MAKE SURE EVERYONE CAN SEE THEM.
OH, I WILL, CHRISTOPHER.

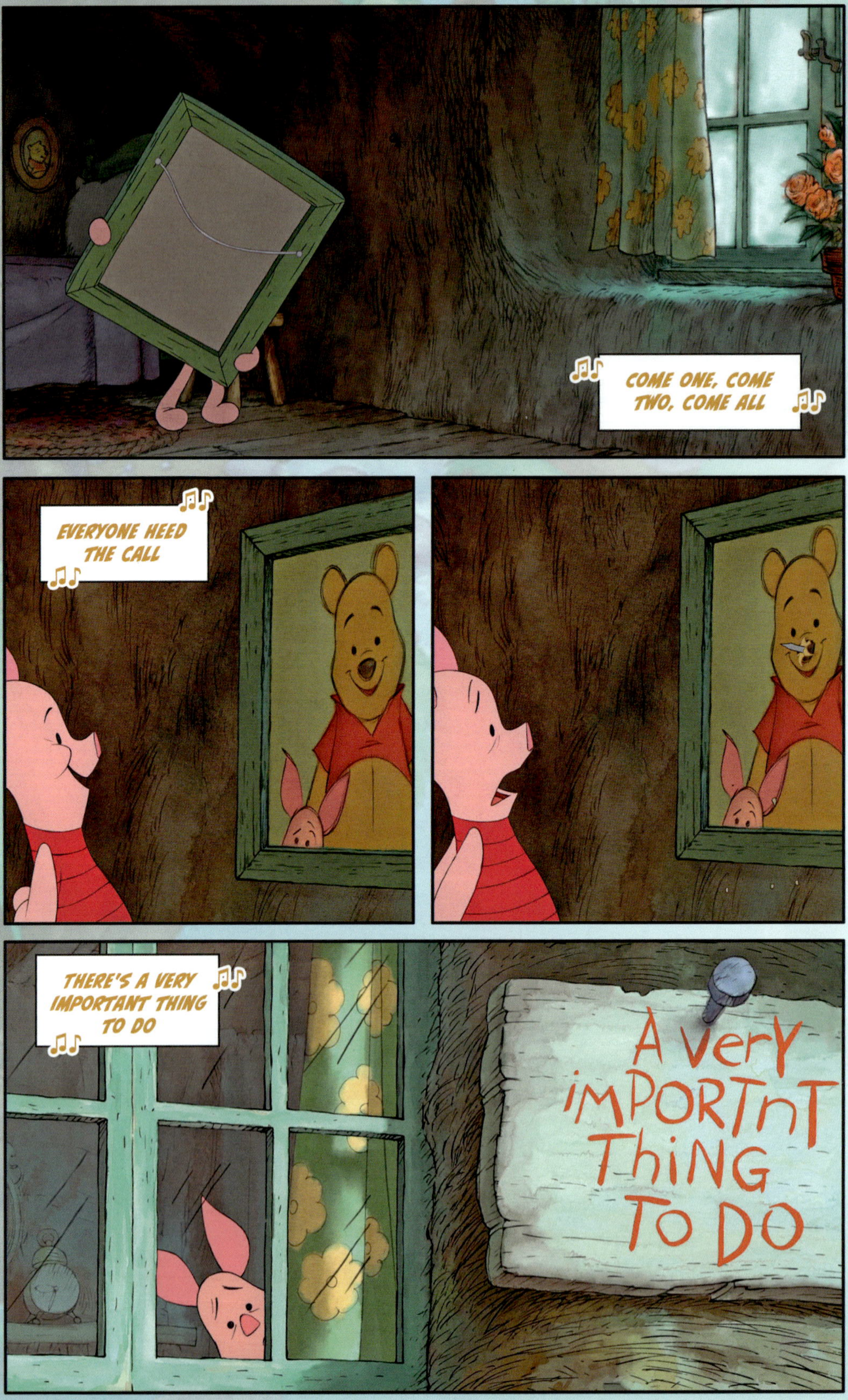
COME ONE, COME TWO, COME ALL
EVERYONE HEED THE CALL
THERE'S A VERY IMPORTANT THING TO DO
A very
iMPORTnT
Thing
To Do

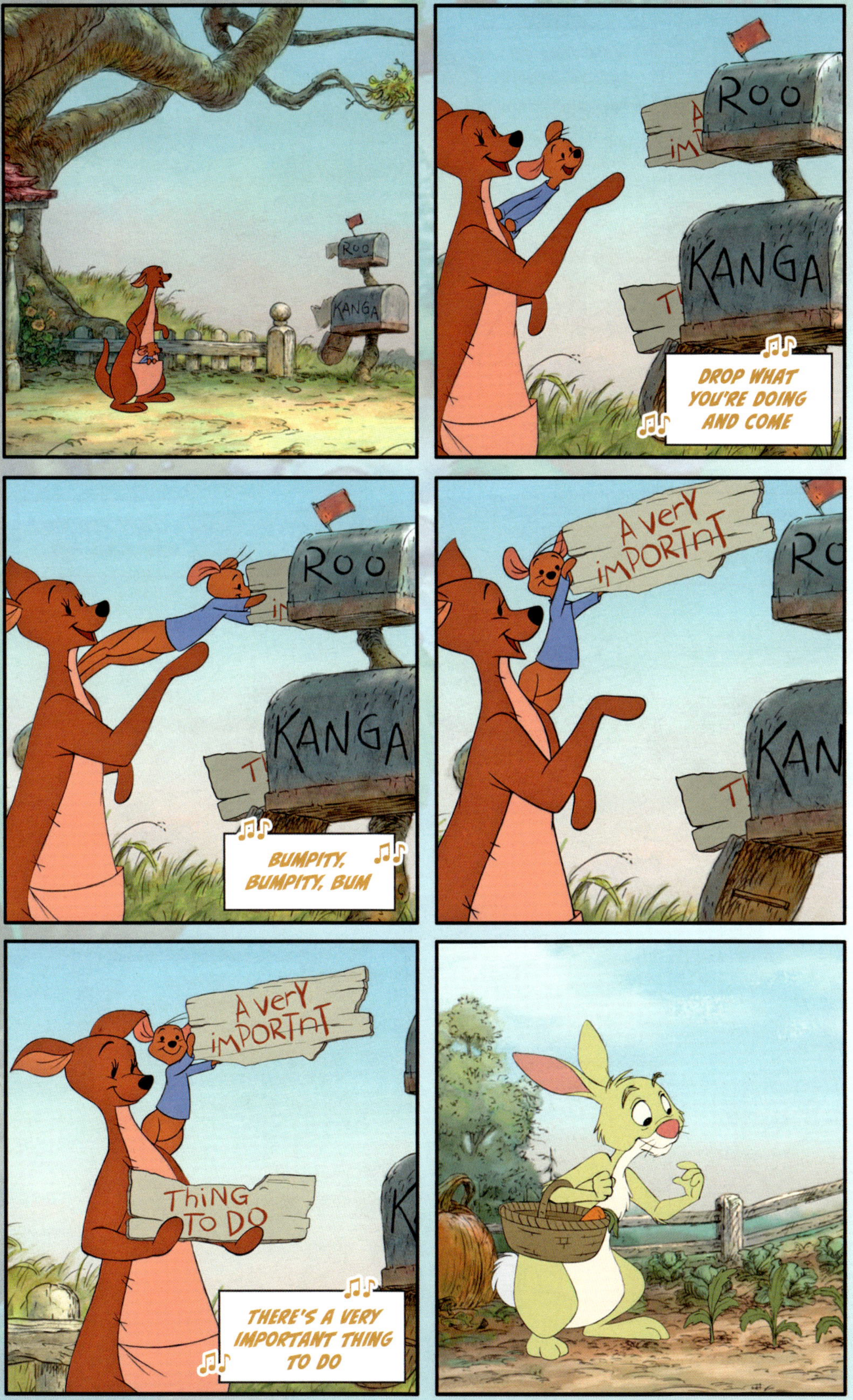
ROO
KANGA
ROO
KANGA
DROP WHAT YOU'RE DOING AND COME
ROO
KANGA
BUMPITY, BUMPITY, BUM
A very IMPORTAT
A very IMPORTAT
ThiNG TO DO
THERE'S A VERY IMPORTANT THING TO DO

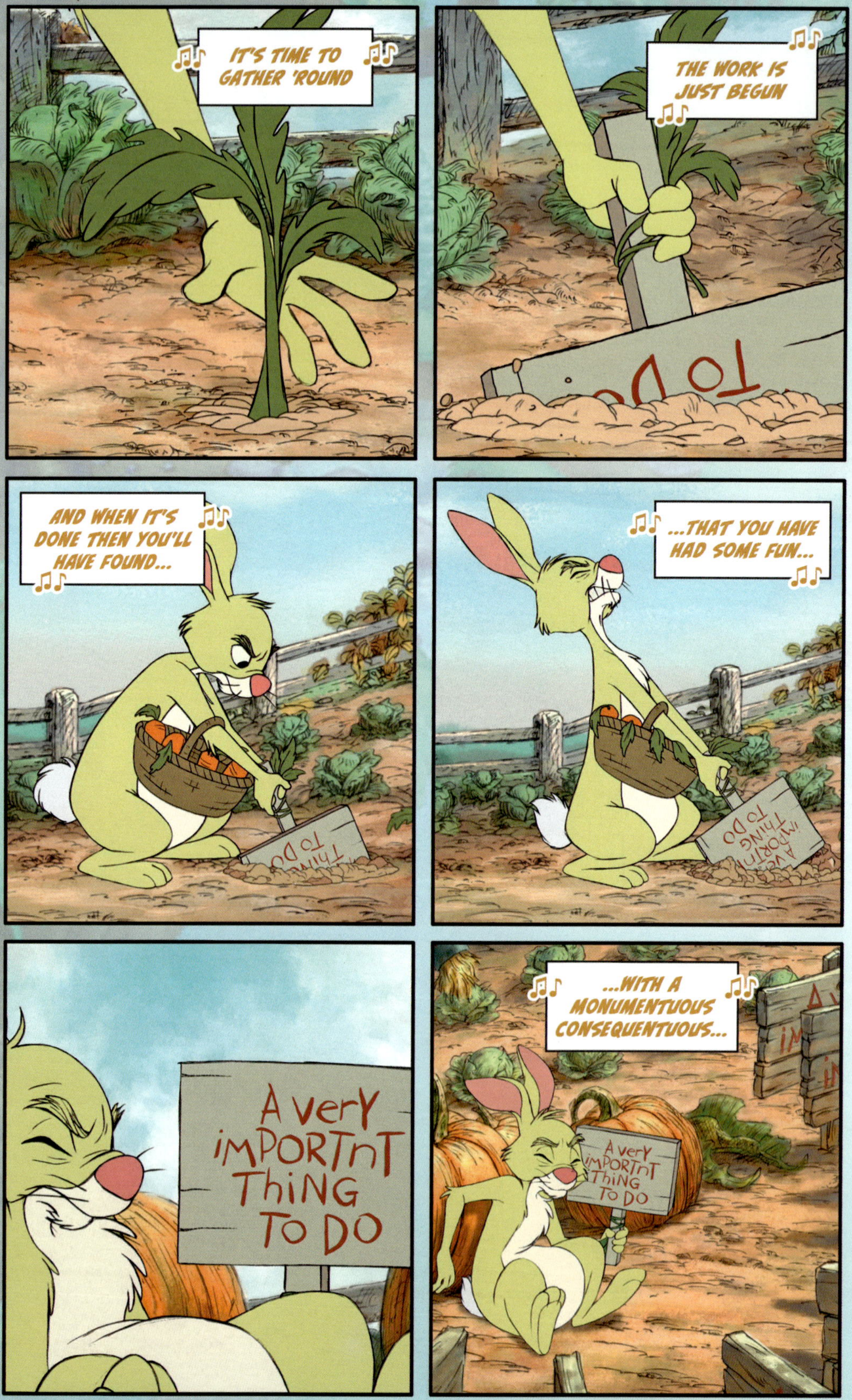
IT'S TIME TO GATHER 'ROUND
THE WORK IS JUST BEGUN
AND WHEN IT'S DONE THEN YOU'LL HAVE FOUND...
...THAT YOU HAVE HAD SOME FUN...
A very imPORTnT Thing TO DO
...WITH A MONUMENTUOUS CONSEQUENTUOUS...
A very imPORTnT Thing TO DO

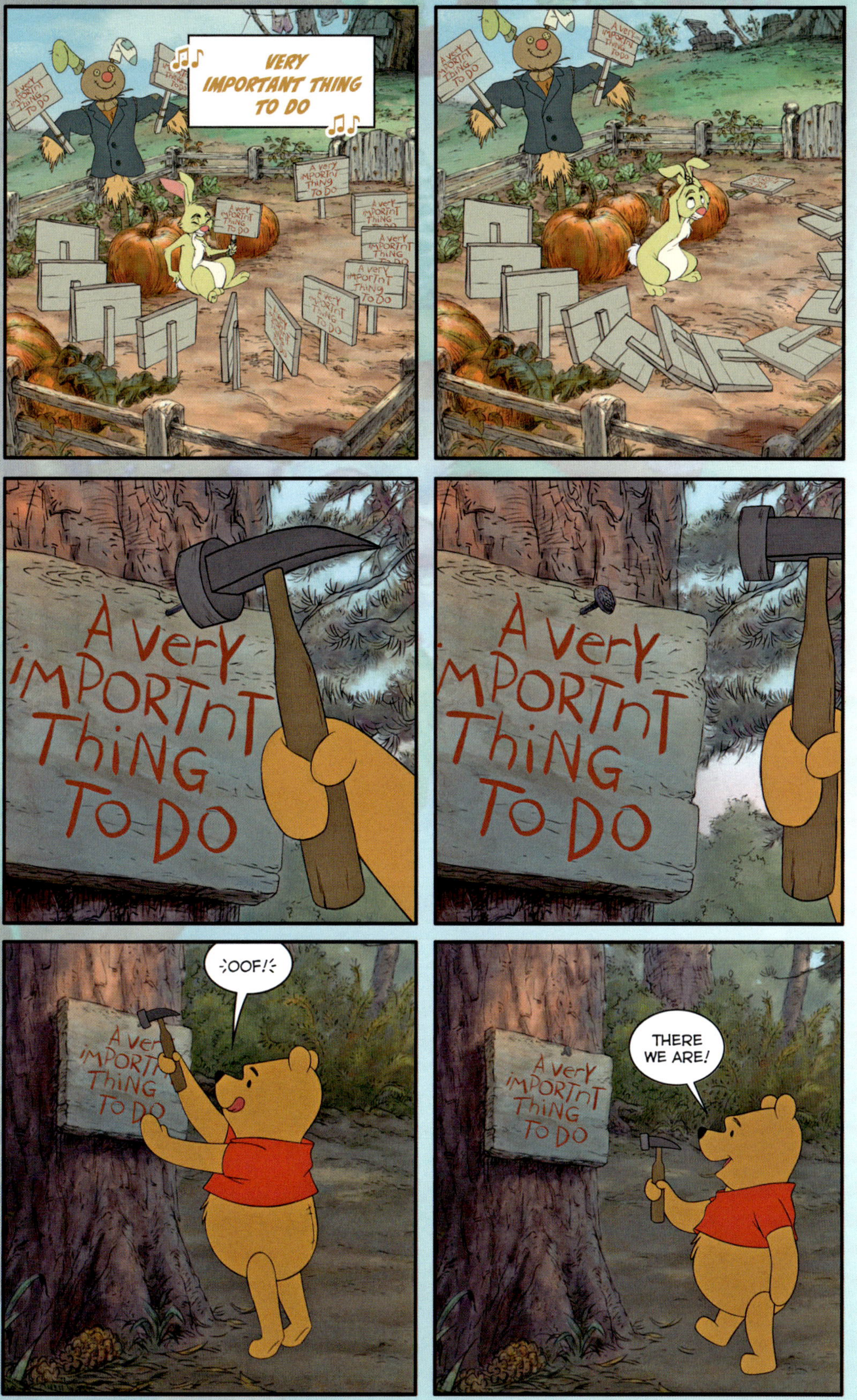
VERY IMPORTANT THING TO DO
A very iMPORTnT Thing To DO
A very iMPORTnT Thing To DO
OOF!
THERE WE ARE!

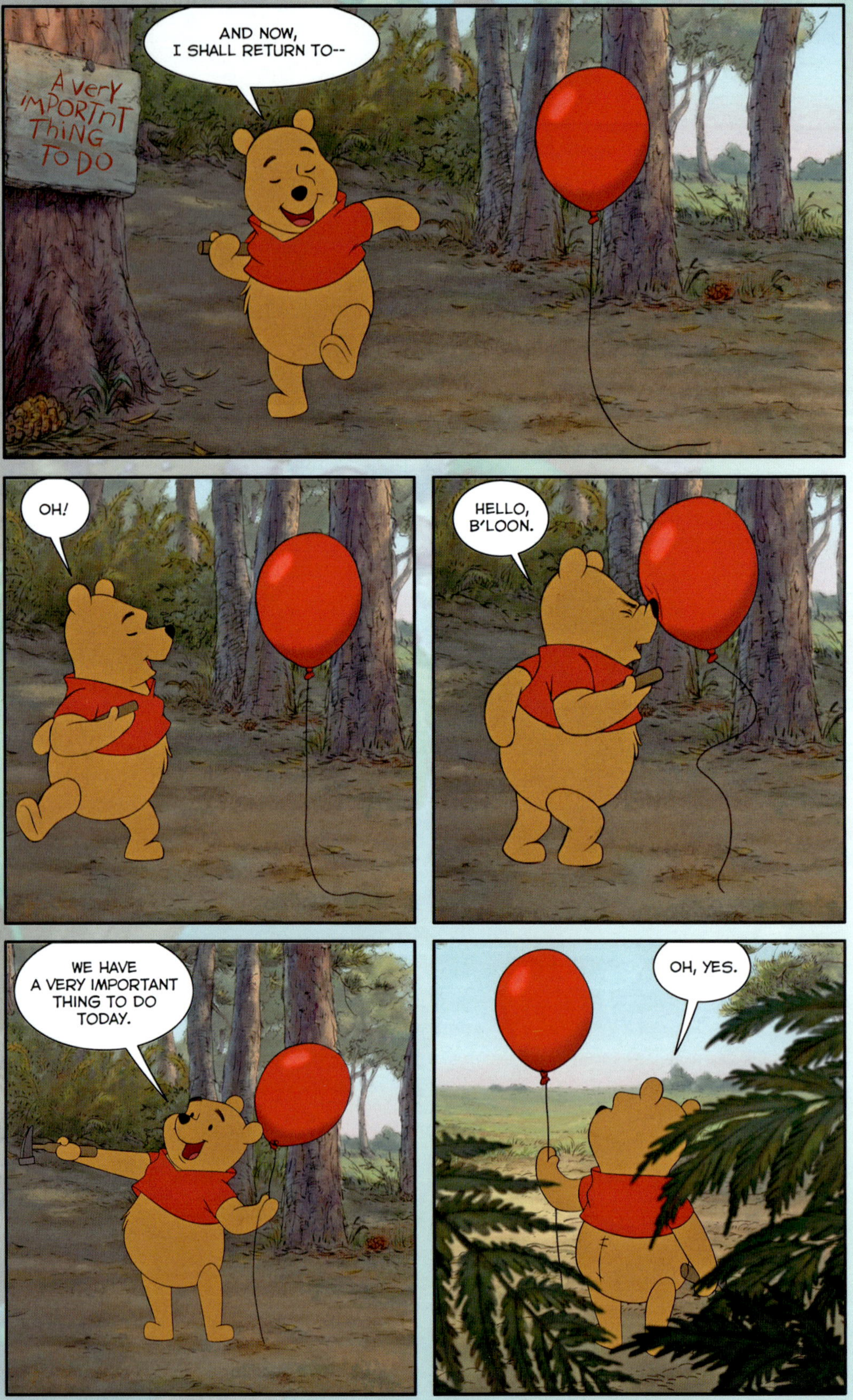
A very IMPORTnT Thing TO DO
AND NOW, I SHALL RETURN TO--
OH!
HELLO, B'LOON.
WE HAVE A VERY IMPORTANT THING TO DO TODAY.
OH, YES.

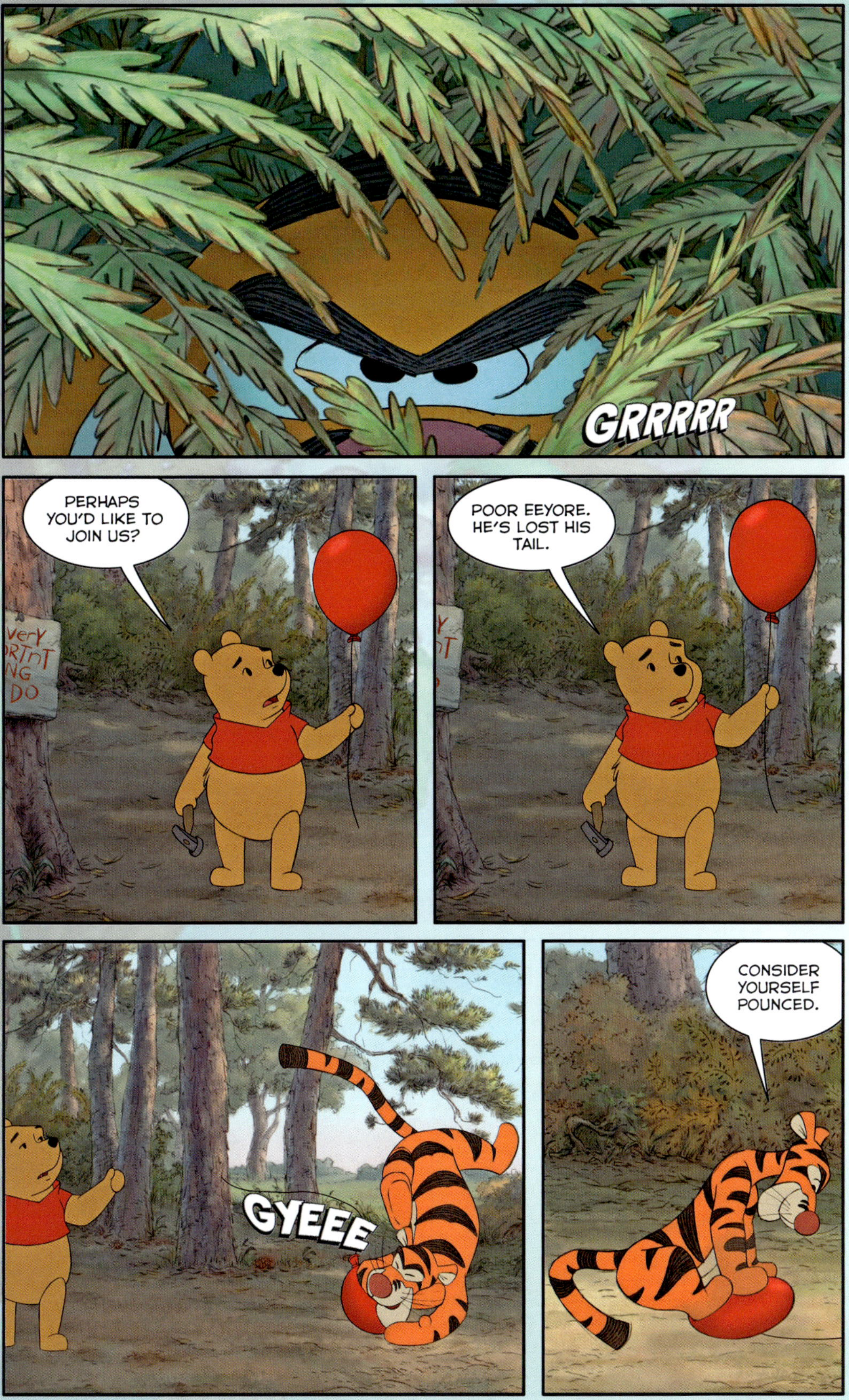
GRRRRR
PERHAPS YOU'D LIKE TO JOIN US?
POOR EEYORE. HE'S LOST HIS TAIL.
GYEEE
CONSIDER YOURSELF POUNCED.

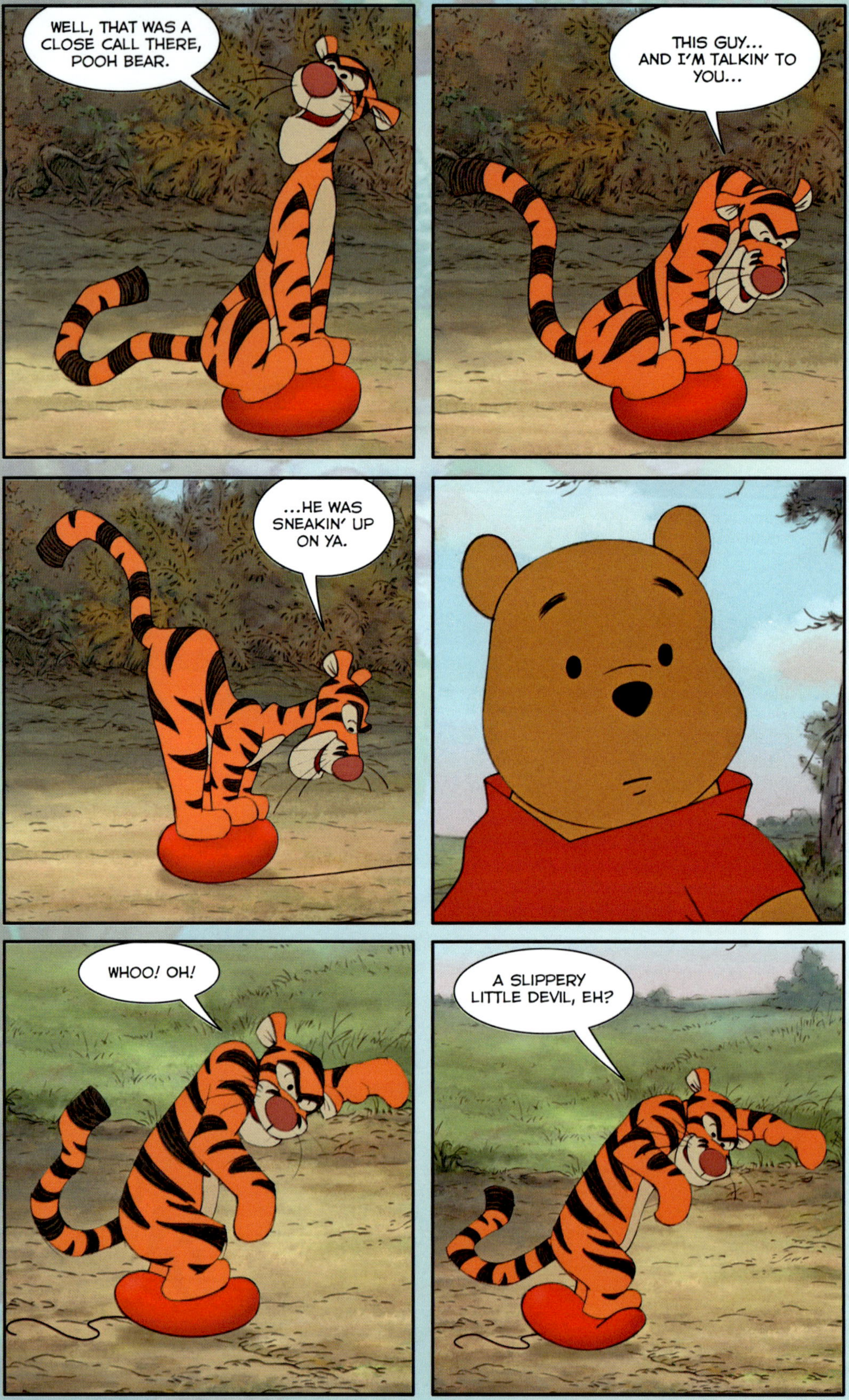
WELL, THAT WAS A CLOSE CALL THERE, POOH BEAR.
THIS GUY... AND I'M TALKIN' TO YOU...
...HE WAS SNEAKIN' UP ON YA.
WHOO! OH!
A SLIPPERY LITTLE DEVIL, EH?

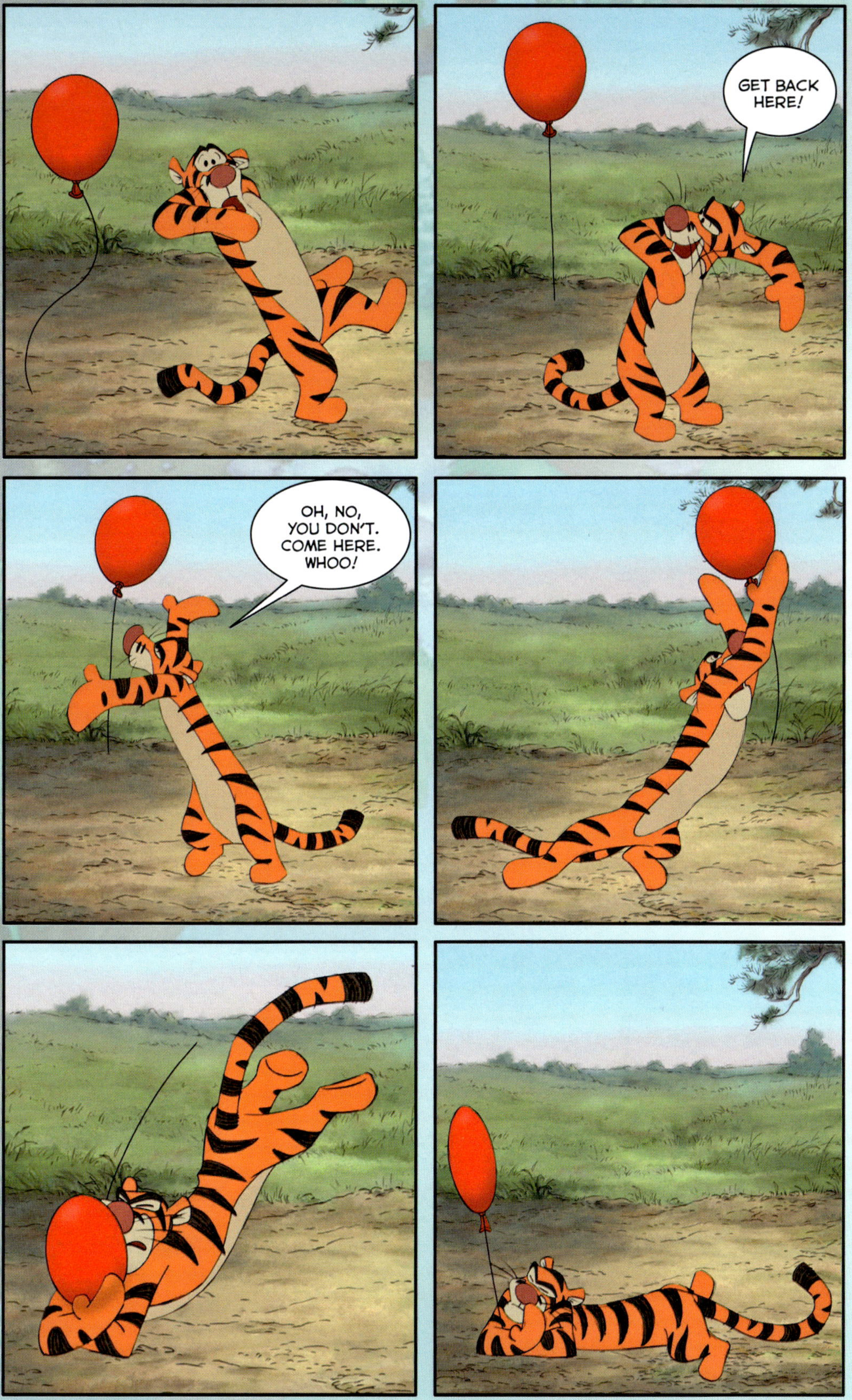
GET BACK HERE!
OH, NO, YOU DON'T. COME HERE. WHOO!

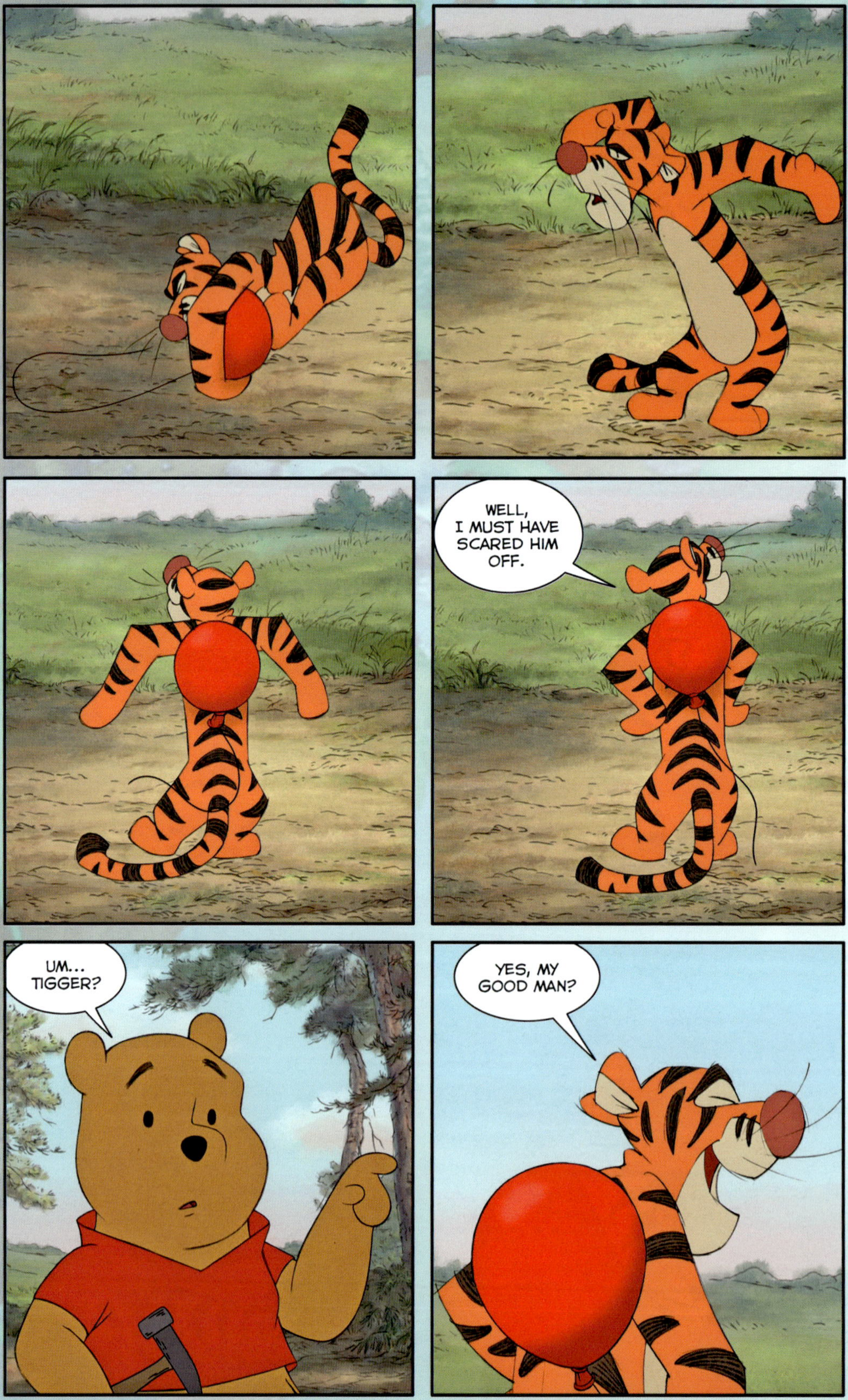
WELL, I MUST HAVE SCARED HIM OFF.
UM... TIGGER?
YES, MY GOOD MAN?

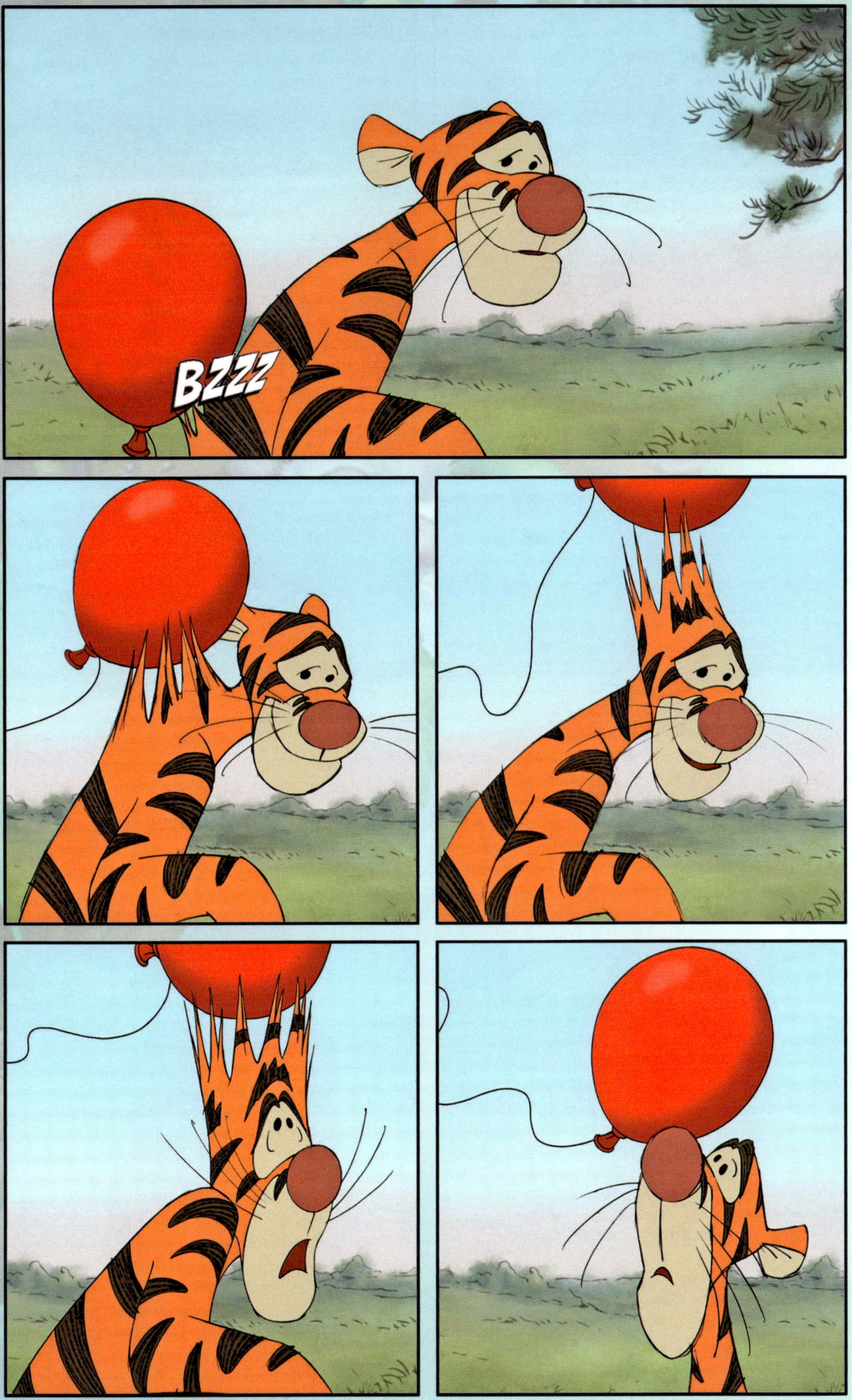
BZZZ

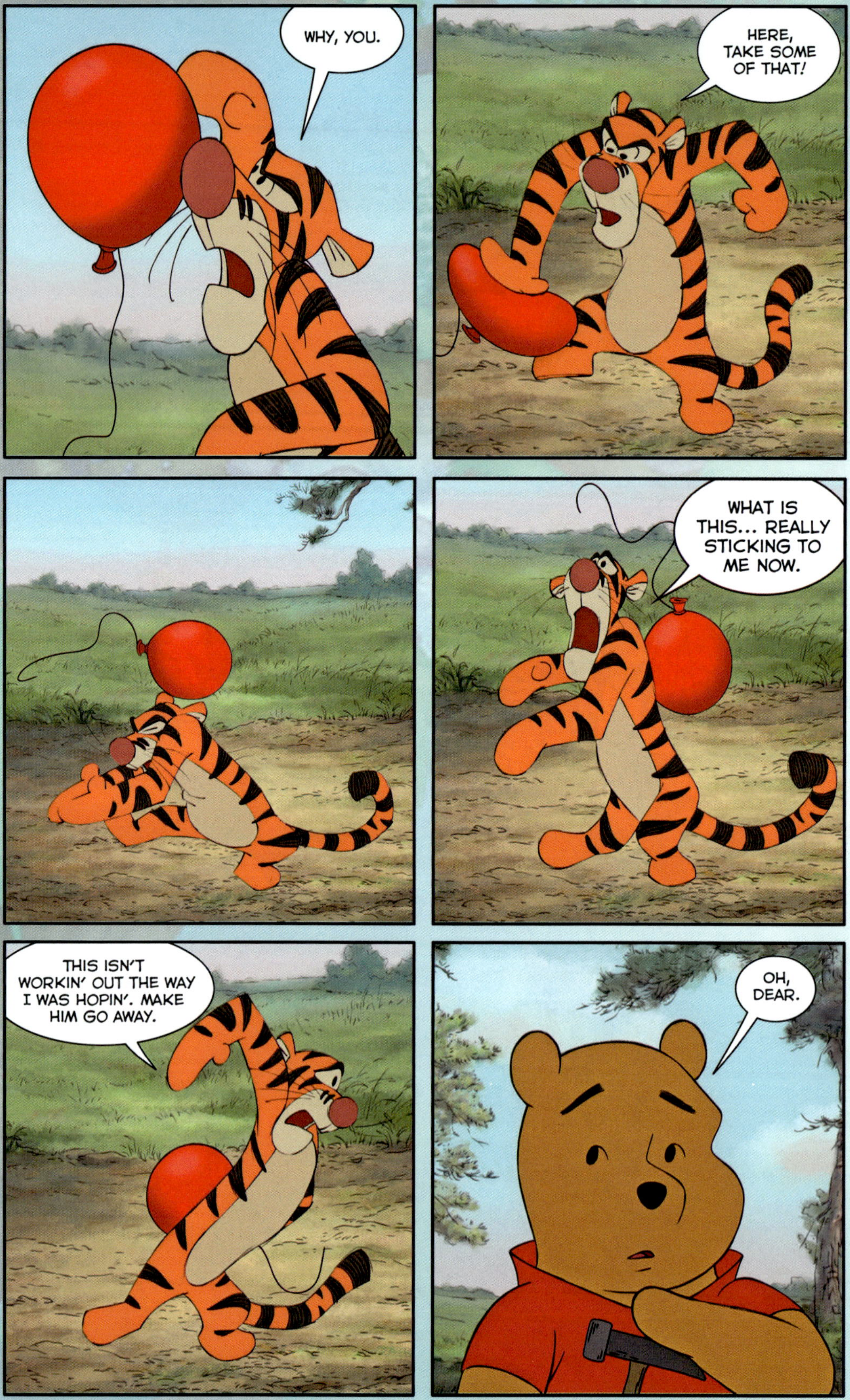
WHY, YOU.
HERE, TAKE SOME OF THAT!
WHAT IS THIS... REALLY STICKING TO ME NOW.
THIS ISN'T WORKIN' OUT THE WAY I WAS HOPIN'. MAKE HIM GO AWAY.
OH, DEAR.

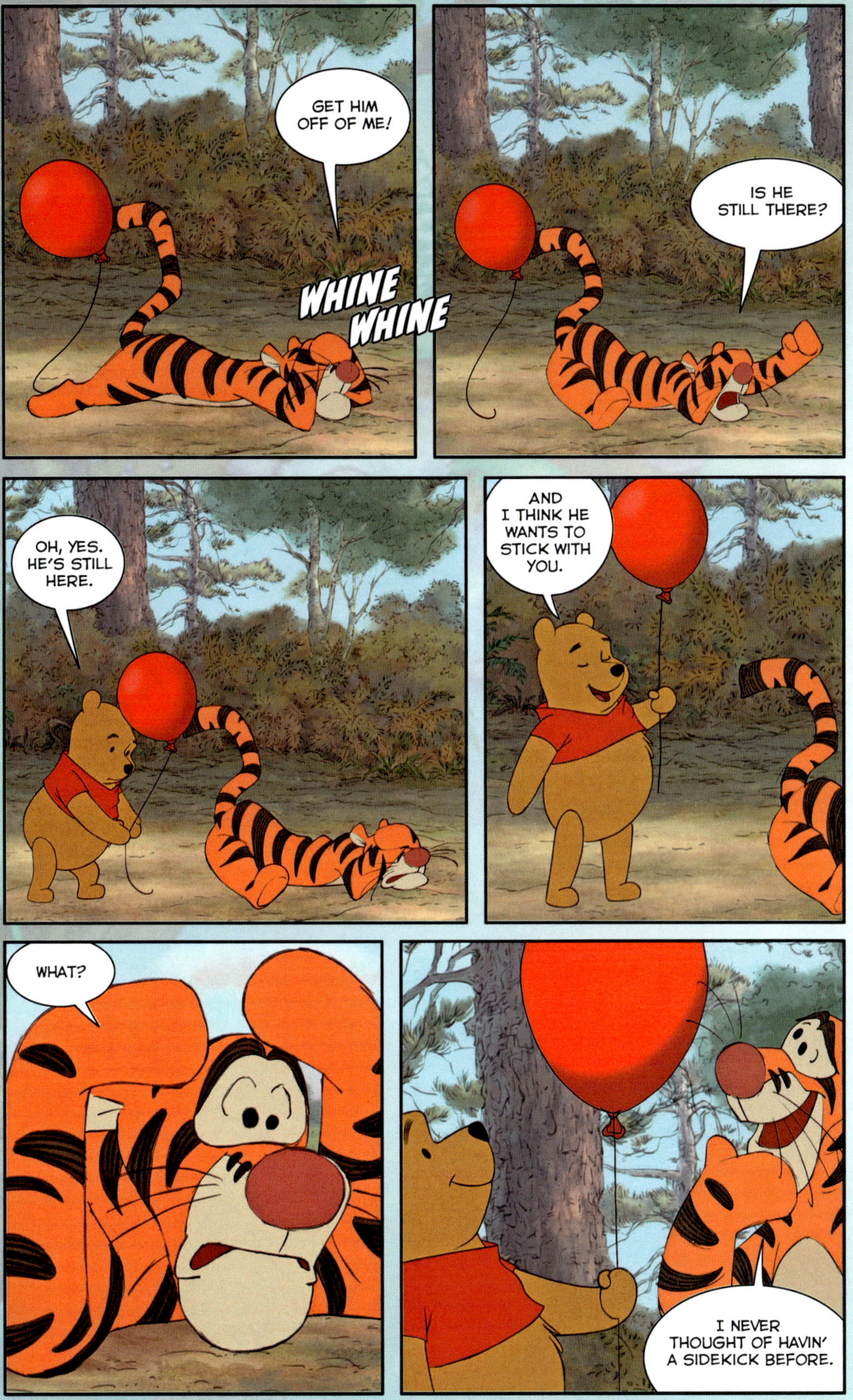
GET HIM OFF OF ME!
WHINE WHINE
IS HE STILL THERE?
OH, YES. HE'S STILL HERE.
AND I THINK HE WANTS TO STICK WITH YOU.
WHAT?
I NEVER THOUGHT OF HAVIN' A SIDEKICK BEFORE.

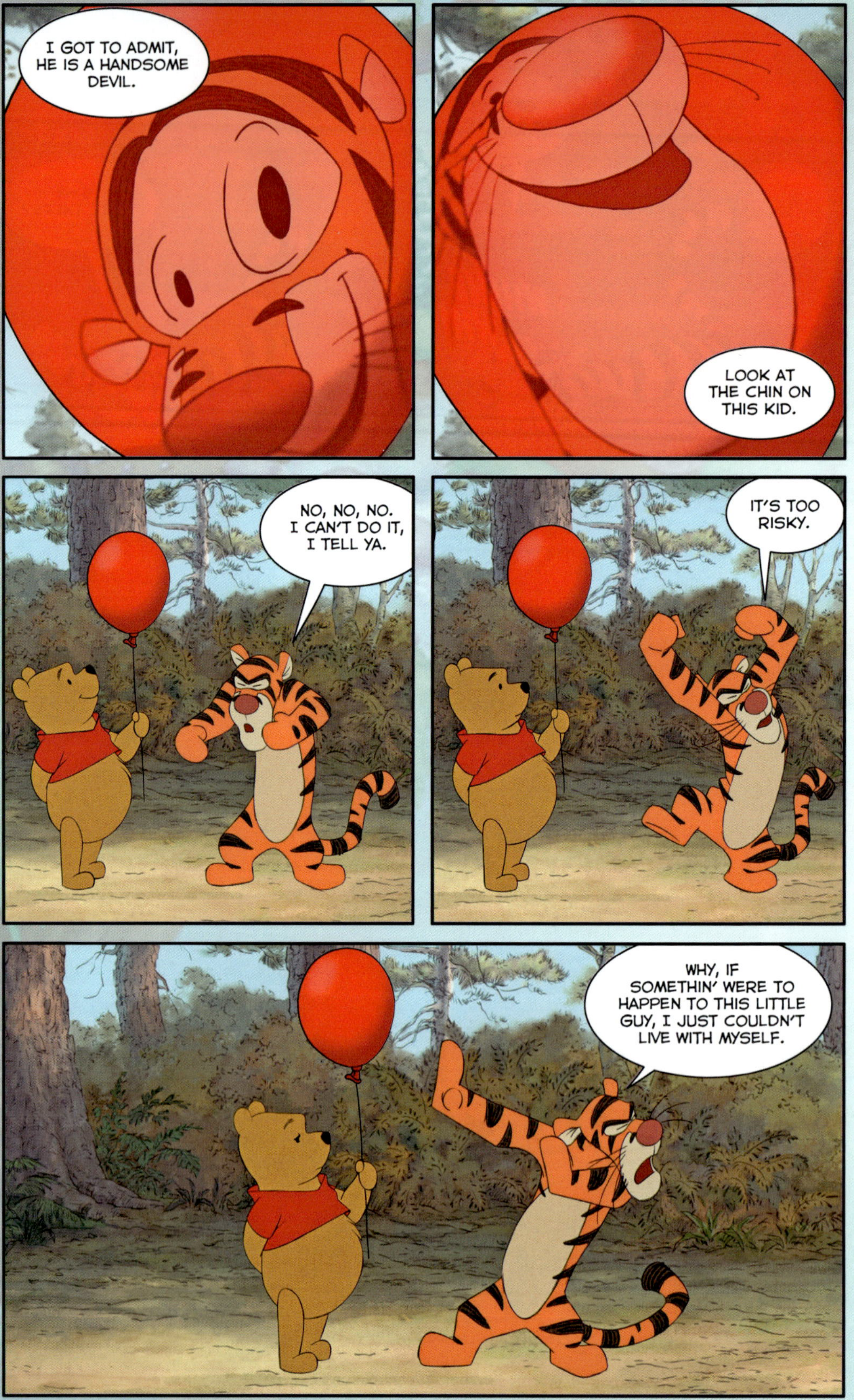
I GOT TO ADMIT, HE IS A HANDSOME DEVIL.
LOOK AT THE CHIN ON THIS KID.
NO, NO, NO. I CAN'T DO IT, I TELL YA.
IT'S TOO RISKY.
WHY, IF SOMETHIN' WERE TO HAPPEN TO THIS LITTLE GUY, I JUST COULDN'T LIVE WITH MYSELF.

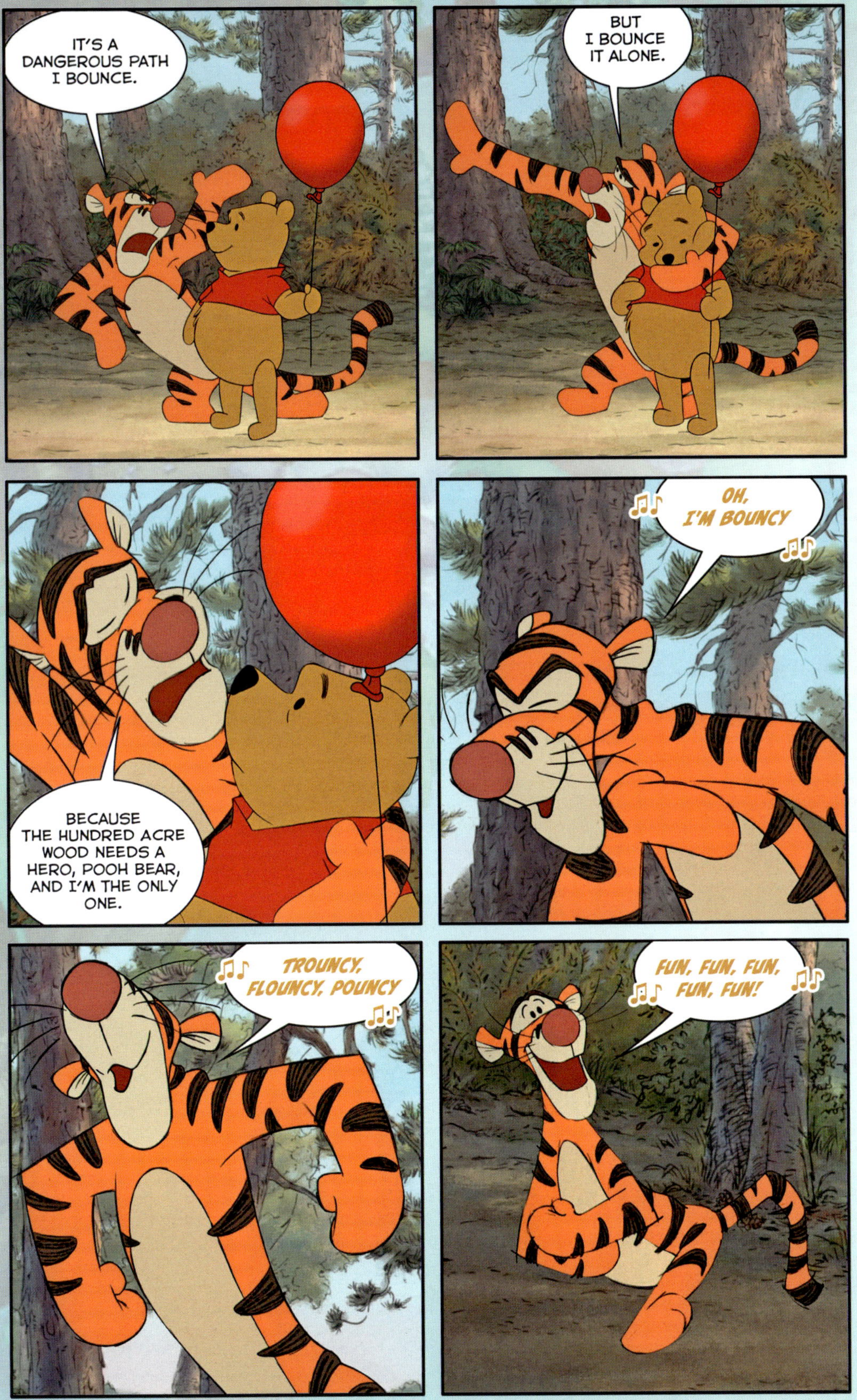
IT'S A DANGEROUS PATH I BOUNCE.
BUT I BOUNCE IT ALONE.
BECAUSE THE HUNDRED ACRE WOOD NEEDS A HERO, POOH BEAR, AND I'M THE ONLY ONE.
OH, I'M BOUNCY
TROUNCY, FLOUNCY, POUNCY
FUN, FUN, FUN, FUN, FUN!

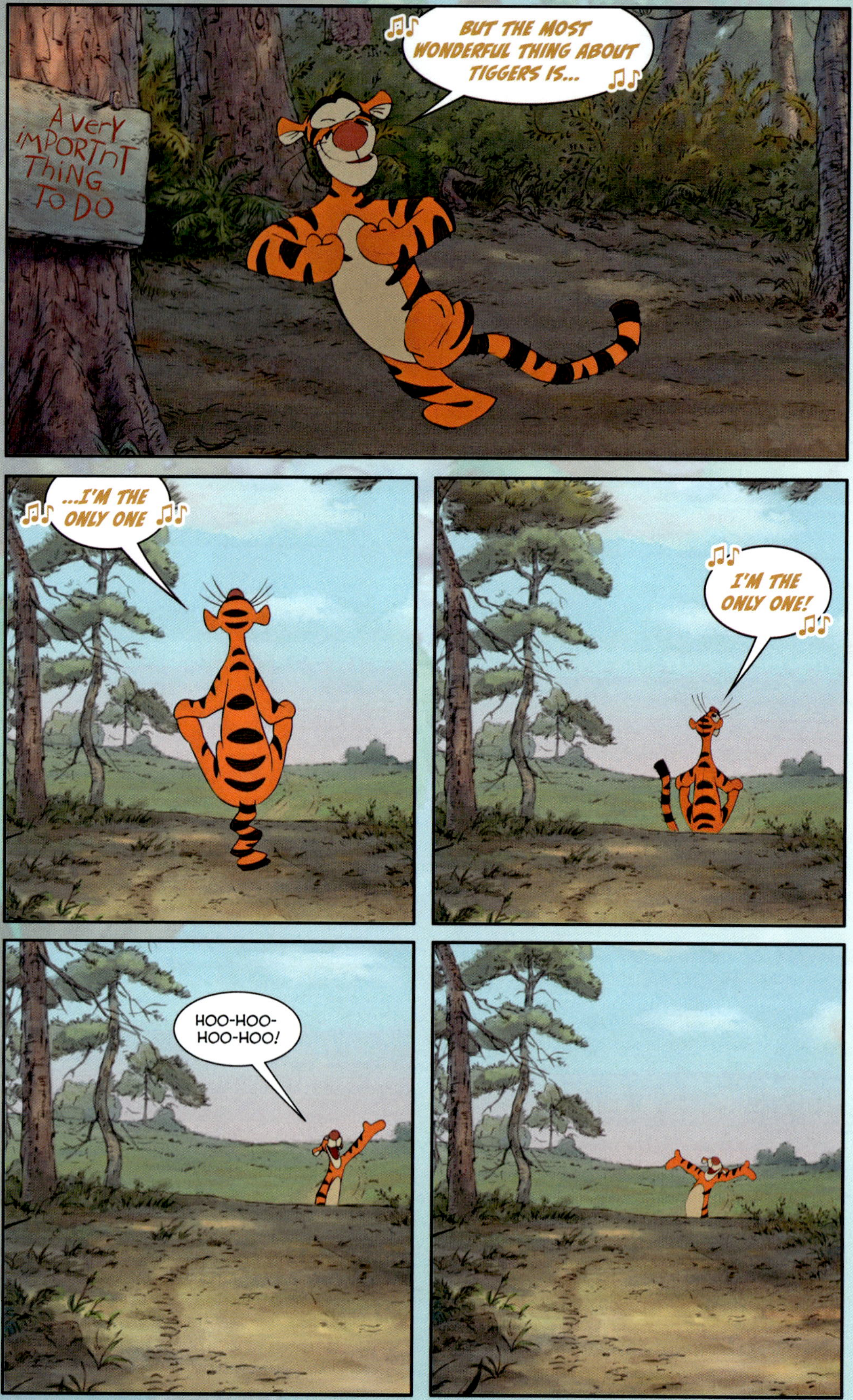
A very importnt thing to do
BUT THE MOST WONDERFUL THING ABOUT TIGGERS IS...
...I'M THE ONLY ONE
I'M THE ONLY ONE!
HOO-HOO-HOO-HOO!

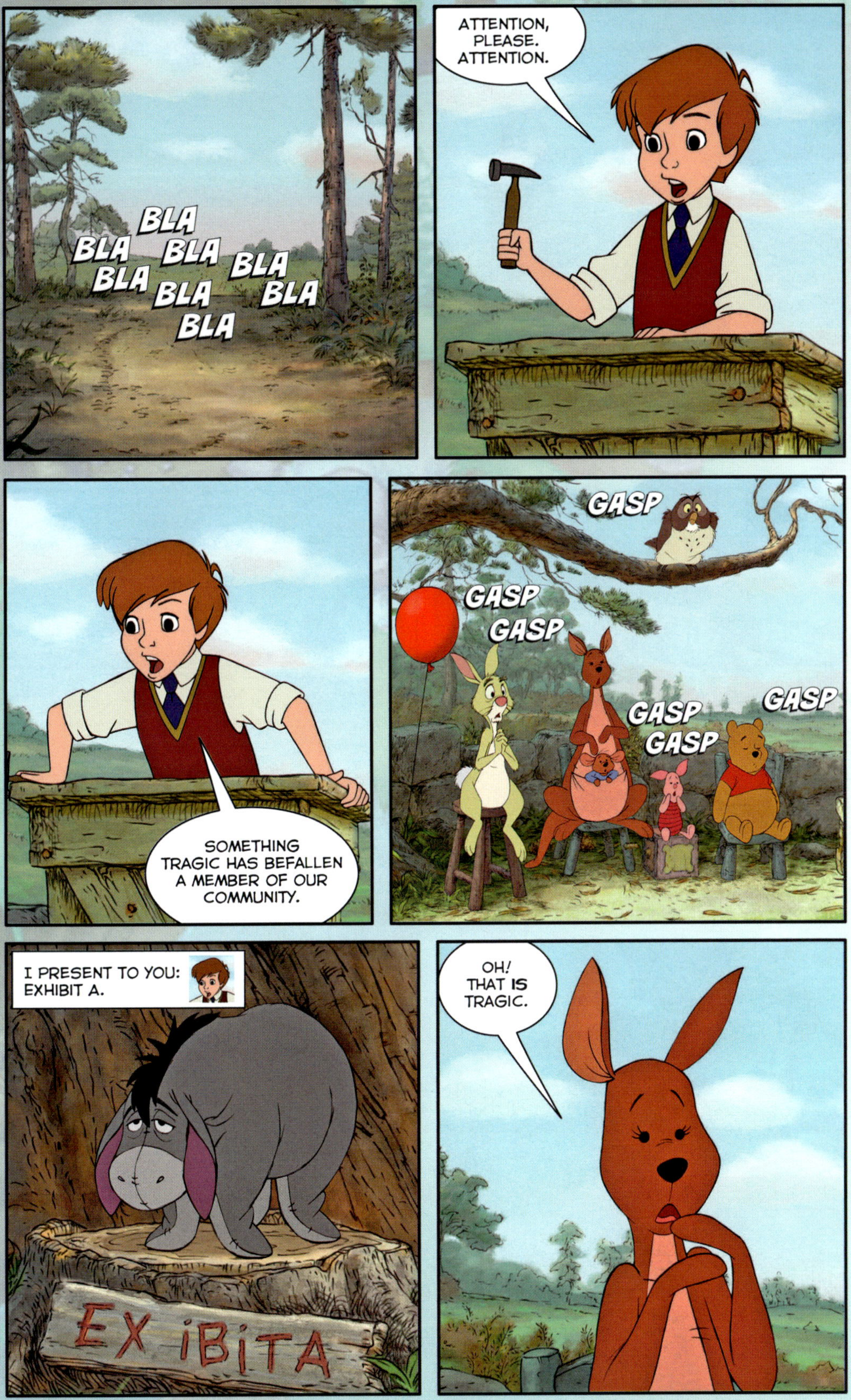
BLA BLA BLA BLA BLA BLA BLA BLA
ATTENTION, PLEASE. ATTENTION.
SOMETHING TRAGIC HAS BEFALLEN A MEMBER OF OUR COMMUNITY.
GASP
GASP
GASP
GASP
GASP
GASP
I PRESENT TO YOU: EXHIBIT A.
EX iBiTA
OH! THAT **IS** TRAGIC.

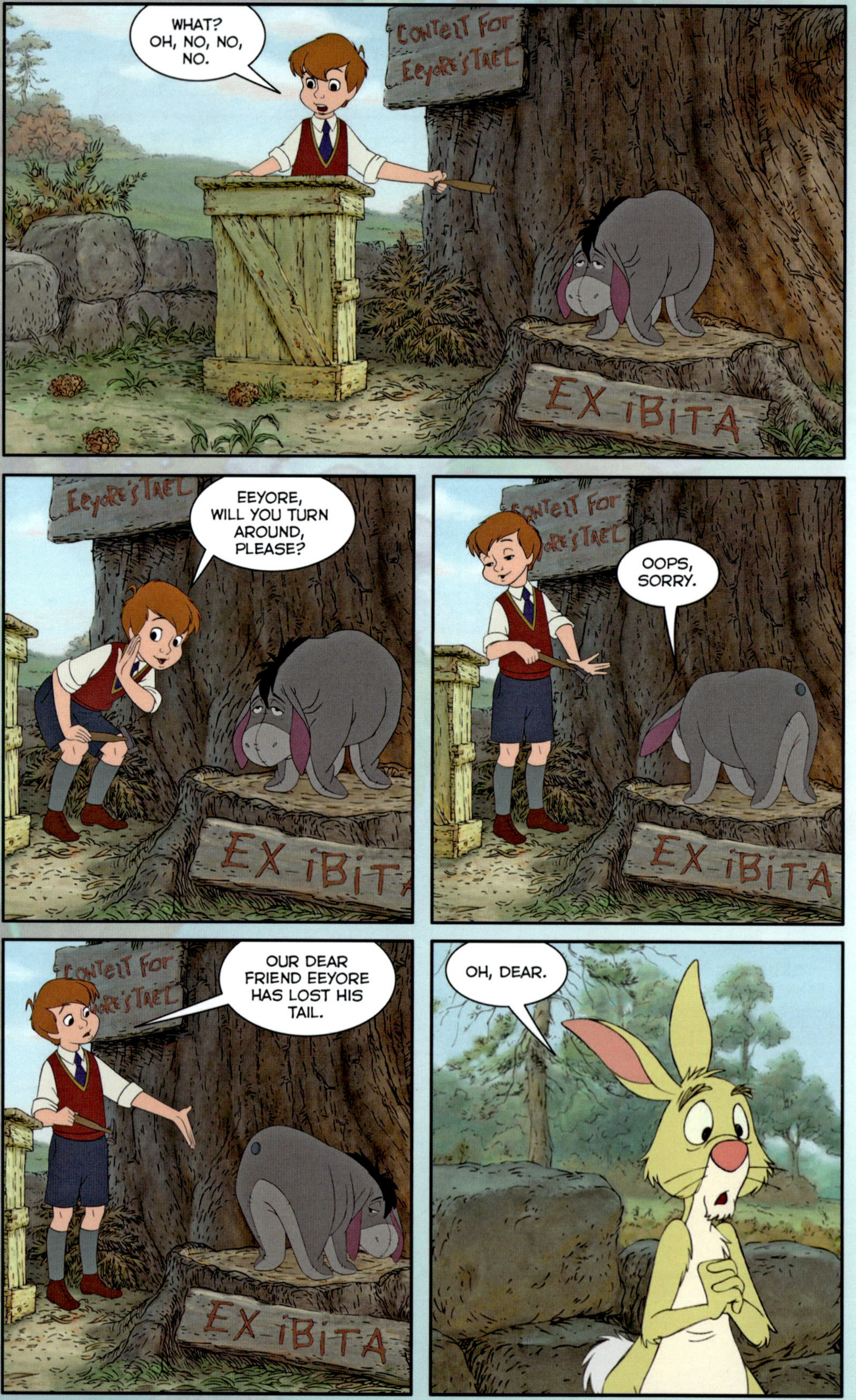

WHAT? OH, NO, NO, NO.
CONTEIT FOR EEYORE'S TAEL
EX iBITA
EEYORE, WILL YOU TURN AROUND, PLEASE?
OOPS, SORRY.
OUR DEAR FRIEND EEYORE HAS LOST HIS TAIL.
OH, DEAR.

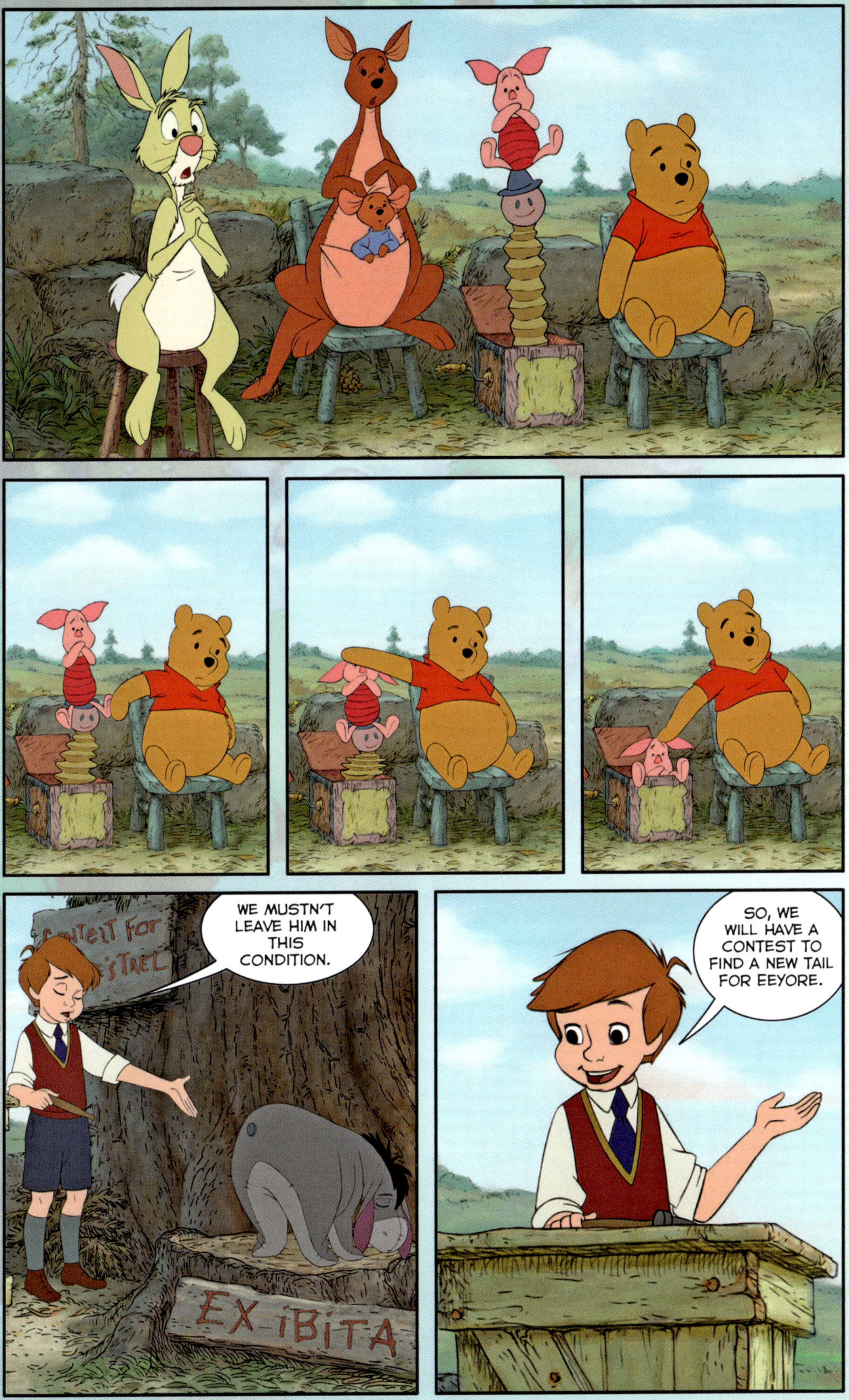
WE MUSTN'T LEAVE HIM IN THIS CONDITION.
EX iBiTA
SO, WE WILL HAVE A CONTEST TO FIND A NEW TAIL FOR EEYORE.

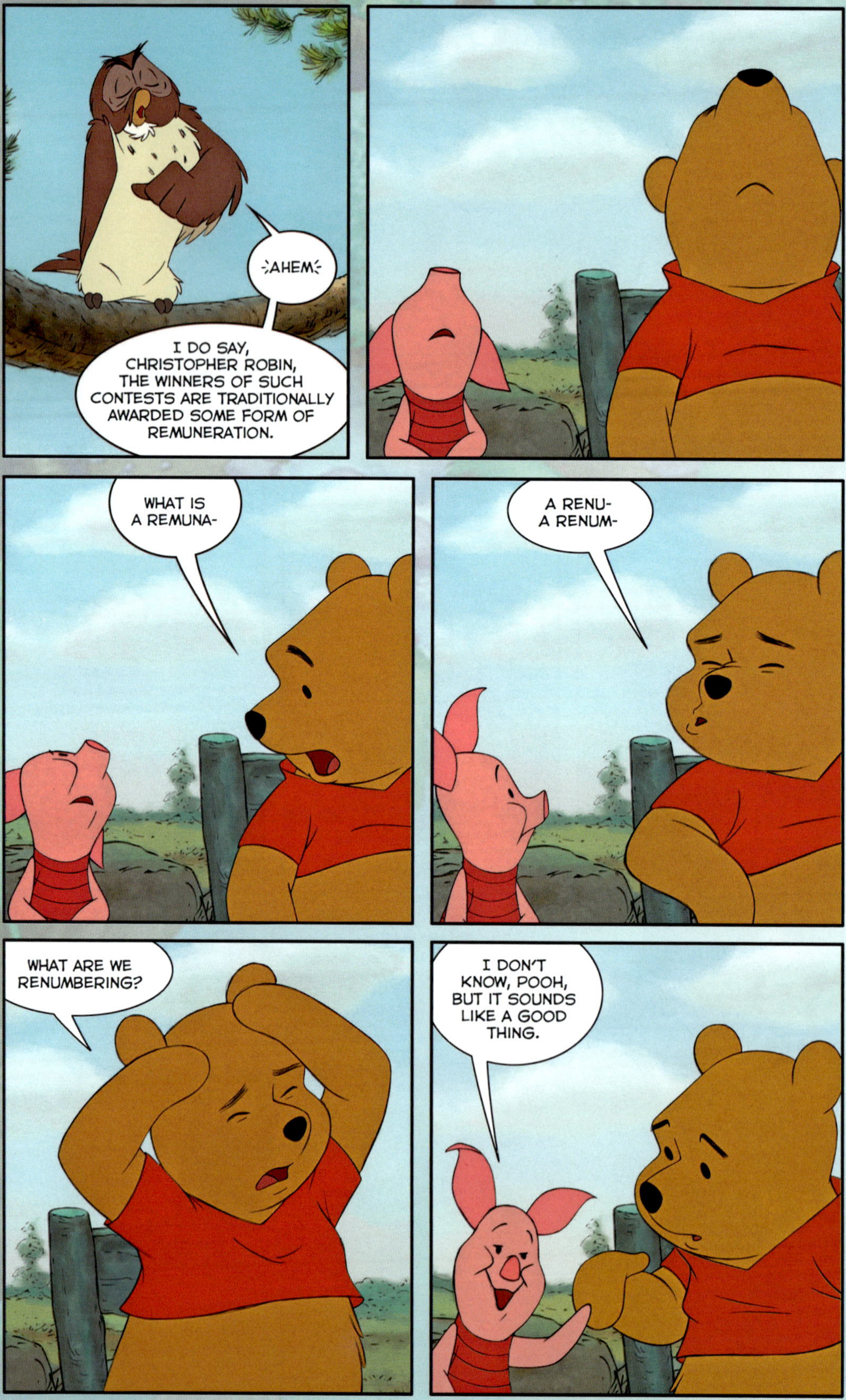
AHEM
I DO SAY, CHRISTOPHER ROBIN, THE WINNERS OF SUCH CONTESTS ARE TRADITIONALLY AWARDED SOME FORM OF REMUNERATION.
WHAT IS A REMUNA-
A RENU- A RENUM-
WHAT ARE WE RENUMBERING?
I DON'T KNOW, POOH, BUT IT SOUNDS LIKE A GOOD THING.

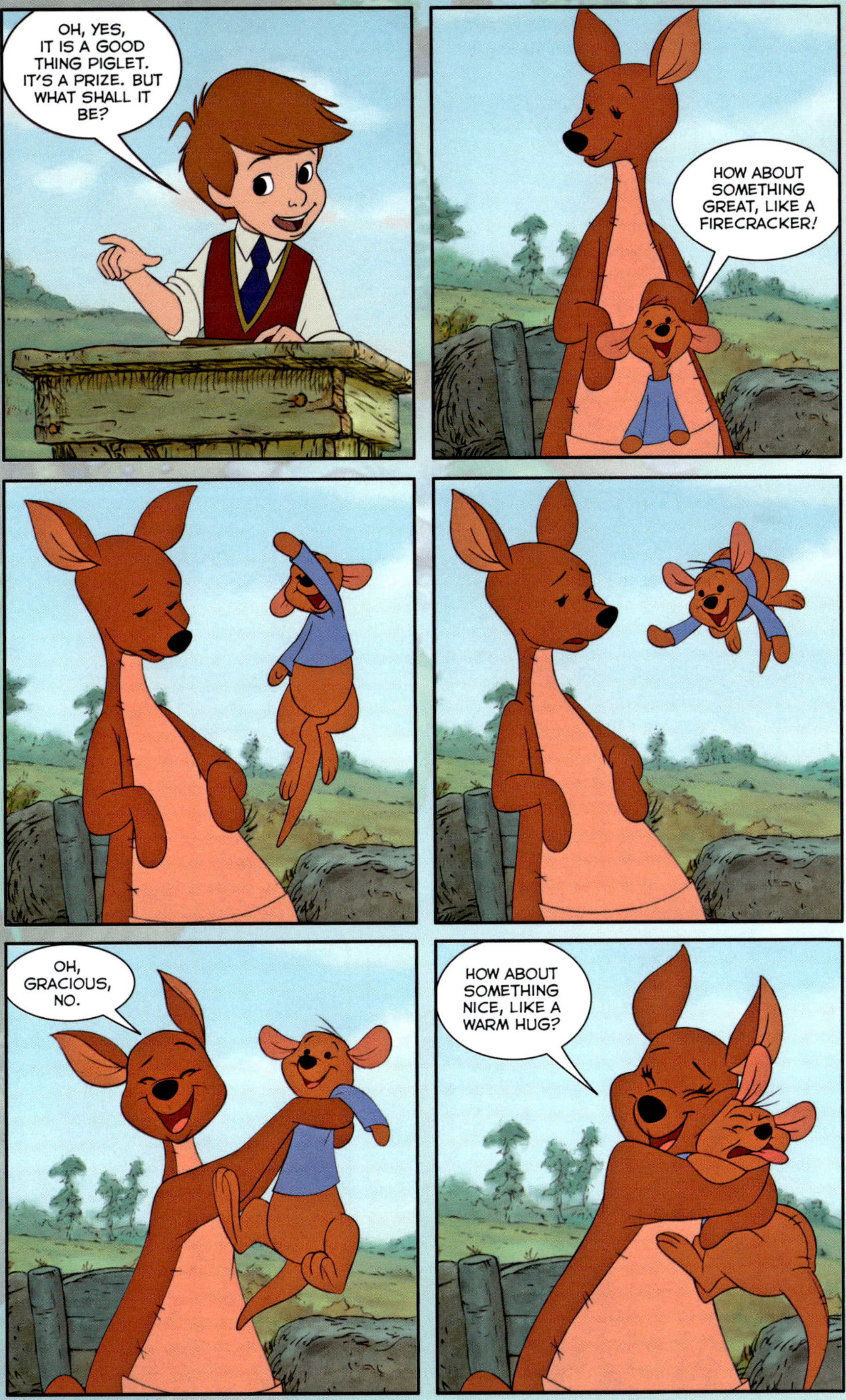
OH, YES, IT IS A GOOD THING PIGLET. IT'S A PRIZE. BUT WHAT SHALL IT BE?
HOW ABOUT SOMETHING GREAT, LIKE A FIRECRACKER!
OH, GRACIOUS, NO.
HOW ABOUT SOMETHING NICE, LIKE A WARM HUG?

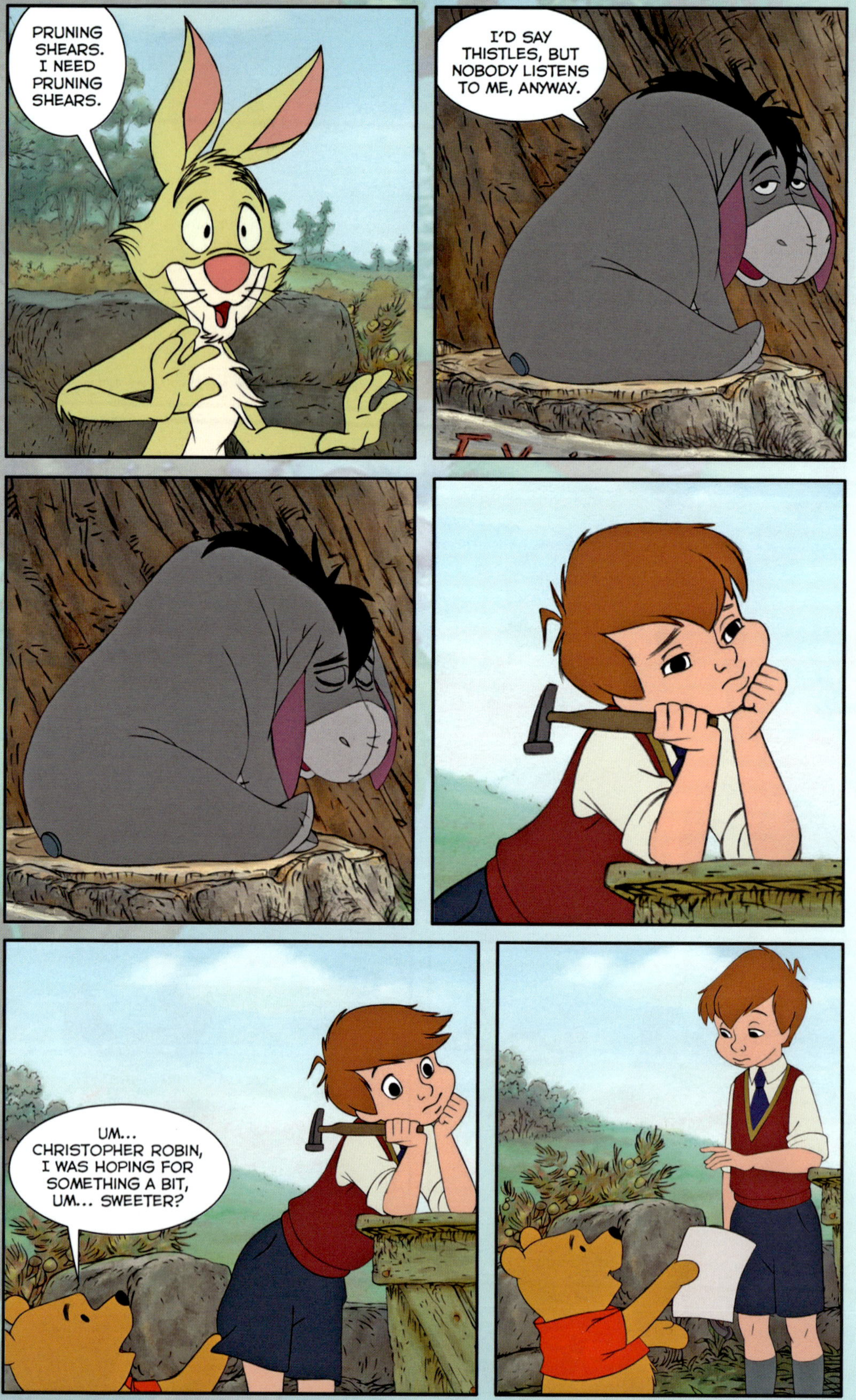
PRUNING SHEARS. I NEED PRUNING SHEARS.
I'D SAY THISTLES, BUT NOBODY LISTENS TO ME, ANYWAY.
UM... CHRISTOPHER ROBIN, I WAS HOPING FOR SOMETHING A BIT, UM... SWEETER?

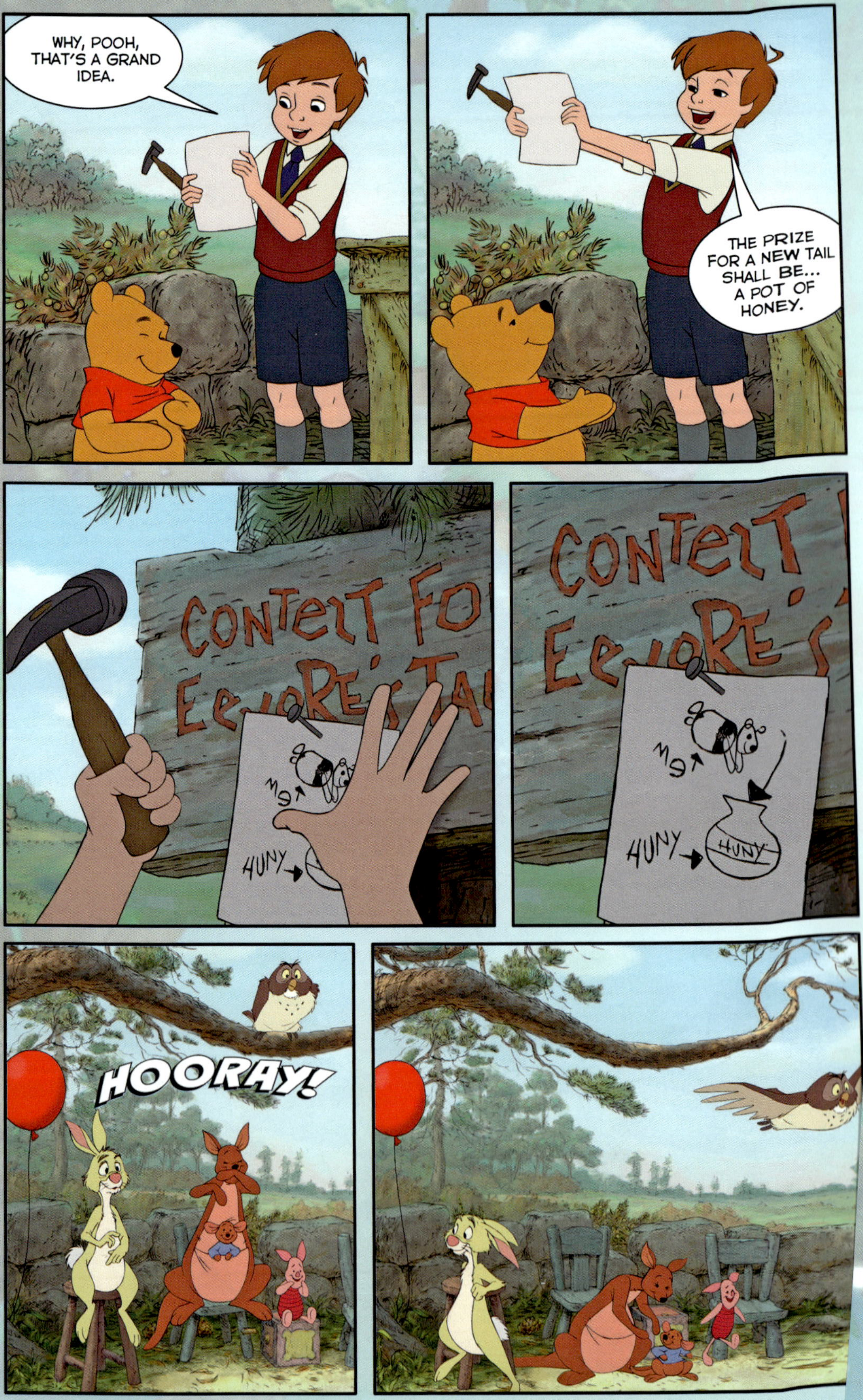
WHY, POOH, THAT'S A GRAND IDEA.
THE PRIZE FOR A NEW TAIL SHALL BE... A POT OF HONEY.
HOORAY!

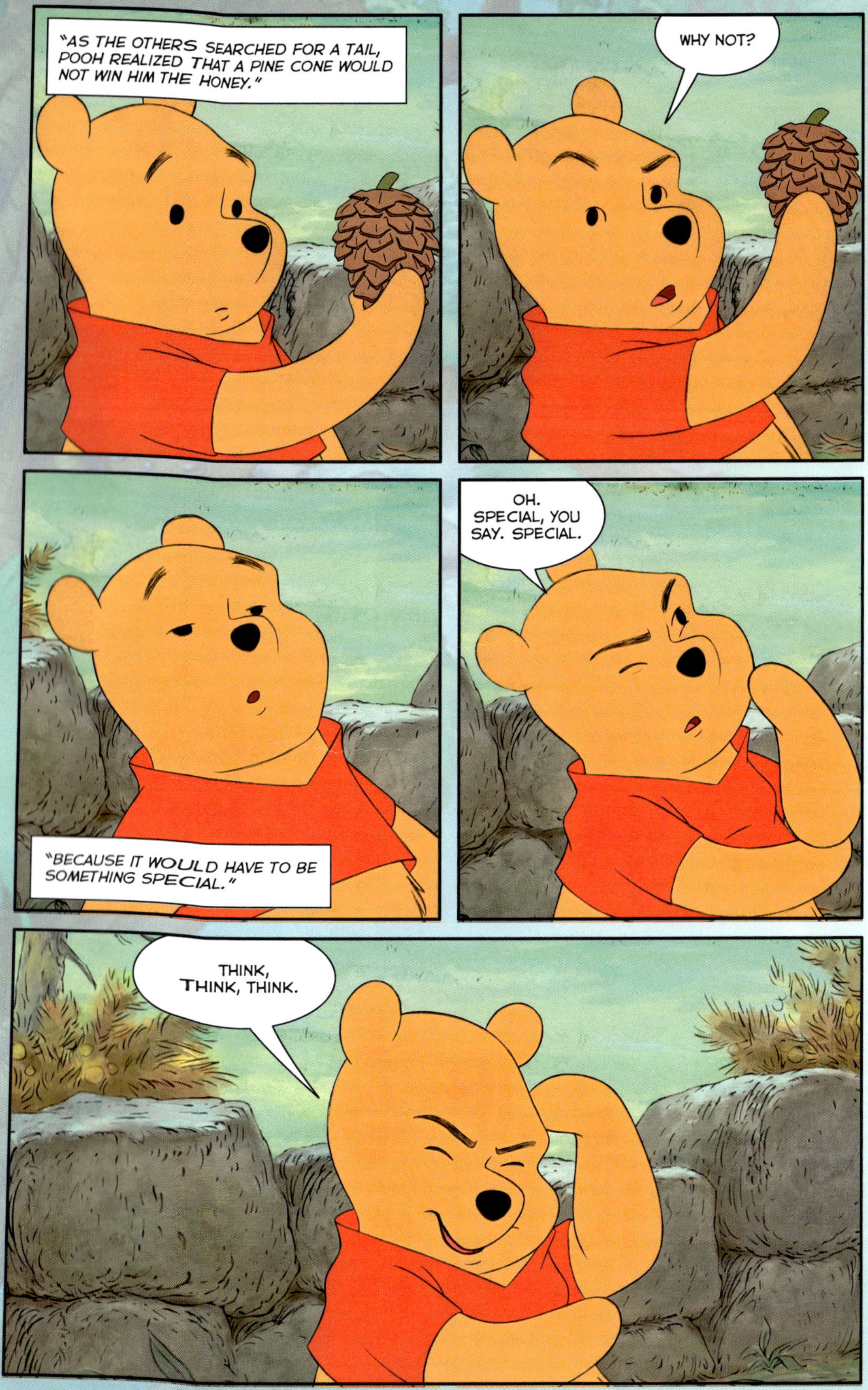
"AS THE OTHERS SEARCHED FOR A TAIL, POOH REALIZED THAT A PINE CONE WOULD NOT WIN HIM THE HONEY."
WHY NOT?
"BECAUSE IT WOULD HAVE TO BE SOMETHING SPECIAL."
OH. SPECIAL, YOU SAY. SPECIAL.
THINK, THINK, THINK.

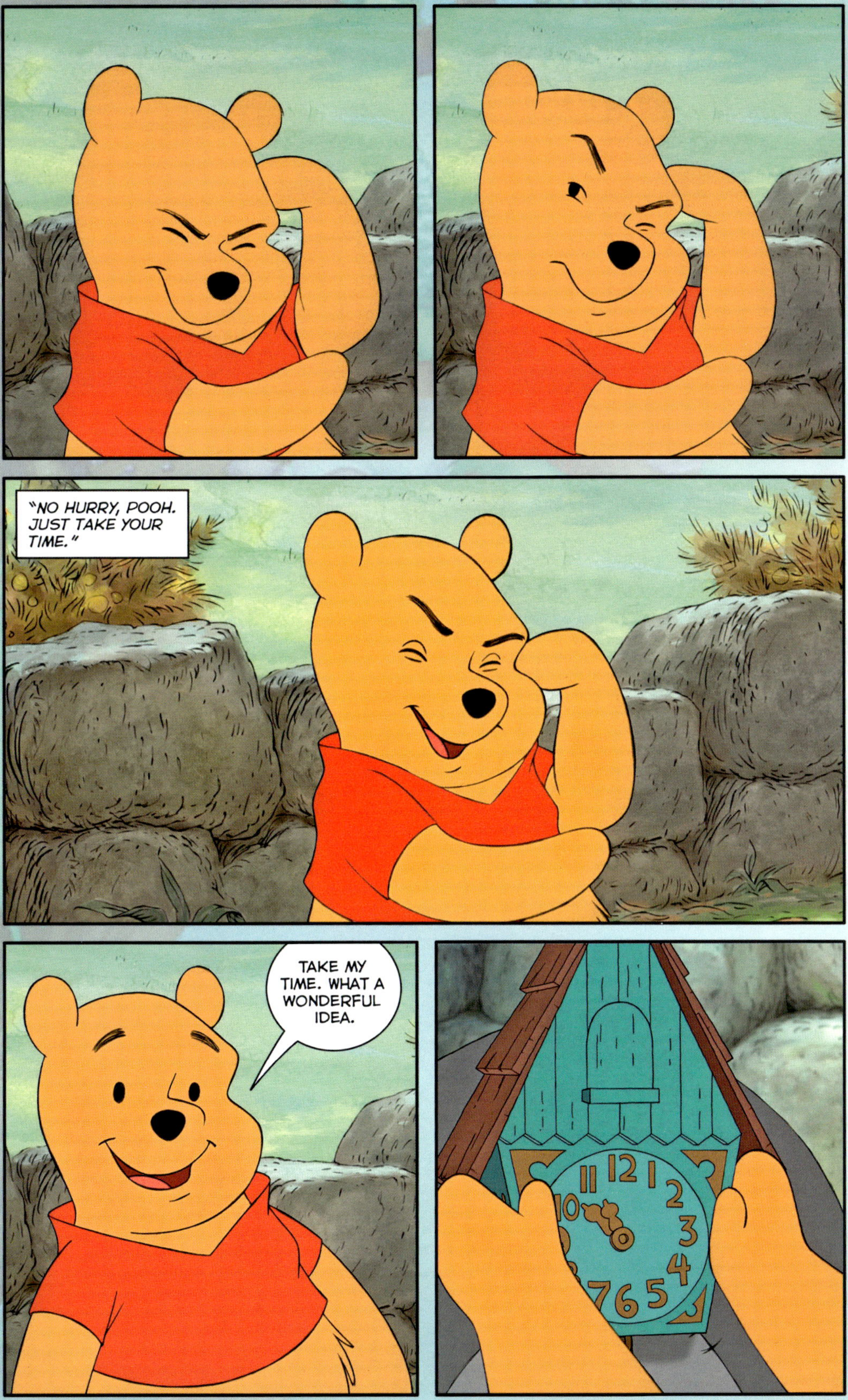
"NO HURRY, POOH. JUST TAKE YOUR TIME."
TAKE MY TIME. WHAT A WONDERFUL IDEA.

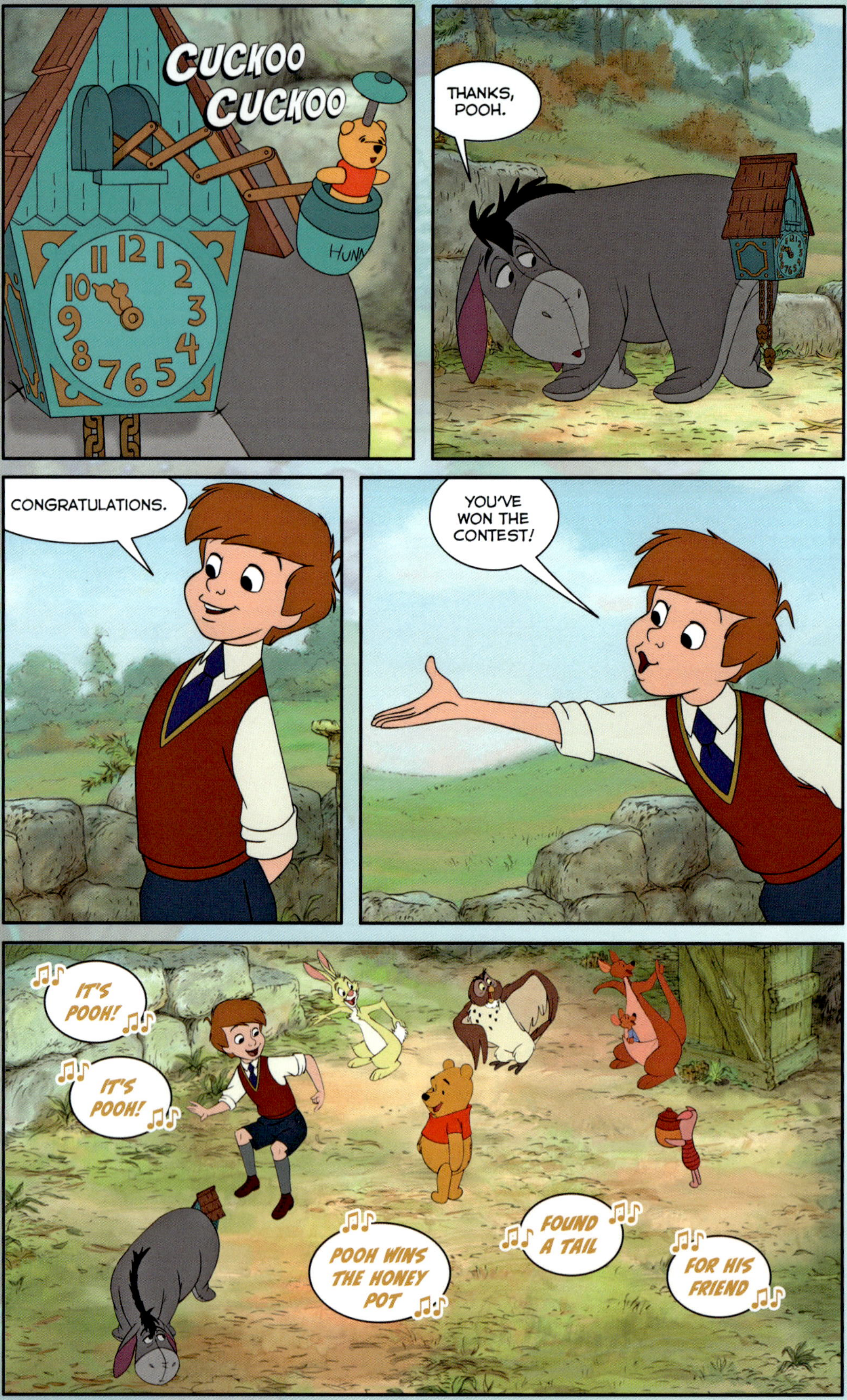

CUCKOO CUCKOO
HUNN
THANKS, POOH.
CONGRATULATIONS.
YOU'VE WON THE CONTEST!
IT'S POOH!
IT'S POOH!
POOH WINS THE HONEY POT
FOUND A TAIL
FOR HIS FRIEND

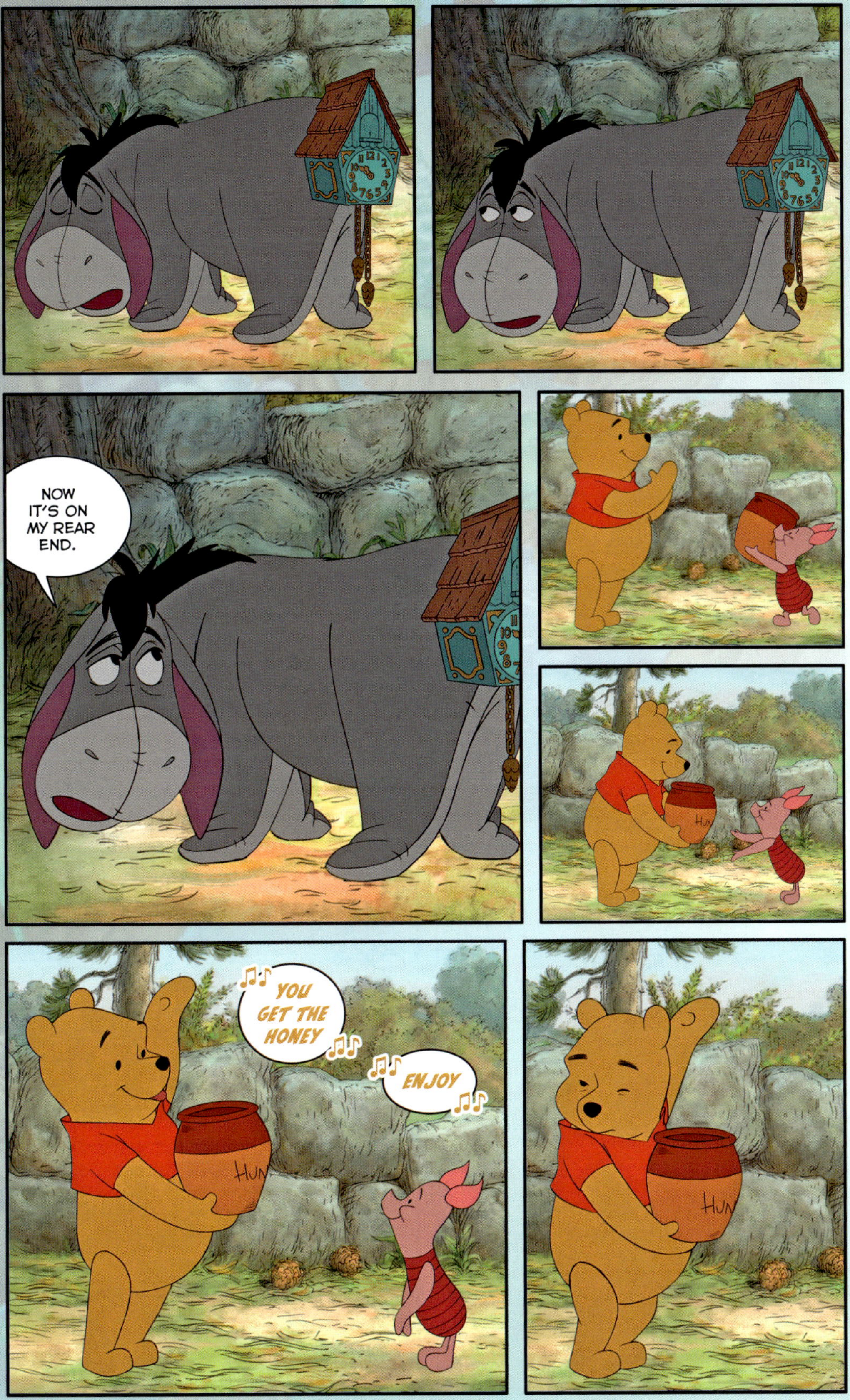
NOW IT'S ON MY REAR END.
YOU GET THE HONEY
ENJOY

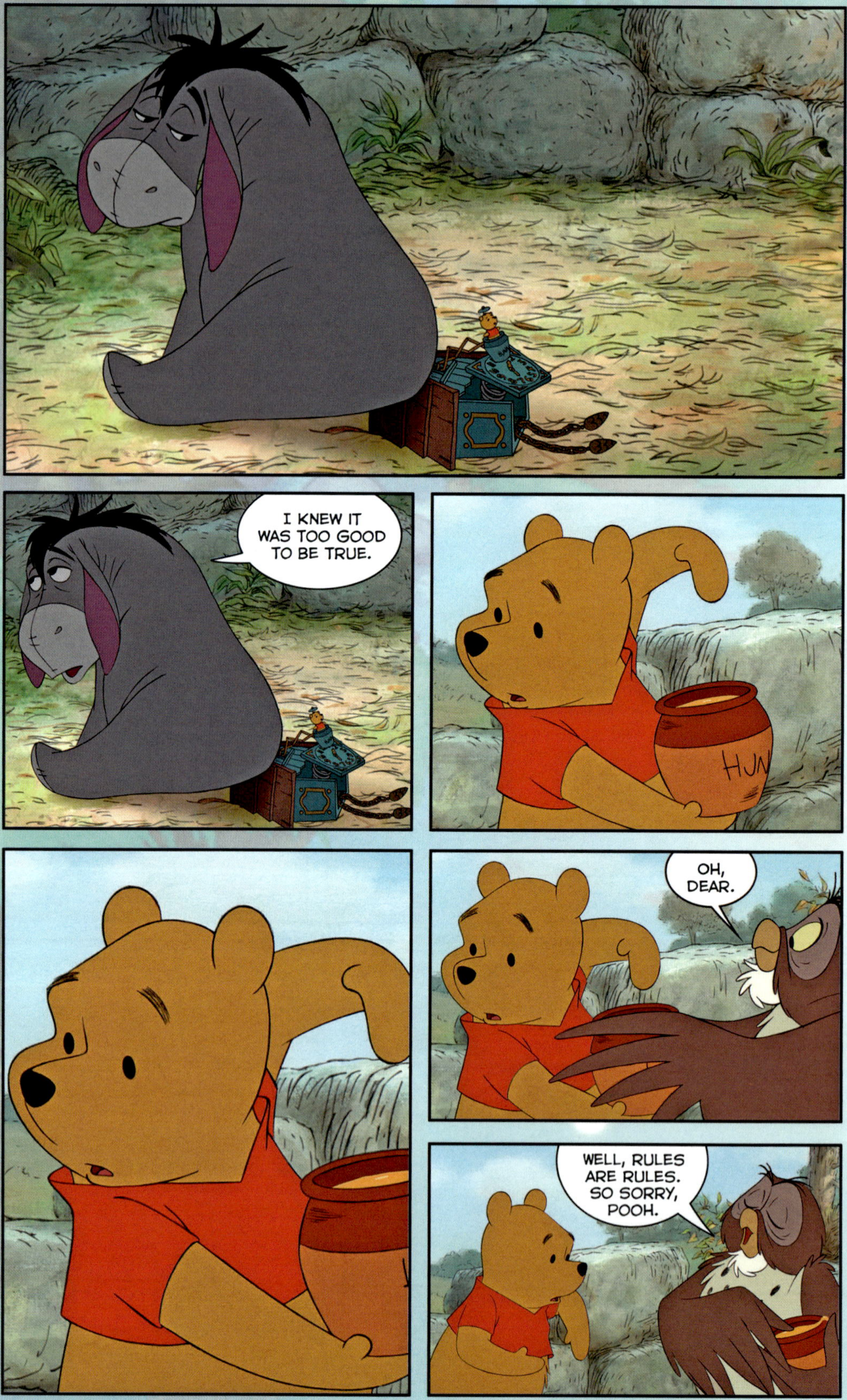
I KNEW IT WAS TOO GOOD TO BE TRUE.
OH, DEAR.
WELL, RULES ARE RULES. SO SORRY, POOH.

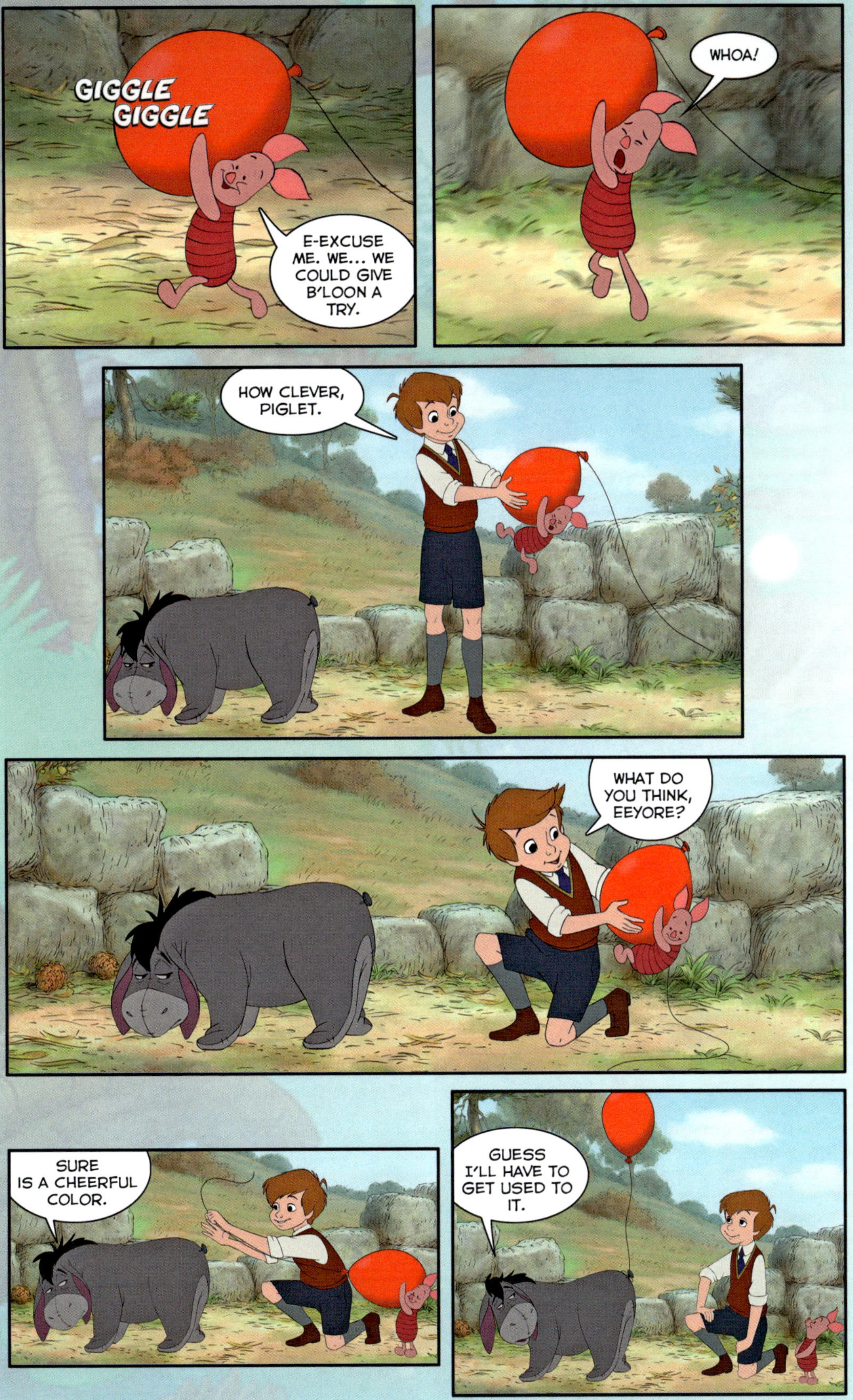
GIGGLE GIGGLE
E-EXCUSE ME. WE... WE COULD GIVE B'LOON A TRY.
WHOA!
HOW CLEVER, PIGLET.
WHAT DO YOU THINK, EEYORE?
SURE IS A CHEERFUL COLOR.
GUESS I'LL HAVE TO GET USED TO IT.

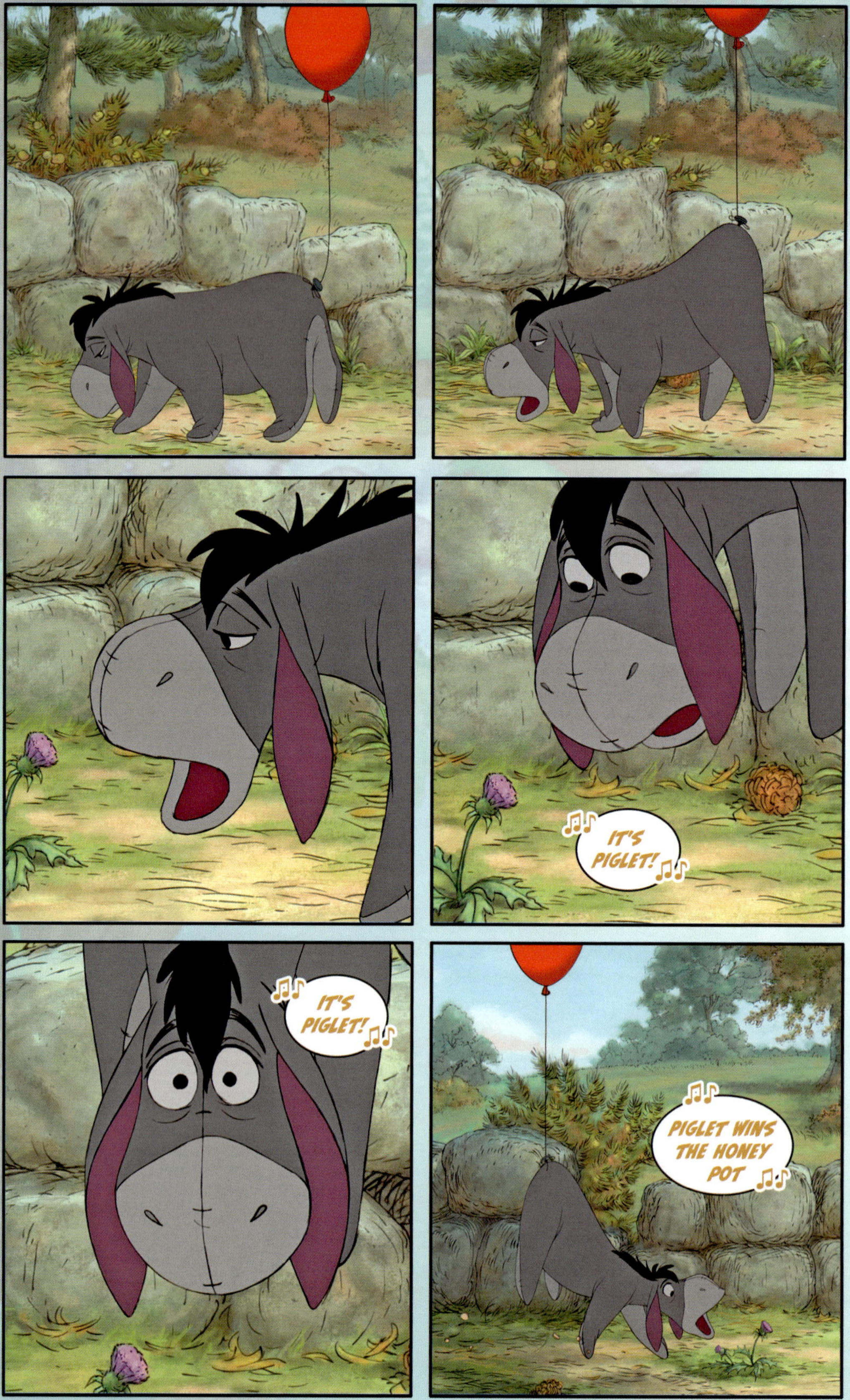
IT'S PIGLET!
IT'S PIGLET!
PIGLET WINS THE HONEY POT

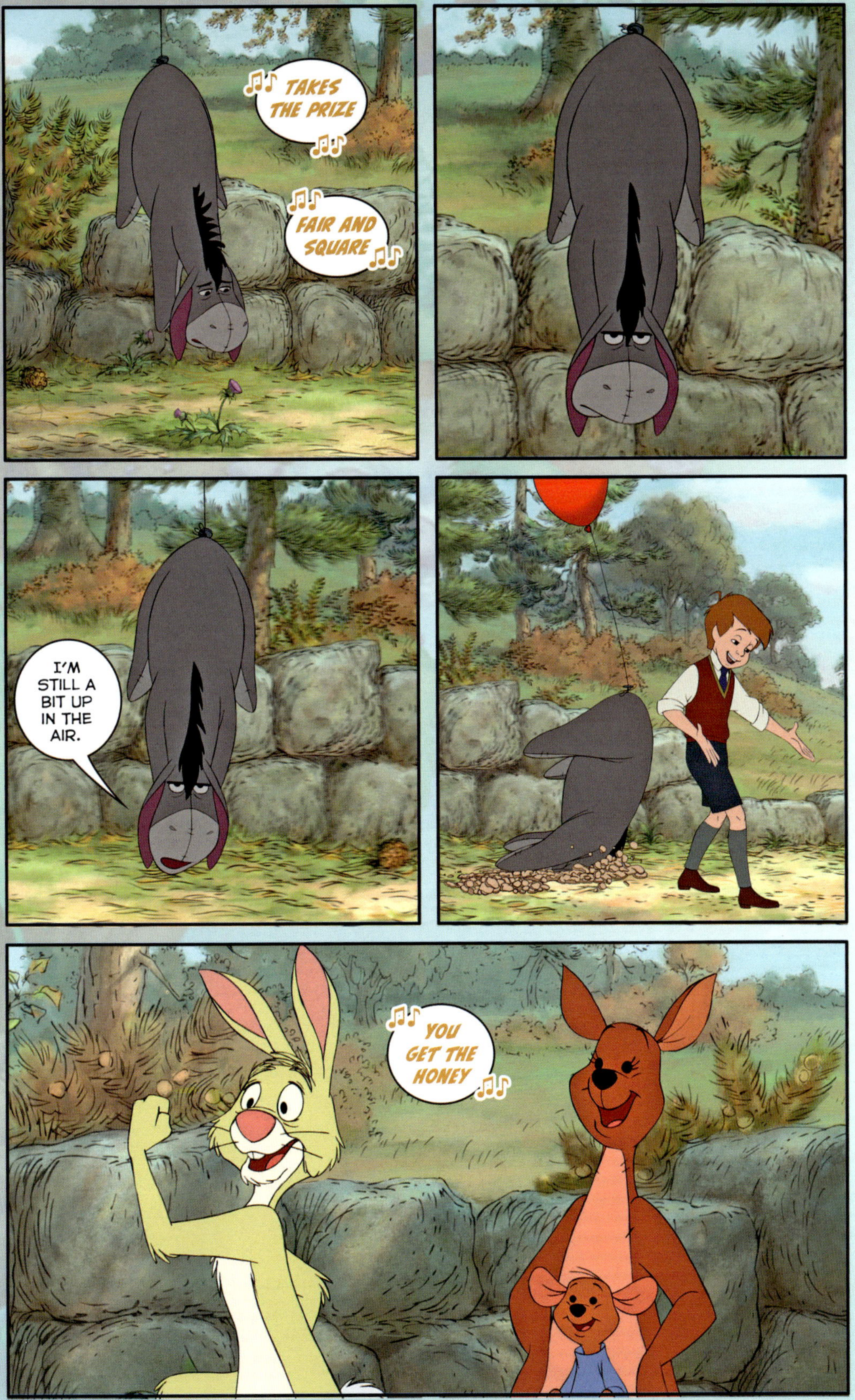
TAKES THE PRIZE
FAIR AND SQUARE
I'M STILL A BIT UP IN THE AIR.
YOU GET THE HONEY

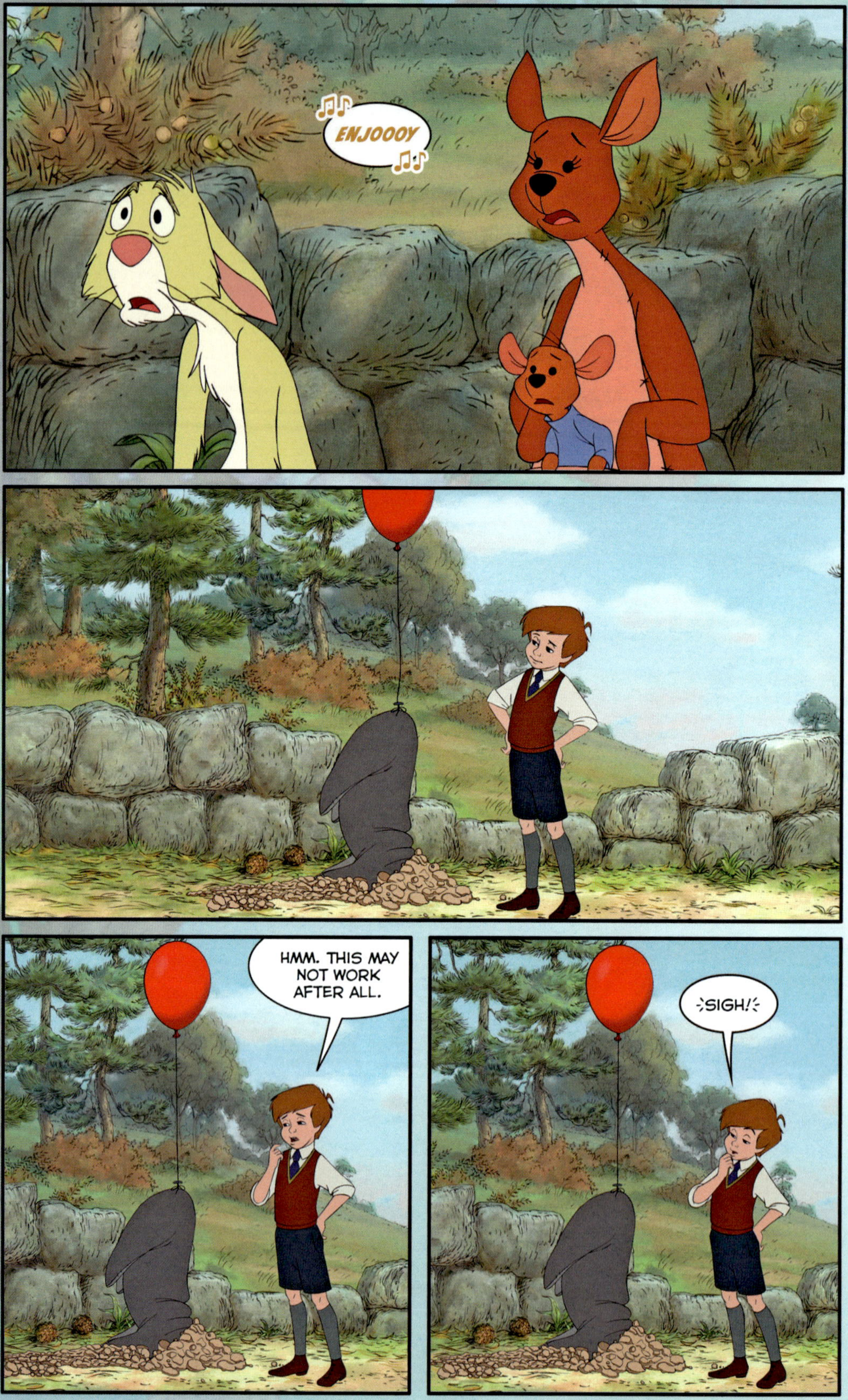
ENJOOOY
HMM. THIS MAY NOT WORK AFTER ALL.
SIGH!

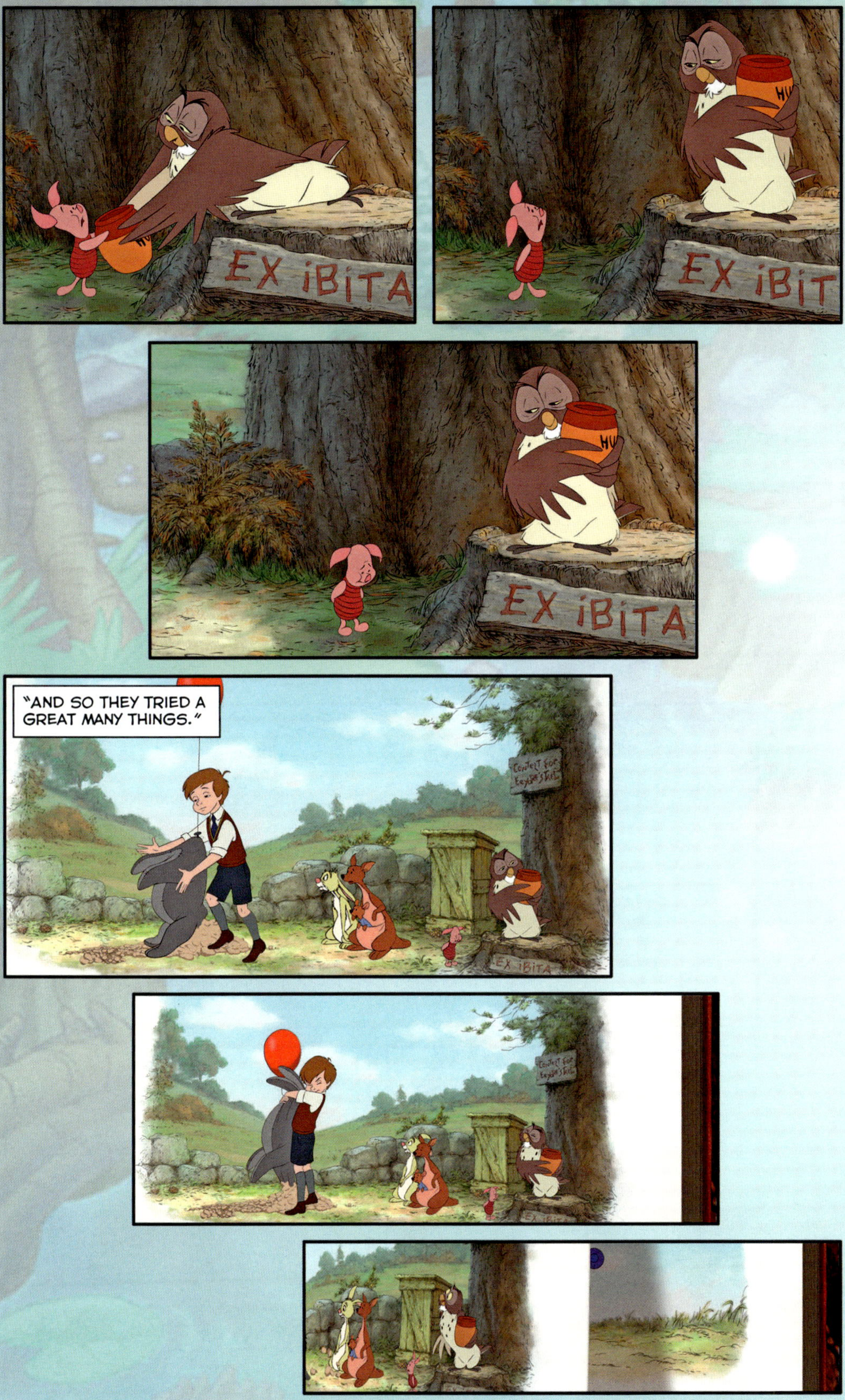
EX iBITA
EX iBIT
EX iBITA
"AND SO THEY TRIED A GREAT MANY THINGS."

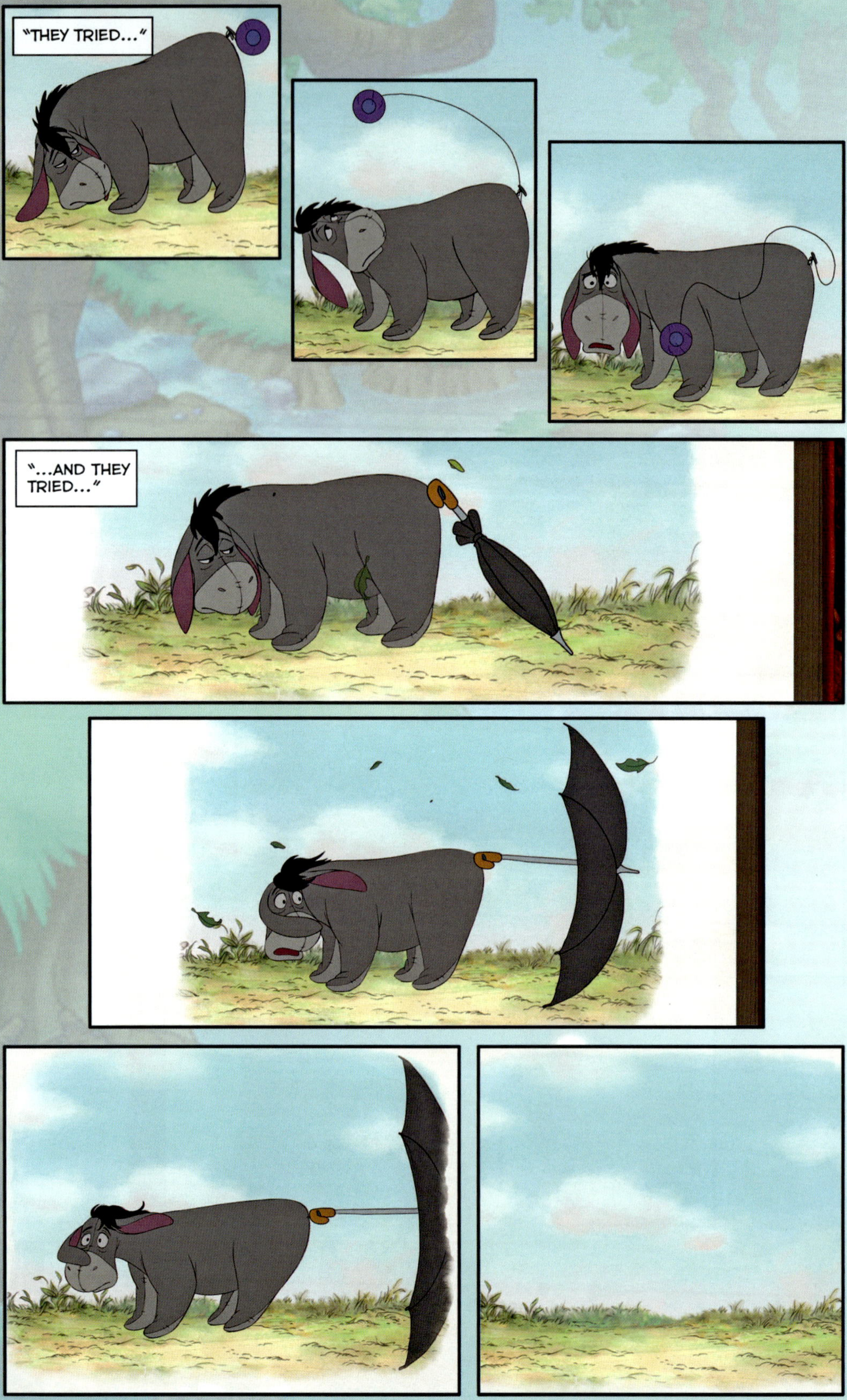
"THEY TRIED..."
"...AND THEY TRIED..."

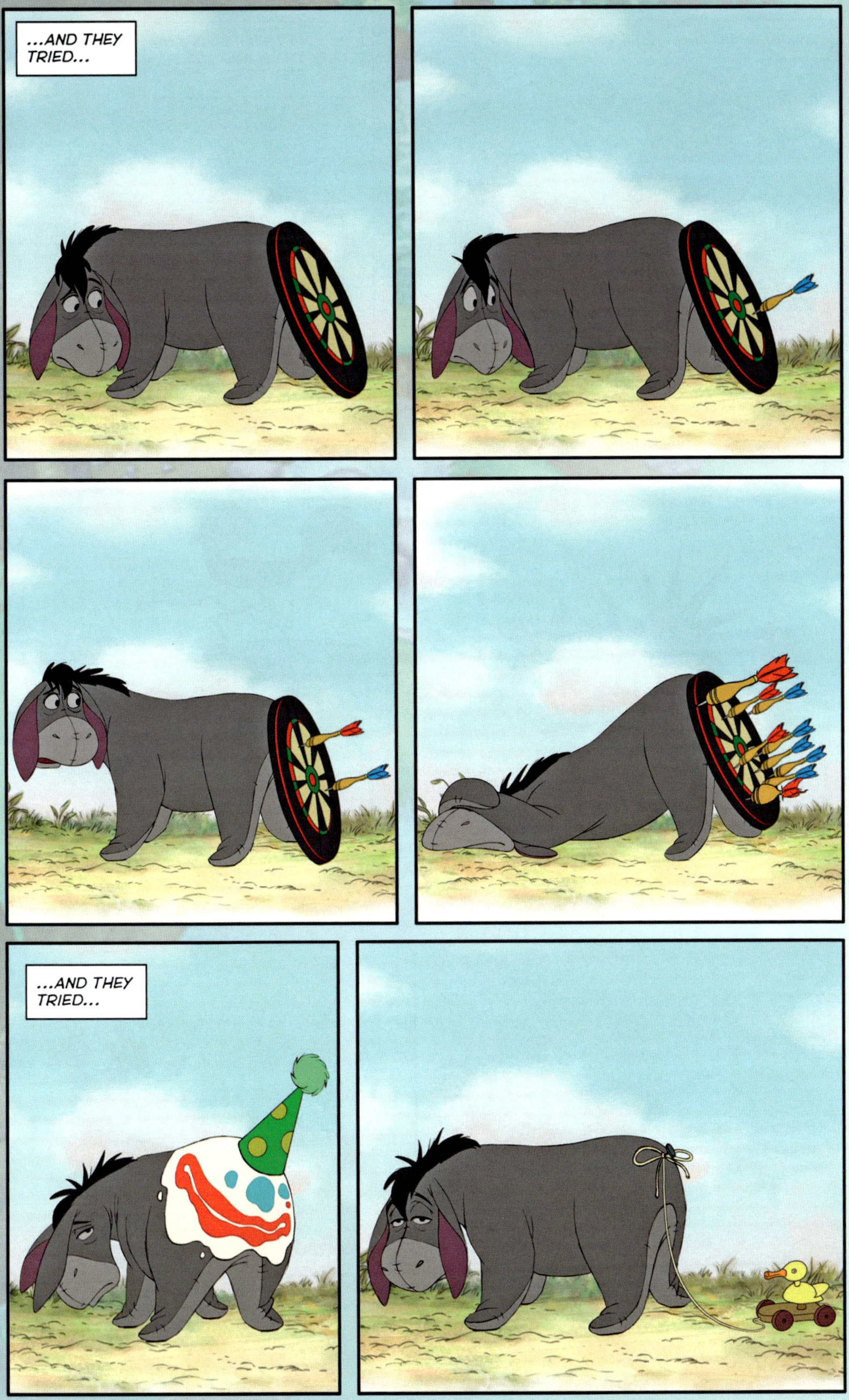
...AND THEY TRIED...
...AND THEY TRIED...

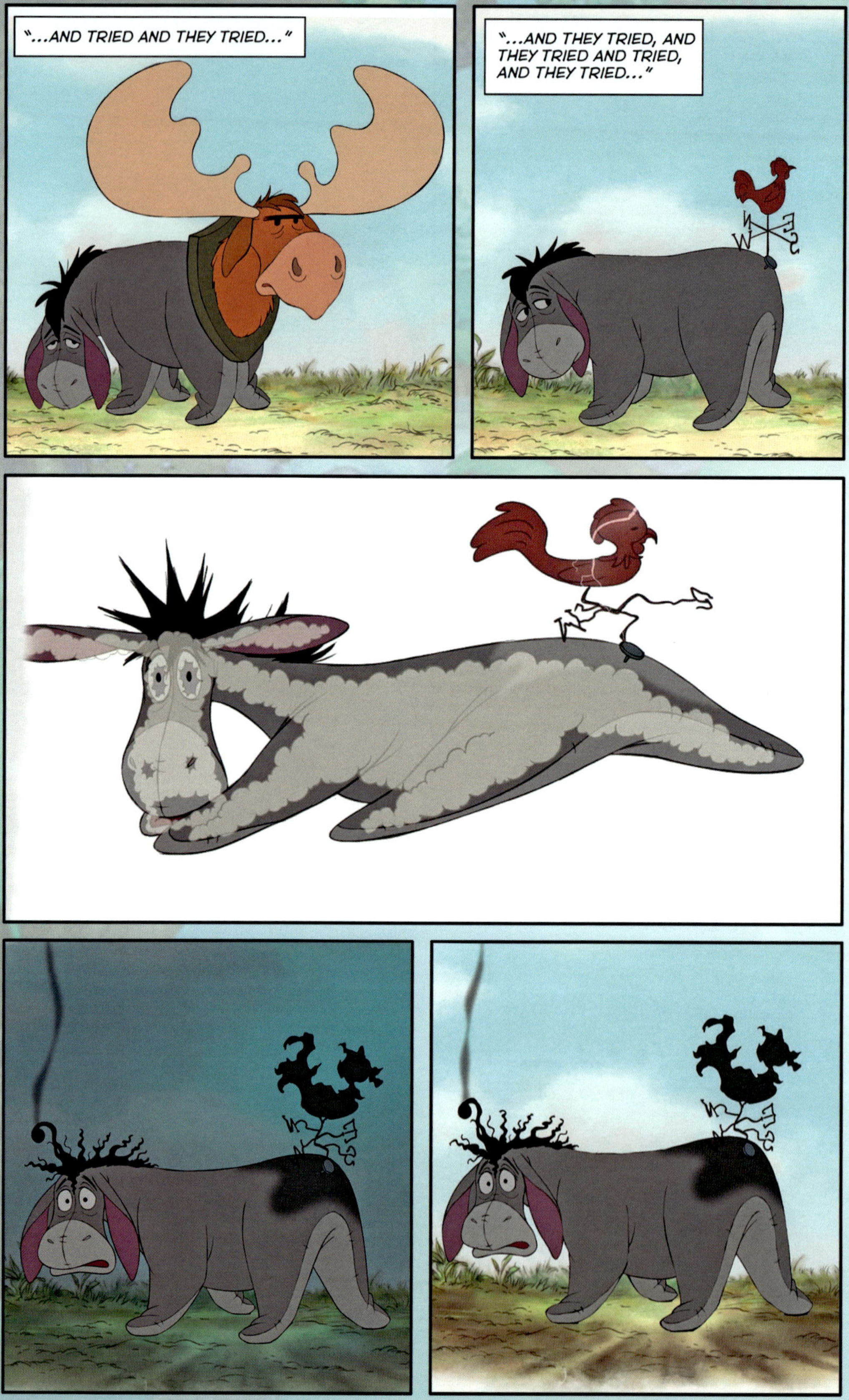
"...AND TRIED AND THEY TRIED..."
"...AND THEY TRIED, AND THEY TRIED AND TRIED, AND THEY TRIED..."

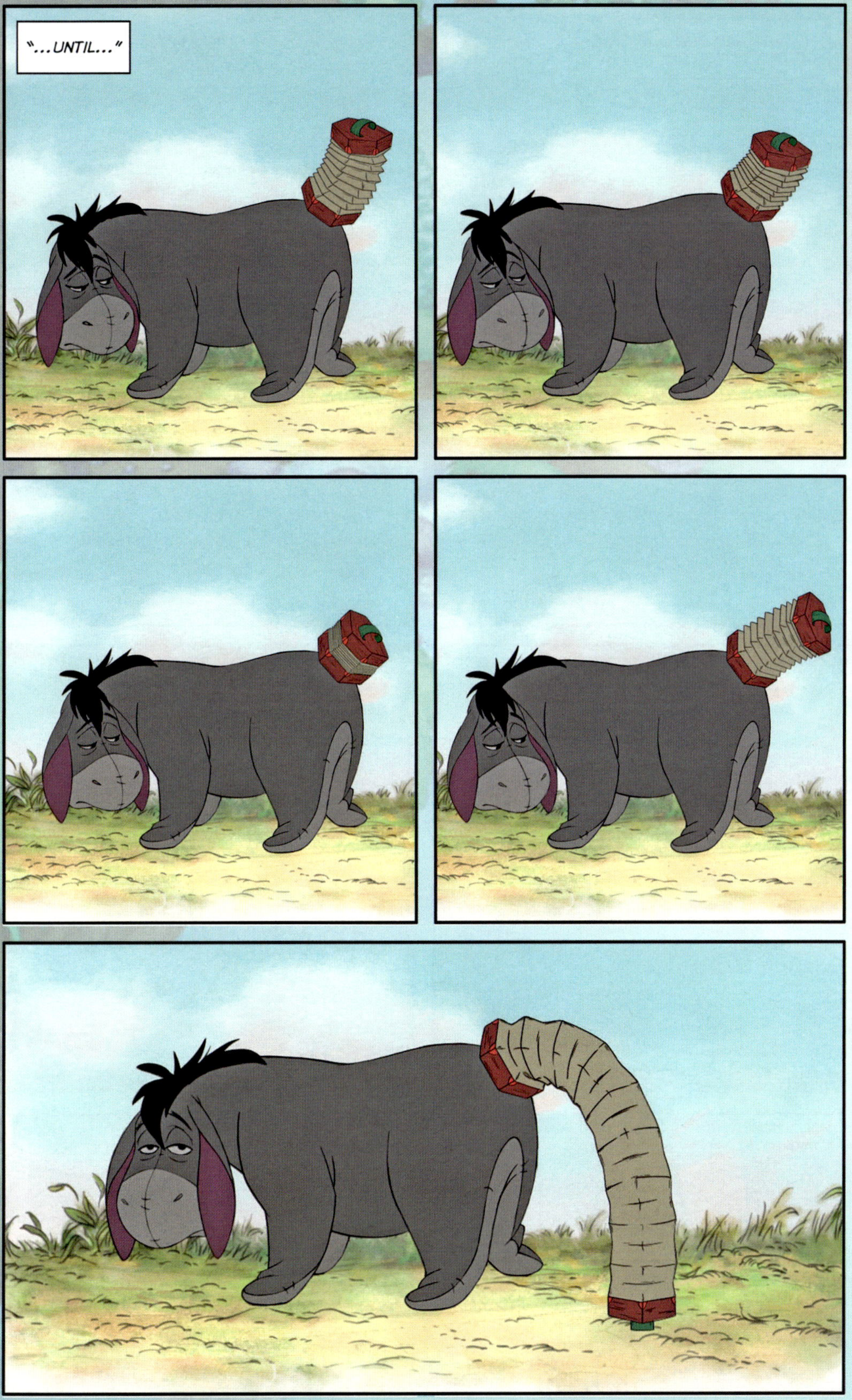
"...UNTIL..."

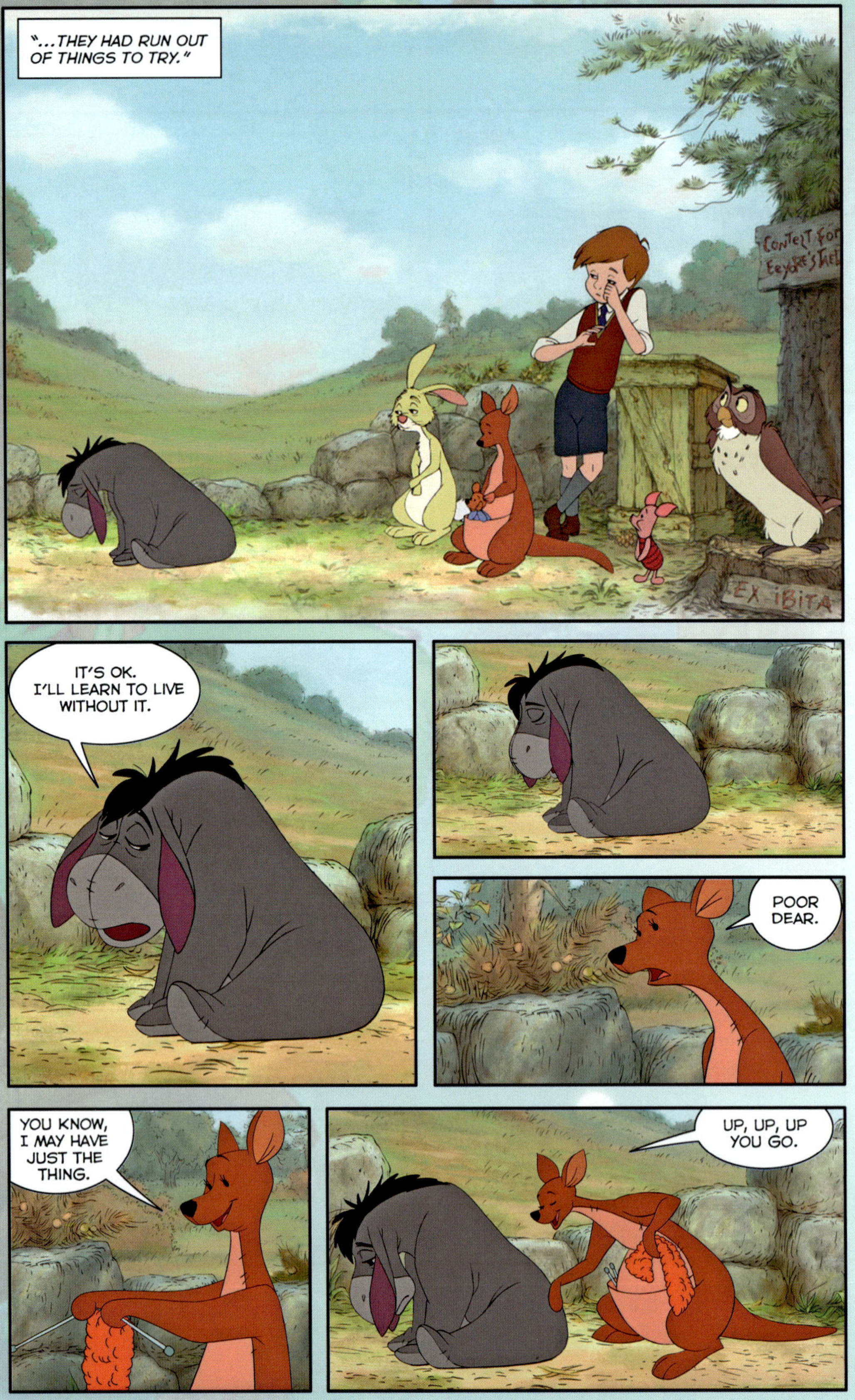
"...THEY HAD RUN OUT OF THINGS TO TRY."
CONTEST FOR EEYORE'S TAIL
EX IBITA
IT'S OK. I'LL LEARN TO LIVE WITHOUT IT.
POOR DEAR.
YOU KNOW, I MAY HAVE JUST THE THING.
UP, UP, UP YOU GO.

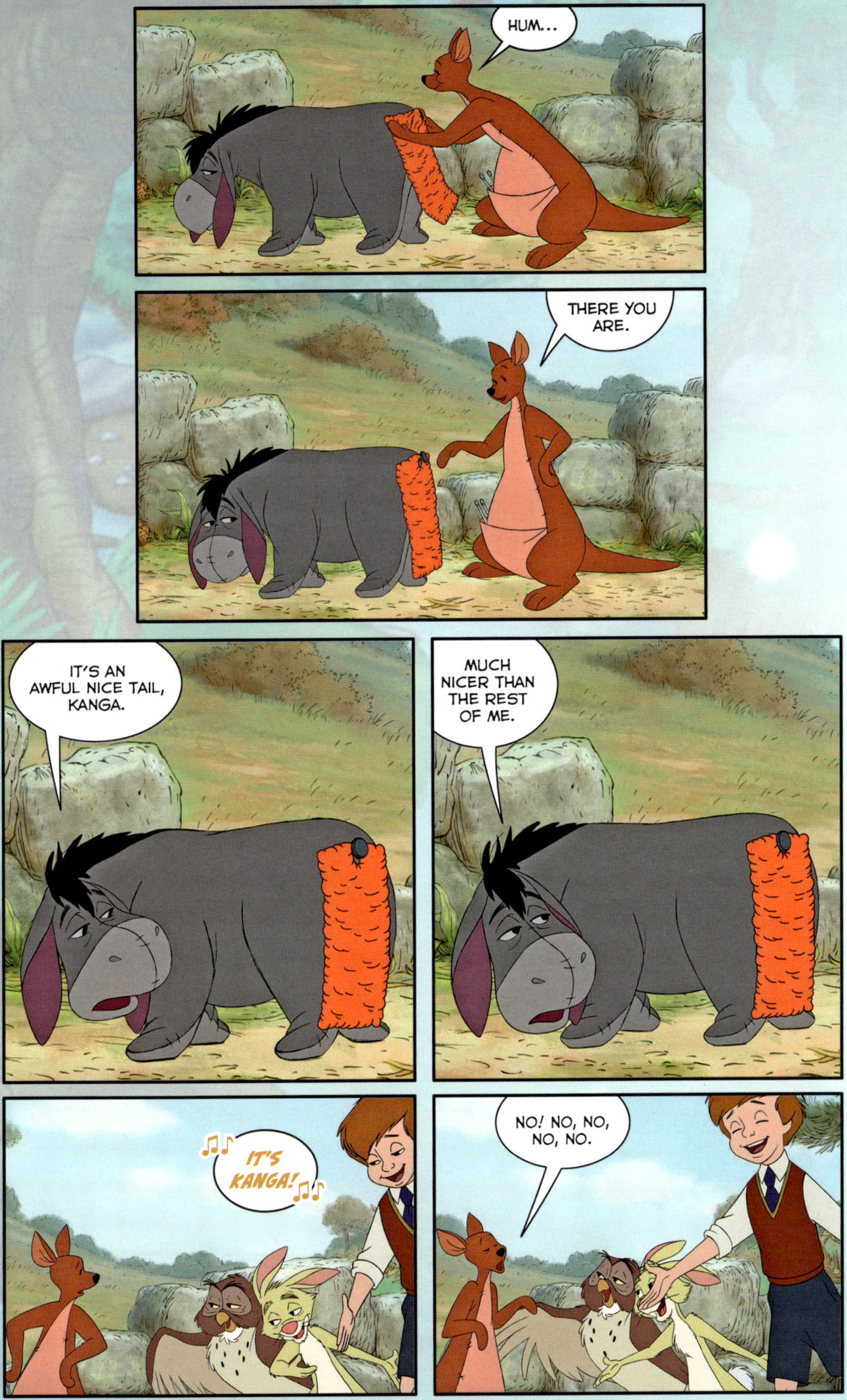
HUM...
THERE YOU ARE.
IT'S AN AWFUL NICE TAIL, KANGA.
MUCH NICER THAN THE REST OF ME.
IT'S KANGA!
NO! NO, NO, NO, NO.

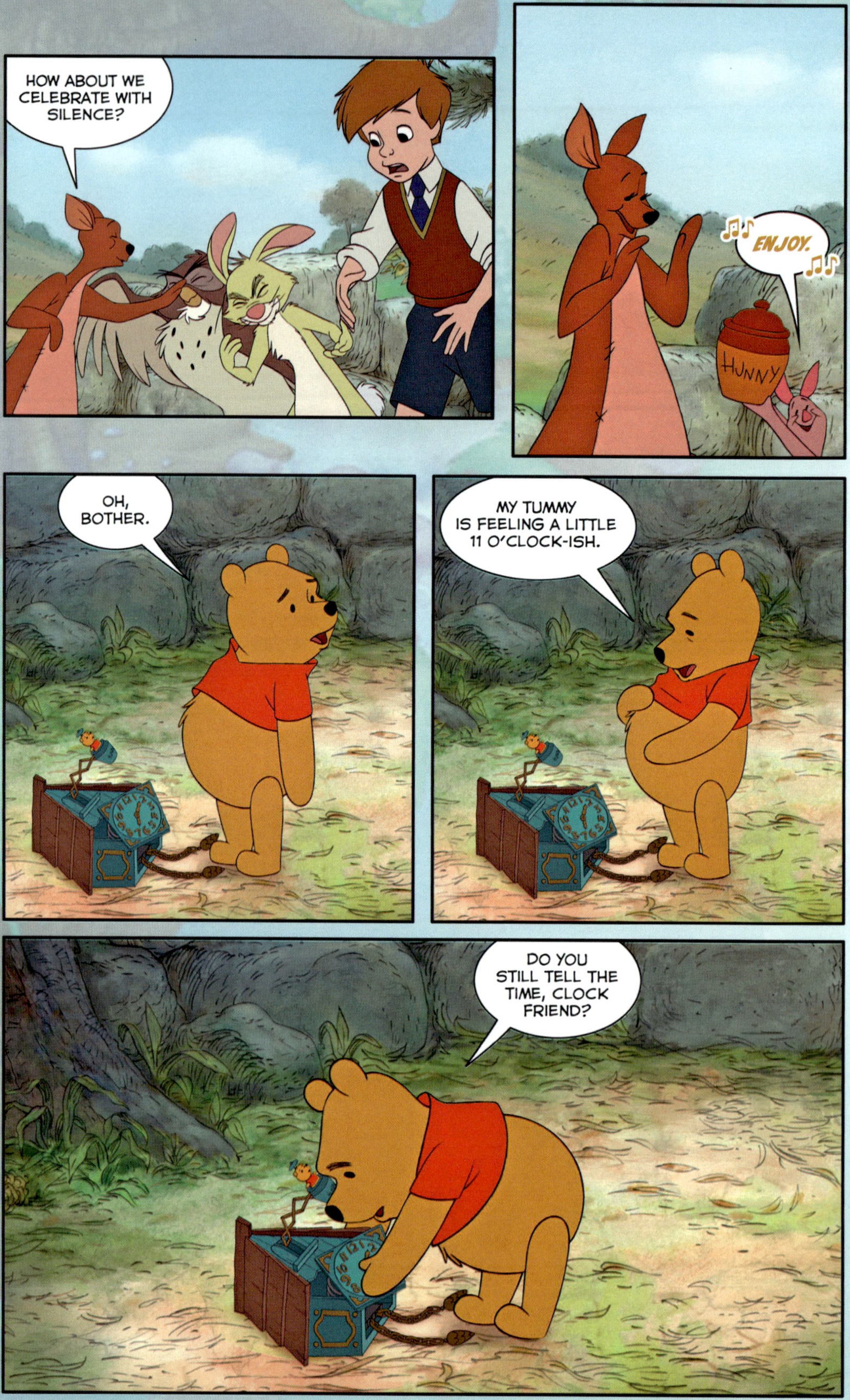
HOW ABOUT WE CELEBRATE WITH SILENCE?
ENJOY.
HUNNY
OH, BOTHER.
MY TUMMY IS FEELING A LITTLE 11 O'CLOCK-ISH.
DO YOU STILL TELL THE TIME, CLOCK FRIEND?

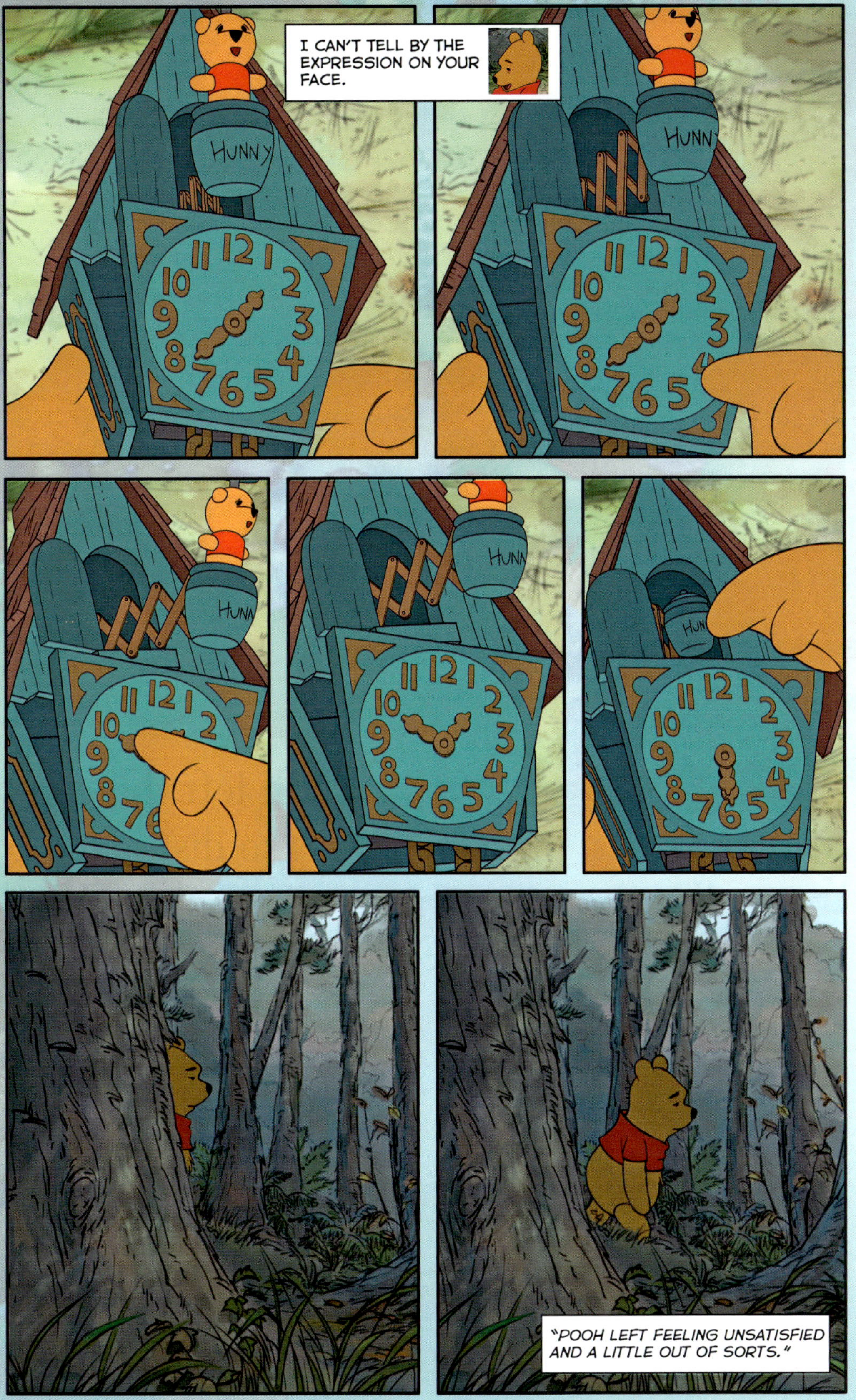
I CAN'T TELL BY THE EXPRESSION ON YOUR FACE.
HUNNY
"POOH LEFT FEELING UNSATISFIED AND A LITTLE OUT OF SORTS."

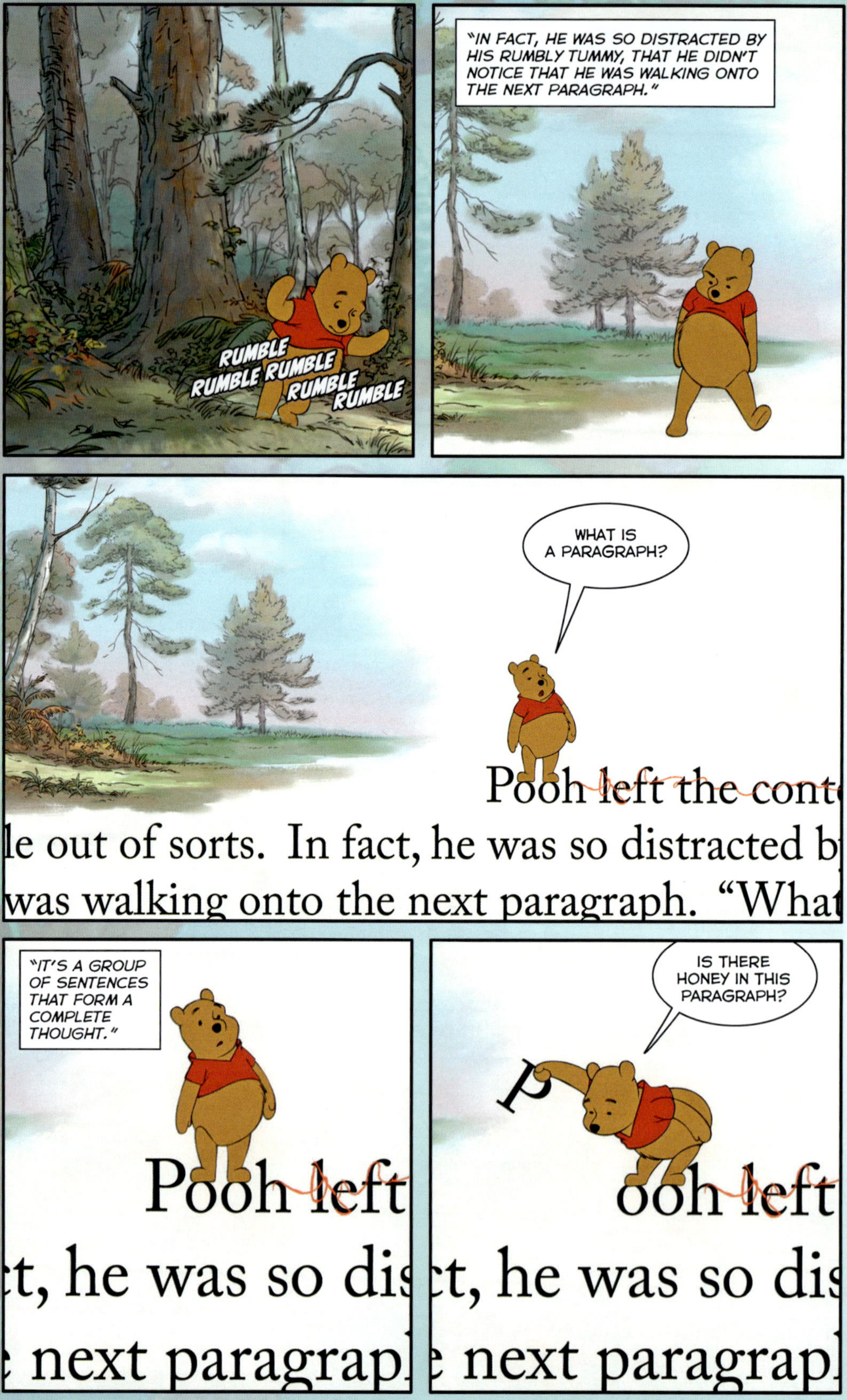
RUMBLE
RUMBLE RUMBLE
RUMBLE
RUMBLE
"IN FACT, HE WAS SO DISTRACTED BY HIS RUMBLY TUMMY, THAT HE DIDN'T NOTICE THAT HE WAS WALKING ONTO THE NEXT PARAGRAPH."
WHAT IS A PARAGRAPH?
Pooh left the cont
le out of sorts. In fact, he was so distracted b
was walking onto the next paragraph. "What
"IT'S A GROUP OF SENTENCES THAT FORM A COMPLETE THOUGHT."
Pooh left
t, he was so dis
next paragrap
IS THERE HONEY IN THIS PARAGRAPH?
P
ooh left
t, he was so dis
next paragrap

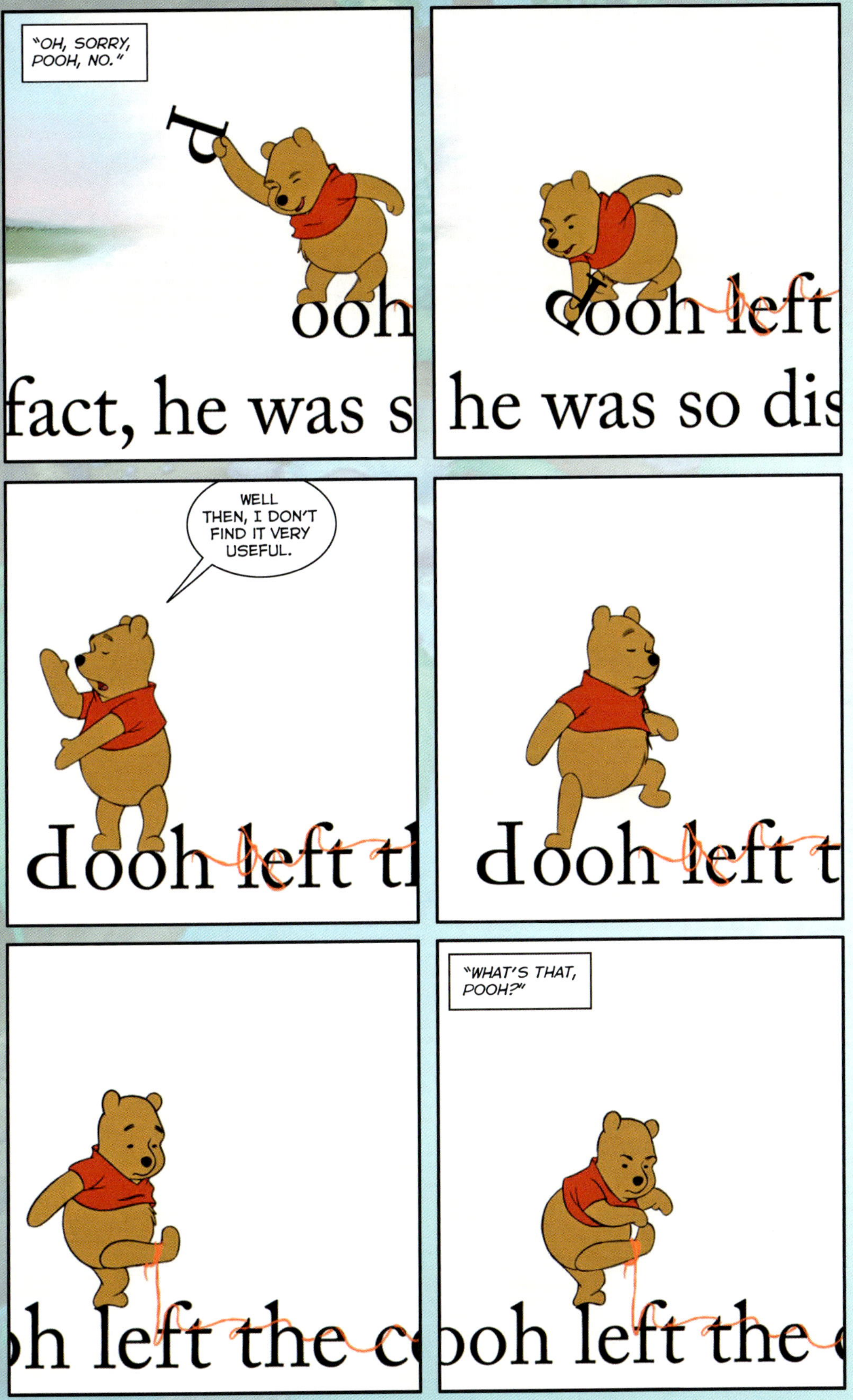
"OH, SORRY, POOH, NO."
ooh
fact, he was s
dooh left
he was so dis
WELL THEN, I DON'T FIND IT VERY USEFUL.
dooh left tl
dooh left t
oh left the c
"WHAT'S THAT, POOH?"
ooh left the

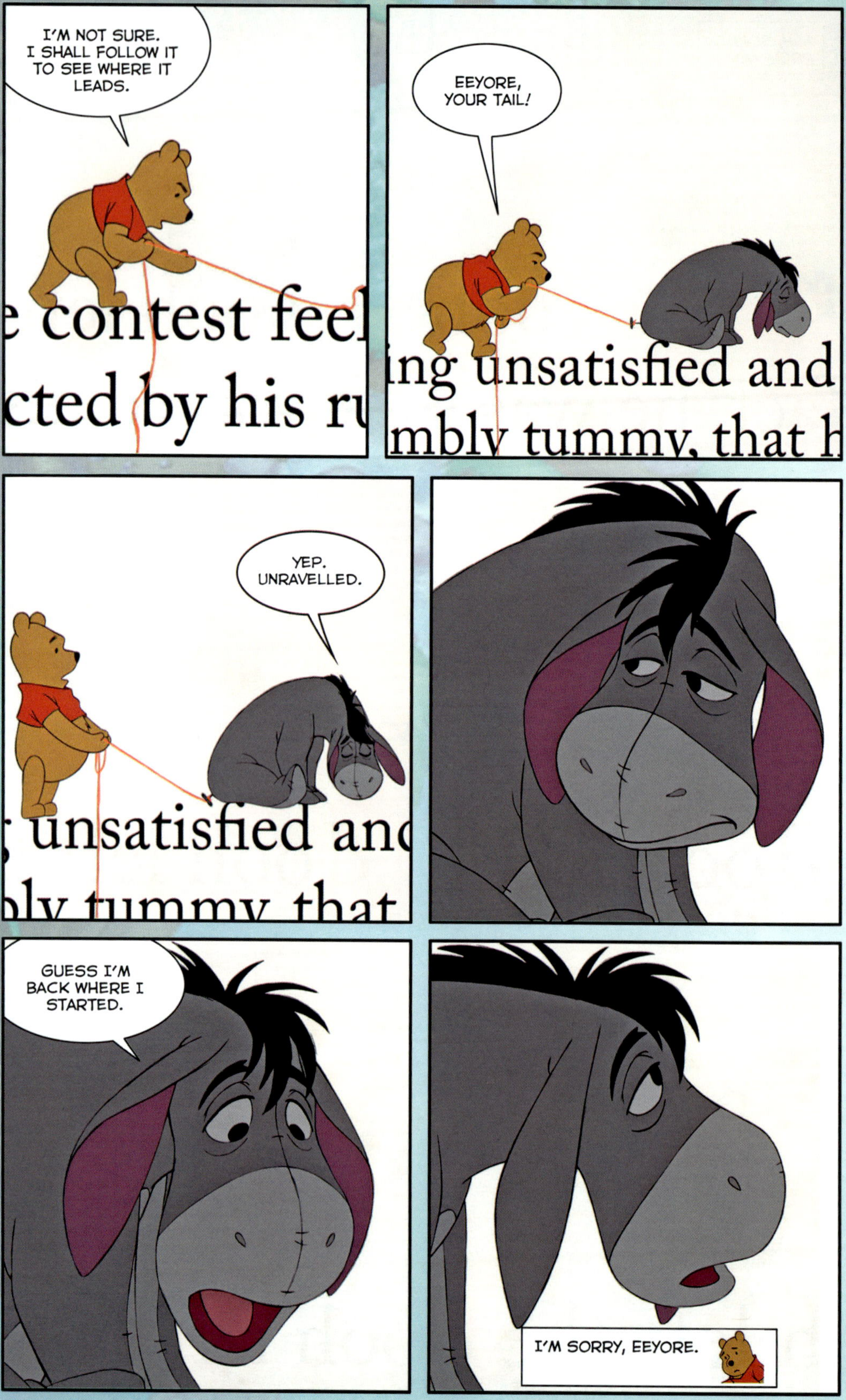
I'M NOT SURE. I SHALL FOLLOW IT TO SEE WHERE IT LEADS.
e contest feel
cted by his ru
EEYORE, YOUR TAIL!
ing unsatisfied and
mbly tummy, that h
YEP. UNRAVELLED.
unsatisfied and
bly tummy that
GUESS I'M BACK WHERE I STARTED.
I'M SORRY, EEYORE.

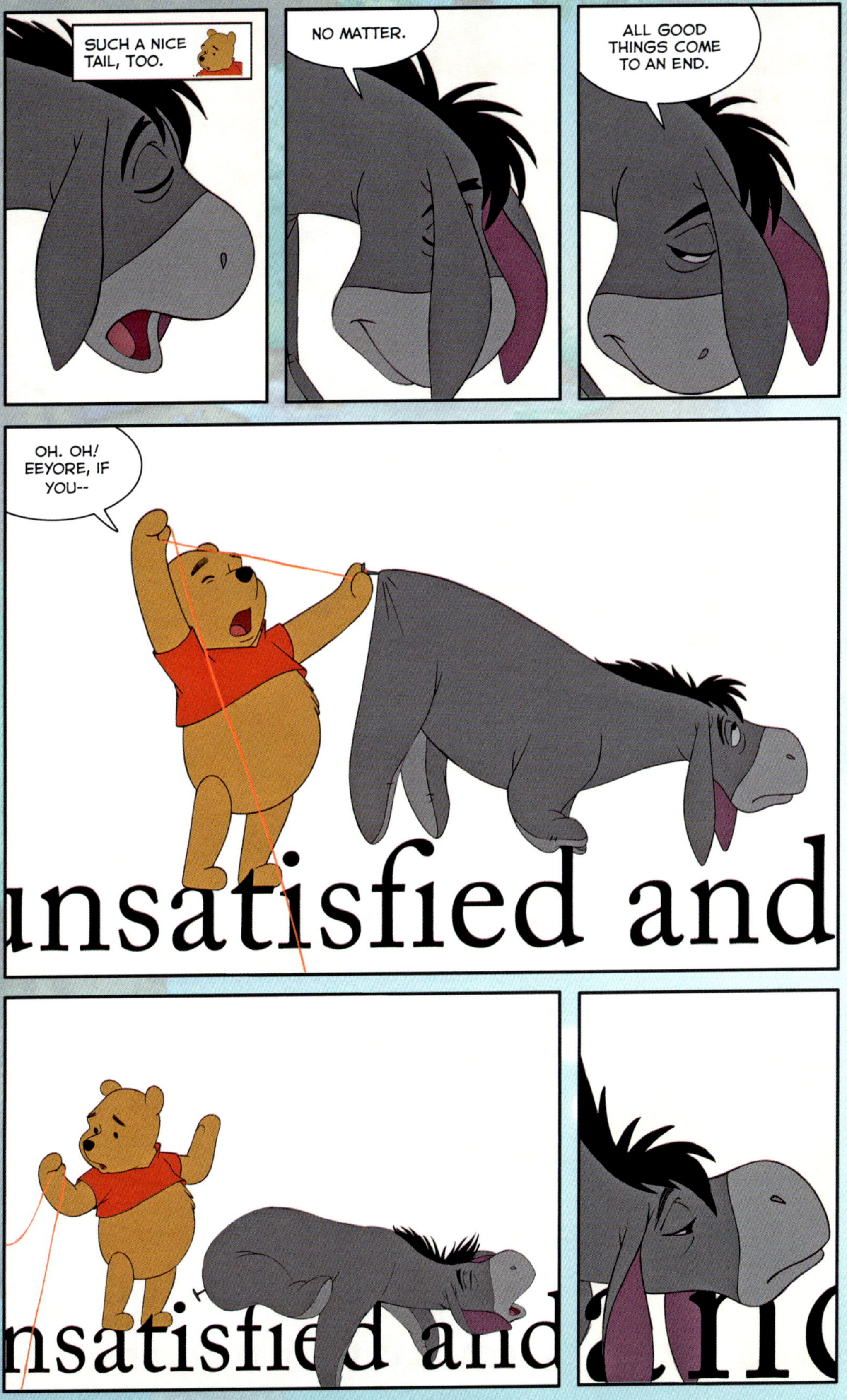

SUCH A NICE TAIL, TOO.
NO MATTER.
ALL GOOD THINGS COME TO AN END.
OH. OH! EEYORE, IF YOU--
nsatisfied and
nsatisfied and

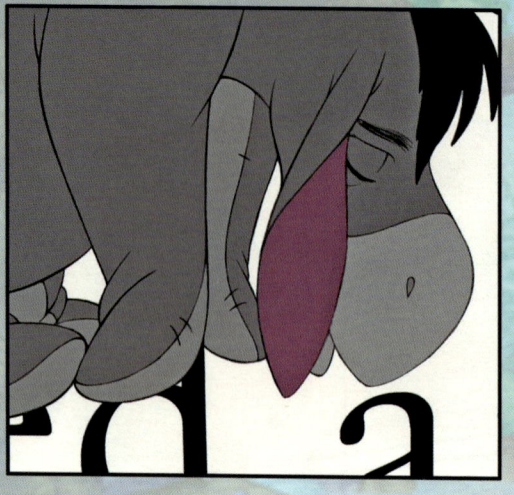

unsatisf

dooh left the contest feeling unsatis
acted by his rumbly tummy, that he   Winnie-the-Pooh
"What's a paragraph?" asked Pooh.   "I wish that parag
o. "Then I don't find it very useful."   "My good friend
                                            some. He loves t

"OH, MY GOODNESS."

dooh left the contest feeling unsatis
so distracted by his rumbly tummy, that he   Winnie-the-Pooh
graph. "What's a paragraph?" asked Pooh.   "I wish that parag
think so. "Then I don't find it very useful."   "My good friend

dooh le
cted by his rumbly tummy, that he

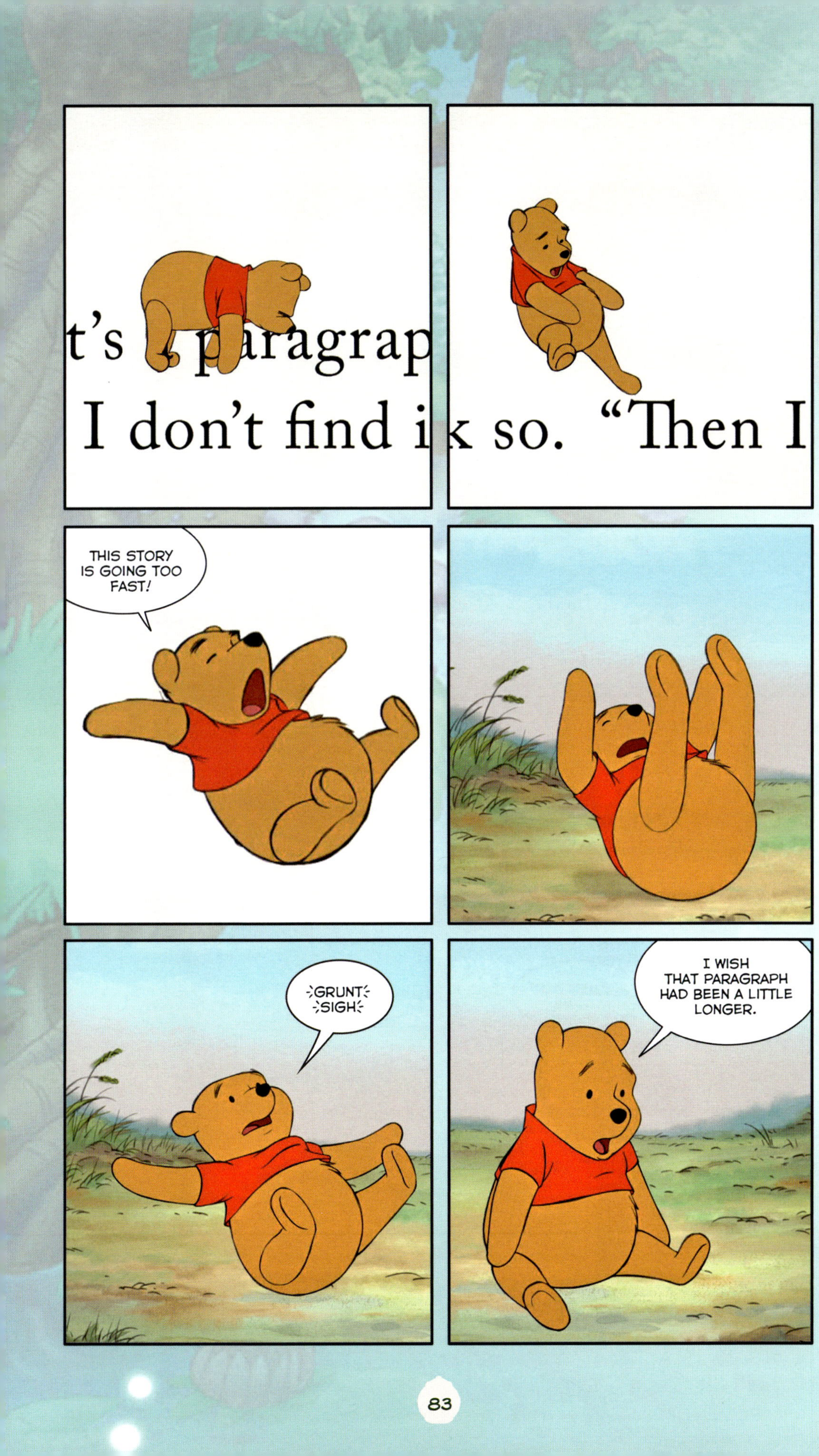
t's paragrap
I don't find i
k so. “Then I
THIS STORY IS GOING TOO FAST!
-GRUNT-
-SIGH-
I WISH THAT PARAGRAPH HAD BEEN A LITTLE LONGER.

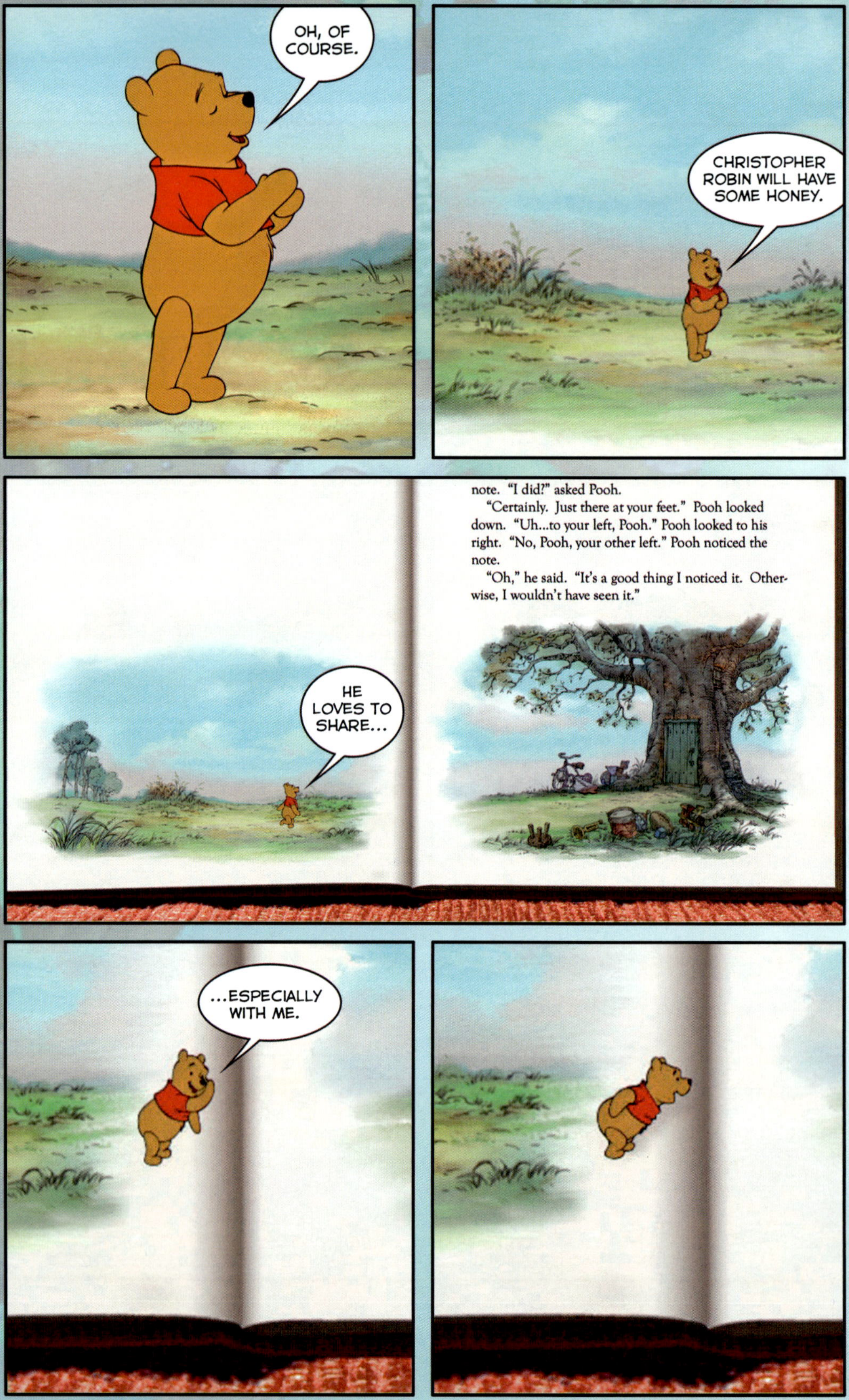
OH, OF COURSE.
CHRISTOPHER ROBIN WILL HAVE SOME HONEY.
HE LOVES TO SHARE...
note. "I did?" asked Pooh.
"Certainly. Just there at your feet." Pooh looked down. "Uh...to your left, Pooh." Pooh looked to his right. "No, Pooh, your other left." Pooh noticed the note.
"Oh," he said. "It's a good thing I noticed it. Otherwise, I wouldn't have seen it."
...ESPECIALLY WITH ME.

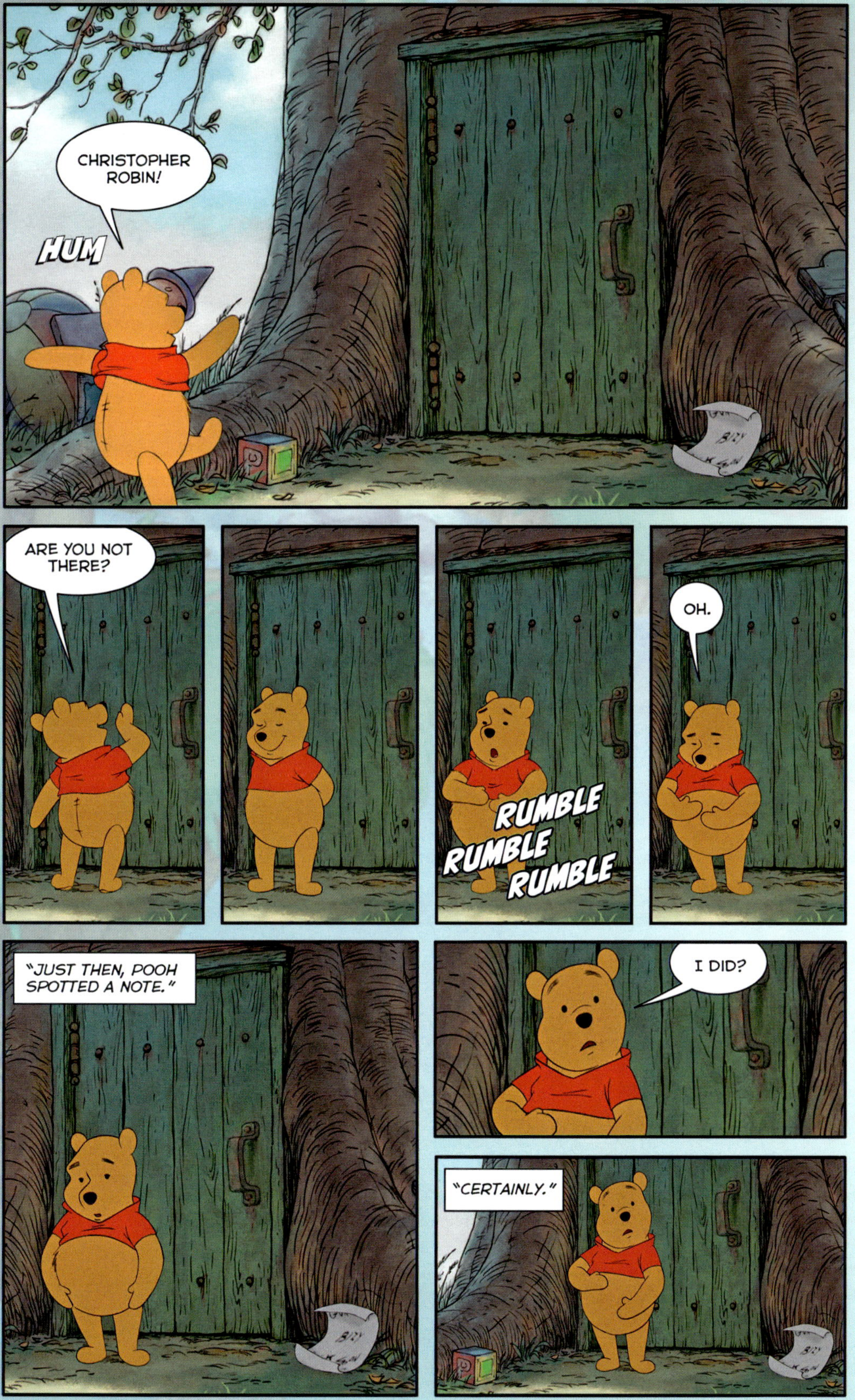
CHRISTOPHER ROBIN!
HUM
ARE YOU NOT THERE?
RUMBLE
RUMBLE
RUMBLE
OH.
"JUST THEN, POOH SPOTTED A NOTE."
I DID?
"CERTAINLY."

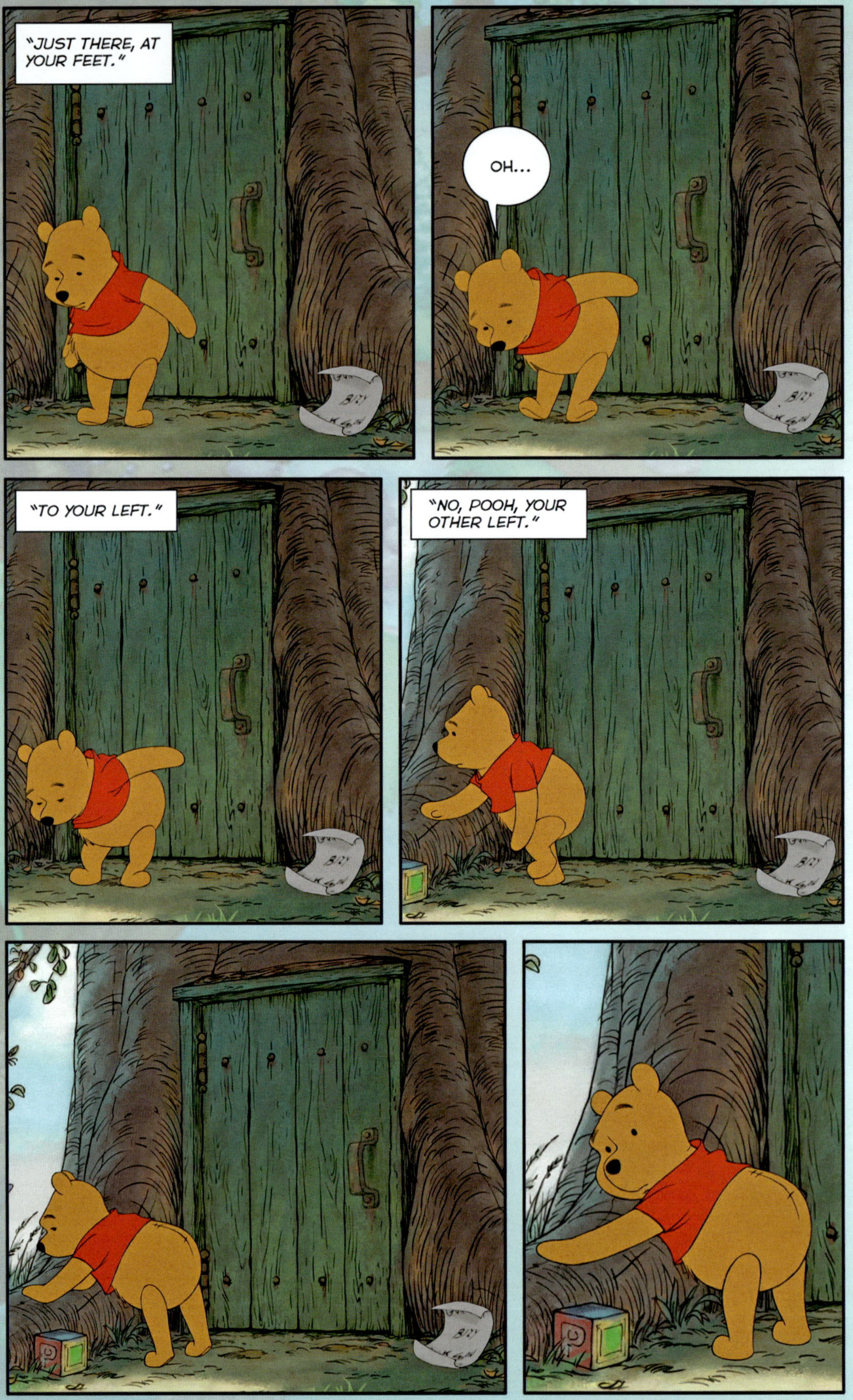
"JUST THERE, AT YOUR FEET."
OH...
"TO YOUR LEFT."
"NO, POOH, YOUR OTHER LEFT."

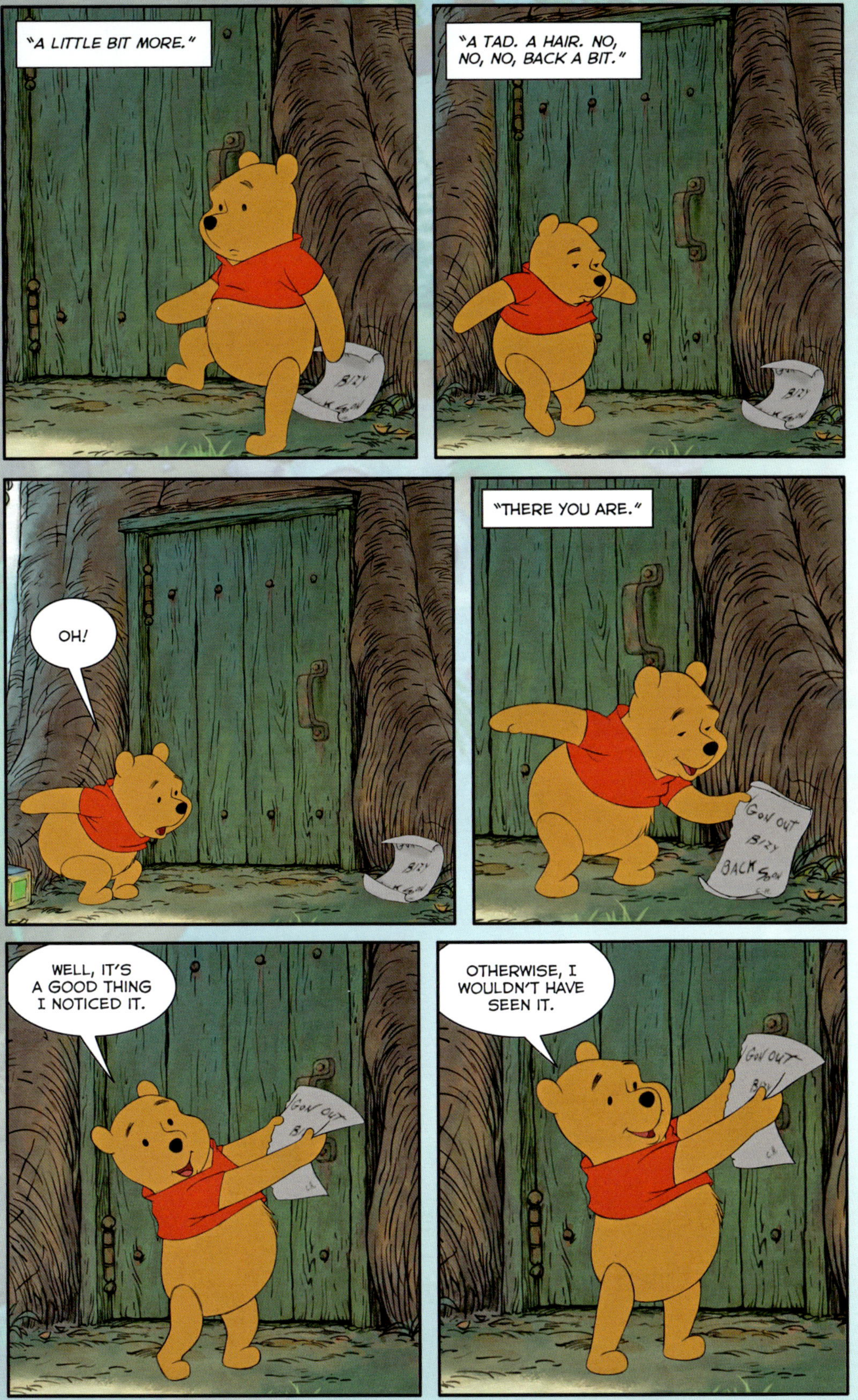
"A LITTLE BIT MORE."
"A TAD. A HAIR. NO, NO, NO, BACK A BIT."
OH!
"THERE YOU ARE."
GON OUT
BIZY
BACK SOON
WELL, IT'S A GOOD THING I NOTICED IT.
OTHERWISE, I WOULDN'T HAVE SEEN IT.

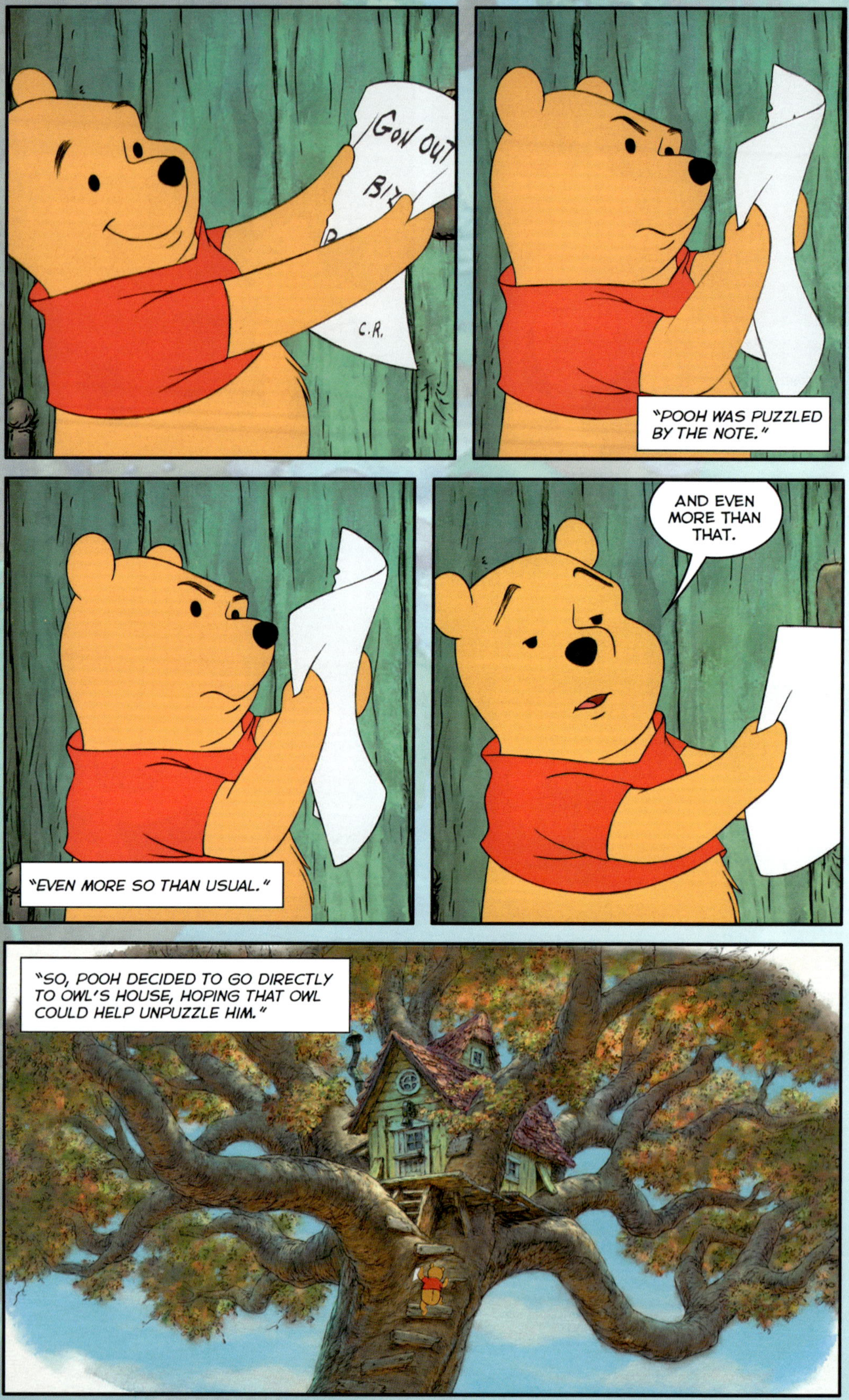
GON OUT
BIZ
C.R.
"POOH WAS PUZZLED BY THE NOTE."
"EVEN MORE SO THAN USUAL."
AND EVEN MORE THAN THAT.
"SO, POOH DECIDED TO GO DIRECTLY TO OWL'S HOUSE, HOPING THAT OWL COULD HELP UNPUZZLE HIM."

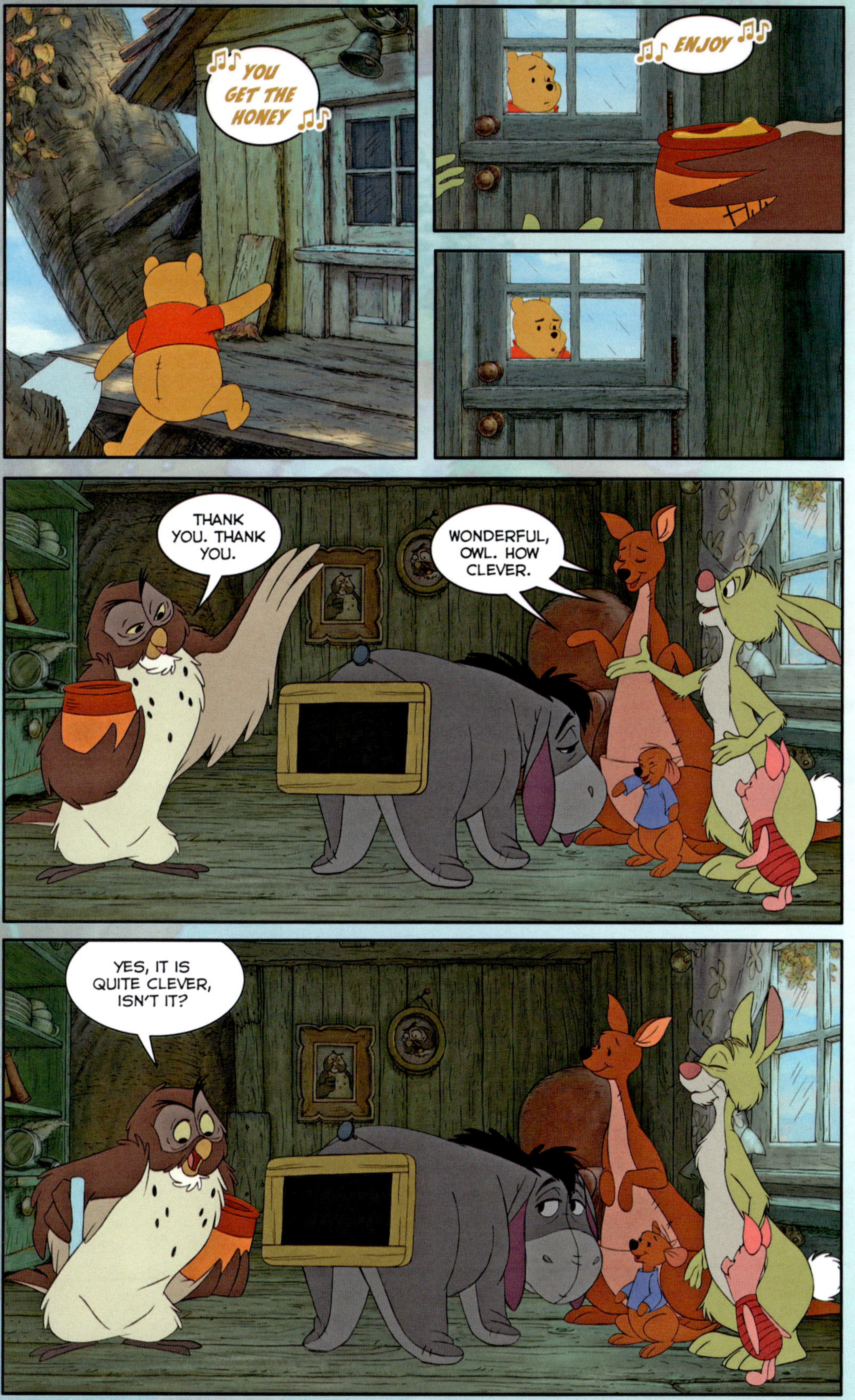

YOU GET THE HONEY
ENJOY
THANK YOU. THANK YOU.
WONDERFUL, OWL. HOW CLEVER.
YES, IT IS QUITE CLEVER, ISN'T IT?

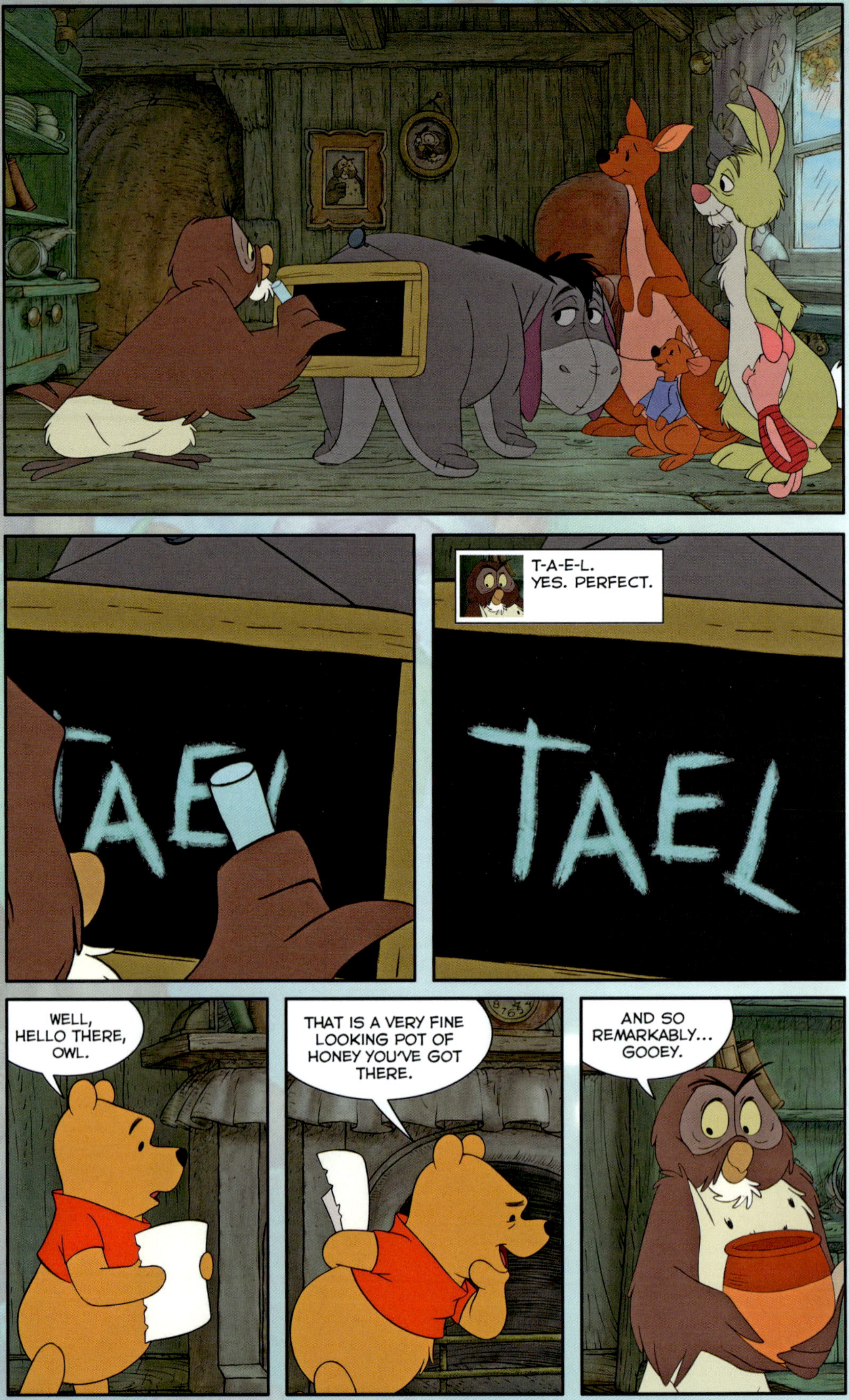

TAEL
T-A-E-L.
YES. PERFECT.
TAEL
WELL, HELLO THERE, OWL.
THAT IS A VERY FINE LOOKING POT OF HONEY YOU'VE GOT THERE.
AND SO REMARKABLY... GOOEY.

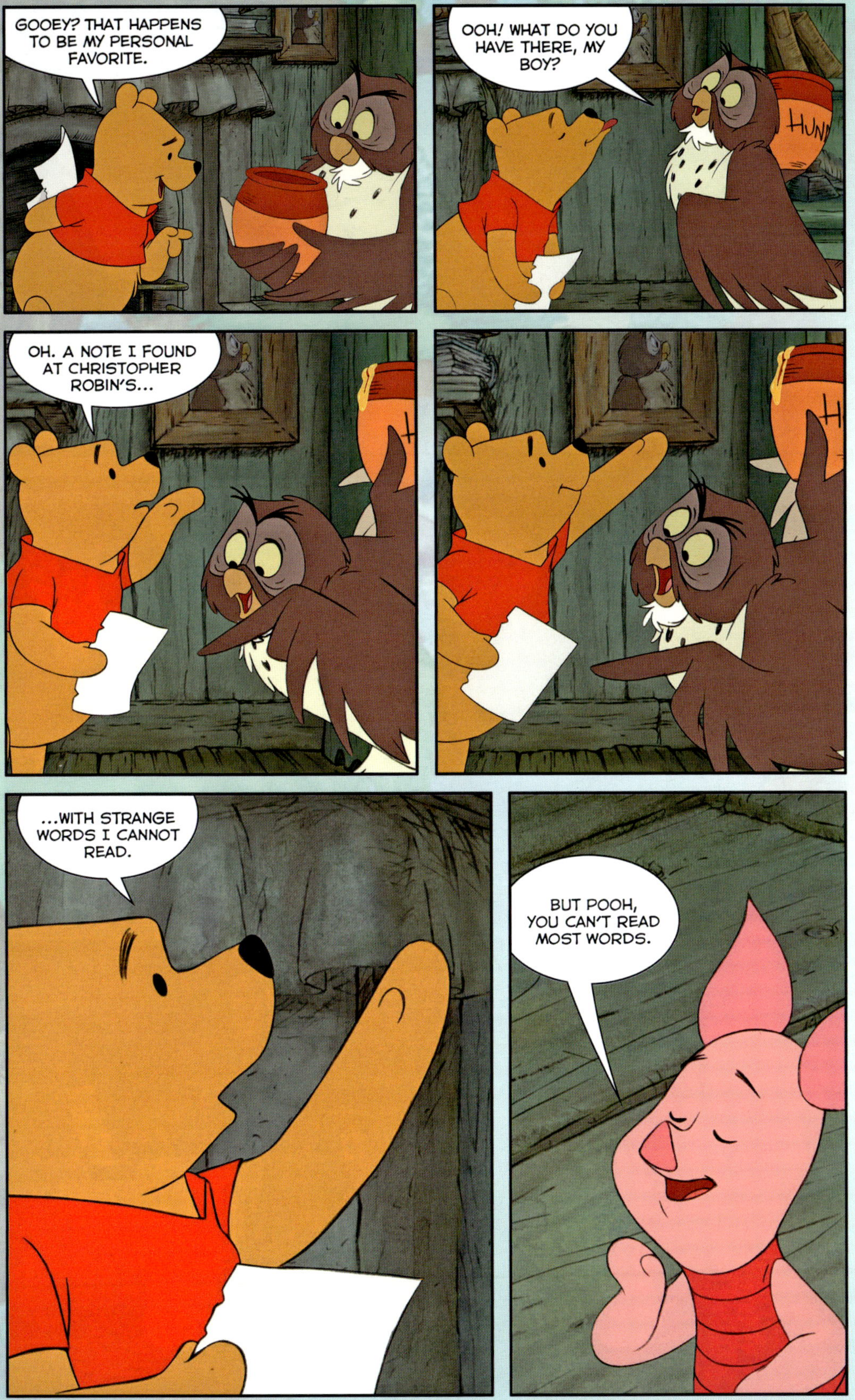
GOOEY? THAT HAPPENS TO BE MY PERSONAL FAVORITE.
OOH! WHAT DO YOU HAVE THERE, MY BOY?
HUNNY
OH. A NOTE I FOUND AT CHRISTOPHER ROBIN'S...
...WITH STRANGE WORDS I CANNOT READ.
BUT POOH, YOU CAN'T READ MOST WORDS.

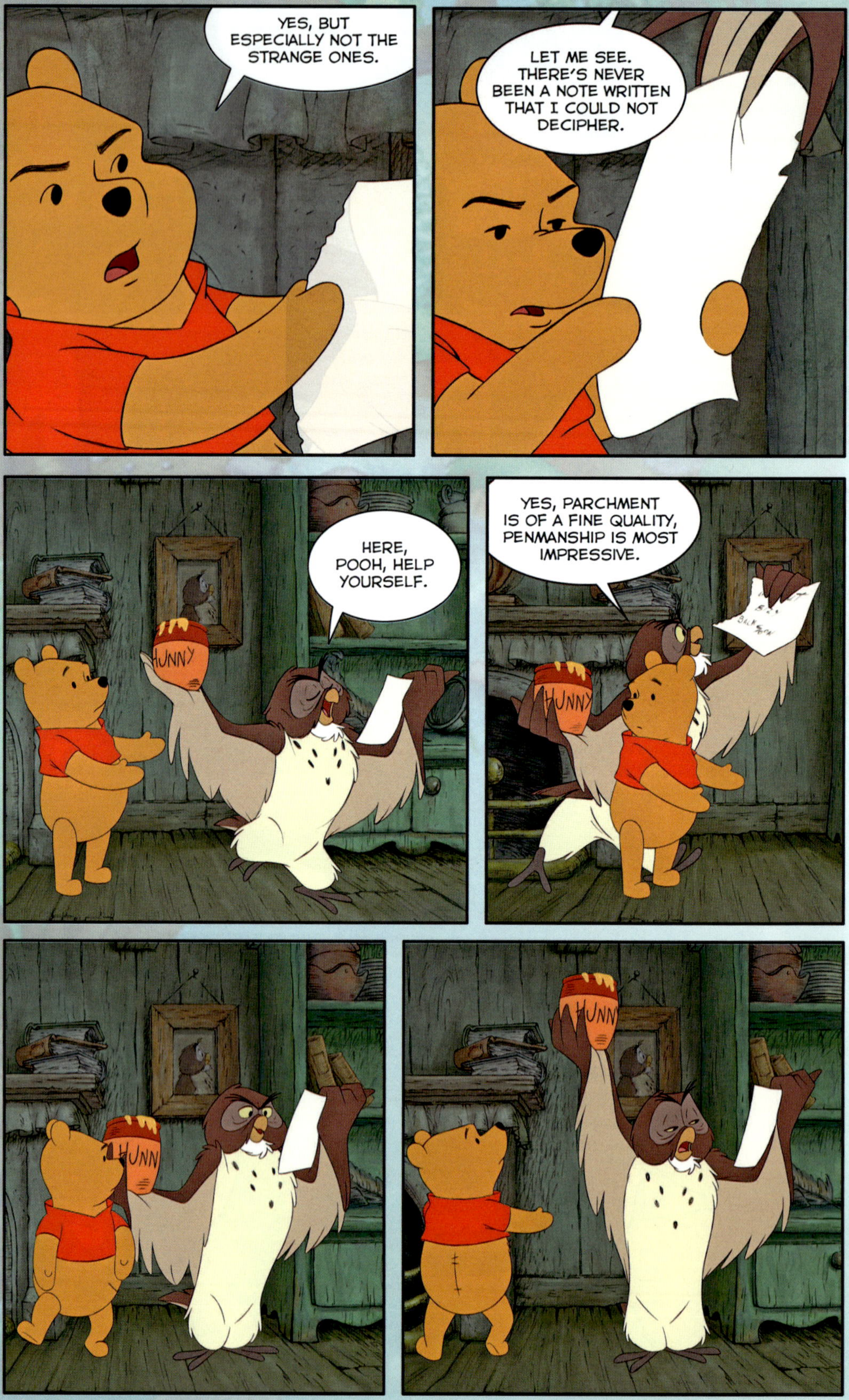
YES, BUT ESPECIALLY NOT THE STRANGE ONES.
LET ME SEE. THERE'S NEVER BEEN A NOTE WRITTEN THAT I COULD NOT DECIPHER.
HERE, POOH, HELP YOURSELF.
HUNNY
YES, PARCHMENT IS OF A FINE QUALITY, PENMANSHIP IS MOST IMPRESSIVE.
HUNNY
HUNN
HUNN

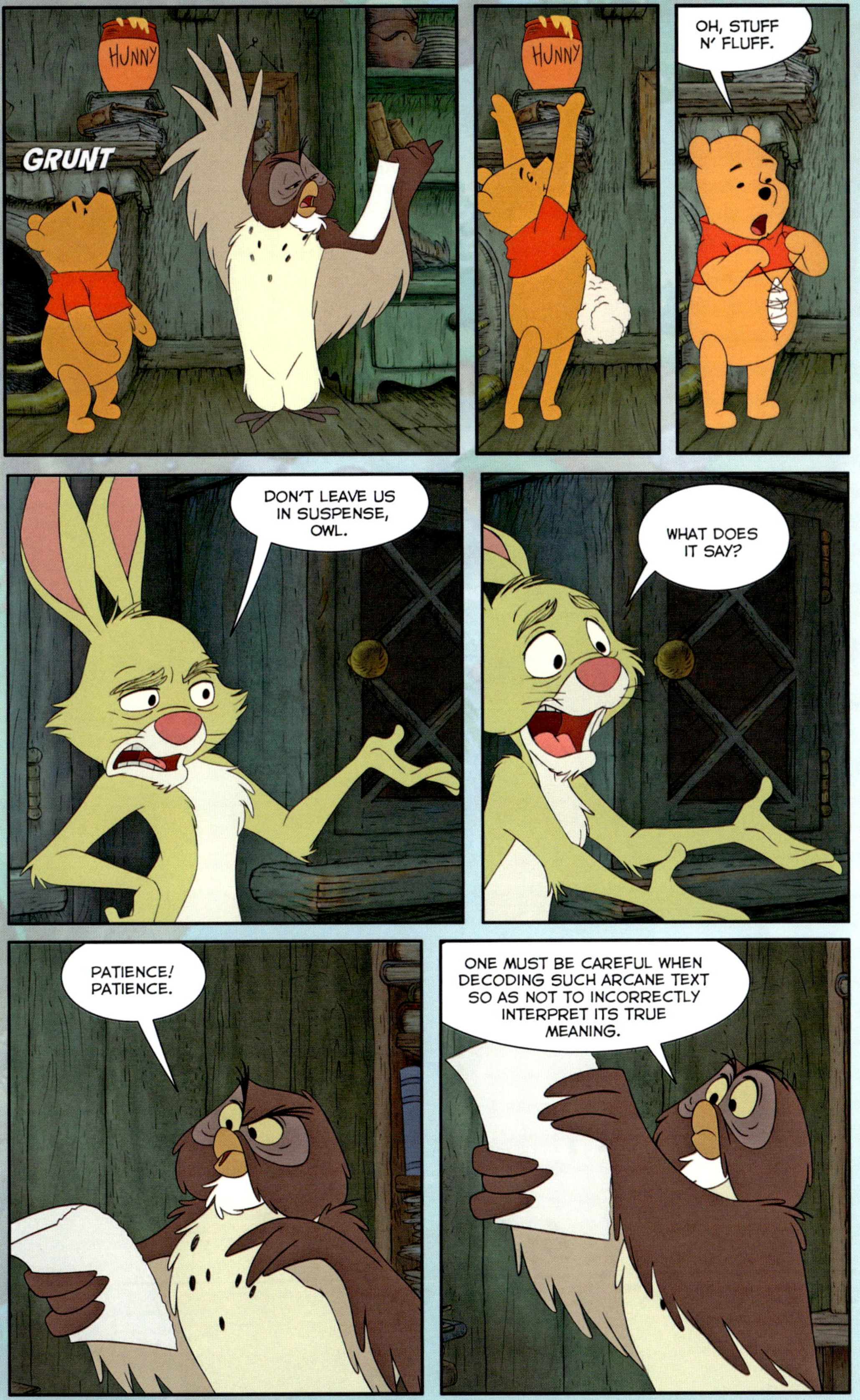
HUNNY
GRUNT
HUNNY
OH, STUFF N' FLUFF.
DON'T LEAVE US IN SUSPENSE, OWL.
WHAT DOES IT SAY?
PATIENCE! PATIENCE.
ONE MUST BE CAREFUL WHEN DECODING SUCH ARCANE TEXT SO AS NOT TO INCORRECTLY INTERPRET ITS TRUE MEANING.

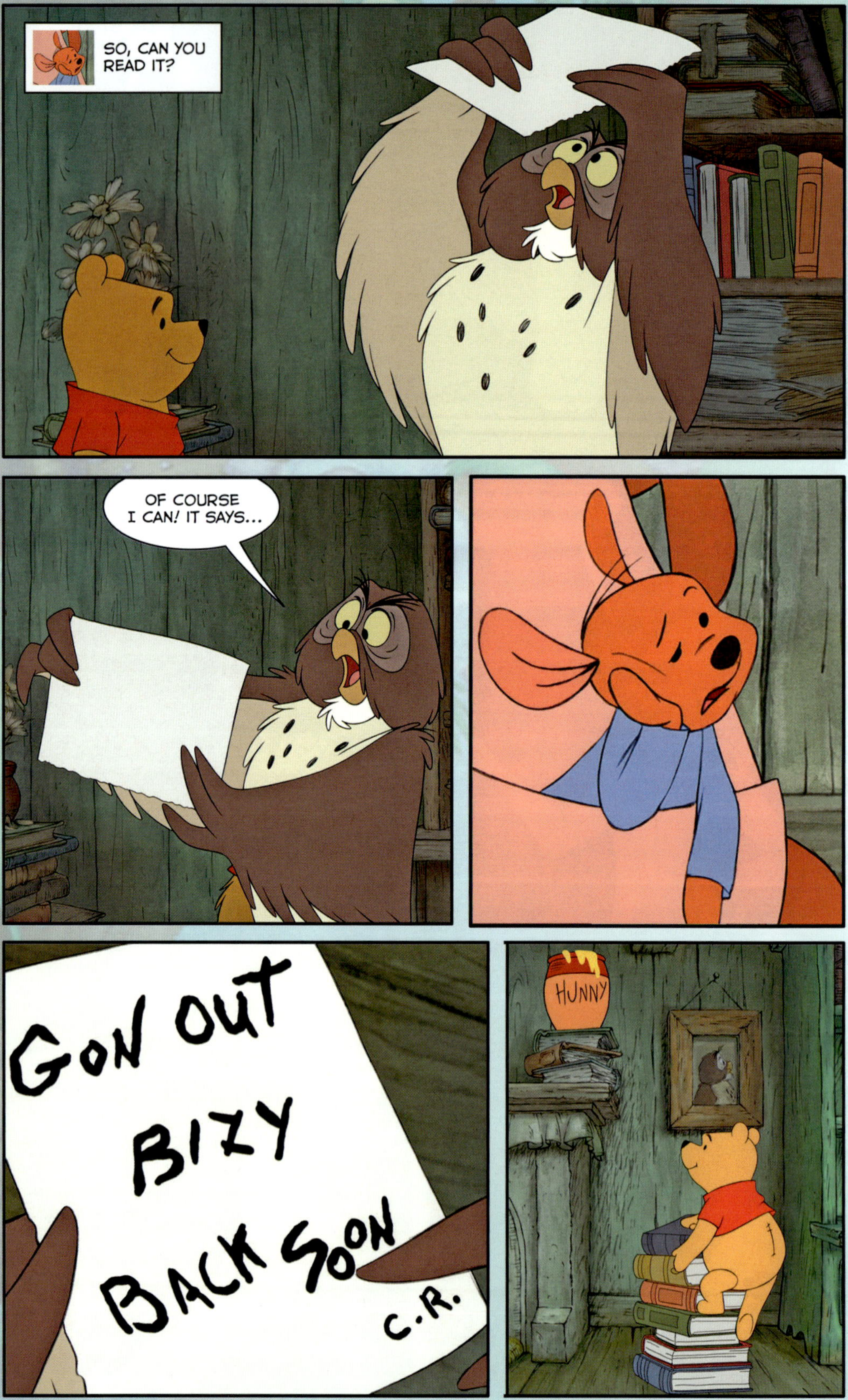
SO, CAN YOU READ IT?
OF COURSE I CAN! IT SAYS...
GON OUT
BIZY
BACK SOON
C.R.
HUNNY

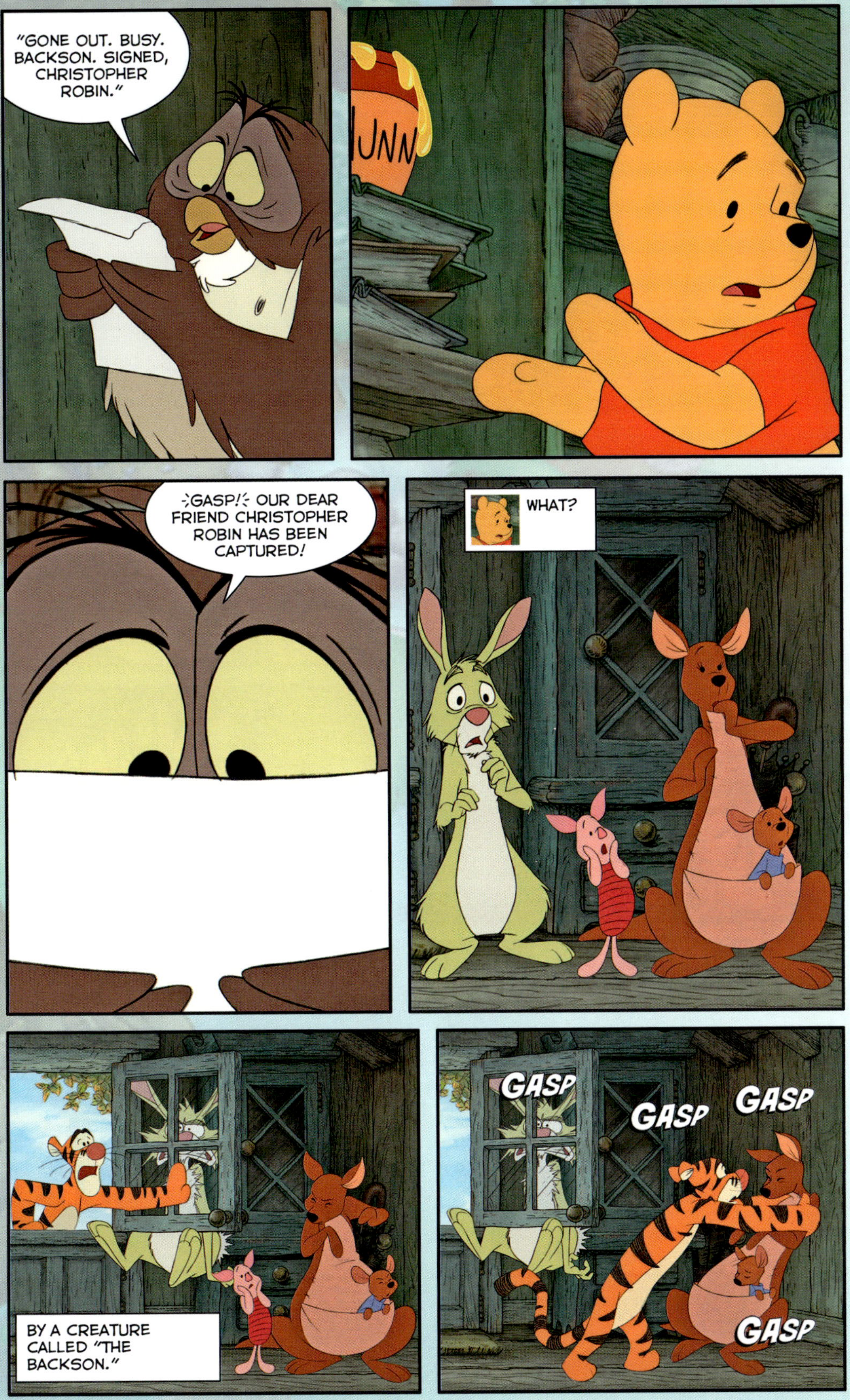
"GONE OUT. BUSY. BACKSON. SIGNED, CHRISTOPHER ROBIN."
HUNN
GASP! OUR DEAR FRIEND CHRISTOPHER ROBIN HAS BEEN CAPTURED!
WHAT?
BY A CREATURE CALLED "THE BACKSON."
GASP
GASP
GASP
GASP

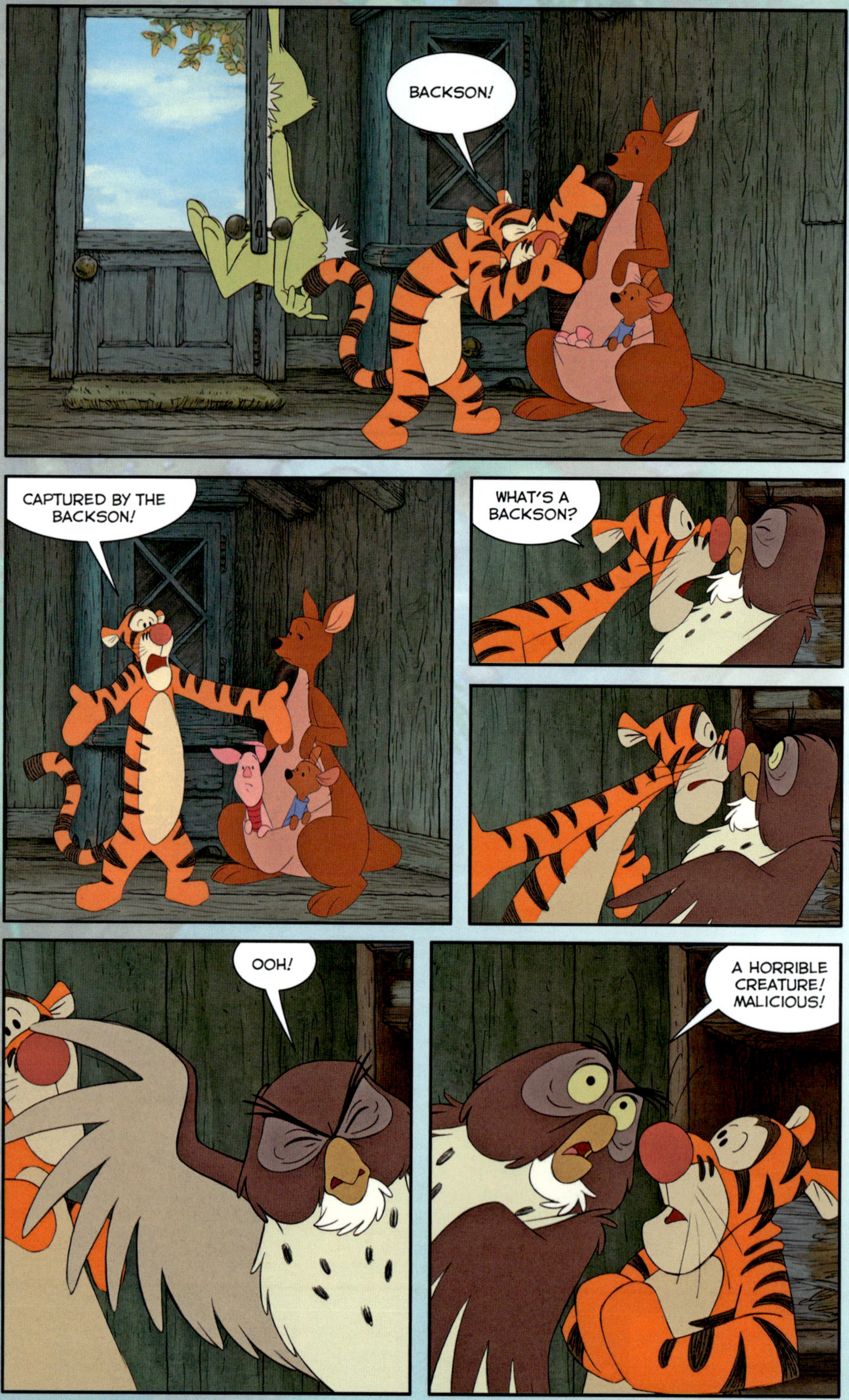
BACKSON!
CAPTURED BY THE BACKSON!
WHAT'S A BACKSON?
OOH!
A HORRIBLE CREATURE! MALICIOUS!

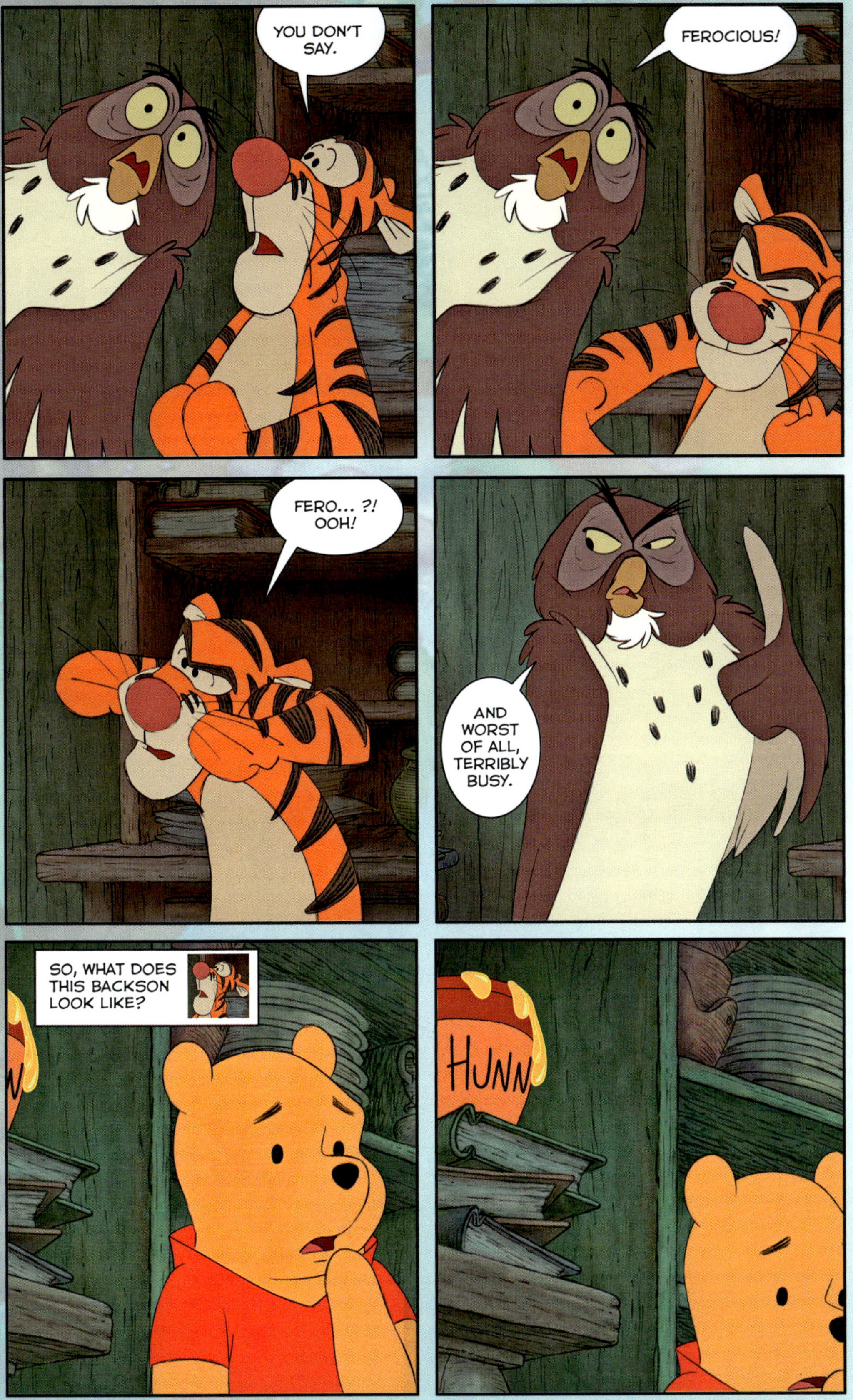
YOU DON'T SAY.
FEROCIOUS!
FERO... ?! OOH!
AND WORST OF ALL, TERRIBLY BUSY.
SO, WHAT DOES THIS BACKSON LOOK LIKE?
HUNN

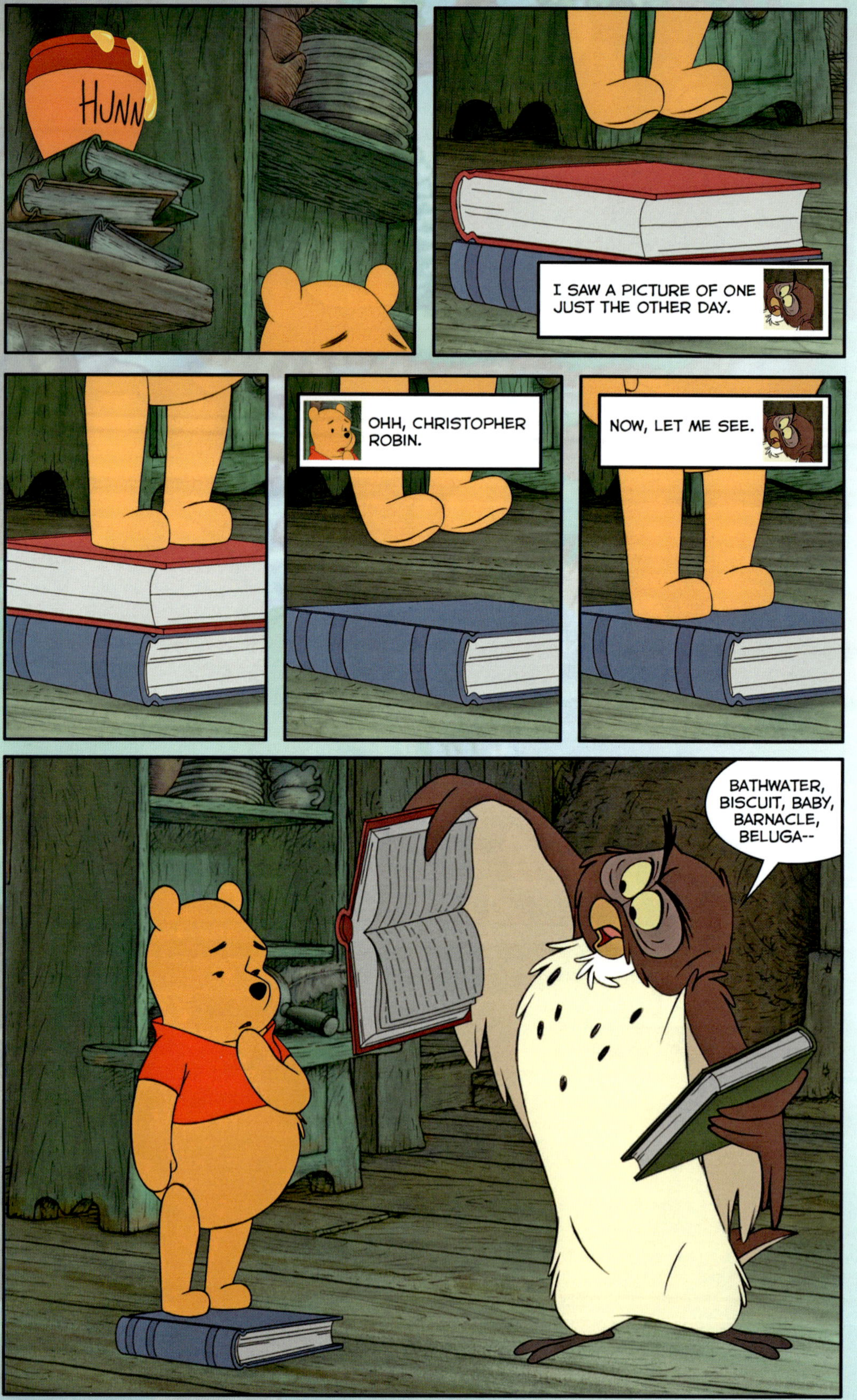
HUNN
I SAW A PICTURE OF ONE JUST THE OTHER DAY.
OHH, CHRISTOPHER ROBIN.
NOW, LET ME SEE.
BATHWATER, BISCUIT, BABY, BARNACLE, BELUGA--

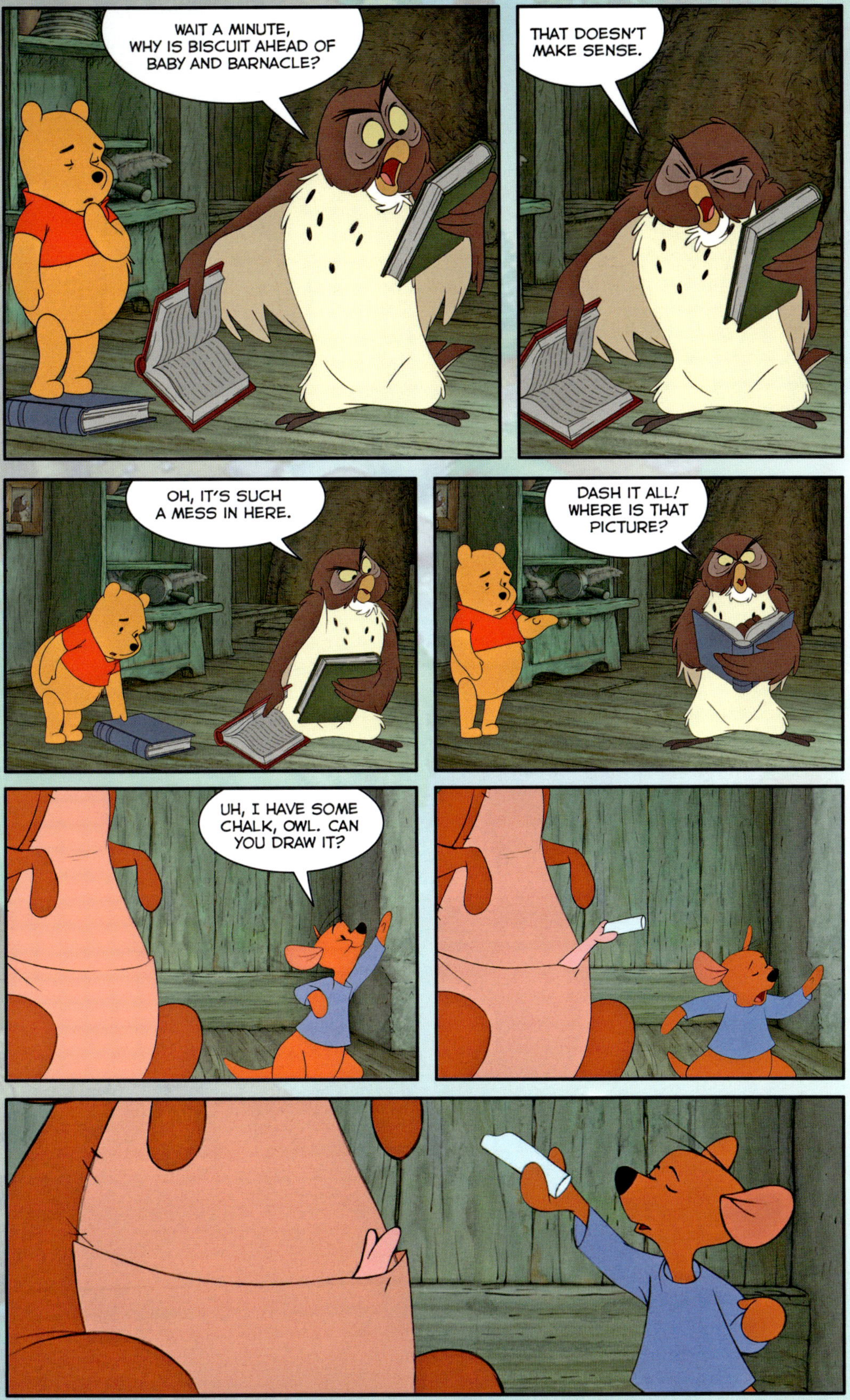
WAIT A MINUTE, WHY IS BISCUIT AHEAD OF BABY AND BARNACLE?
THAT DOESN'T MAKE SENSE.
OH, IT'S SUCH A MESS IN HERE.
DASH IT ALL! WHERE IS THAT PICTURE?
UH, I HAVE SOME CHALK, OWL. CAN YOU DRAW IT?

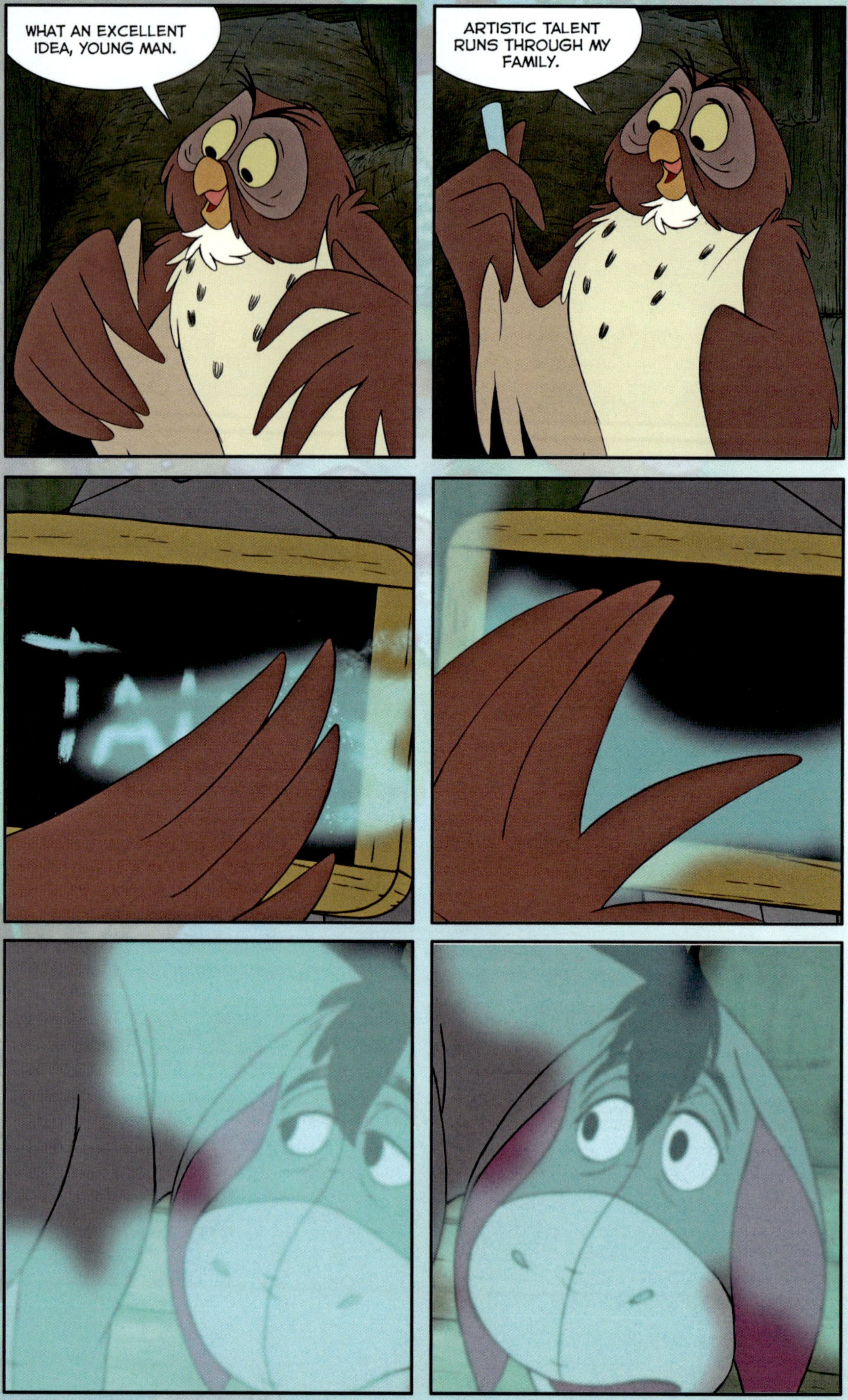
WHAT AN EXCELLENT IDEA, YOUNG MAN.
ARTISTIC TALENT RUNS THROUGH MY FAMILY.

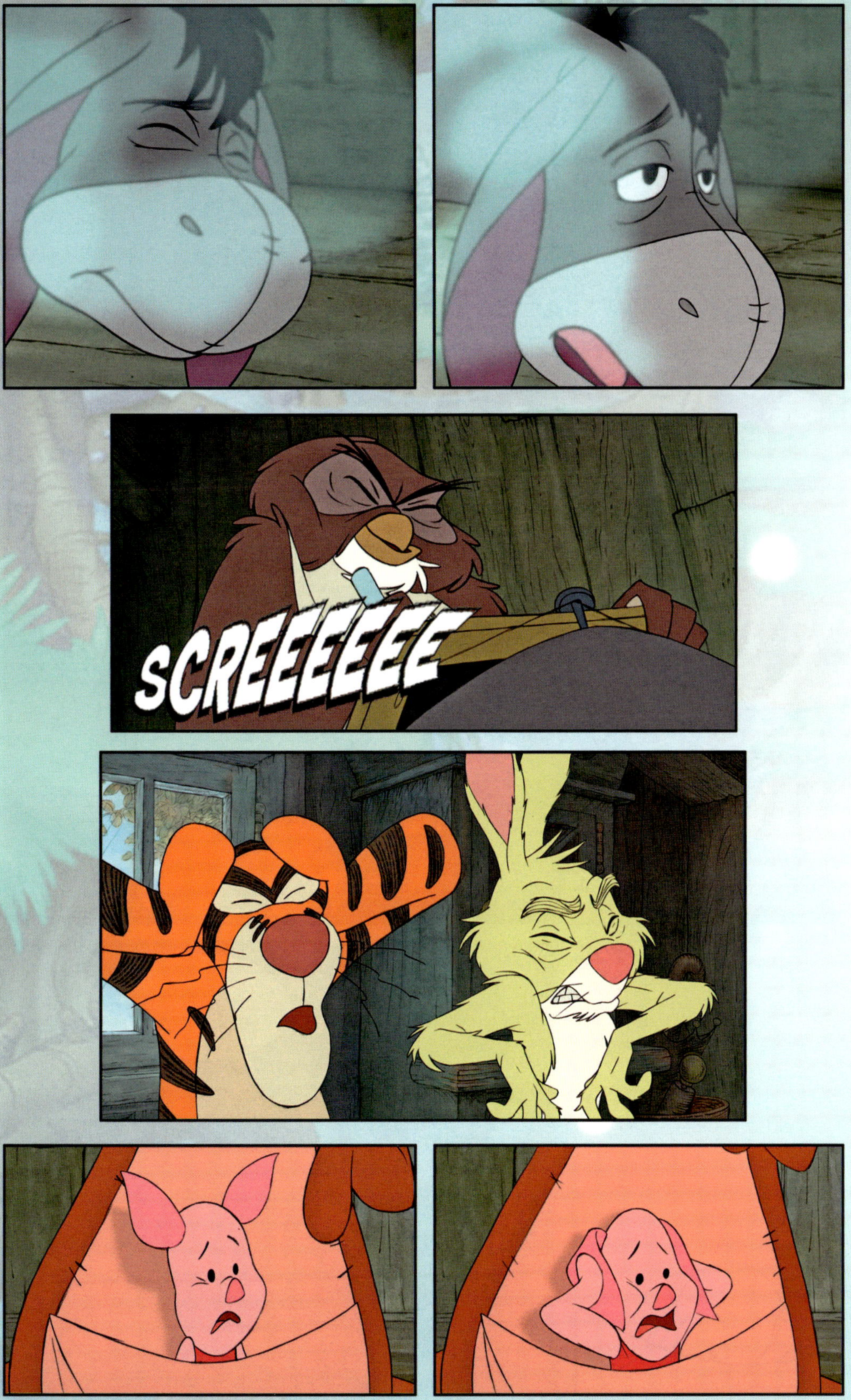
SCREEEEEE

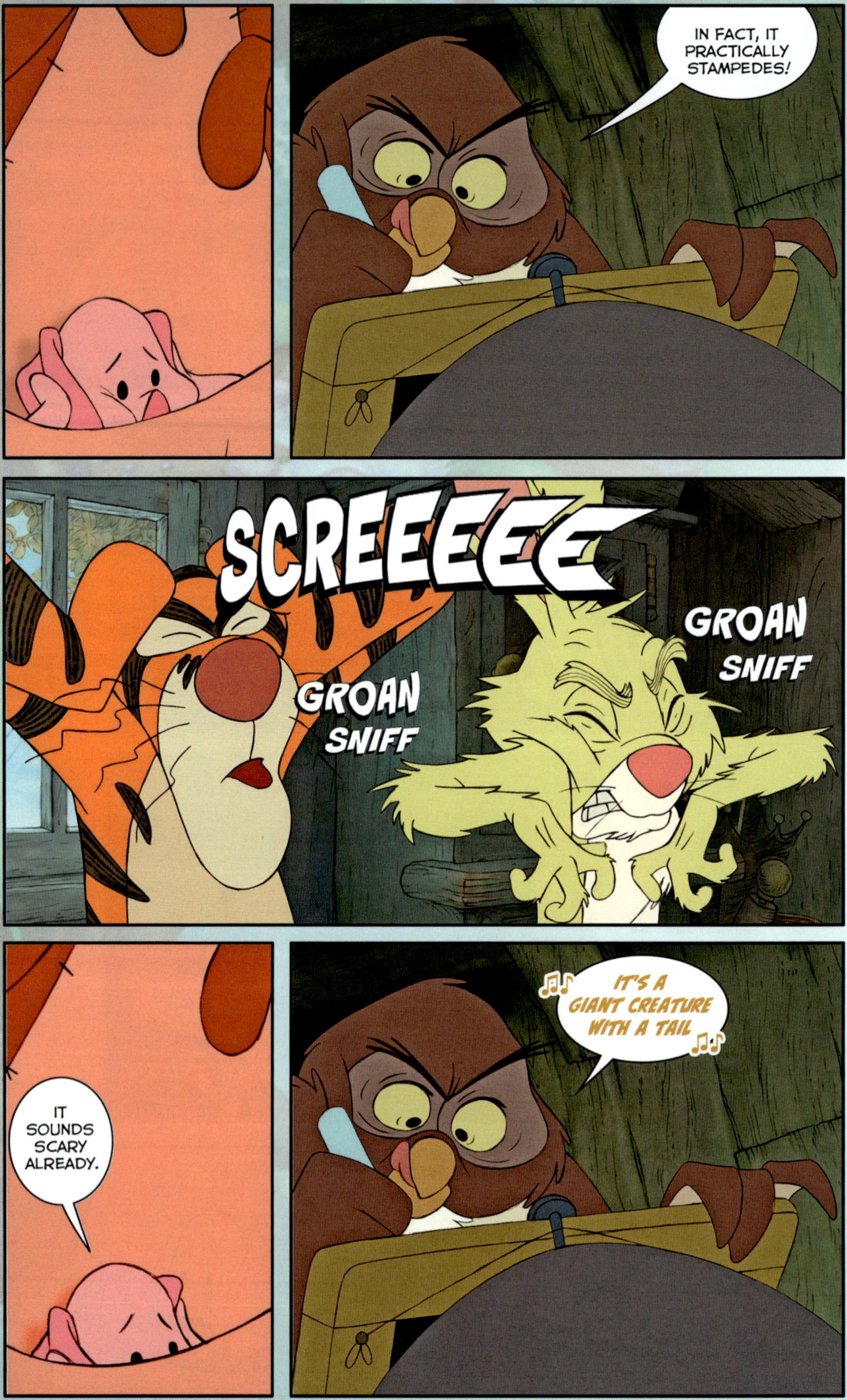
IN FACT, IT PRACTICALLY STAMPEDES!
SCREEEEEE
GROAN SNIFF
GROAN SNIFF
IT SOUNDS SCARY ALREADY.
IT'S A GIANT CREATURE WITH A TAIL

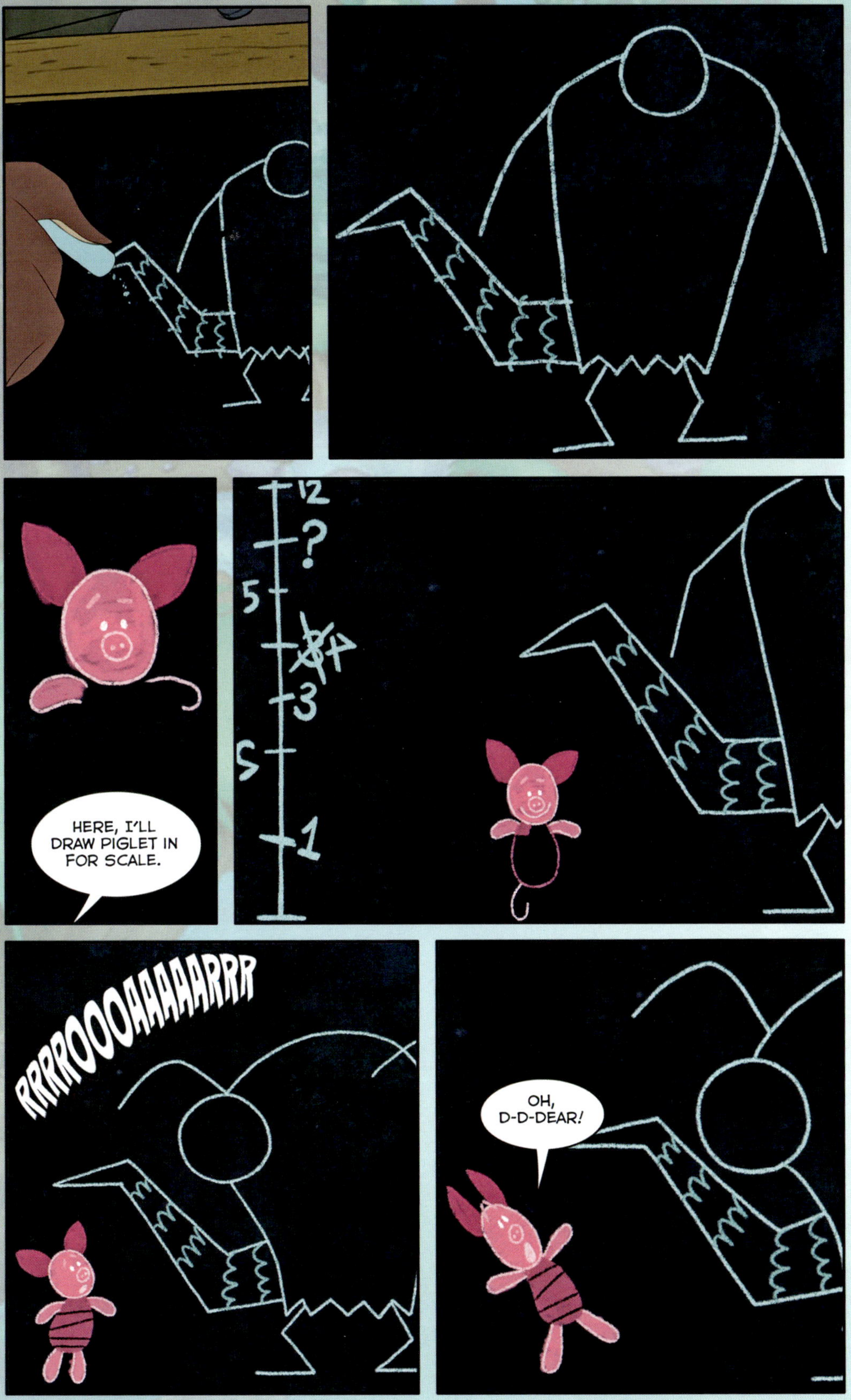

12
?
5
3
5
1
HERE, I'LL DRAW PIGLET IN FOR SCALE.
RRRROOOAAAAARRR
OH, D-D-DEAR!

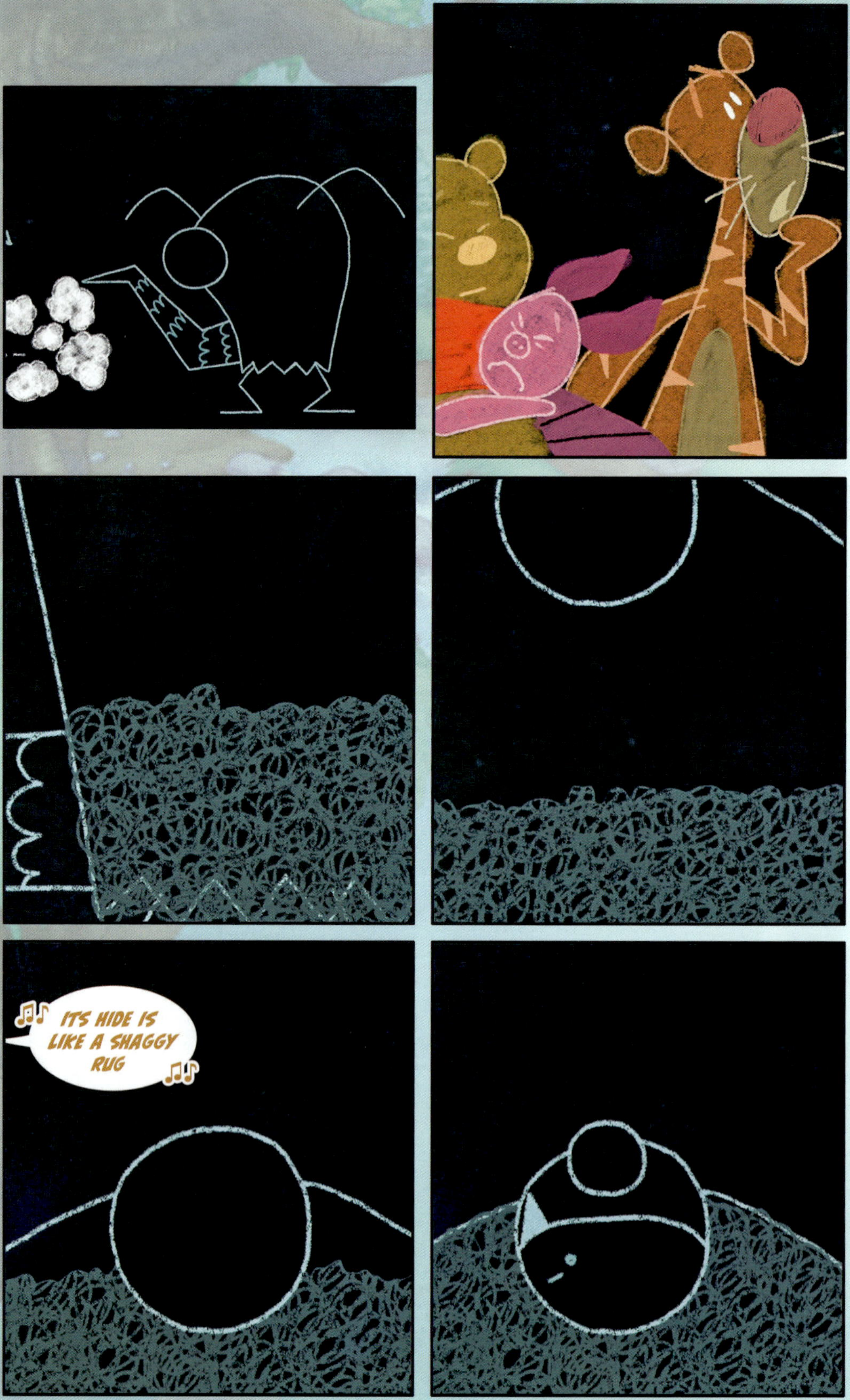
ITS HIDE IS LIKE A SHAGGY RUG

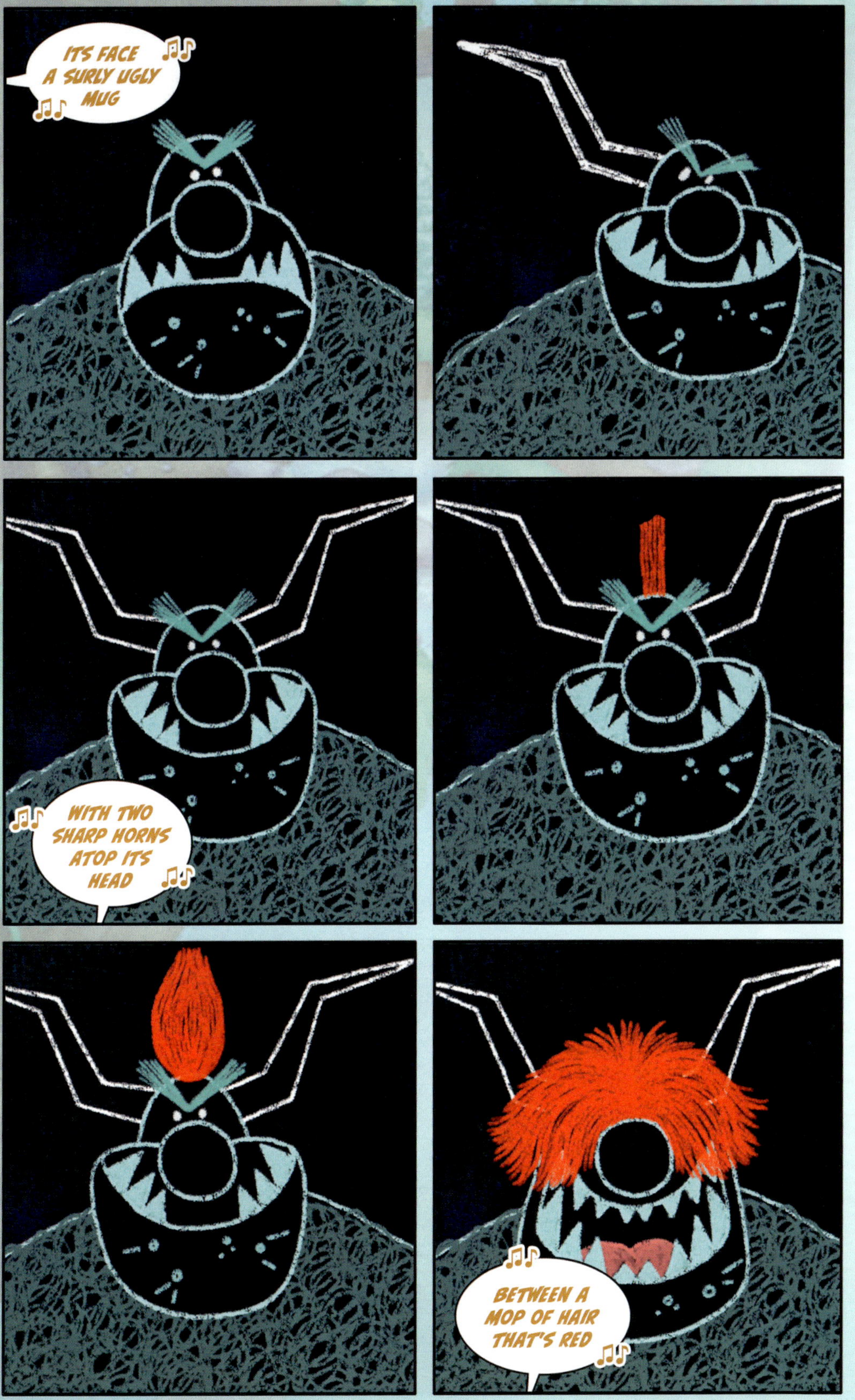
ITS FACE A SURLY UGLY MUG
WITH TWO SHARP HORNS ATOP ITS HEAD
BETWEEN A MOP OF HAIR THAT'S RED

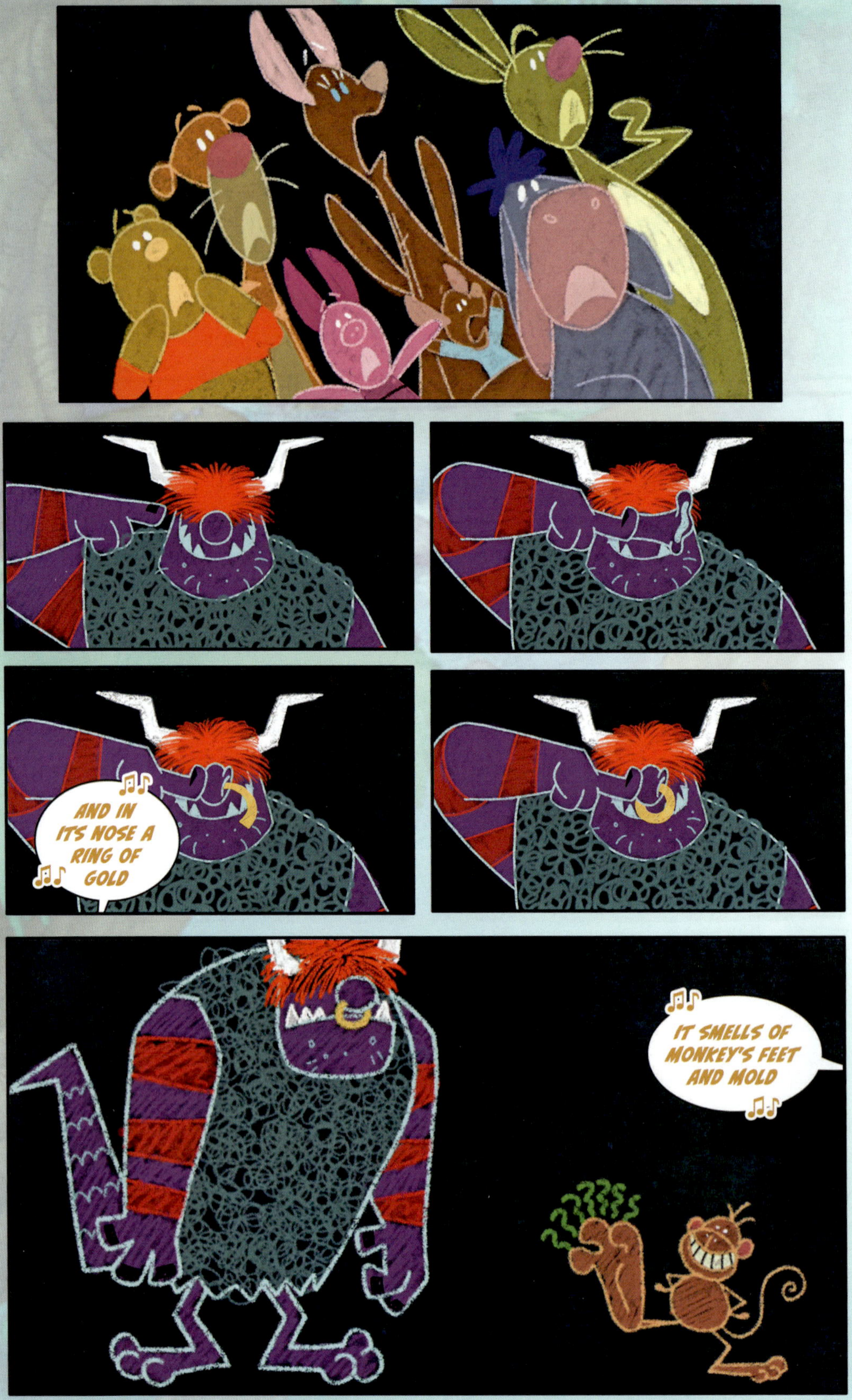
AND IN ITS NOSE A RING OF GOLD
IT SMELLS OF MONKEY'S FEET AND MOLD

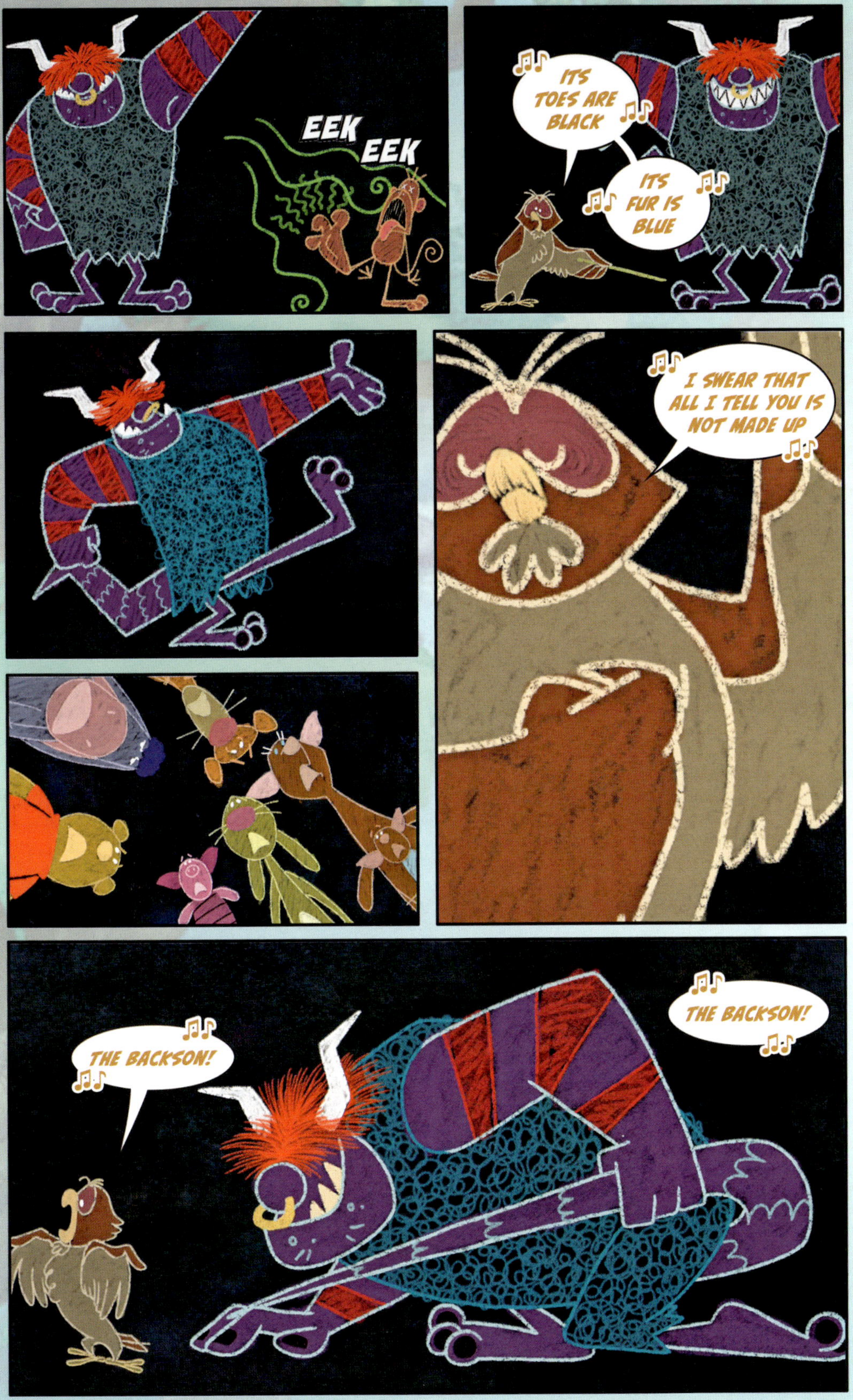
EEK
EEK
ITS TOES ARE BLACK
ITS FUR IS BLUE
I SWEAR THAT ALL I TELL YOU IS NOT MADE UP
THE BACKSON!
THE BACKSON!

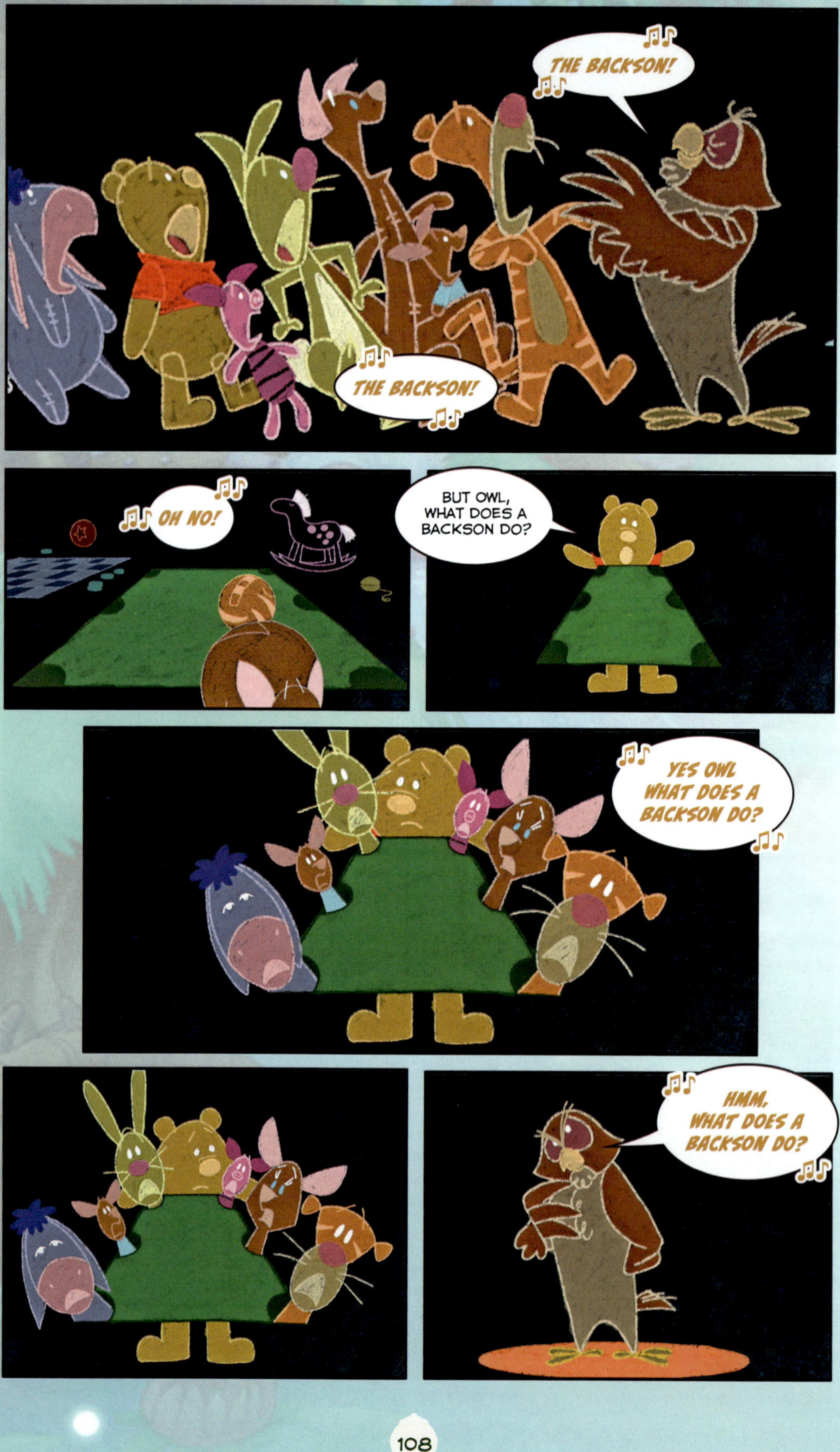
THE BACKSON!
THE BACKSON!
OH NO!
BUT OWL, WHAT DOES A BACKSON DO?
YES OWL WHAT DOES A BACKSON DO?
HMM, WHAT DOES A BACKSON DO?

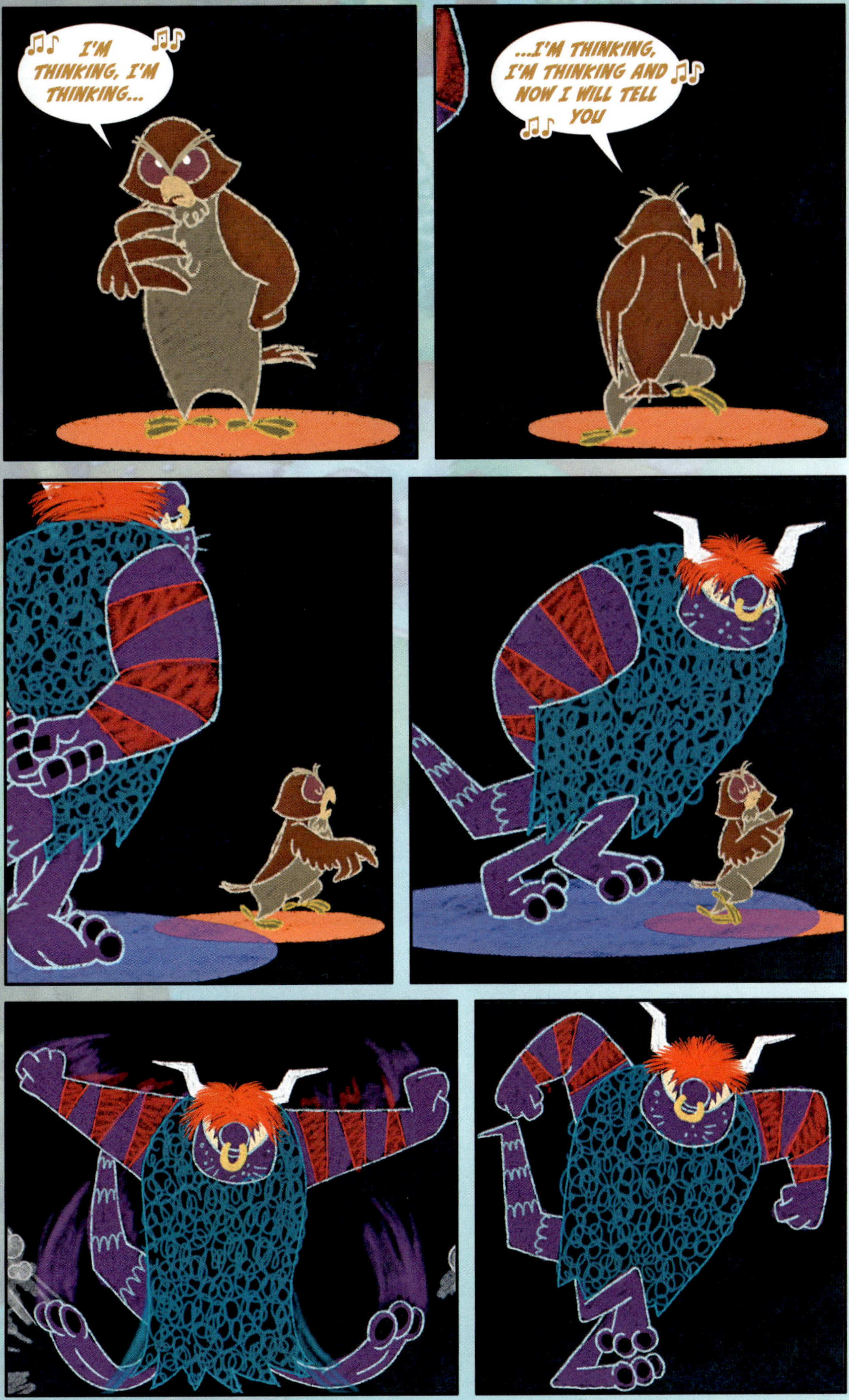
I'M THINKING, I'M THINKING...
...I'M THINKING, I'M THINKING AND NOW I WILL TELL YOU

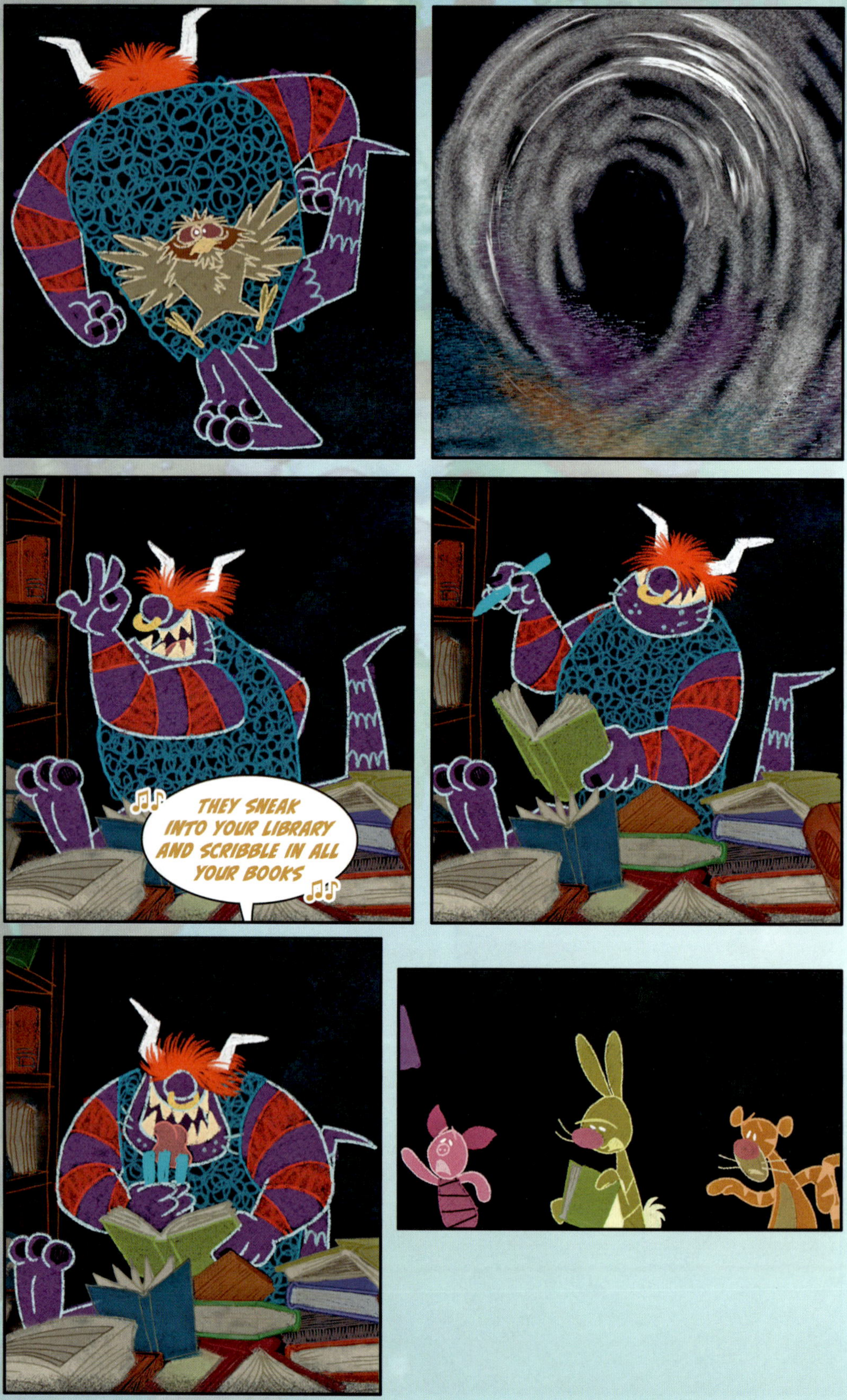
THEY SNEAK INTO YOUR LIBRARY AND SCRIBBLE IN ALL YOUR BOOKS

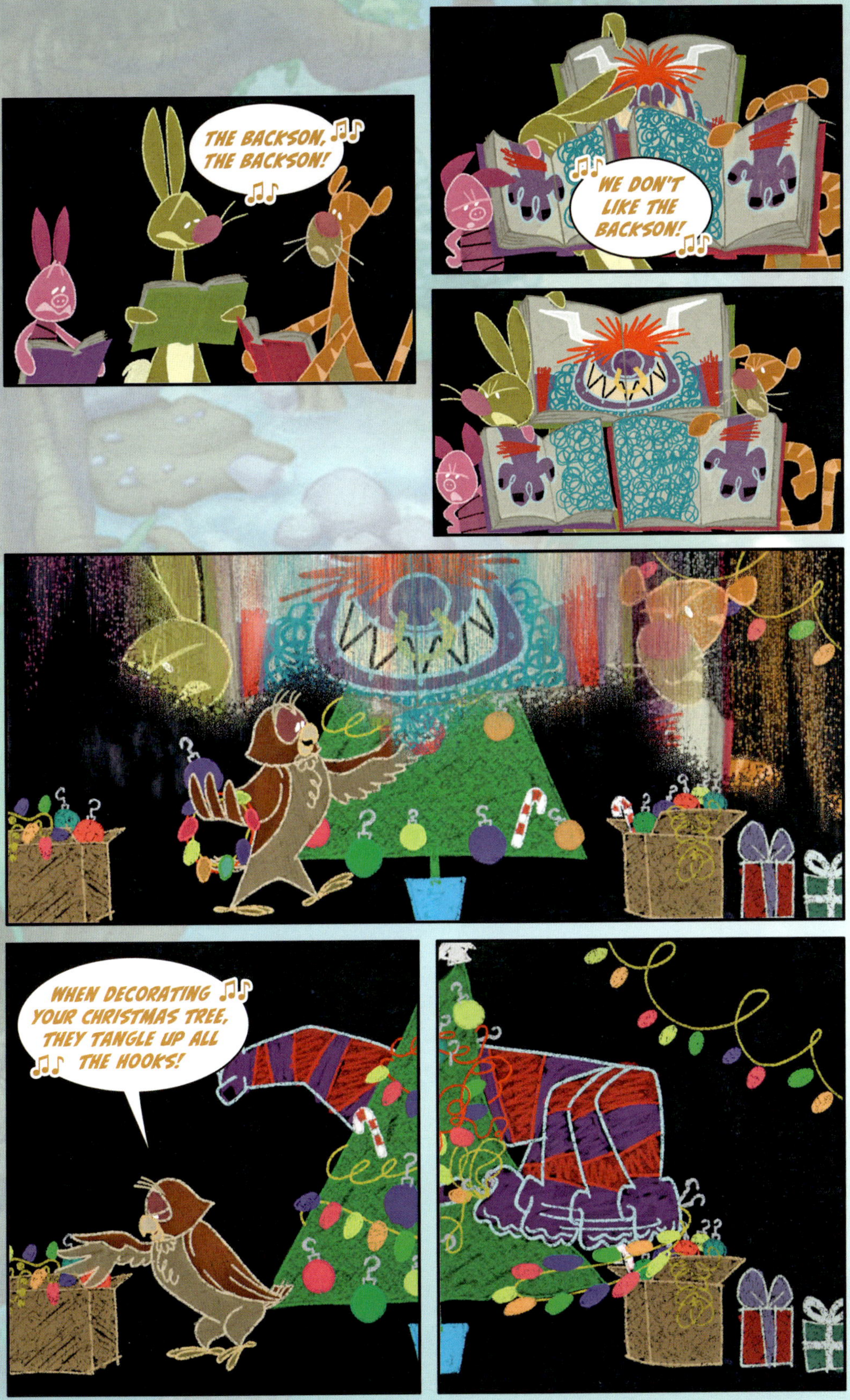
THE BACKSON, THE BACKSON!
WE DON'T LIKE THE BACKSON!
WHEN DECORATING YOUR CHRISTMAS TREE, THEY TANGLE UP ALL THE HOOKS!

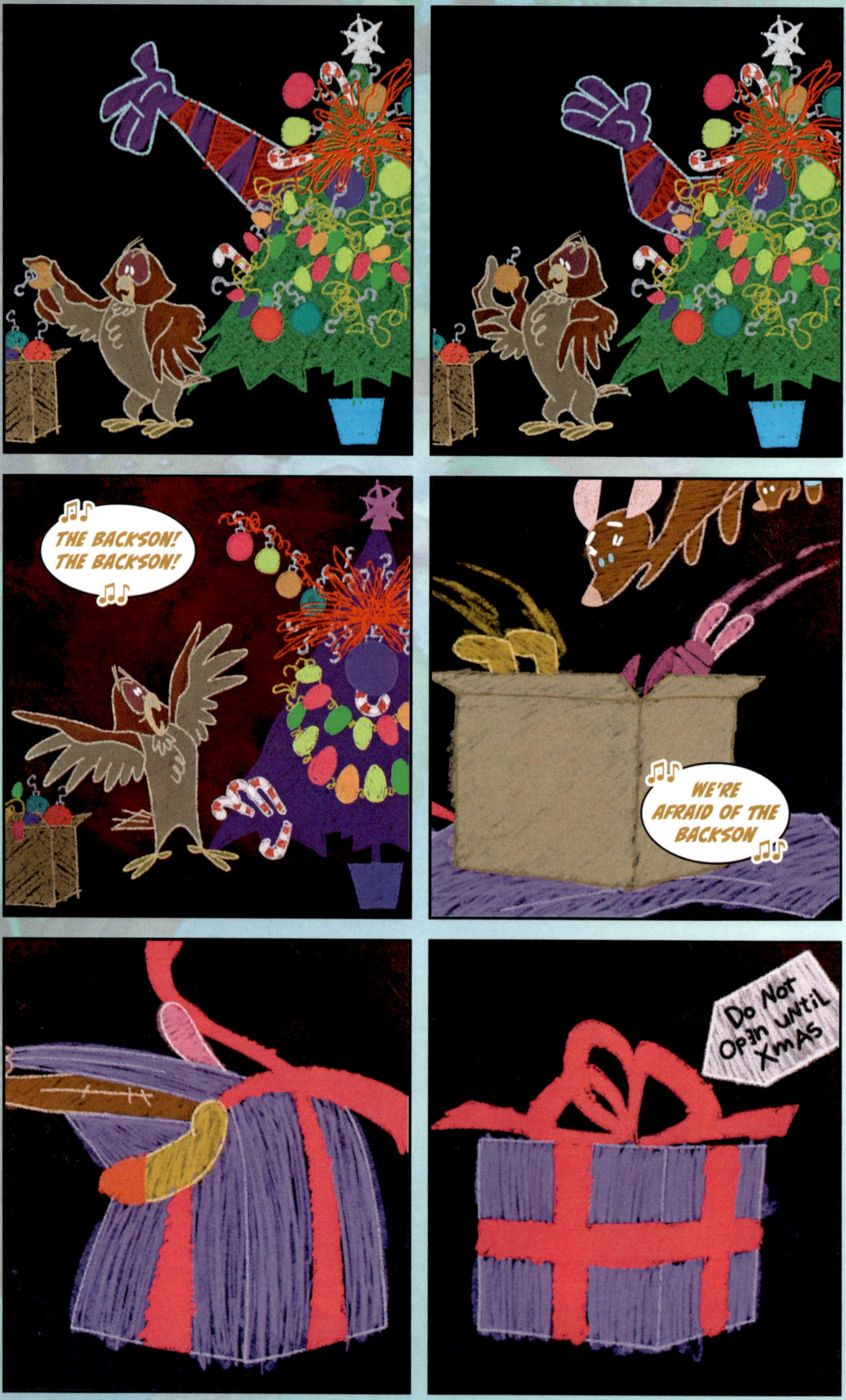
THE BACKSON! THE BACKSON!
WE'RE AFRAID OF THE BACKSON
Do Not Open until XmAS

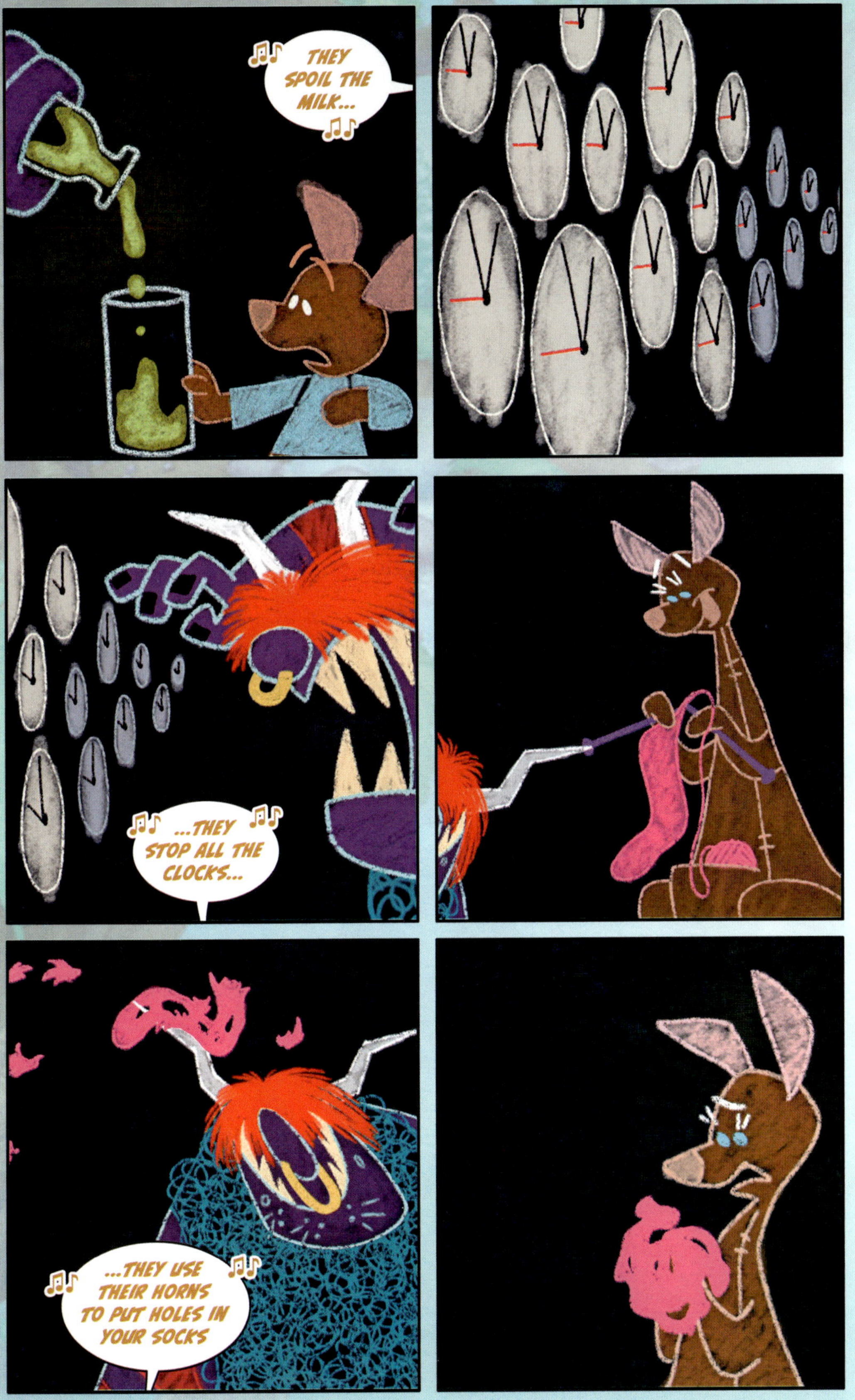
THEY SPOIL THE MILK...
...THEY STOP ALL THE CLOCKS...
...THEY USE THEIR HORNS TO PUT HOLES IN YOUR SOCKS

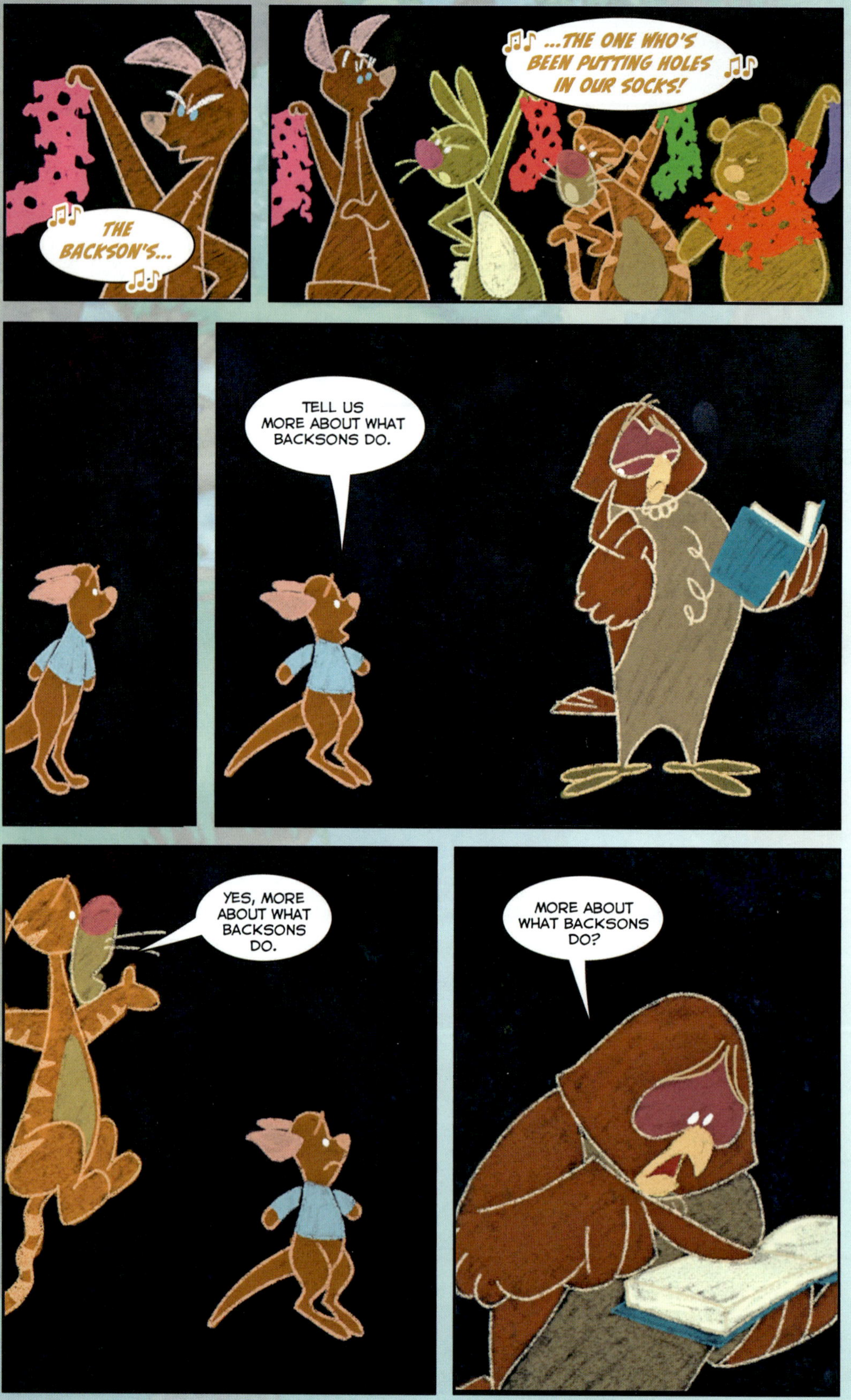
THE BACKSON'S...
...THE ONE WHO'S BEEN PUTTING HOLES IN OUR SOCKS!
TELL US MORE ABOUT WHAT BACKSONS DO.
YES, MORE ABOUT WHAT BACKSONS DO.
MORE ABOUT WHAT BACKSONS DO?

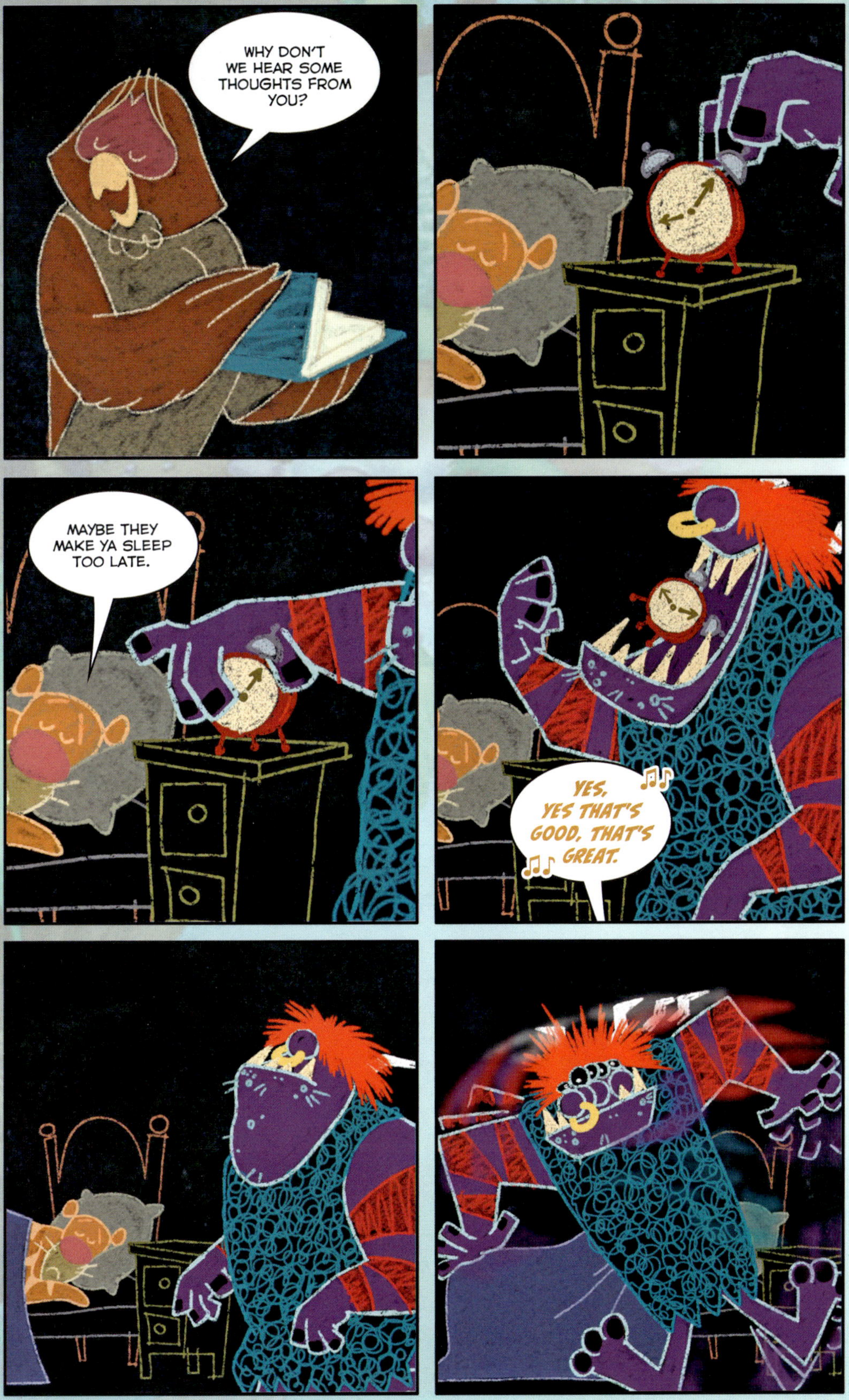
WHY DON'T WE HEAR SOME THOUGHTS FROM YOU?
MAYBE THEY MAKE YA SLEEP TOO LATE.
YES, YES THAT'S GOOD, THAT'S GREAT.

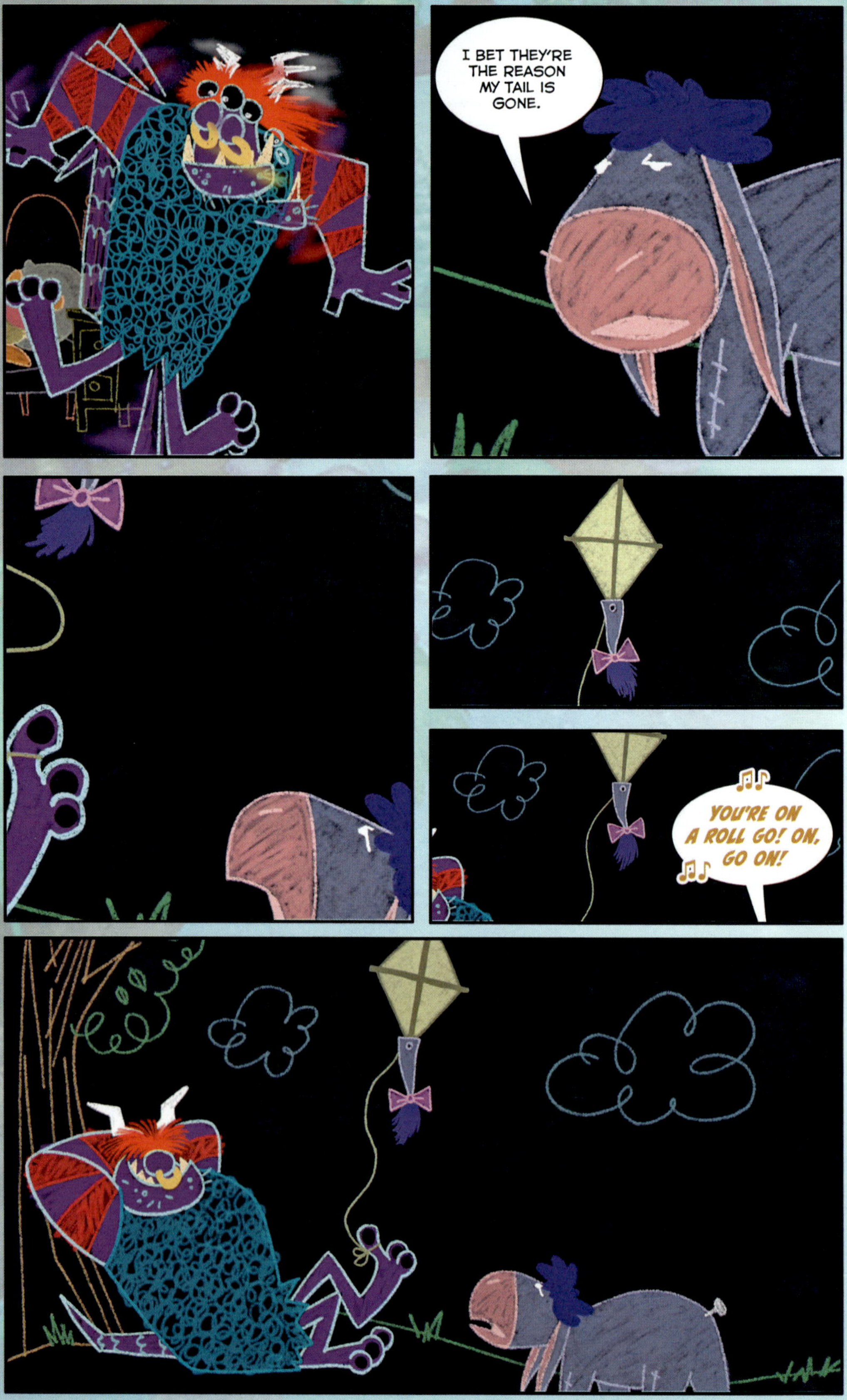
I BET THEY'RE THE REASON MY TAIL IS GONE.
YOU'RE ON A ROLL GO! ON, GO ON!

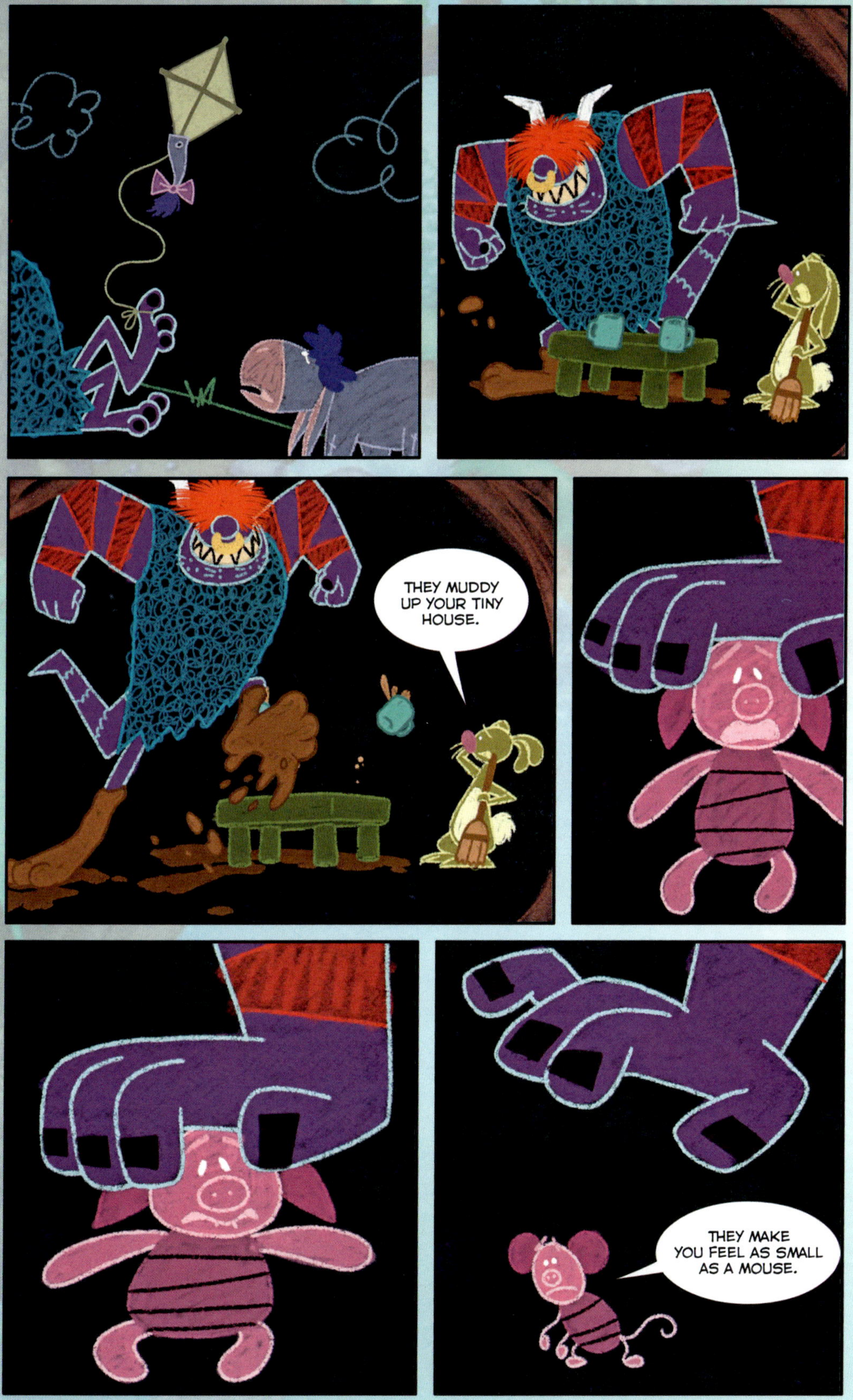
THEY MUDDY UP YOUR TINY HOUSE.
THEY MAKE YOU FEEL AS SMALL AS A MOUSE.

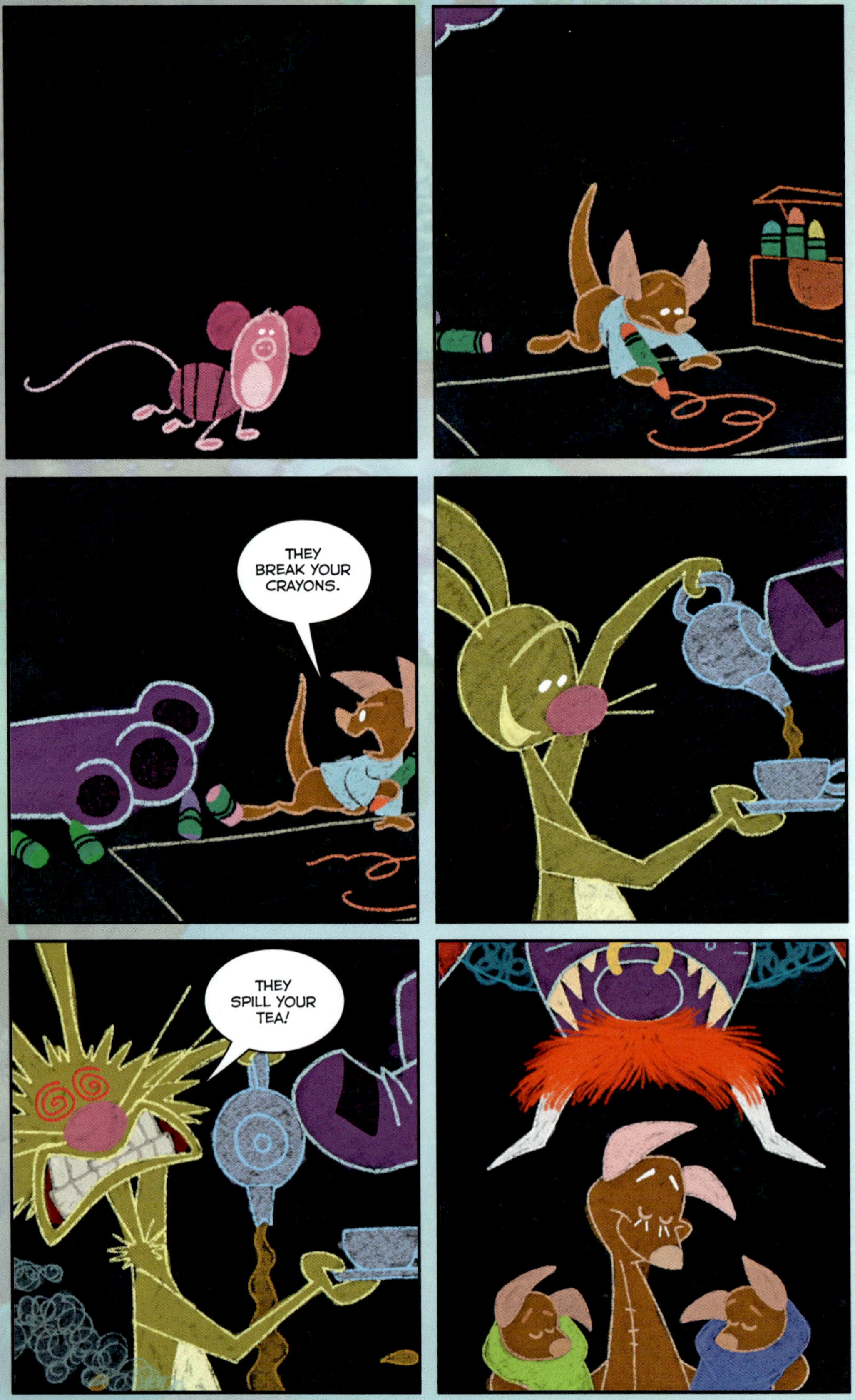
THEY BREAK YOUR CRAYONS.
THEY SPILL YOUR TEA!

THEY WAKE UP BABIES AT ONE AND THREE.
THEY MADE ME CATCH THE COLD I CAUGHT.
THEY MADE ME LOSE MY TRAIN OF THOUGHT.

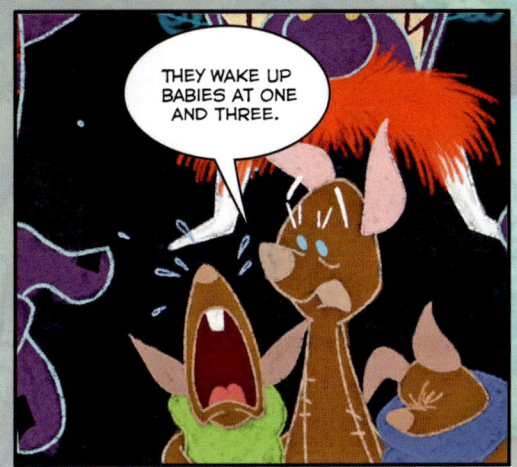

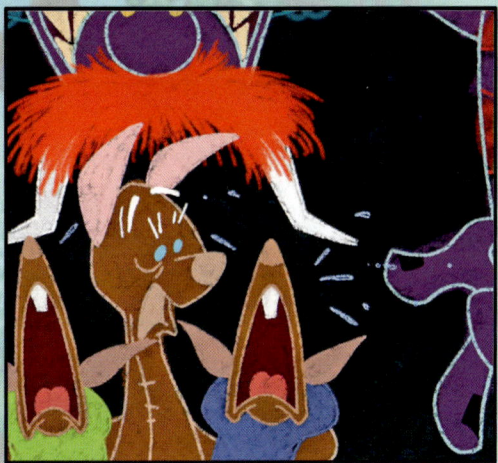

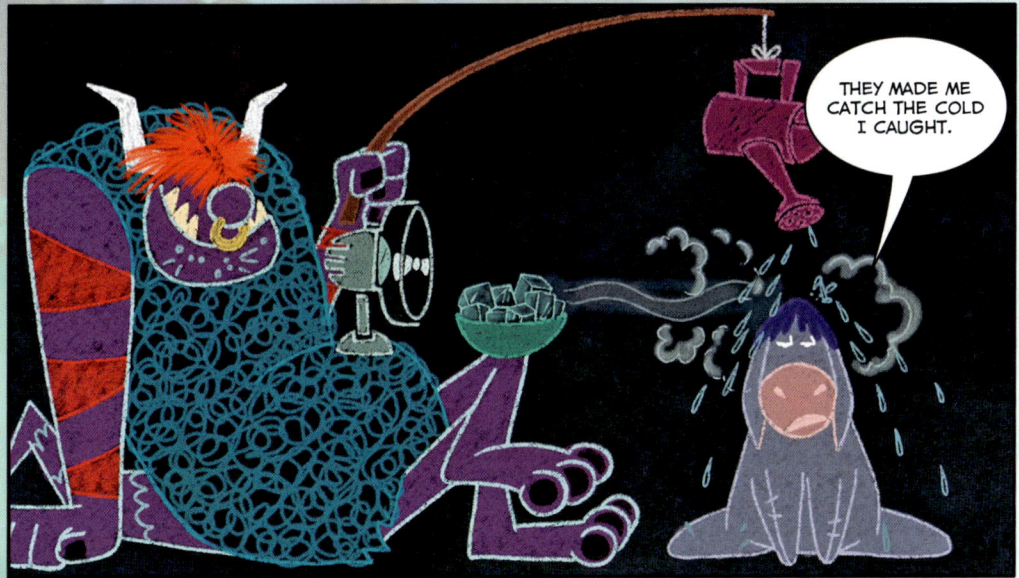

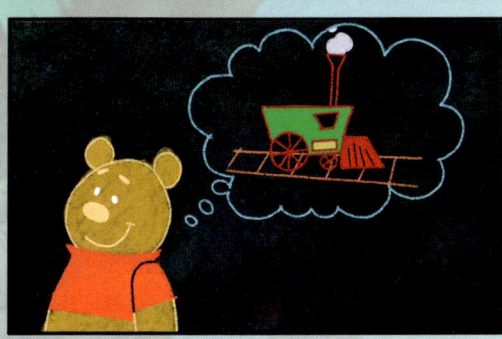

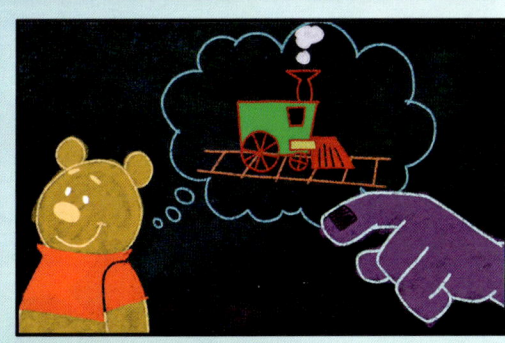

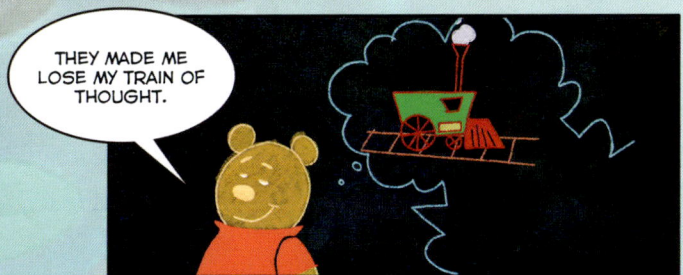

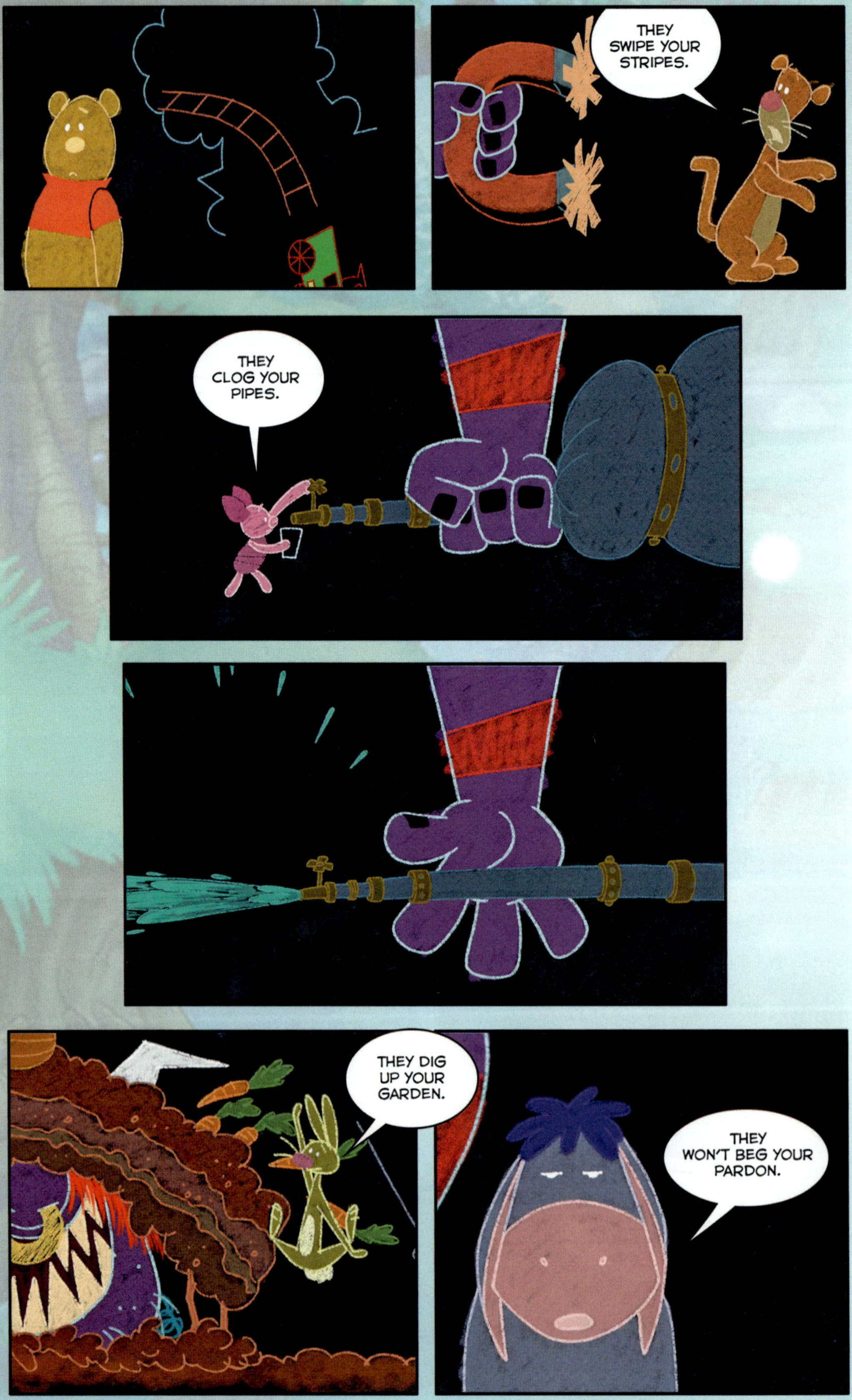
THEY SWIPE YOUR STRIPES.
THEY CLOG YOUR PIPES.
THEY DIG UP YOUR GARDEN.
THEY WON'T BEG YOUR PARDON.

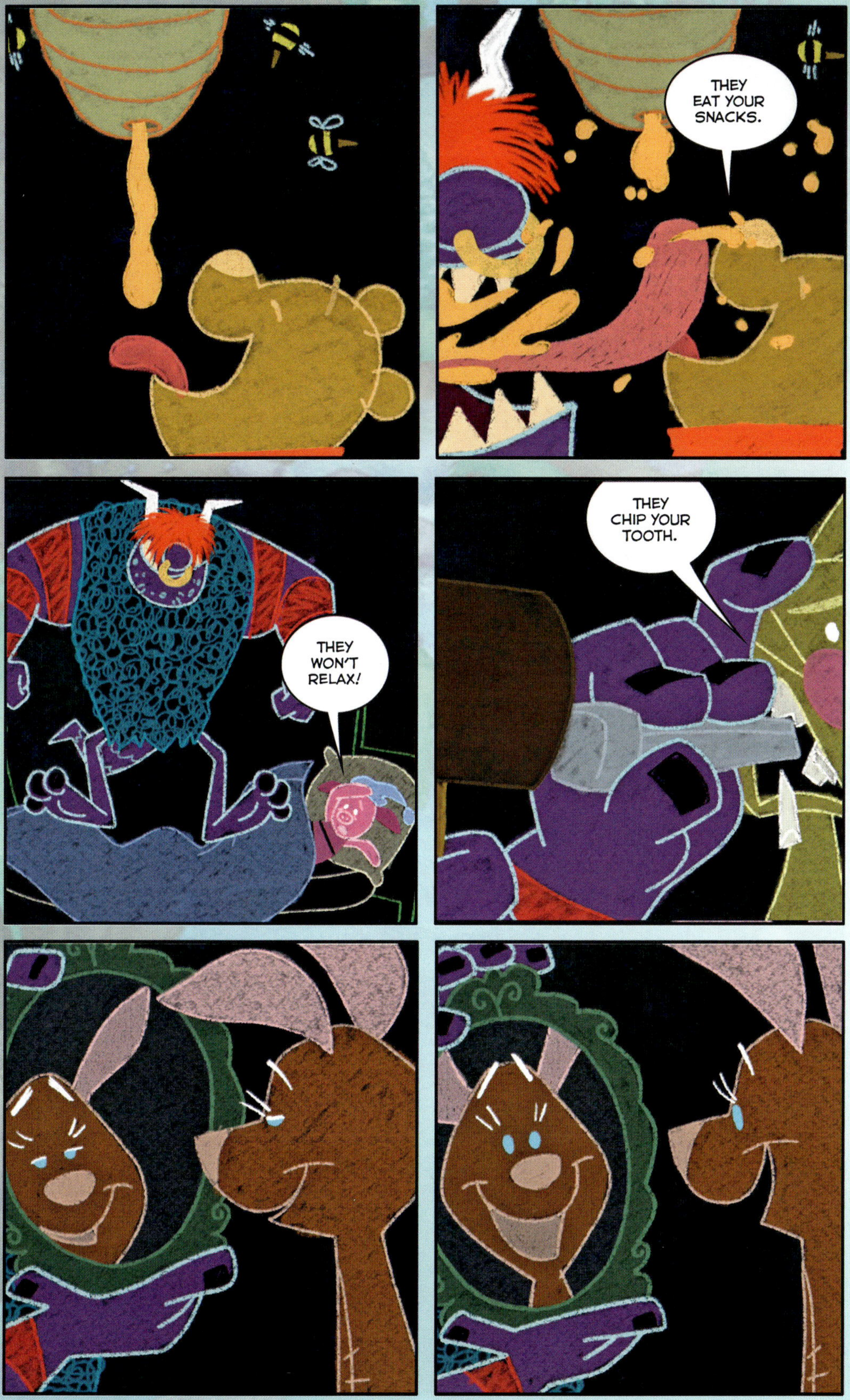
THEY EAT YOUR SNACKS.
THEY WON'T RELAX!
THEY CHIP YOUR TOOTH.

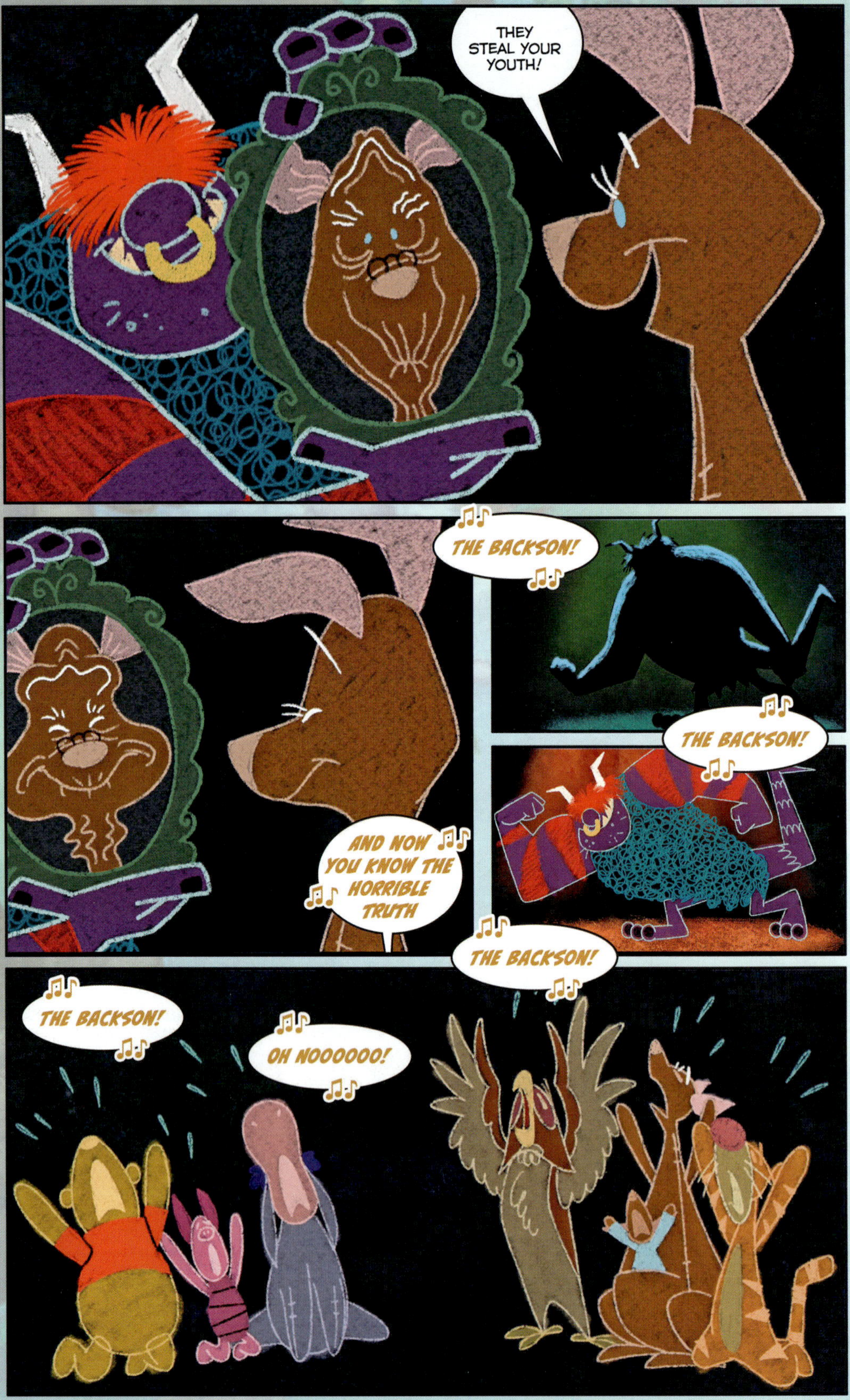
THEY STEAL YOUR YOUTH!
AND NOW YOU KNOW THE HORRIBLE TRUTH
THE BACKSON!
THE BACKSON!
THE BACKSON!
THE BACKSON!
OH NOOOOOO!

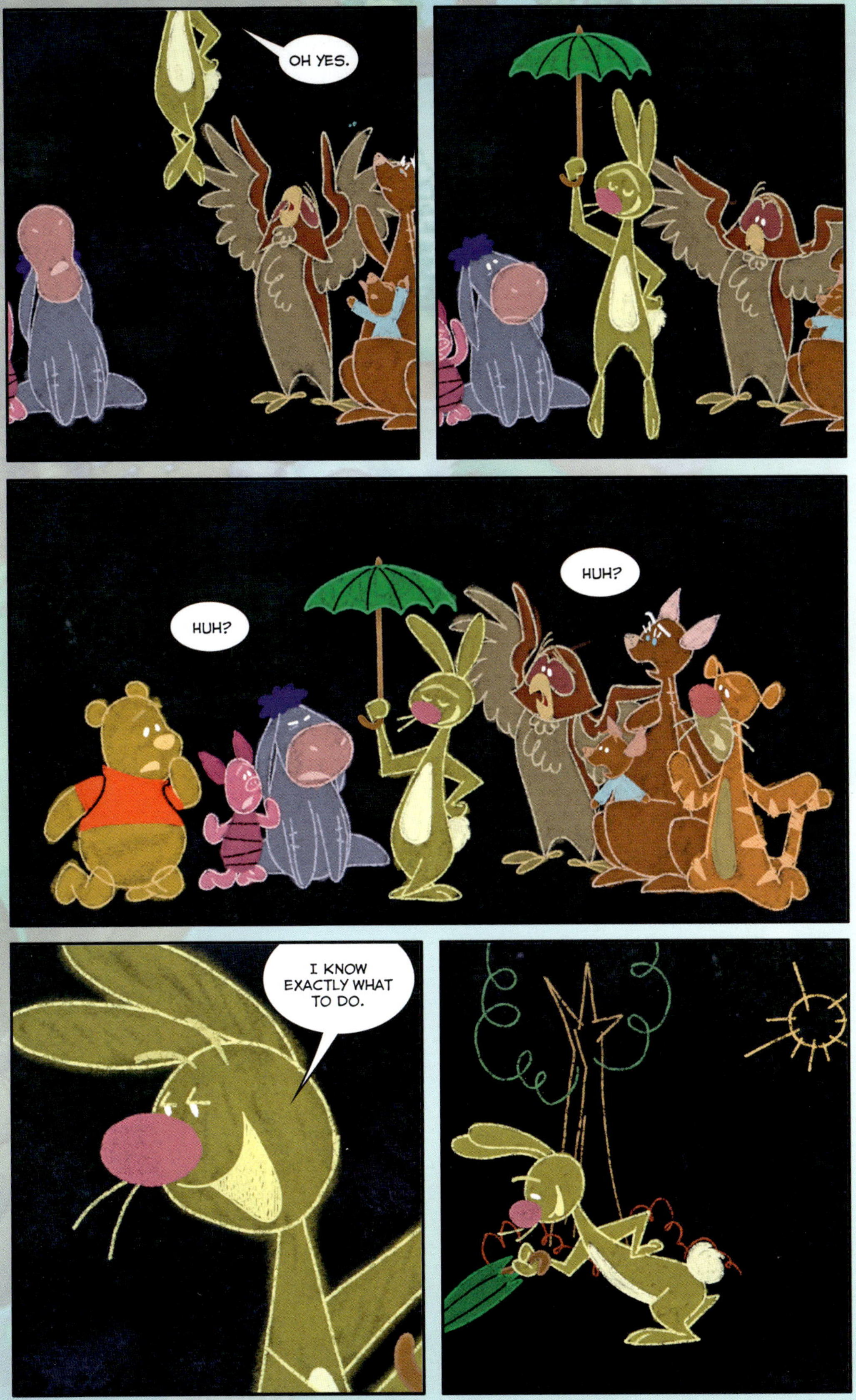
OH YES.
HUH?
HUH?
I KNOW EXACTLY WHAT TO DO.

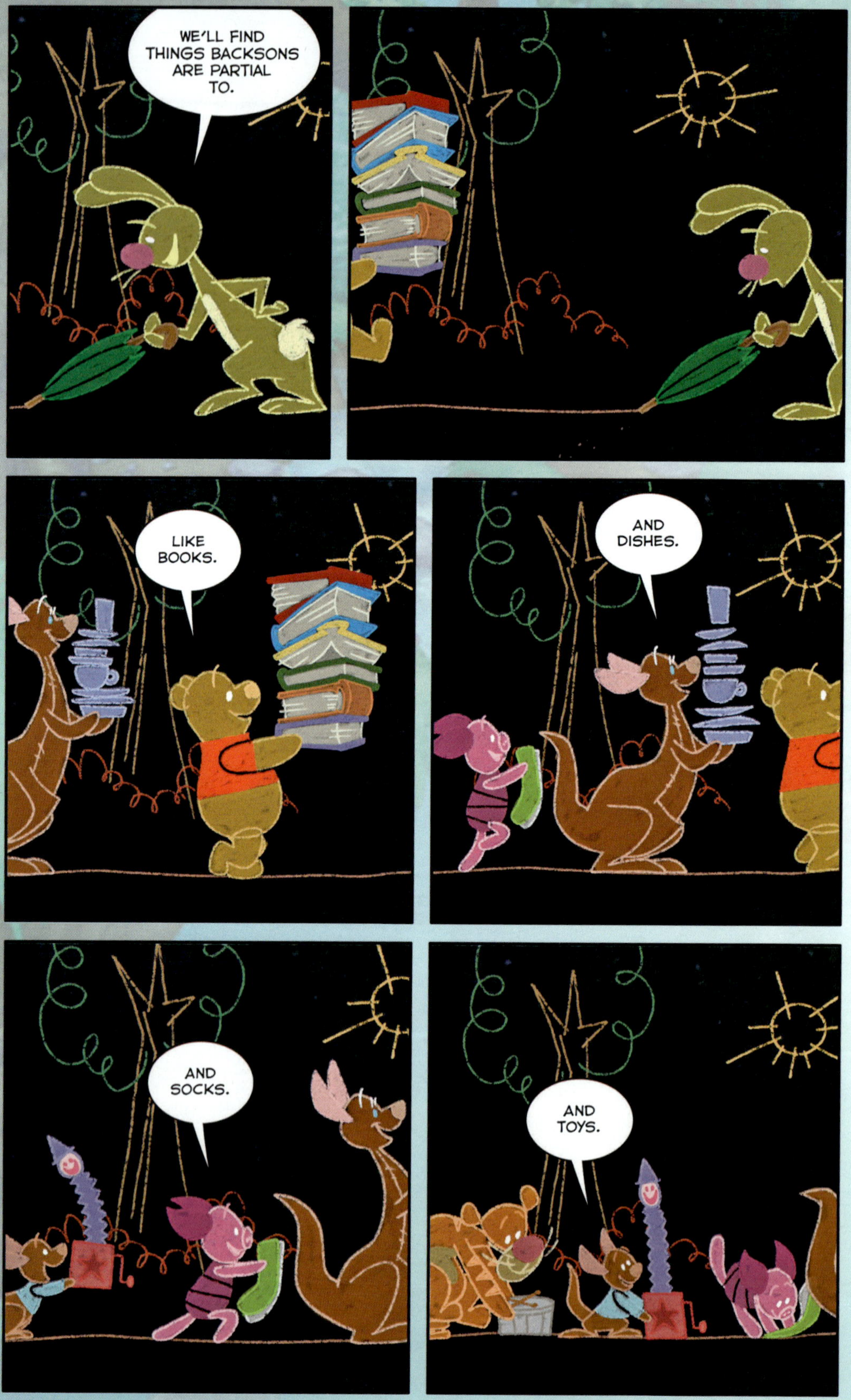
WE'LL FIND THINGS BACKSONS ARE PARTIAL TO.
LIKE BOOKS.
AND DISHES.
AND SOCKS.
AND TOYS.

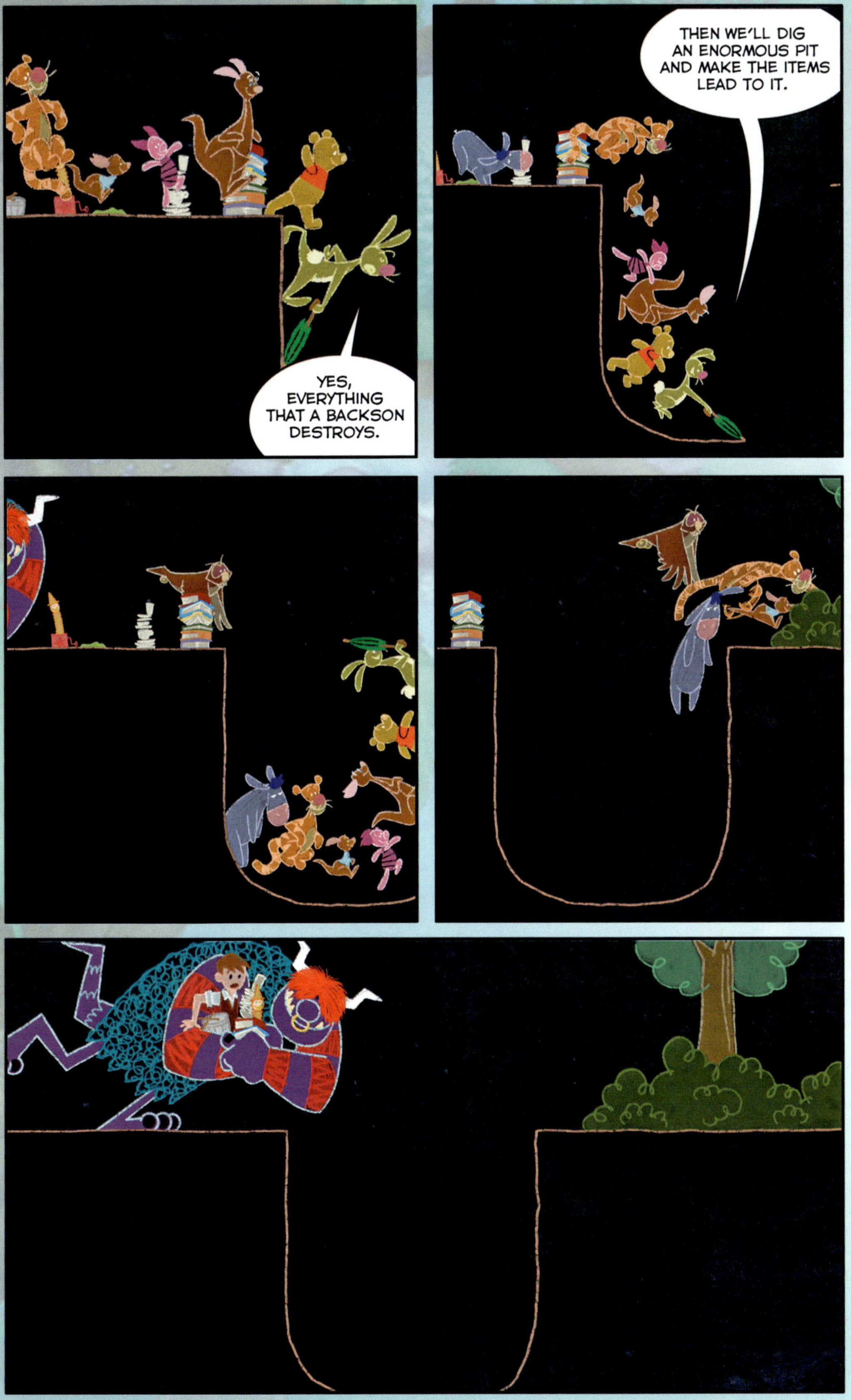
YES, EVERYTHING THAT A BACKSON DESTROYS.
THEN WE'LL DIG AN ENORMOUS PIT AND MAKE THE ITEMS LEAD TO IT.

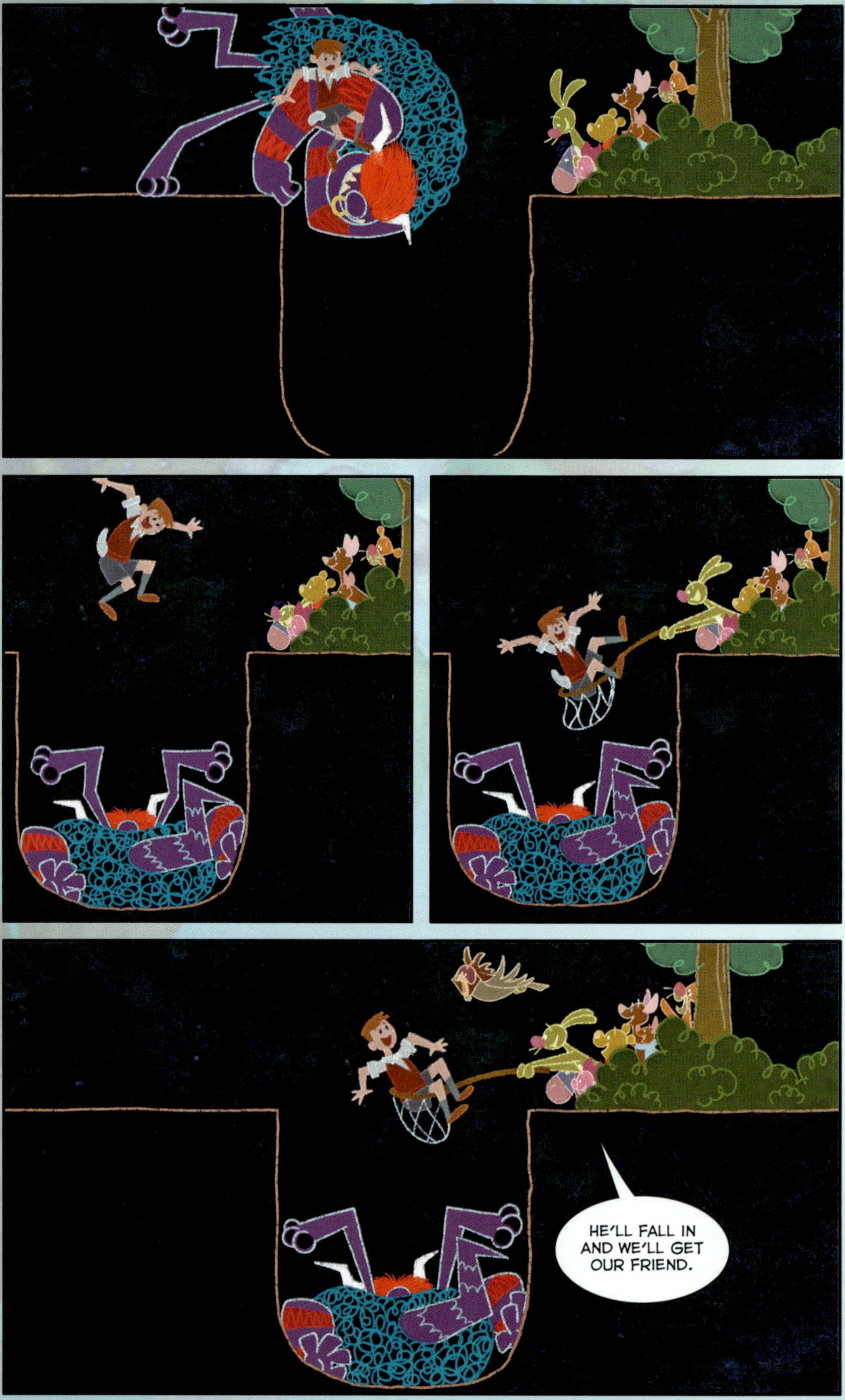
HE'LL FALL IN
AND WE'LL GET
OUR FRIEND.

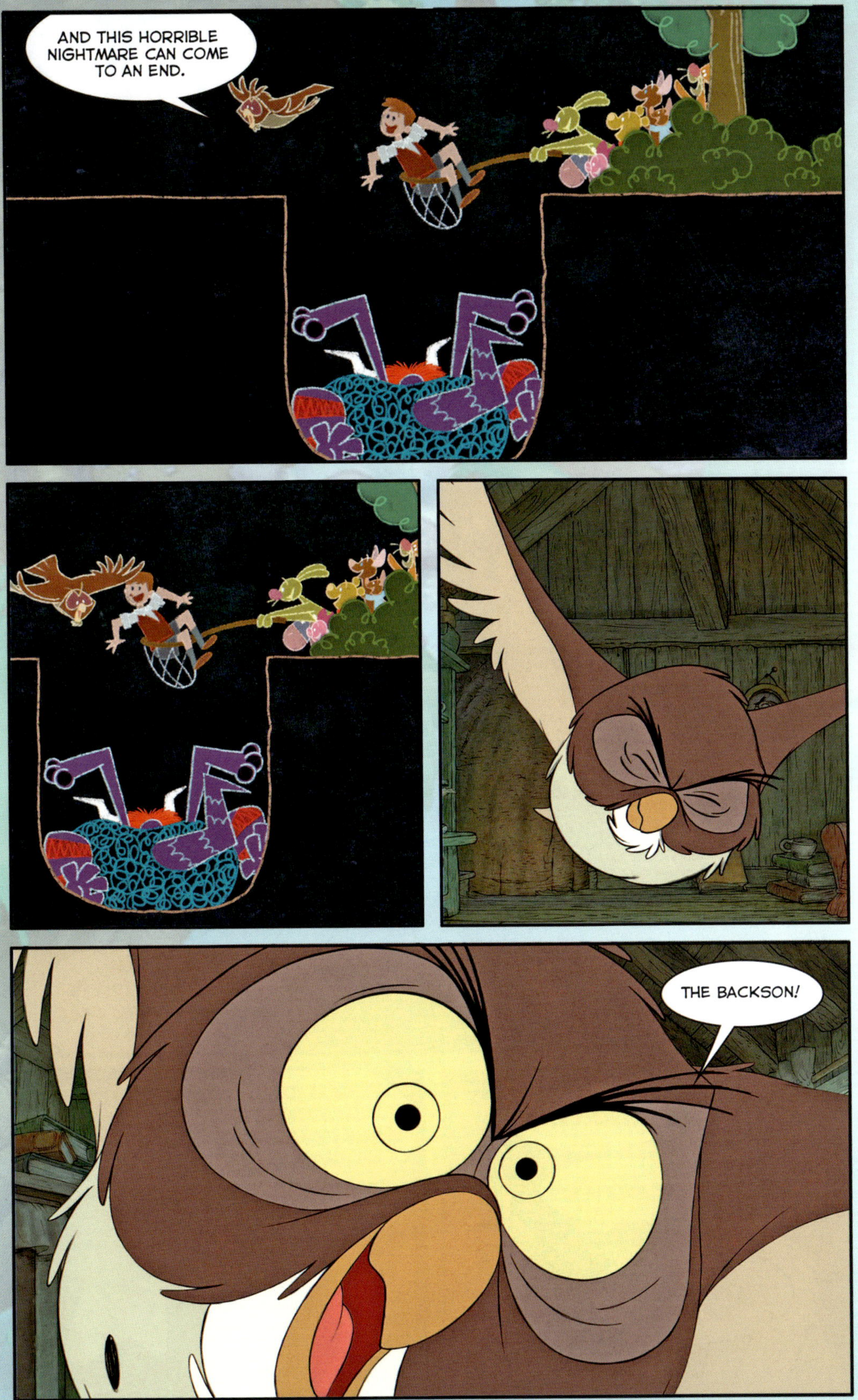
AND THIS HORRIBLE NIGHTMARE CAN COME TO AN END.
THE BACKSON!

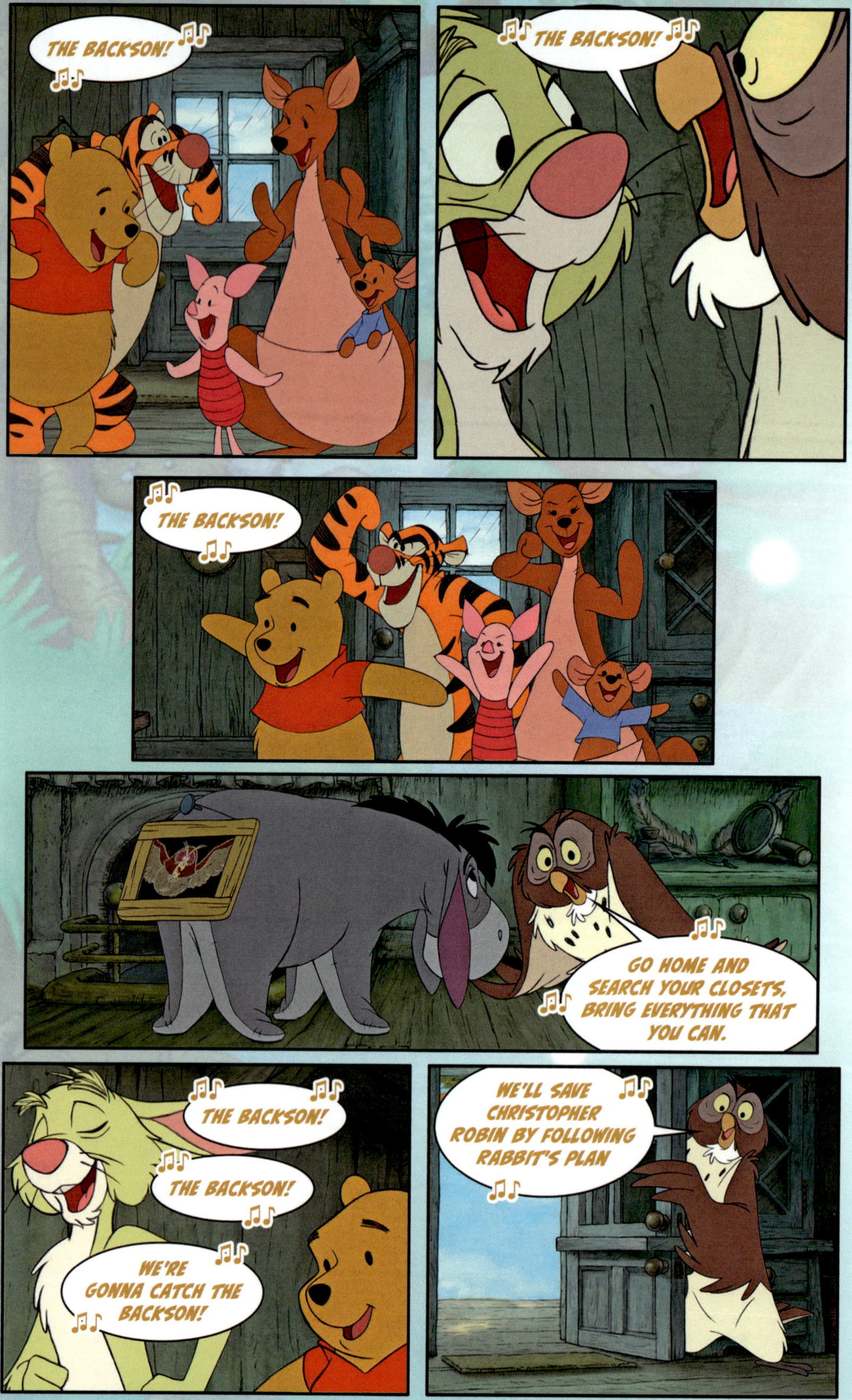
THE BACKSON!
THE BACKSON!
THE BACKSON!
GO HOME AND SEARCH YOUR CLOSETS, BRING EVERYTHING THAT YOU CAN.
THE BACKSON!
THE BACKSON!
WE'RE GONNA CATCH THE BACKSON!
WE'LL SAVE CHRISTOPHER ROBIN BY FOLLOWING RABBIT'S PLAN

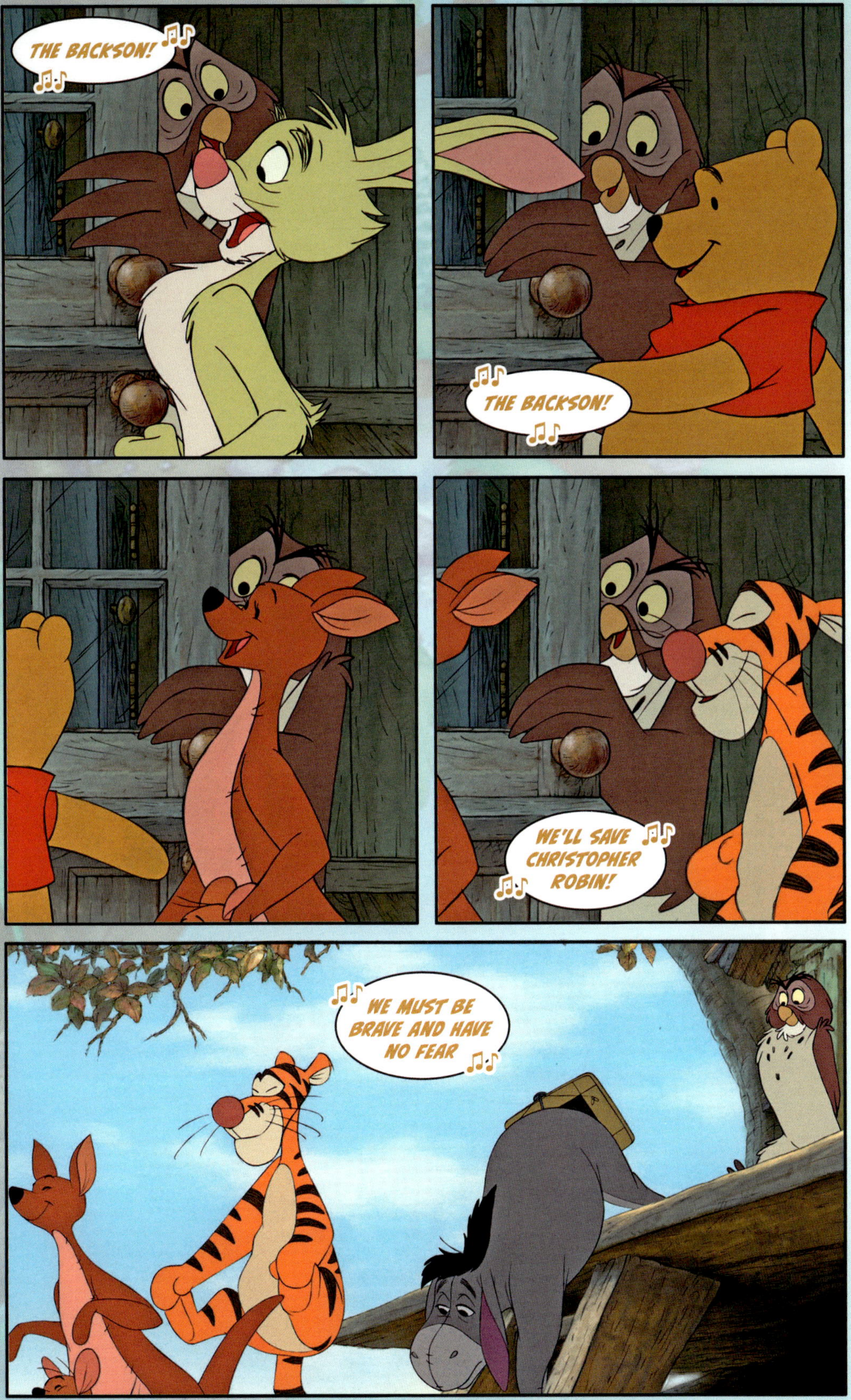
THE BACKSON!
THE BACKSON!
WE'LL SAVE CHRISTOPHER ROBIN!
WE MUST BE BRAVE AND HAVE NO FEAR

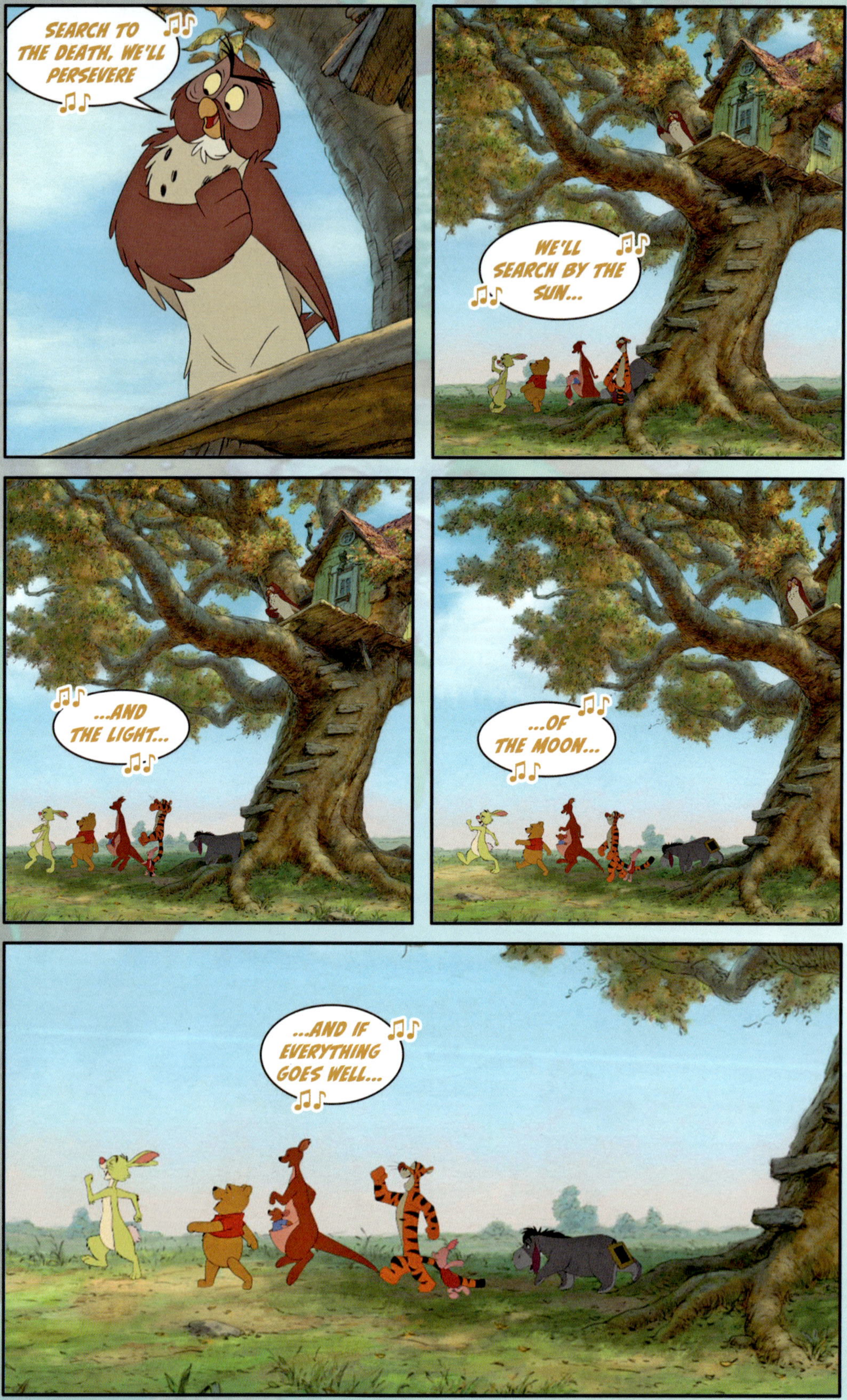
SEARCH TO THE DEATH, WE'LL PERSEVERE
WE'LL SEARCH BY THE SUN...
...AND THE LIGHT...
...OF THE MOON...
...AND IF EVERYTHING GOES WELL...

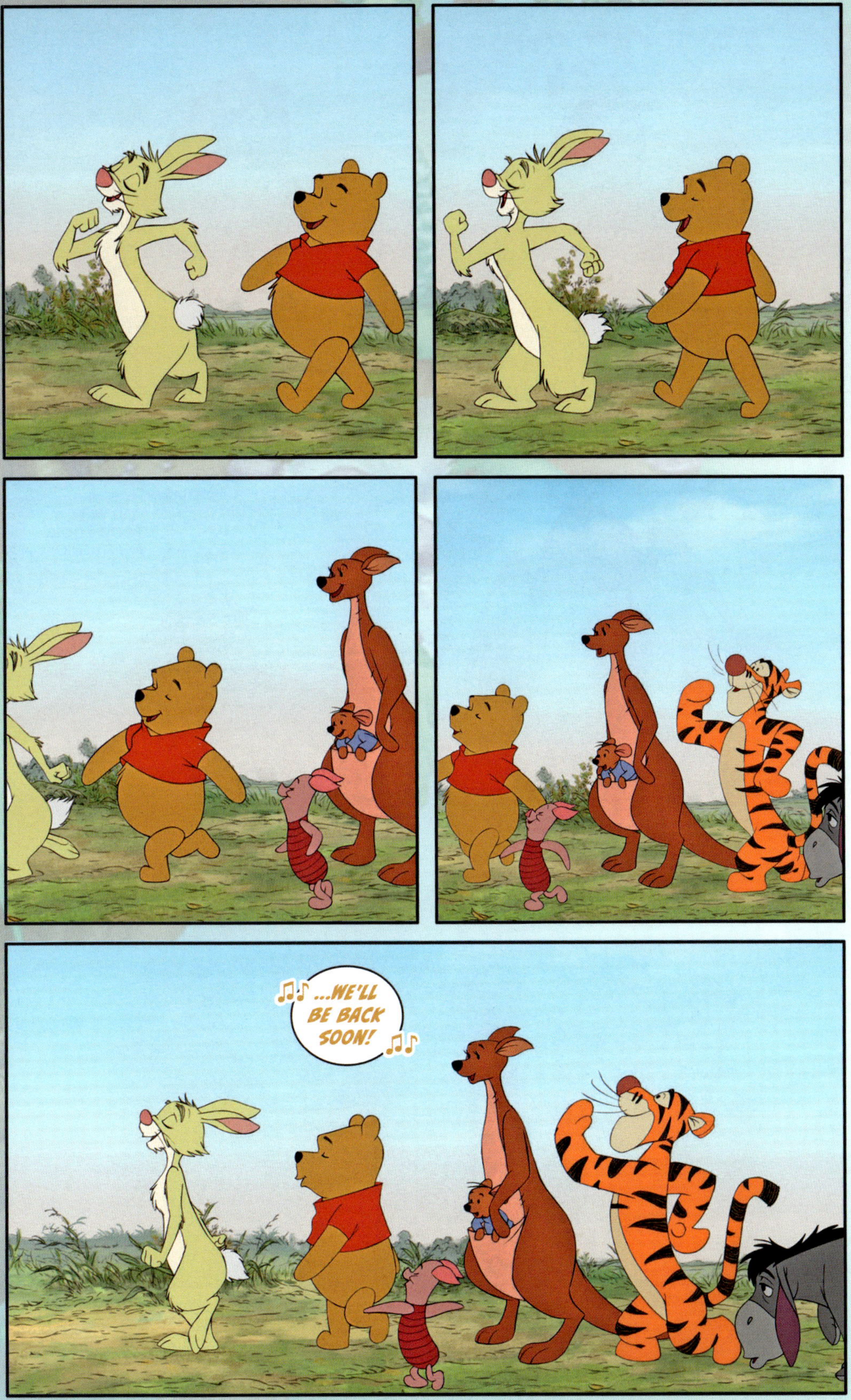

...WE'LL BE BACK SOON!

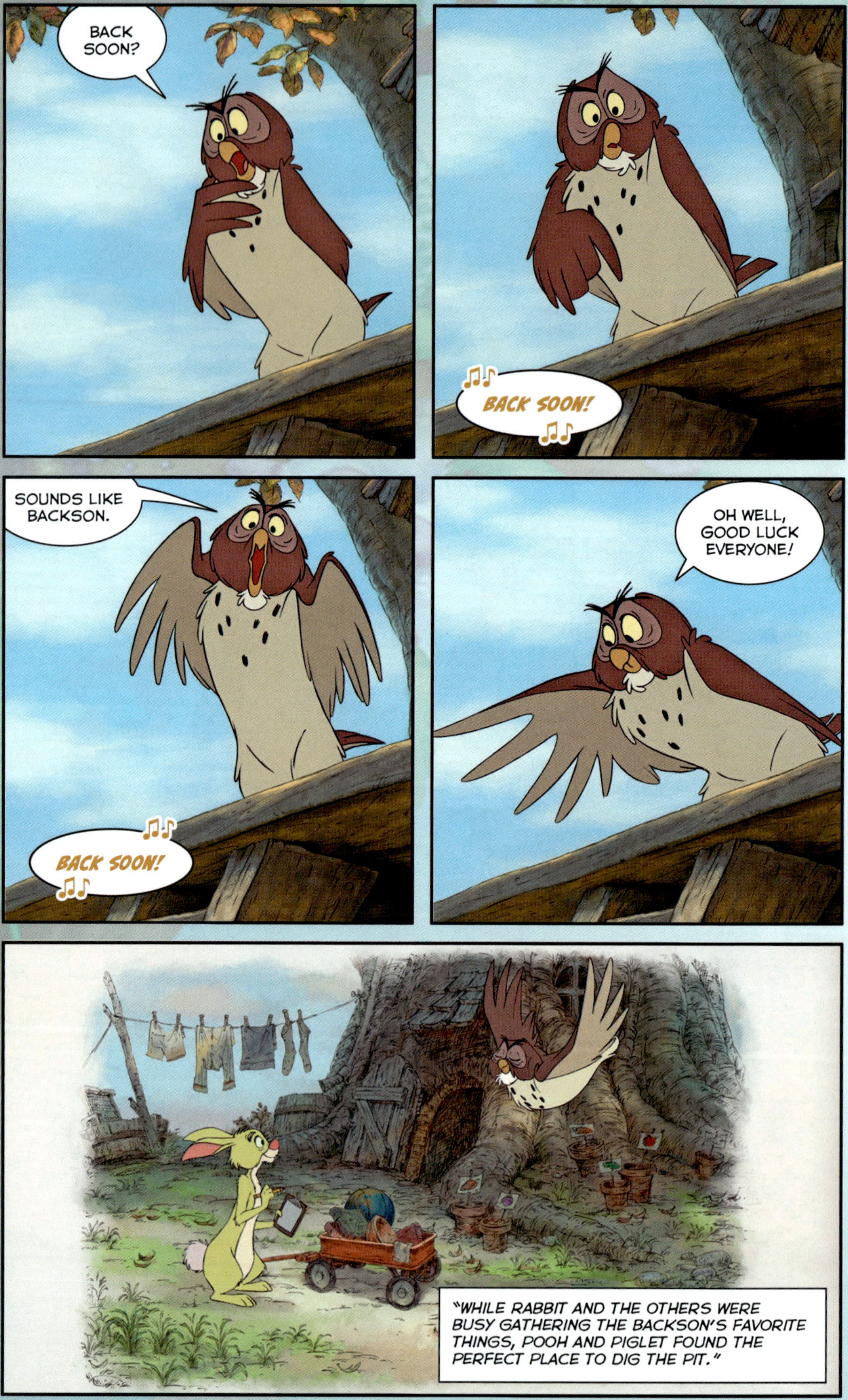
BACK SOON?
BACK SOON!
SOUNDS LIKE BACKSON.
BACK SOON!
OH WELL, GOOD LUCK EVERYONE!
"WHILE RABBIT AND THE OTHERS WERE BUSY GATHERING THE BACKSON'S FAVORITE THINGS, POOH AND PIGLET FOUND THE PERFECT PLACE TO DIG THE PIT."

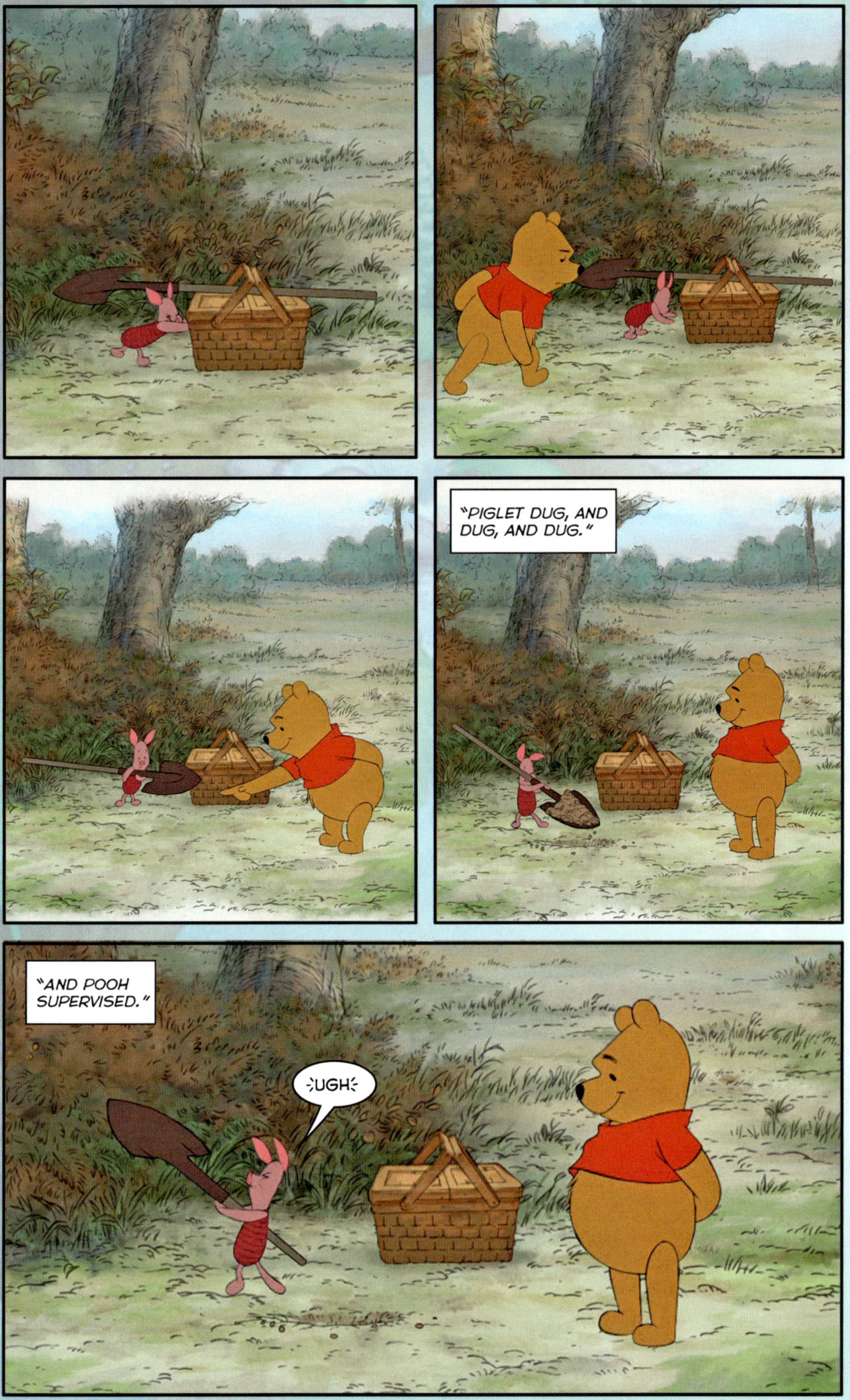
"PIGLET DUG, AND DUG, AND DUG."
"AND POOH SUPERVISED."
UGH

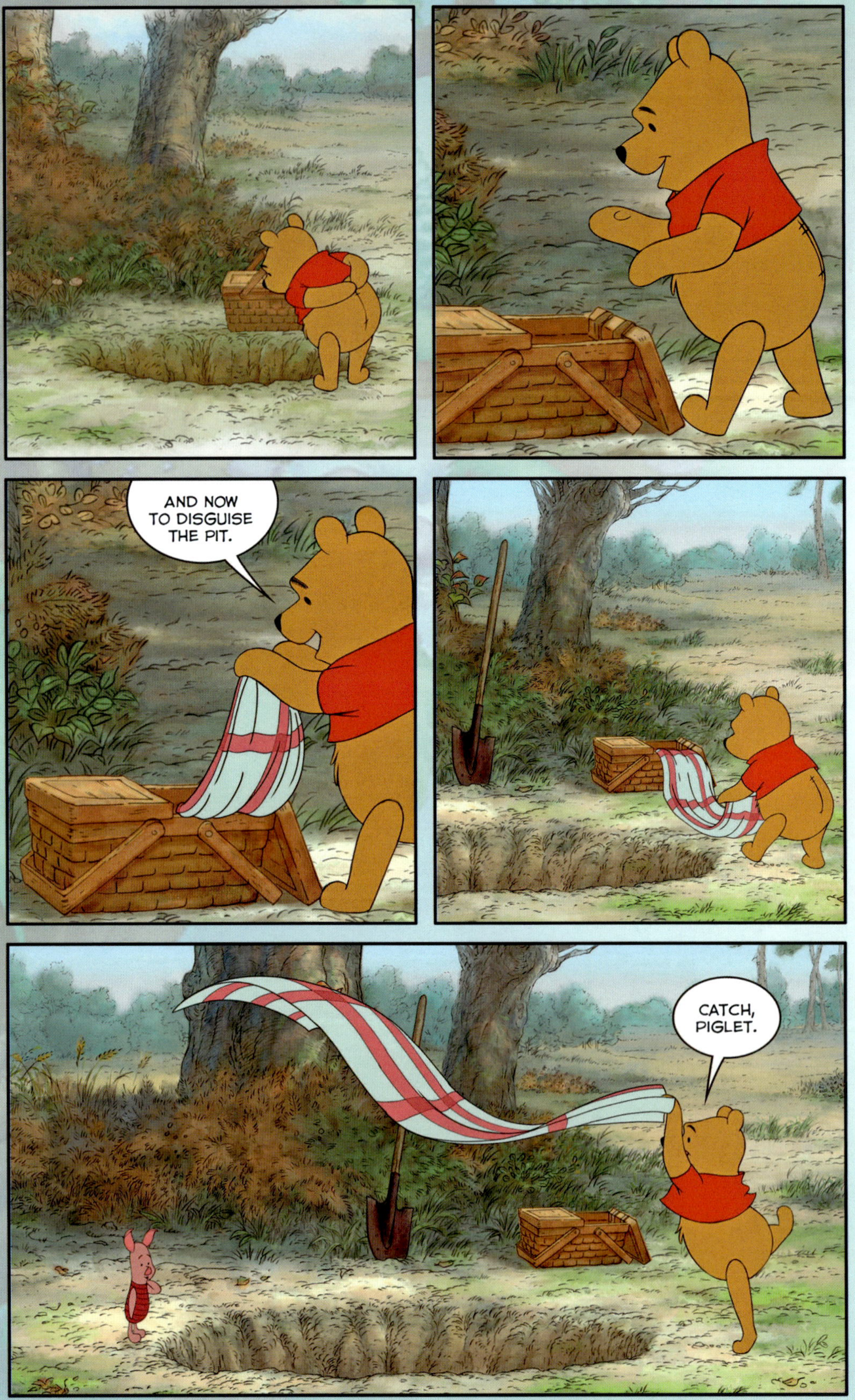
AND NOW TO DISGUISE THE PIT.
CATCH, PIGLET.

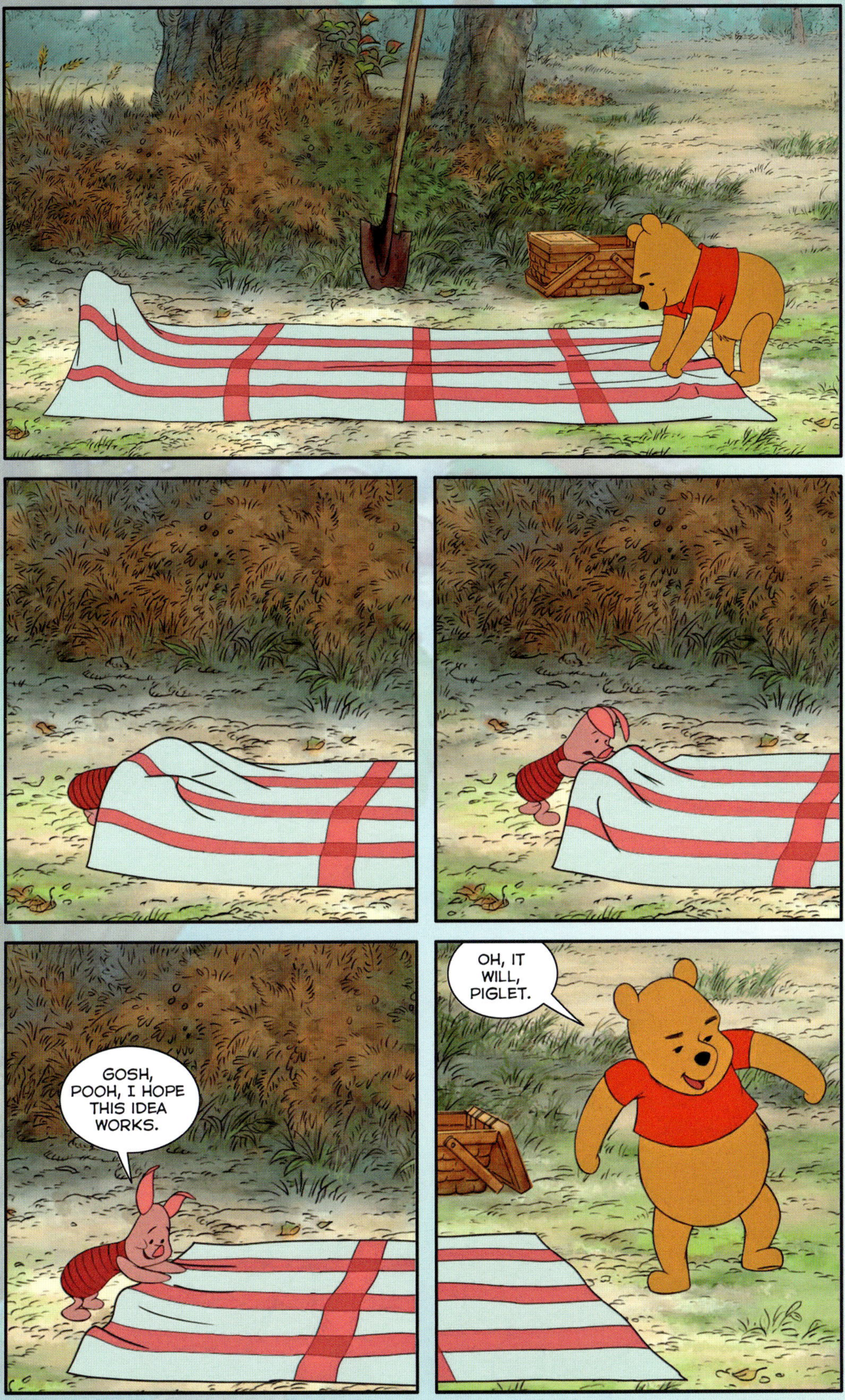
GOSH, POOH, I HOPE THIS IDEA WORKS.
OH, IT WILL, PIGLET.

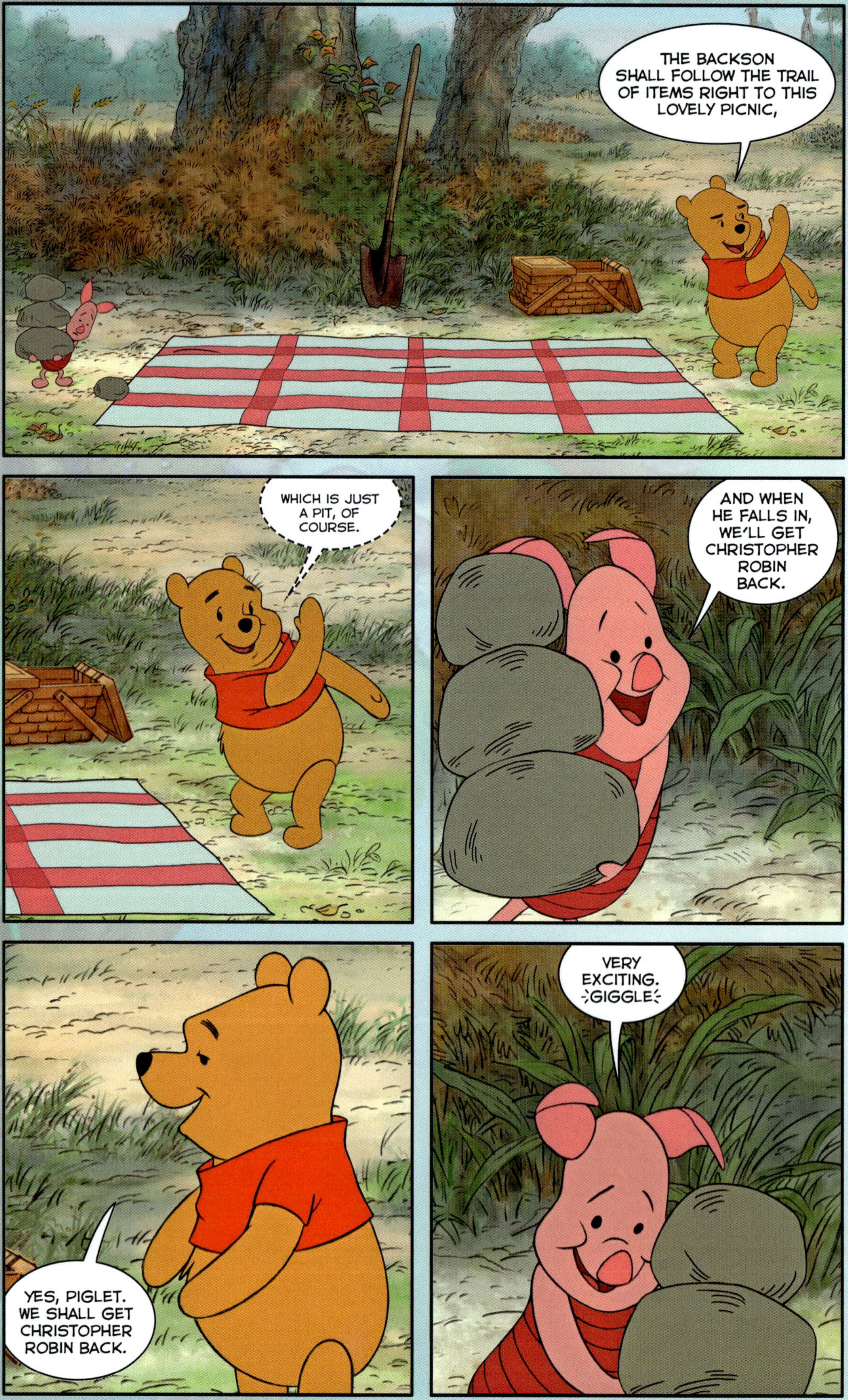
THE BACKSON SHALL FOLLOW THE TRAIL OF ITEMS RIGHT TO THIS LOVELY PICNIC,
WHICH IS JUST A PIT, OF COURSE.
AND WHEN HE FALLS IN, WE'LL GET CHRISTOPHER ROBIN BACK.
YES, PIGLET. WE SHALL GET CHRISTOPHER ROBIN BACK.
VERY EXCITING. GIGGLE

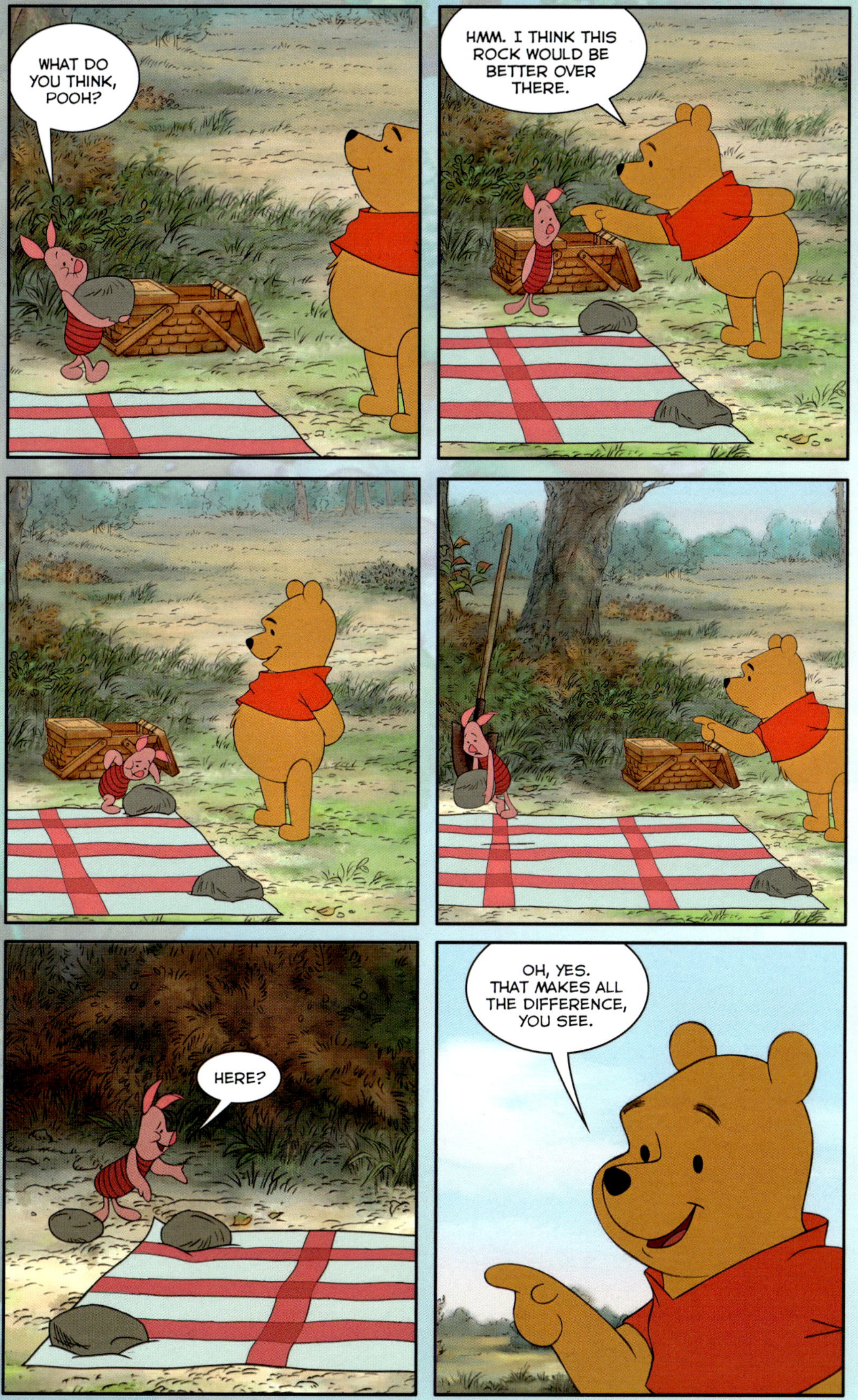
WHAT DO YOU THINK, POOH?
HMM. I THINK THIS ROCK WOULD BE BETTER OVER THERE.
HERE?
OH, YES. THAT MAKES ALL THE DIFFERENCE, YOU SEE.

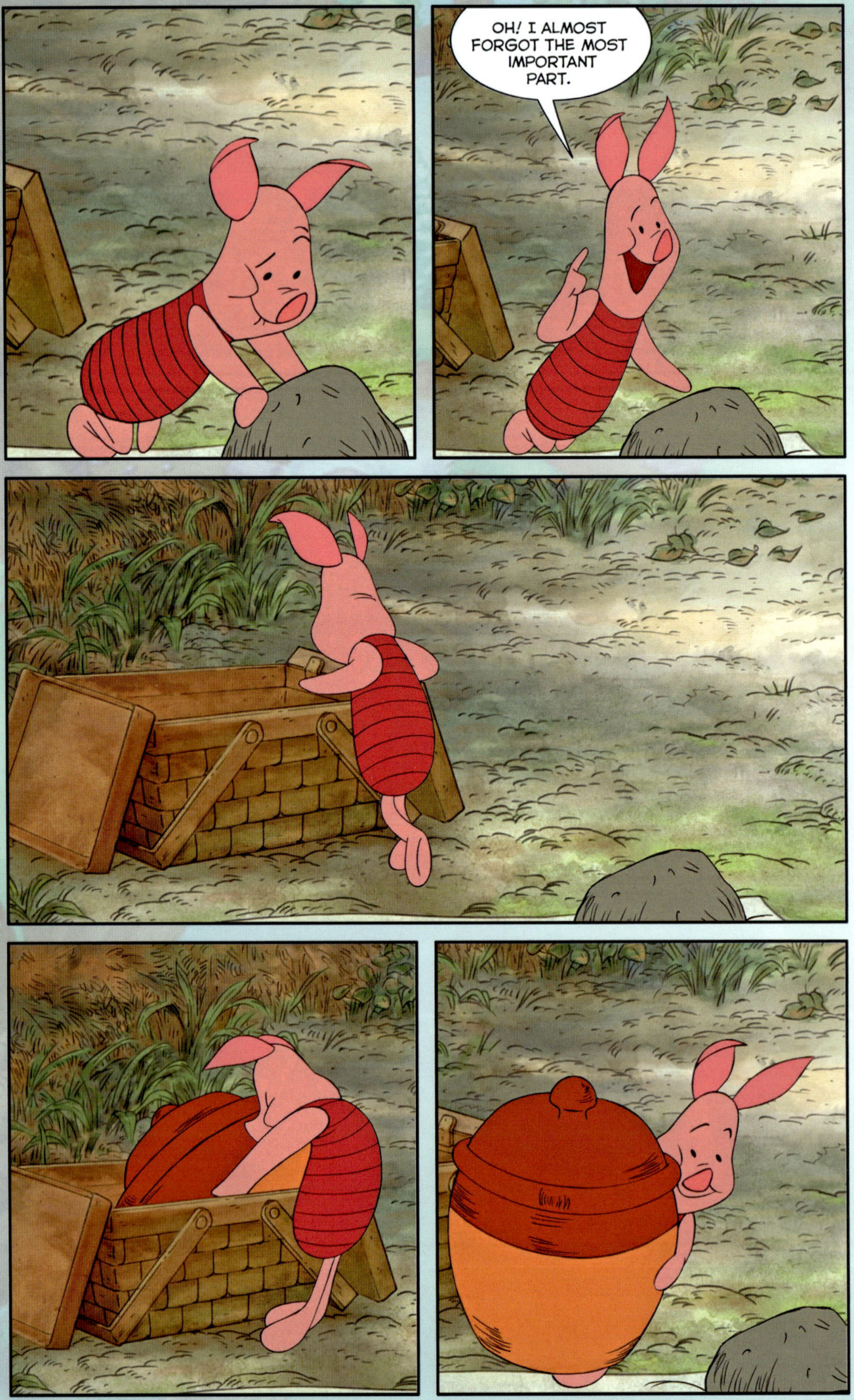
OH! I ALMOST FORGOT THE MOST IMPORTANT PART.

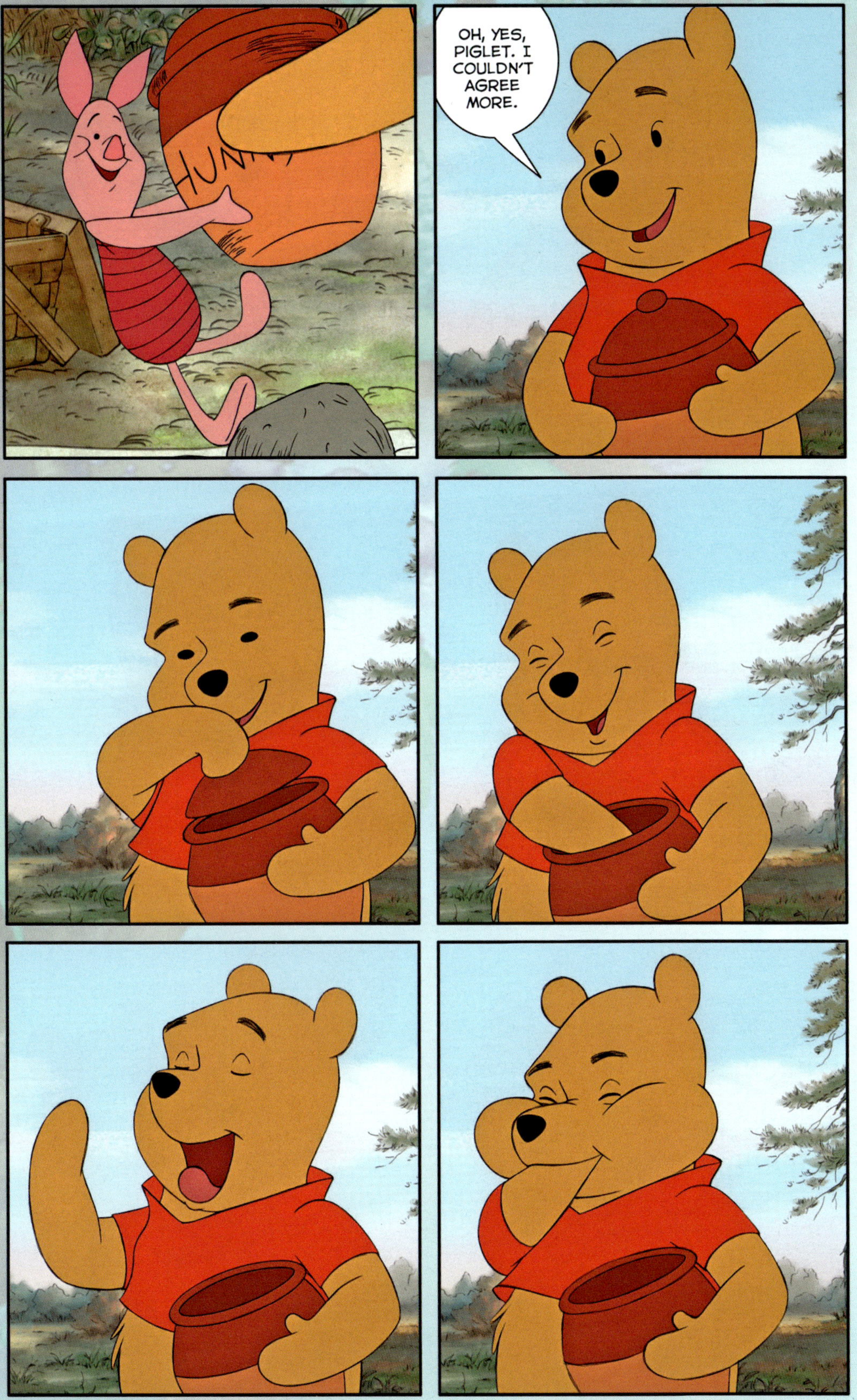
HUNNY
OH, YES, PIGLET. I COULDN'T AGREE MORE.

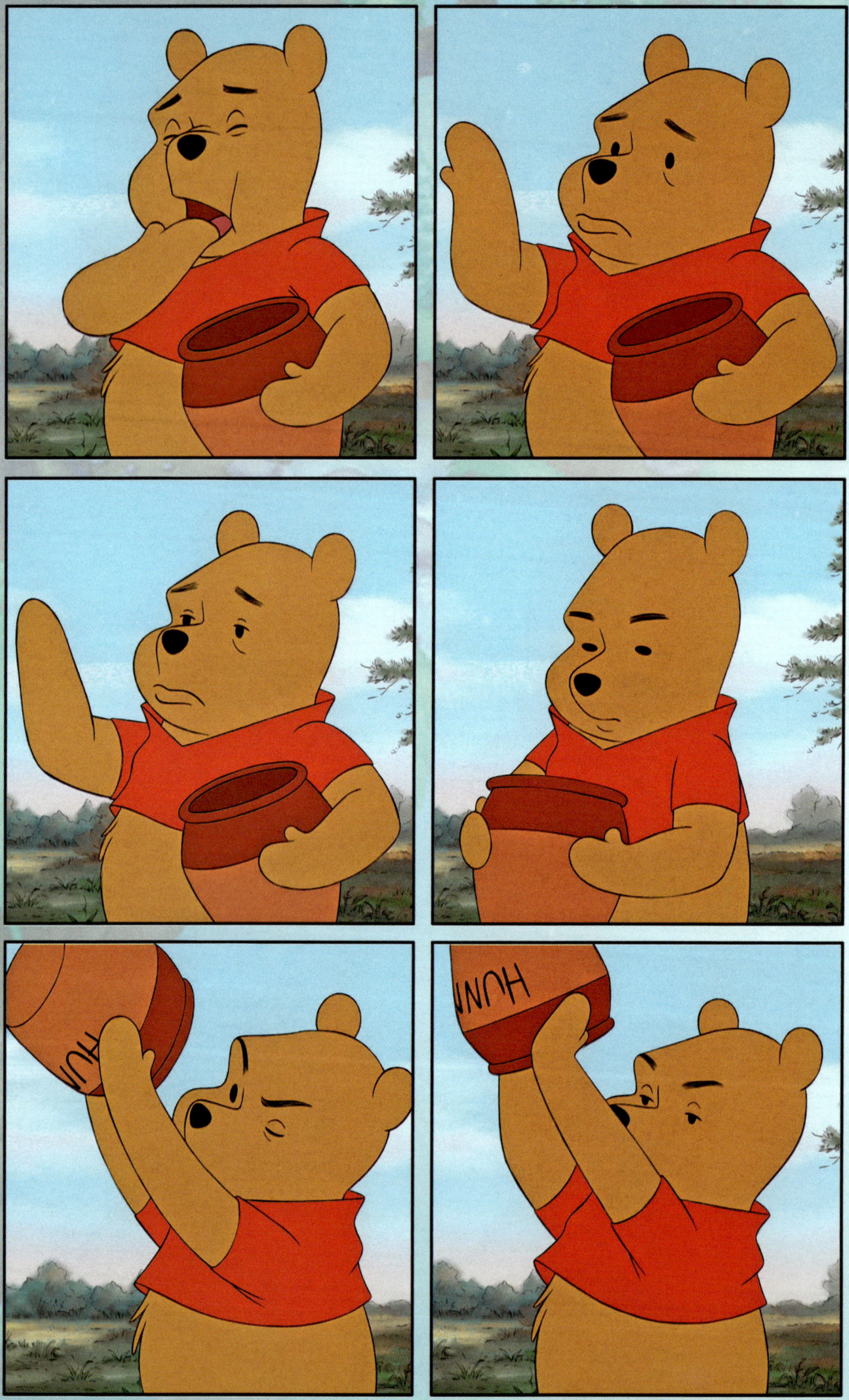

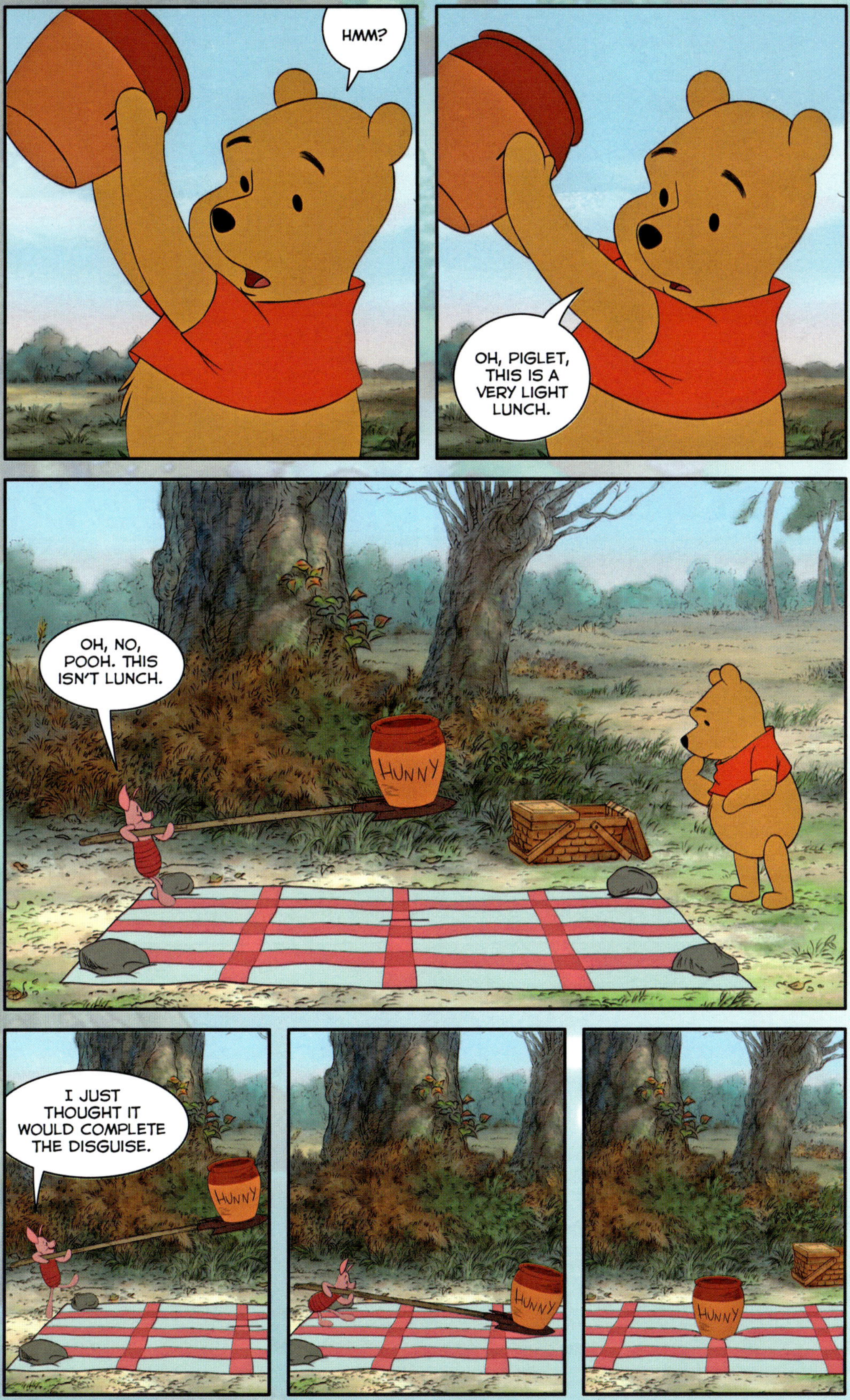
HMM?
OH, PIGLET, THIS IS A VERY LIGHT LUNCH.
OH, NO, POOH. THIS ISN'T LUNCH.
HUNNY
I JUST THOUGHT IT WOULD COMPLETE THE DISGUISE.
HUNNY
HUNNY
HUNNY

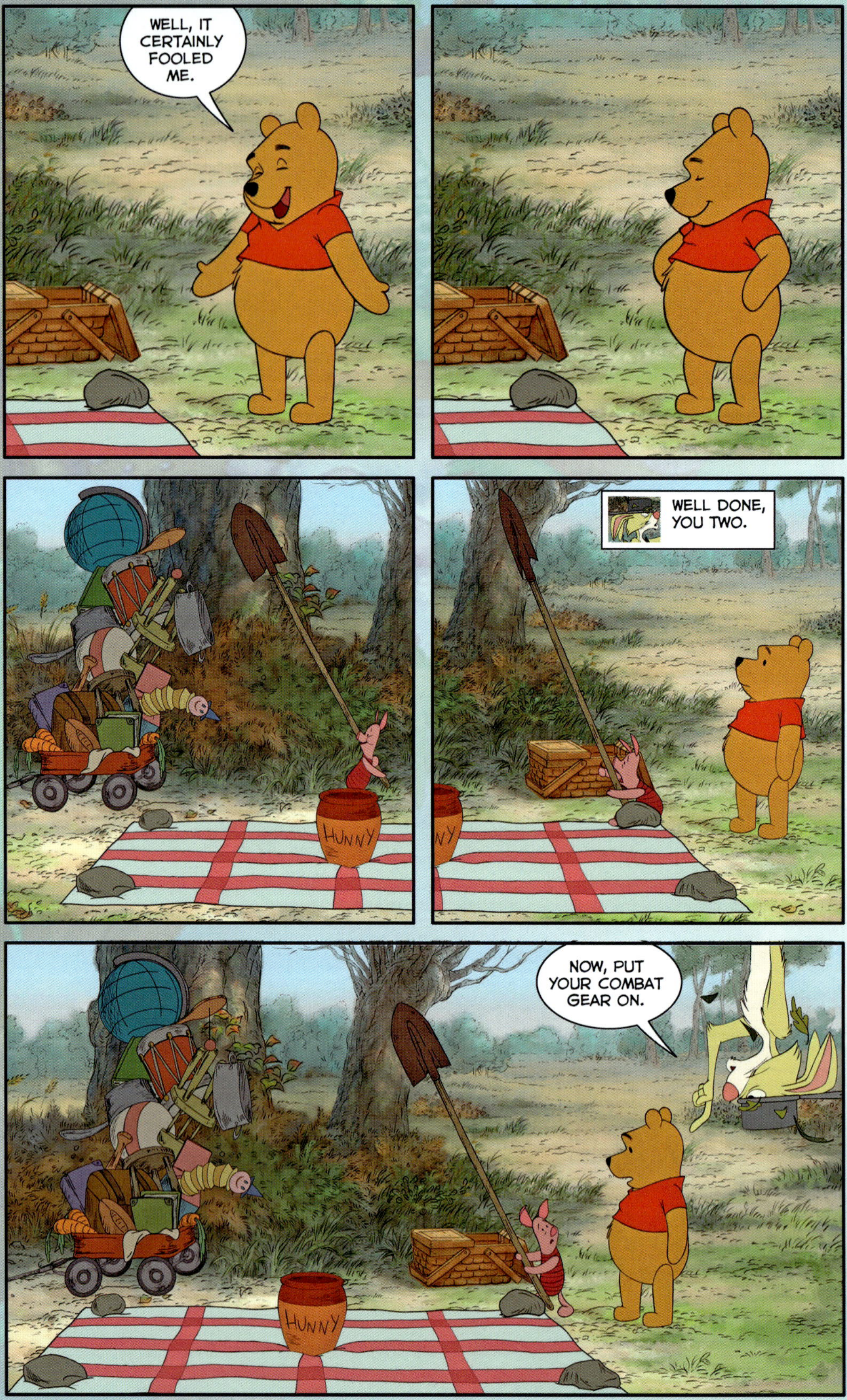
WELL, IT CERTAINLY FOOLED ME.
WELL DONE, YOU TWO.
NOW, PUT YOUR COMBAT GEAR ON.
HUNNY
HUNNY

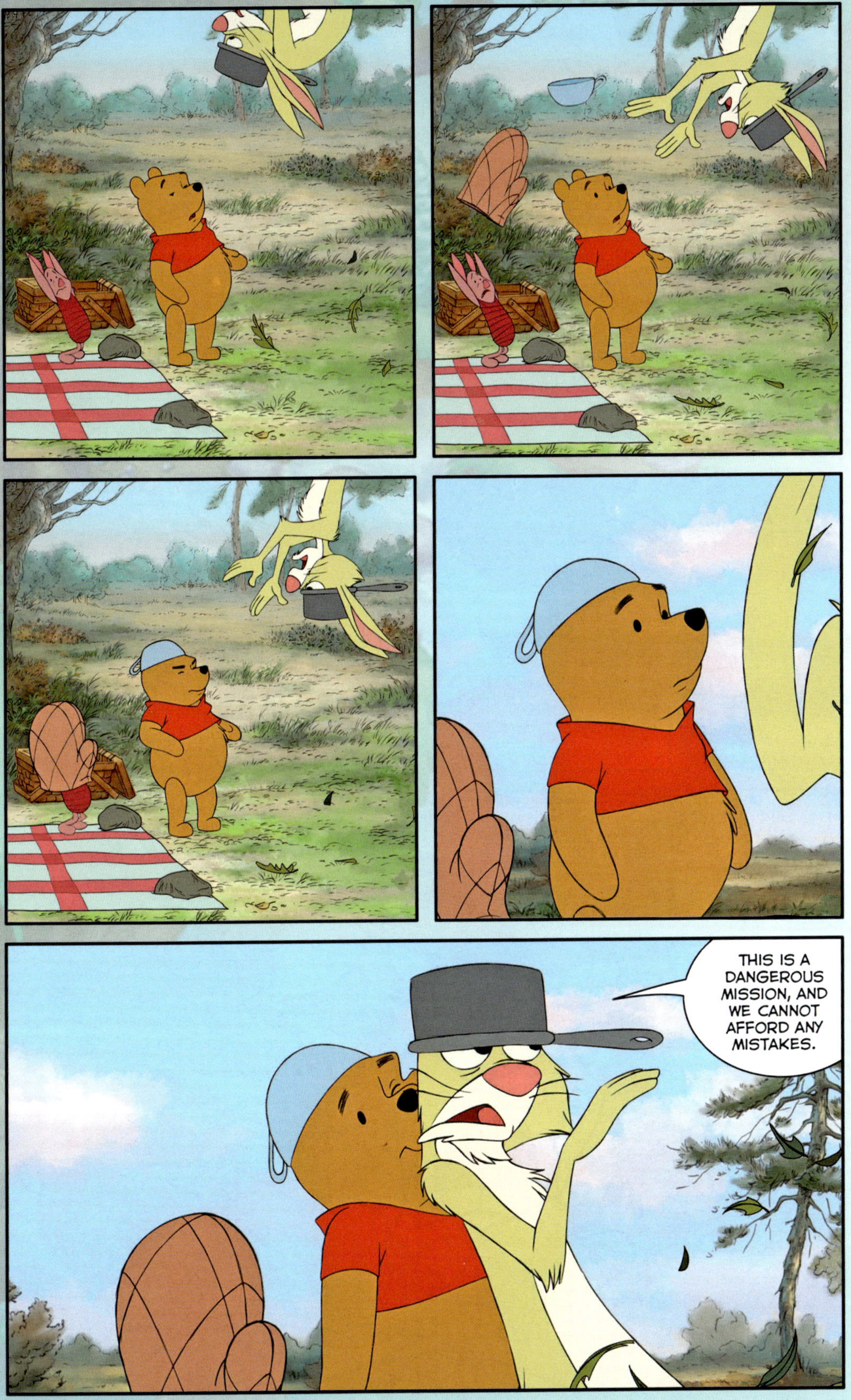
THIS IS A DANGEROUS MISSION, AND WE CANNOT AFFORD ANY MISTAKES.

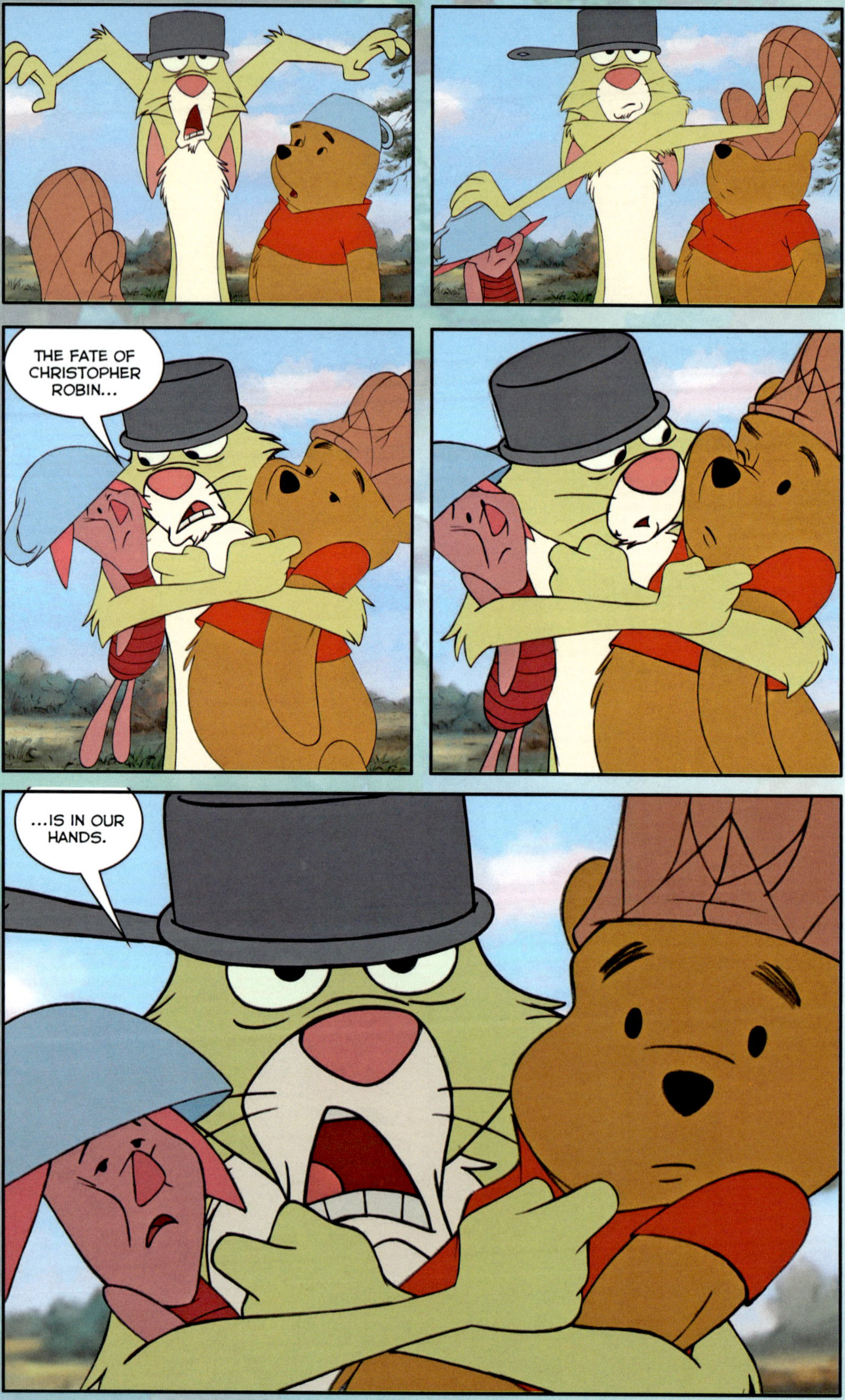
THE FATE OF CHRISTOPHER ROBIN...
...IS IN OUR HANDS.

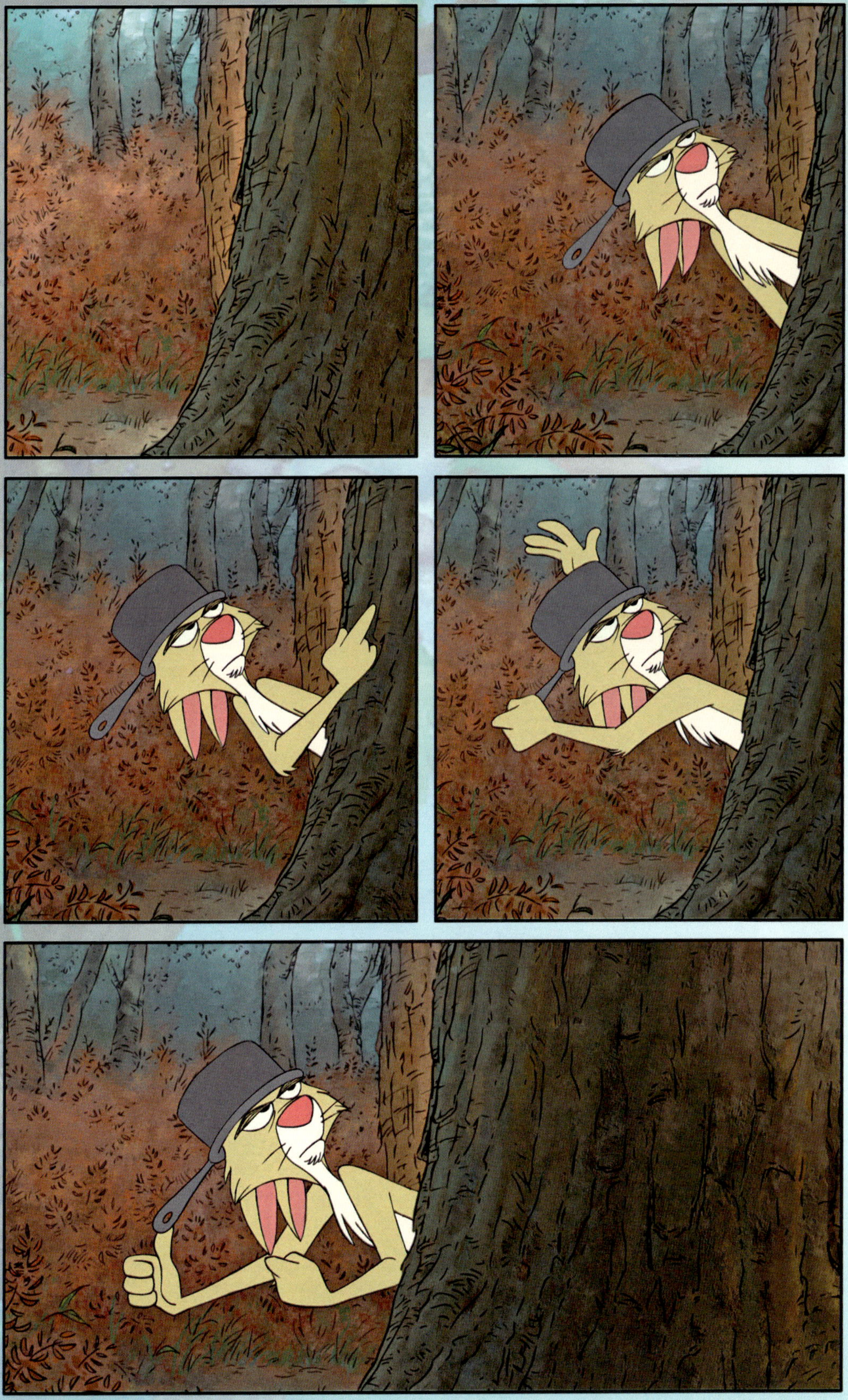

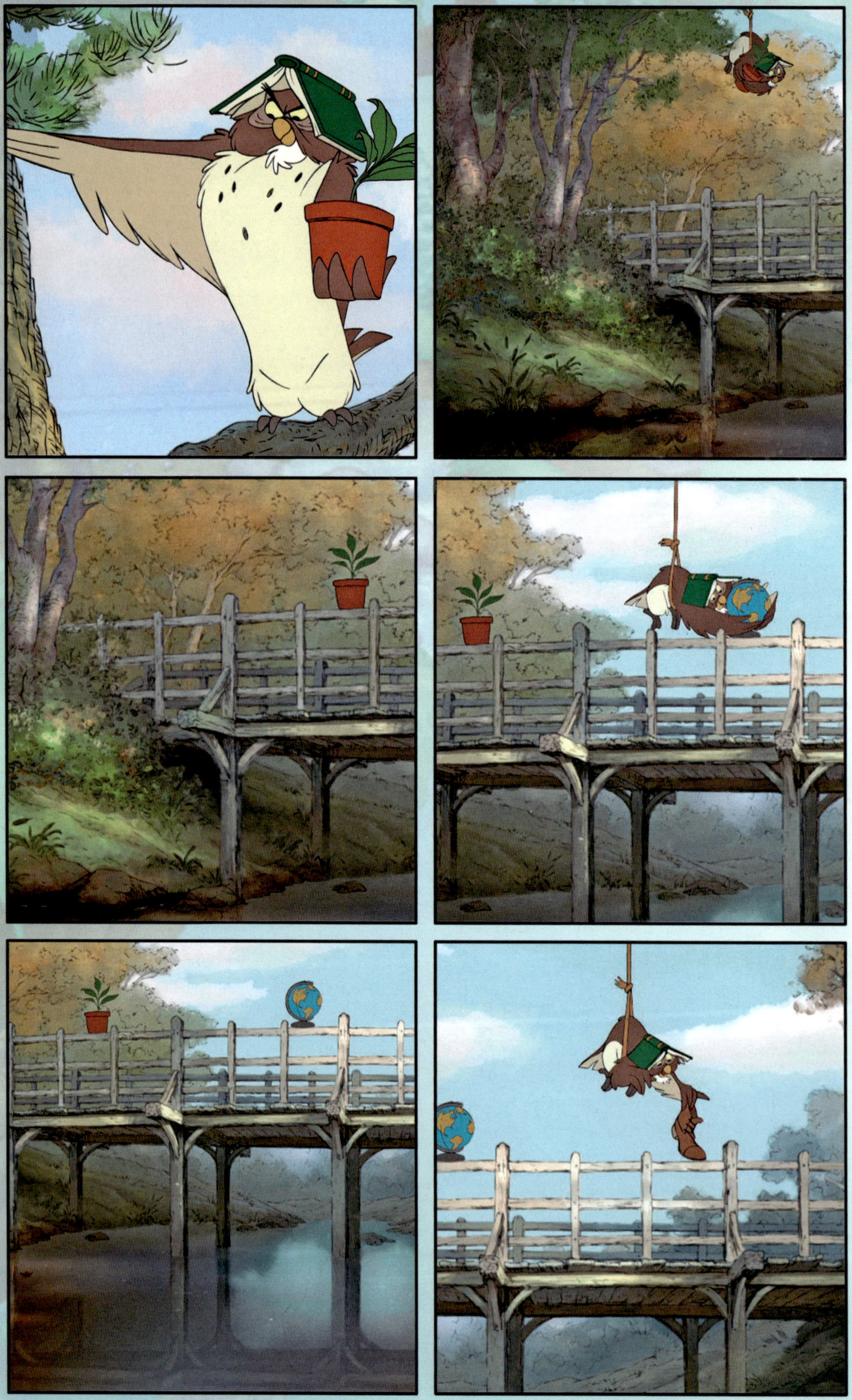

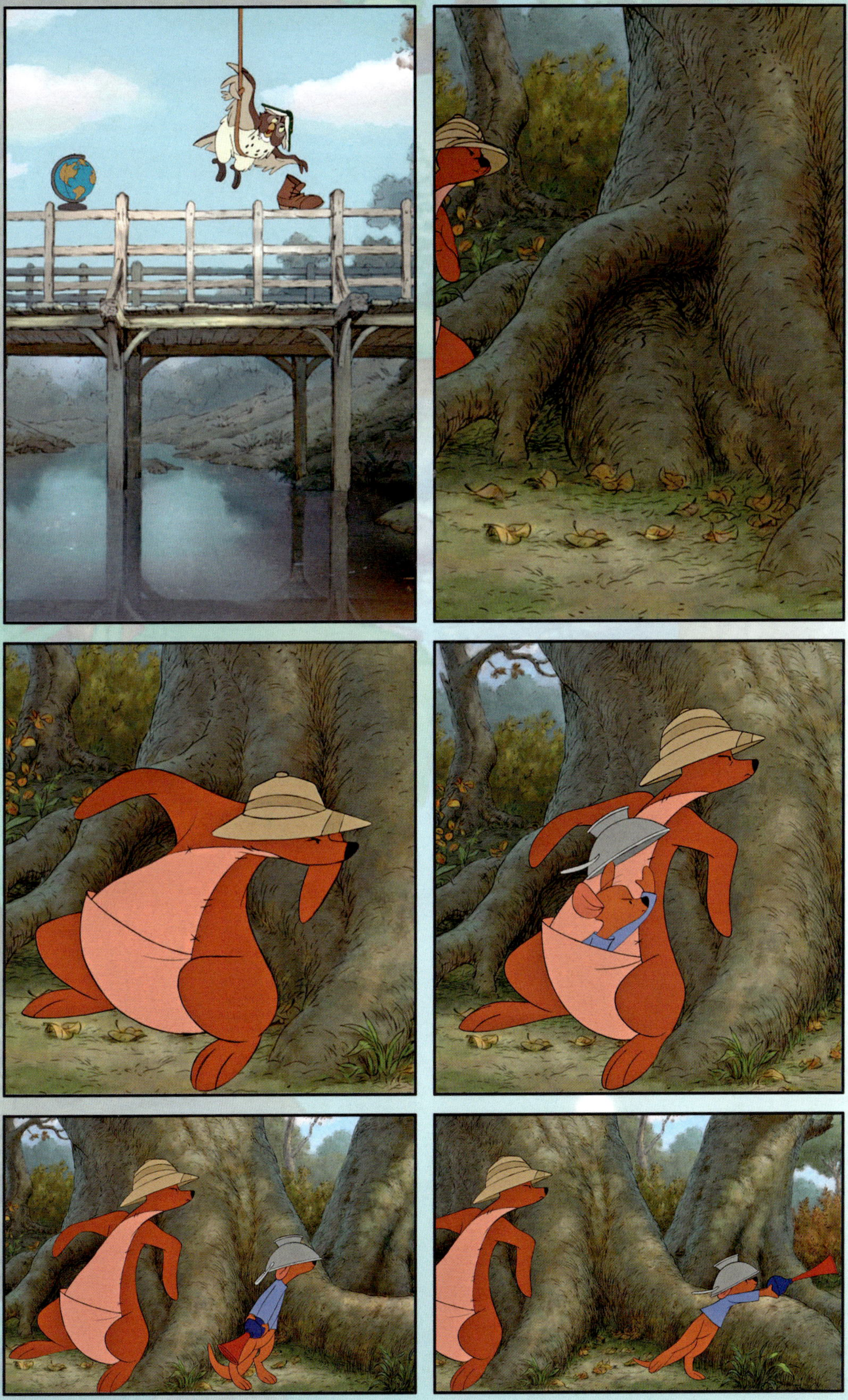

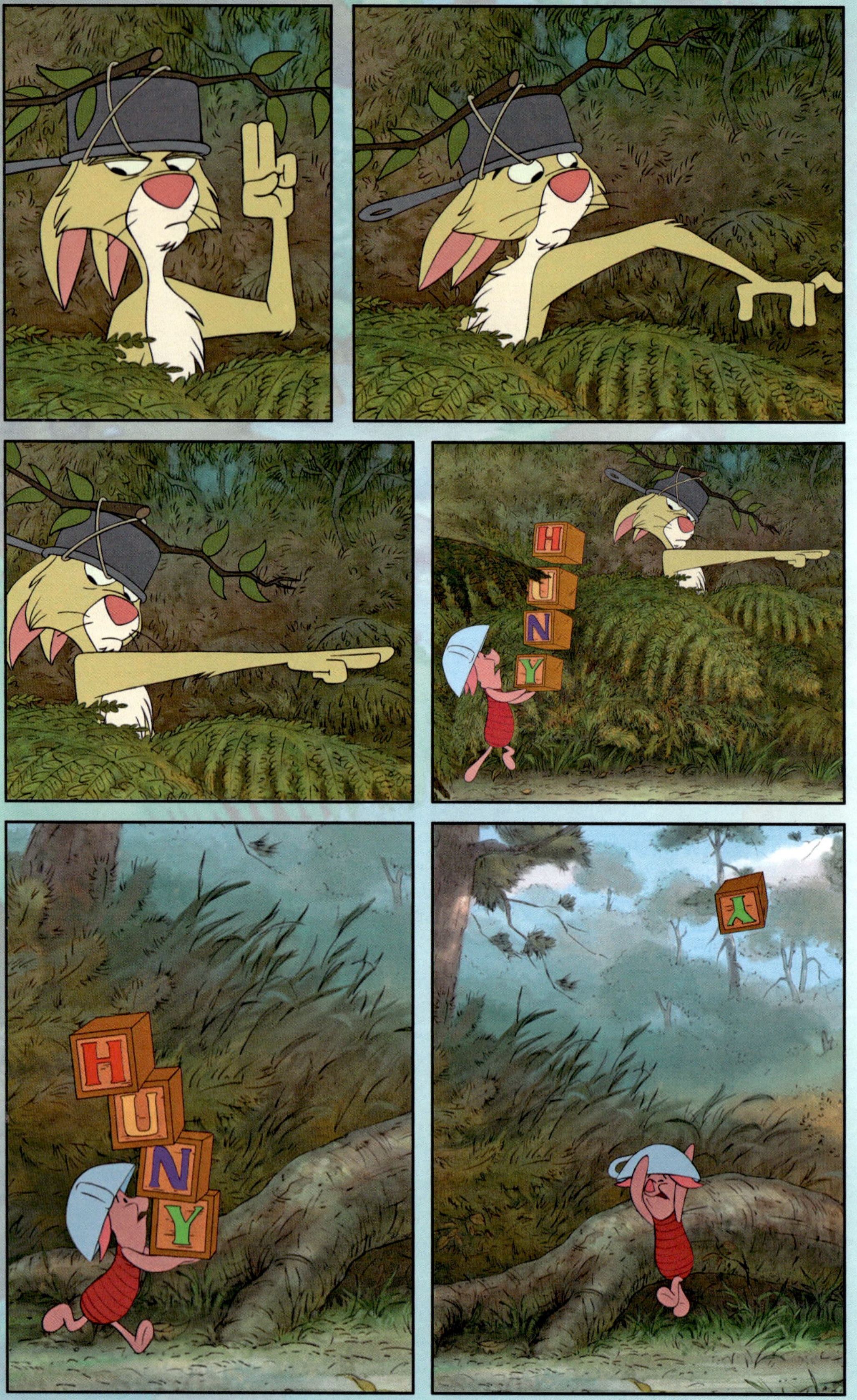
HUNY
HUNY
Y

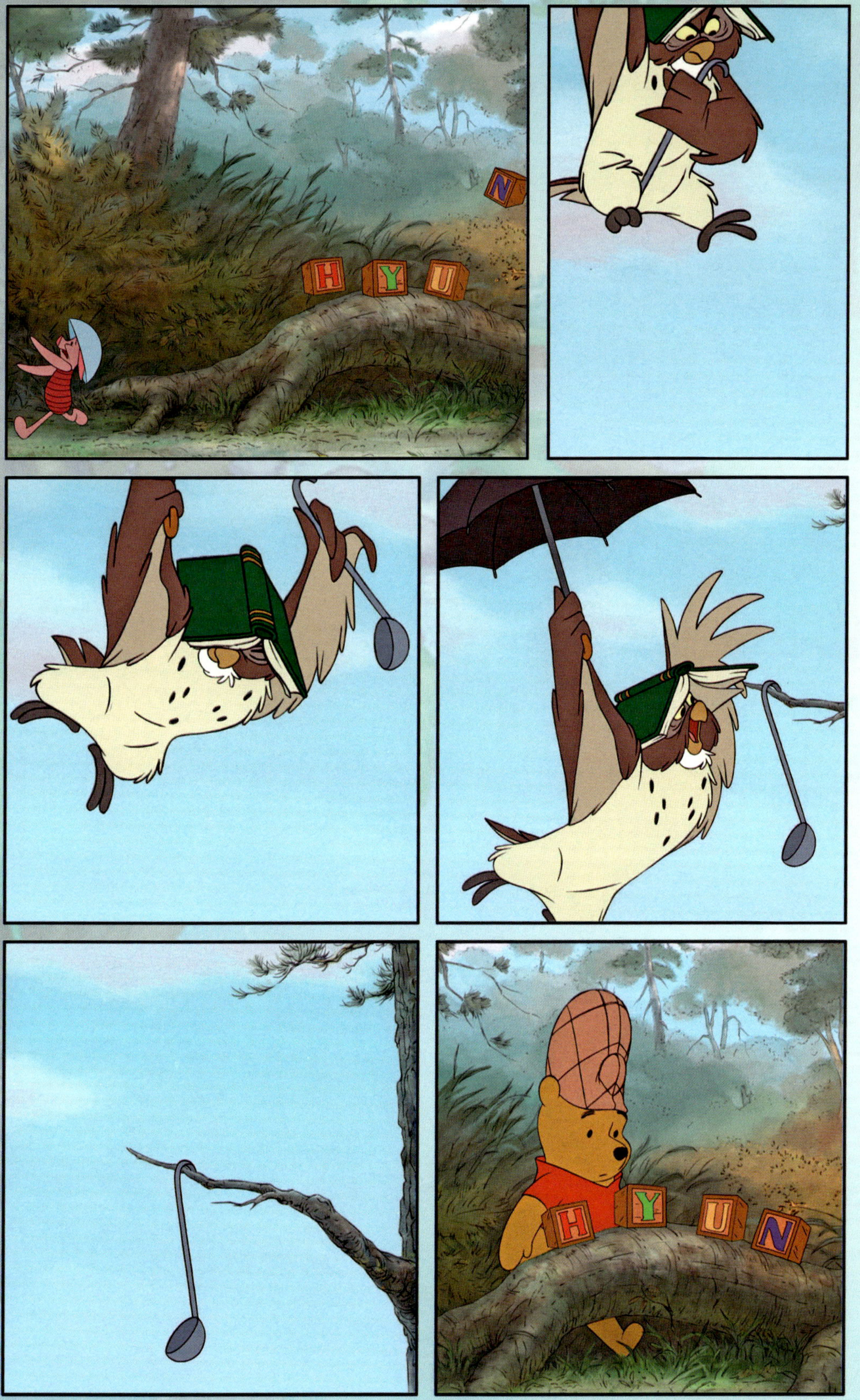
H Y U N

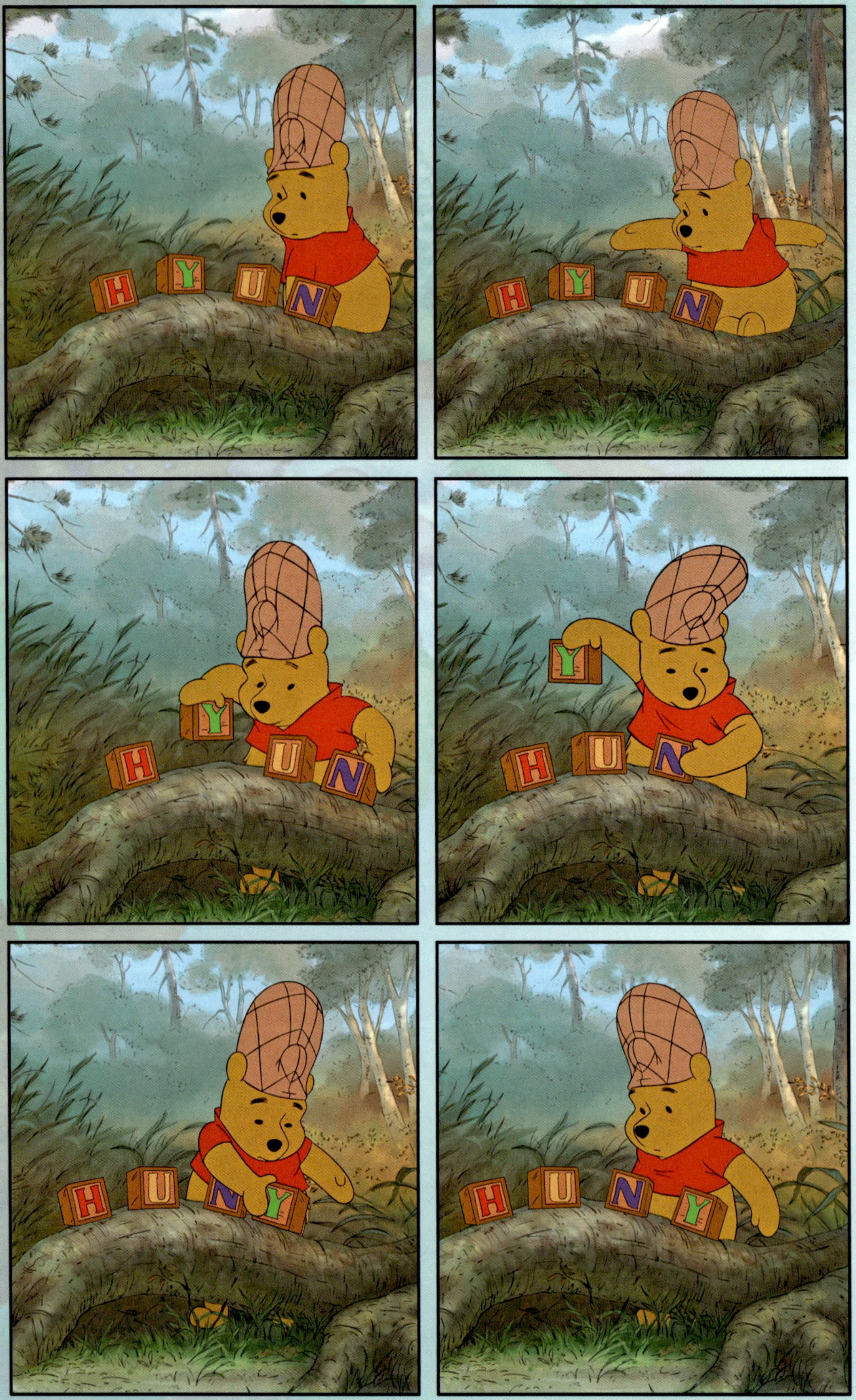

H Y U N
H Y U N
H Y U N
Y H U N
H U N Y
H U N Y

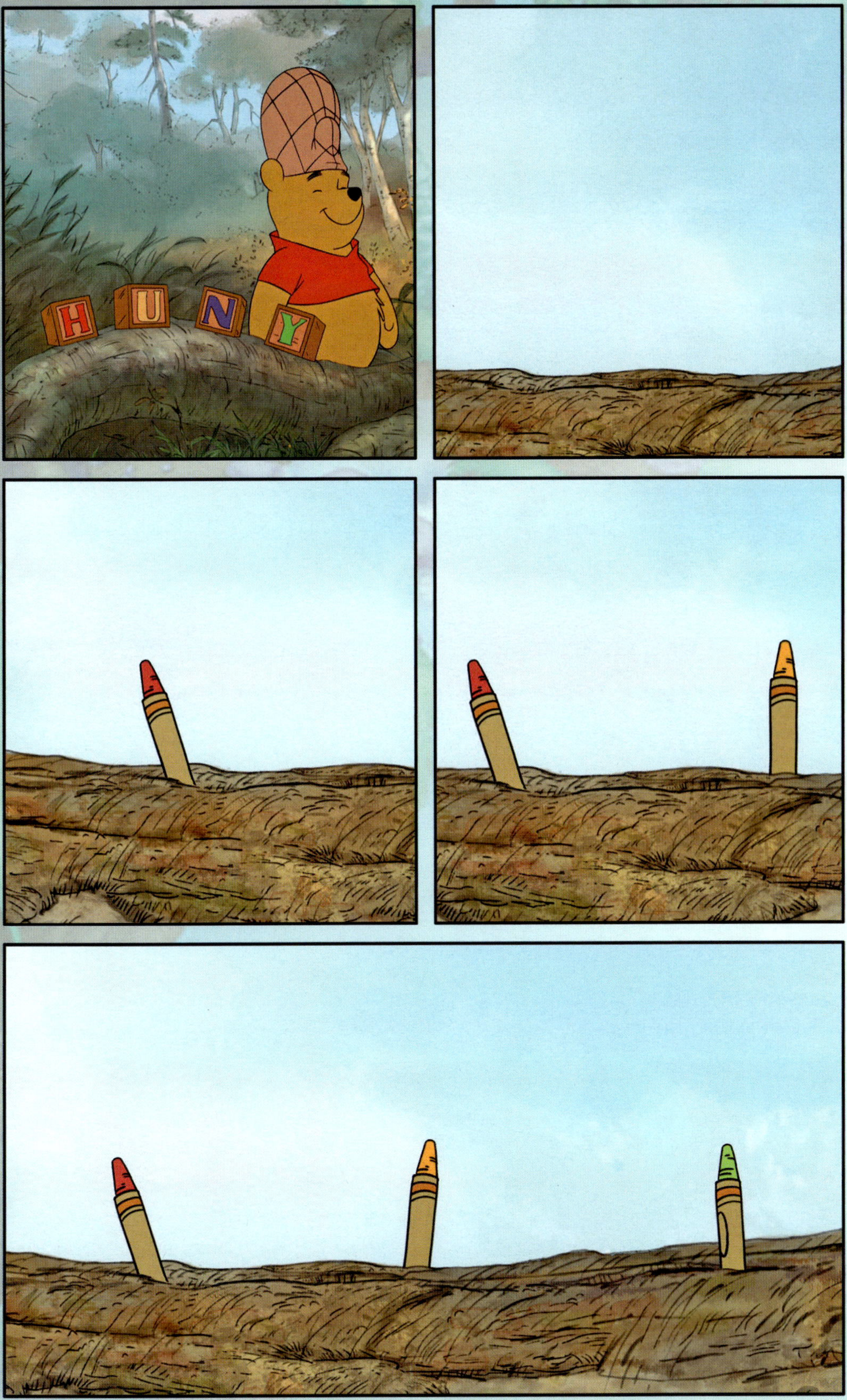
H U N Y

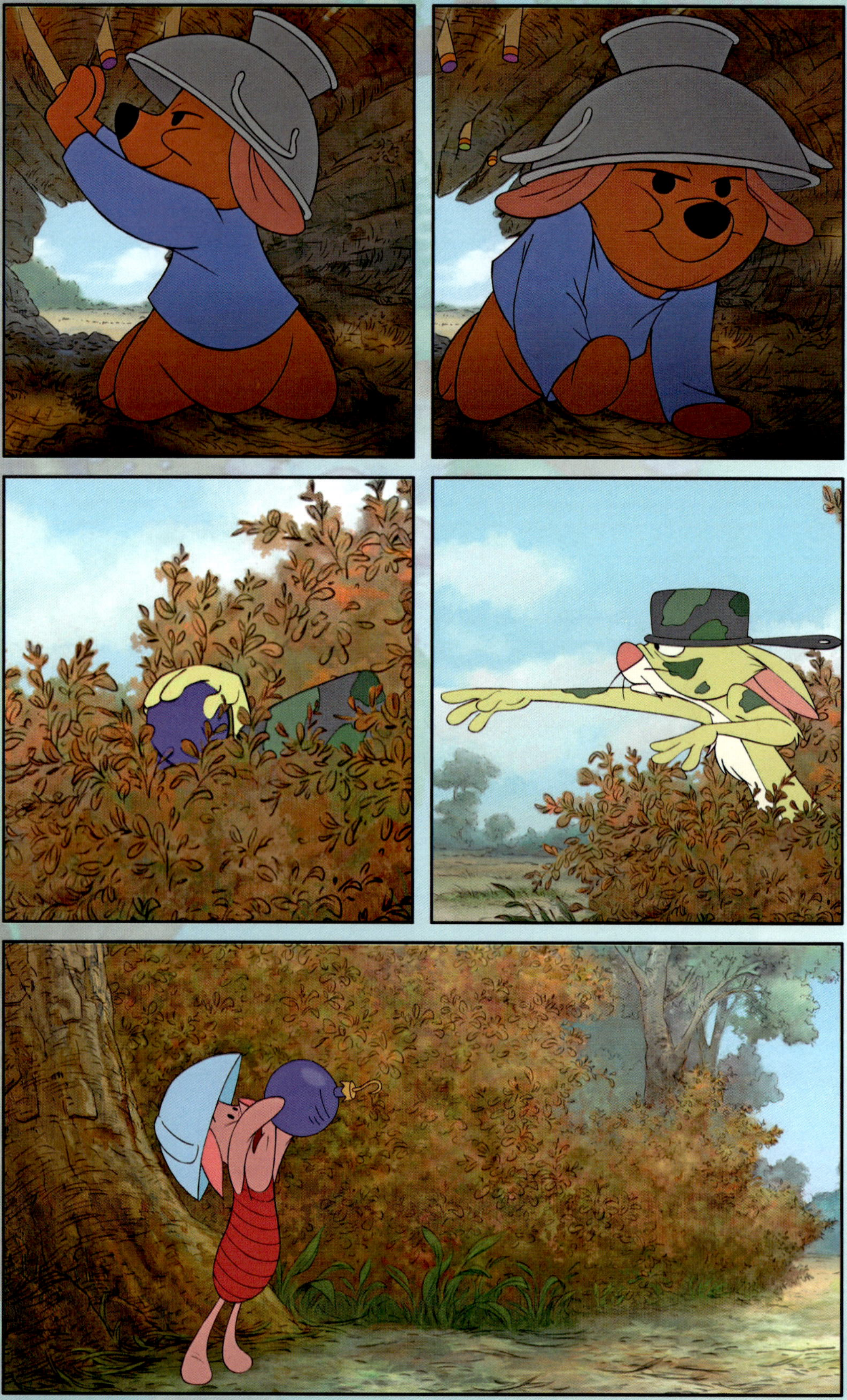

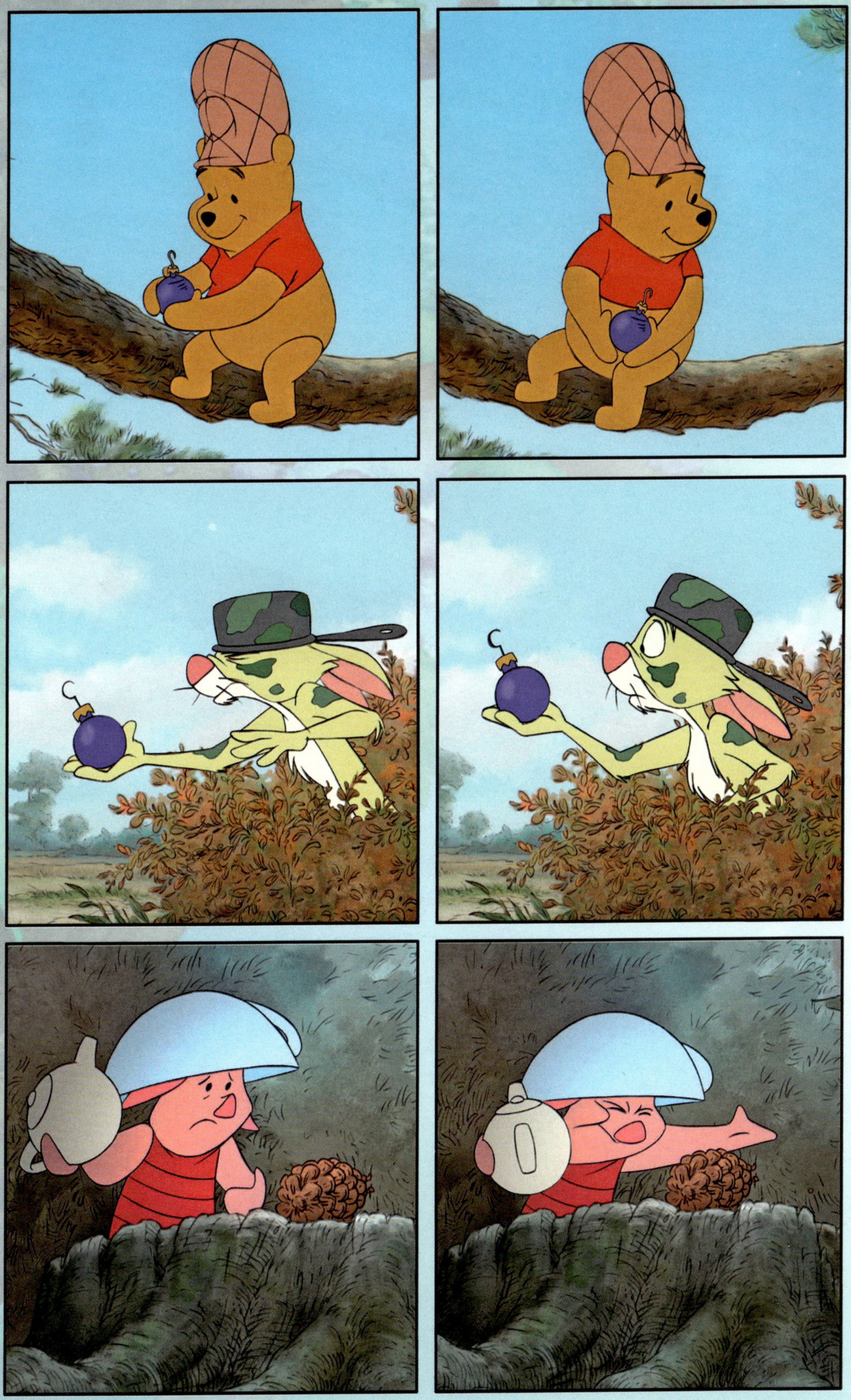

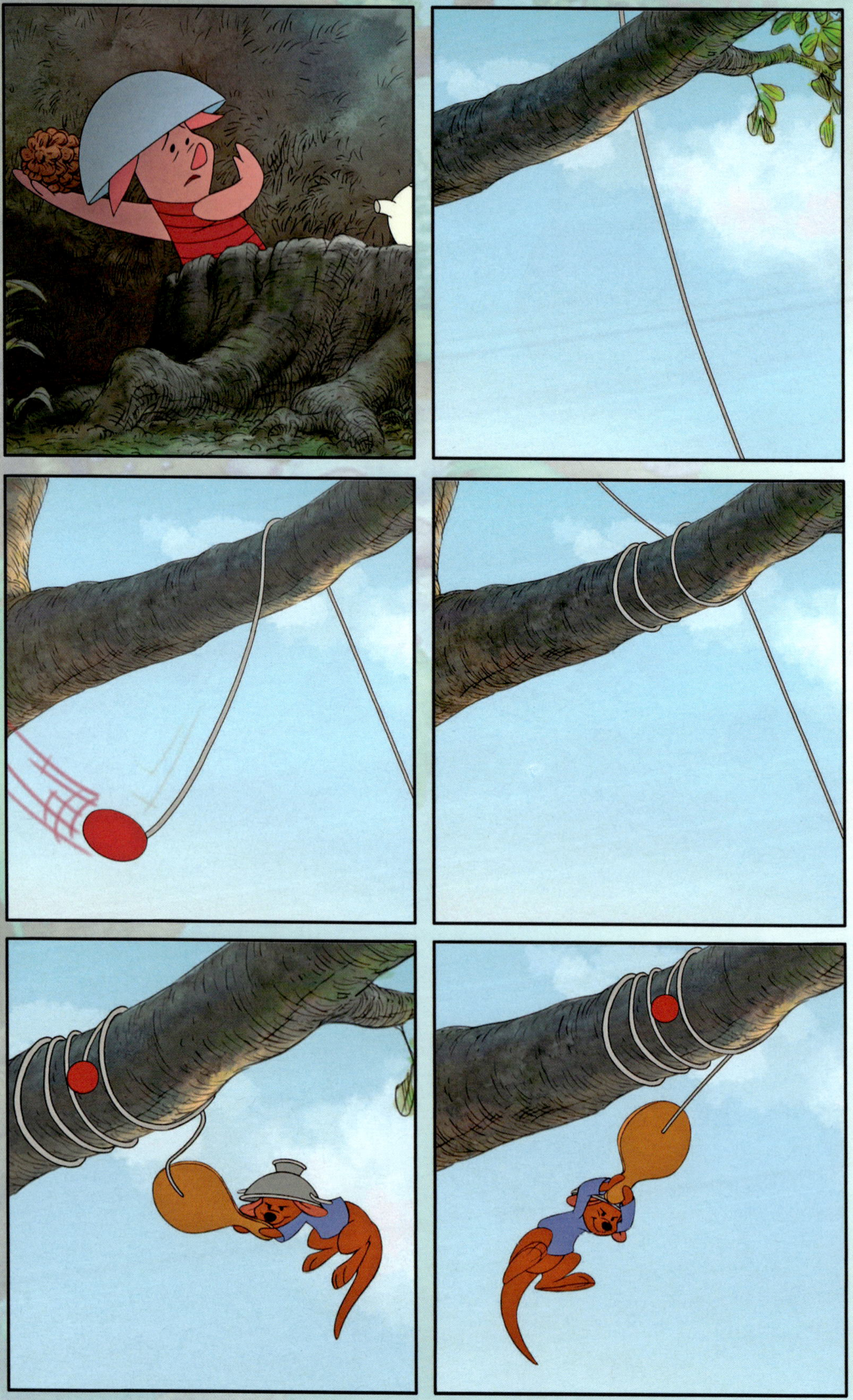

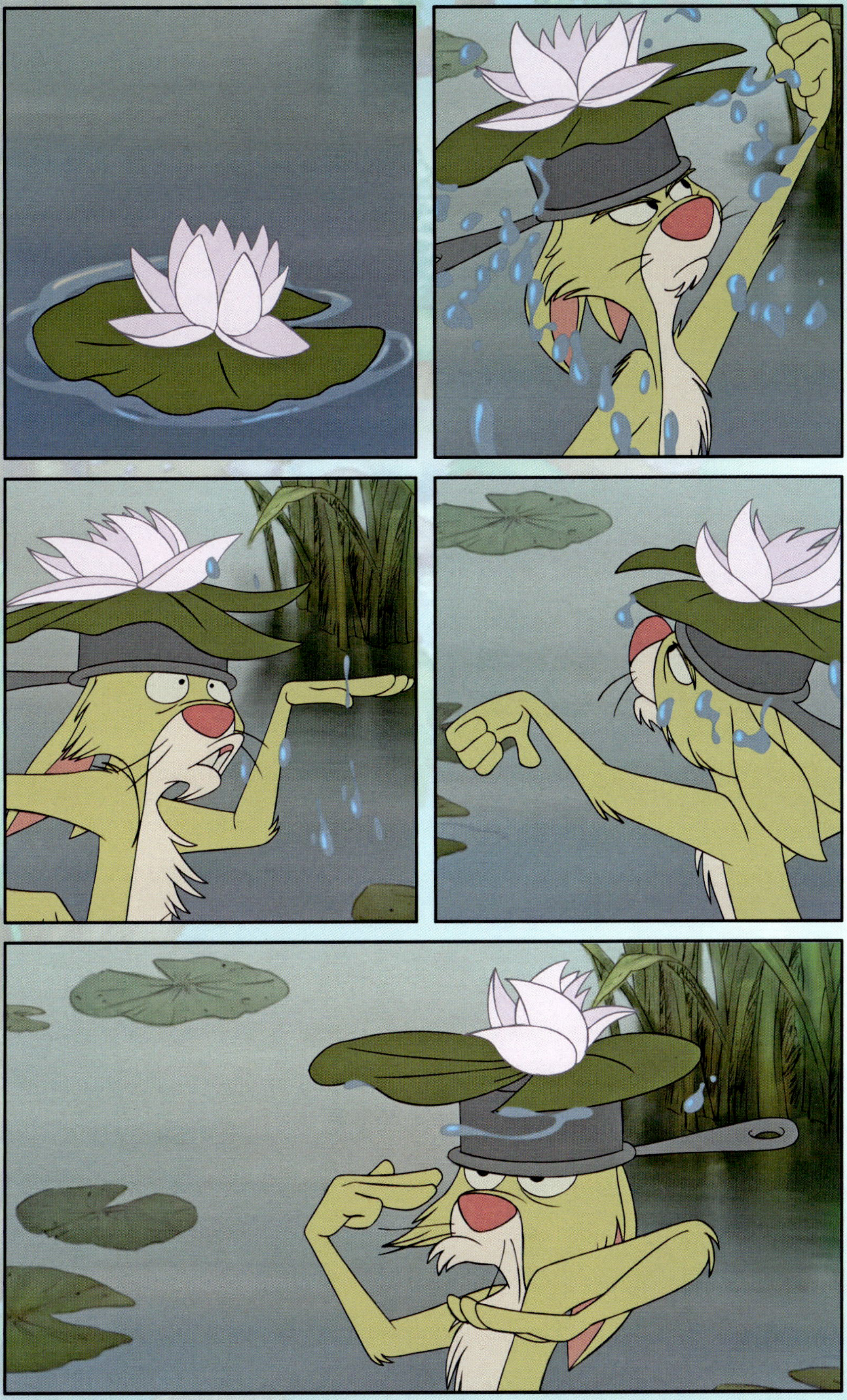

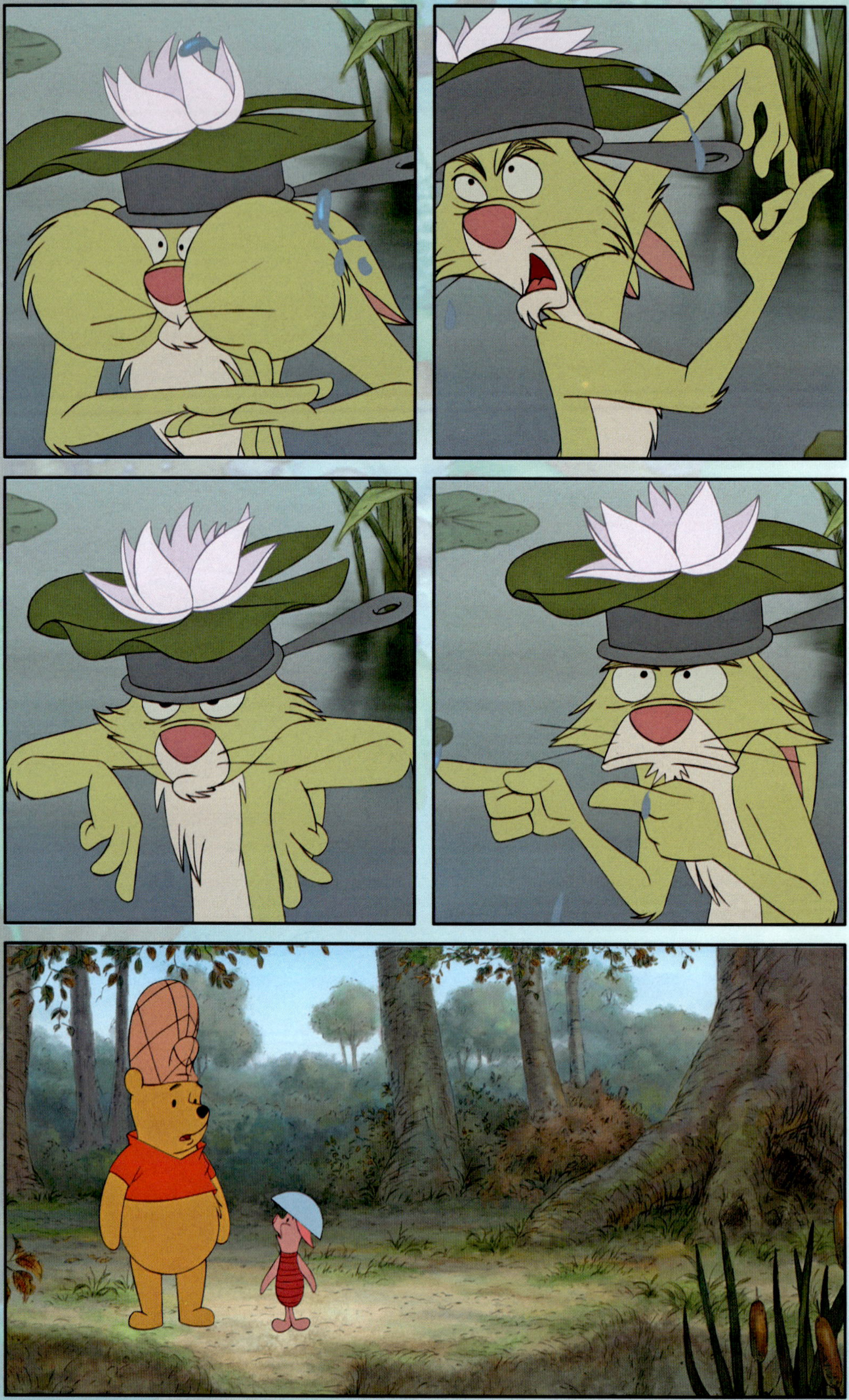

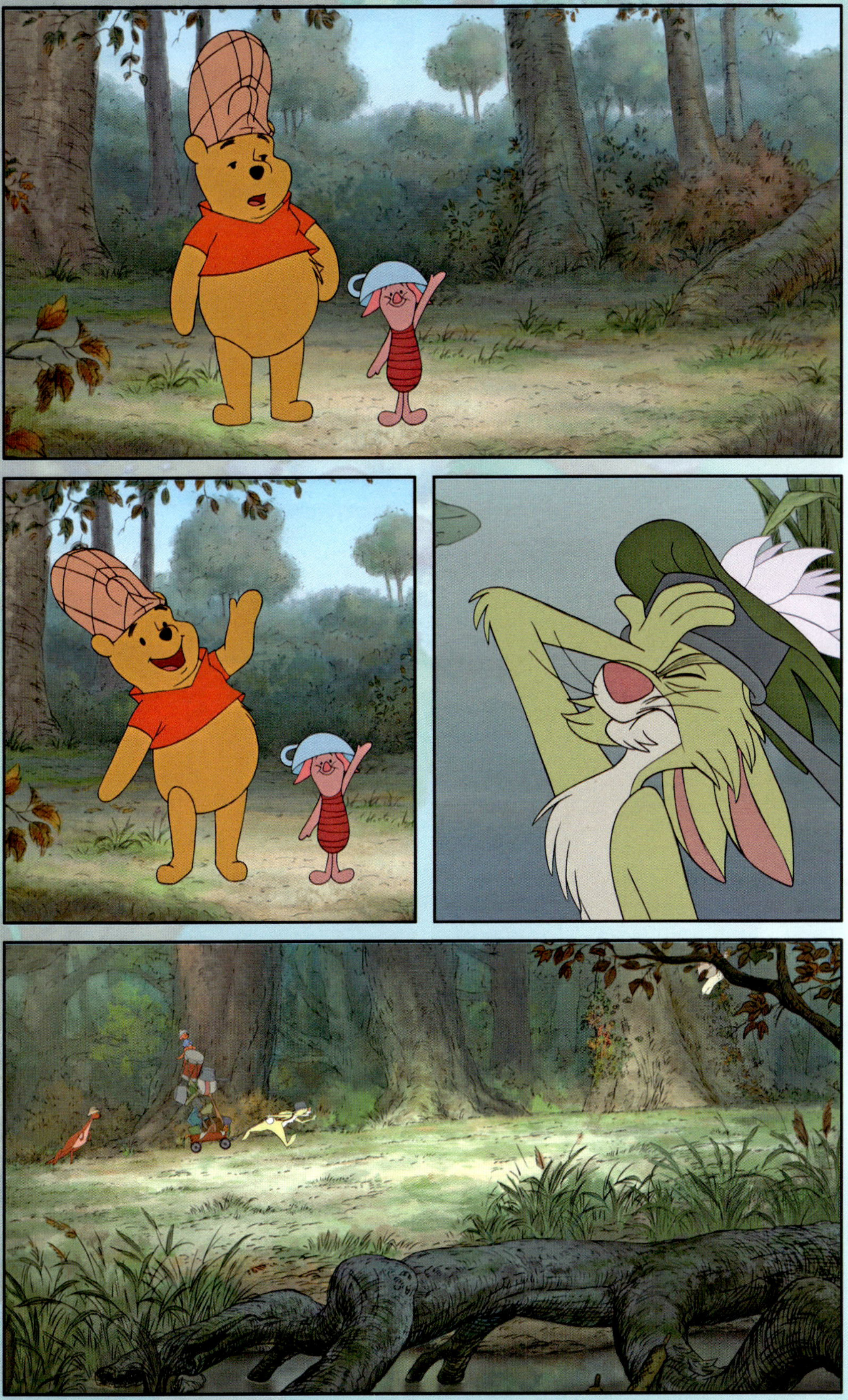

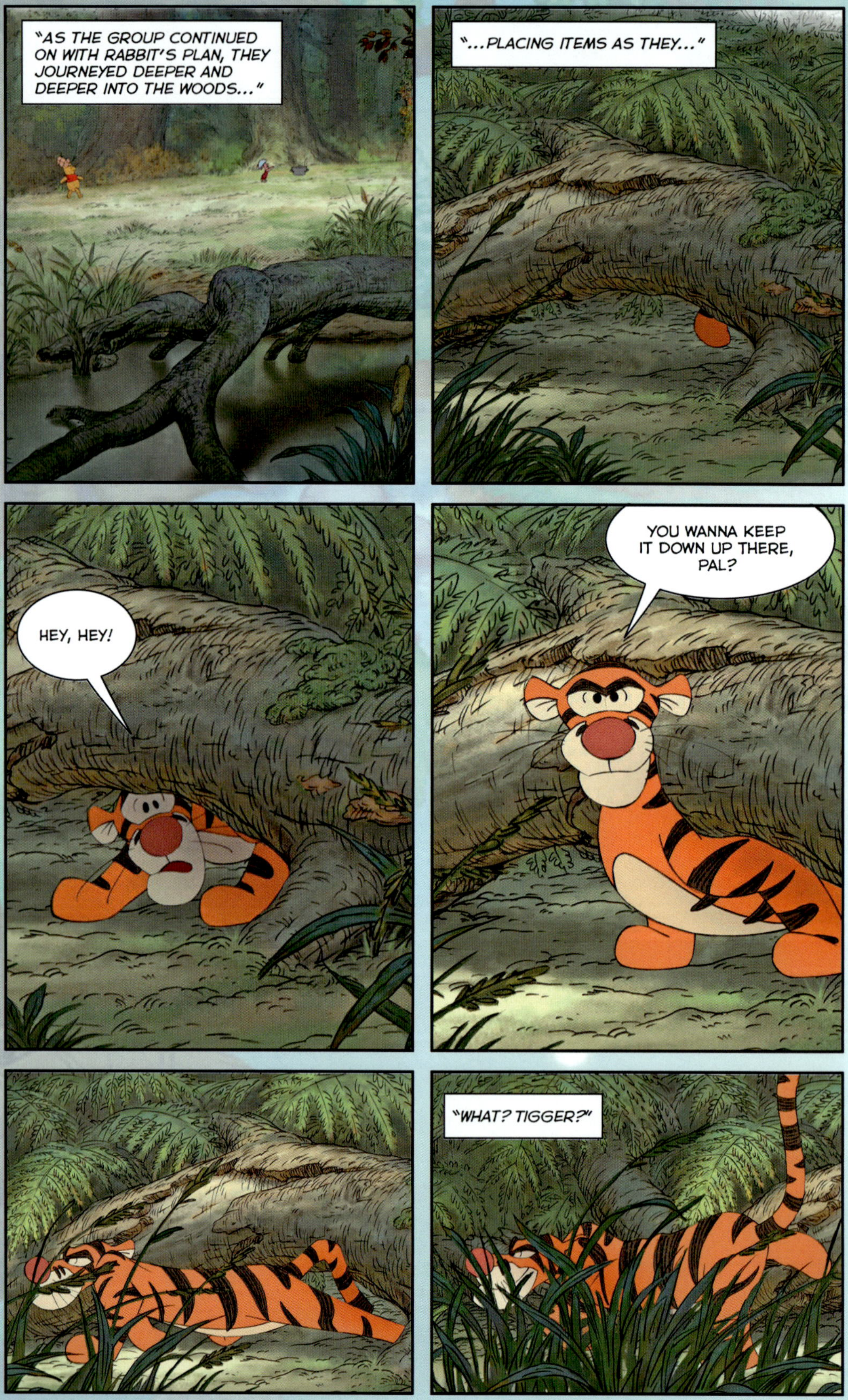
"AS THE GROUP CONTINUED ON WITH RABBIT'S PLAN, THEY JOURNEYED DEEPER AND DEEPER INTO THE WOODS..."
"...PLACING ITEMS AS THEY..."
HEY, HEY!
YOU WANNA KEEP IT DOWN UP THERE, PAL?
"WHAT? TIGGER?"

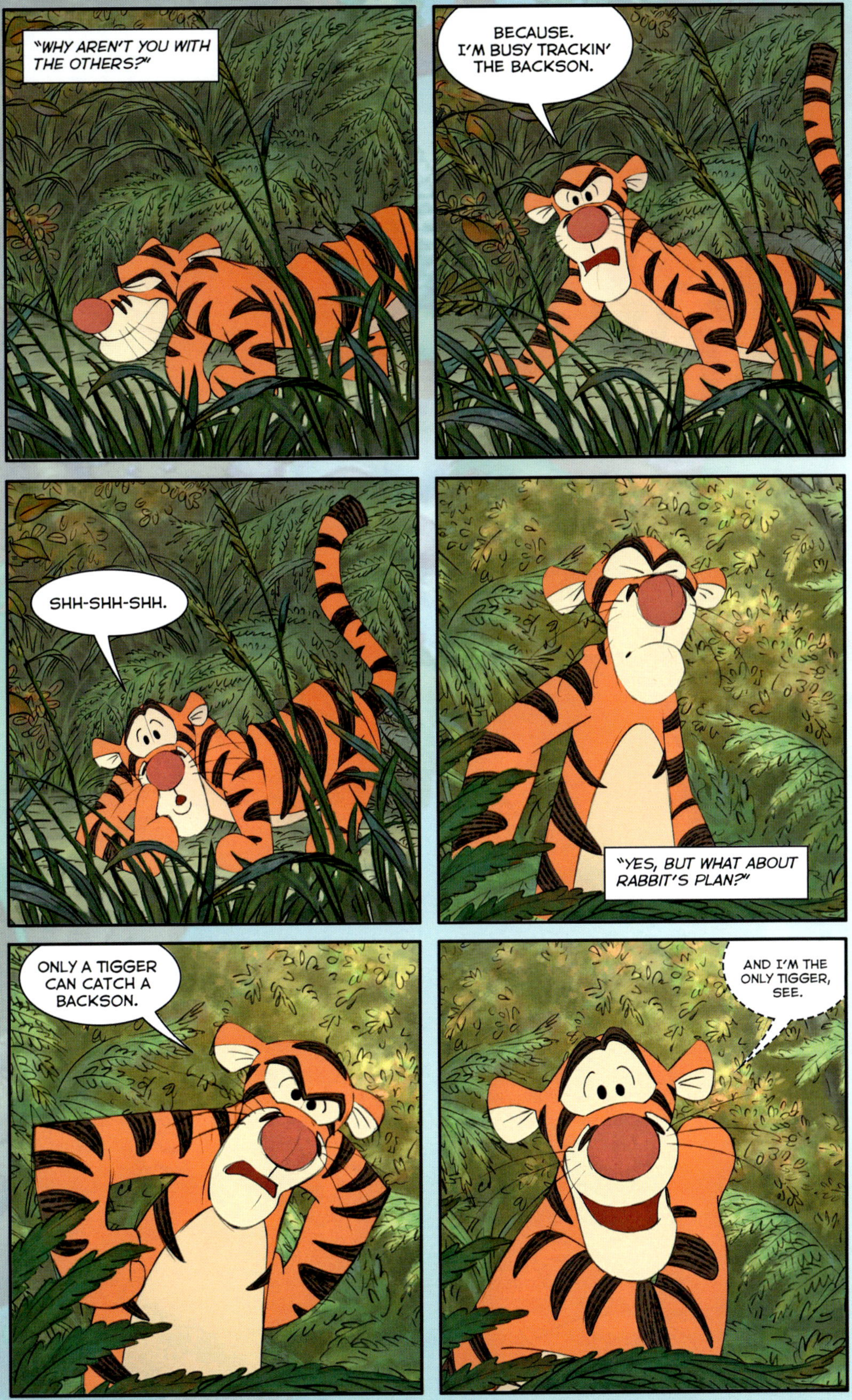
"WHY AREN'T YOU WITH THE OTHERS?"
BECAUSE. I'M BUSY TRACKIN' THE BACKSON.
SHH-SHH-SHH.
"YES, BUT WHAT ABOUT RABBIT'S PLAN?"
ONLY A TIGGER CAN CATCH A BACKSON.
AND I'M THE ONLY TIGGER, SEE.

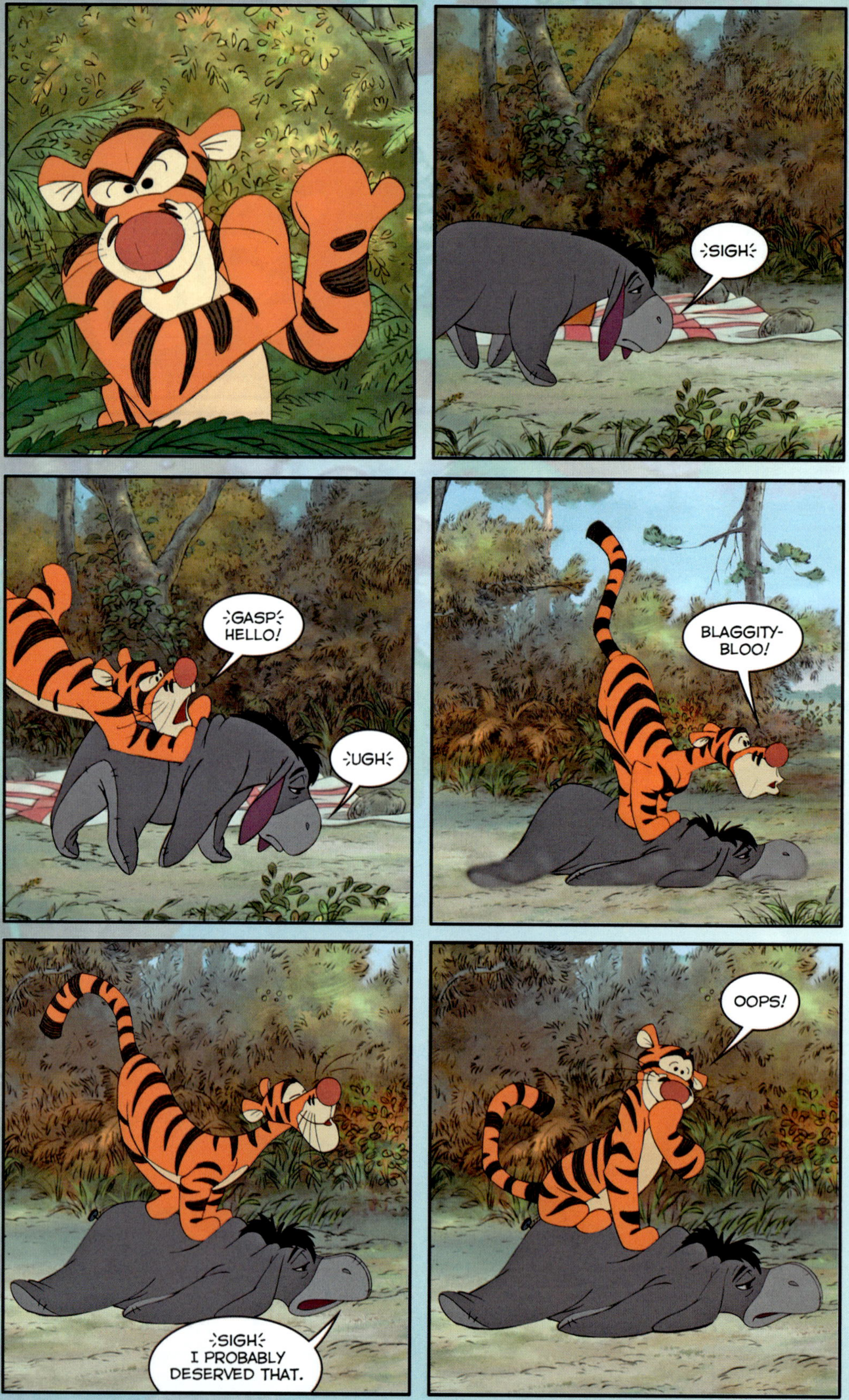

SIGH
GASP HELLO!
UGH
BLAGGITY-BLOO!
SIGH I PROBABLY DESERVED THAT.
OOPS!

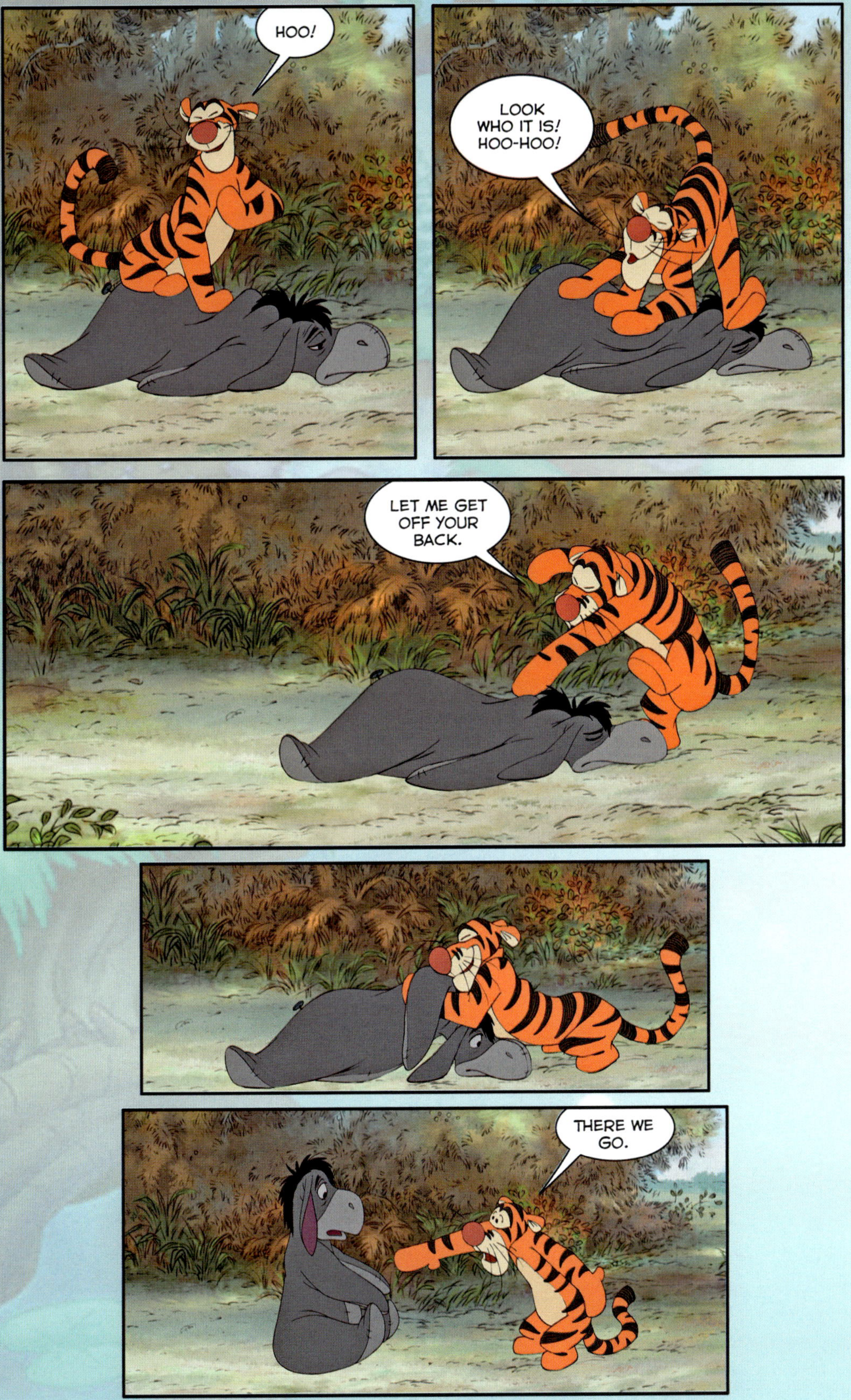
HOO!
LOOK WHO IT IS! HOO-HOO!
LET ME GET OFF YOUR BACK.
THERE WE GO.

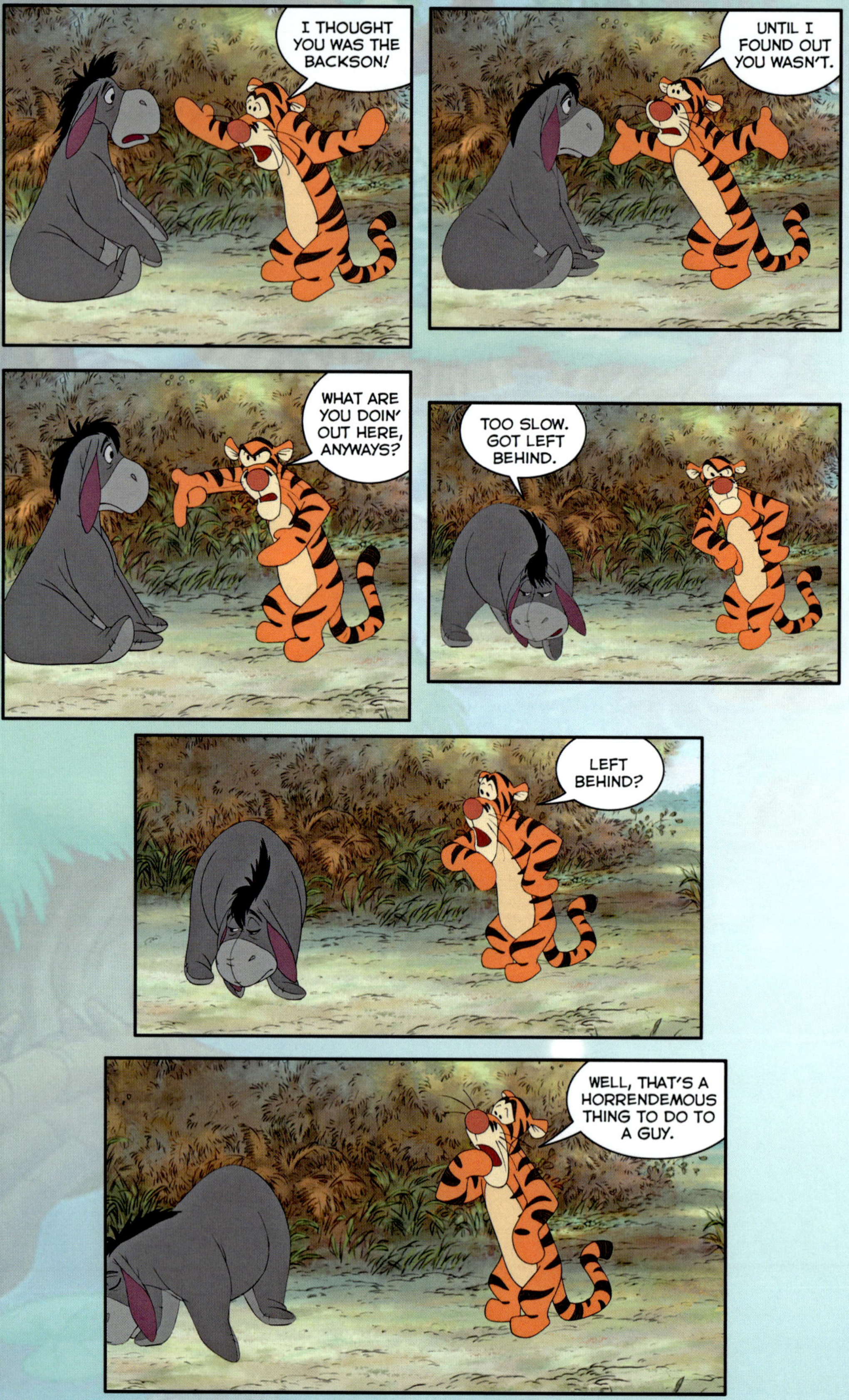
I THOUGHT YOU WAS THE BACKSON!
UNTIL I FOUND OUT YOU WASN'T.
WHAT ARE YOU DOIN' OUT HERE, ANYWAYS?
TOO SLOW. GOT LEFT BEHIND.
LEFT BEHIND?
WELL, THAT'S A HORRENDEMOUS THING TO DO TO A GUY.

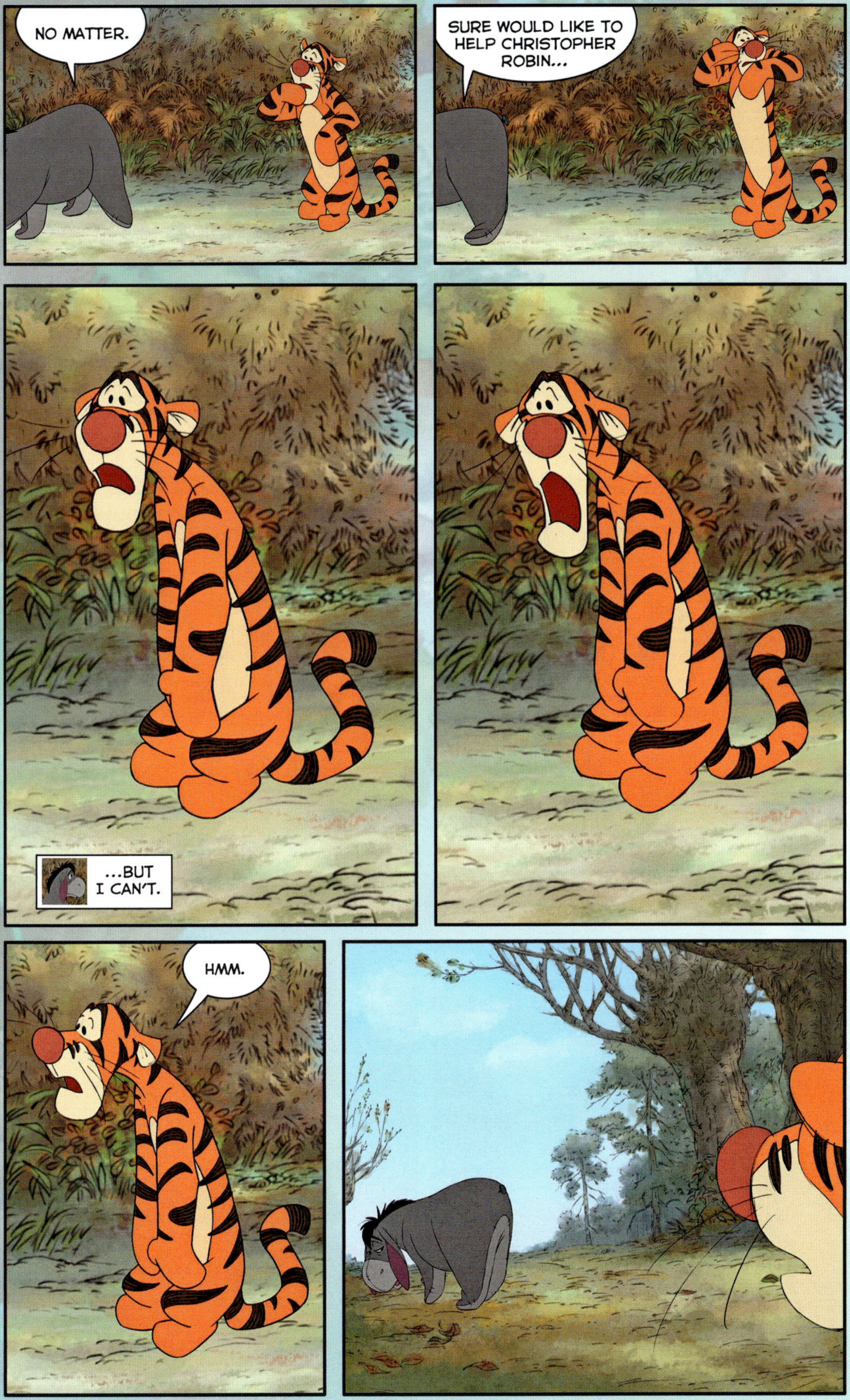
NO MATTER.
SURE WOULD LIKE TO HELP CHRISTOPHER ROBIN...
...BUT I CAN'T.
HMM.

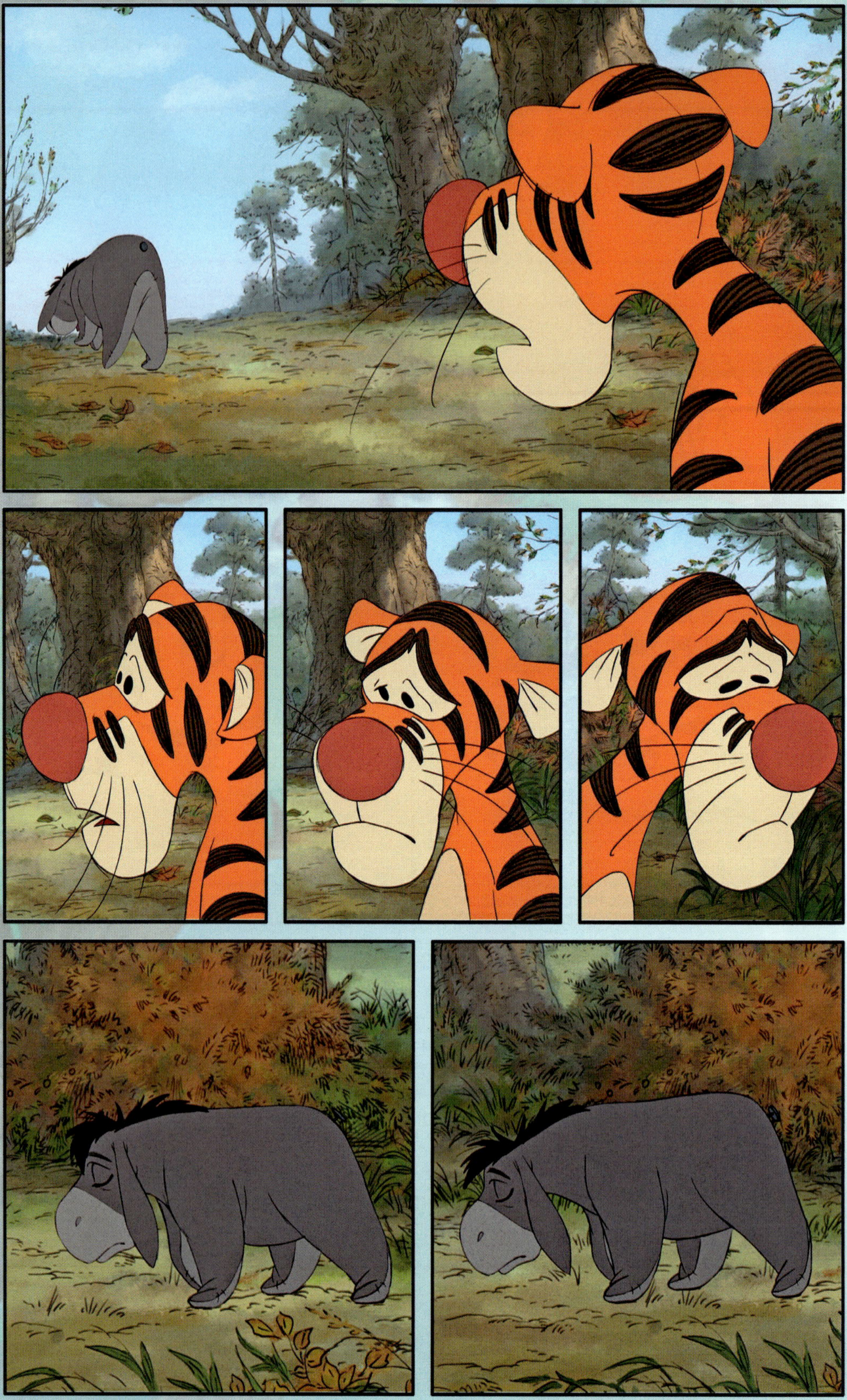

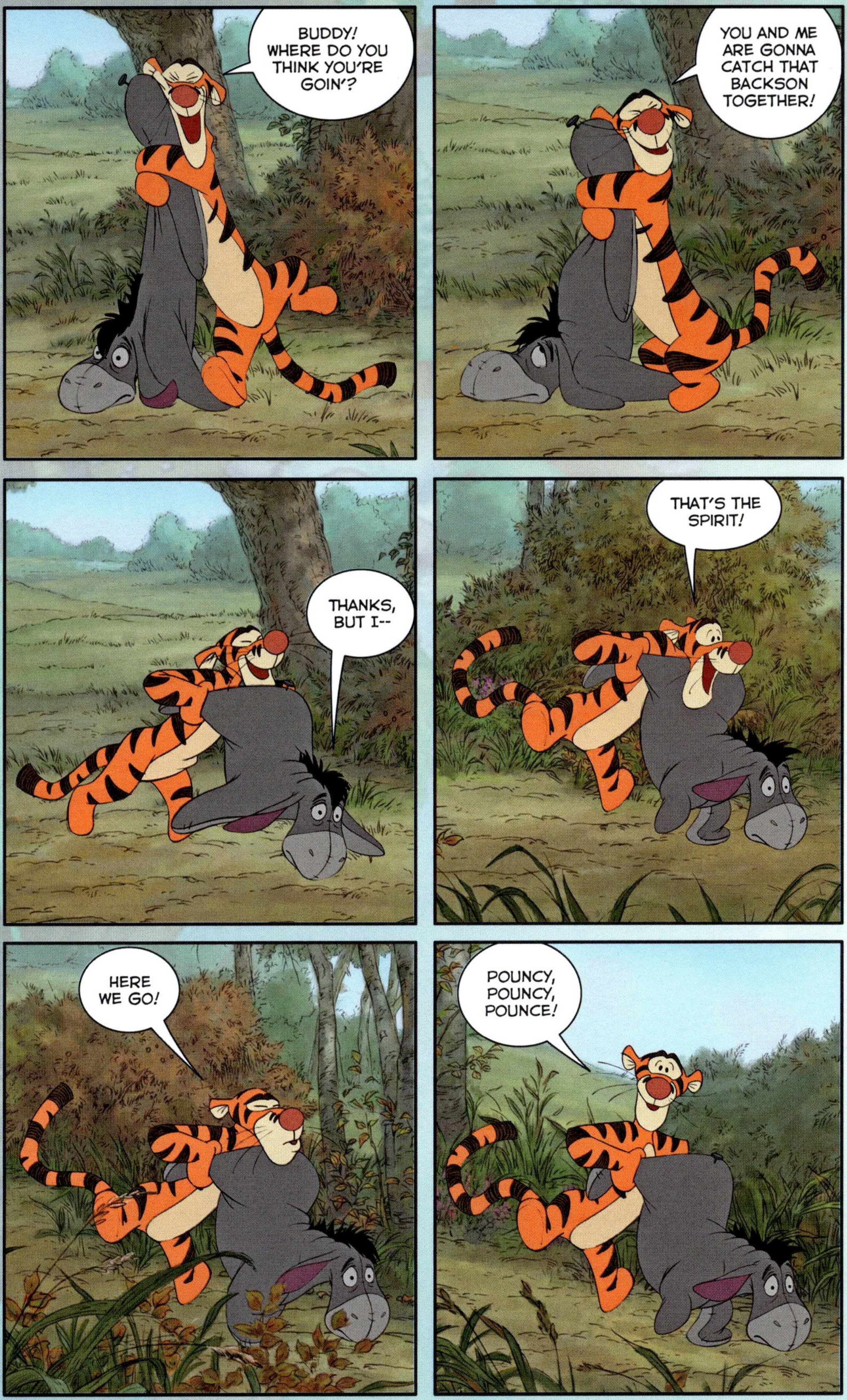
BUDDY! WHERE DO YOU THINK YOU'RE GOIN'?
YOU AND ME ARE GONNA CATCH THAT BACKSON TOGETHER!
THANKS, BUT I--
THAT'S THE SPIRIT!
HERE WE GO!
POUNCY, POUNCY, POUNCE!

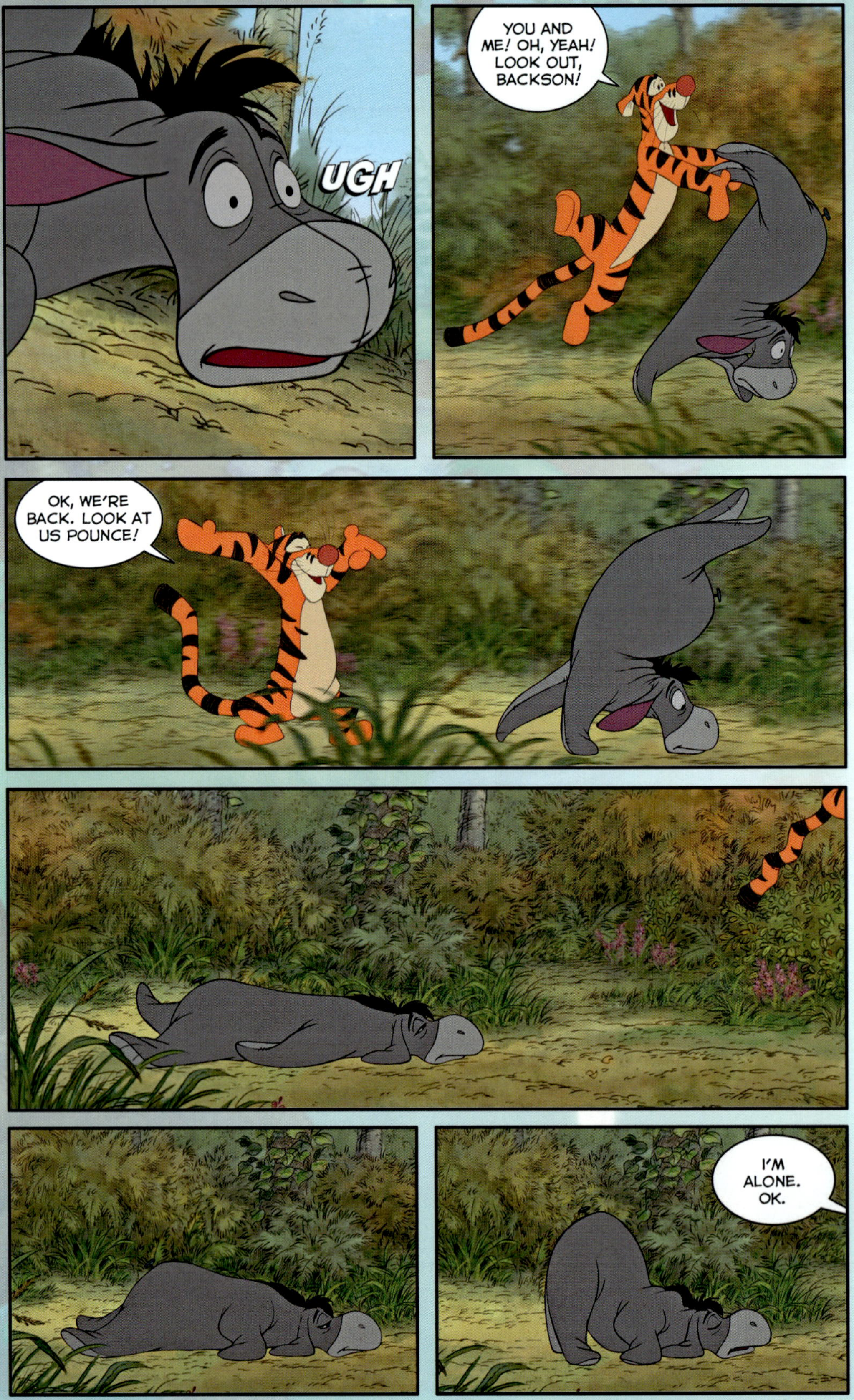
UGH
YOU AND ME! OH, YEAH! LOOK OUT, BACKSON!
OK, WE'RE BACK. LOOK AT US POUNCE!
I'M ALONE. OK.

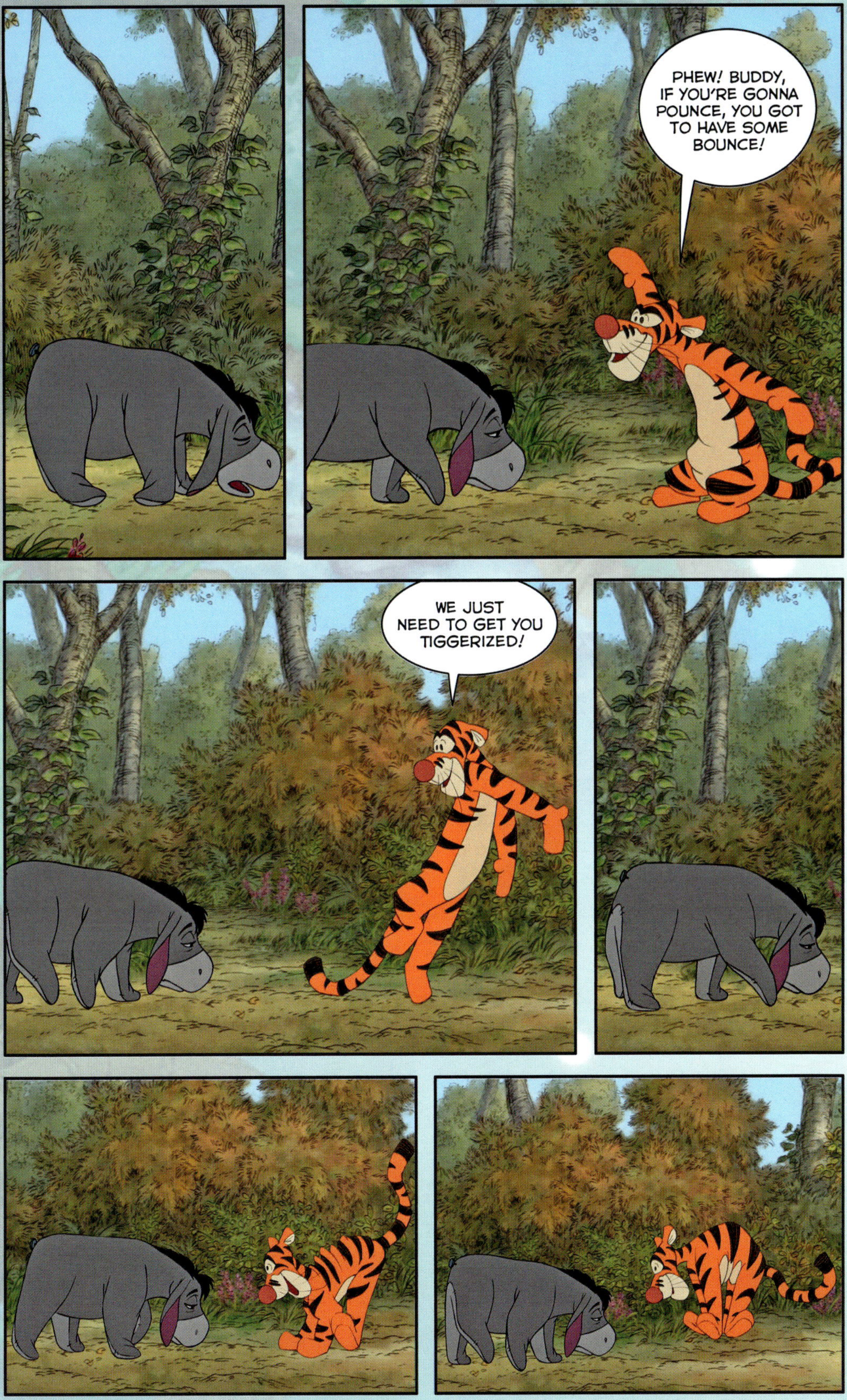
PHEW! BUDDY, IF YOU'RE GONNA POUNCE, YOU GOT TO HAVE SOME BOUNCE!
WE JUST NEED TO GET YOU TIGGERIZED!

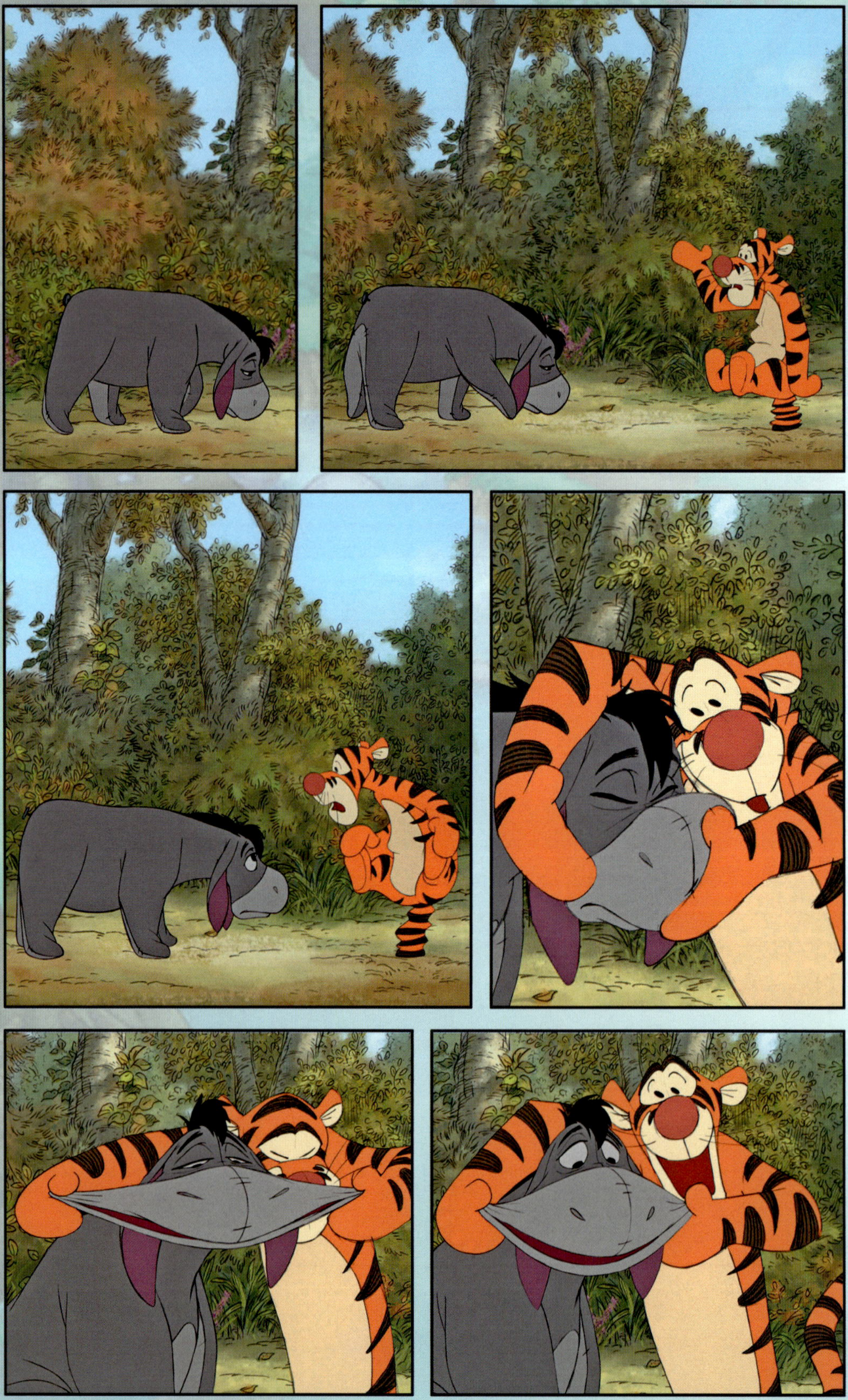

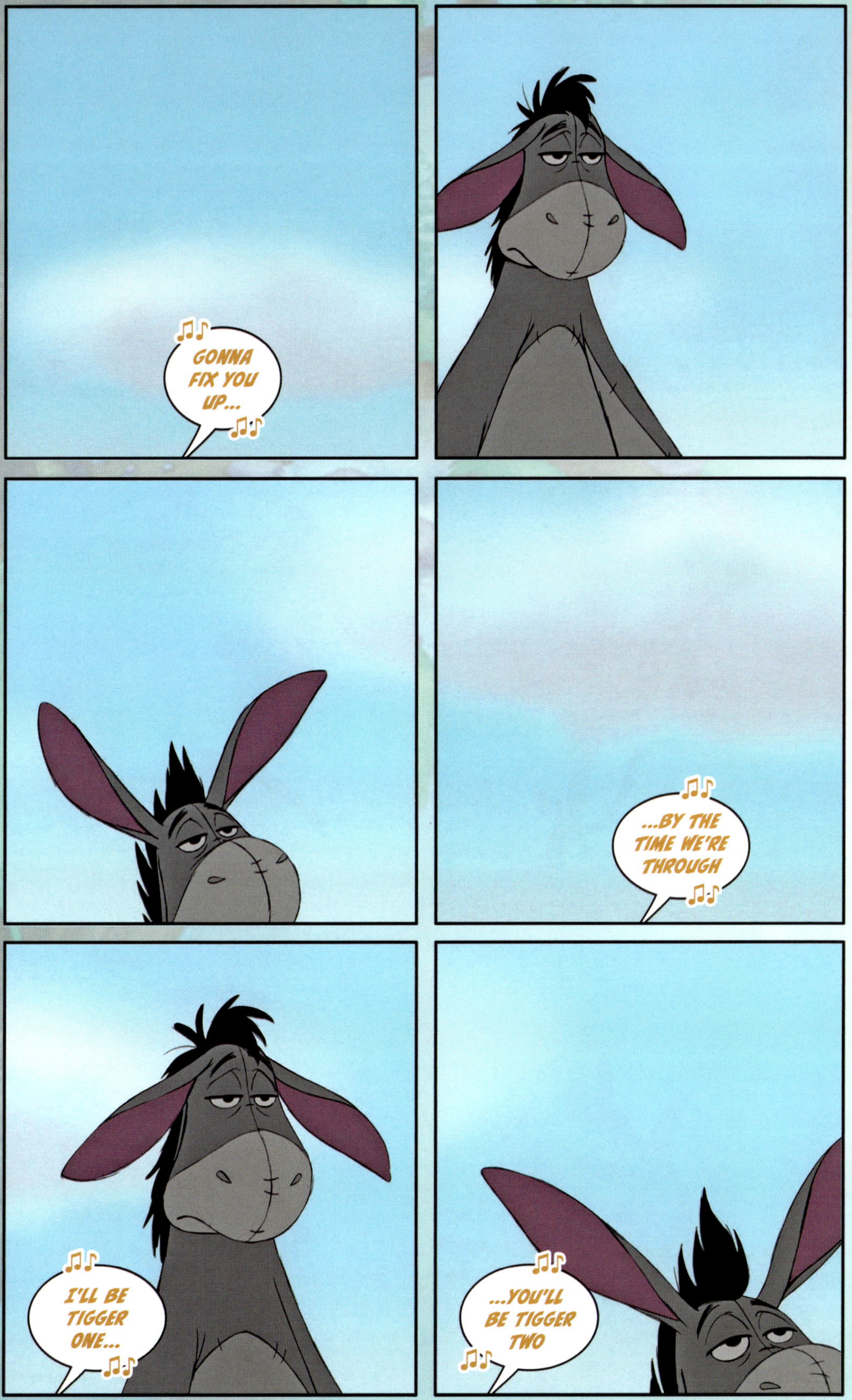
GONNA FIX YOU UP...
...BY THE TIME WE'RE THROUGH
I'LL BE TIGGER ONE...
...YOU'LL BE TIGGER TWO

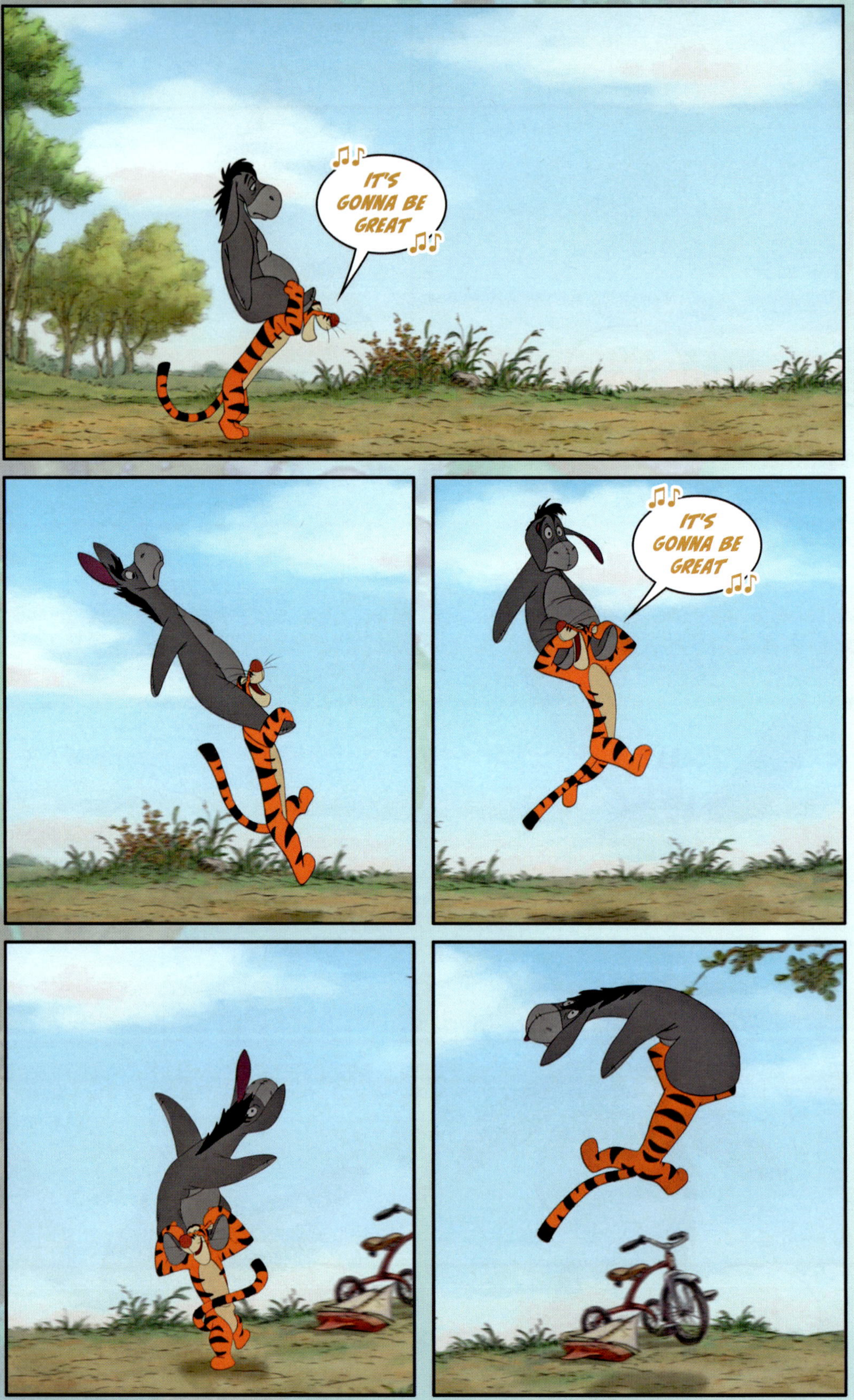
IT'S GONNA BE GREAT
IT'S GONNA BE GREAT

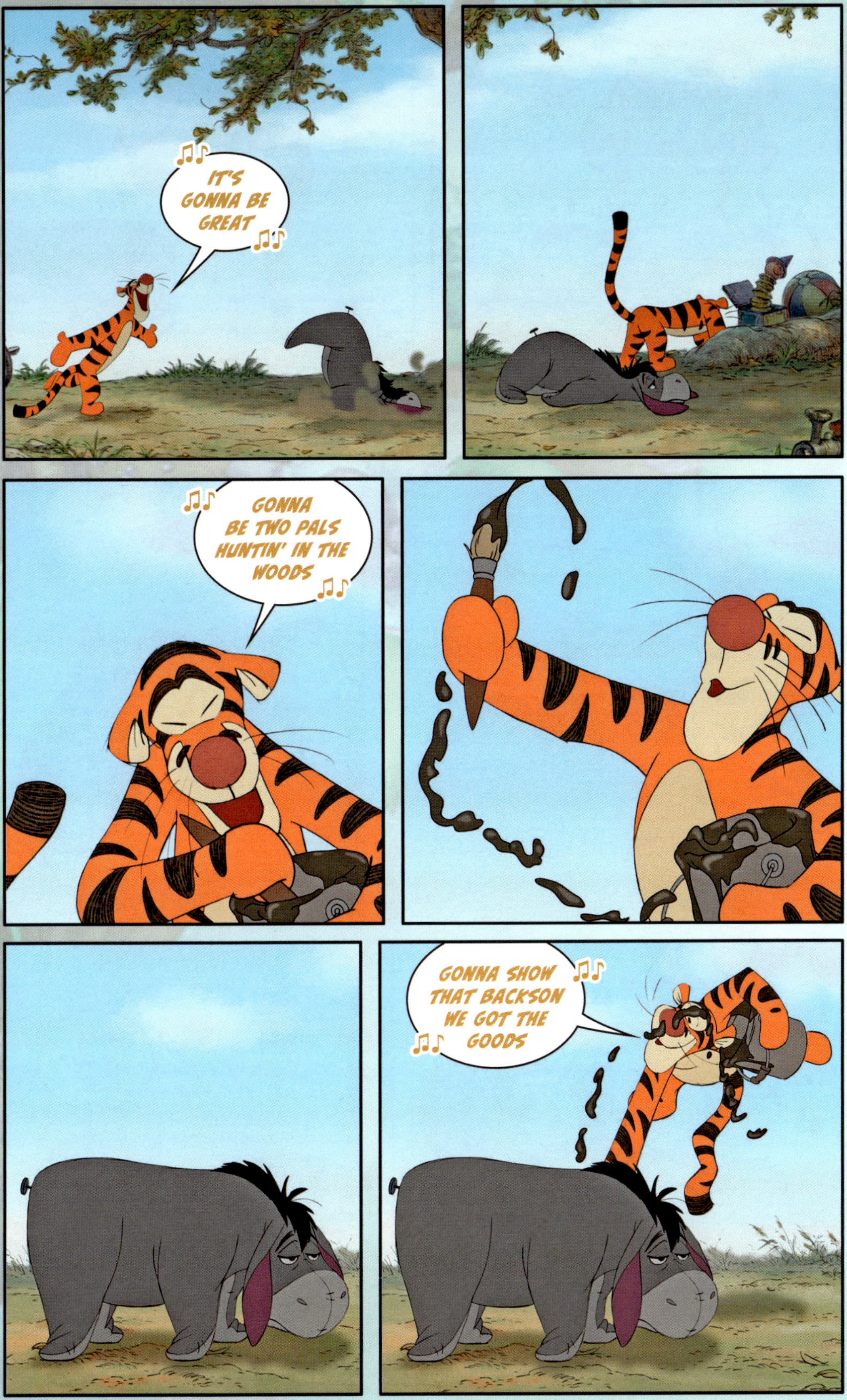
IT'S GONNA BE GREAT
GONNA BE TWO PALS HUNTIN' IN THE WOODS
GONNA SHOW THAT BACKSON WE GOT THE GOODS

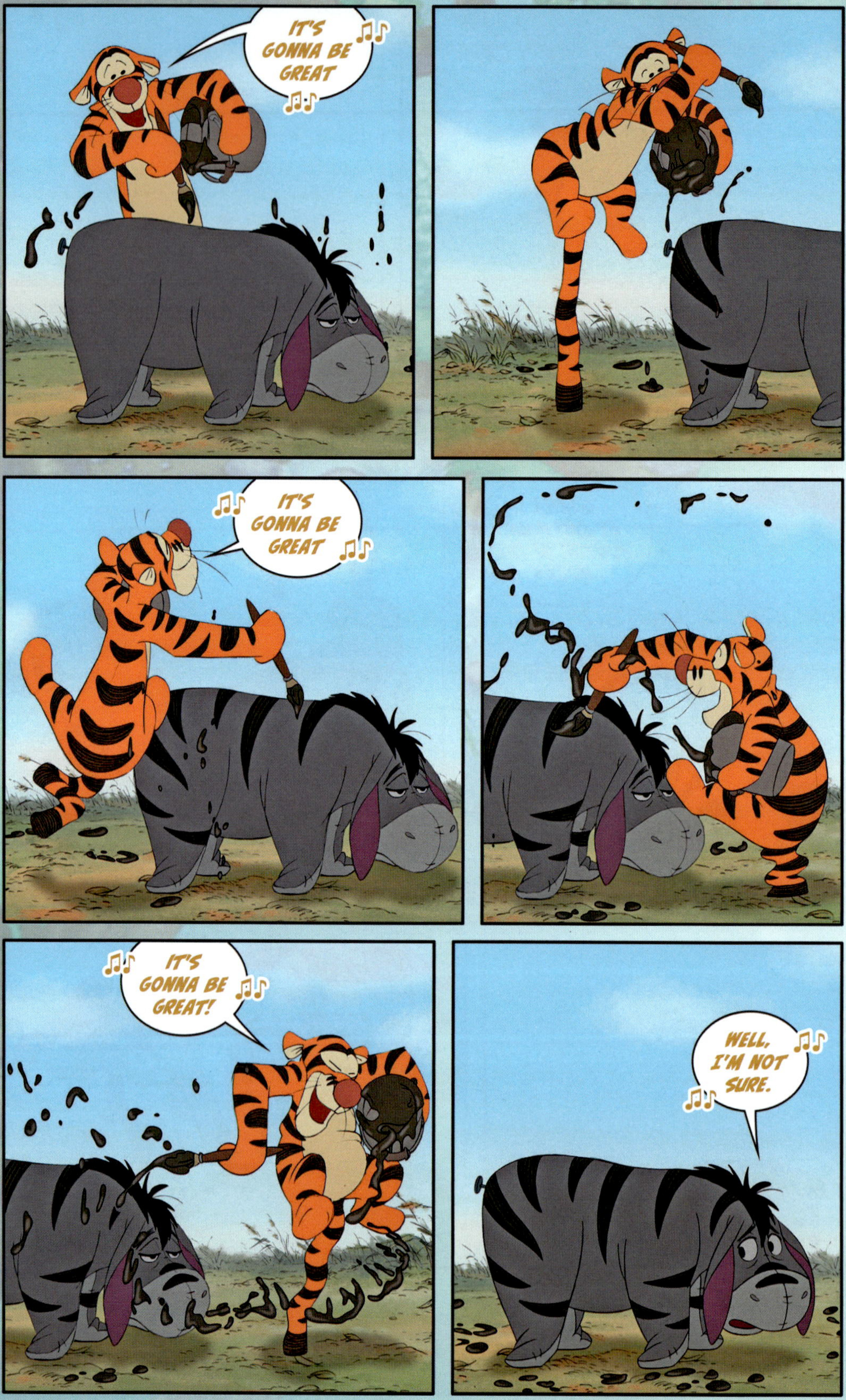
IT'S GONNA BE GREAT
IT'S GONNA BE GREAT
IT'S GONNA BE GREAT!
WELL, I'M NOT SURE.

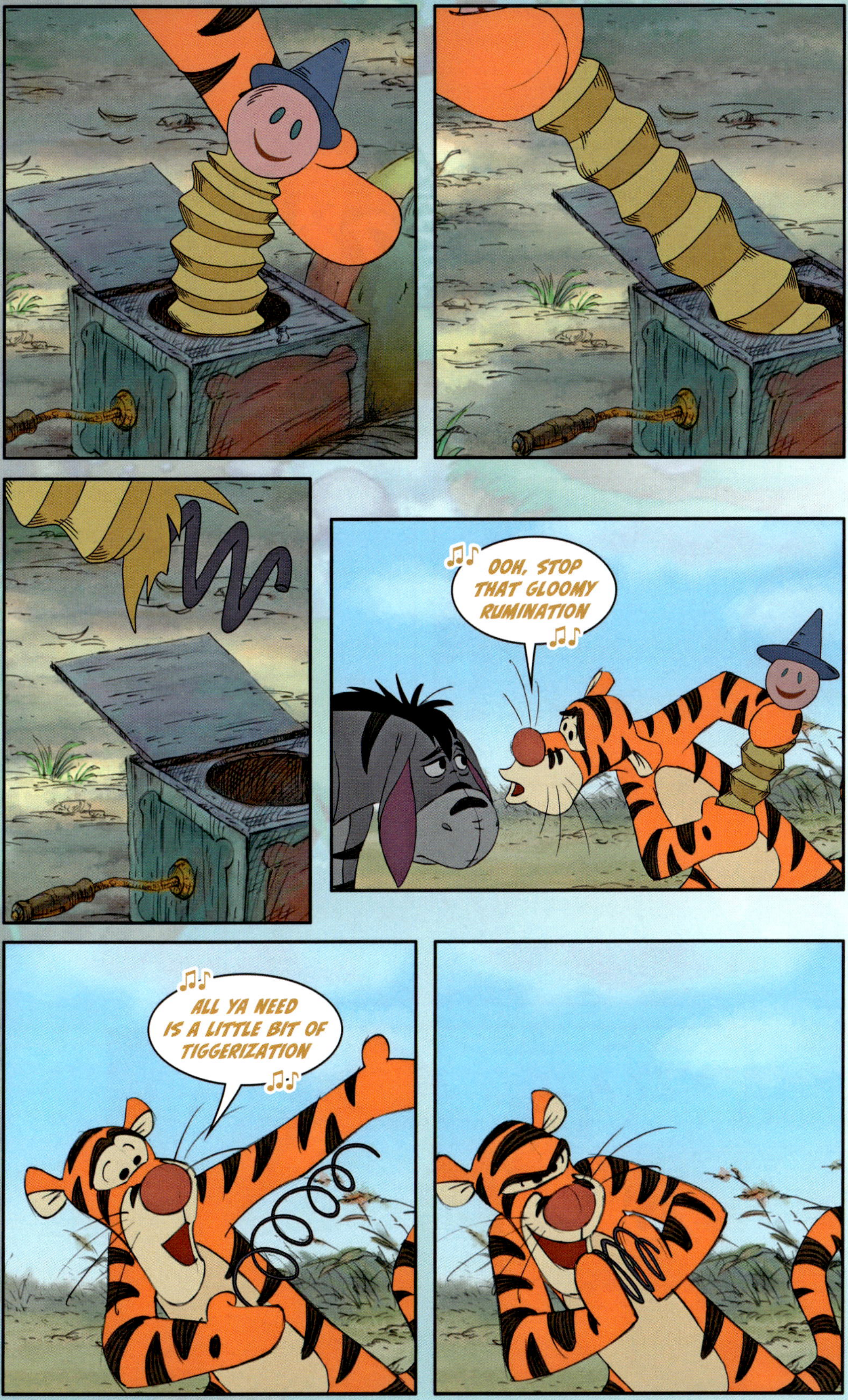
OOH, STOP THAT GLOOMY RUMINATION
ALL YA NEED IS A LITTLE BIT OF TIGGERIZATION

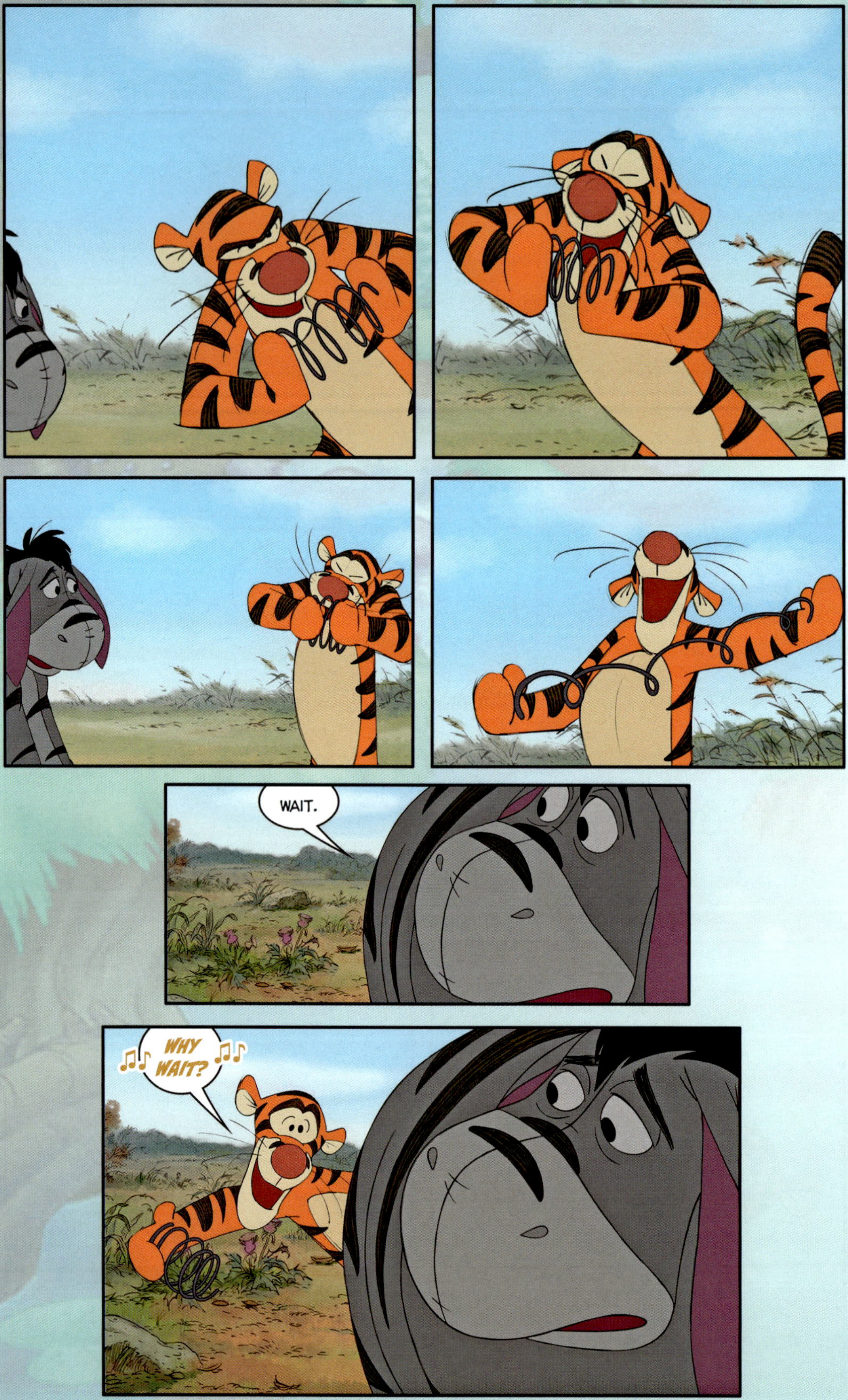
WAIT.
WHY WAIT?

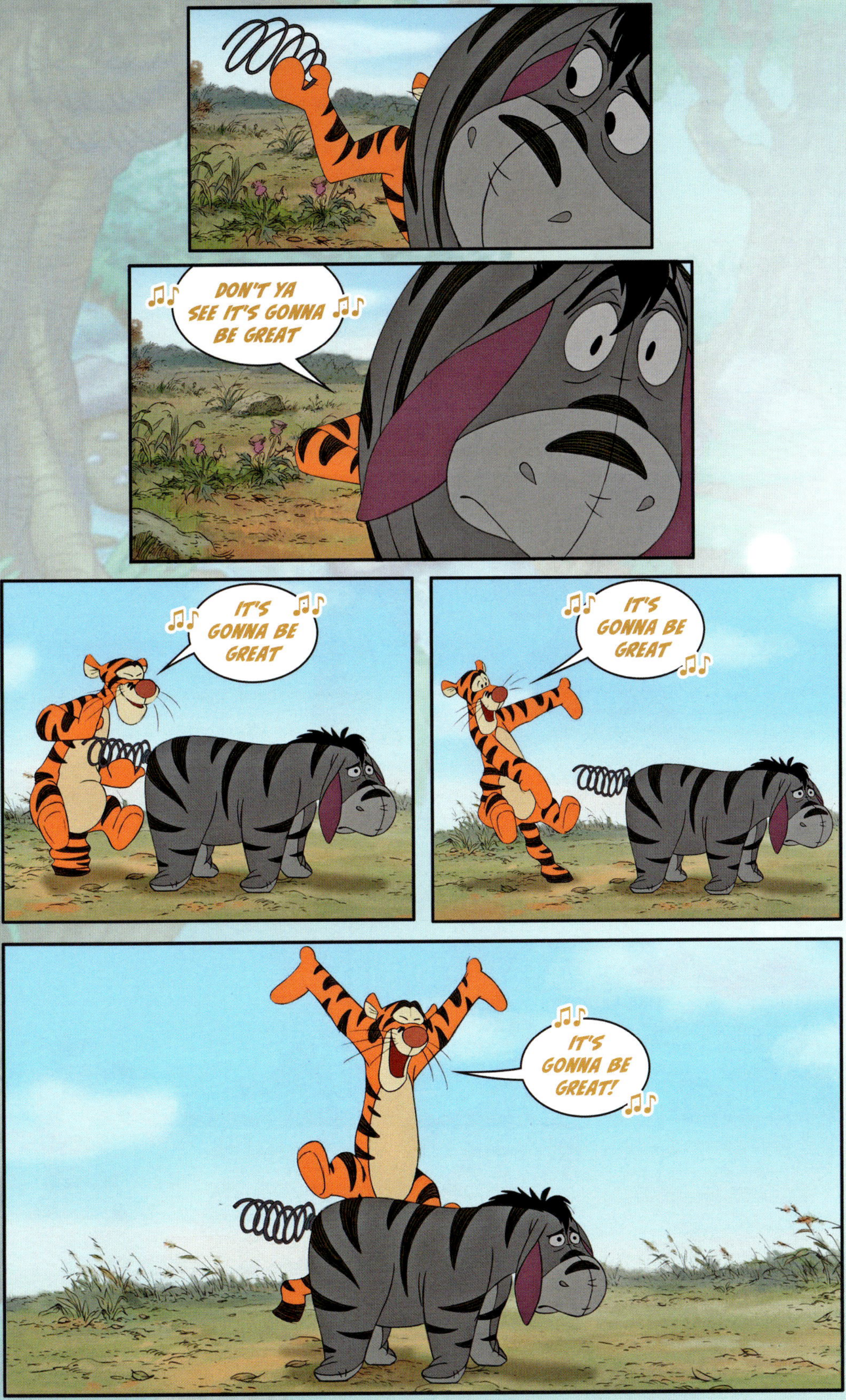
DON'T YA SEE IT'S GONNA BE GREAT
IT'S GONNA BE GREAT
IT'S GONNA BE GREAT
IT'S GONNA BE GREAT!

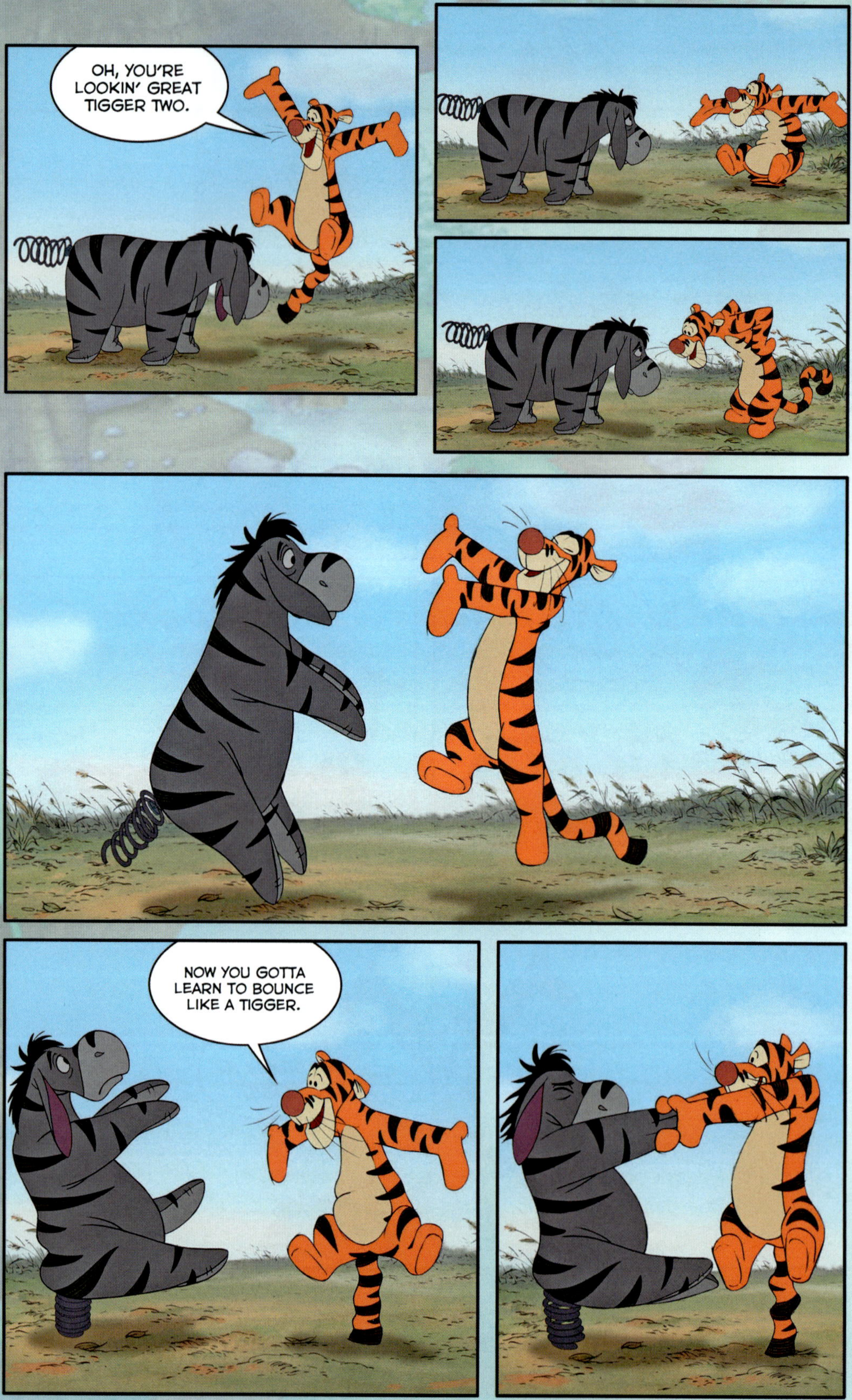
OH, YOU'RE LOOKIN' GREAT TIGGER TWO.
NOW YOU GOTTA LEARN TO BOUNCE LIKE A TIGGER.

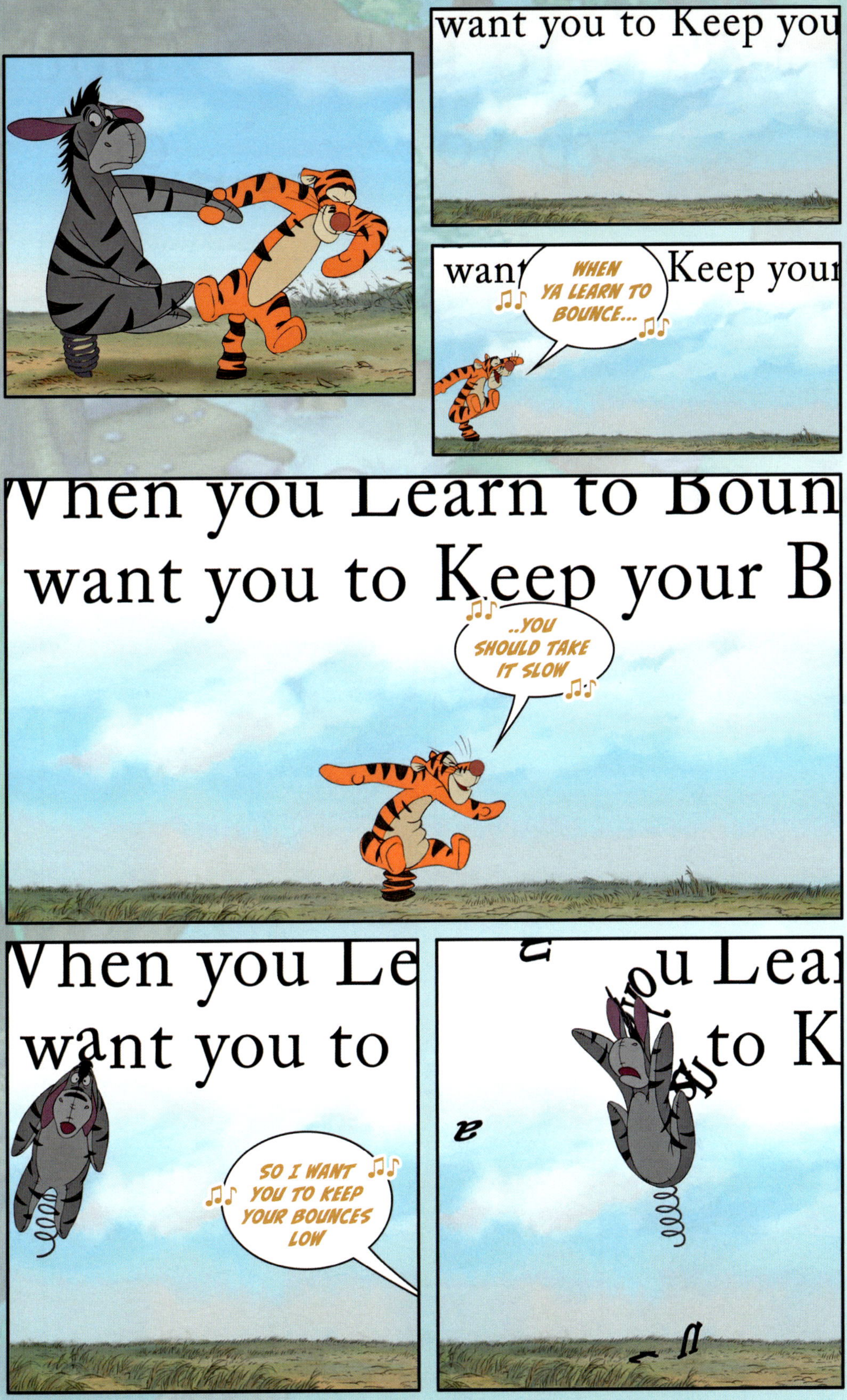
want you to Keep you
want
Keep your
WHEN YA LEARN TO BOUNCE...
When you Learn to Boun
want you to Keep your B
..YOU SHOULD TAKE IT SLOW
When you Le
want you to
SO I WANT YOU TO KEEP YOUR BOUNCES LOW
u Lear
to K

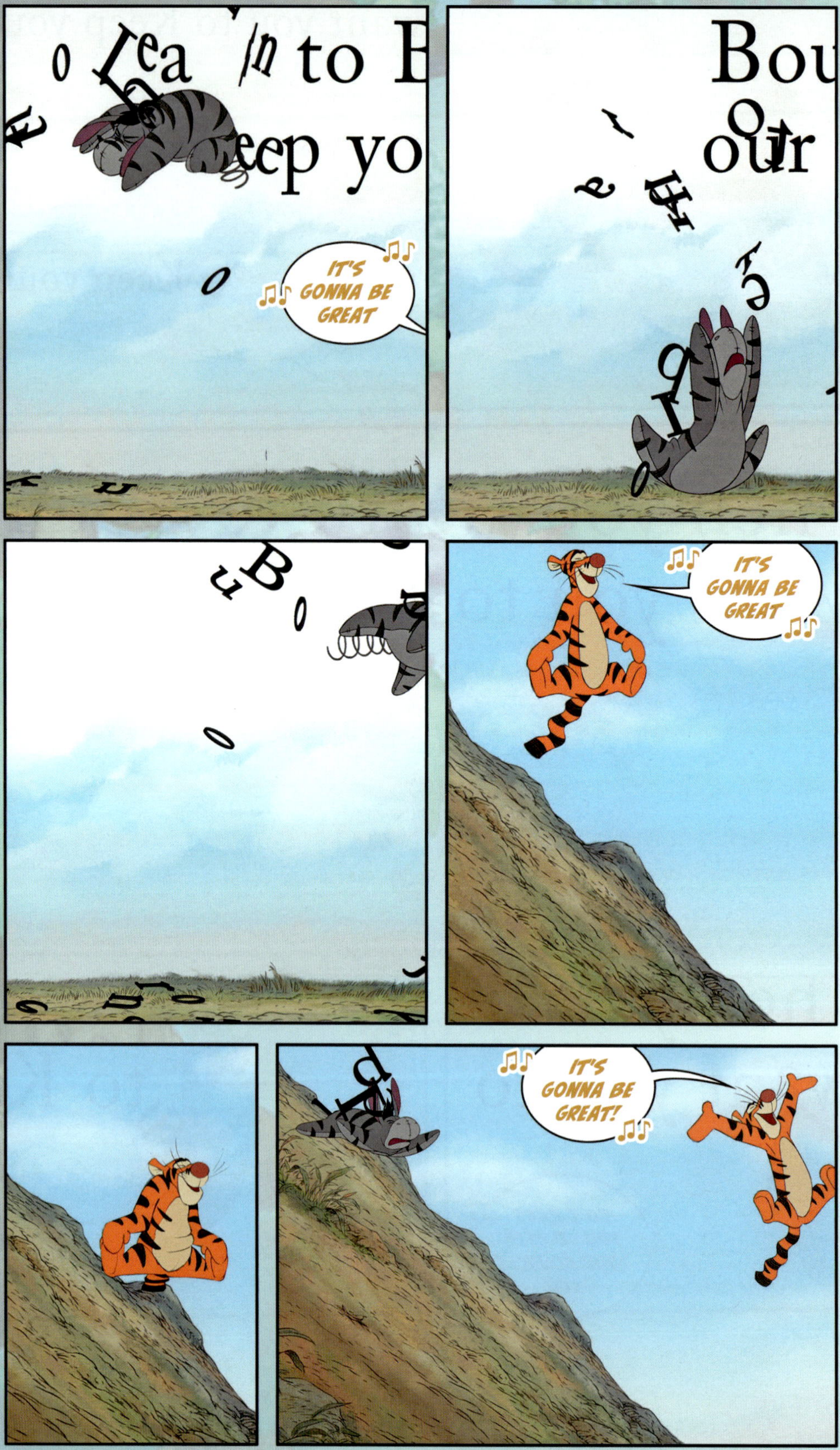
ea
to B
eep yo
IT'S GONNA BE GREAT
Bou
our
IT'S GONNA BE GREAT
IT'S GONNA BE GREAT!

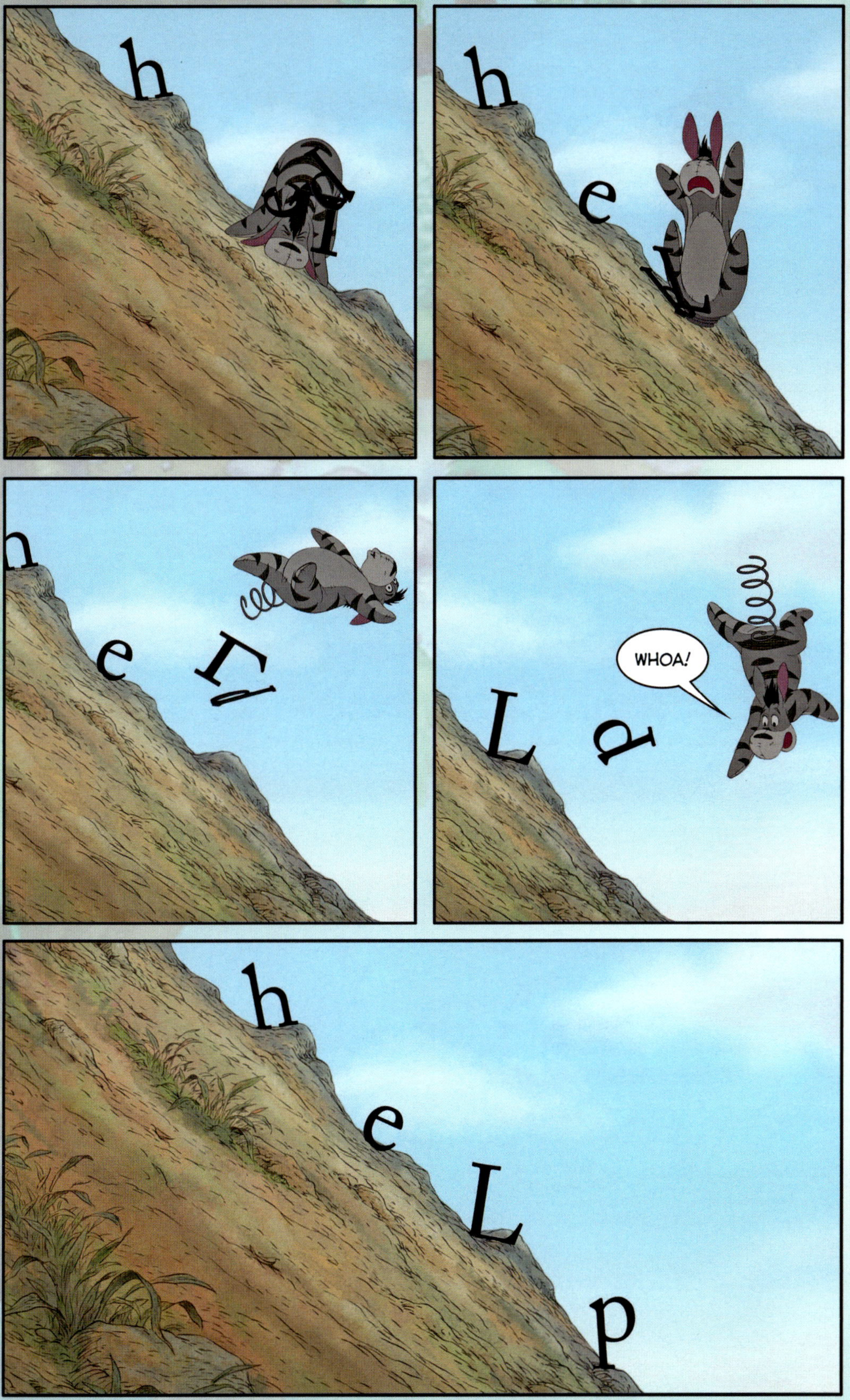
h
h
e
WHOA!
h
e
L
p

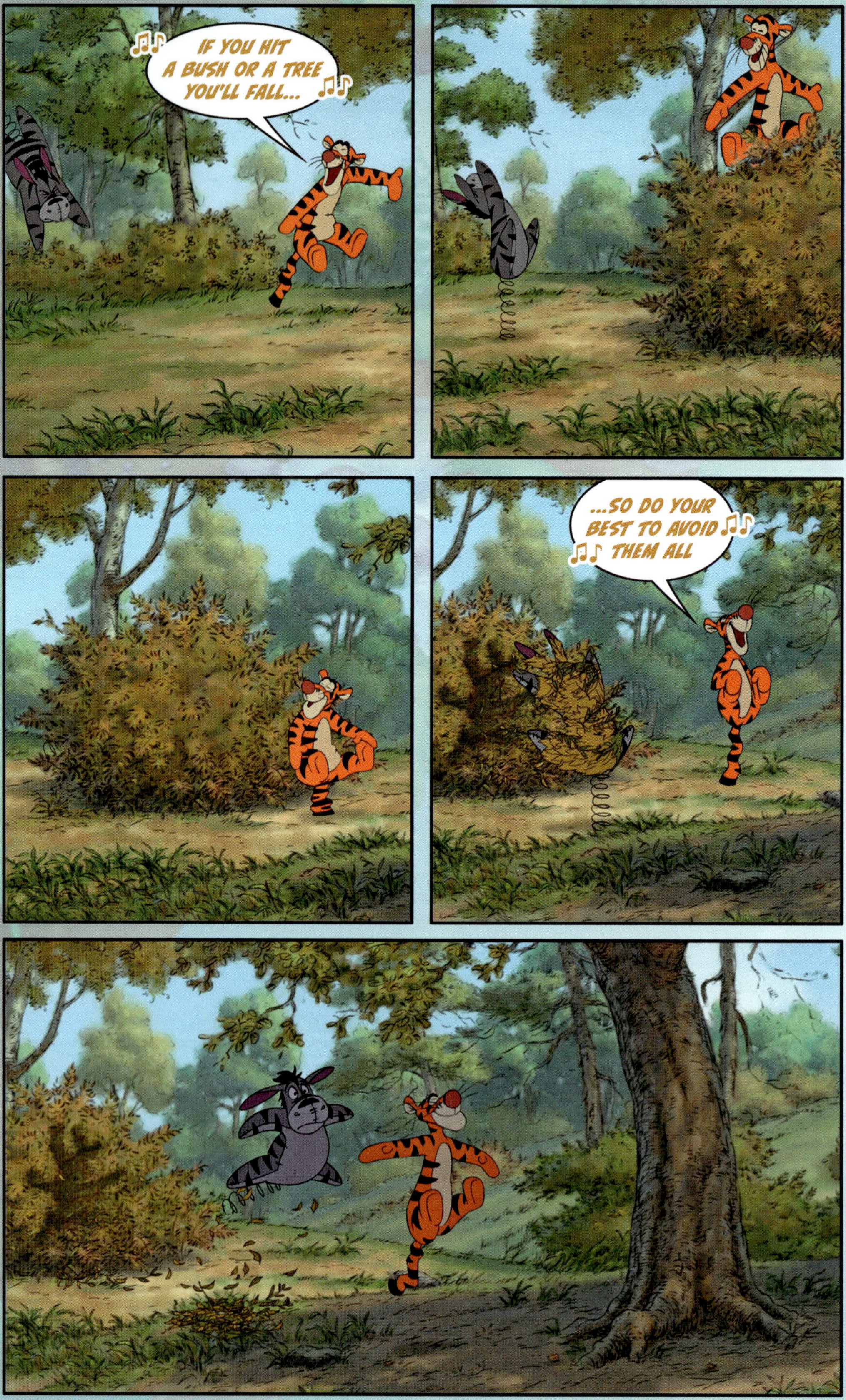
IF YOU HIT A BUSH OR A TREE YOU'LL FALL...
...SO DO YOUR BEST TO AVOID THEM ALL

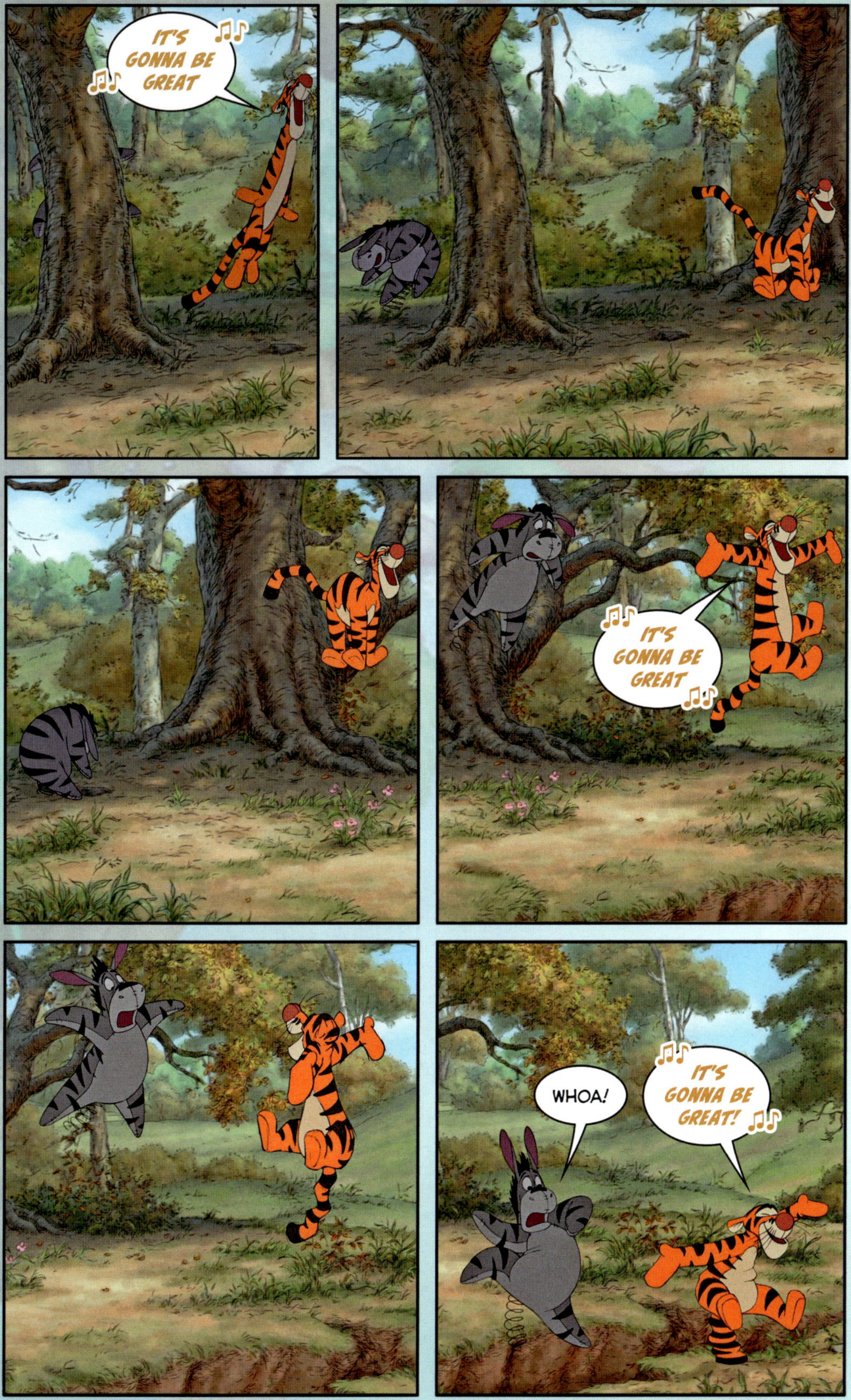
IT'S GONNA BE GREAT
IT'S GONNA BE GREAT
WHOA!
IT'S GONNA BE GREAT!

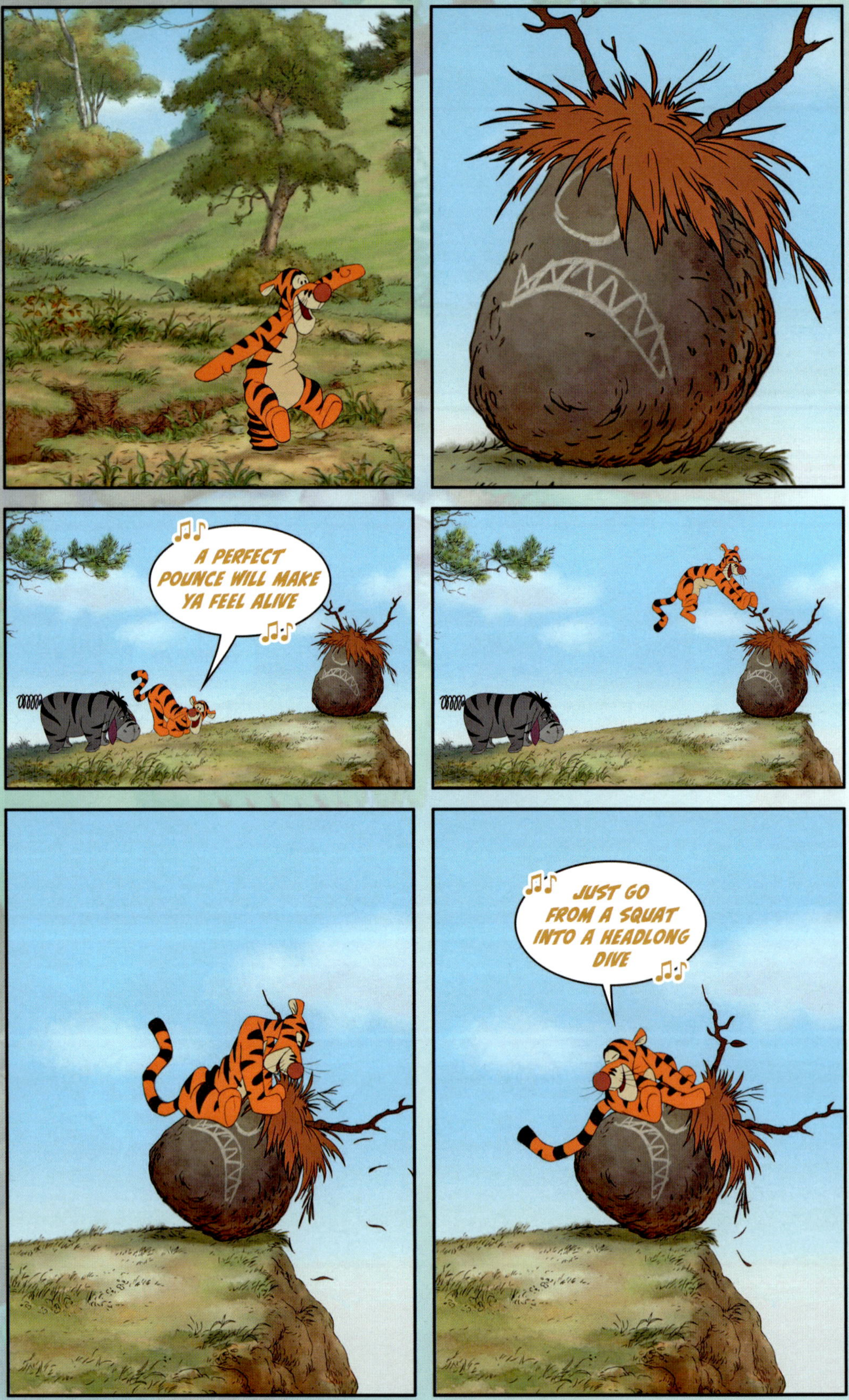
A PERFECT POUNCE WILL MAKE YA FEEL ALIVE
JUST GO FROM A SQUAT INTO A HEADLONG DIVE

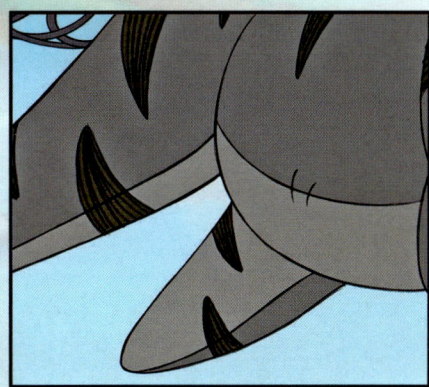

OW, OW, OW.

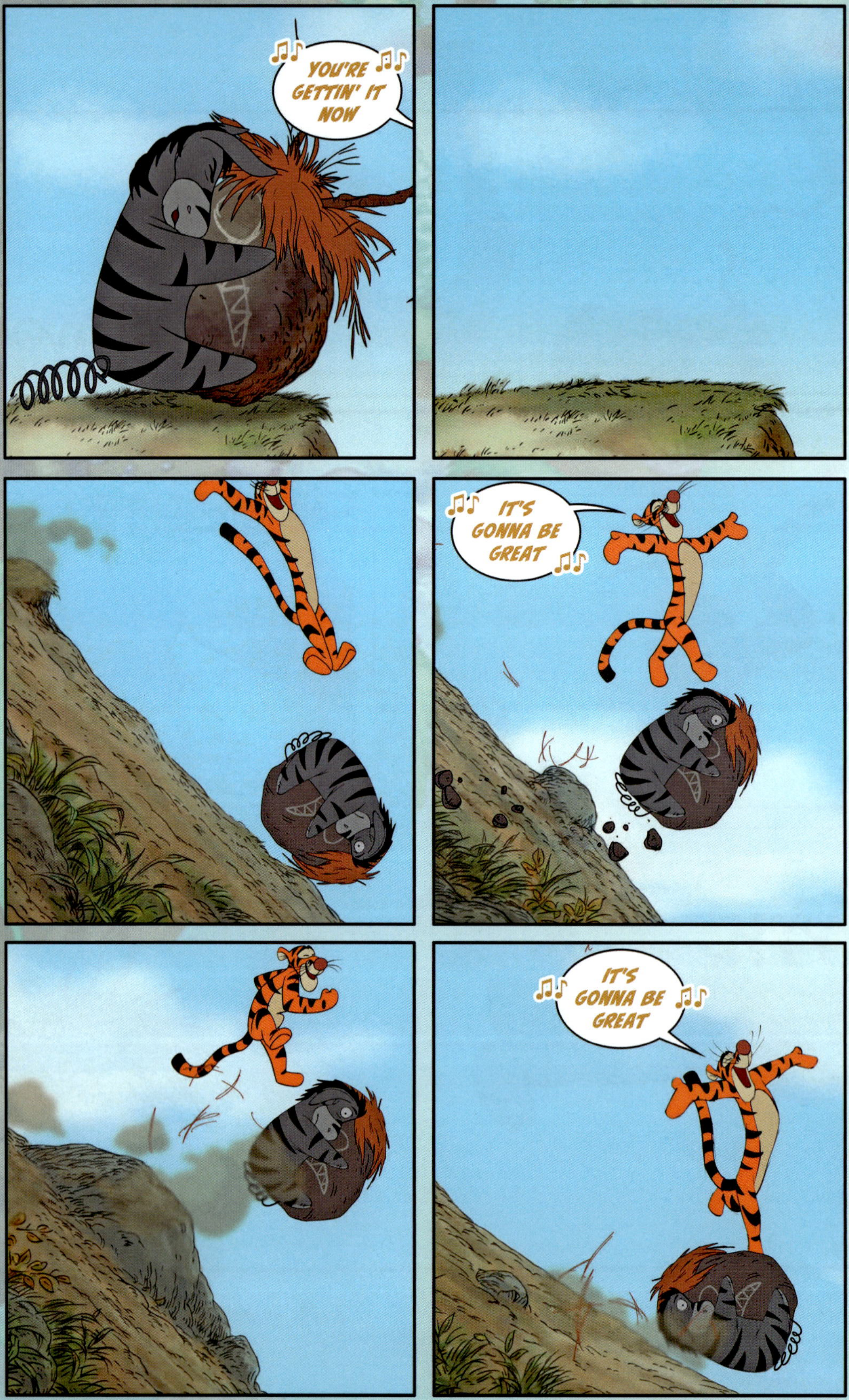
YOU'RE GETTIN' IT NOW
IT'S GONNA BE GREAT
IT'S GONNA BE GREAT

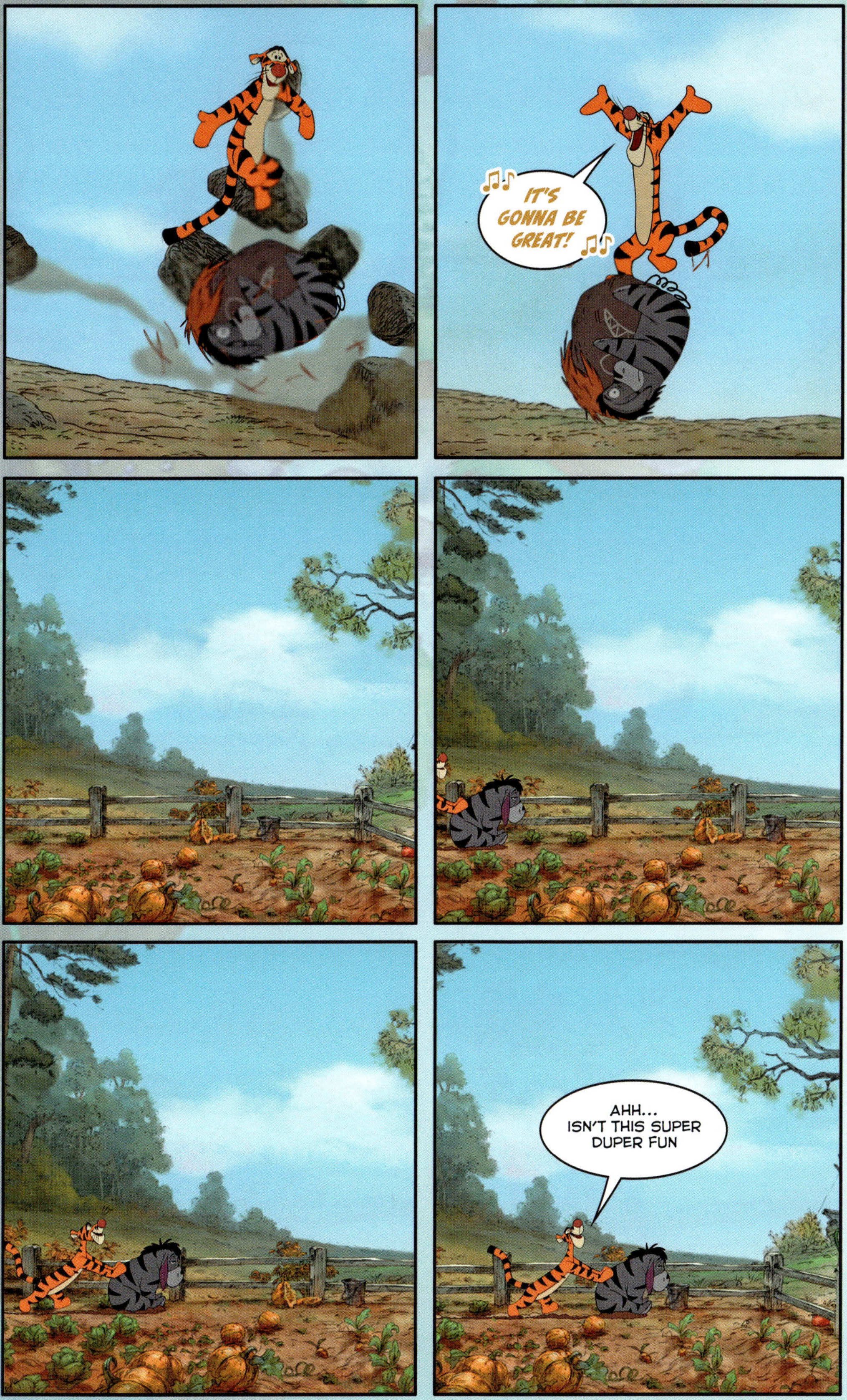
IT'S GONNA BE GREAT!
AHH... ISN'T THIS SUPER DUPER FUN

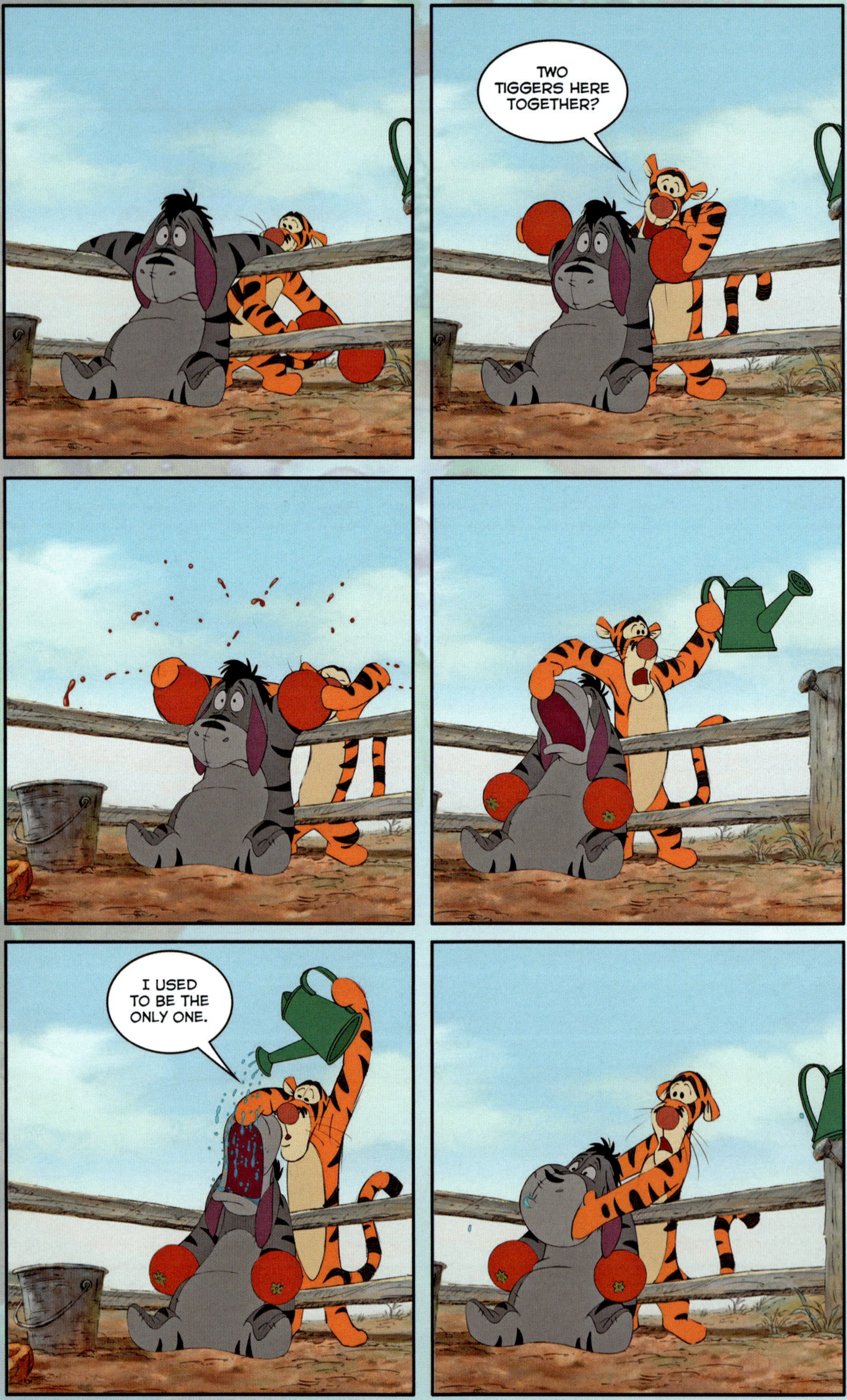
TWO TIGGERS HERE TOGETHER?
I USED TO BE THE ONLY ONE.

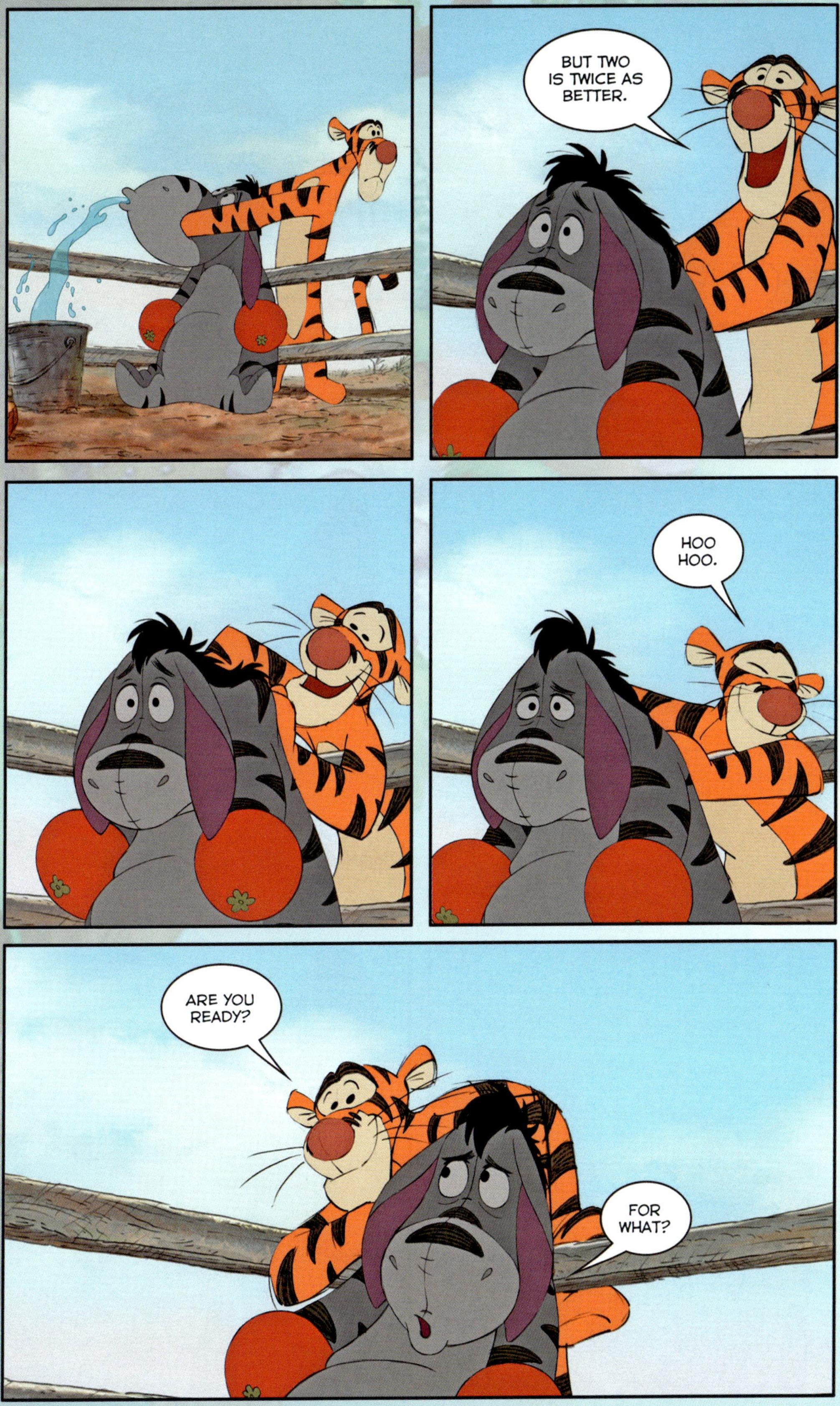
BUT TWO IS TWICE AS BETTER.
HOO HOO.
ARE YOU READY?
FOR WHAT?

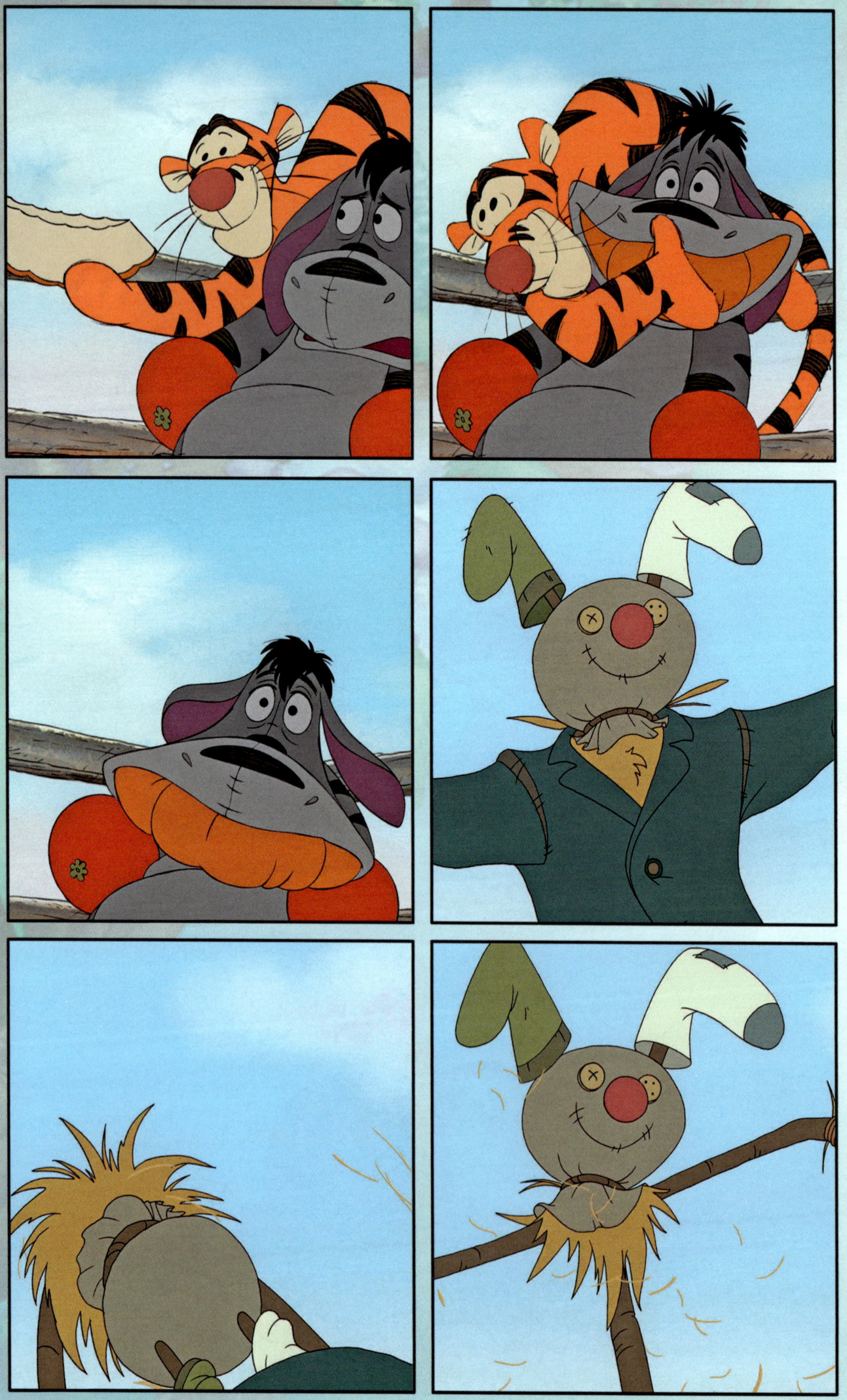

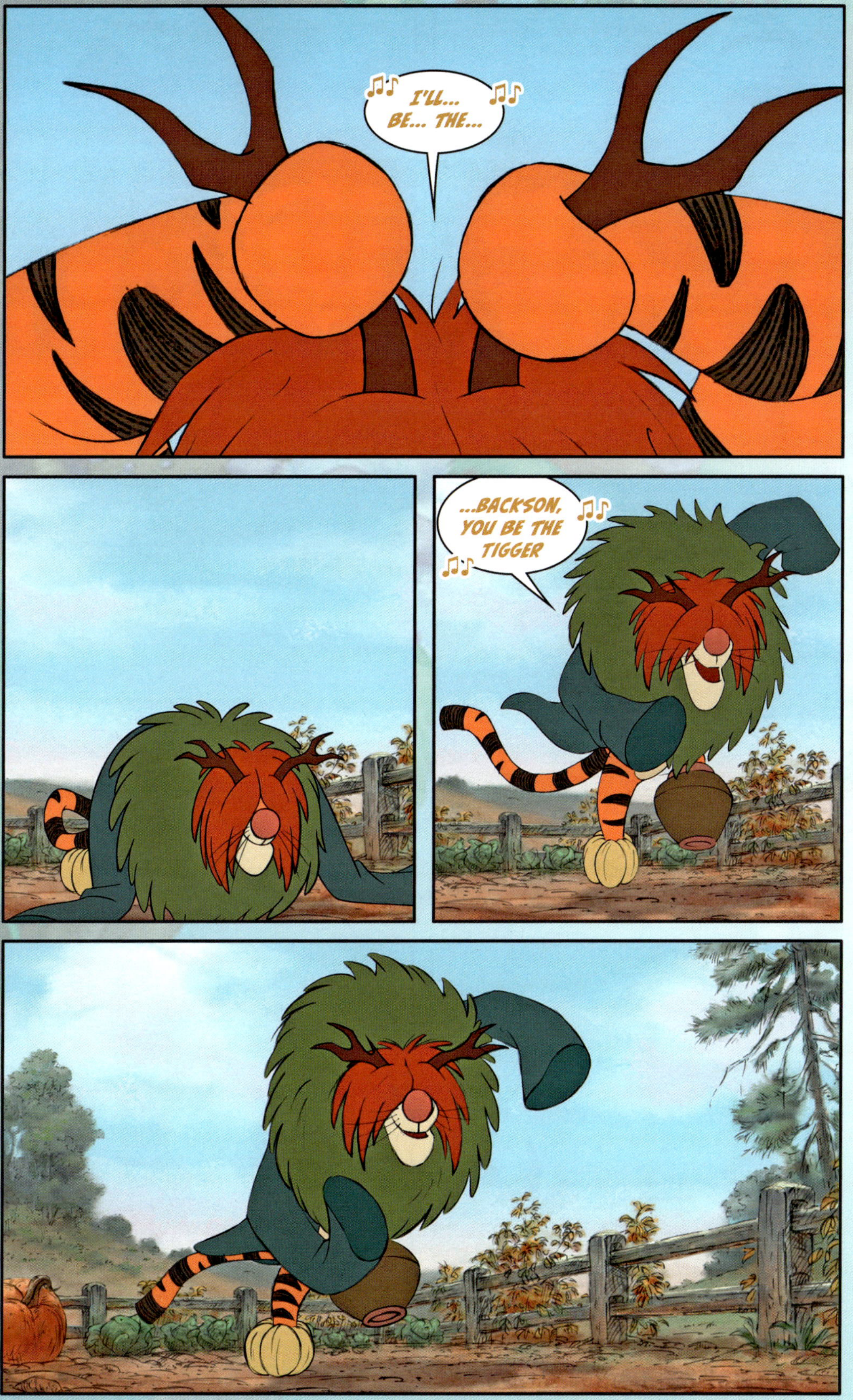
I'LL... BE... THE...
...BACKSON, YOU BE THE TIGGER

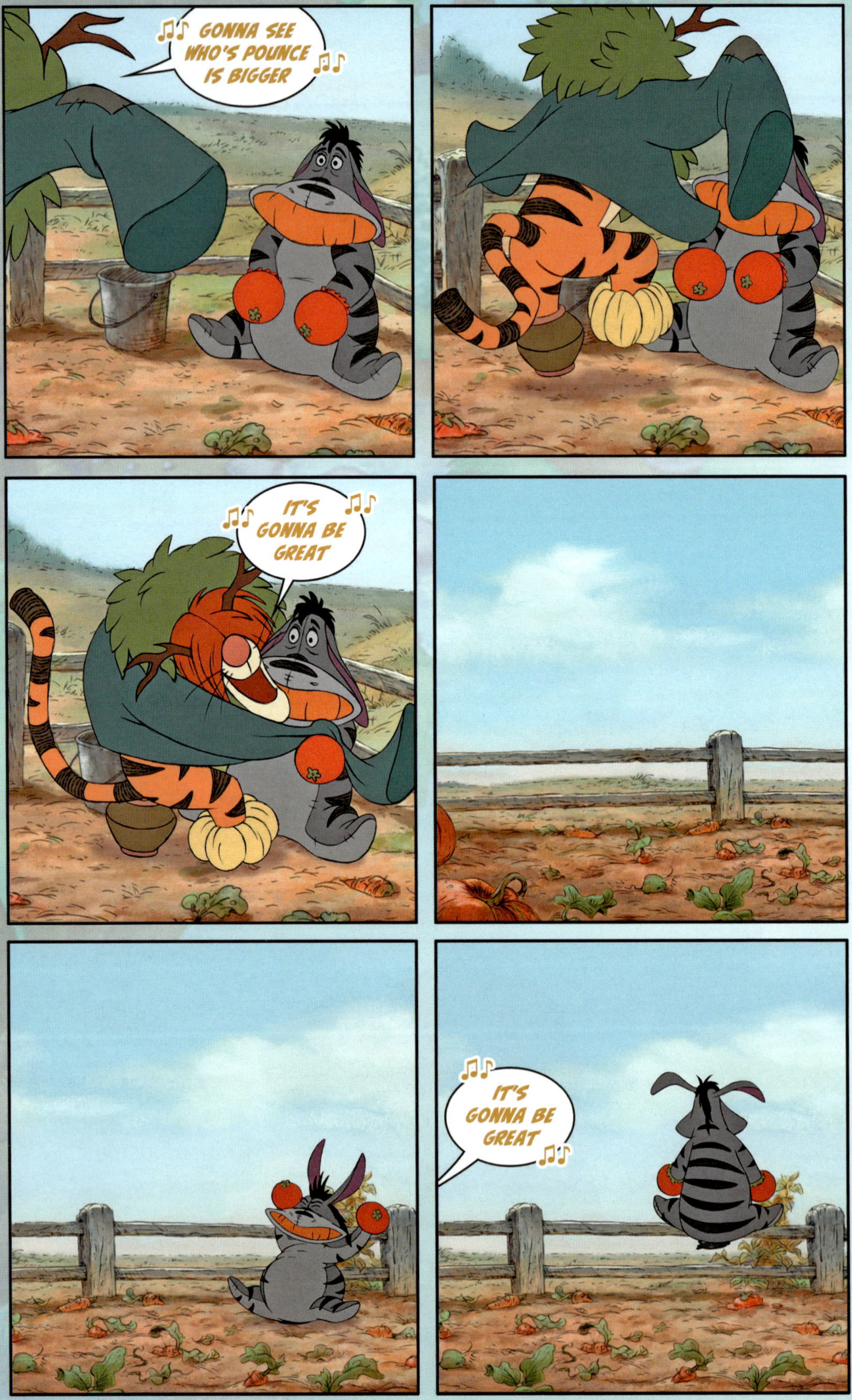
GONNA SEE WHO'S POUNCE IS BIGGER
IT'S GONNA BE GREAT
IT'S GONNA BE GREAT

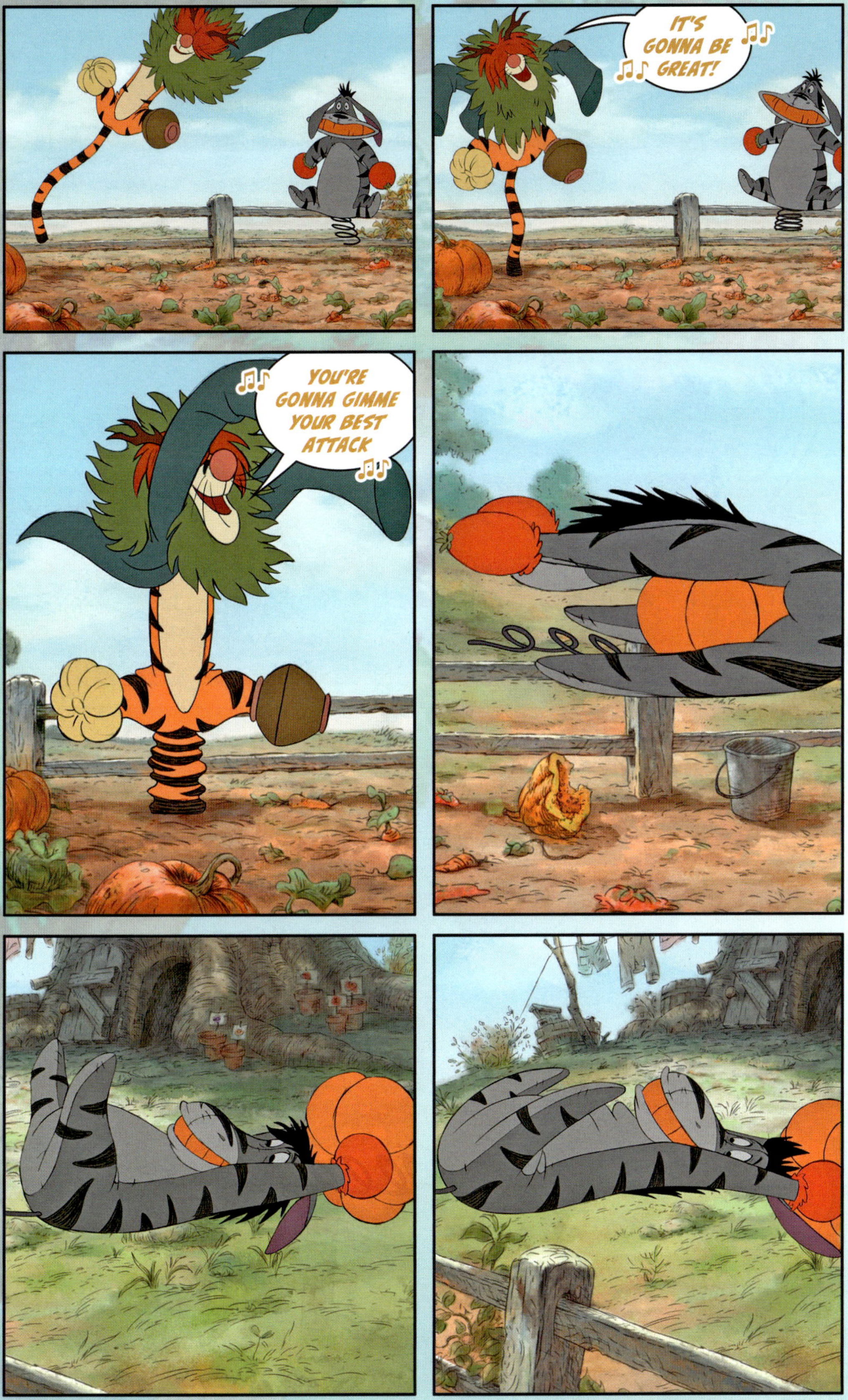
IT'S GONNA BE GREAT!
YOU'RE GONNA GIMME YOUR BEST ATTACK

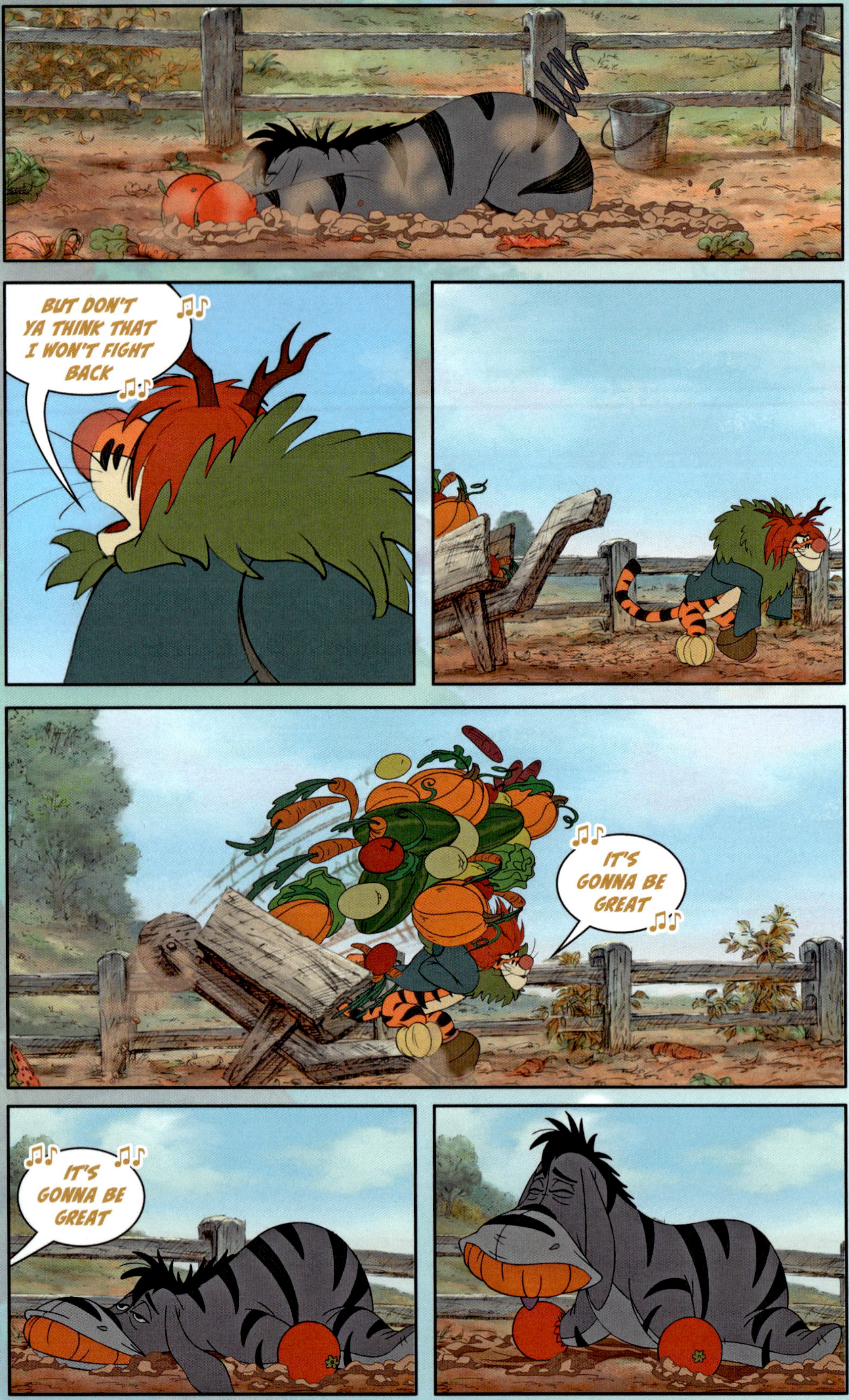
BUT DON'T YA THINK THAT I WON'T FIGHT BACK
IT'S GONNA BE GREAT
IT'S GONNA BE GREAT

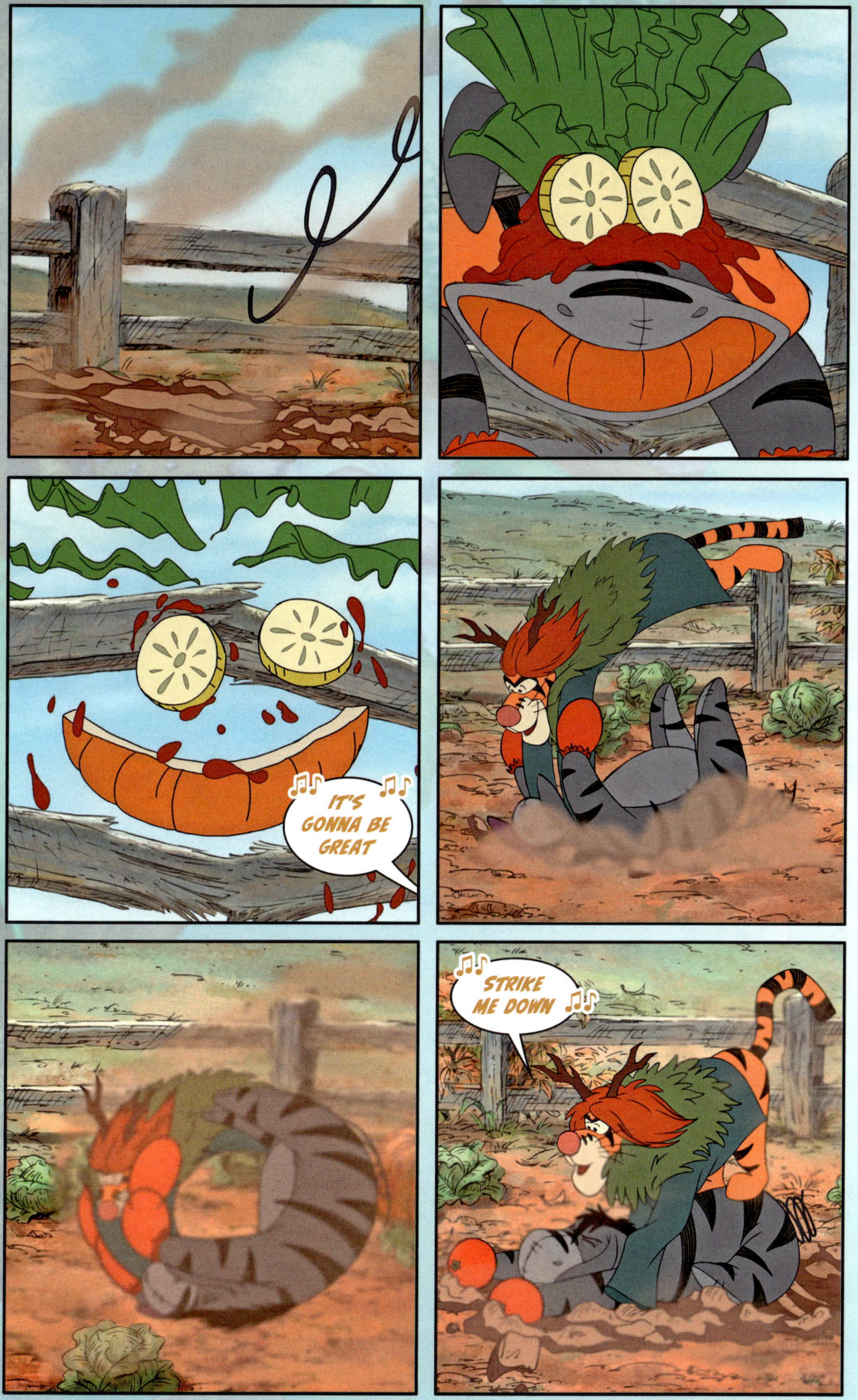
IT'S GONNA BE GREAT
STRIKE ME DOWN

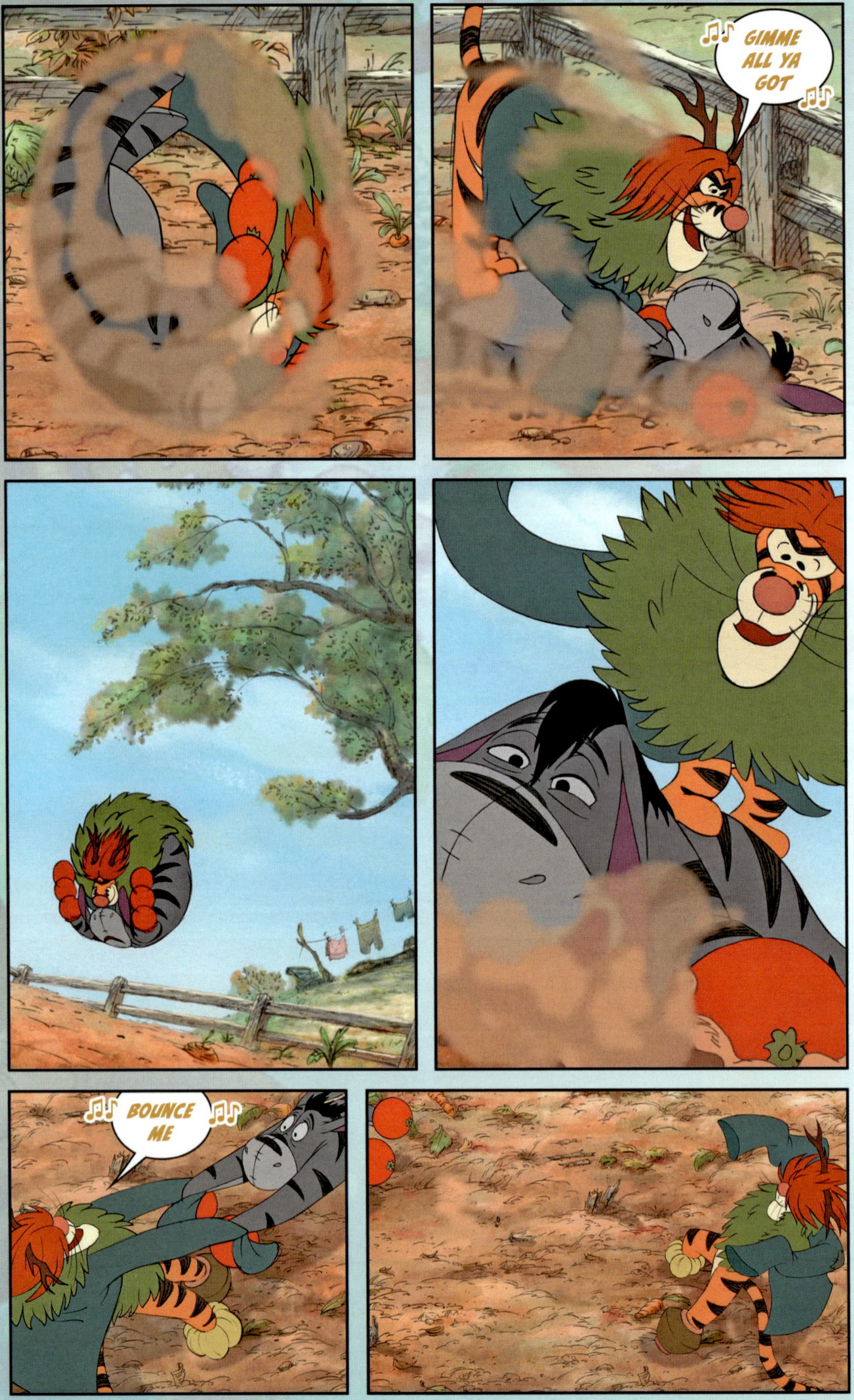
GIMME ALL YA GOT
BOUNCE ME

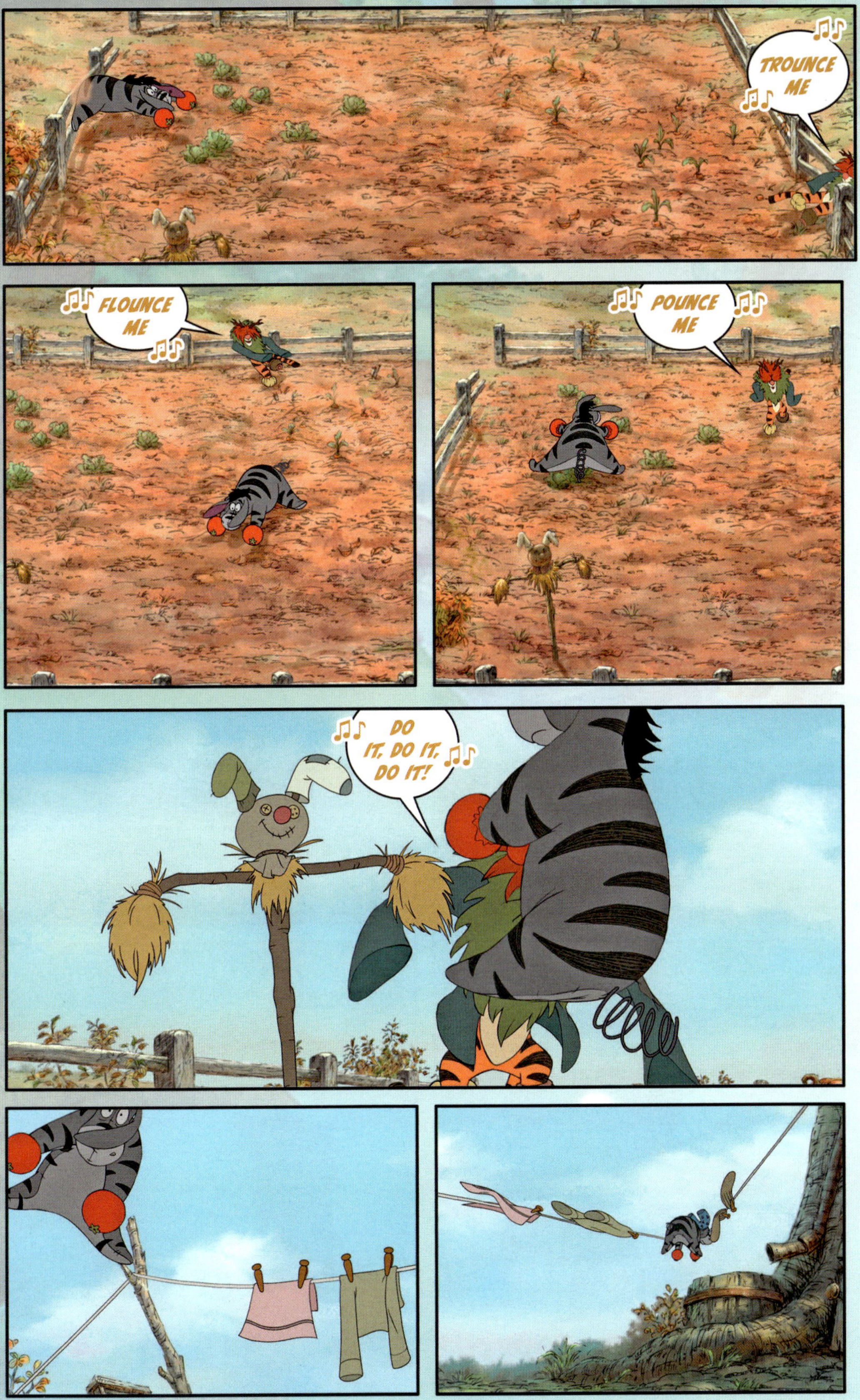
TROUNCE ME
FLOUNCE ME
POUNCE ME
DO IT, DO IT, DO IT!

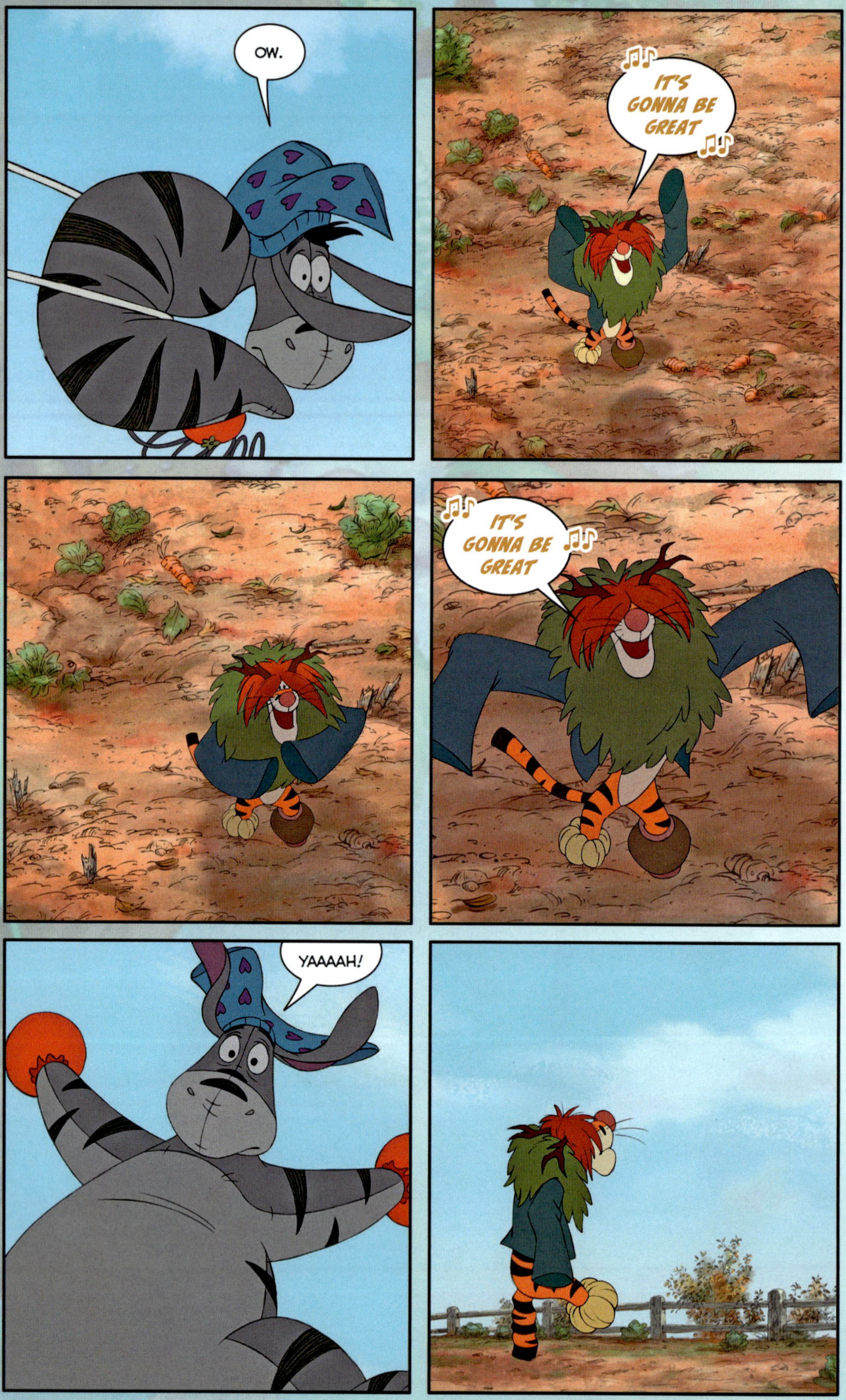
OW.
IT'S GONNA BE GREAT
IT'S GONNA BE GREAT
YAAAAH!

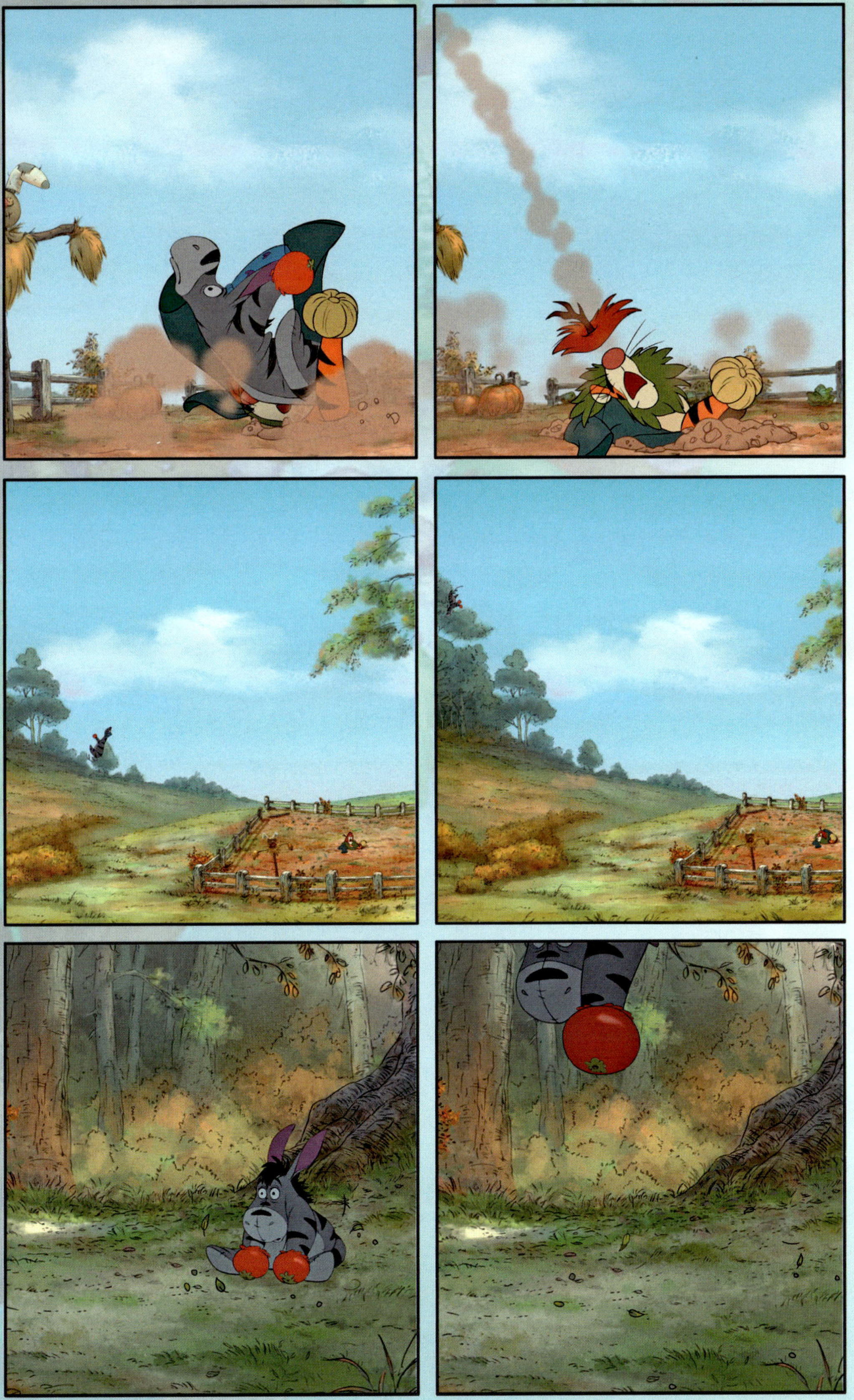

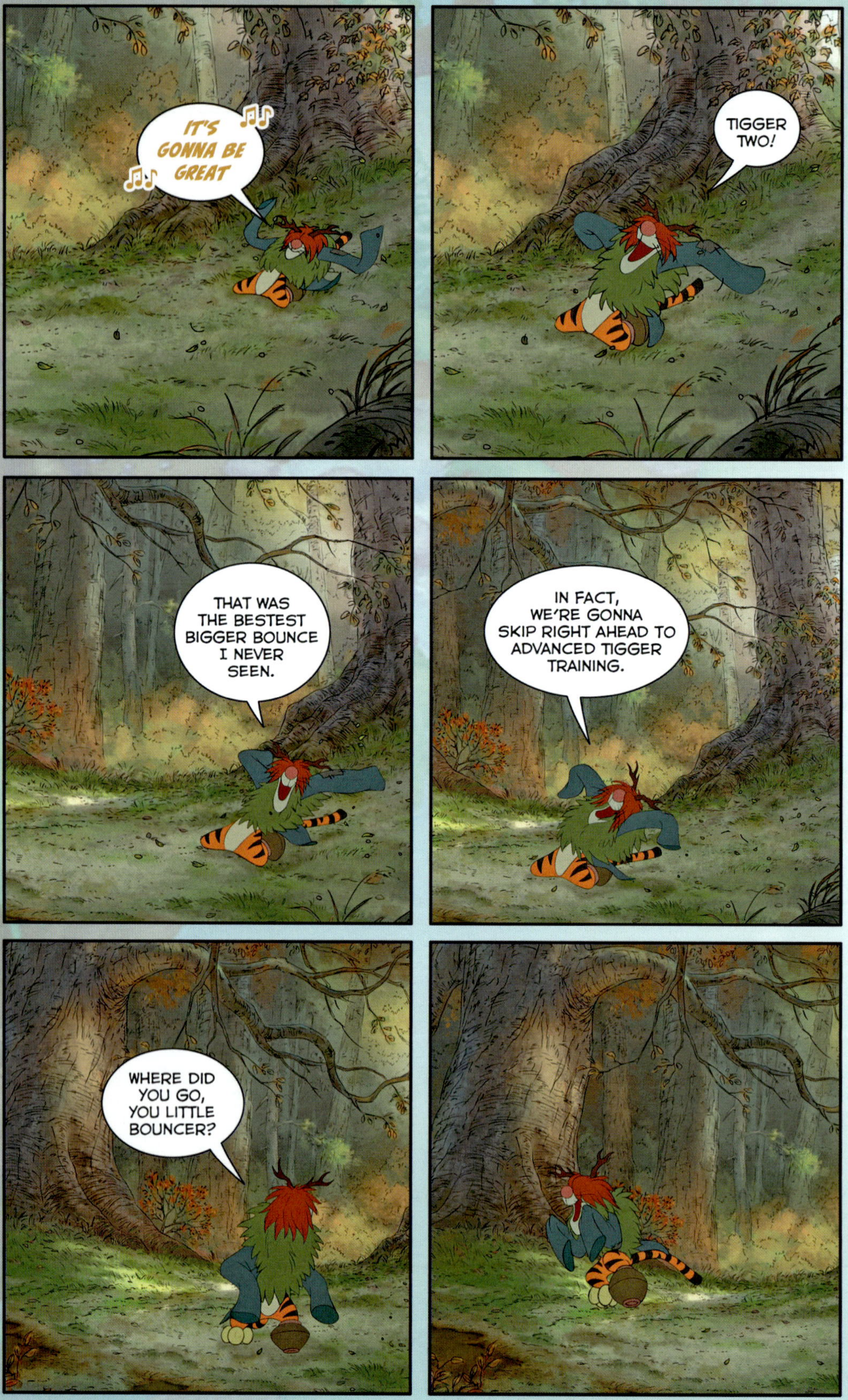
IT'S GONNA BE GREAT
TIGGER TWO!
THAT WAS THE BESTEST BIGGER BOUNCE I NEVER SEEN.
IN FACT, WE'RE GONNA SKIP RIGHT AHEAD TO ADVANCED TIGGER TRAINING.
WHERE DID YOU GO, YOU LITTLE BOUNCER?

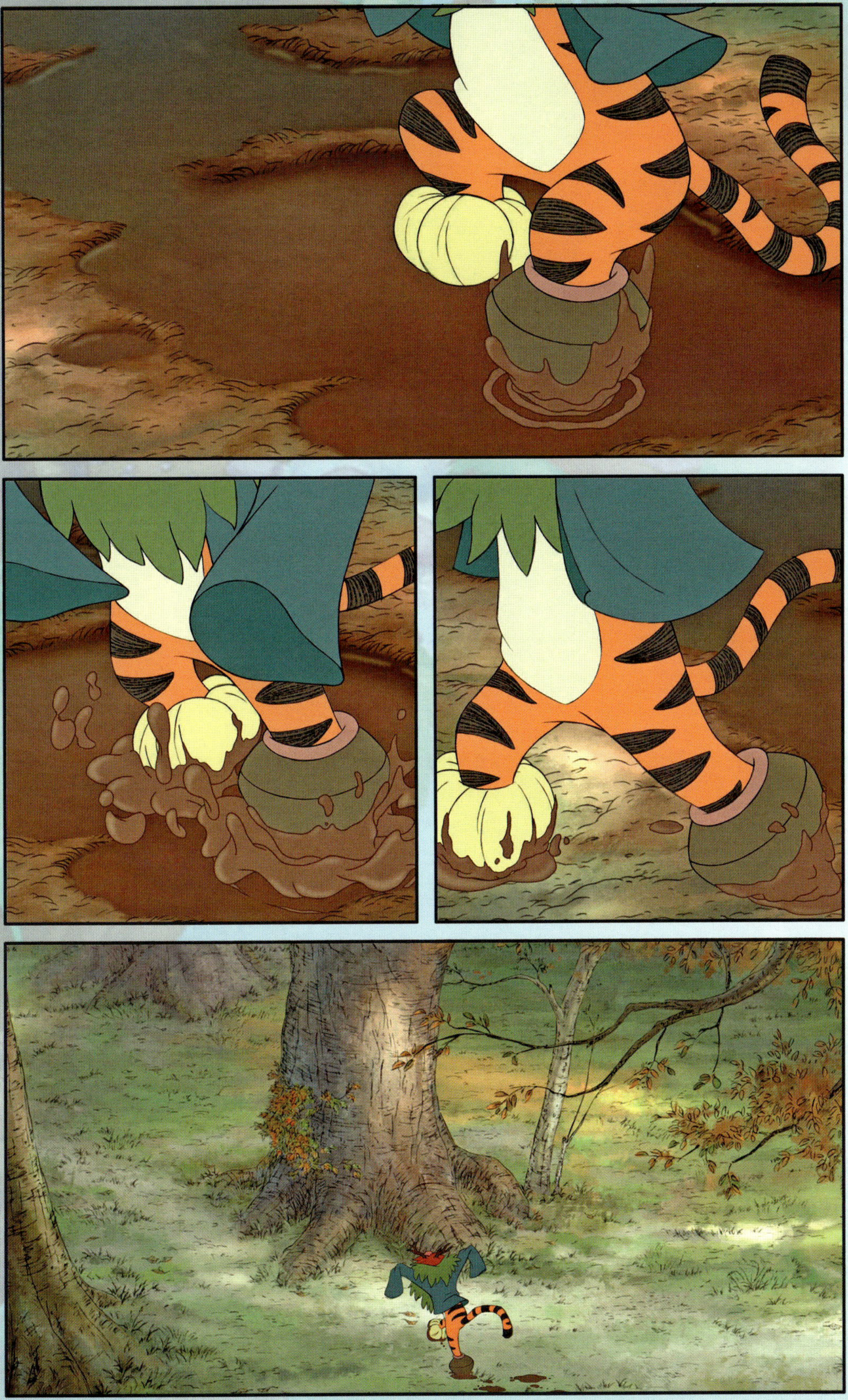

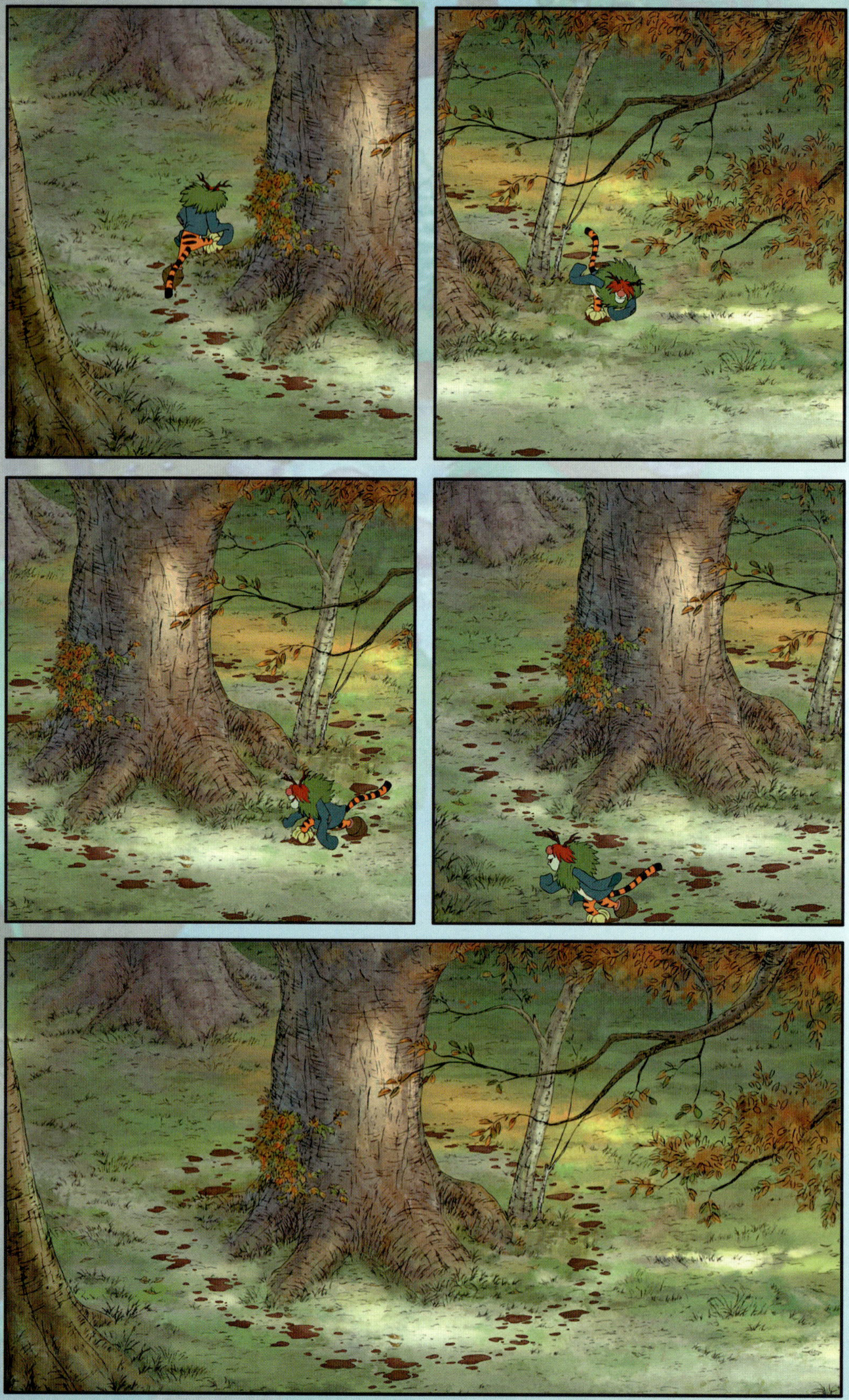

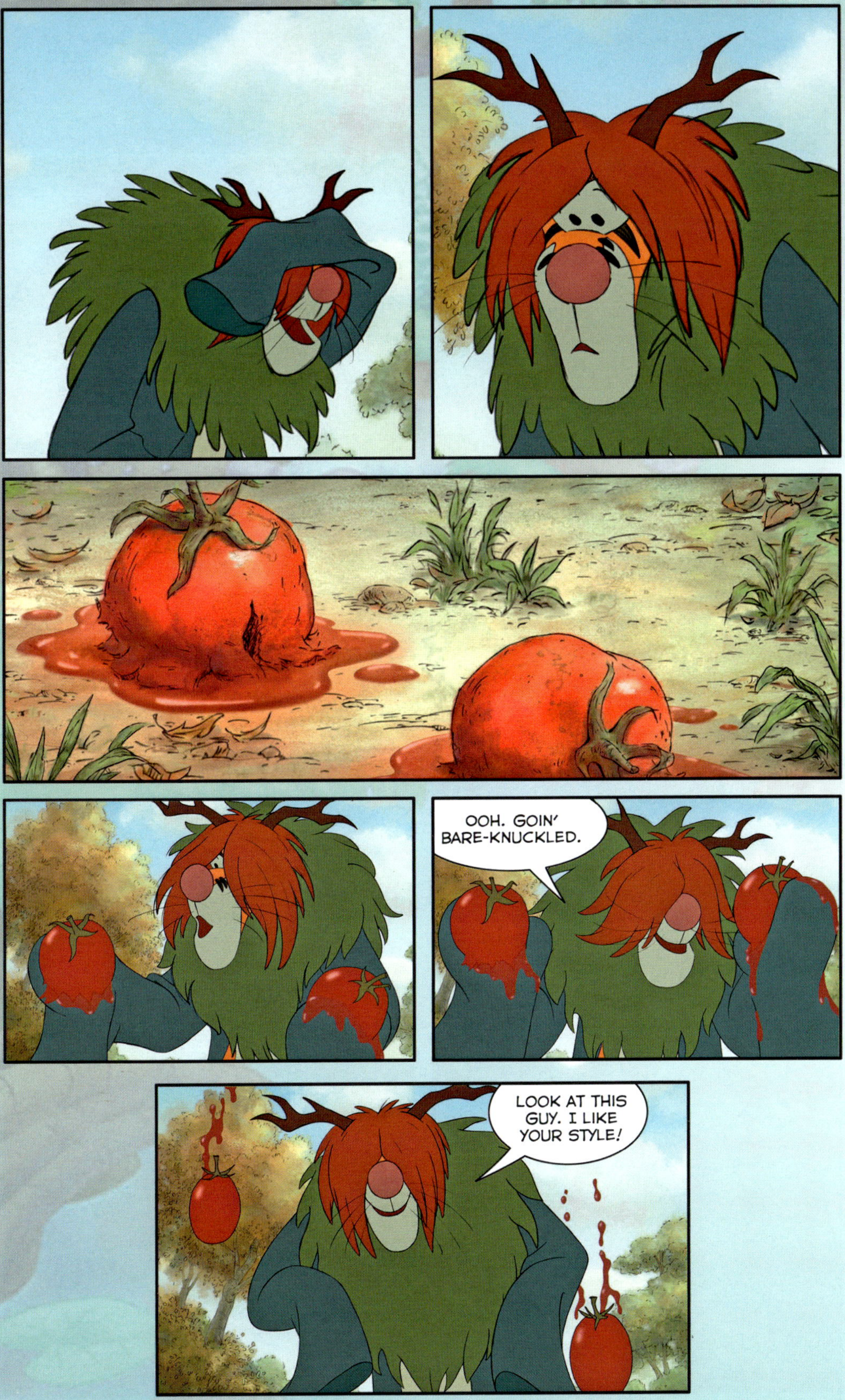
OOH. GOIN' BARE-KNUCKLED.
LOOK AT THIS GUY. I LIKE YOUR STYLE!

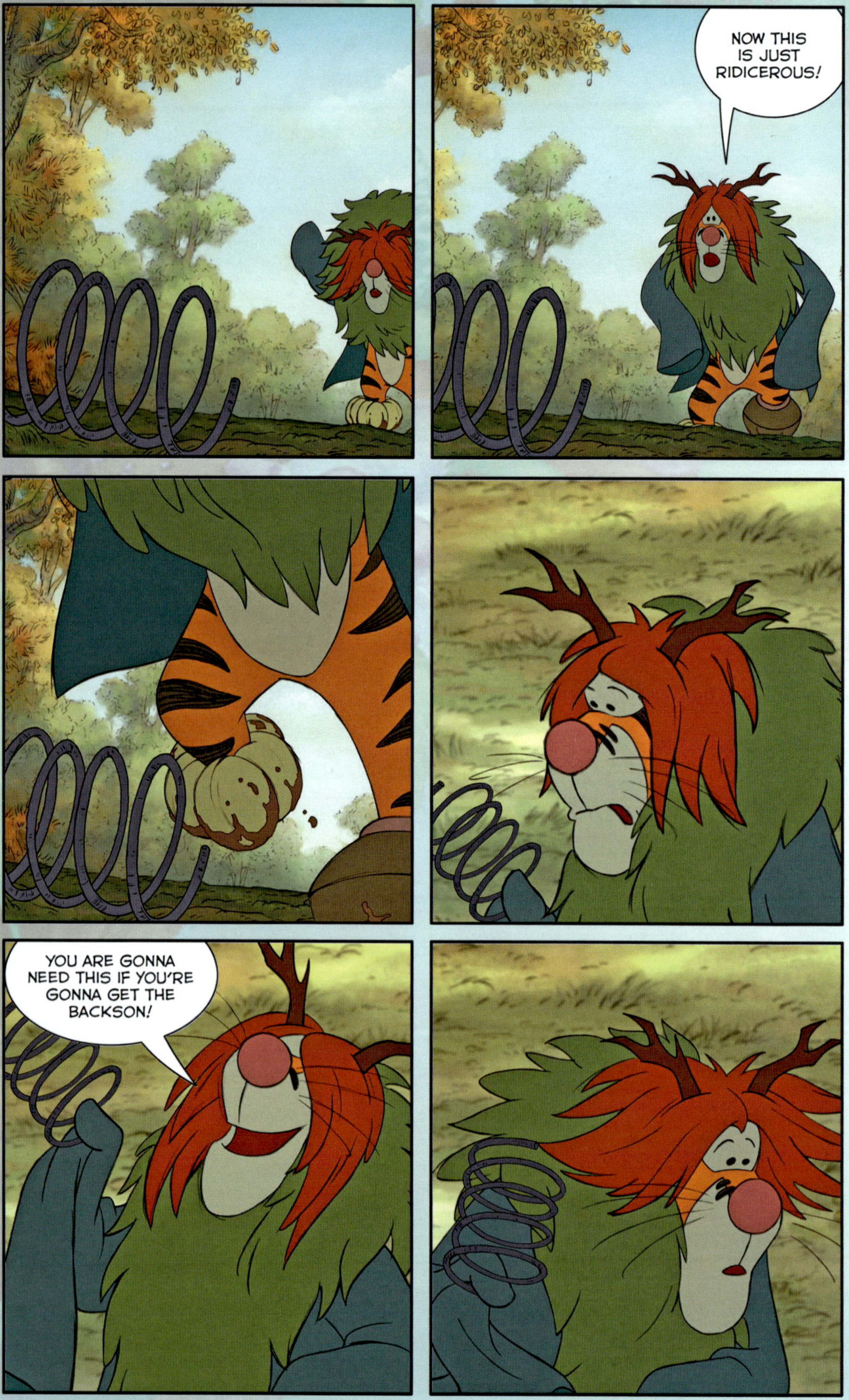
NOW THIS IS JUST RIDICEROUS!
YOU ARE GONNA NEED THIS IF YOU'RE GONNA GET THE BACKSON!

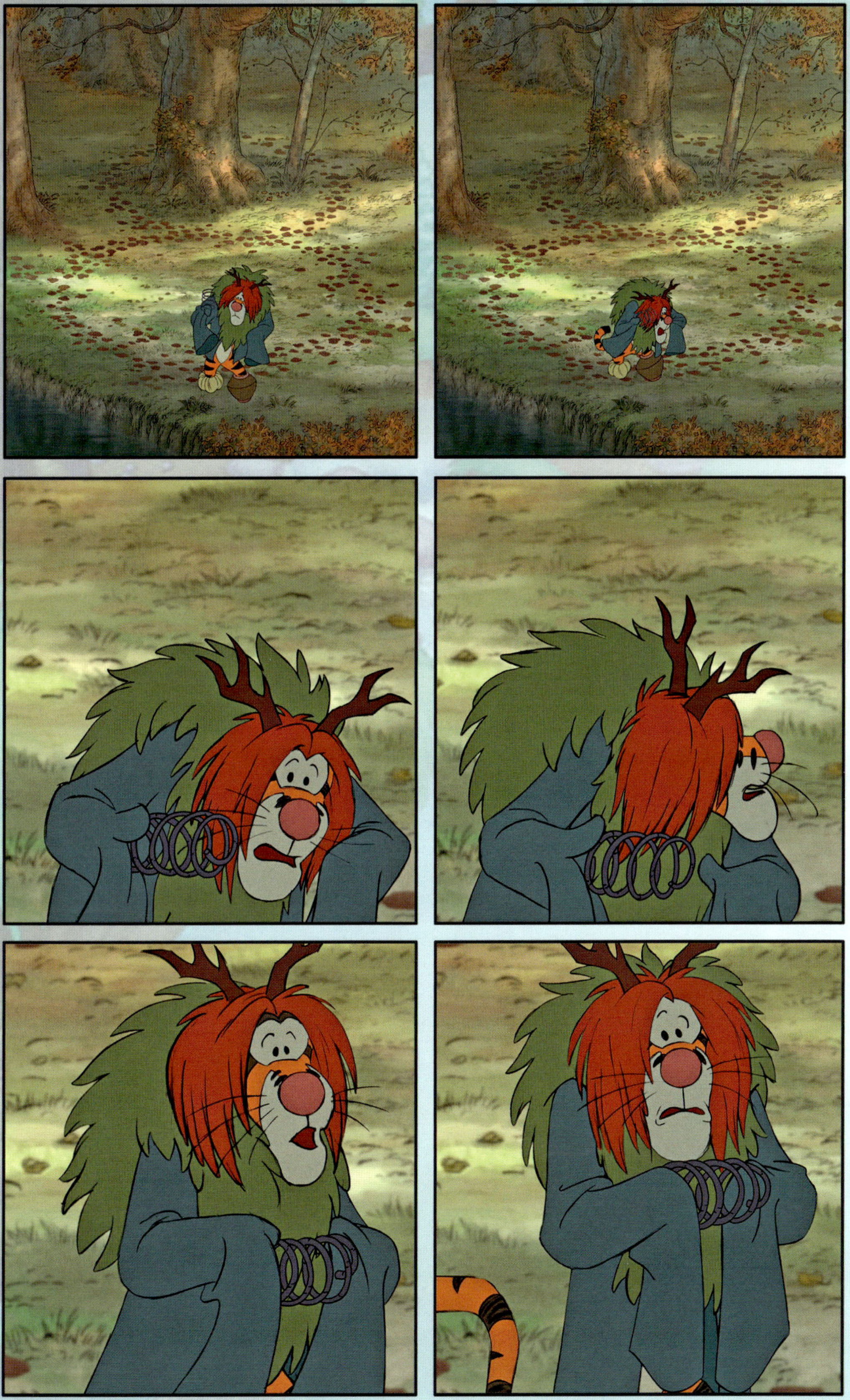

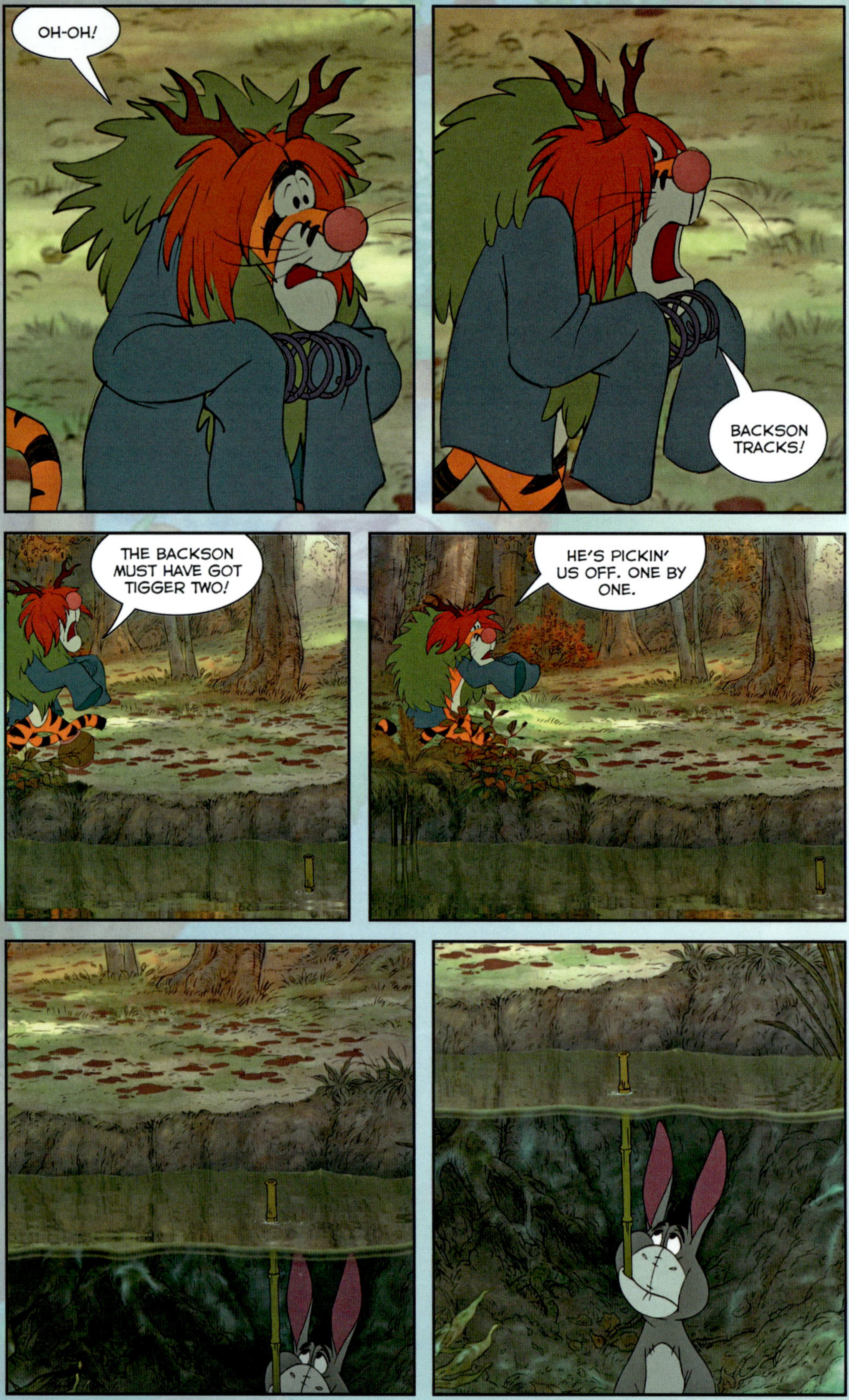
OH-OH!
BACKSON TRACKS!
THE BACKSON MUST HAVE GOT TIGGER TWO!
HE'S PICKIN' US OFF. ONE BY ONE.

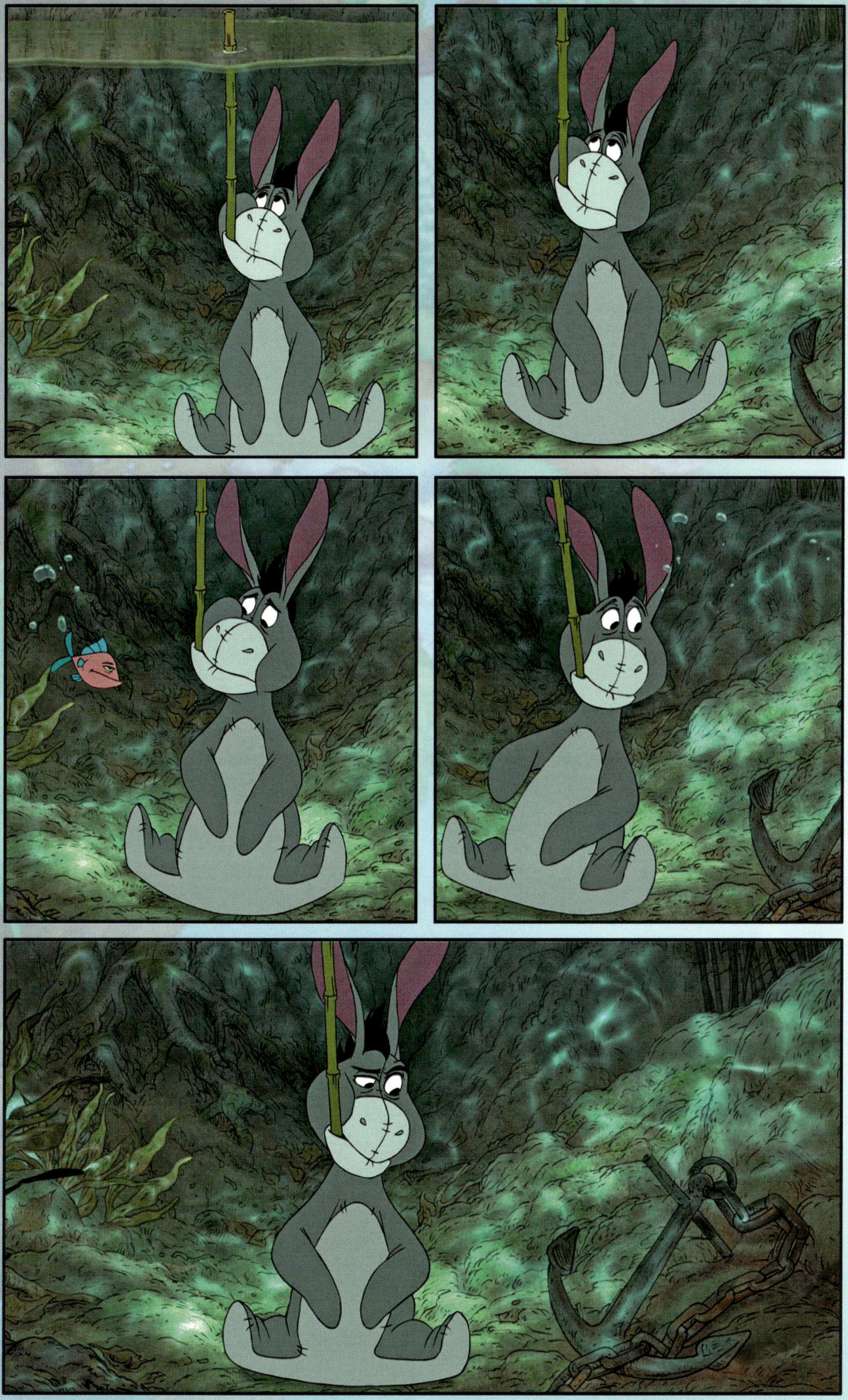

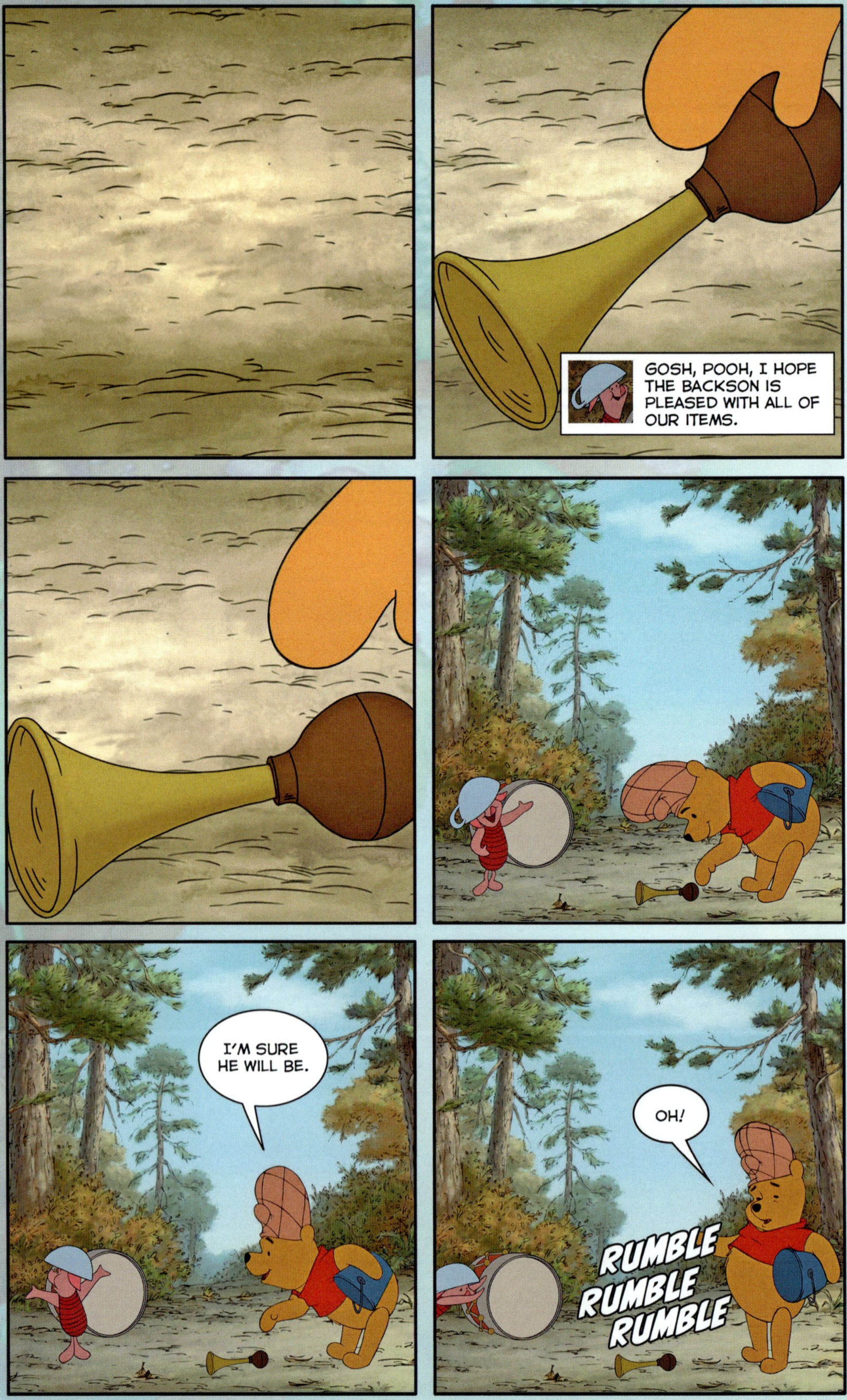
GOSH, POOH, I HOPE THE BACKSON IS PLEASED WITH ALL OF OUR ITEMS.
I'M SURE HE WILL BE.
OH!
RUMBLE RUMBLE RUMBLE

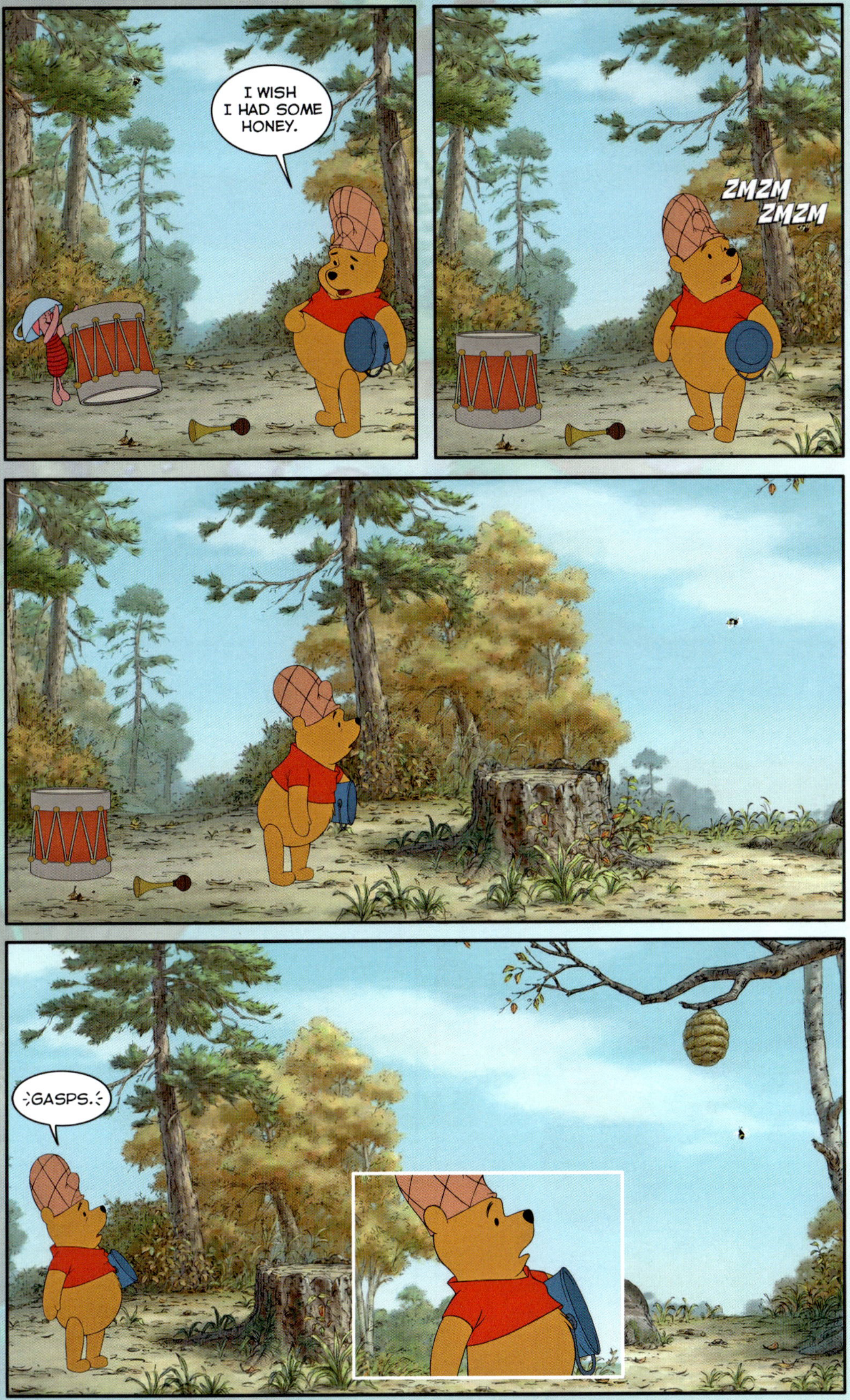
I WISH I HAD SOME HONEY.
ZMZM ZMZM
GASPS.

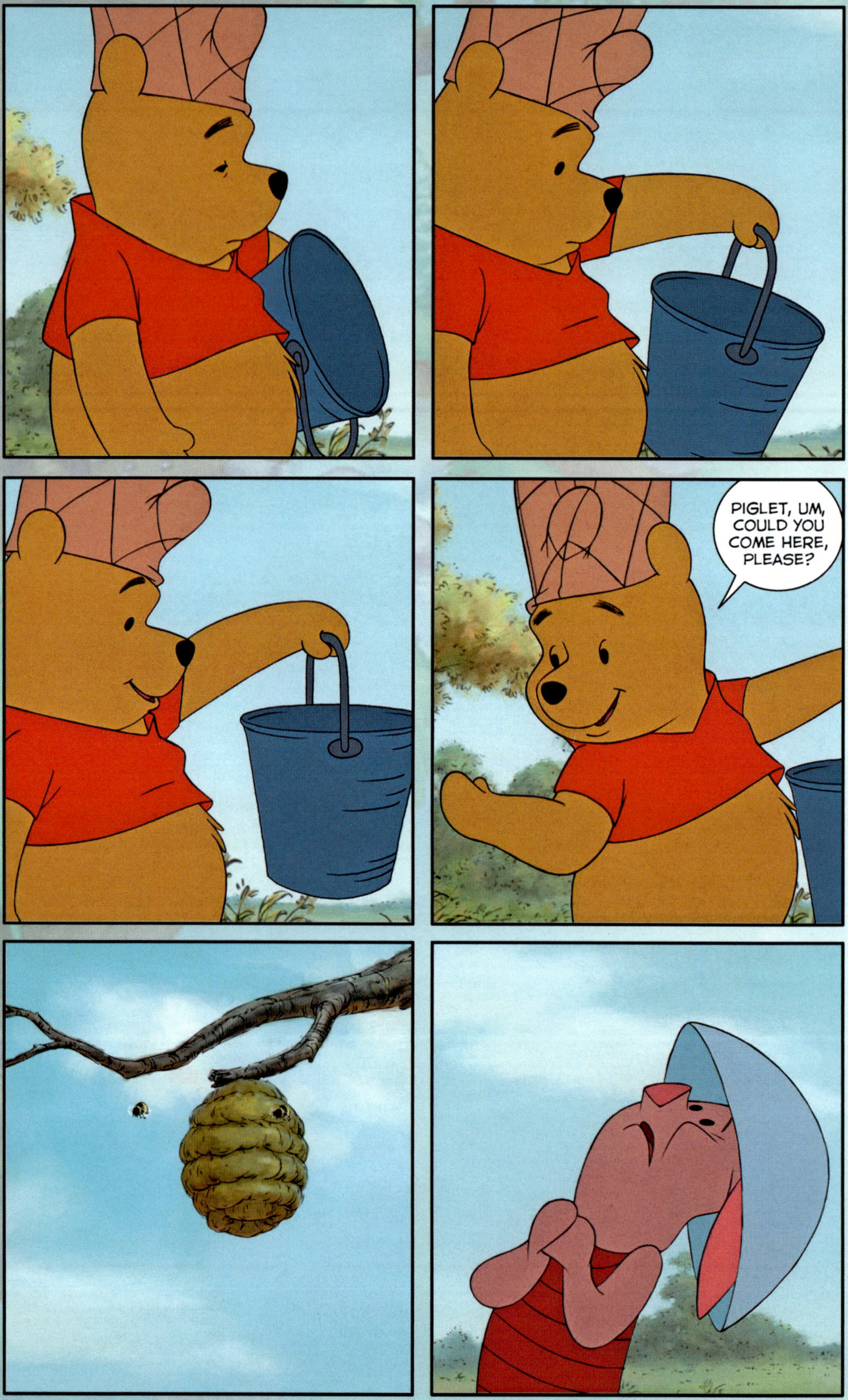
PIGLET, UM, COULD YOU COME HERE, PLEASE?

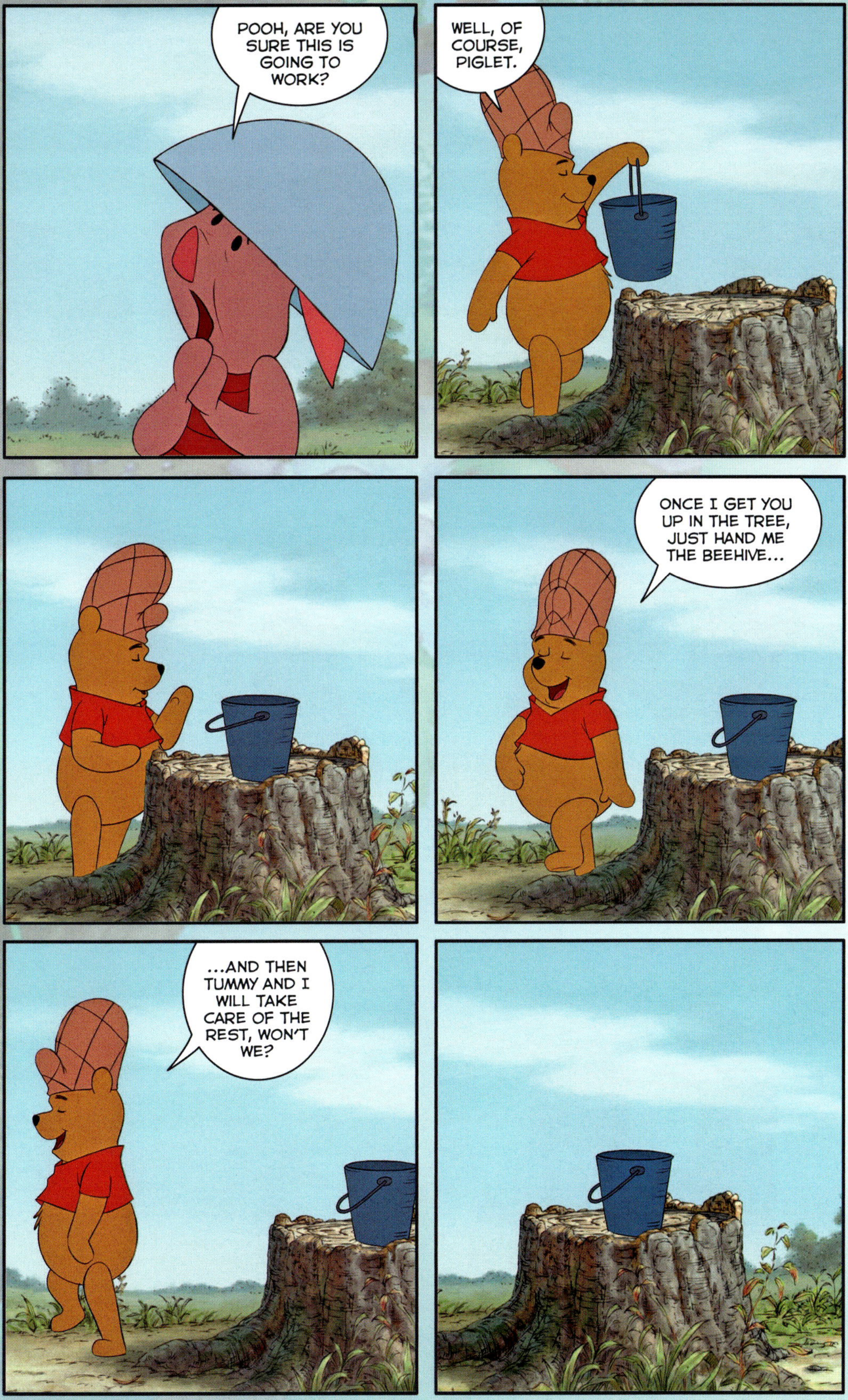
POOH, ARE YOU SURE THIS IS GOING TO WORK?
WELL, OF COURSE, PIGLET.
ONCE I GET YOU UP IN THE TREE, JUST HAND ME THE BEEHIVE...
...AND THEN TUMMY AND I WILL TAKE CARE OF THE REST, WON'T WE?

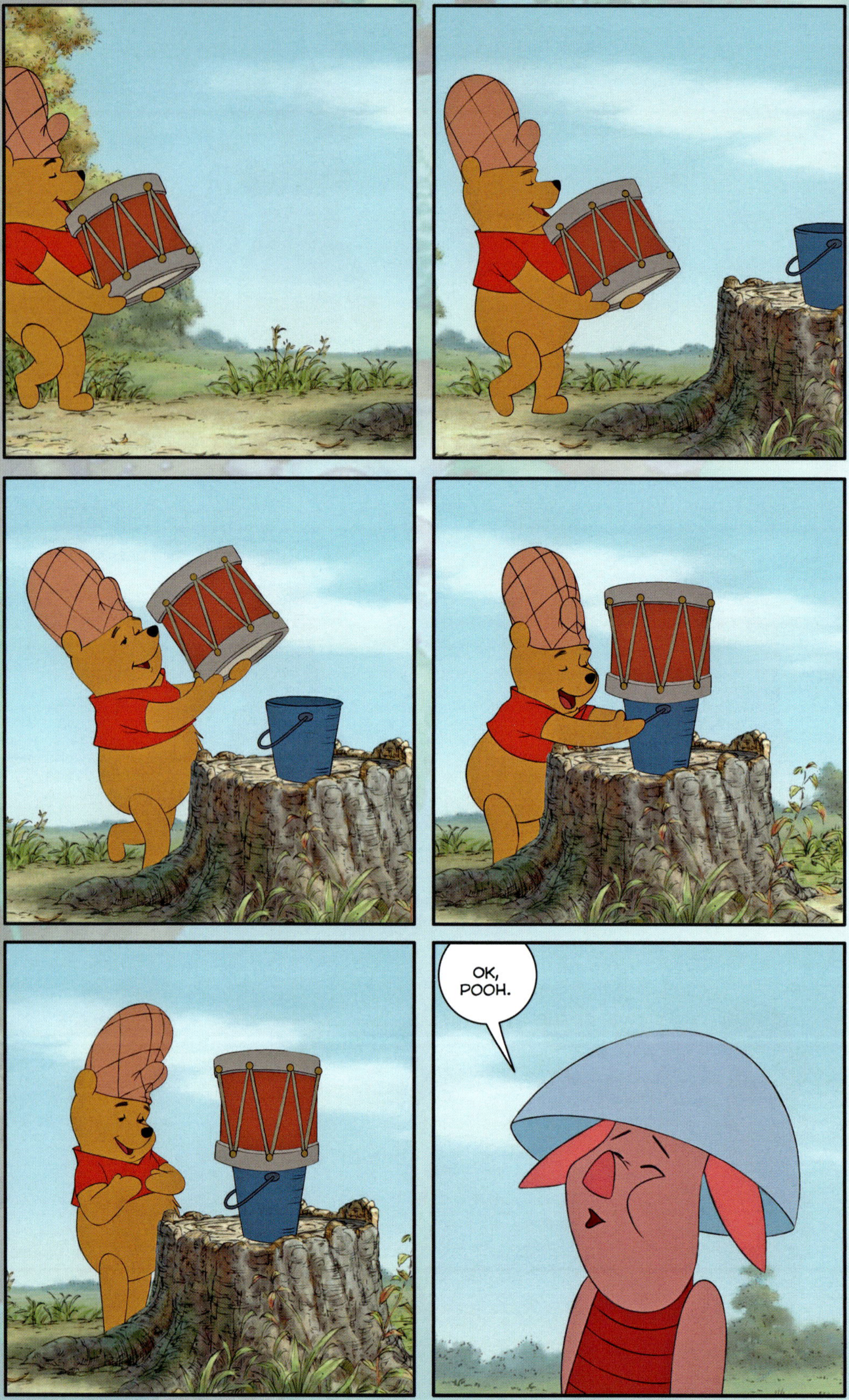
OK, POOH.

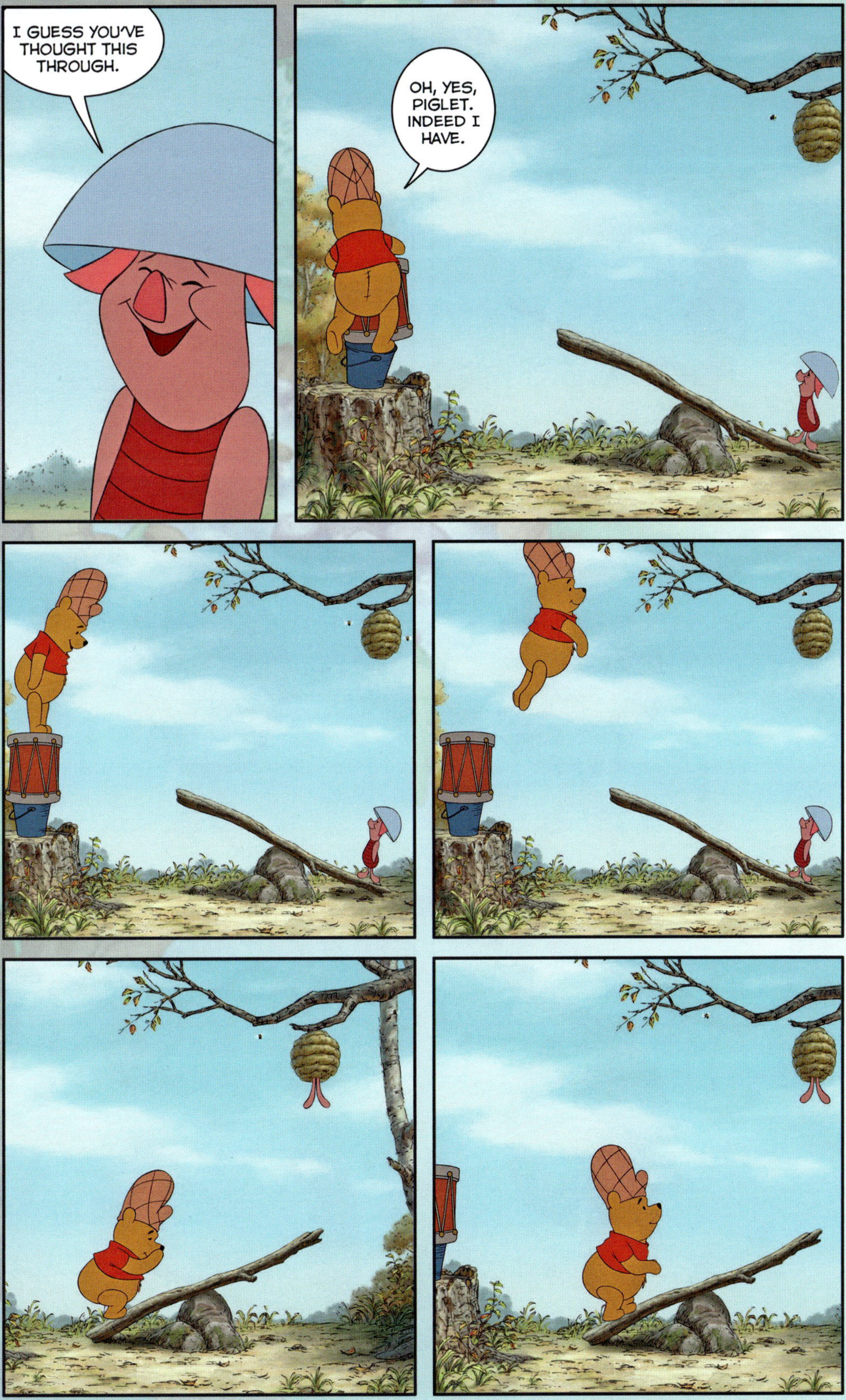
I GUESS YOU'VE THOUGHT THIS THROUGH.
OH, YES, PIGLET. INDEED I HAVE.

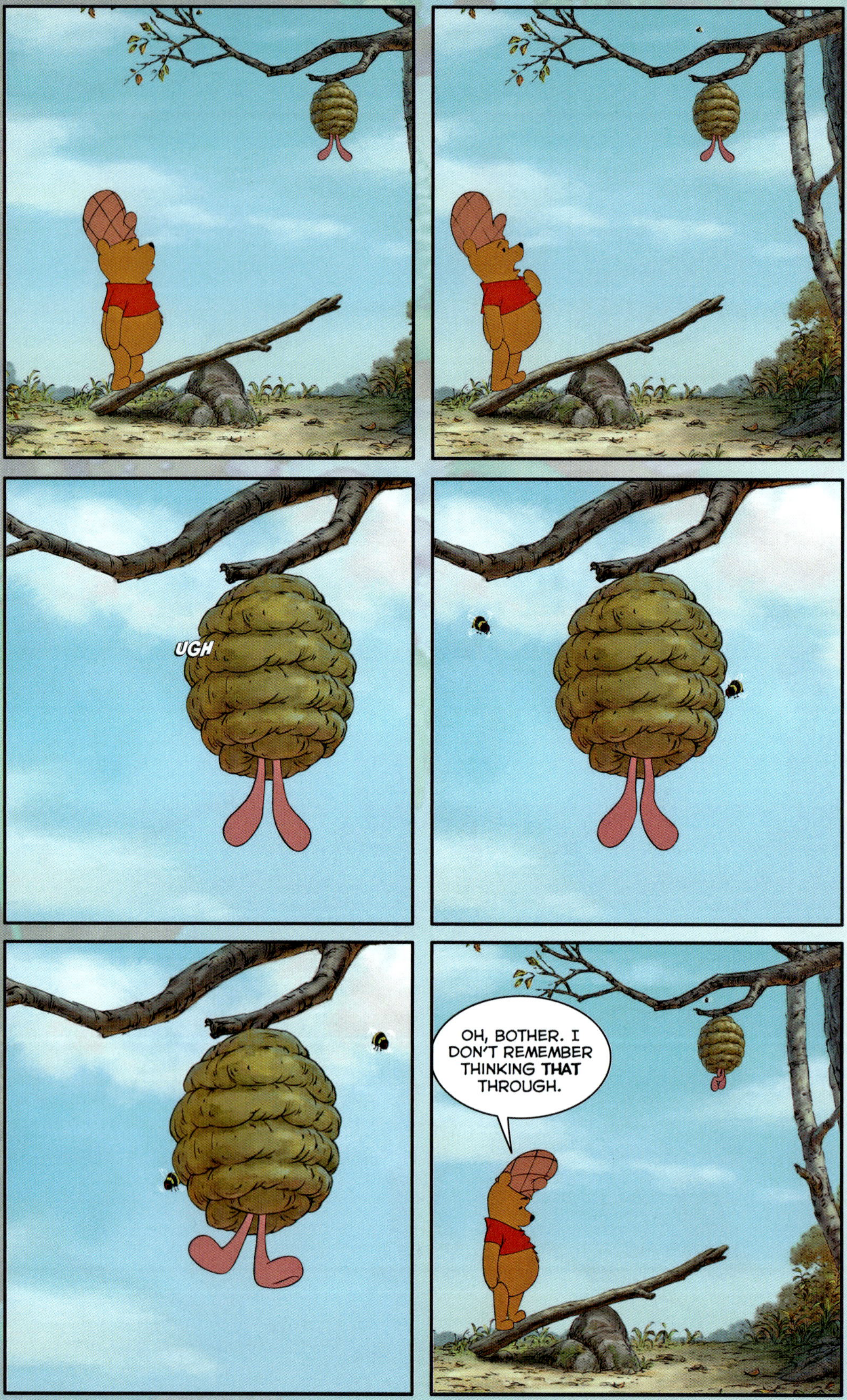
UGH
OH, BOTHER. I DON'T REMEMBER THINKING THAT THROUGH.

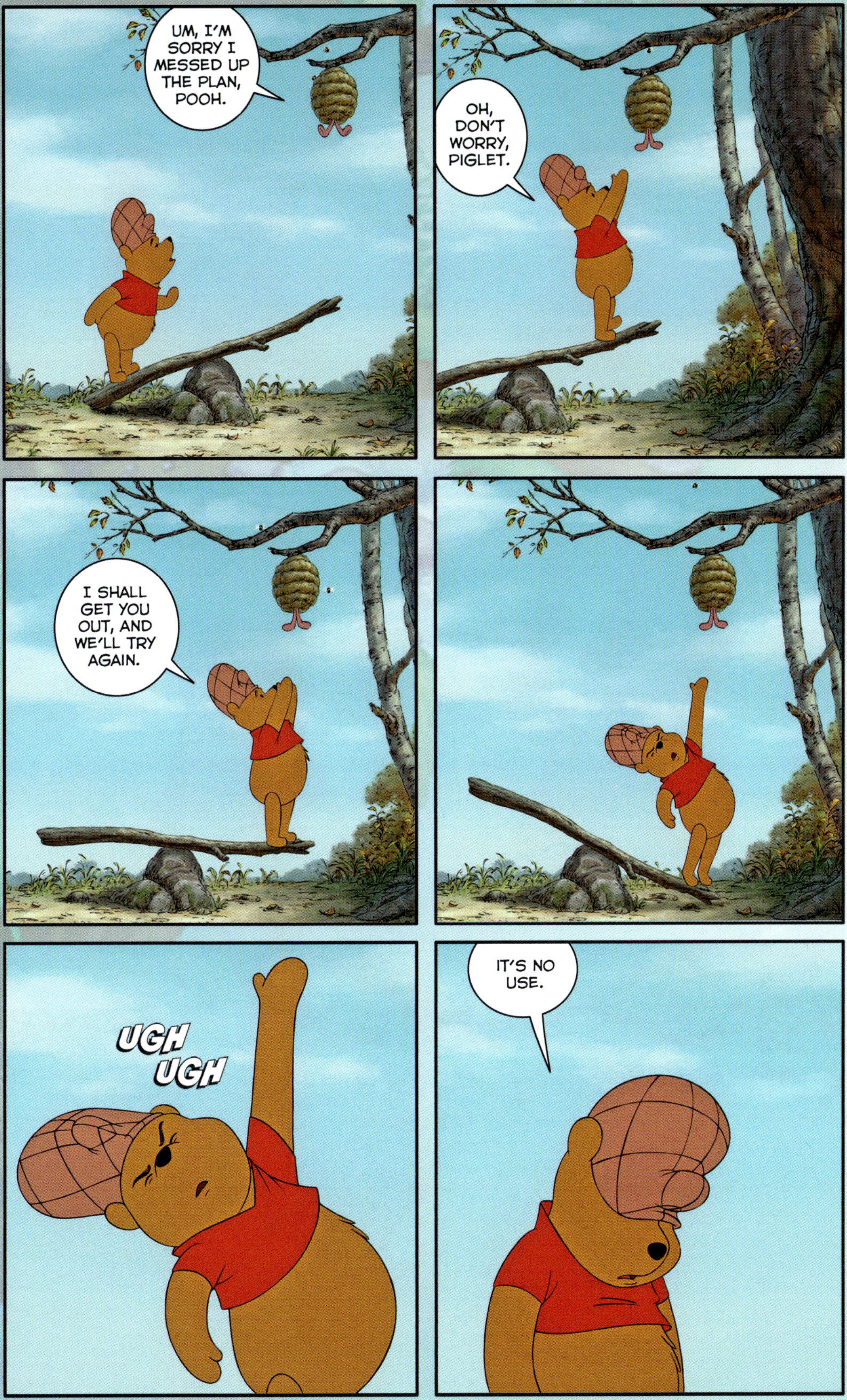
UM, I'M SORRY I MESSED UP THE PLAN, POOH.
OH, DON'T WORRY, PIGLET.
I SHALL GET YOU OUT, AND WE'LL TRY AGAIN.
UGH
UGH
IT'S NO USE.

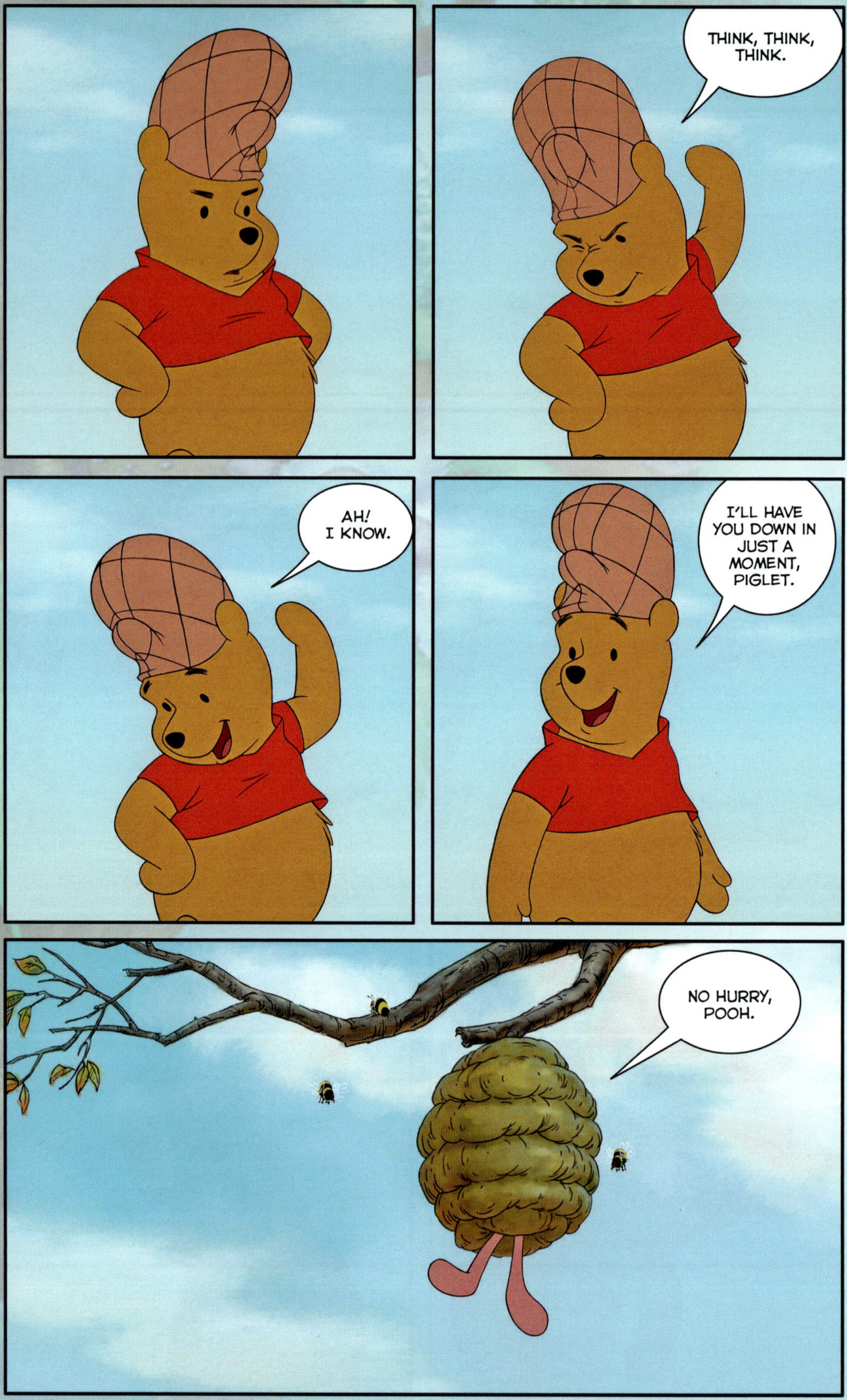
THINK, THINK, THINK.
AH! I KNOW.
I'LL HAVE YOU DOWN IN JUST A MOMENT, PIGLET.
NO HURRY, POOH.

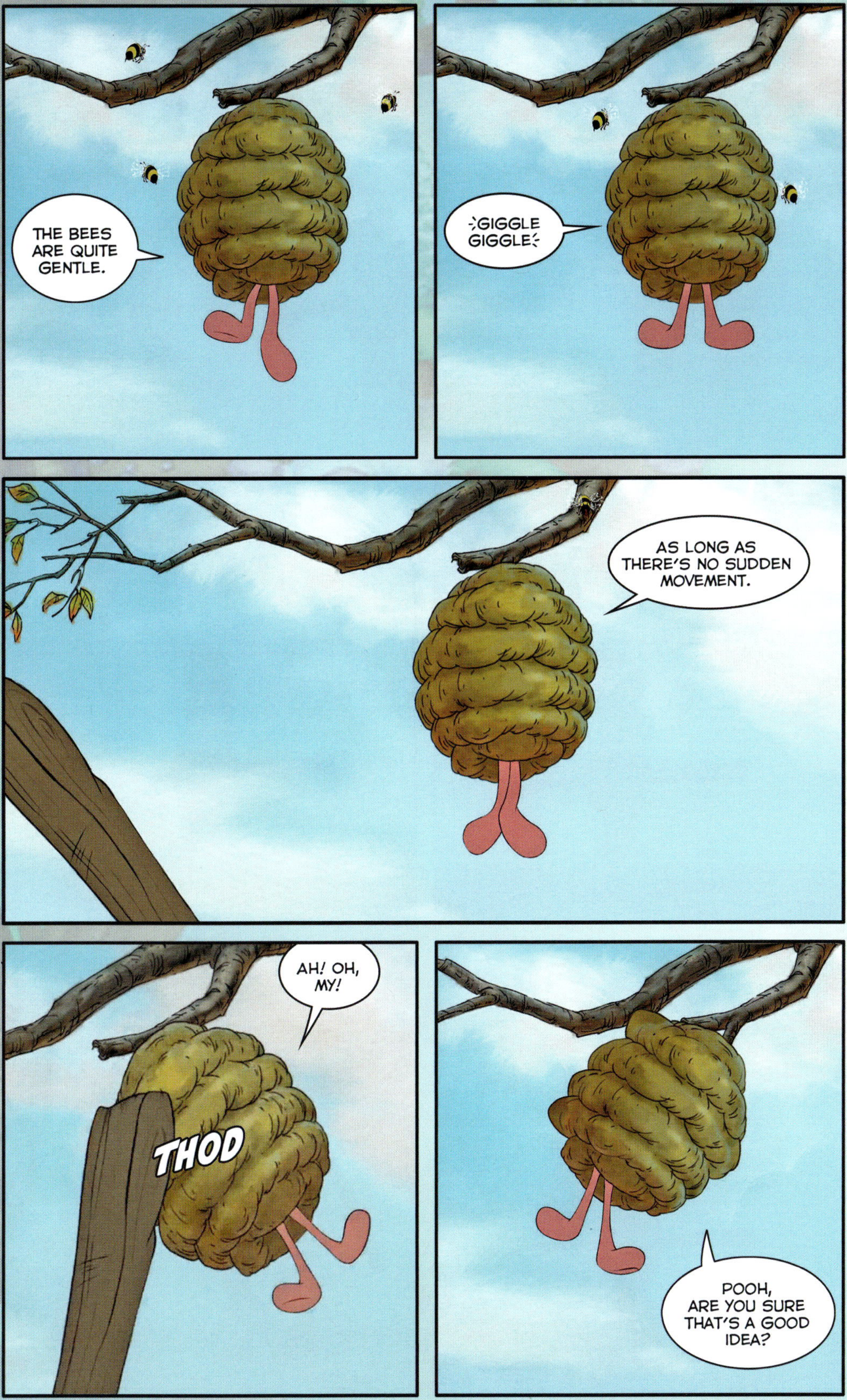
THE BEES ARE QUITE GENTLE.
GIGGLE GIGGLE
AS LONG AS THERE'S NO SUDDEN MOVEMENT.
AH! OH, MY!
THOD
POOH, ARE YOU SURE THAT'S A GOOD IDEA?

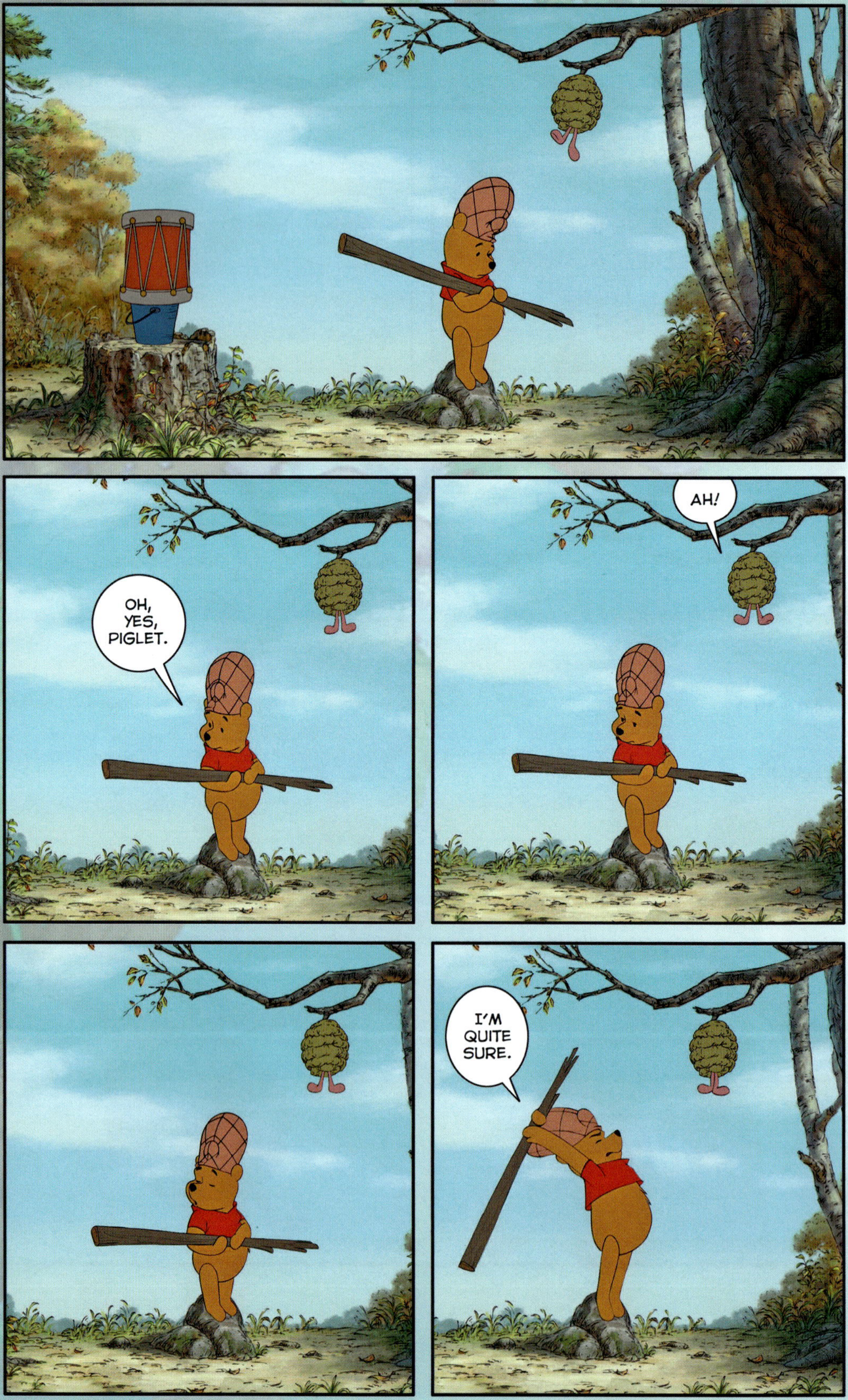
OH, YES, PIGLET.
AH!
I'M QUITE SURE.

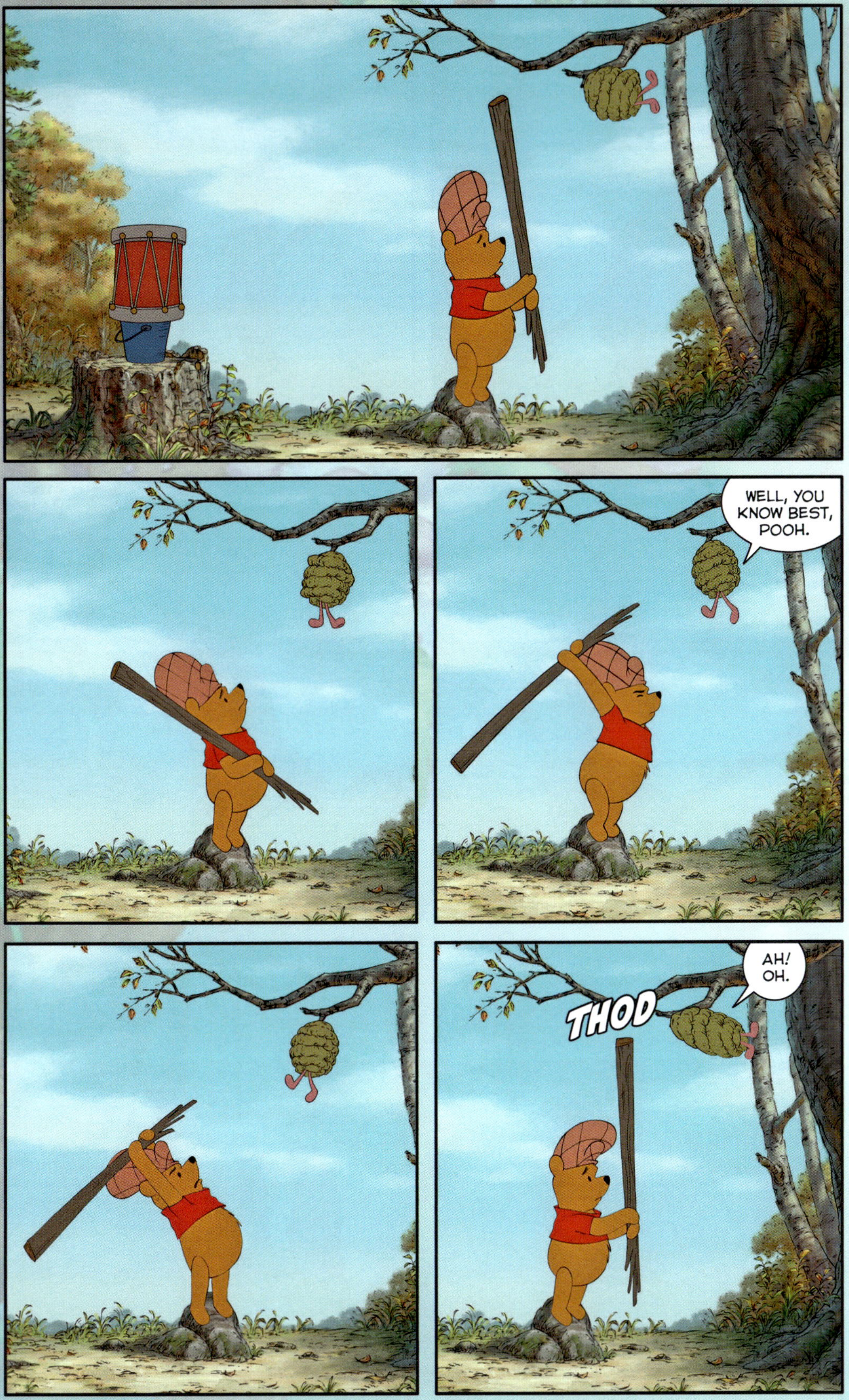
WELL, YOU KNOW BEST, POOH.
THOD
AH! OH.

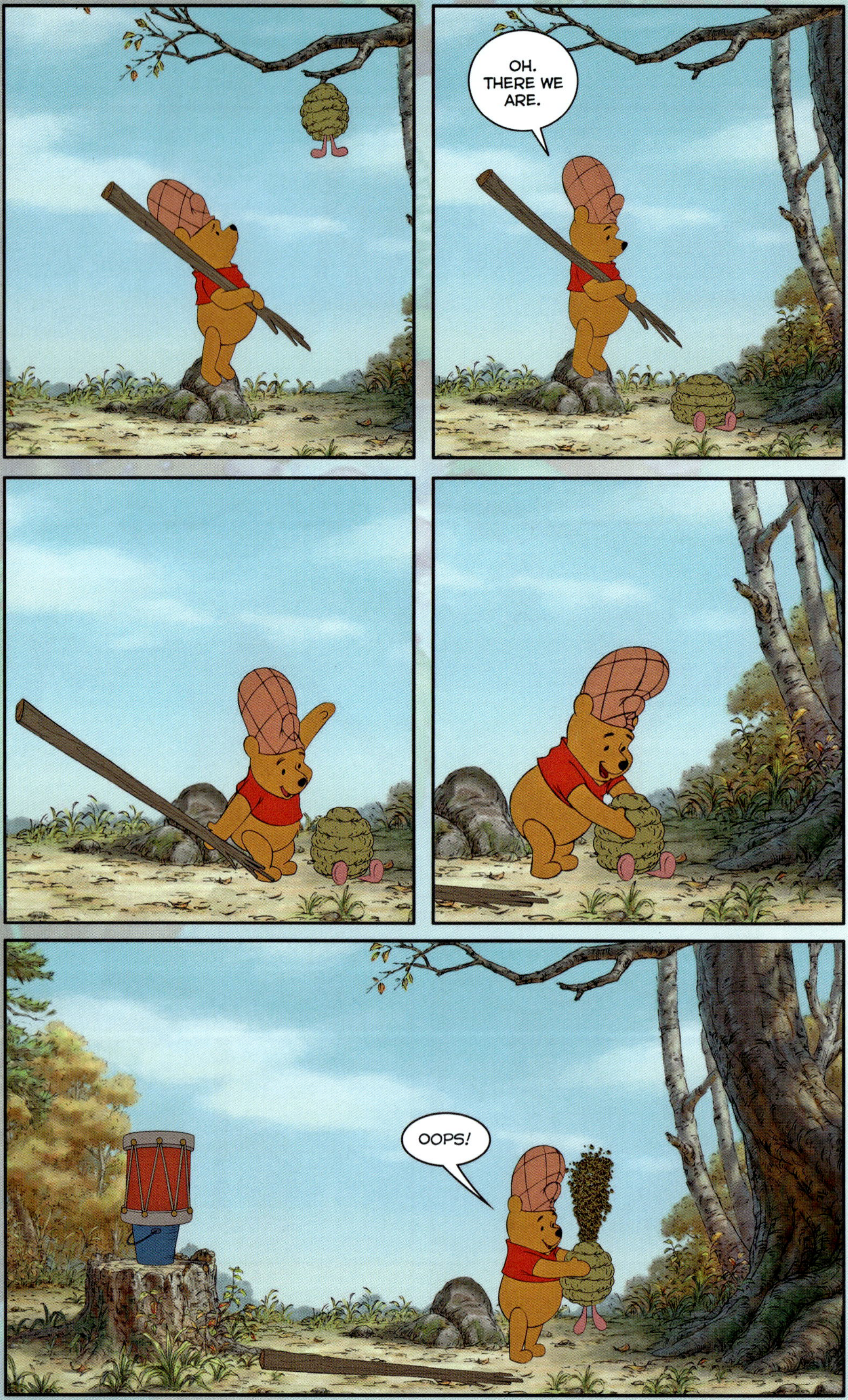
OH. THERE WE ARE.
OOPS!

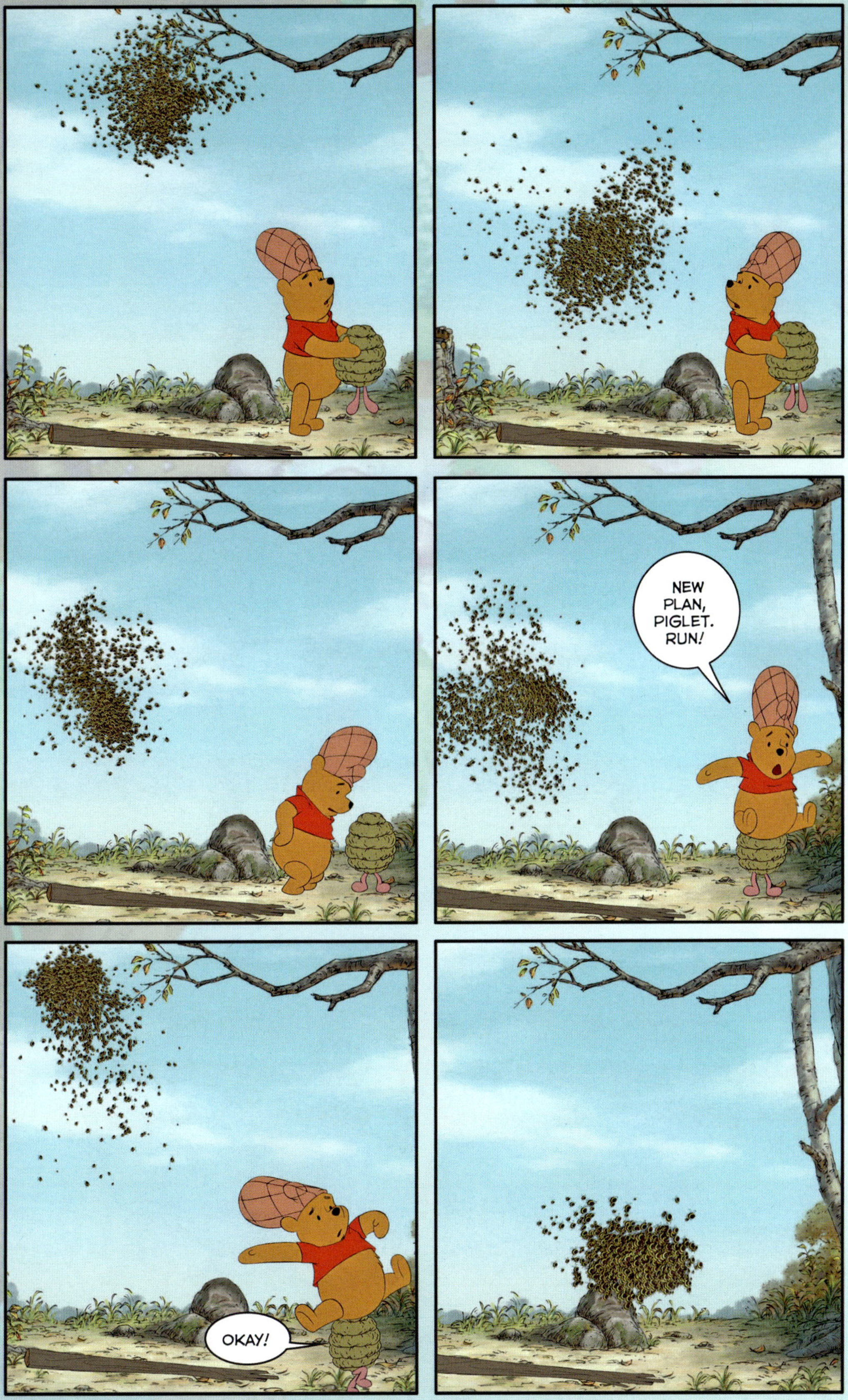
NEW PLAN, PIGLET. RUN!
OKAY!

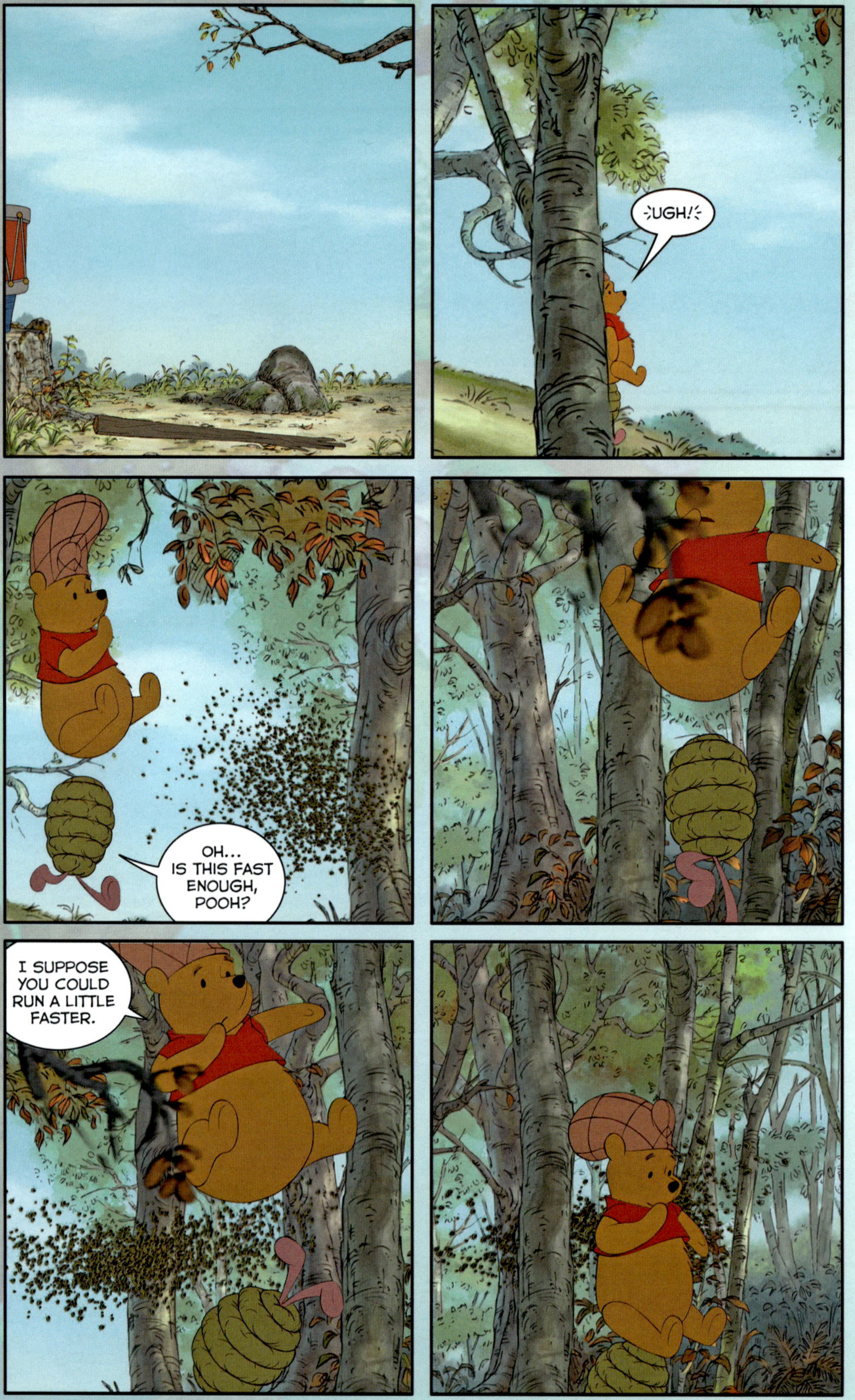
UGH!
OH... IS THIS FAST ENOUGH, POOH?
I SUPPOSE YOU COULD RUN A LITTLE FASTER.

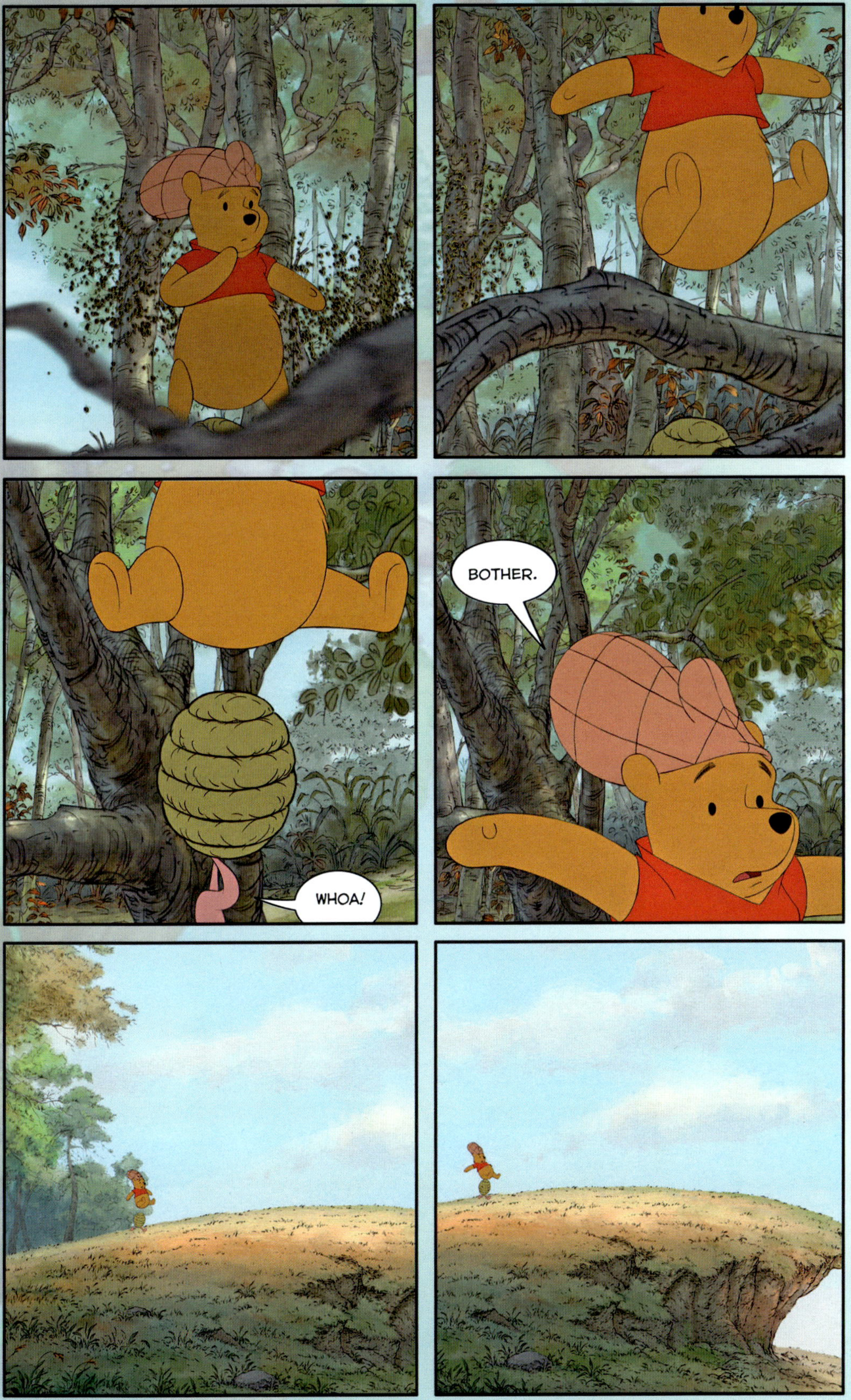
WHOA!
BOTHER.

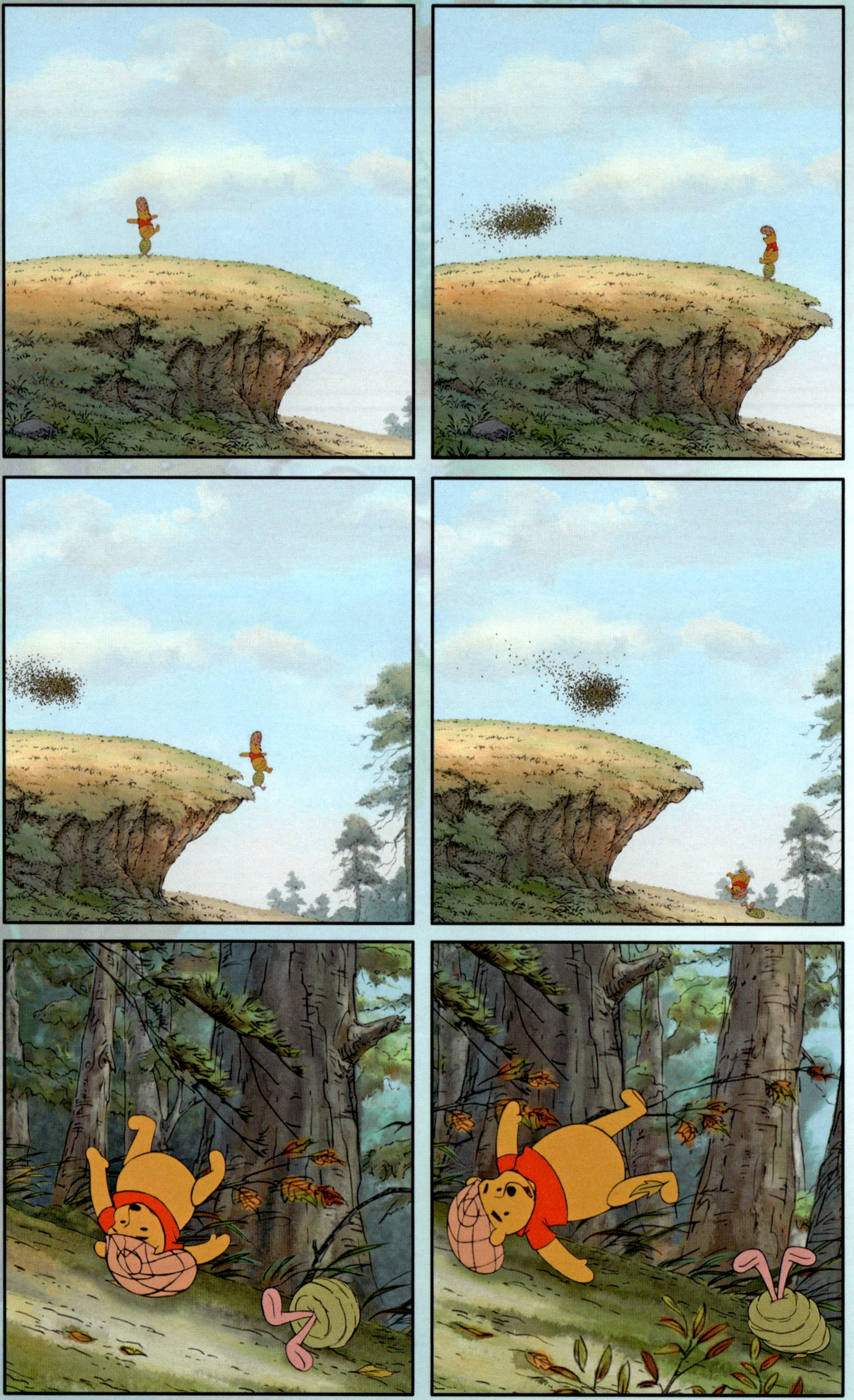

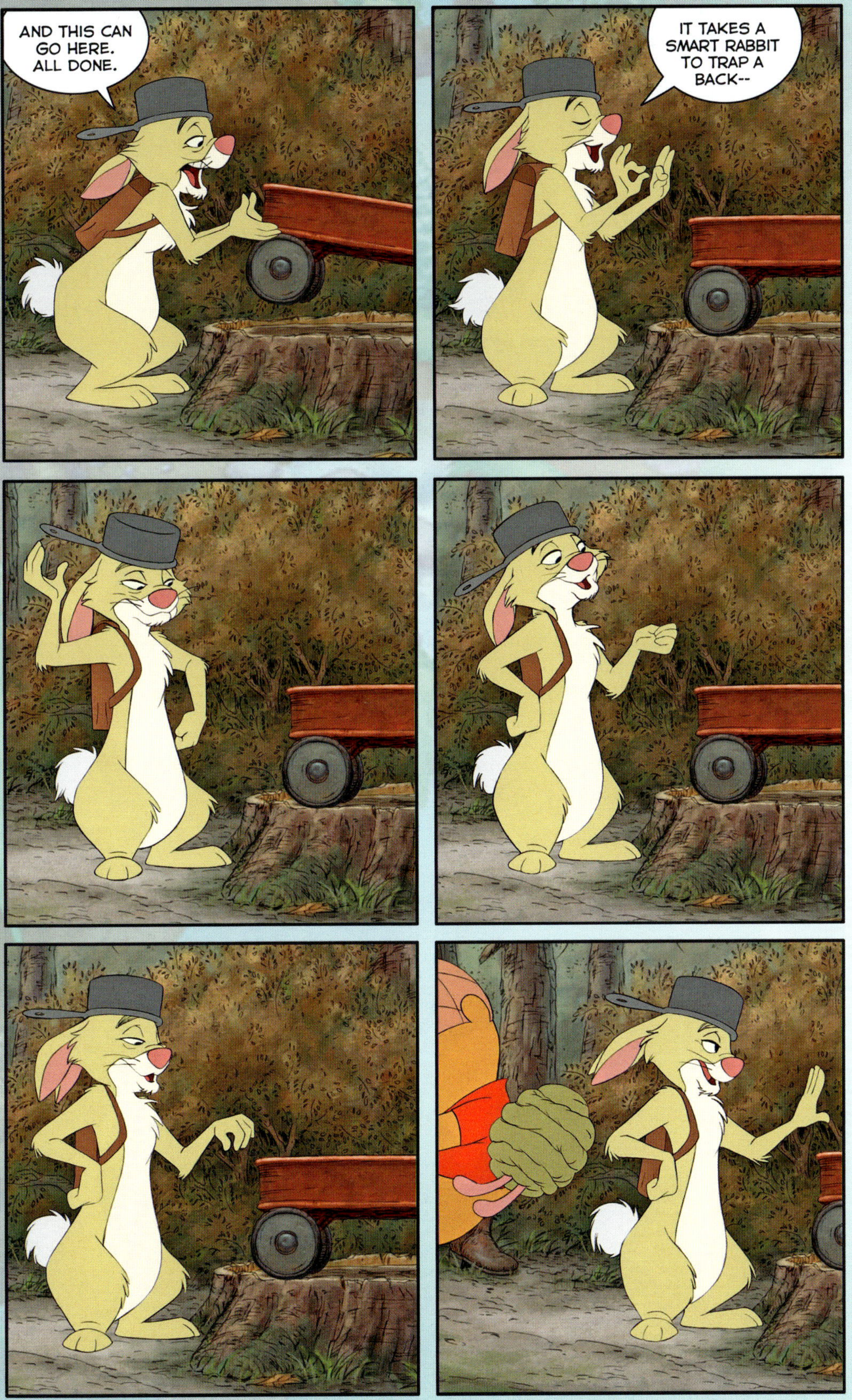
AND THIS CAN GO HERE. ALL DONE.
IT TAKES A SMART RABBIT TO TRAP A BACK--

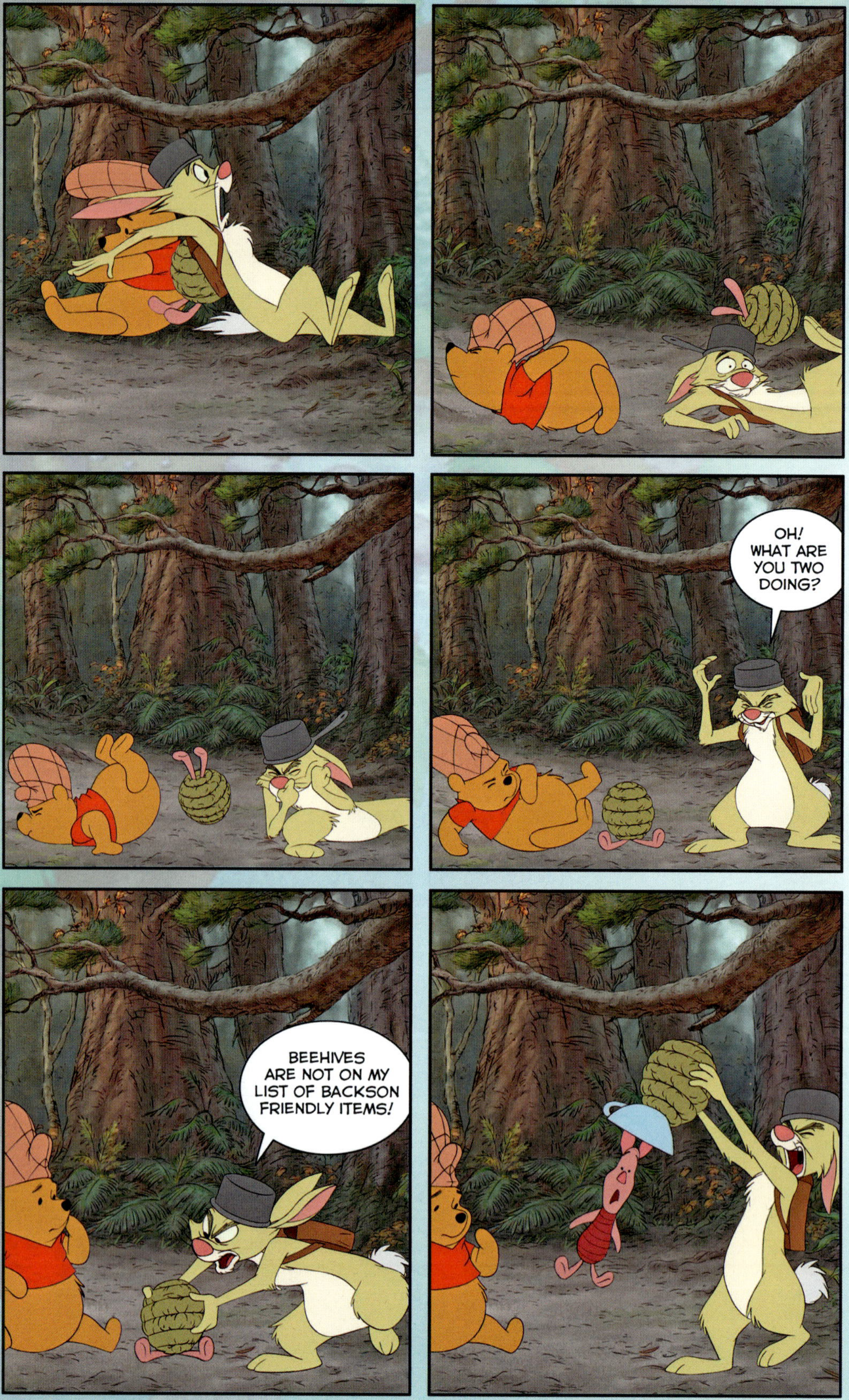
OH! WHAT ARE YOU TWO DOING?
BEEHIVES ARE NOT ON MY LIST OF BACKSON FRIENDLY ITEMS!

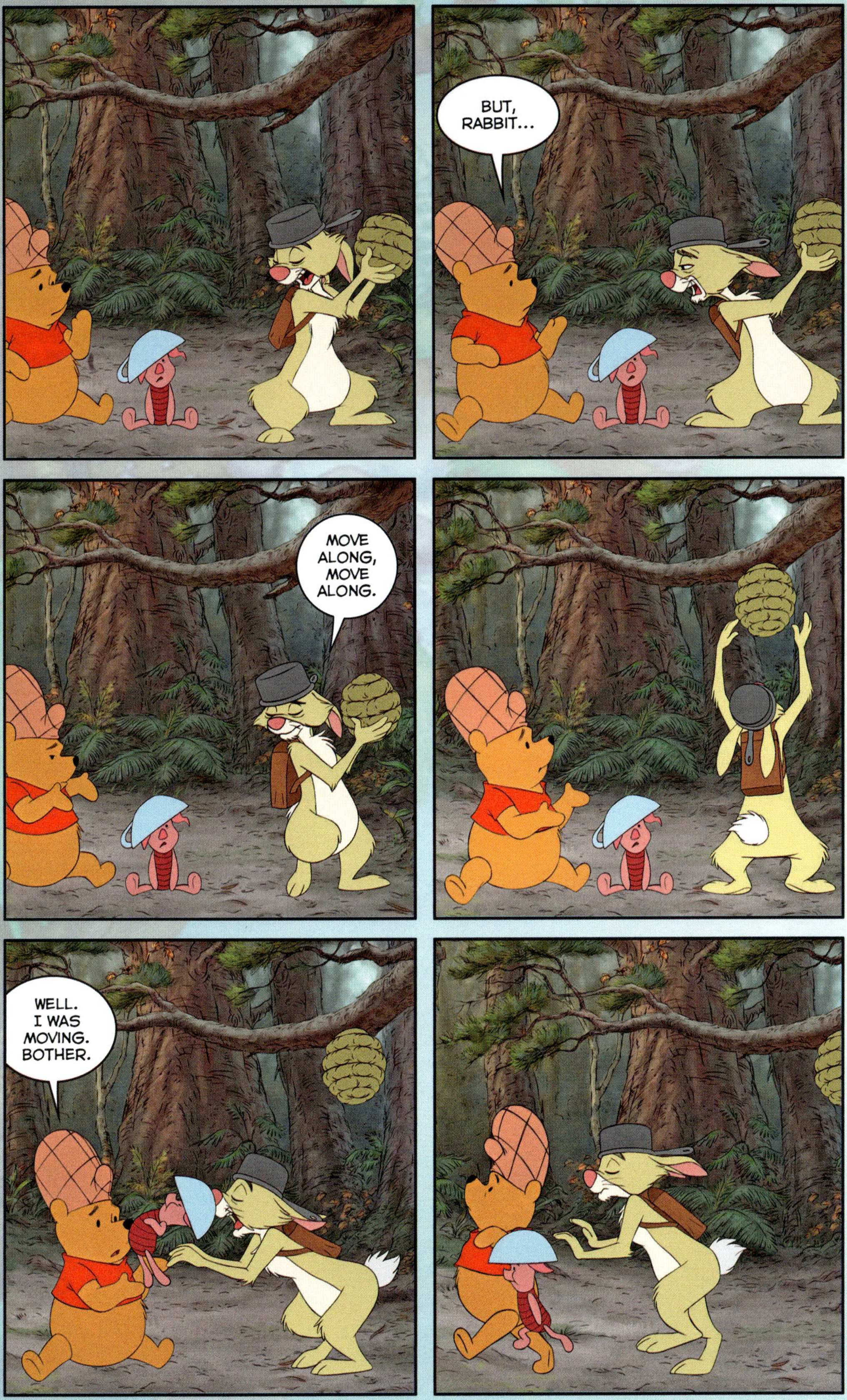
BUT, RABBIT...
MOVE ALONG, MOVE ALONG.
WELL. I WAS MOVING. BOTHER.

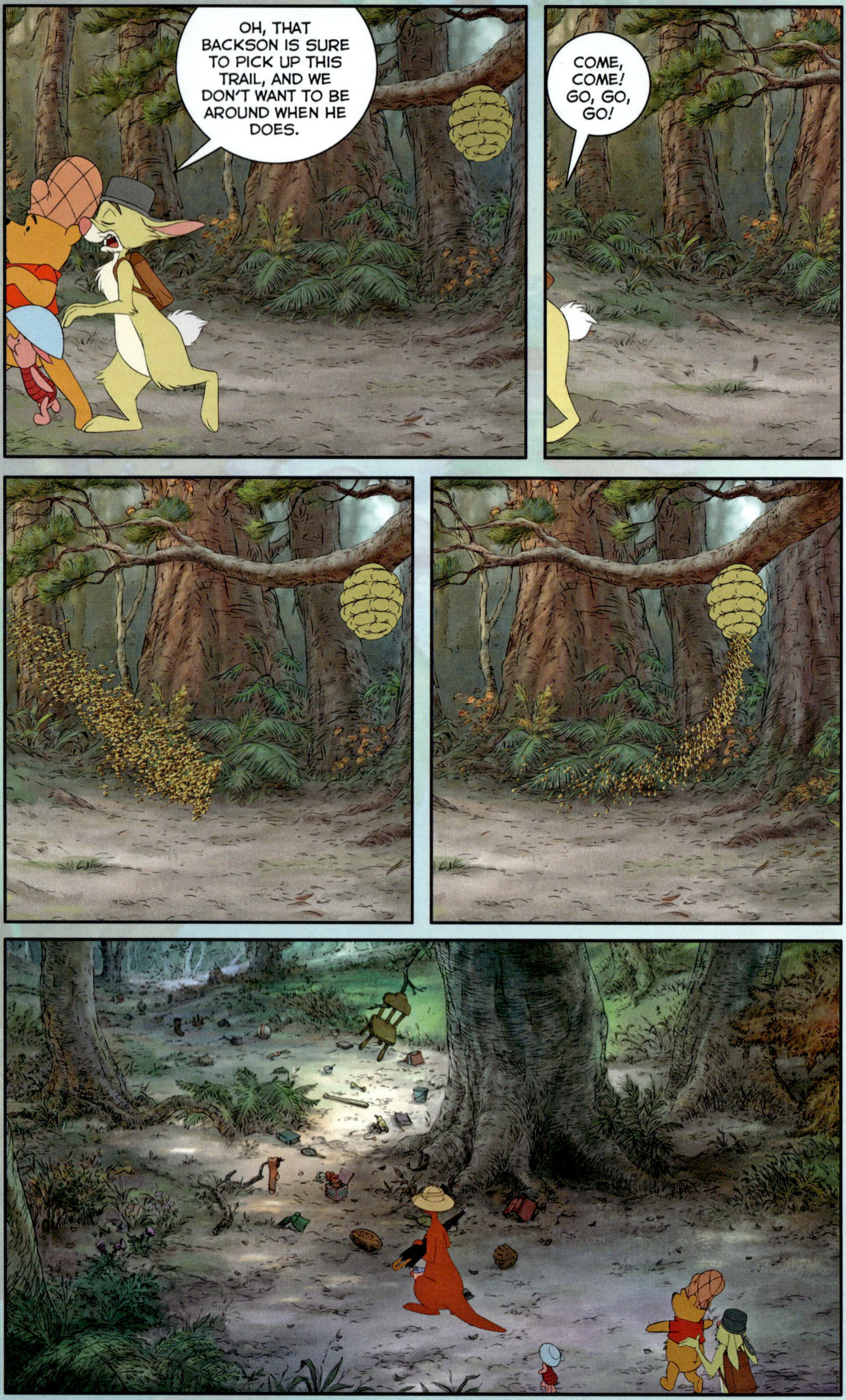
OH, THAT BACKSON IS SURE TO PICK UP THIS TRAIL, AND WE DON'T WANT TO BE AROUND WHEN HE DOES.
COME, COME! GO, GO, GO!

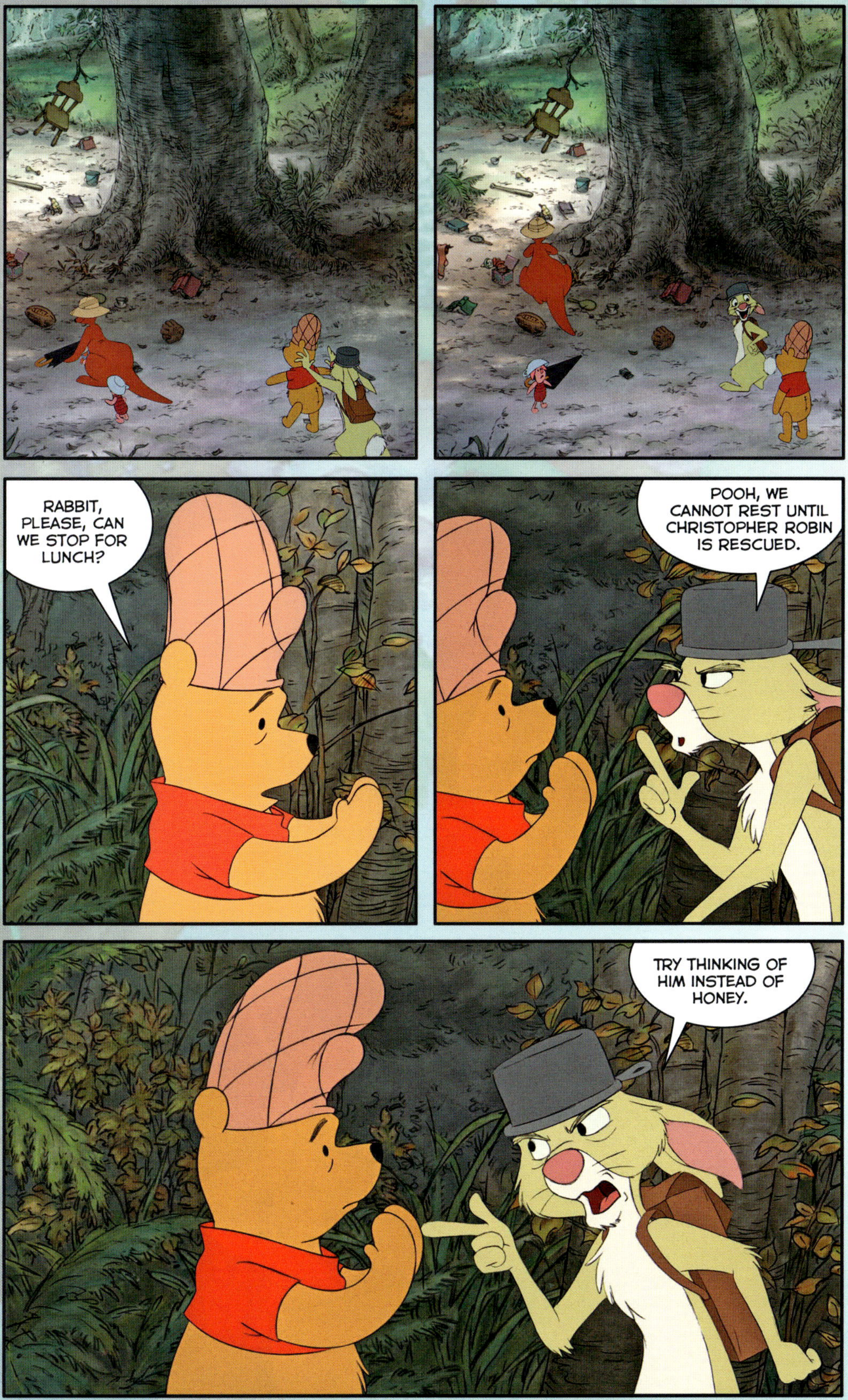
RABBIT, PLEASE, CAN WE STOP FOR LUNCH?
POOH, WE CANNOT REST UNTIL CHRISTOPHER ROBIN IS RESCUED.
TRY THINKING OF HIM INSTEAD OF HONEY.

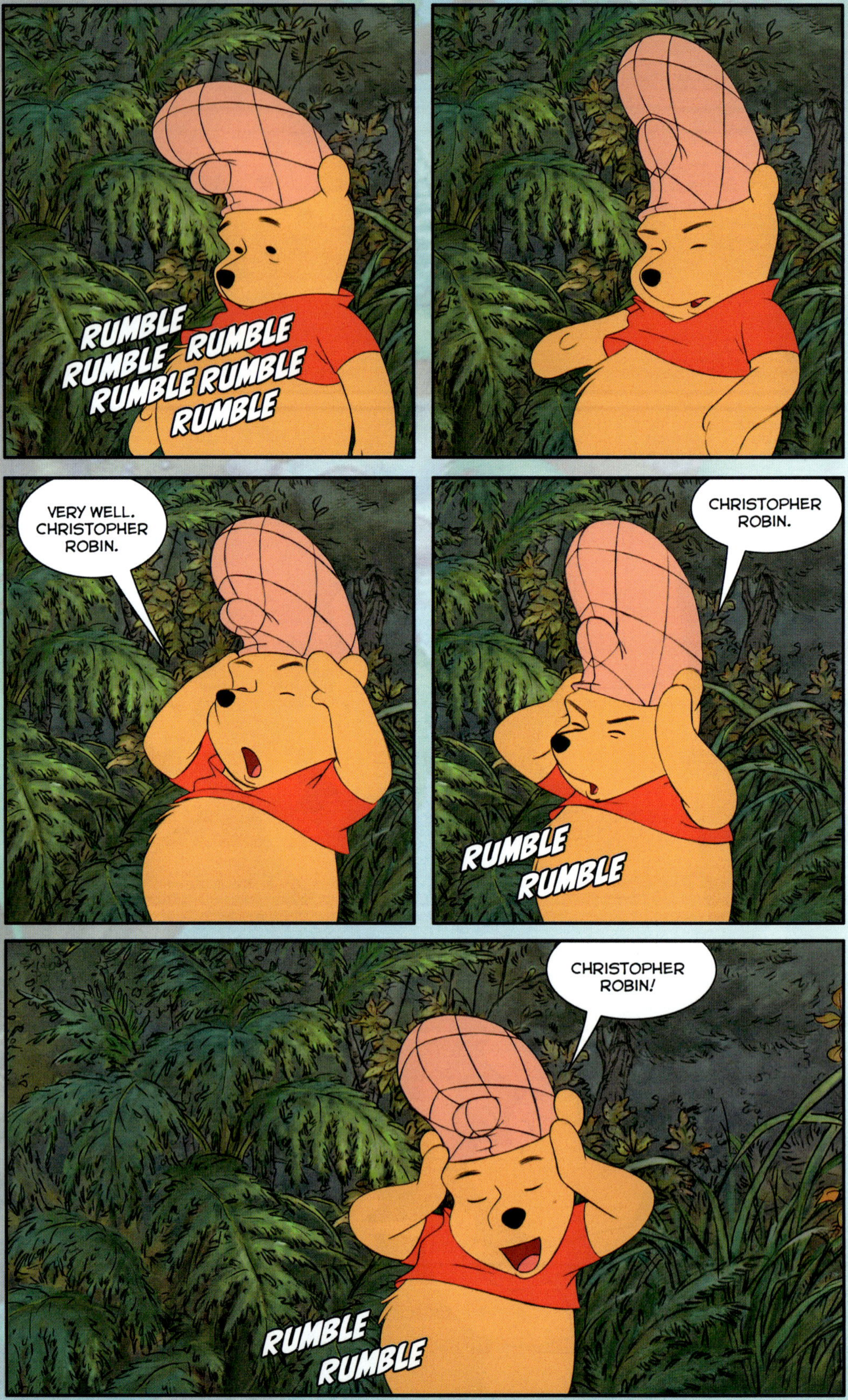
RUMBLE RUMBLE RUMBLE RUMBLE RUMBLE RUMBLE
VERY WELL. CHRISTOPHER ROBIN.
CHRISTOPHER ROBIN.
RUMBLE RUMBLE
CHRISTOPHER ROBIN!
RUMBLE RUMBLE

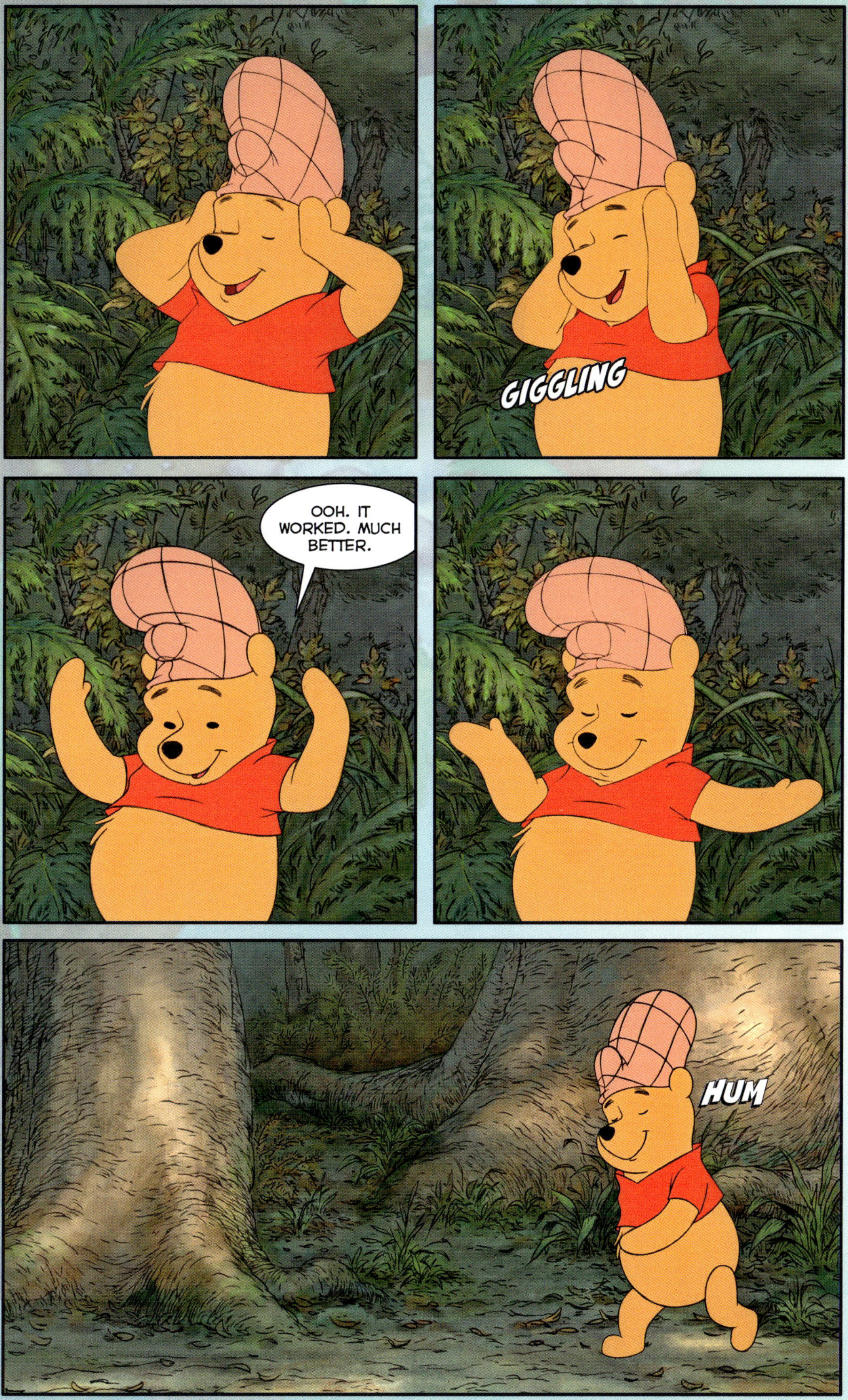
GIGGLING
OOH. IT WORKED. MUCH BETTER.
HUM

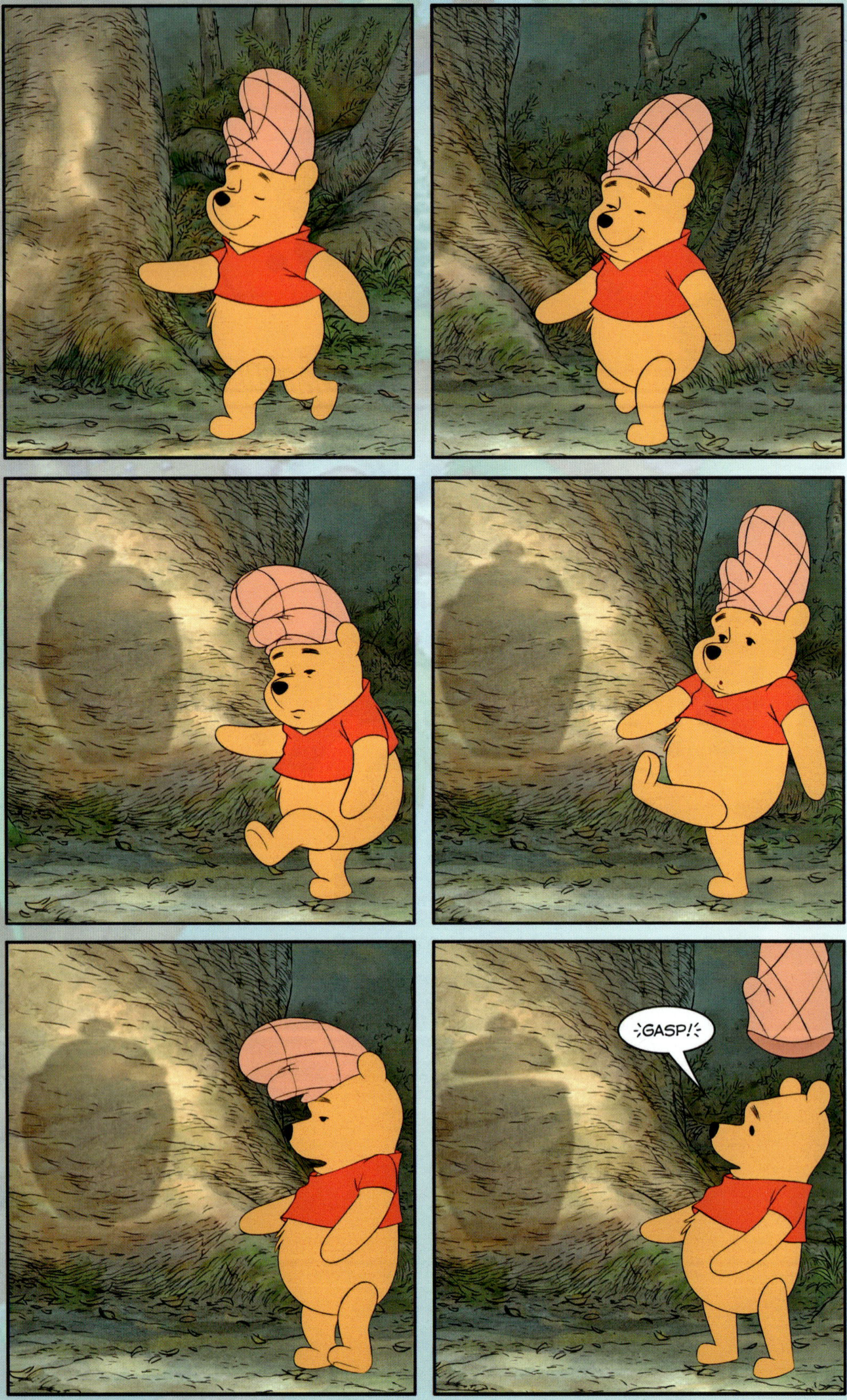
GASP!

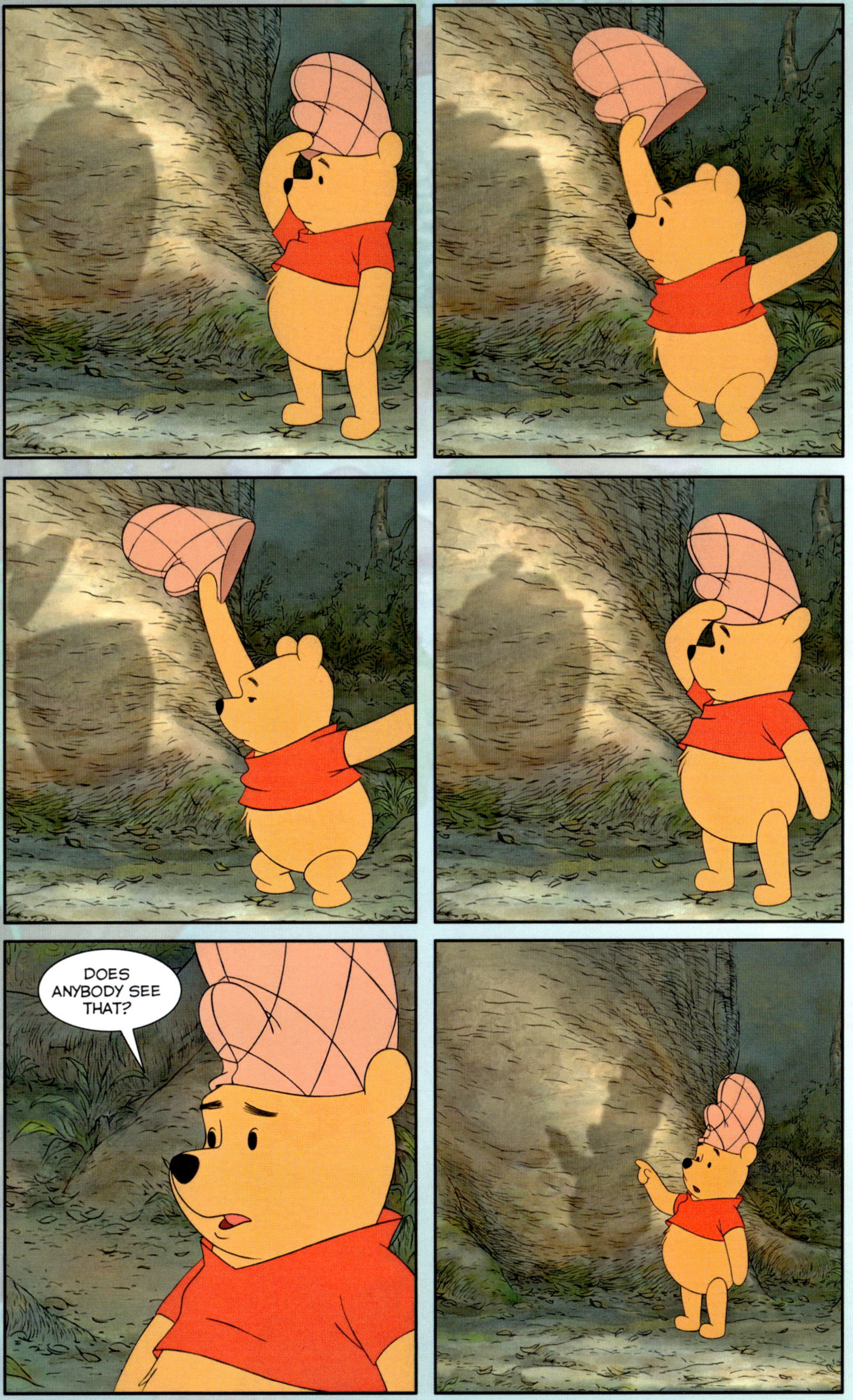
DOES ANYBODY SEE THAT?

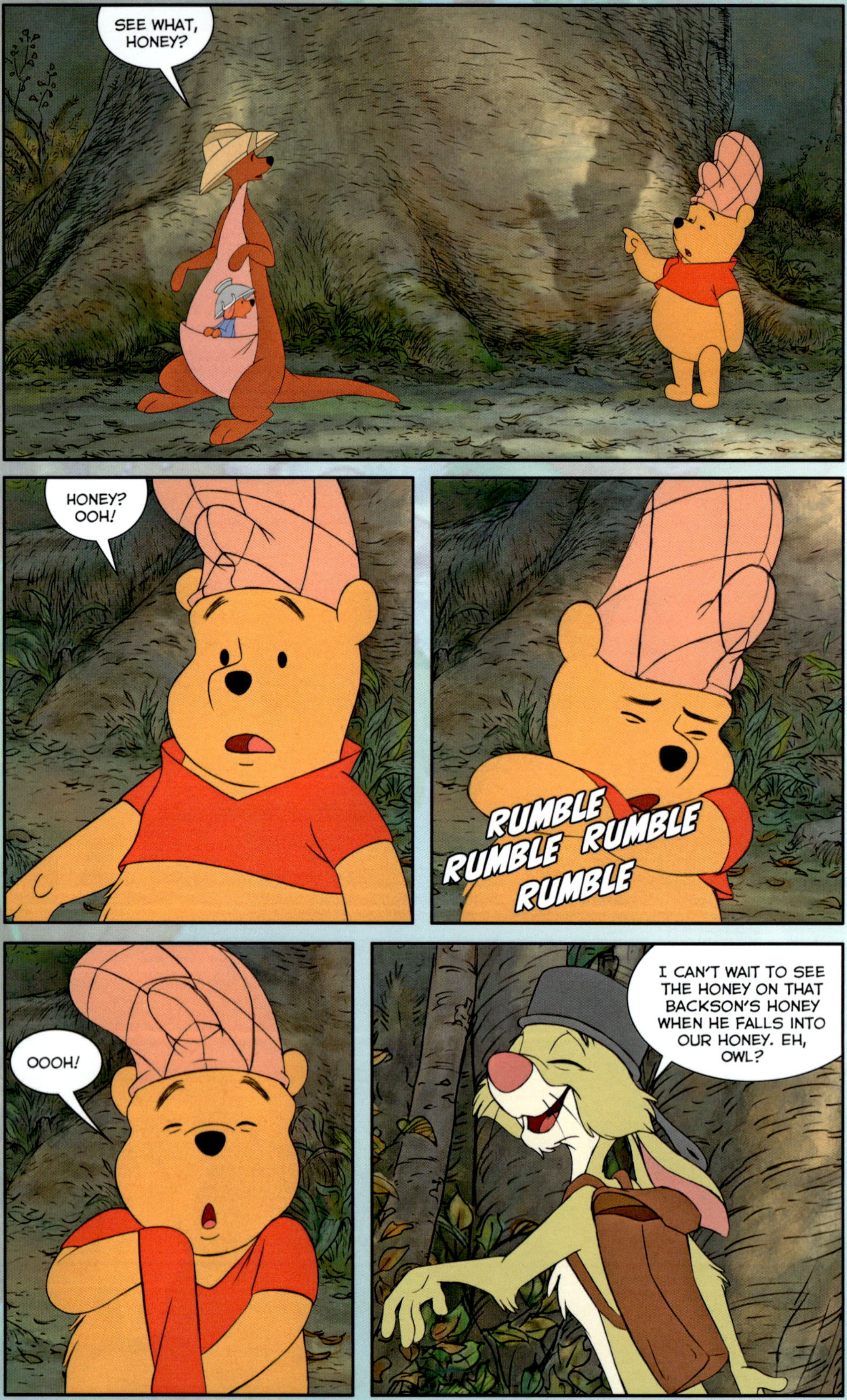
SEE WHAT, HONEY?
HONEY? OOH!
RUMBLE RUMBLE RUMBLE RUMBLE
OOOH!
I CAN'T WAIT TO SEE THE HONEY ON THAT BACKSON'S HONEY WHEN HE FALLS INTO OUR HONEY. EH, OWL?

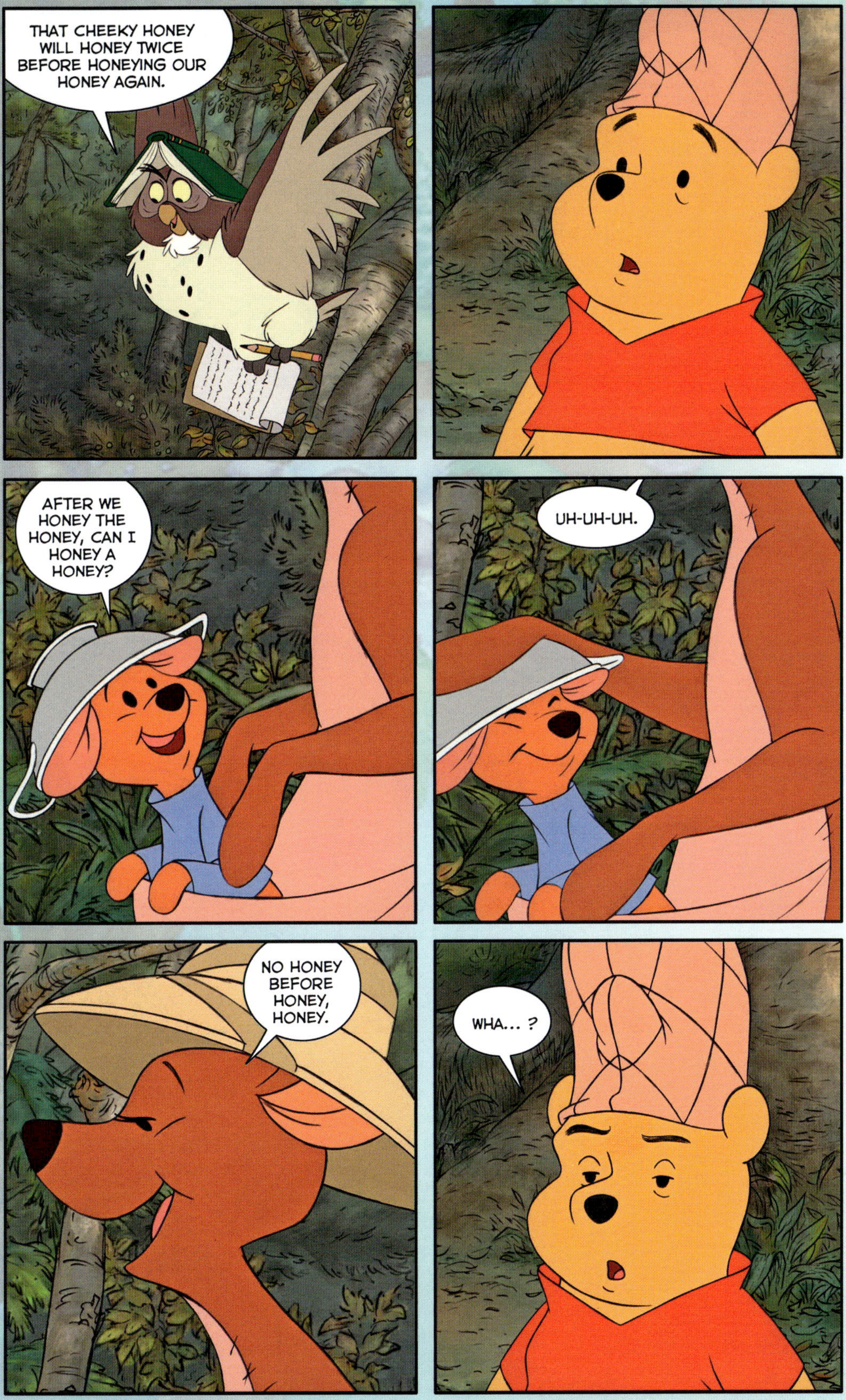
THAT CHEEKY HONEY WILL HONEY TWICE BEFORE HONEYING OUR HONEY AGAIN.
AFTER WE HONEY THE HONEY, CAN I HONEY A HONEY?
UH-UH-UH.
NO HONEY BEFORE HONEY, HONEY.
WHA... ?

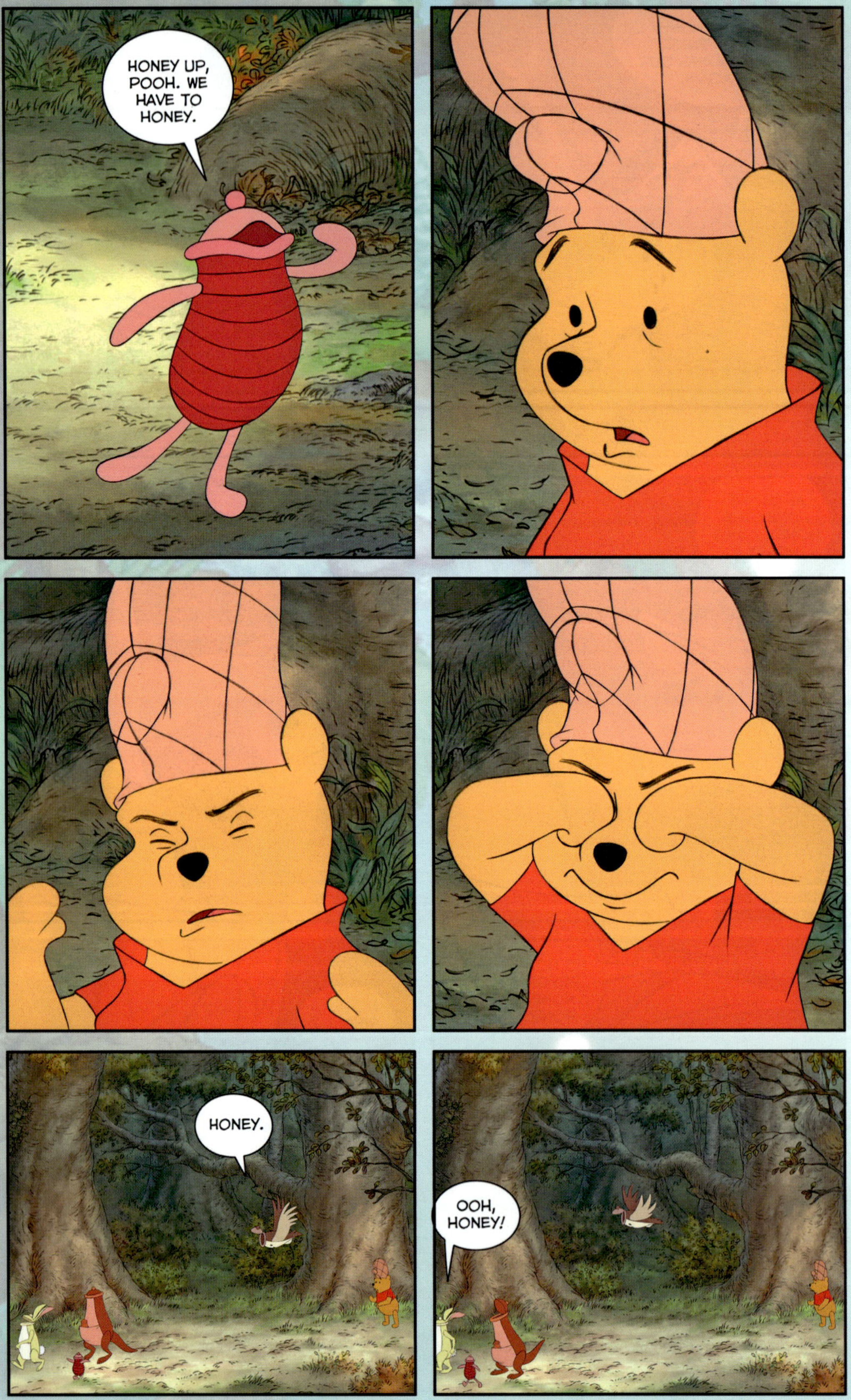
HONEY UP, POOH. WE HAVE TO HONEY.
HONEY.
OOH, HONEY!

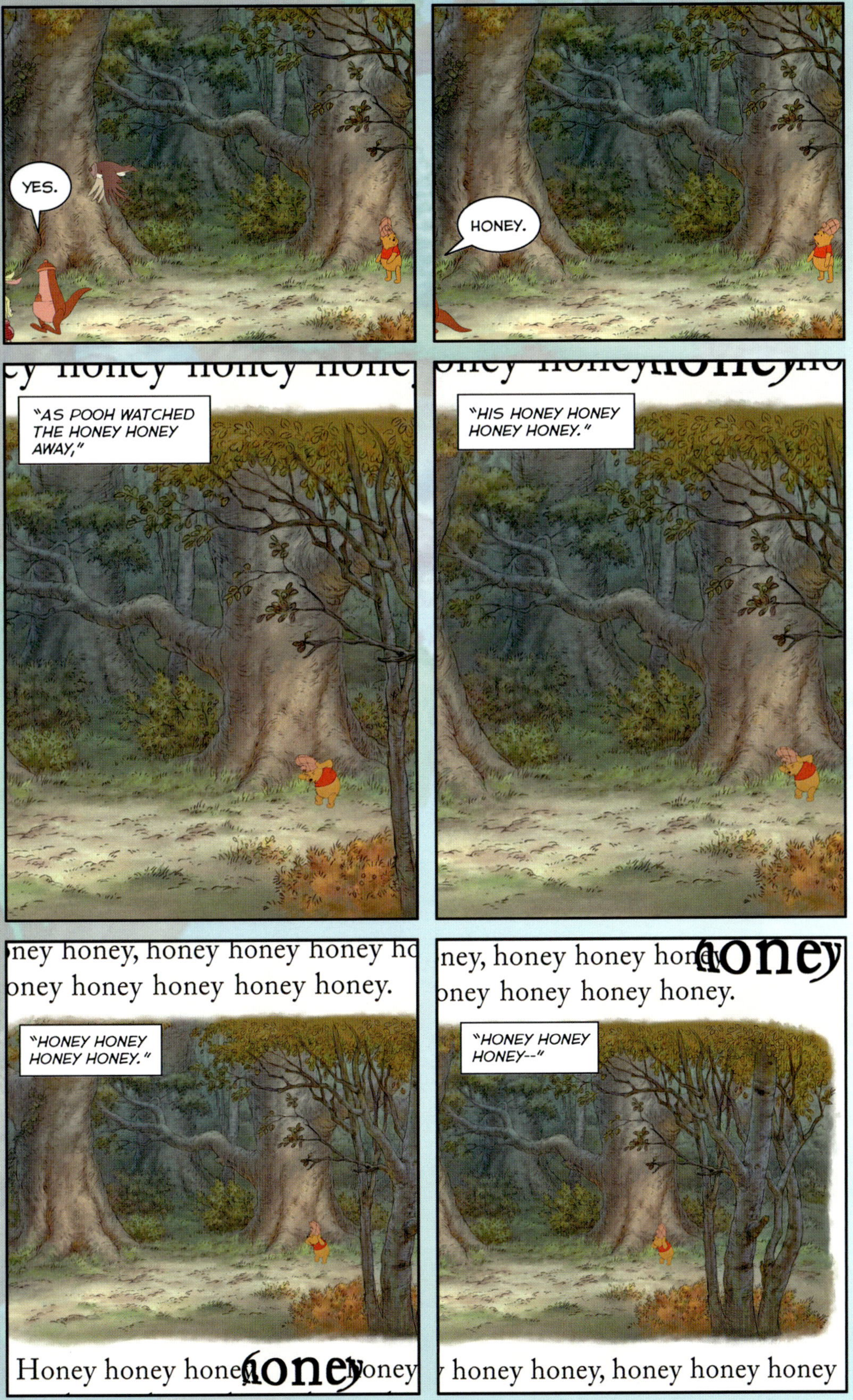
YES.
HONEY.
"AS POOH WATCHED THE HONEY HONEY AWAY,"
"HIS HONEY HONEY HONEY HONEY."
ney honey, honey honey honey ho
oney honey honey honey honey.
"HONEY HONEY HONEY HONEY."
Honey honey honey honey honey
ney, honey honey honey honey
oney honey honey honey.
"HONEY HONEY HONEY--"
y honey honey, honey honey honey

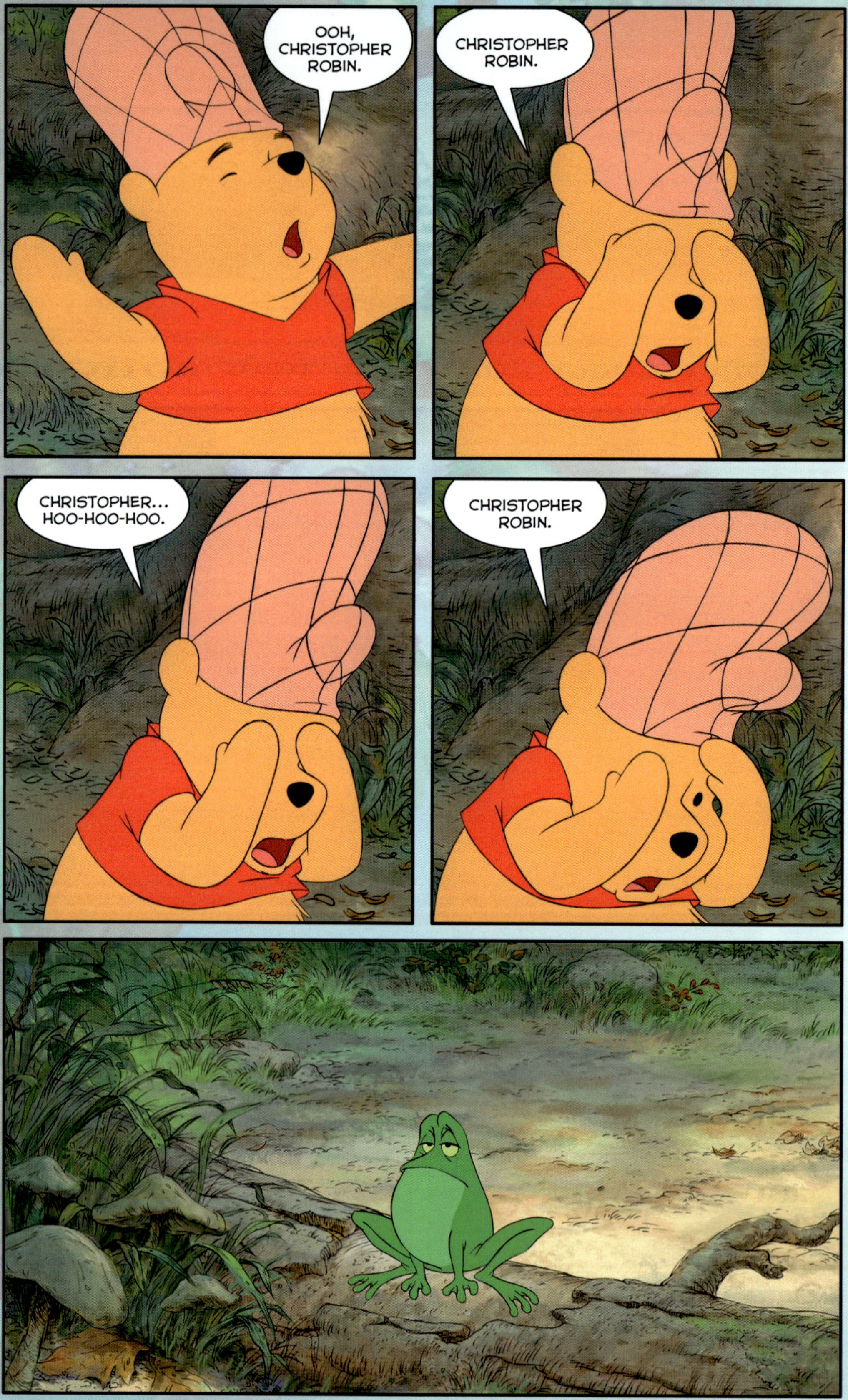
OOH, CHRISTOPHER ROBIN.
CHRISTOPHER ROBIN.
CHRISTOPHER... HOO-HOO-HOO.
CHRISTOPHER ROBIN.

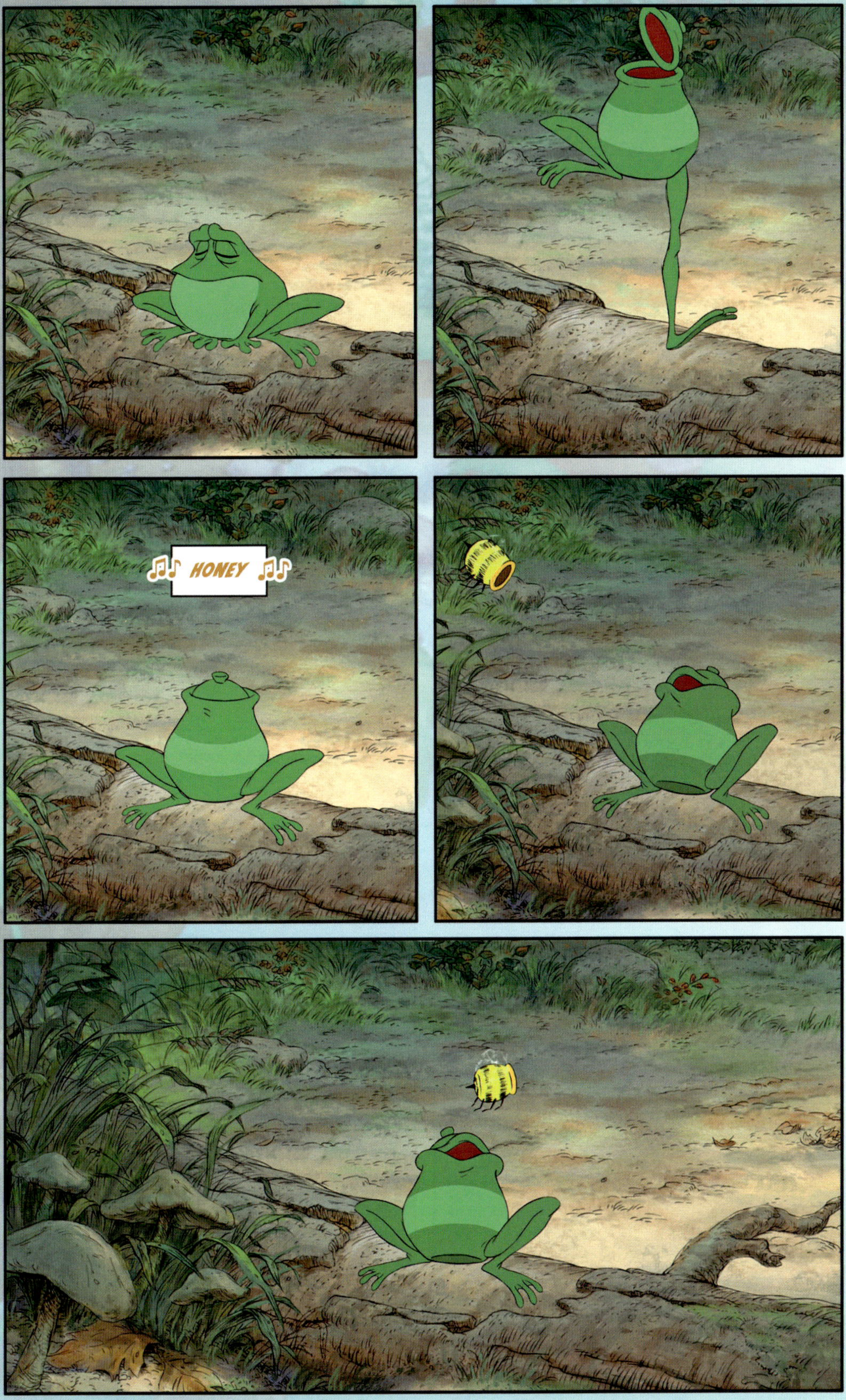
HONEY

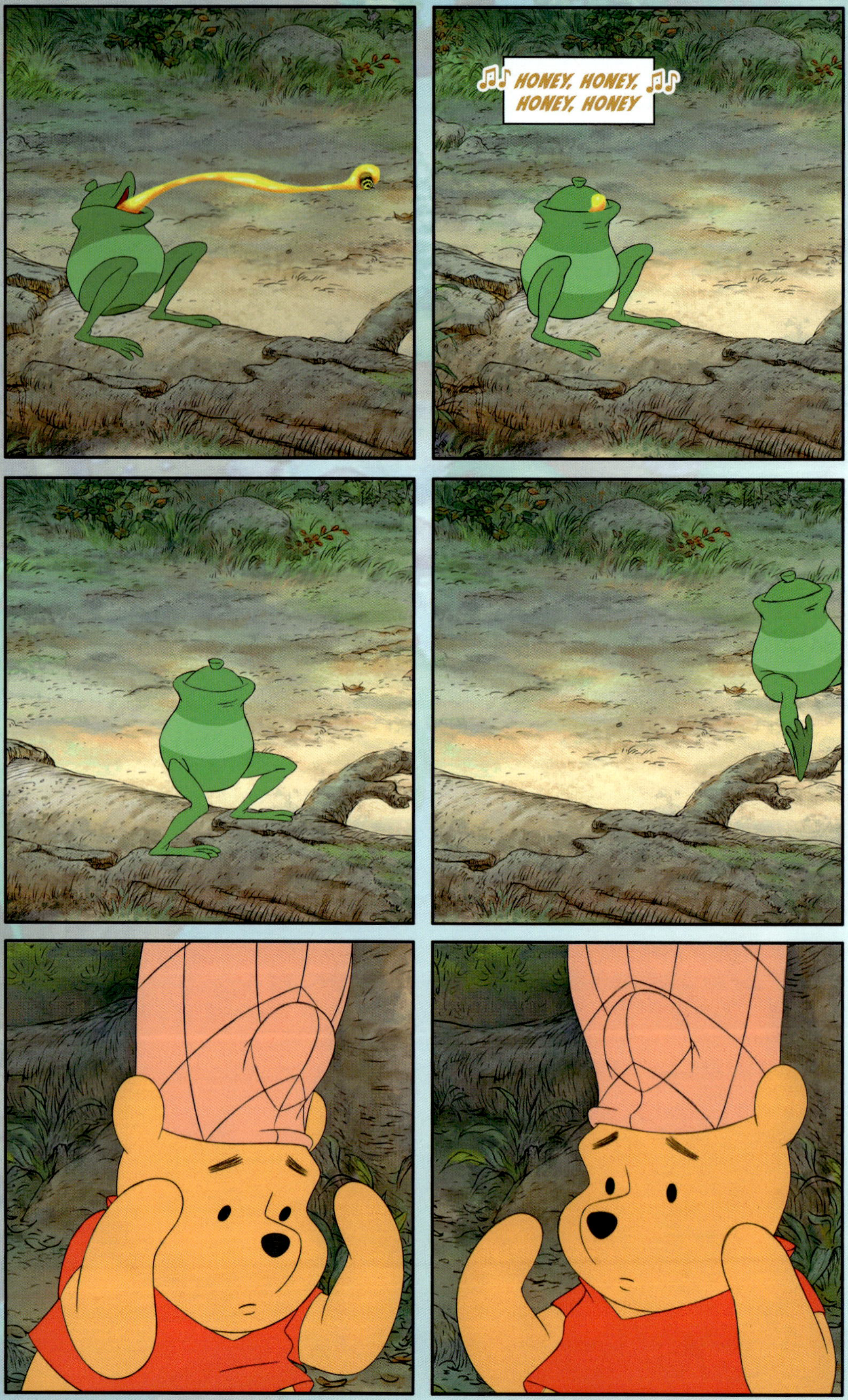
♫♪ HONEY, HONEY, ♫♪
HONEY, HONEY

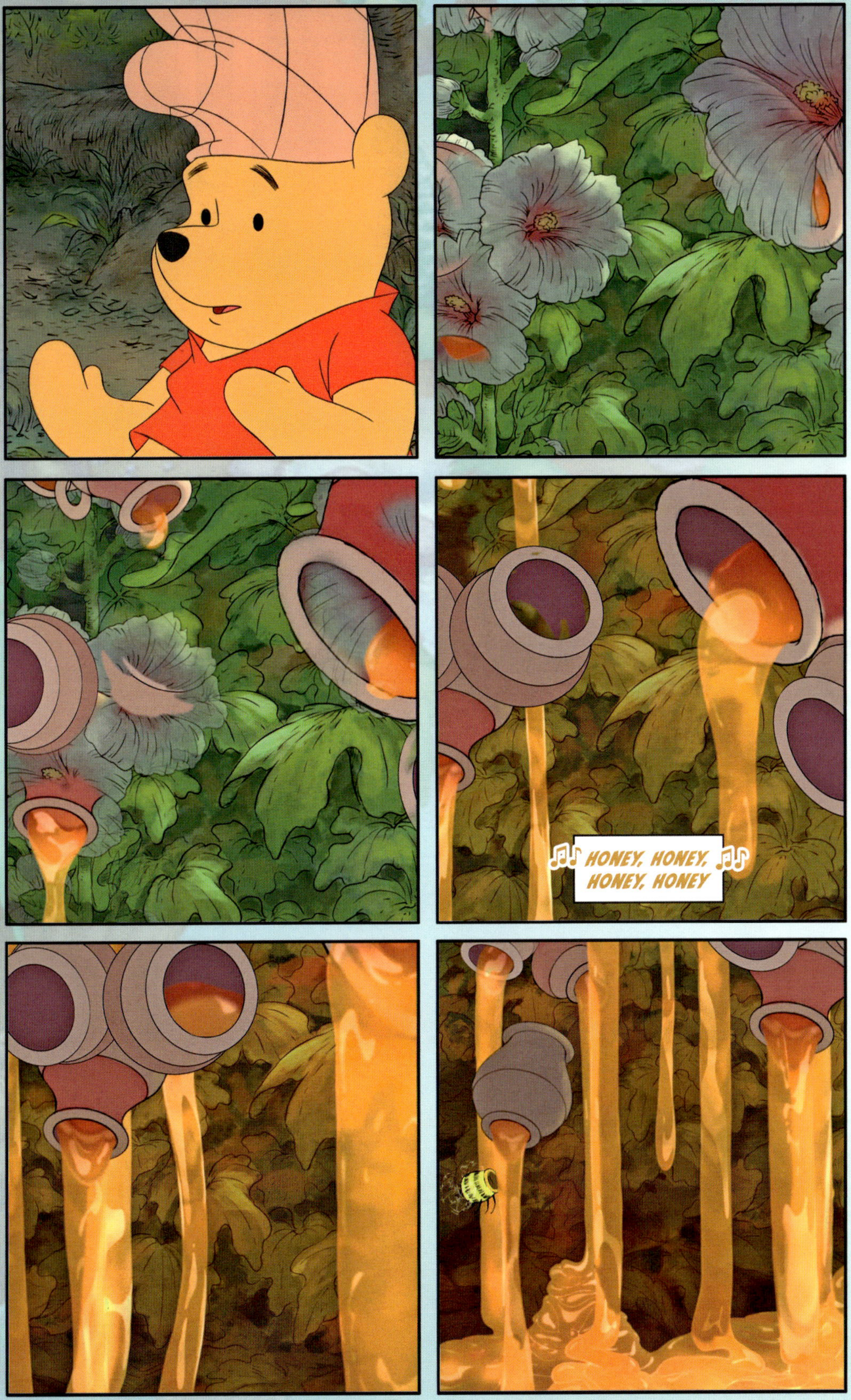
HONEY, HONEY,
HONEY, HONEY

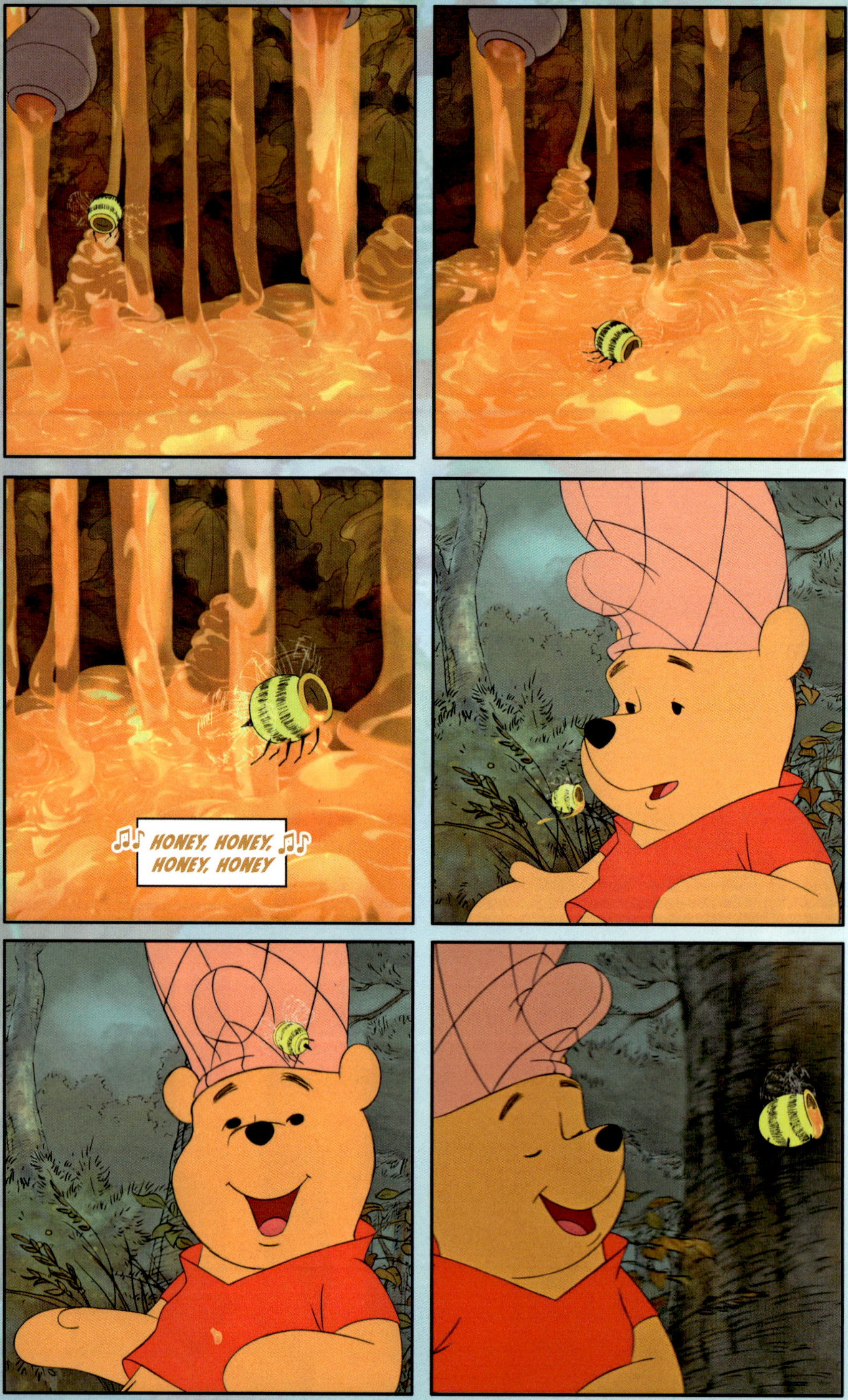

♫♪ HONEY, HONEY, ♫♪
HONEY, HONEY

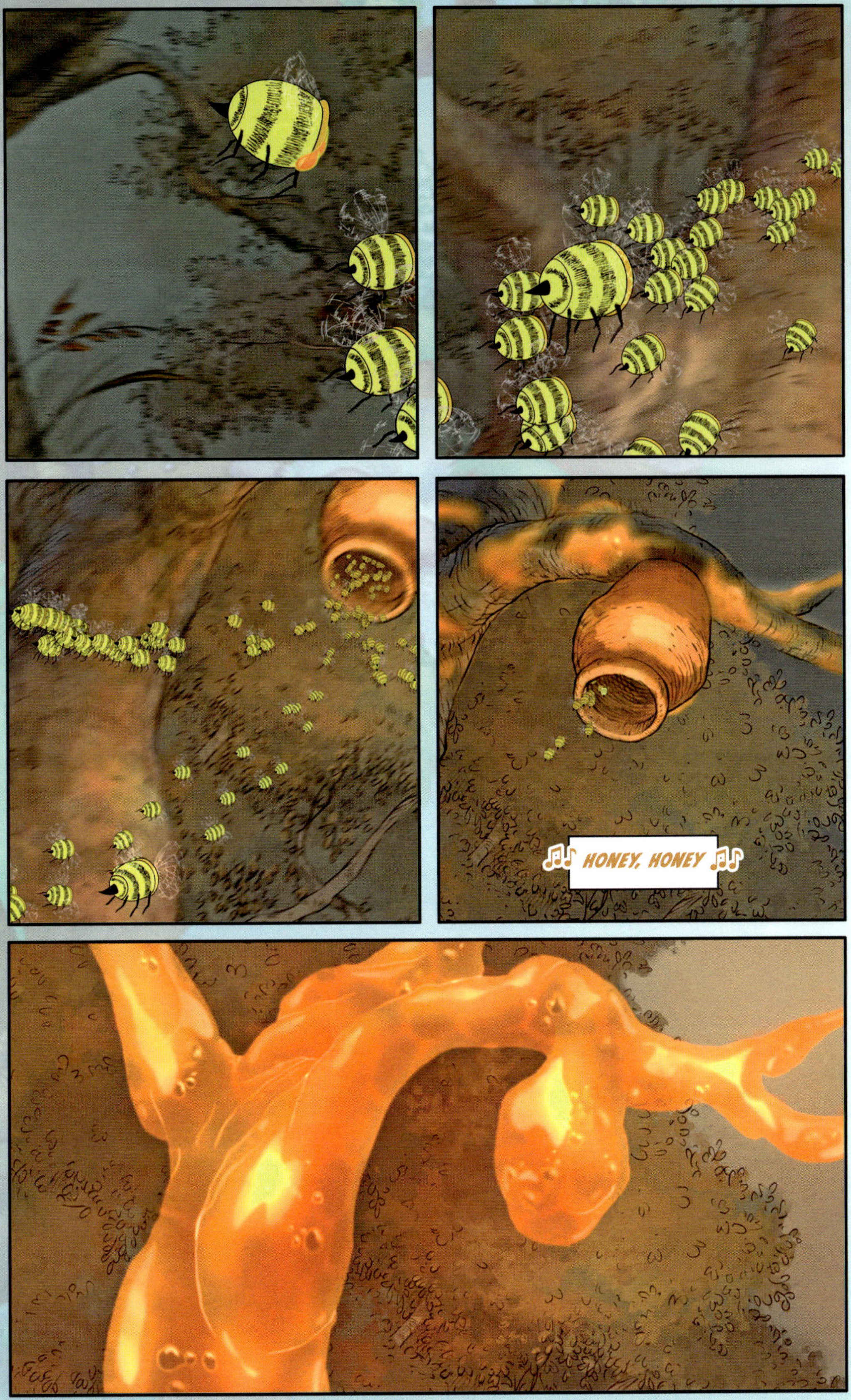
♫♪ HONEY, HONEY ♫♪

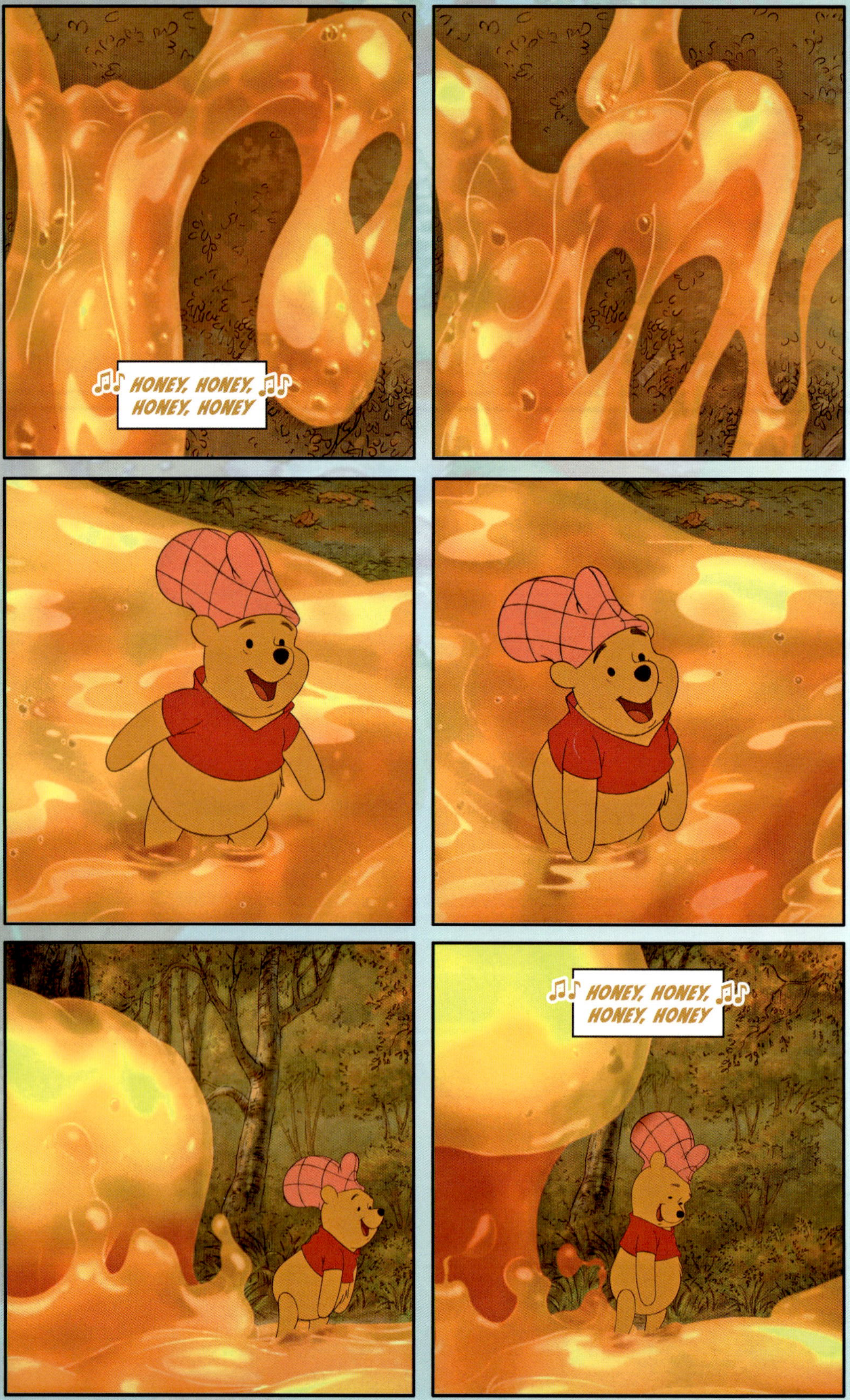
HONEY, HONEY,
HONEY, HONEY
HONEY, HONEY,
HONEY, HONEY

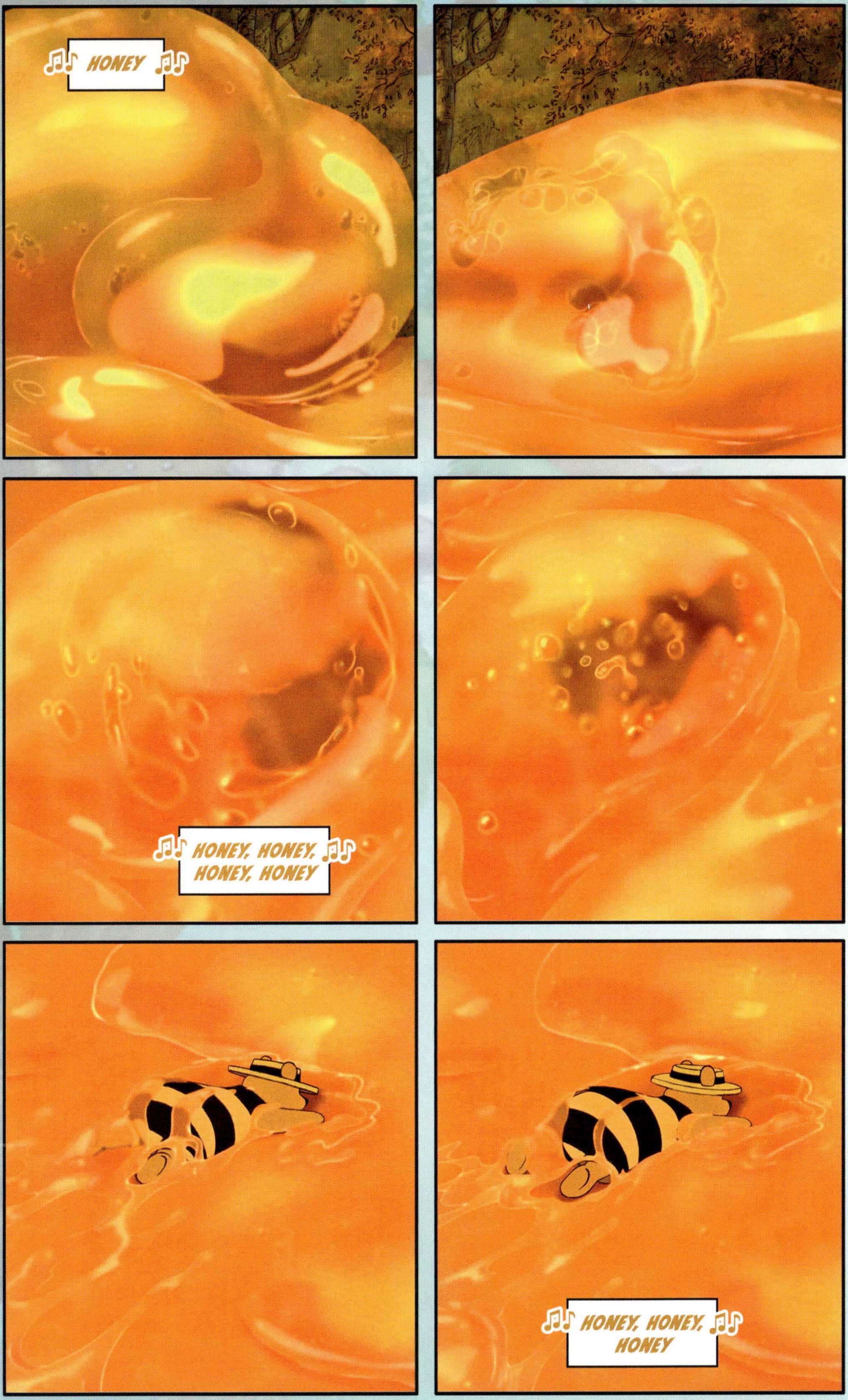
HONEY
HONEY, HONEY, HONEY, HONEY
HONEY, HONEY, HONEY

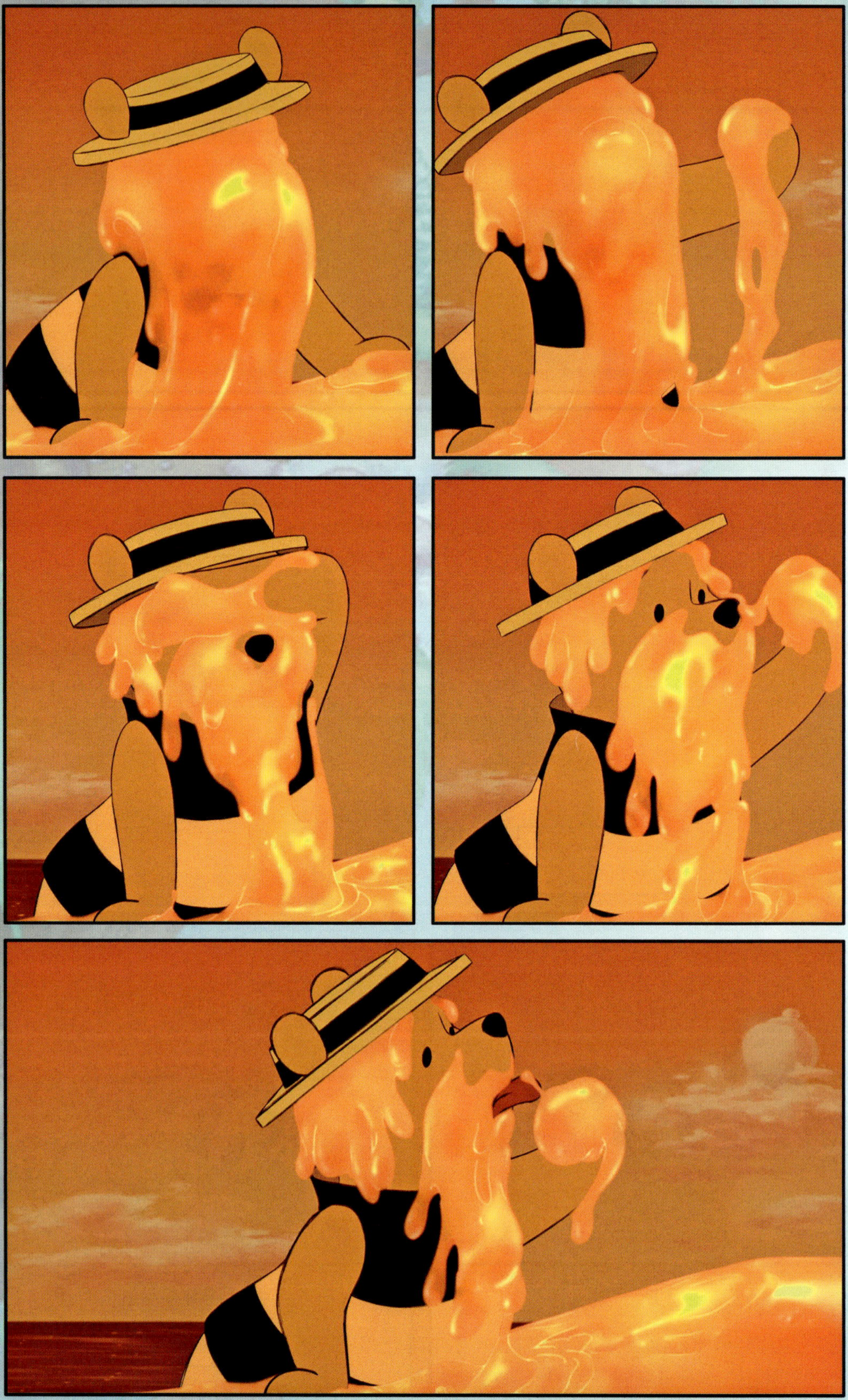

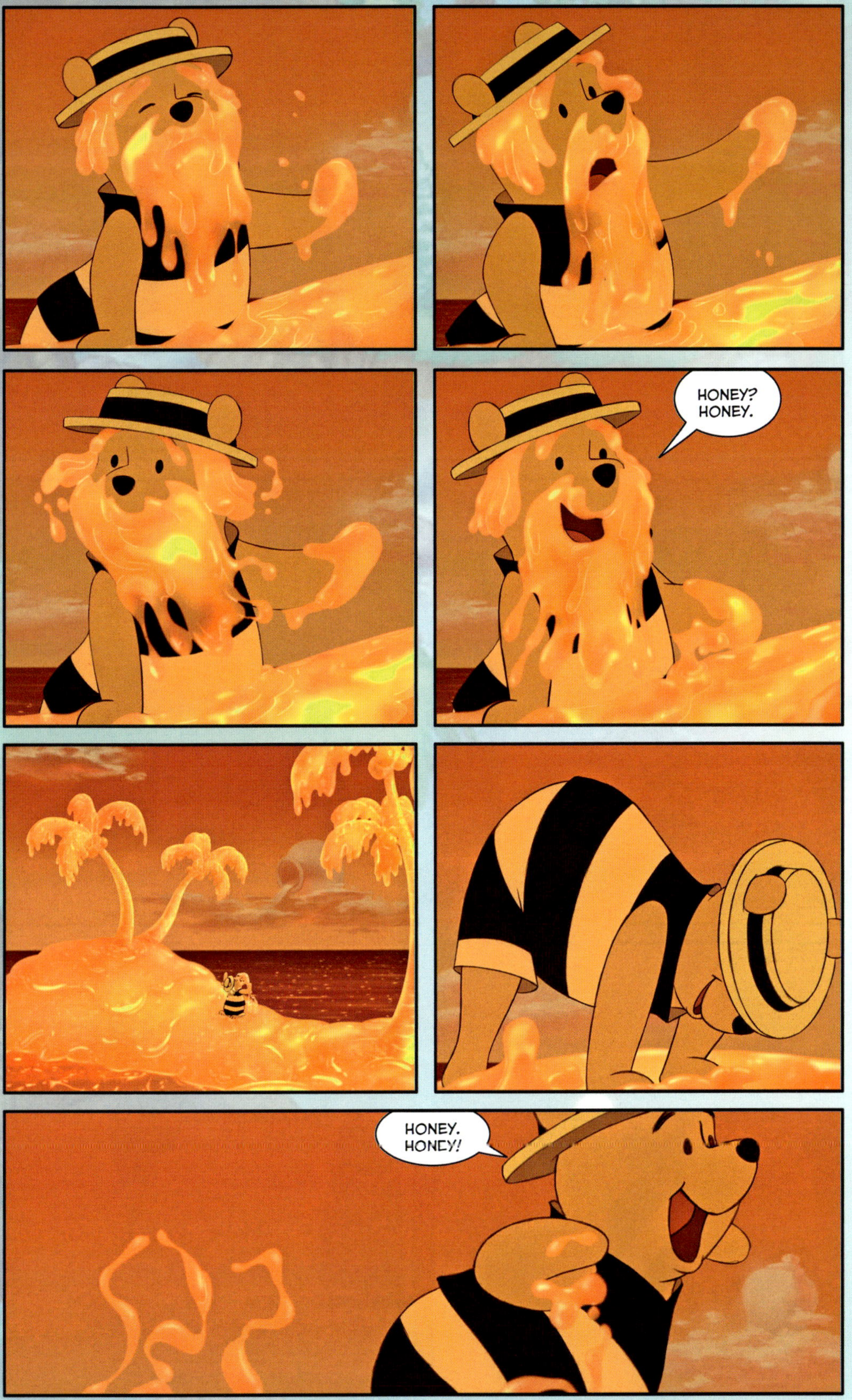
HONEY? HONEY.
HONEY. HONEY!

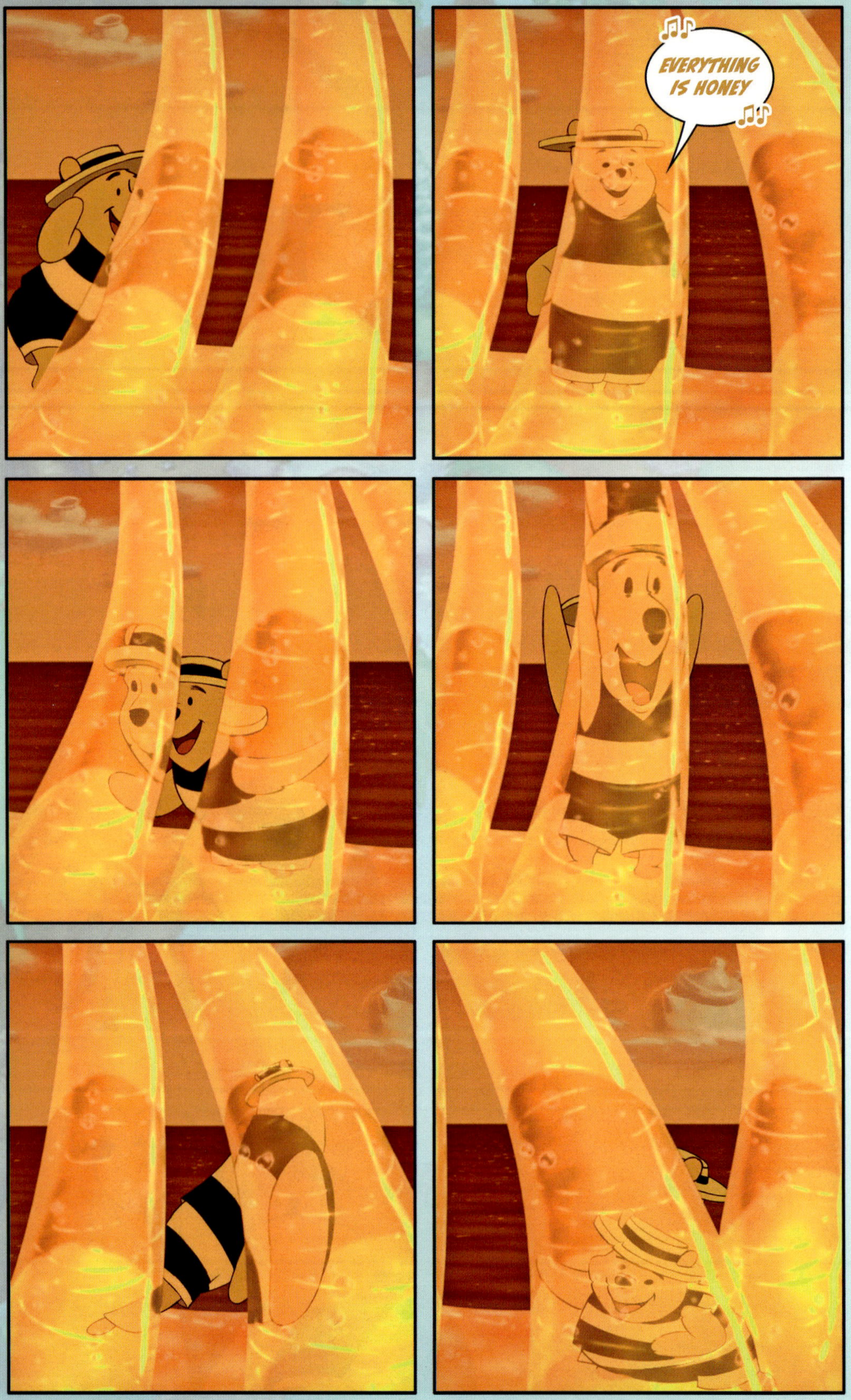
EVERYTHING IS HONEY

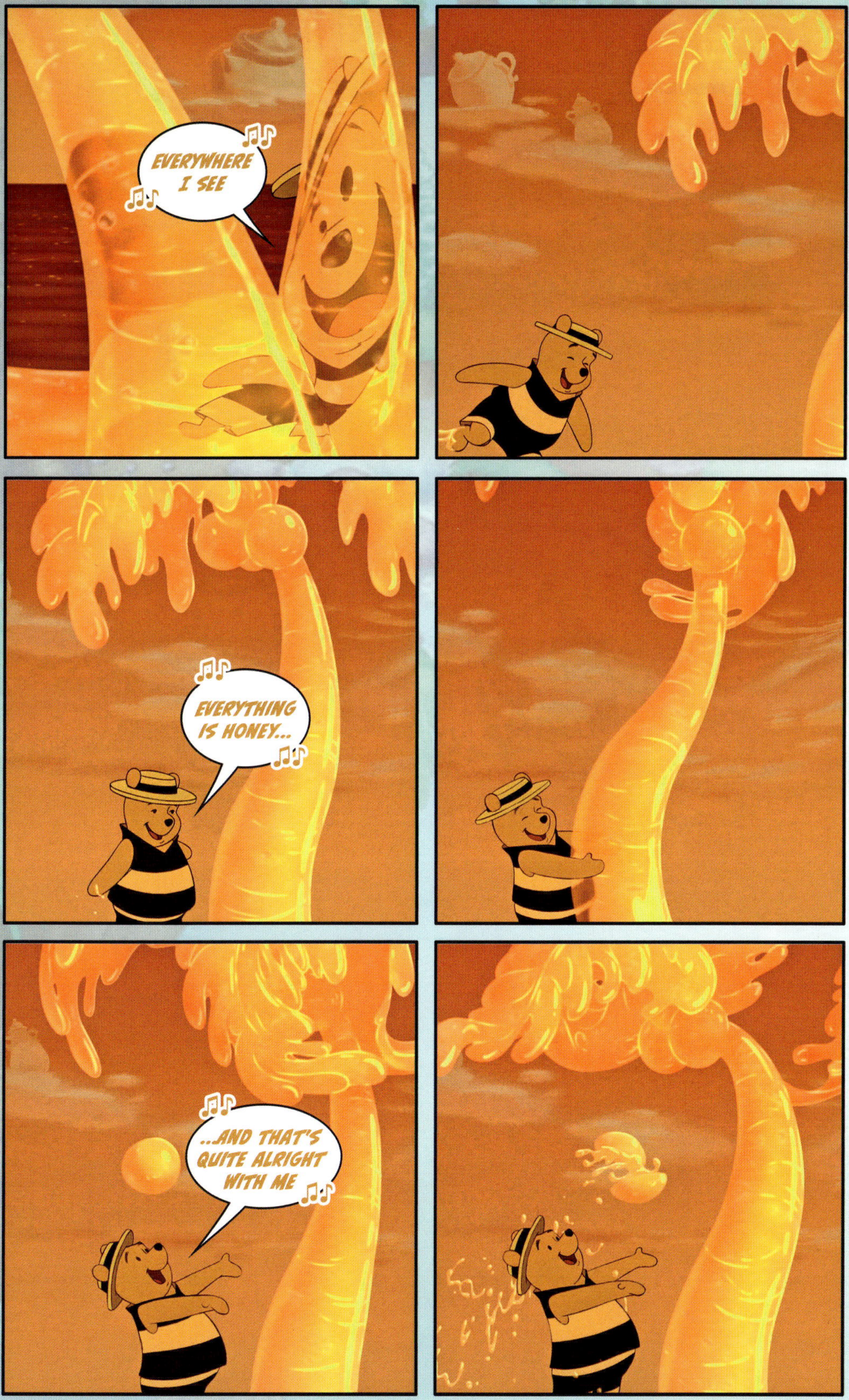
EVERYWHERE I SEE
EVERYTHING IS HONEY...
...AND THAT'S QUITE ALRIGHT WITH ME

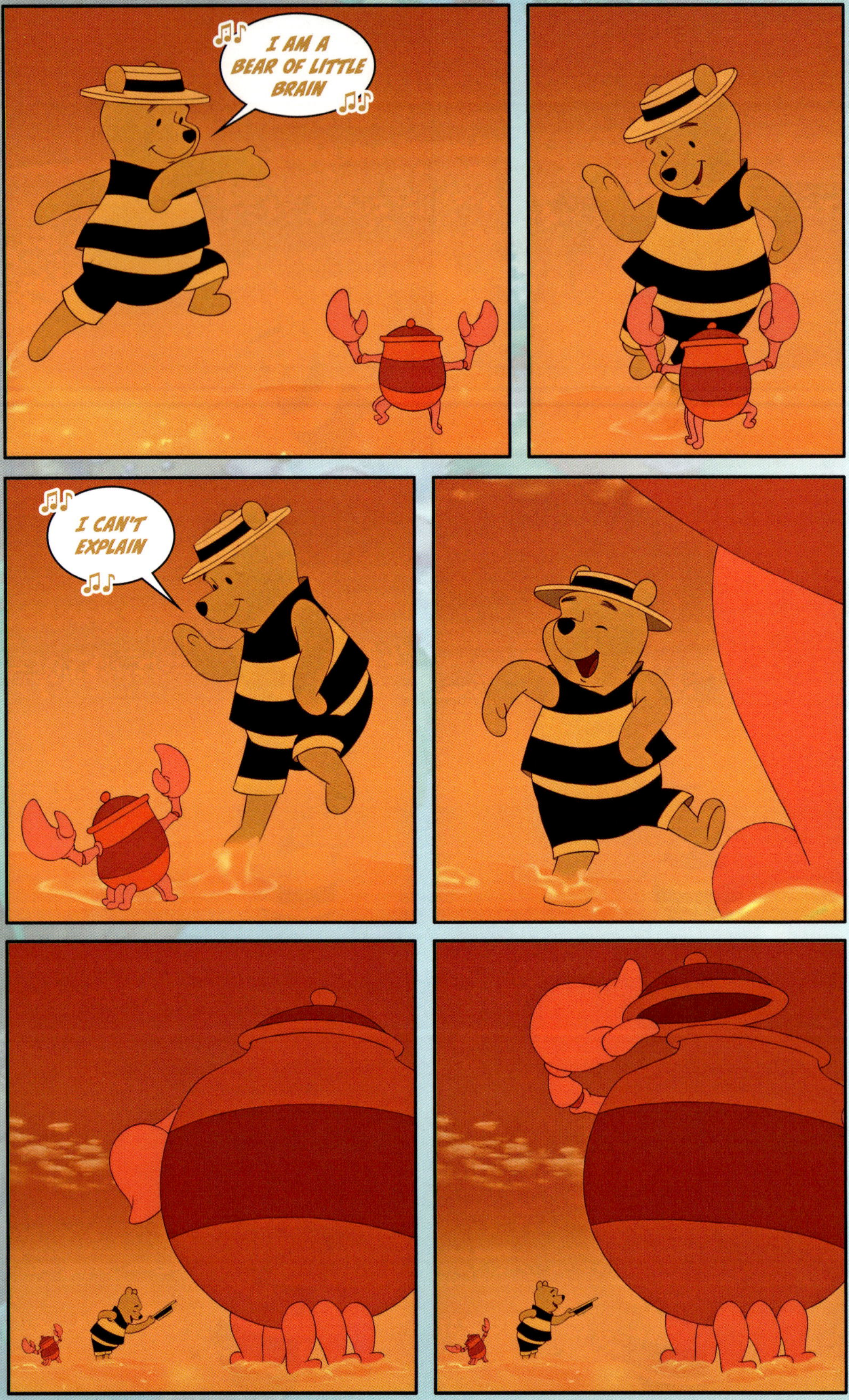
I AM A BEAR OF LITTLE BRAIN
I CAN'T EXPLAIN

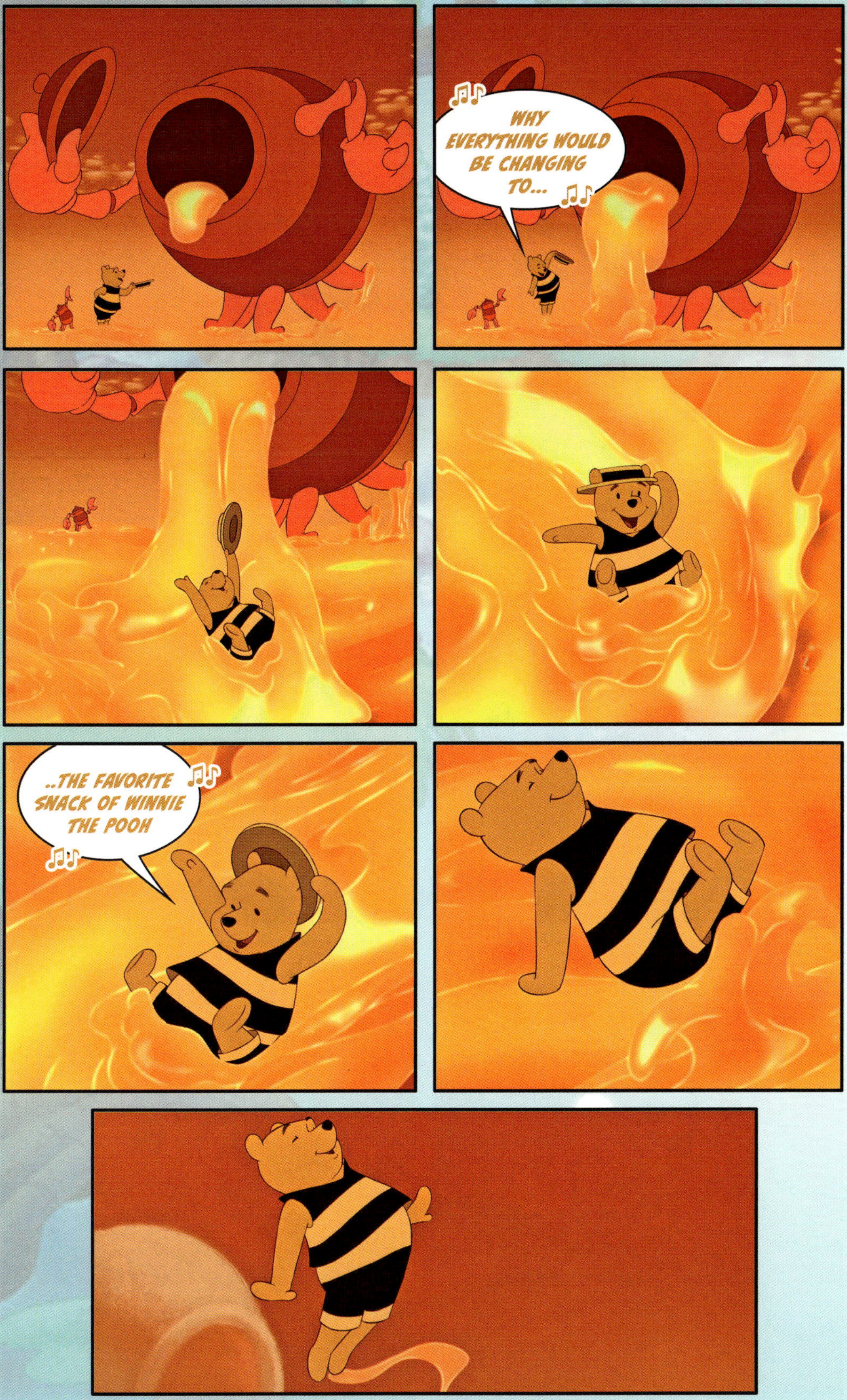
WHY EVERYTHING WOULD BE CHANGING TO...
..THE FAVORITE SNACK OF WINNIE THE POOH

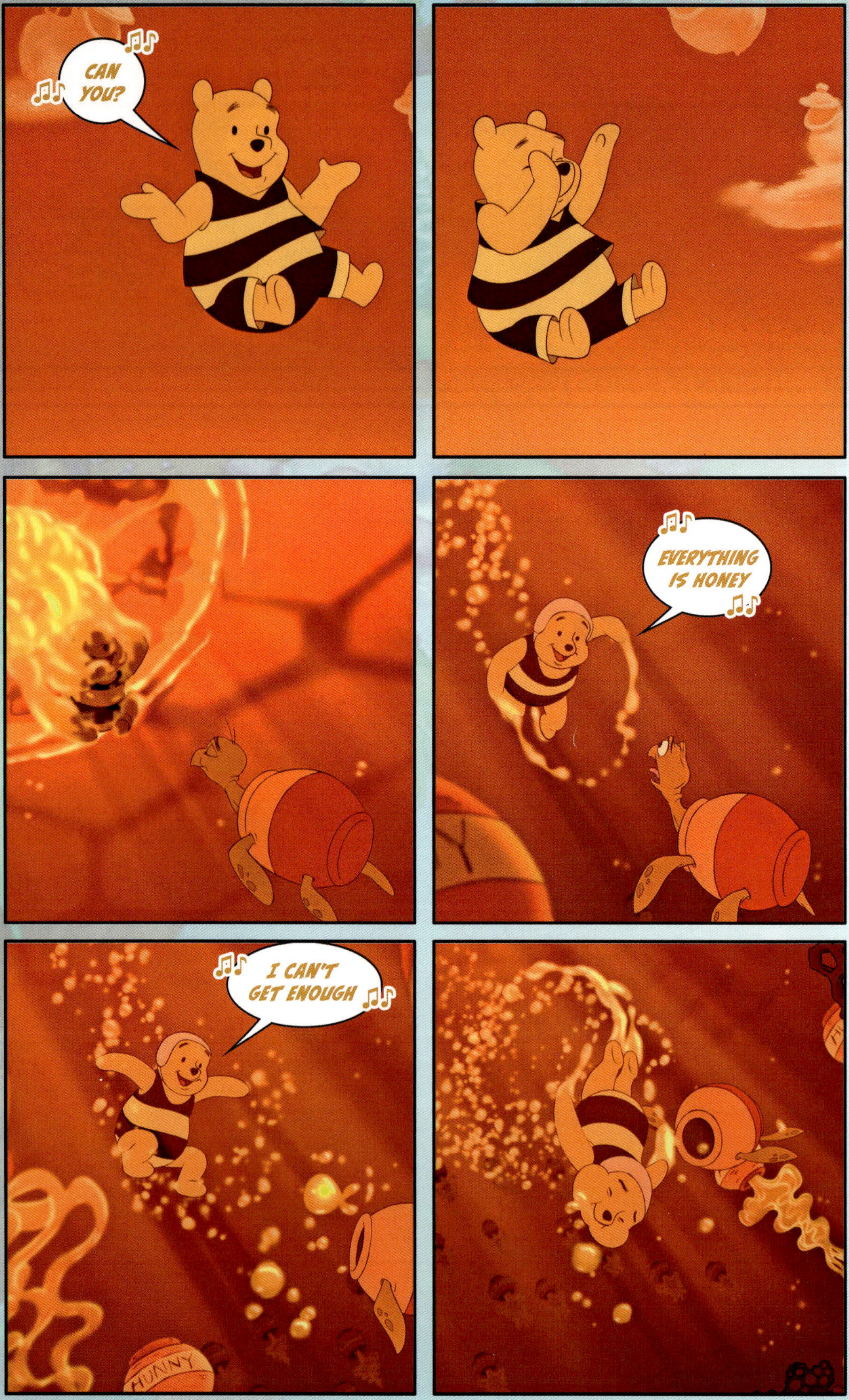
CAN YOU?
EVERYTHING IS HONEY
I CAN'T GET ENOUGH
HUNNY

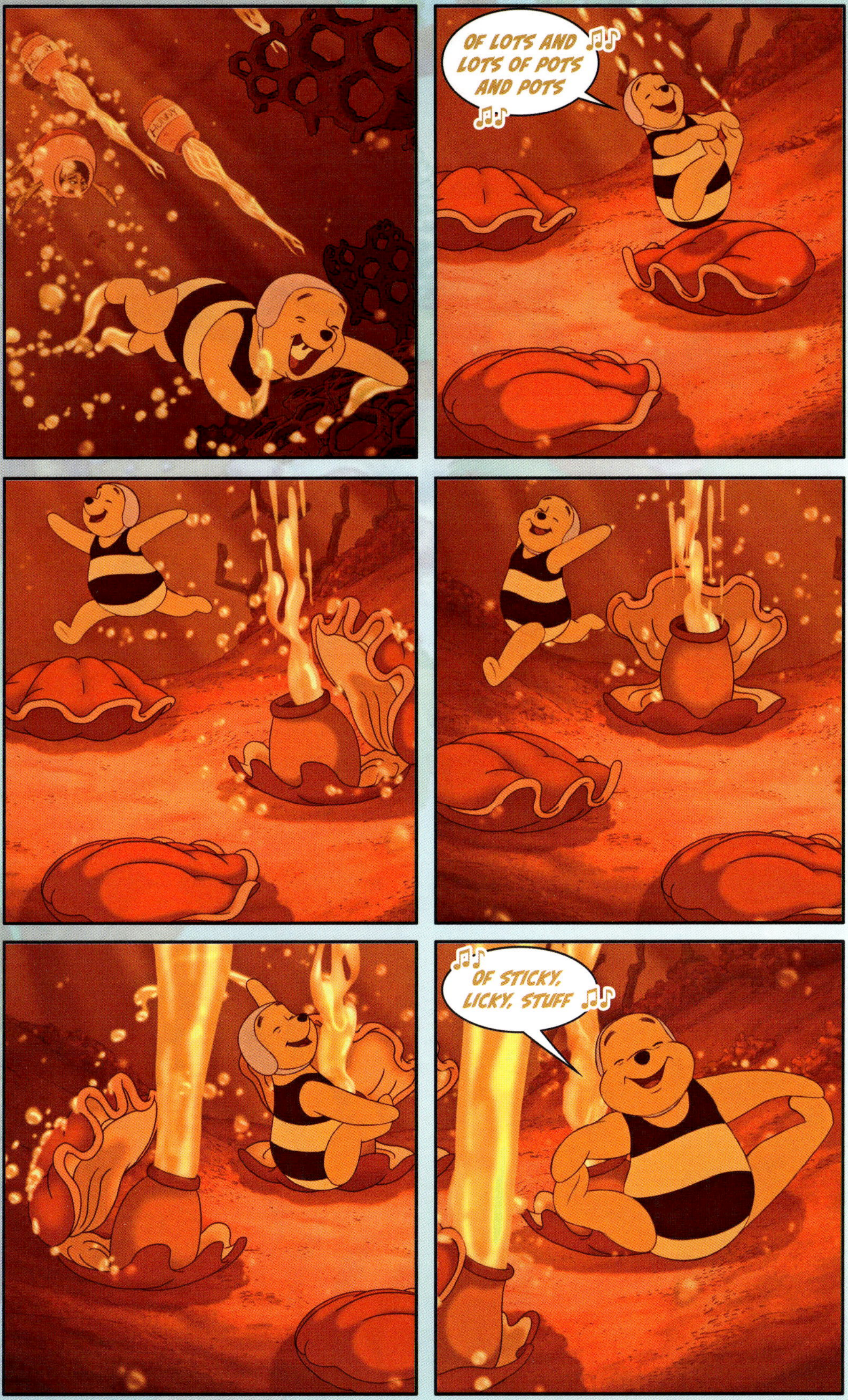
OF LOTS AND LOTS OF POTS AND POTS
OF STICKY, LICKY, STUFF

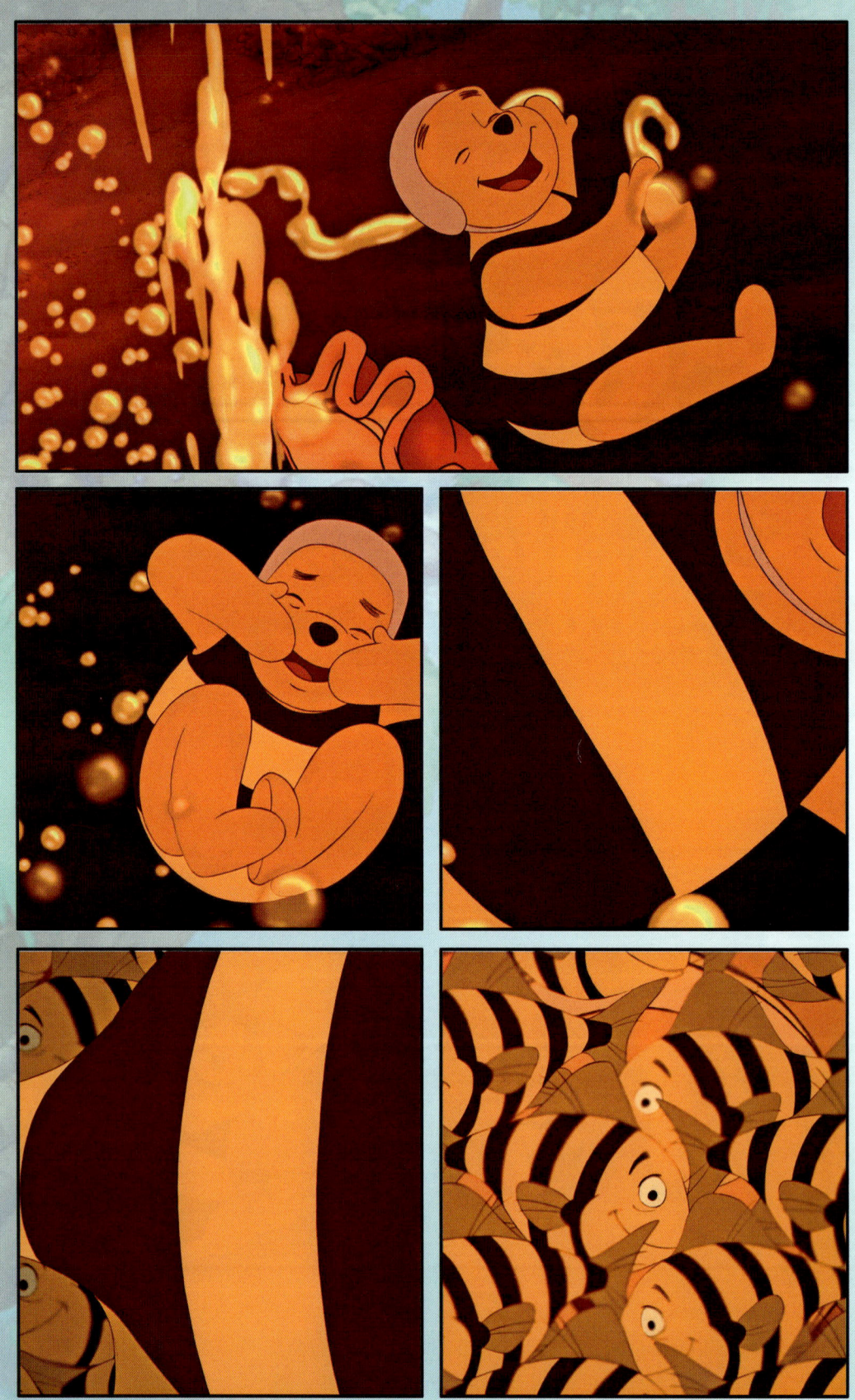

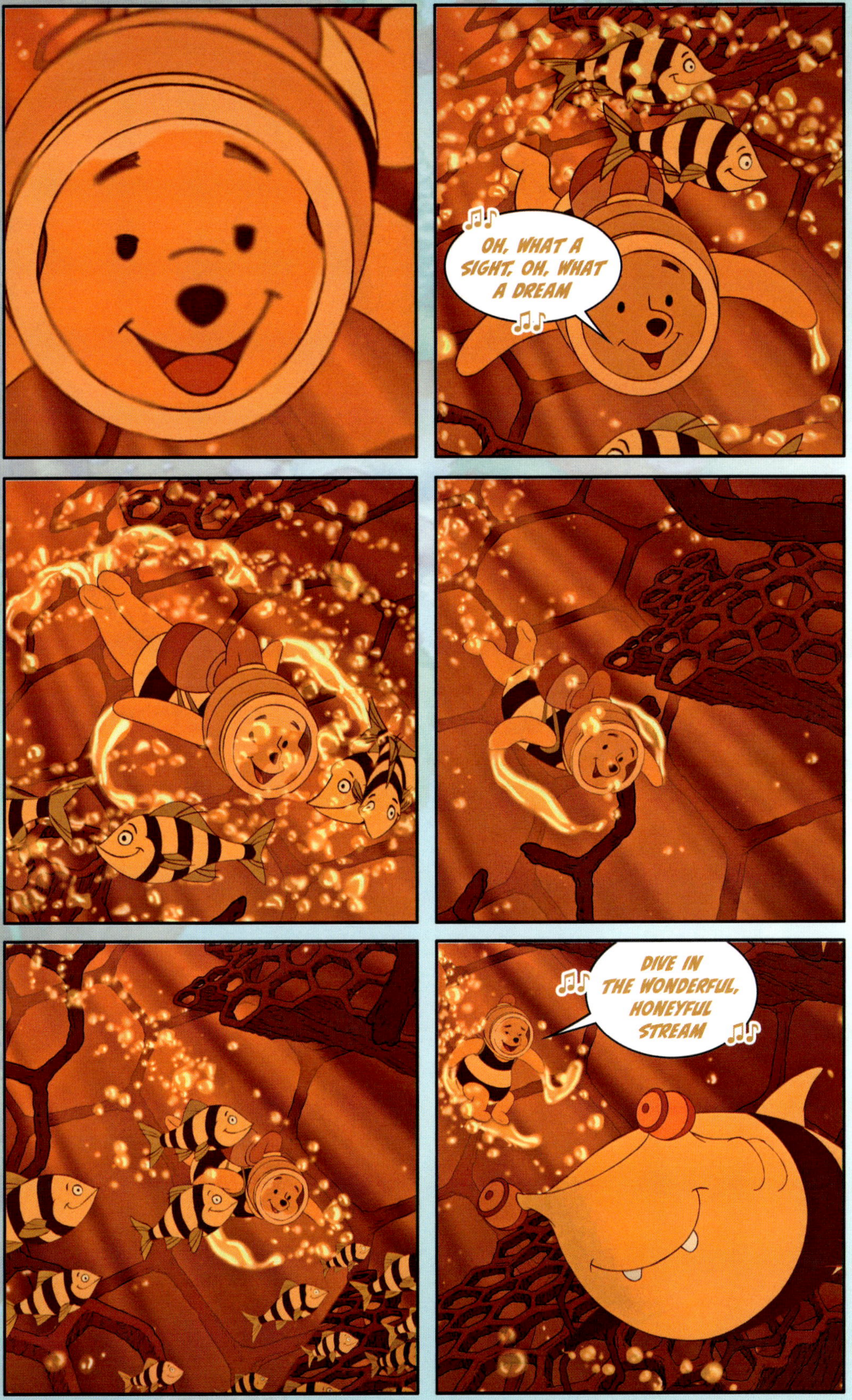
OH, WHAT A SIGHT, OH, WHAT A DREAM
DIVE IN THE WONDERFUL, HONEYFUL STREAM

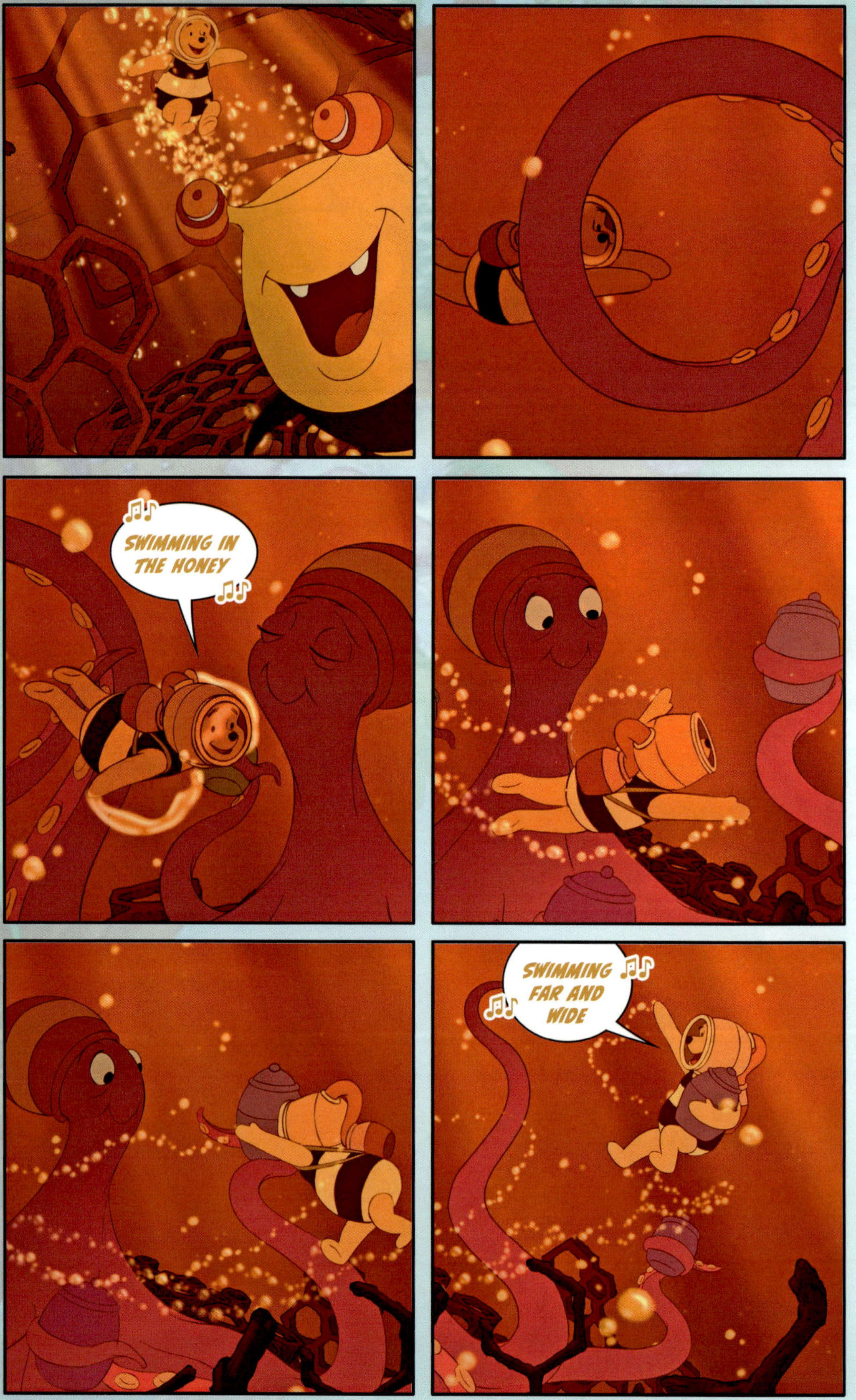
SWIMMING IN THE HONEY
SWIMMING FAR AND WIDE

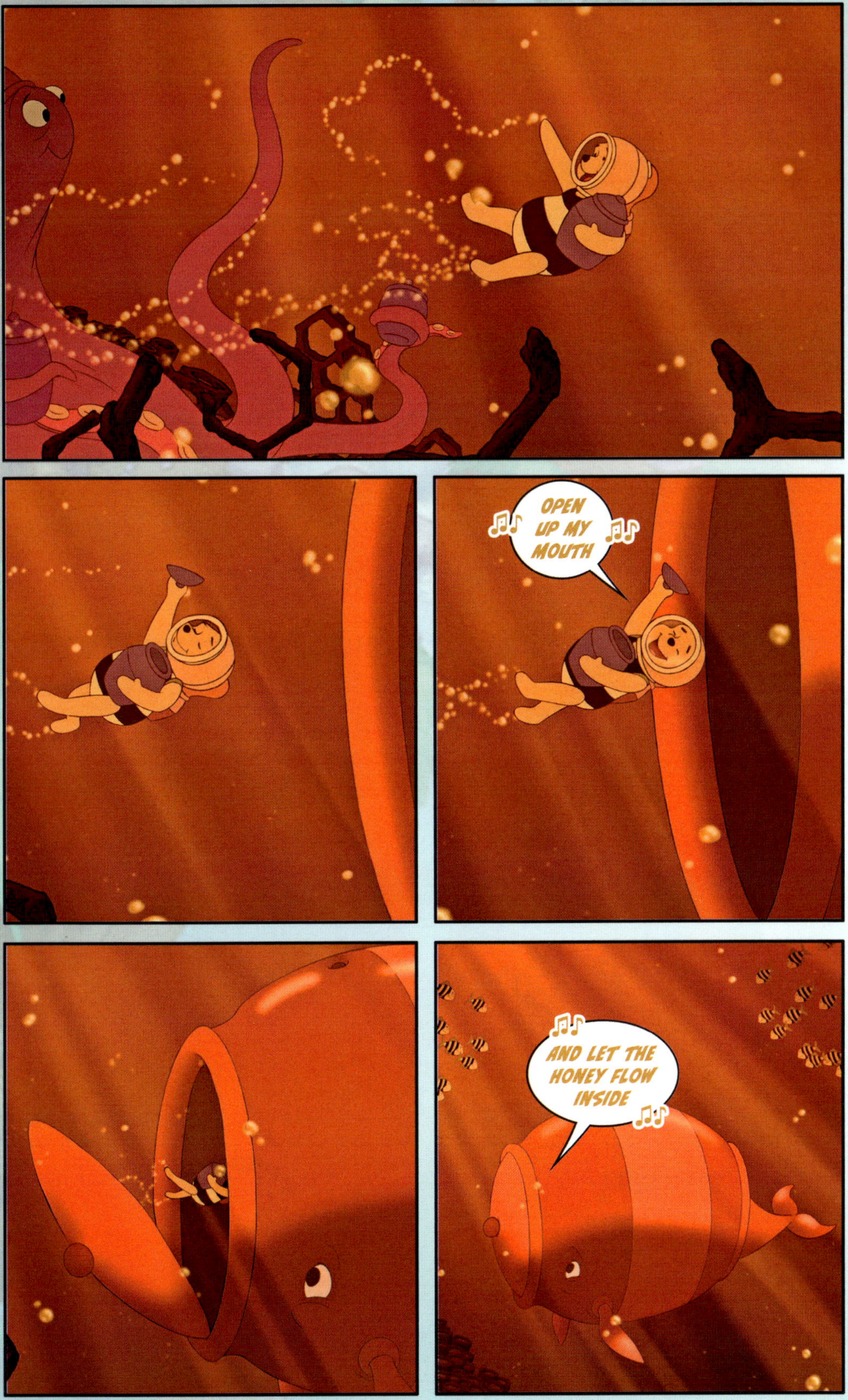
OPEN UP MY MOUTH
AND LET THE HONEY FLOW INSIDE

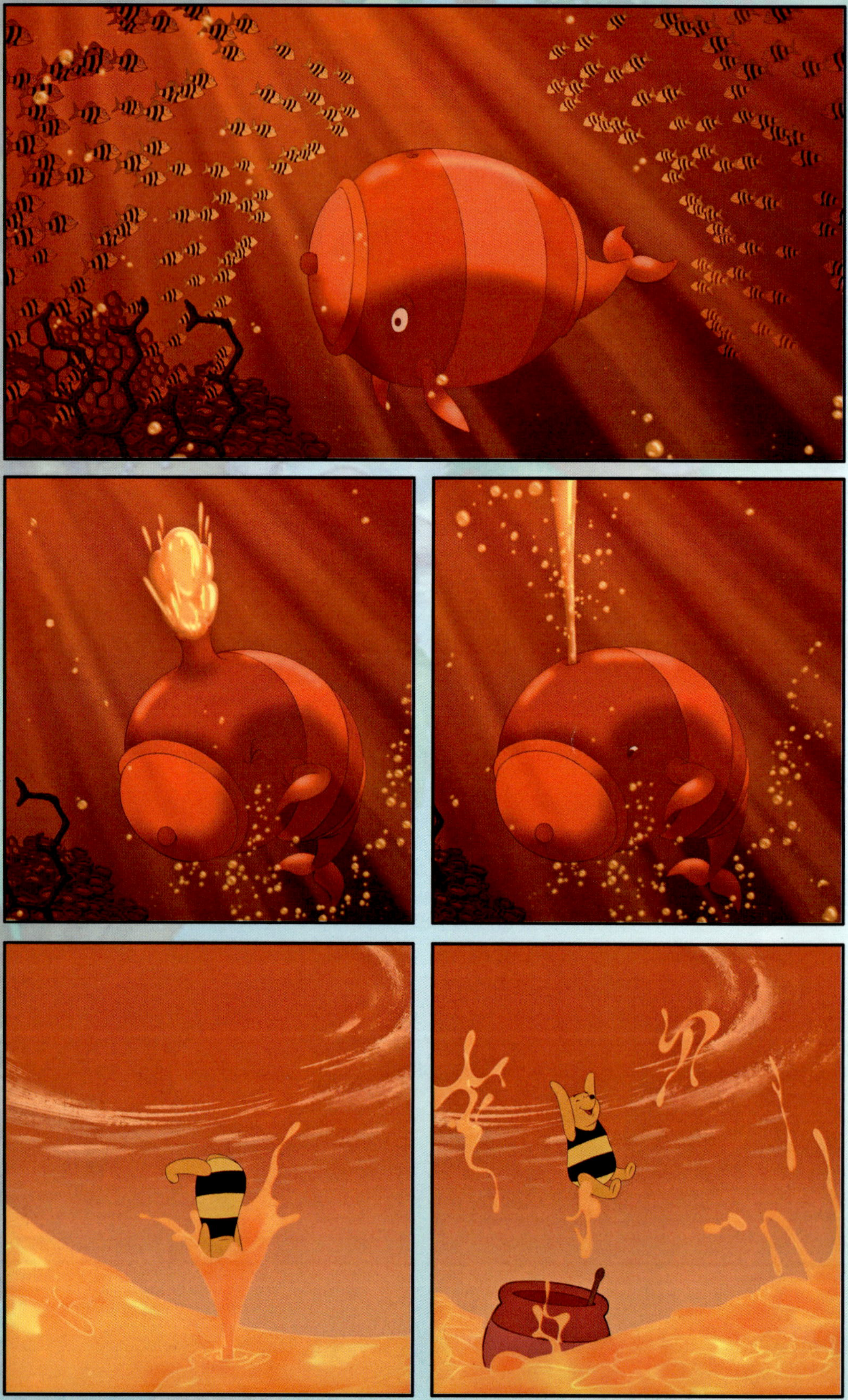

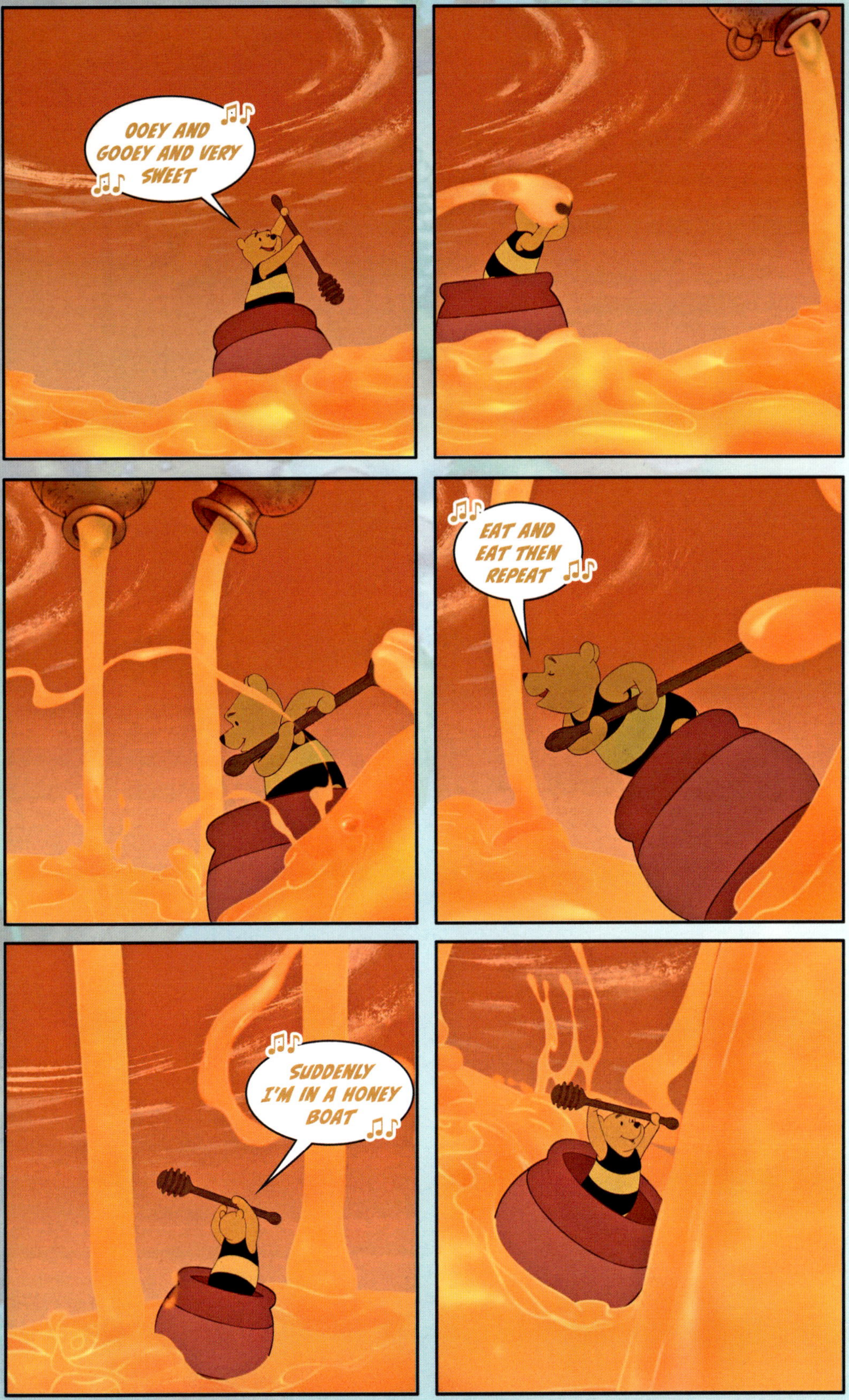
OOEY AND GOOEY AND VERY SWEET
EAT AND EAT THEN REPEAT
SUDDENLY I'M IN A HONEY BOAT

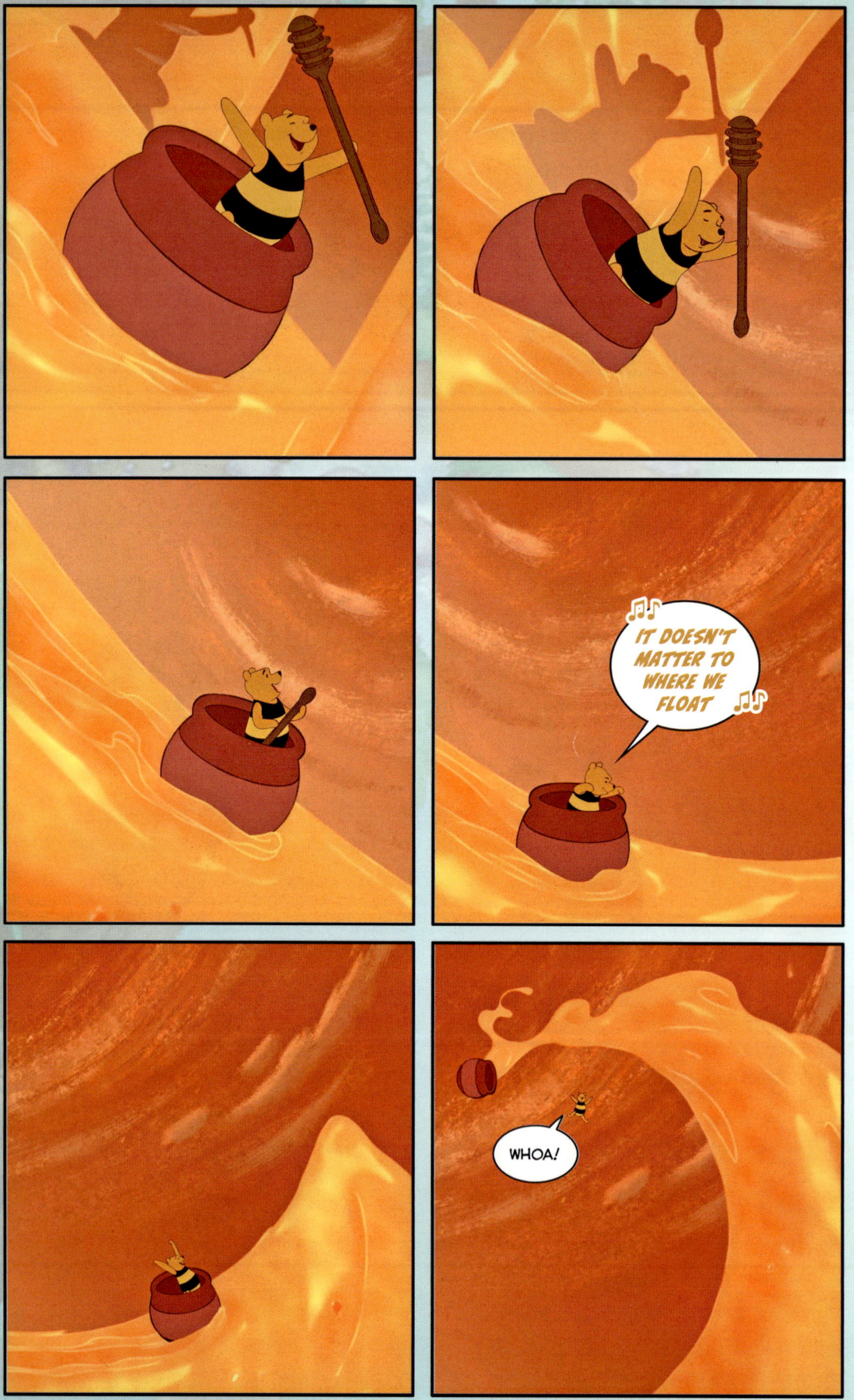
IT DOESN'T MATTER TO WHERE WE FLOAT
WHOA!

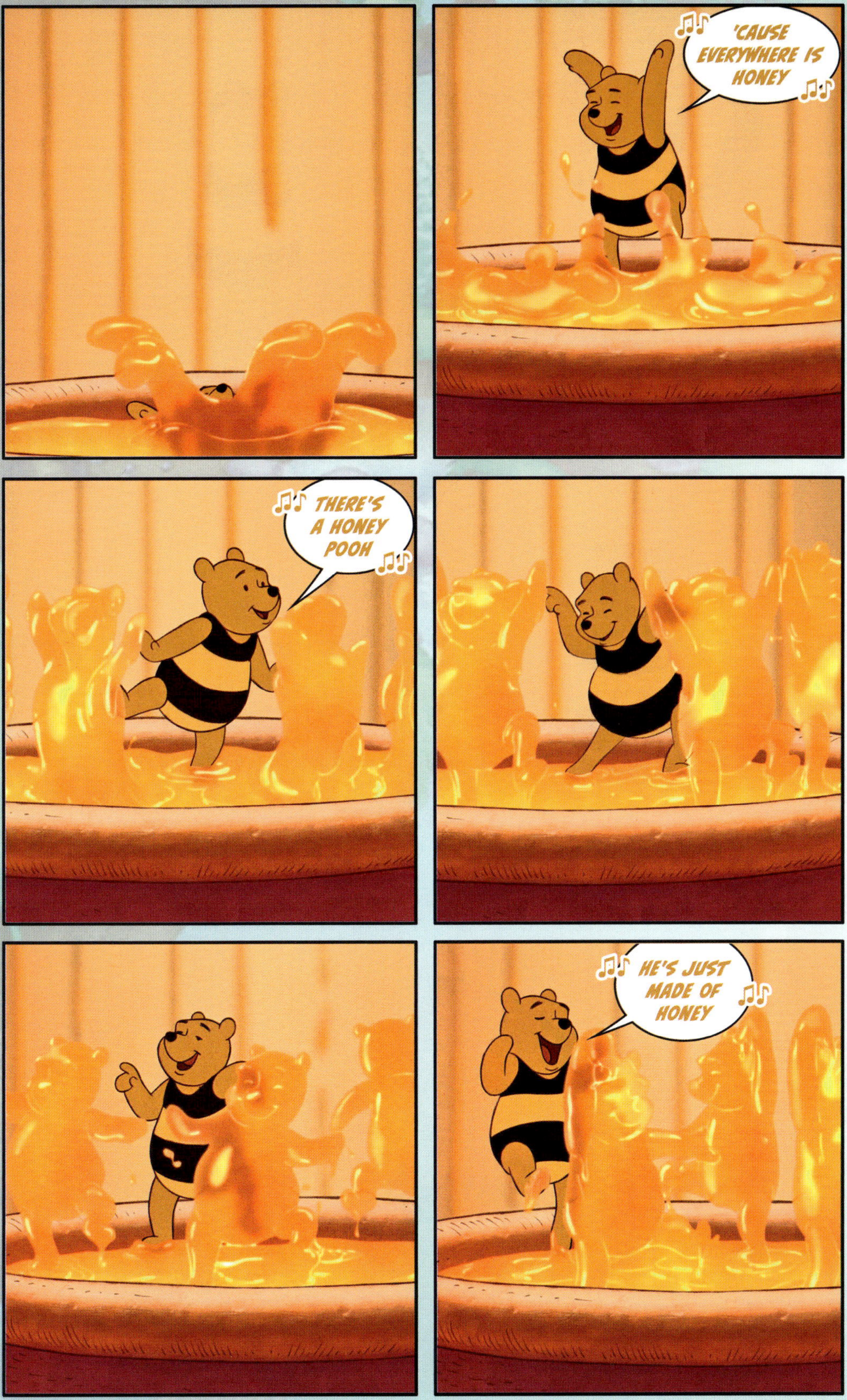
'CAUSE EVERYWHERE IS HONEY
THERE'S A HONEY POOH
HE'S JUST MADE OF HONEY

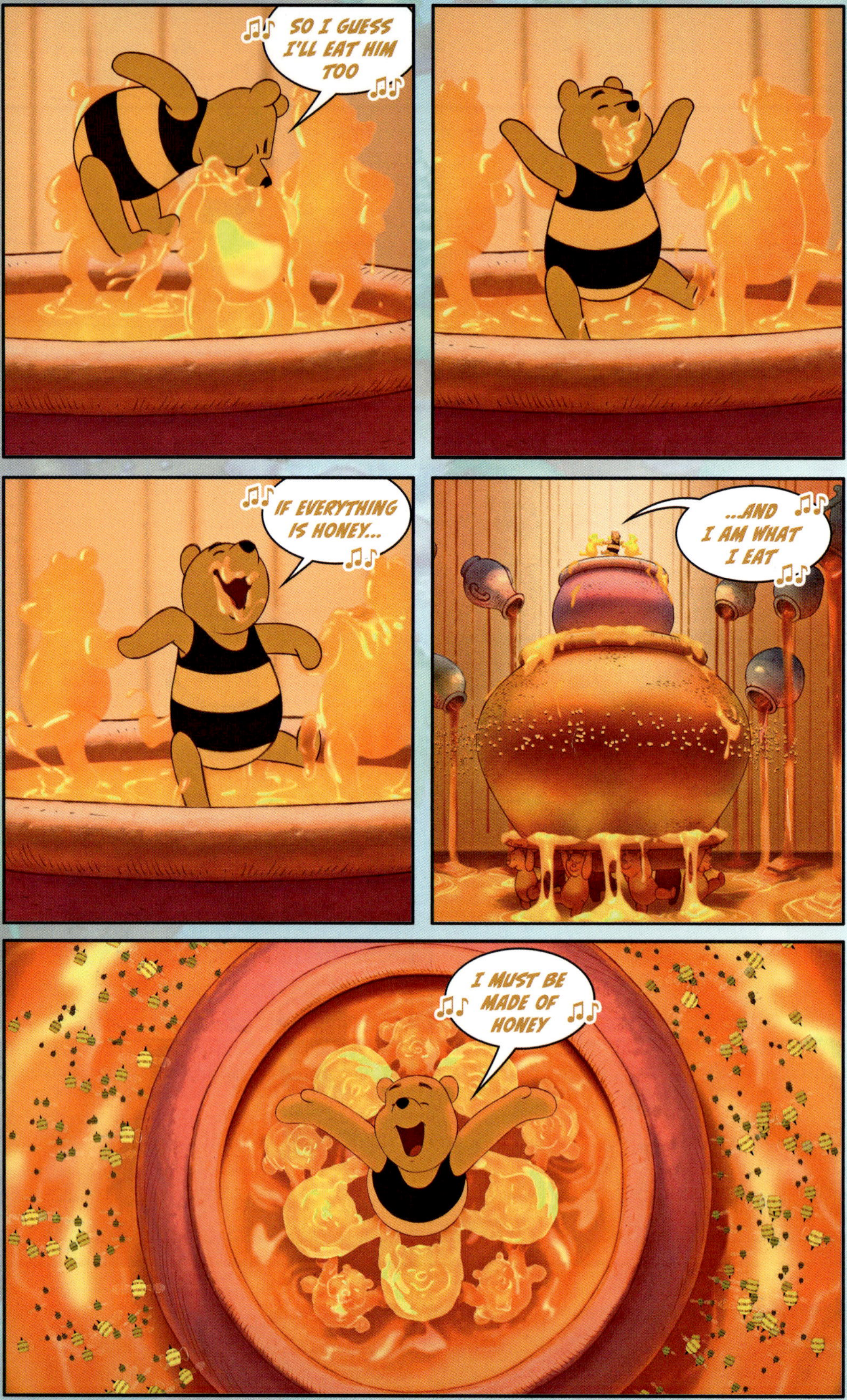
SO I GUESS I'LL EAT HIM TOO
IF EVERYTHING IS HONEY...
...AND I AM WHAT I EAT
I MUST BE MADE OF HONEY

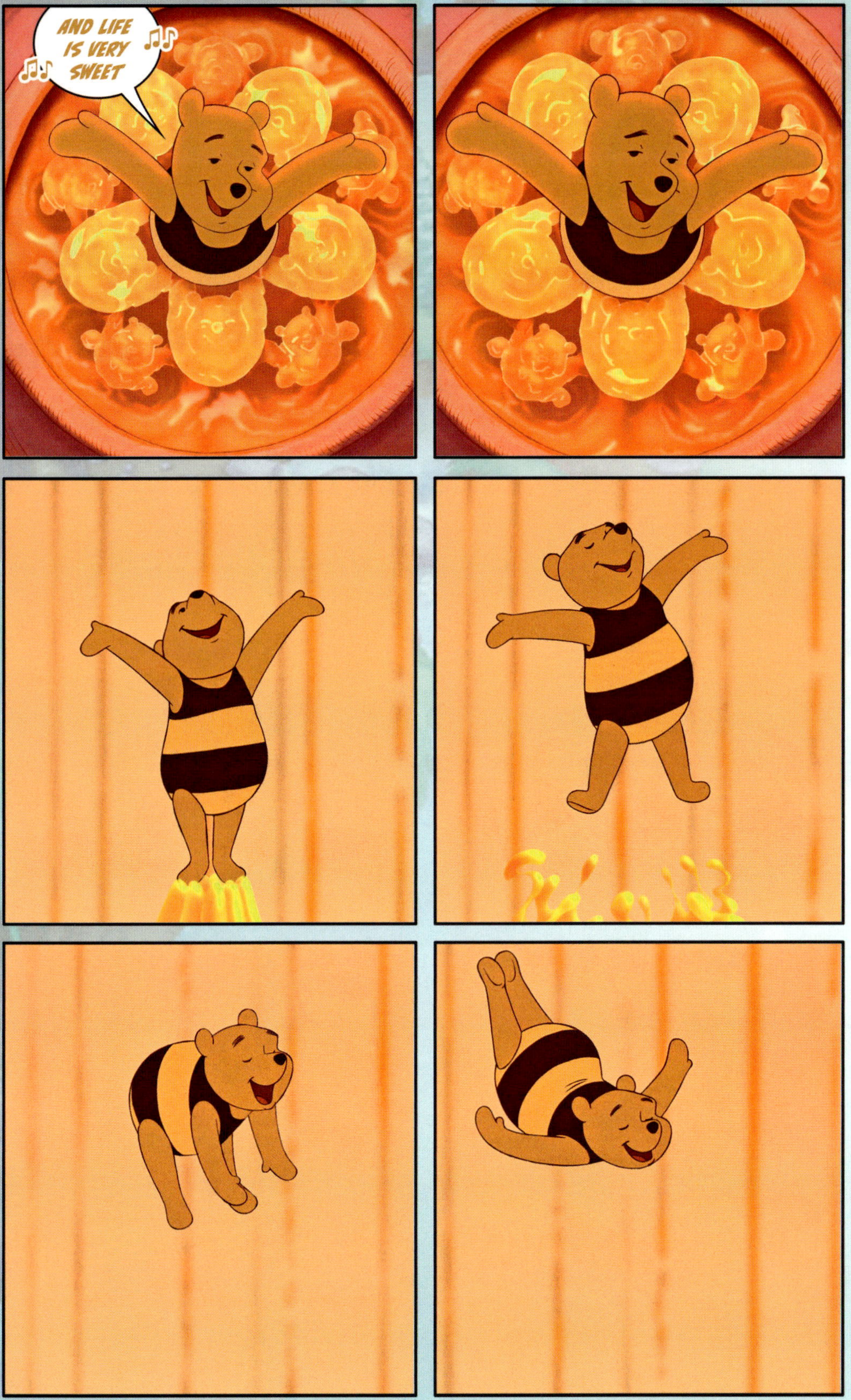
AND LIFE IS VERY SWEET

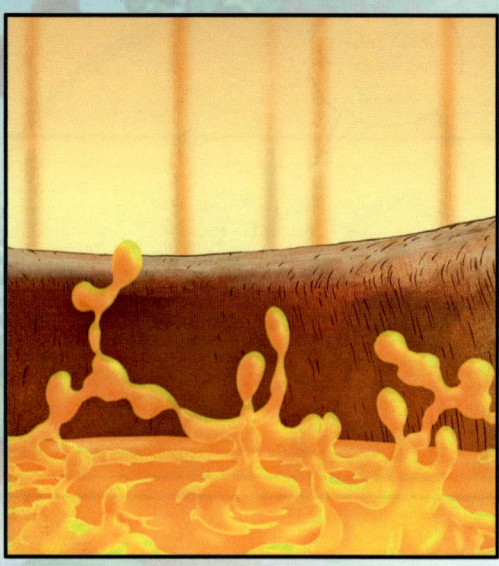
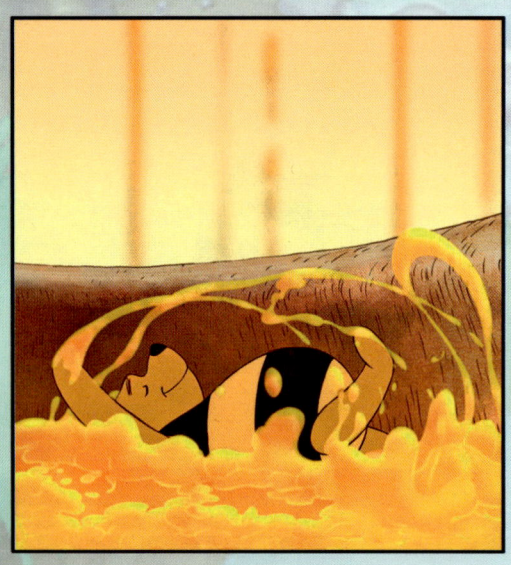

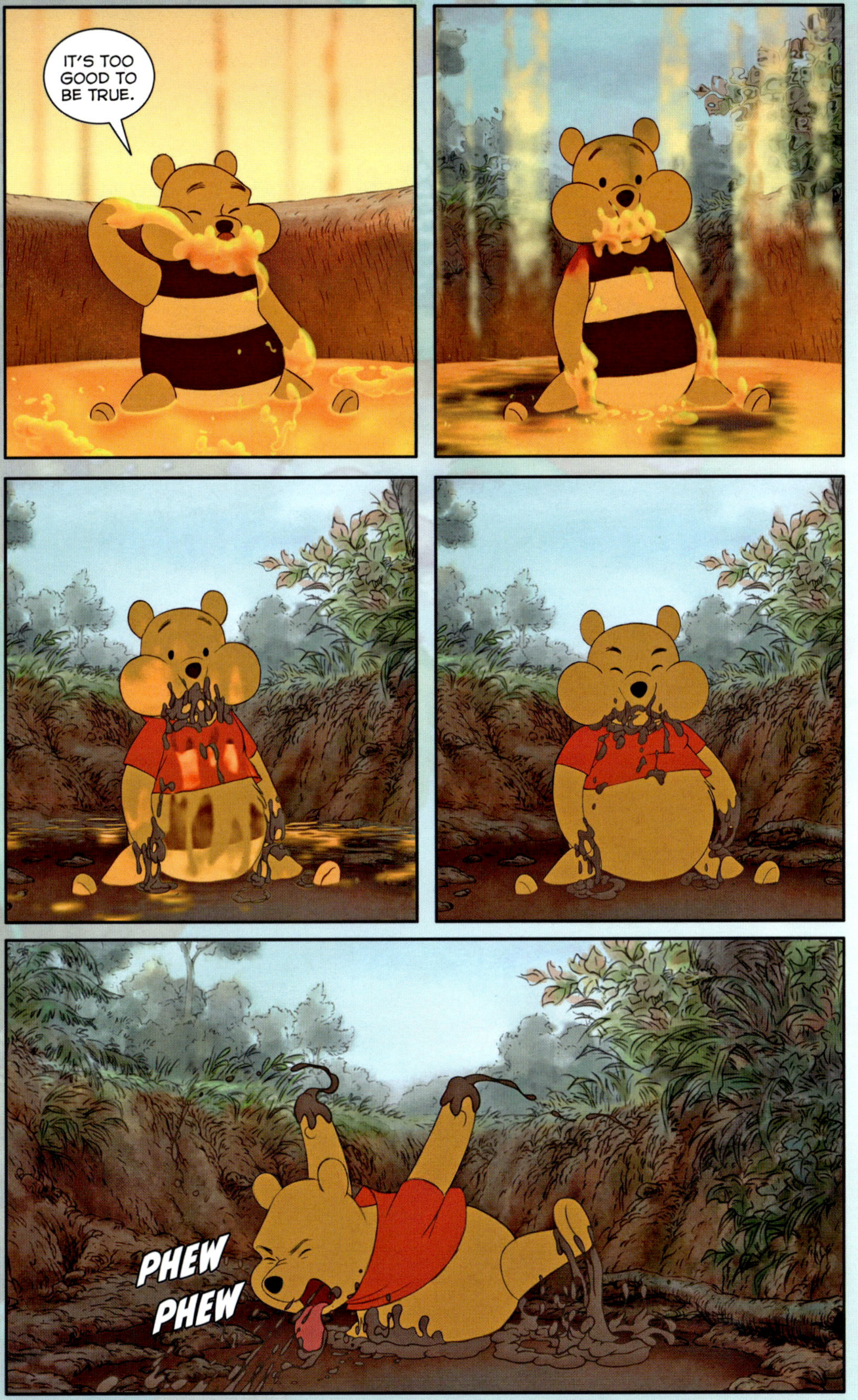

IT'S TOO GOOD TO BE TRUE.
PHEW
PHEW

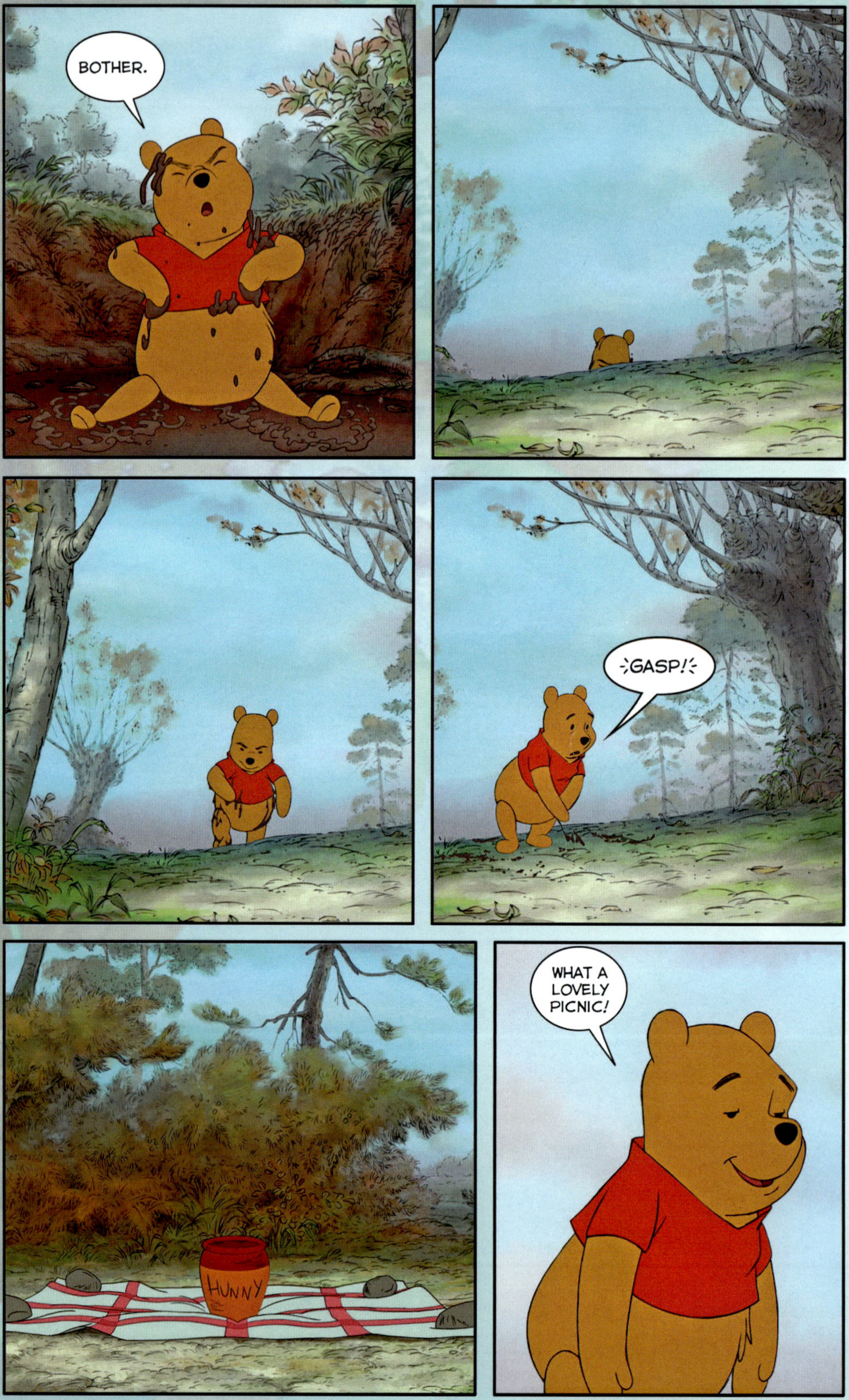
BOTHER.
GASP!
WHAT A LOVELY PICNIC!
HUNNY

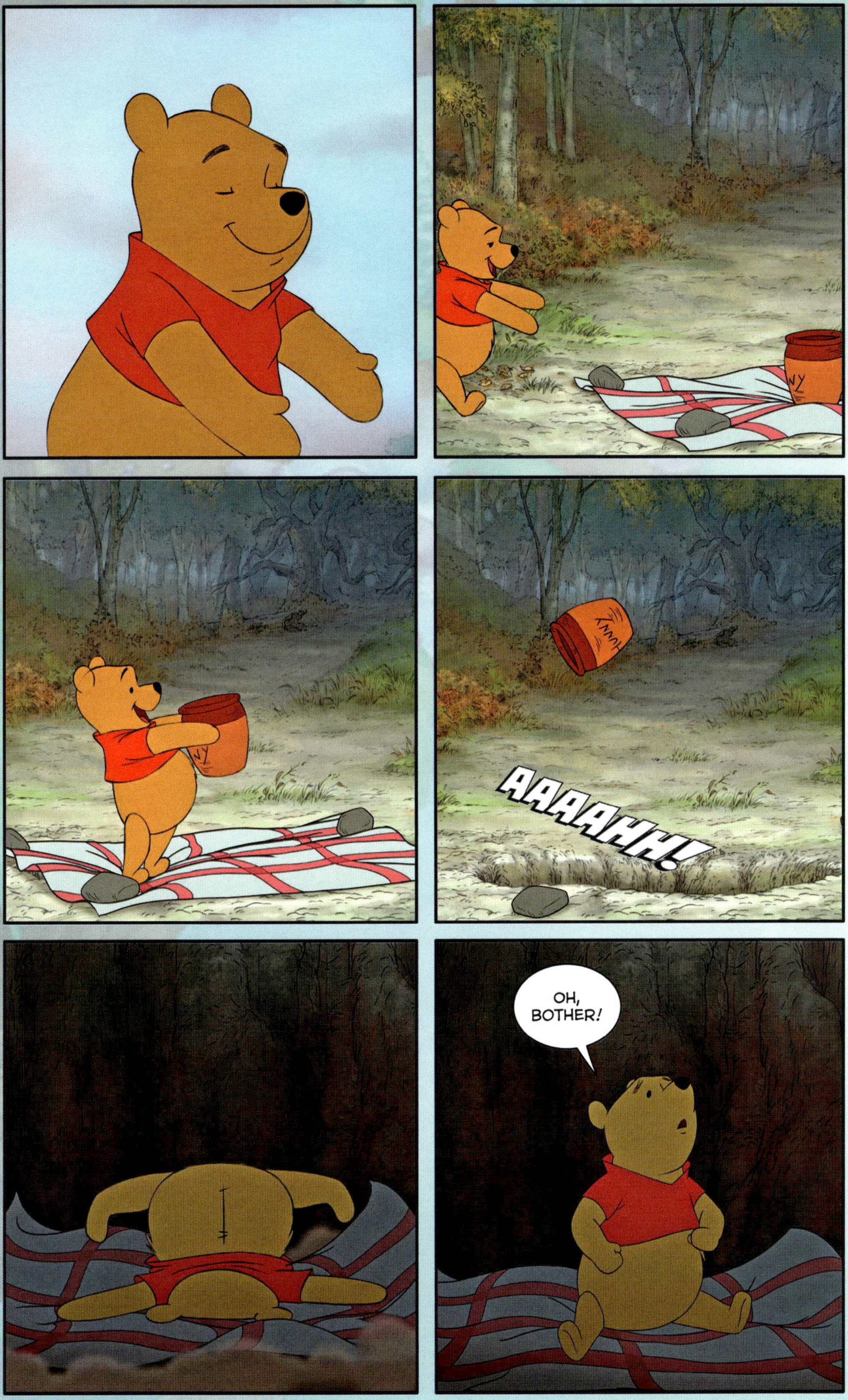
AAAAHH!
OH, BOTHER!

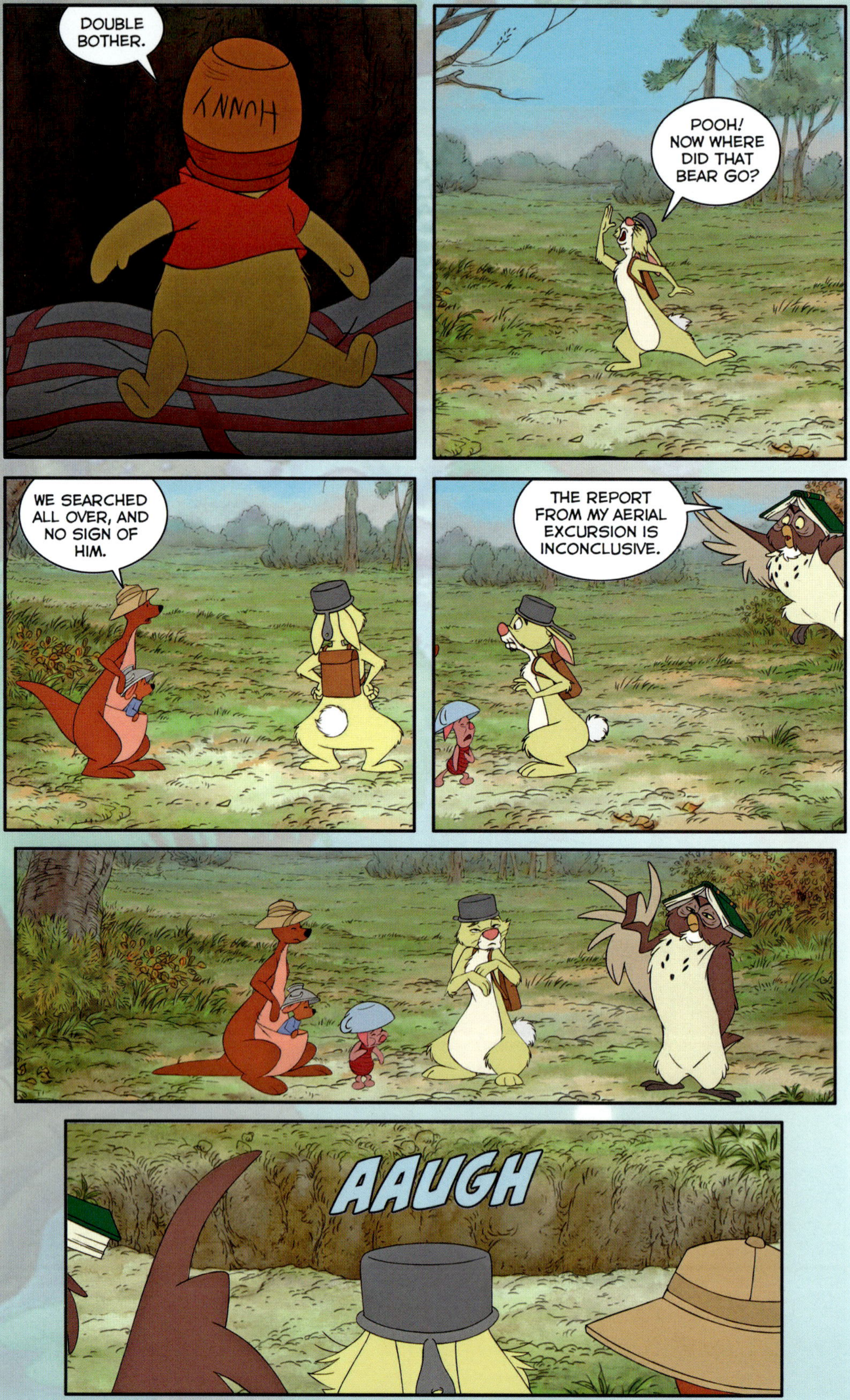

DOUBLE BOTHER.
HUNNY
POOH! NOW WHERE DID THAT BEAR GO?
WE SEARCHED ALL OVER, AND NO SIGN OF HIM.
THE REPORT FROM MY AERIAL EXCURSION IS INCONCLUSIVE.
AAUGH

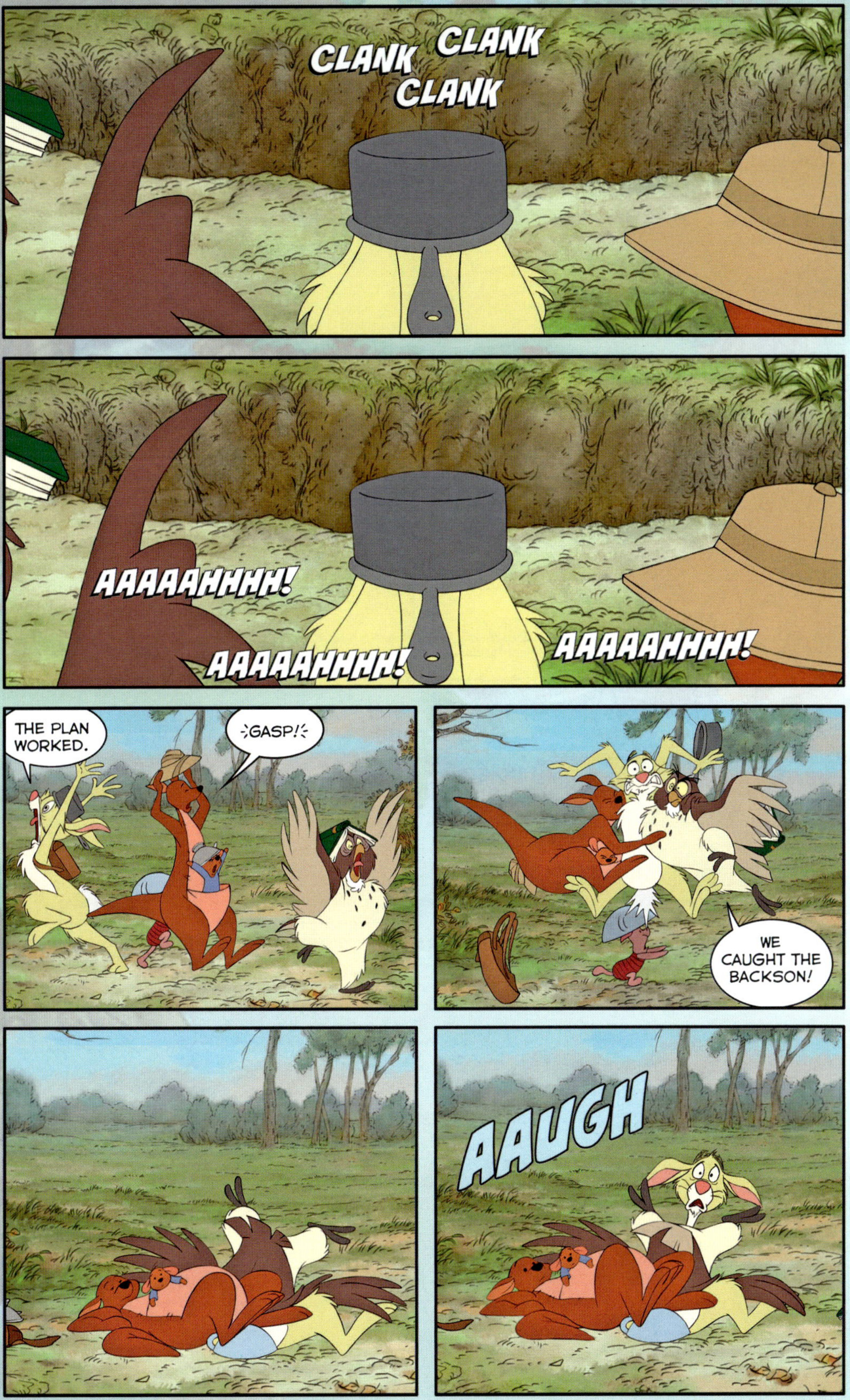
CLANK
CLANK
CLANK
AAAAAHHHH!
AAAAAHHHH!
AAAAAHHHH!
THE PLAN WORKED.
GASP!
WE CAUGHT THE BACKSON!
AAUGH

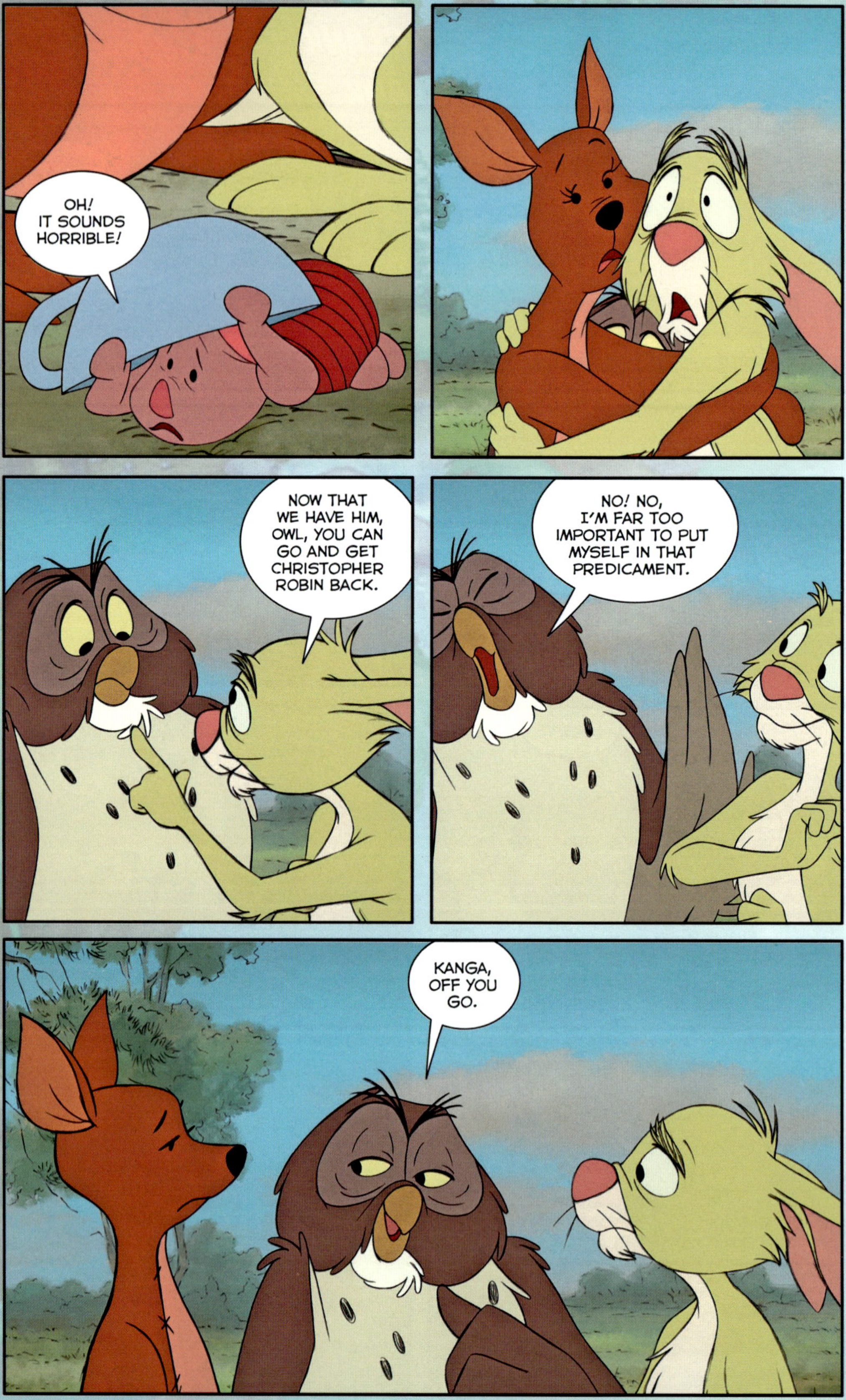
OH! IT SOUNDS HORRIBLE!
NOW THAT WE HAVE HIM, OWL, YOU CAN GO AND GET CHRISTOPHER ROBIN BACK.
NO! NO, I'M FAR TOO IMPORTANT TO PUT MYSELF IN THAT PREDICAMENT.
KANGA, OFF YOU GO.

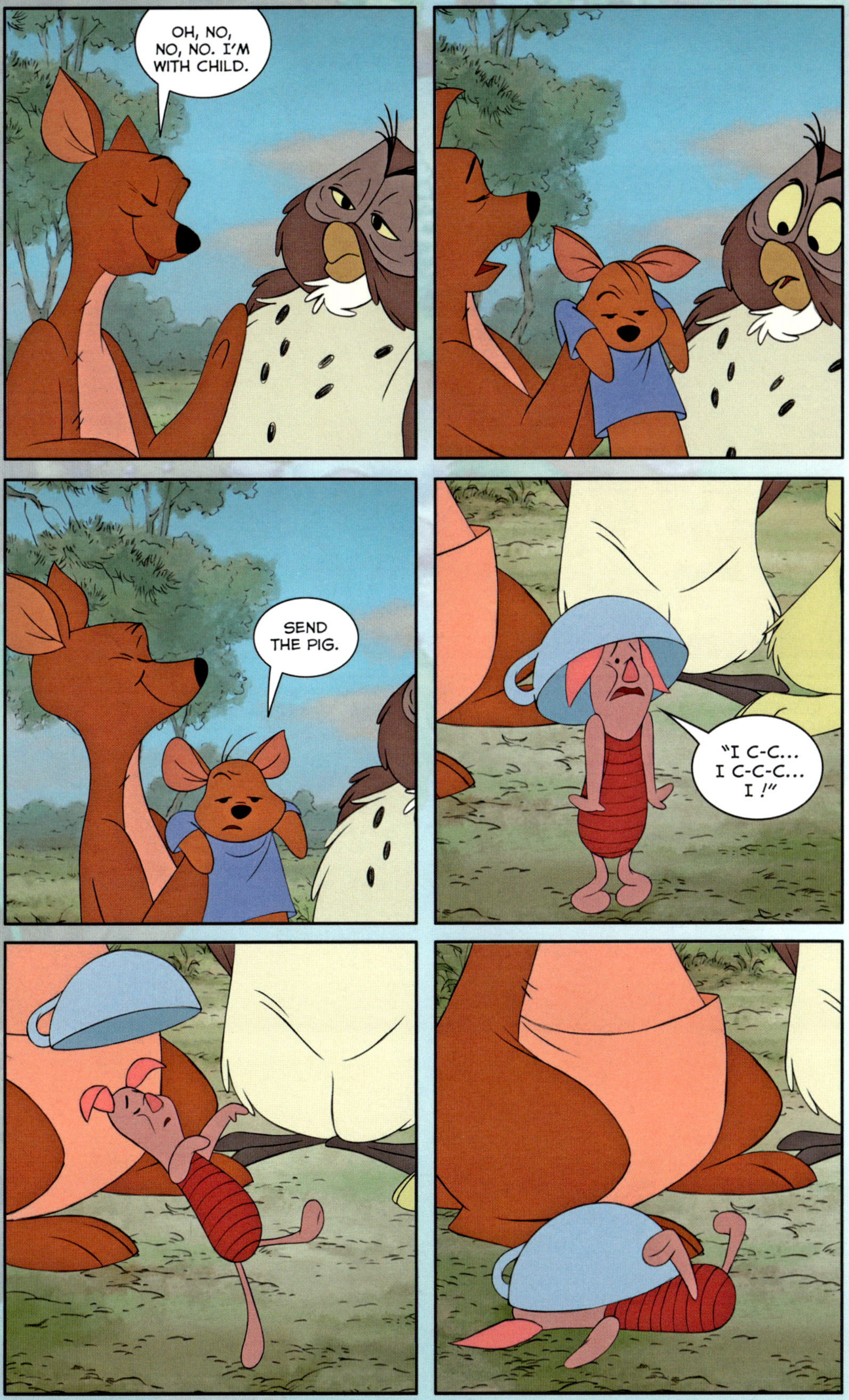
OH, NO, NO, NO. I'M WITH CHILD.
SEND THE PIG.
"I C-C... I C-C-C... I!"

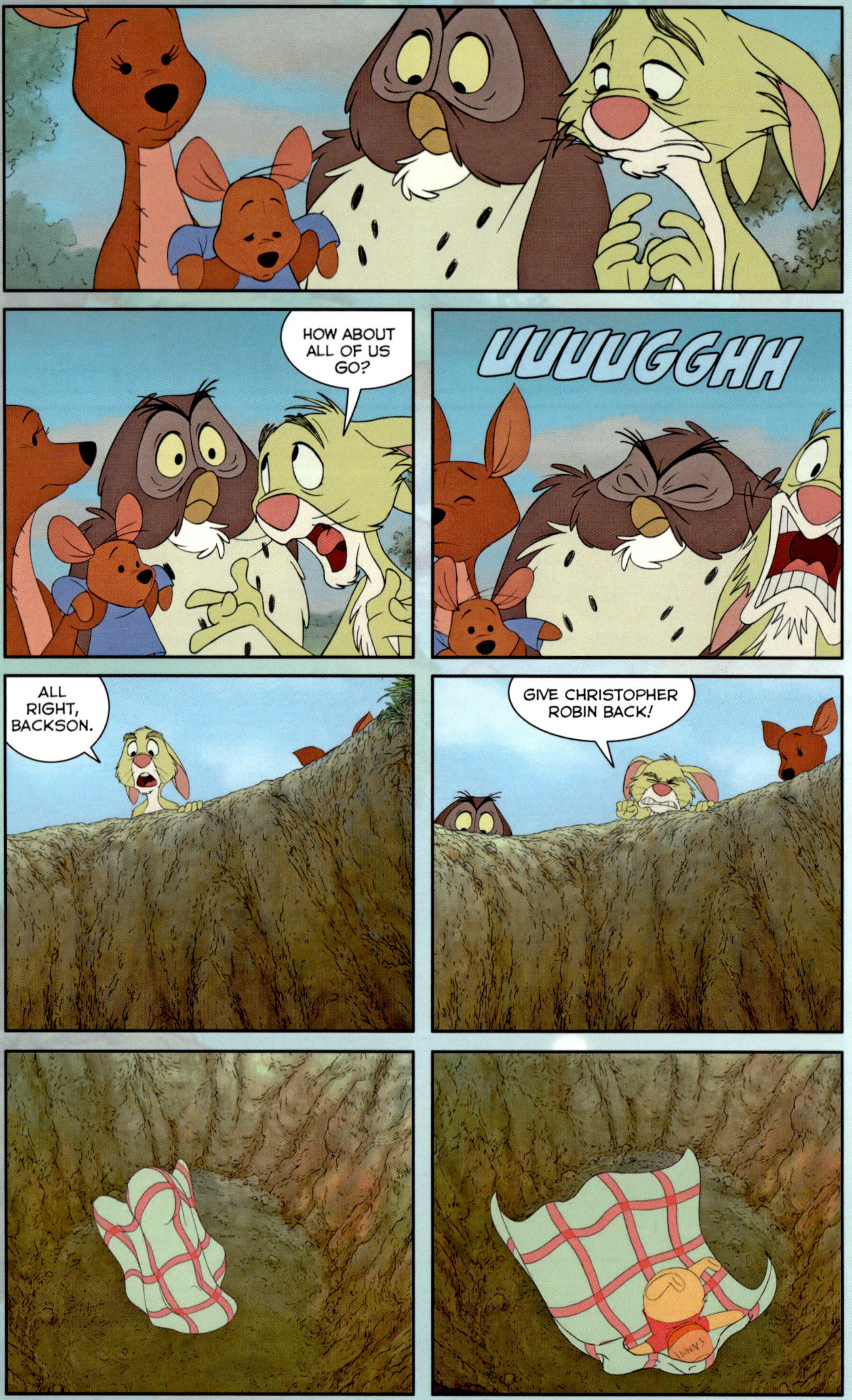
HOW ABOUT ALL OF US GO?
UUUUGGHH
ALL RIGHT, BACKSON.
GIVE CHRISTOPHER ROBIN BACK!

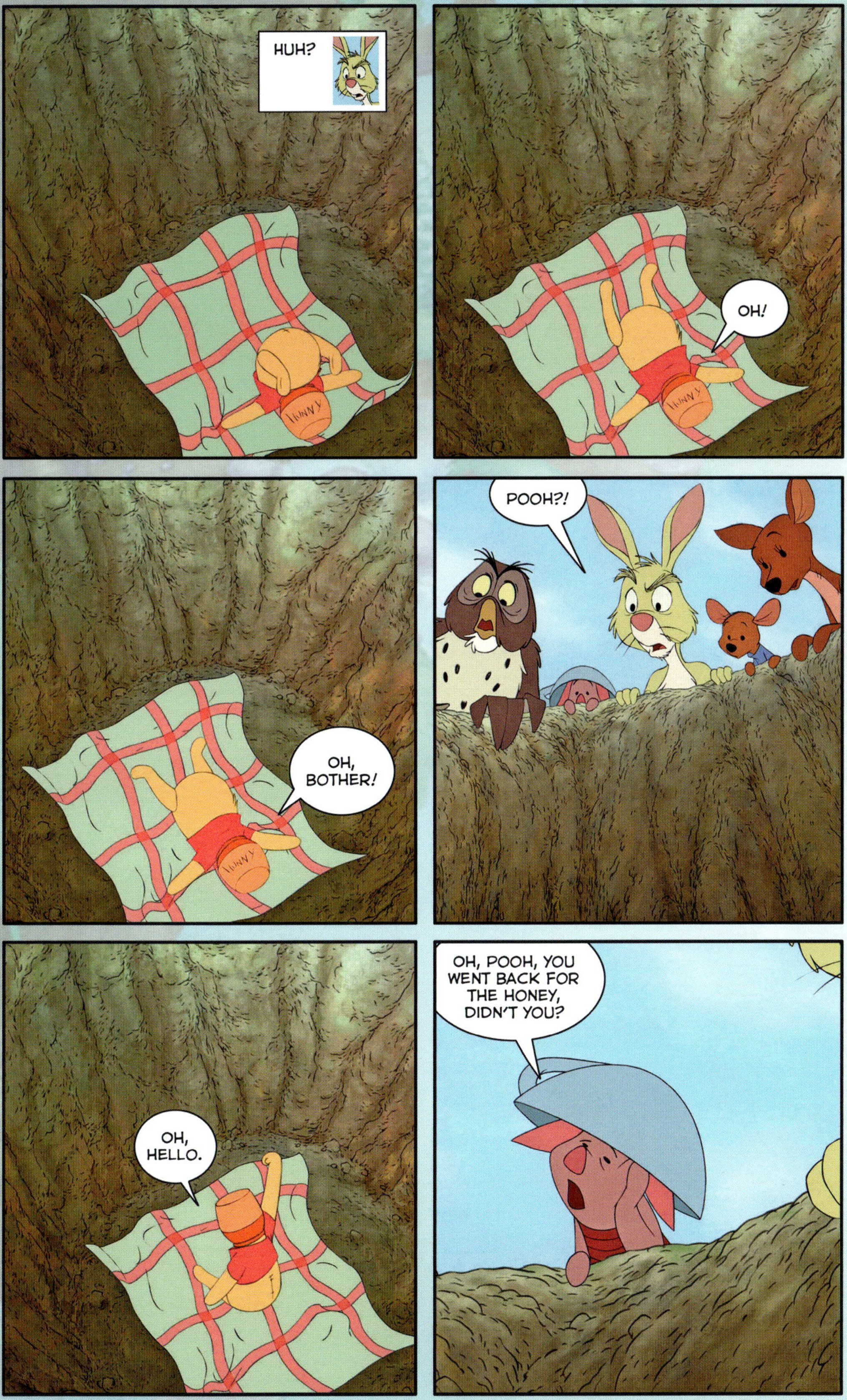
HUH?
OH!
OH, BOTHER!
POOH?!
OH, HELLO.
OH, POOH, YOU WENT BACK FOR THE HONEY, DIDN'T YOU?

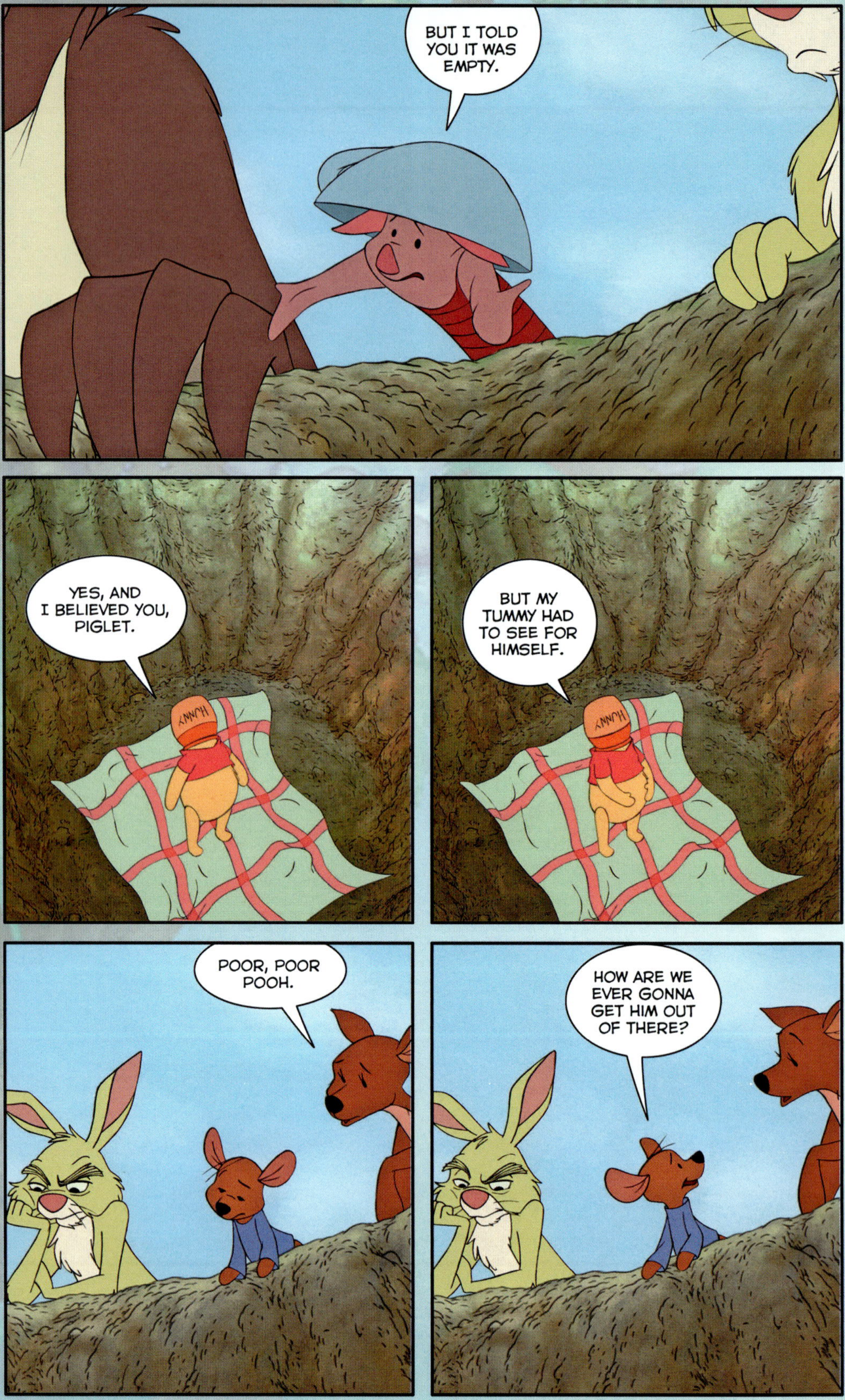
BUT I TOLD YOU IT WAS EMPTY.
YES, AND I BELIEVED YOU, PIGLET.
BUT MY TUMMY HAD TO SEE FOR HIMSELF.
HUNNY
HUNNY
POOR, POOR POOH.
HOW ARE WE EVER GONNA GET HIM OUT OF THERE?

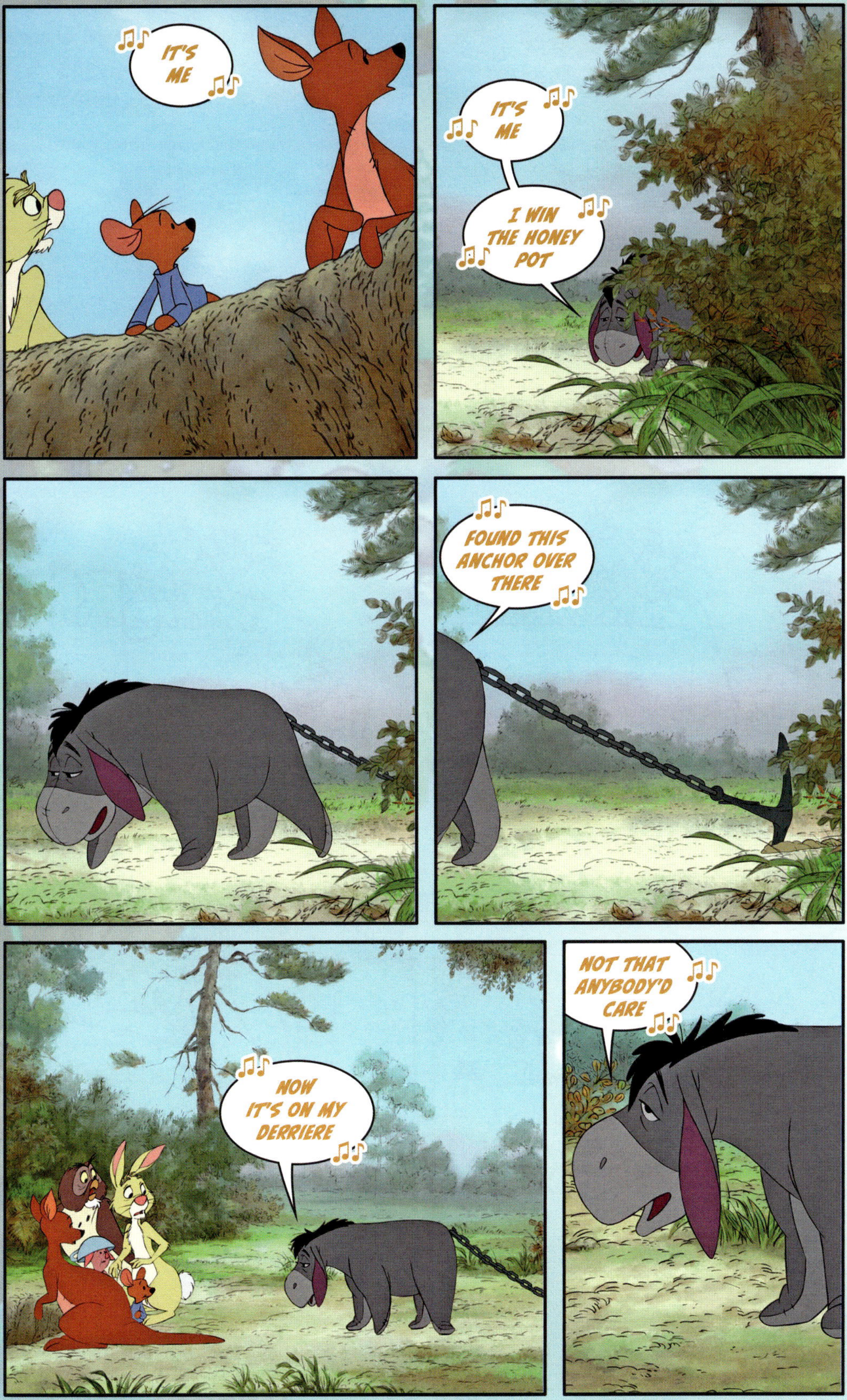
IT'S ME
IT'S ME
I WIN THE HONEY POT
FOUND THIS ANCHOR OVER THERE
NOW IT'S ON MY DERRIERE
NOT THAT ANYBODY'D CARE

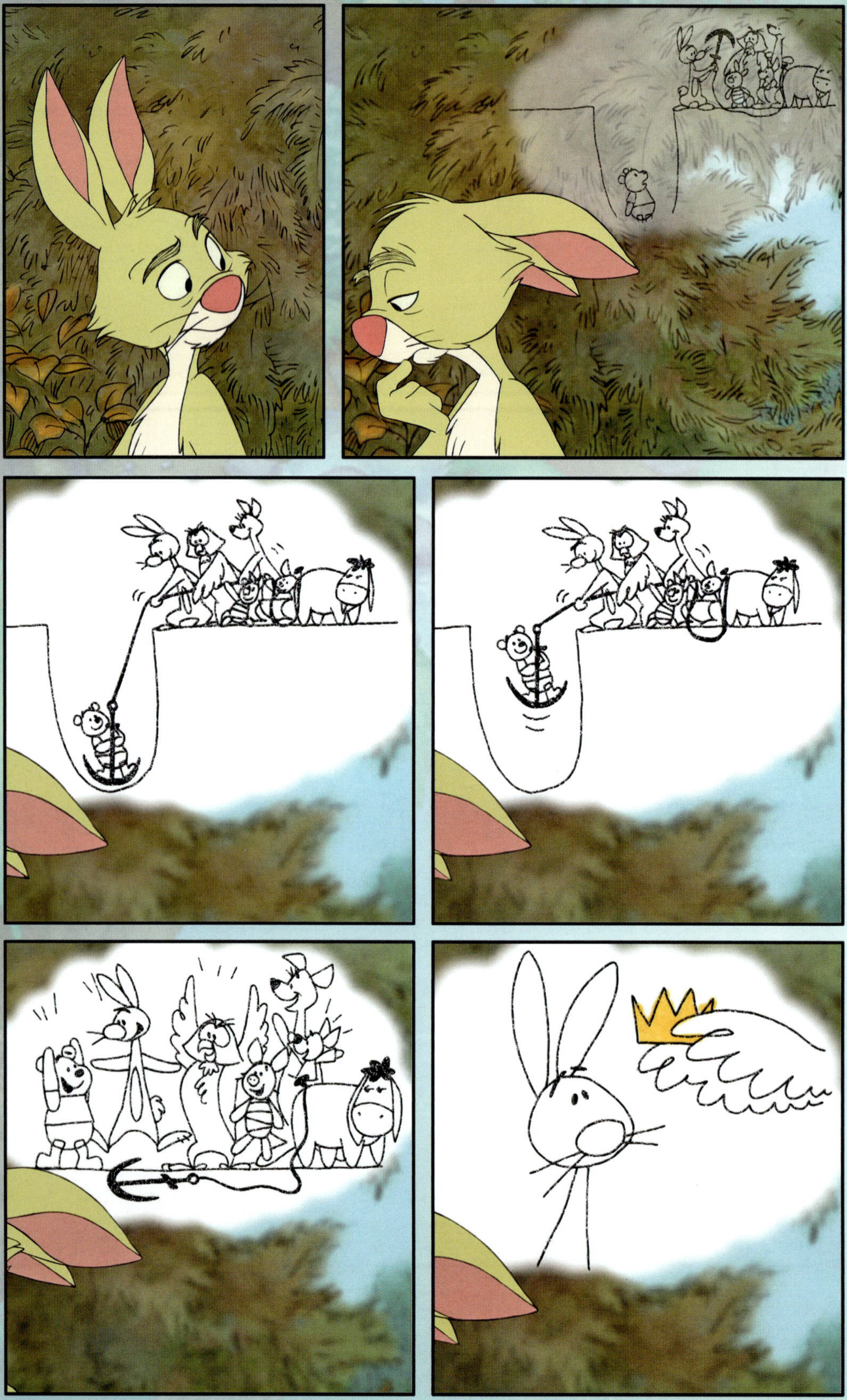

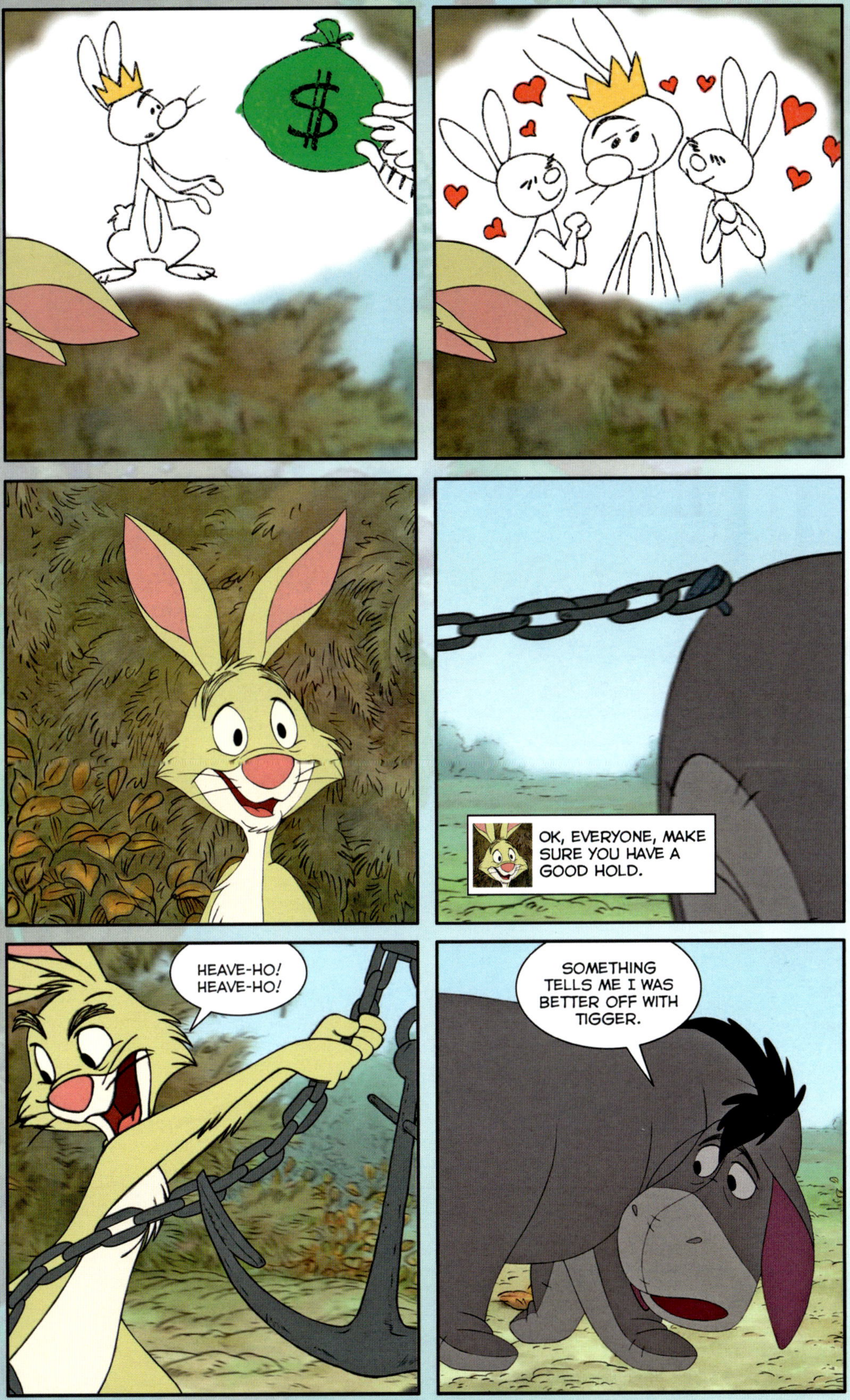
OK, EVERYONE, MAKE SURE YOU HAVE A GOOD HOLD.
HEAVE-HO! HEAVE-HO!
SOMETHING TELLS ME I WAS BETTER OFF WITH TIGGER.

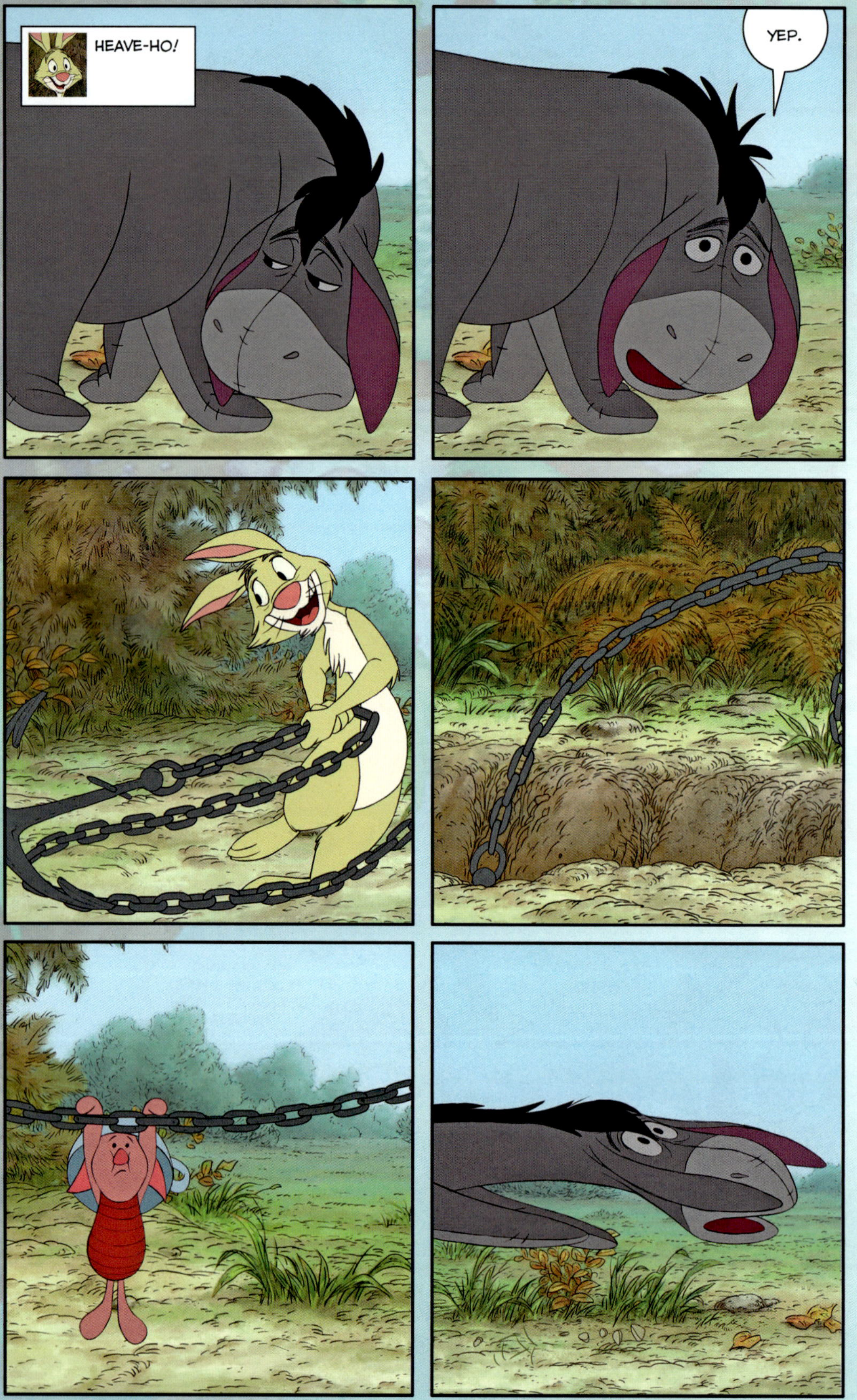
HEAVE-HO!
YEP.

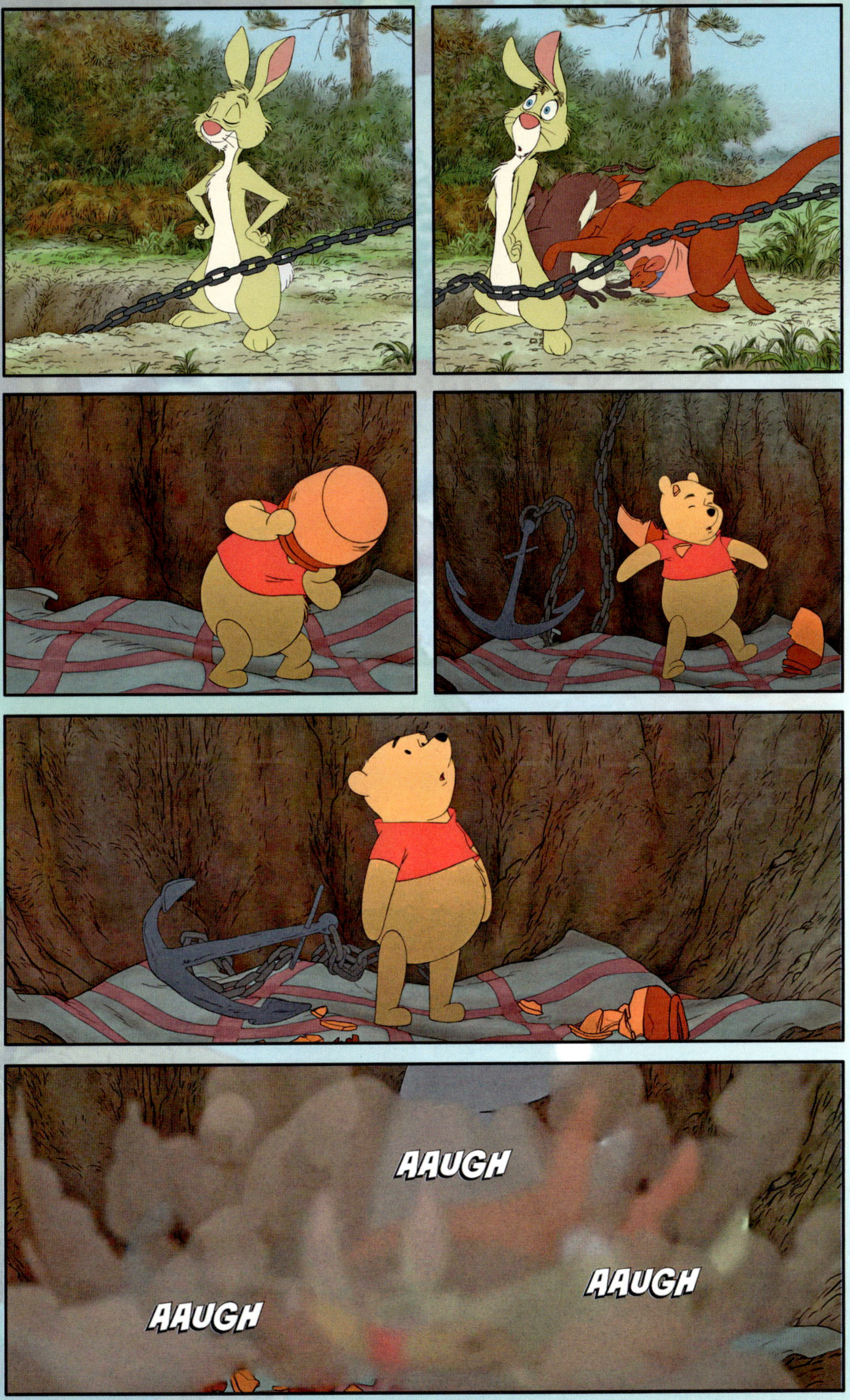
AAUGH
AAUGH
AAUGH

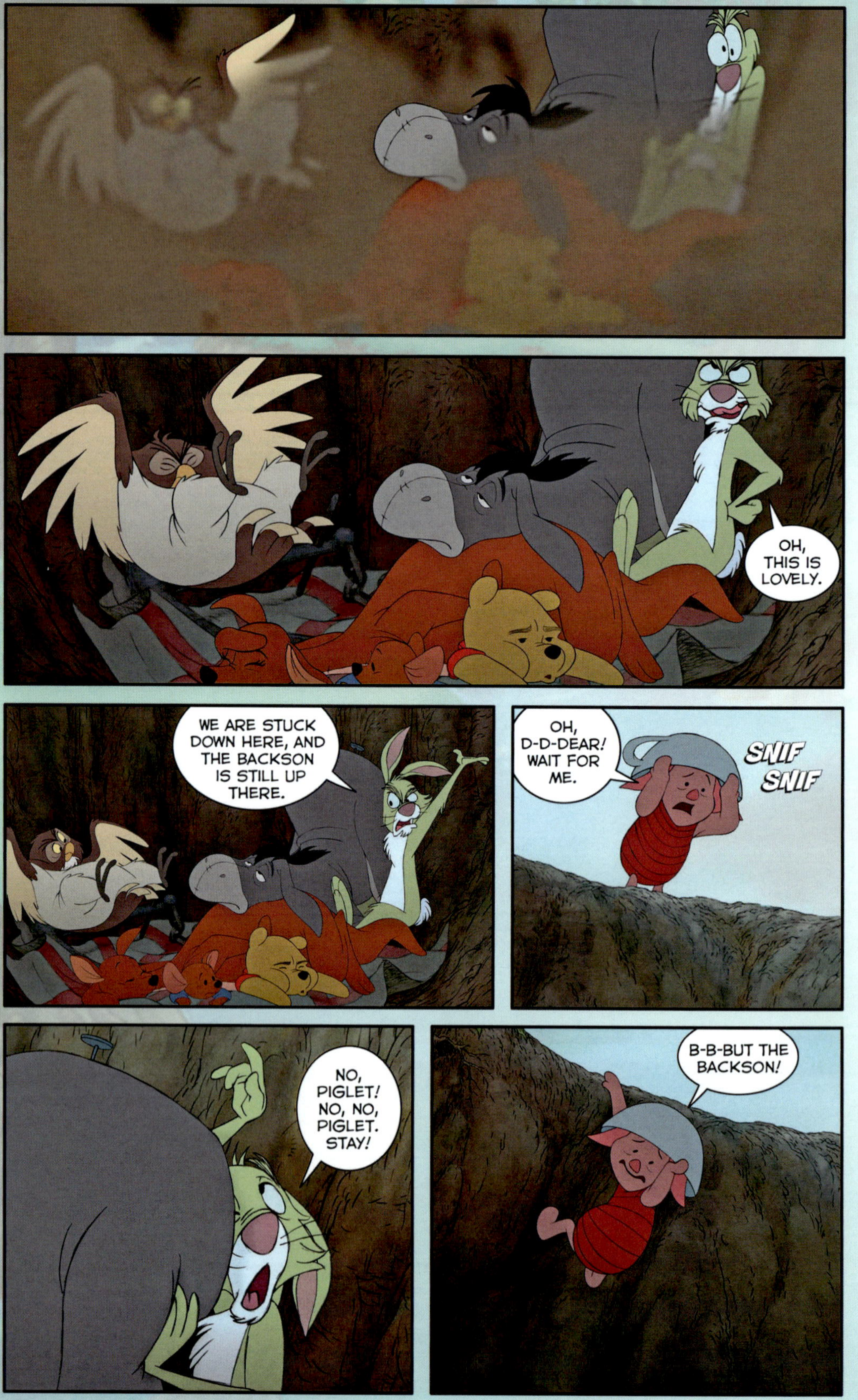
OH, THIS IS LOVELY.
WE ARE STUCK DOWN HERE, AND THE BACKSON IS STILL UP THERE.
OH, D-D-DEAR! WAIT FOR ME.
SNIF SNIF
NO, PIGLET! NO, NO, PIGLET. STAY!
B-B-BUT THE BACKSON!

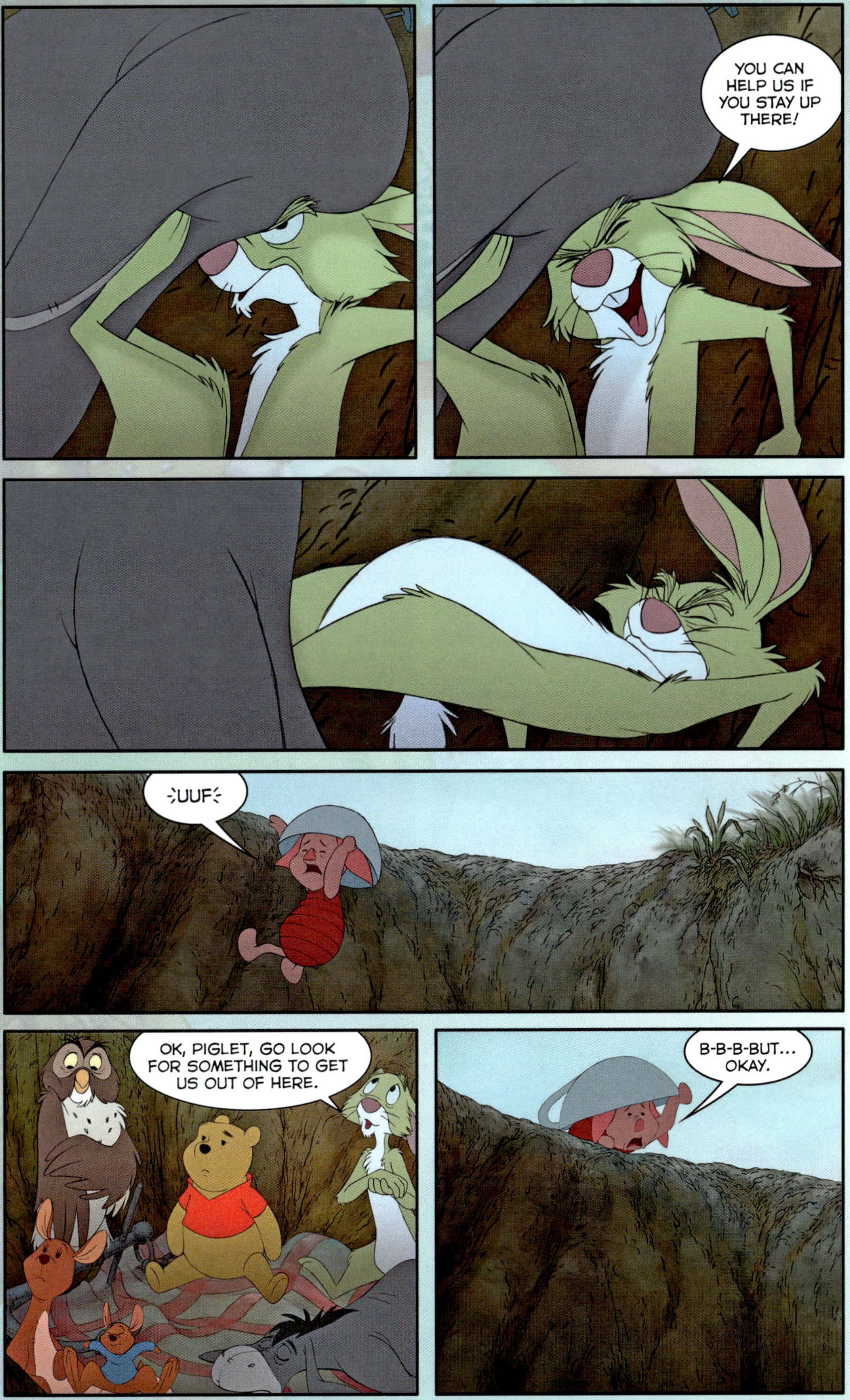
YOU CAN HELP US IF YOU STAY UP THERE!
UUF
OK, PIGLET, GO LOOK FOR SOMETHING TO GET US OUT OF HERE.
B-B-B-BUT... OKAY.

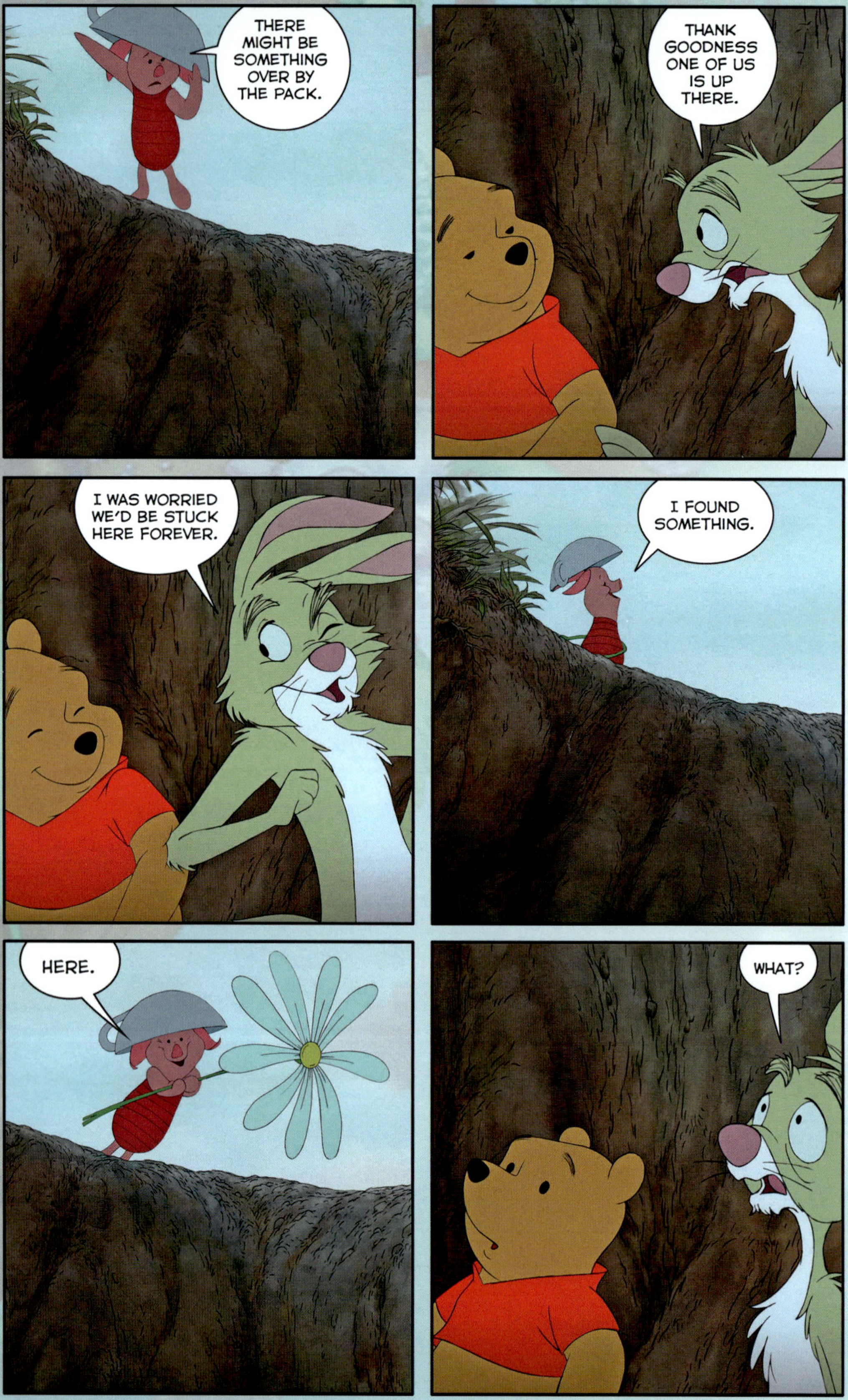
THERE MIGHT BE SOMETHING OVER BY THE PACK.
THANK GOODNESS ONE OF US IS UP THERE.
I WAS WORRIED WE'D BE STUCK HERE FOREVER.
I FOUND SOMETHING.
HERE.
WHAT?

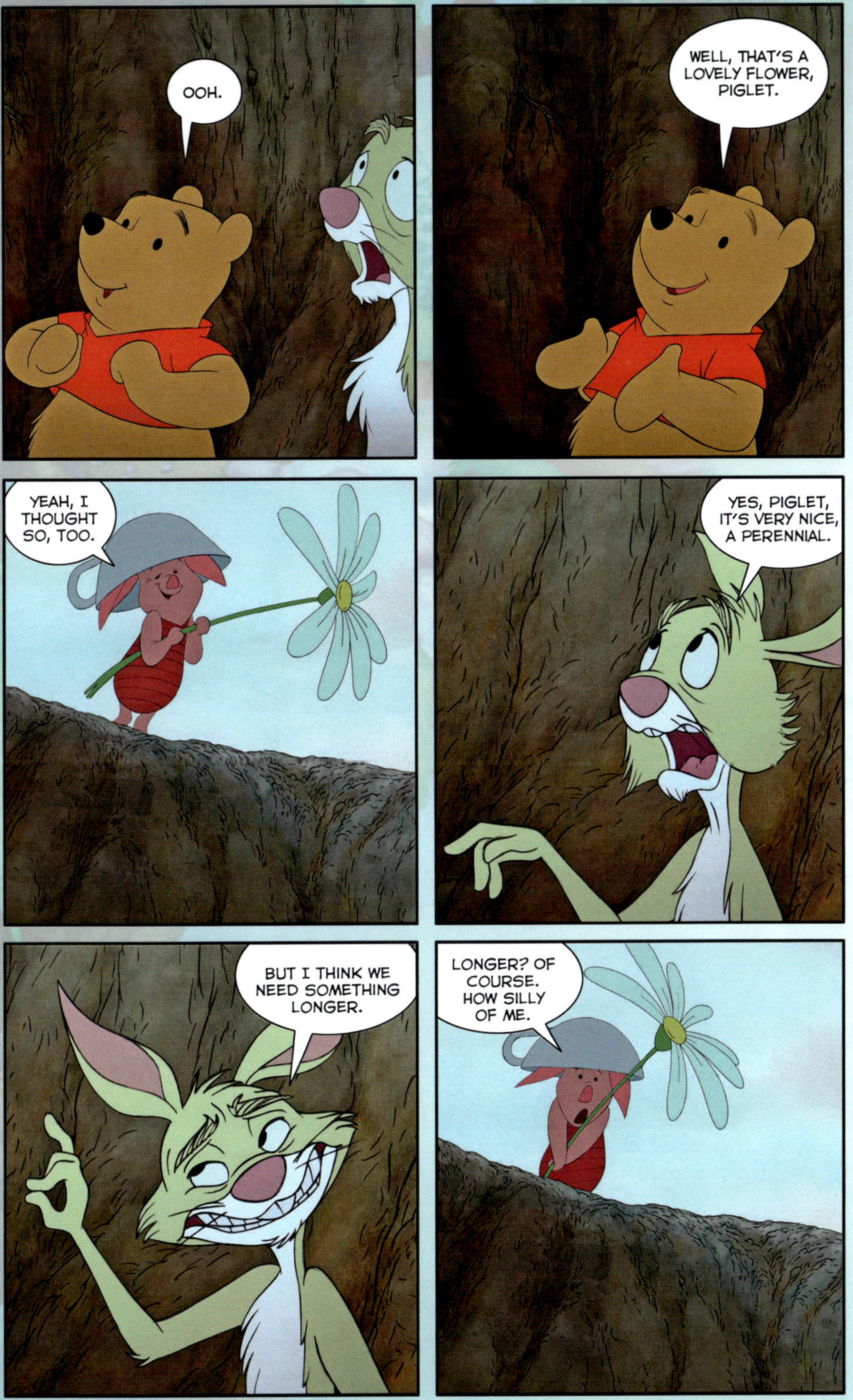
OOH.
WELL, THAT'S A LOVELY FLOWER, PIGLET.
YEAH, I THOUGHT SO, TOO.
YES, PIGLET, IT'S VERY NICE, A PERENNIAL.
BUT I THINK WE NEED SOMETHING LONGER.
LONGER? OF COURSE. HOW SILLY OF ME.

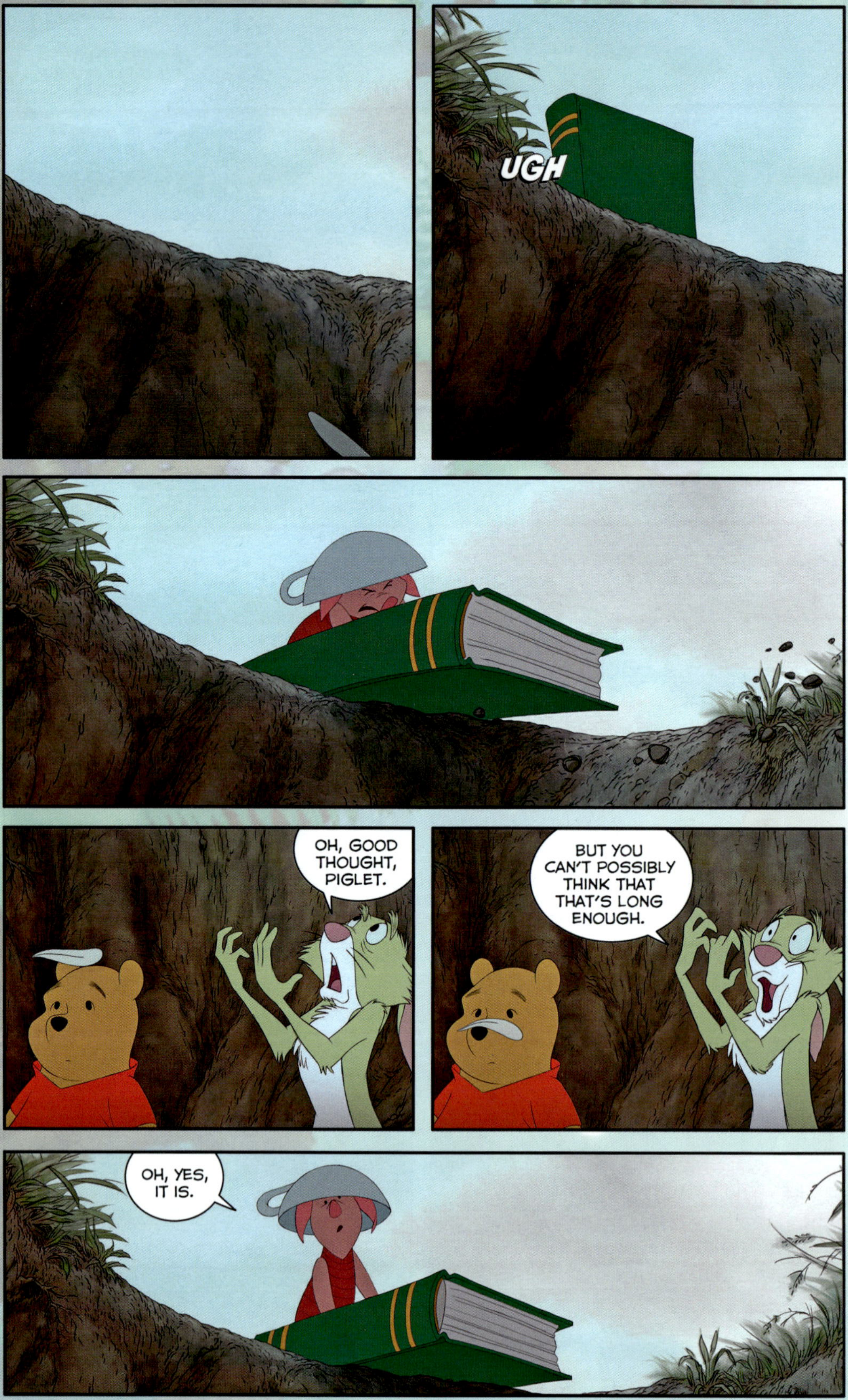
UGH
OH, GOOD THOUGHT, PIGLET.
BUT YOU CAN'T POSSIBLY THINK THAT THAT'S LONG ENOUGH.
OH, YES, IT IS.

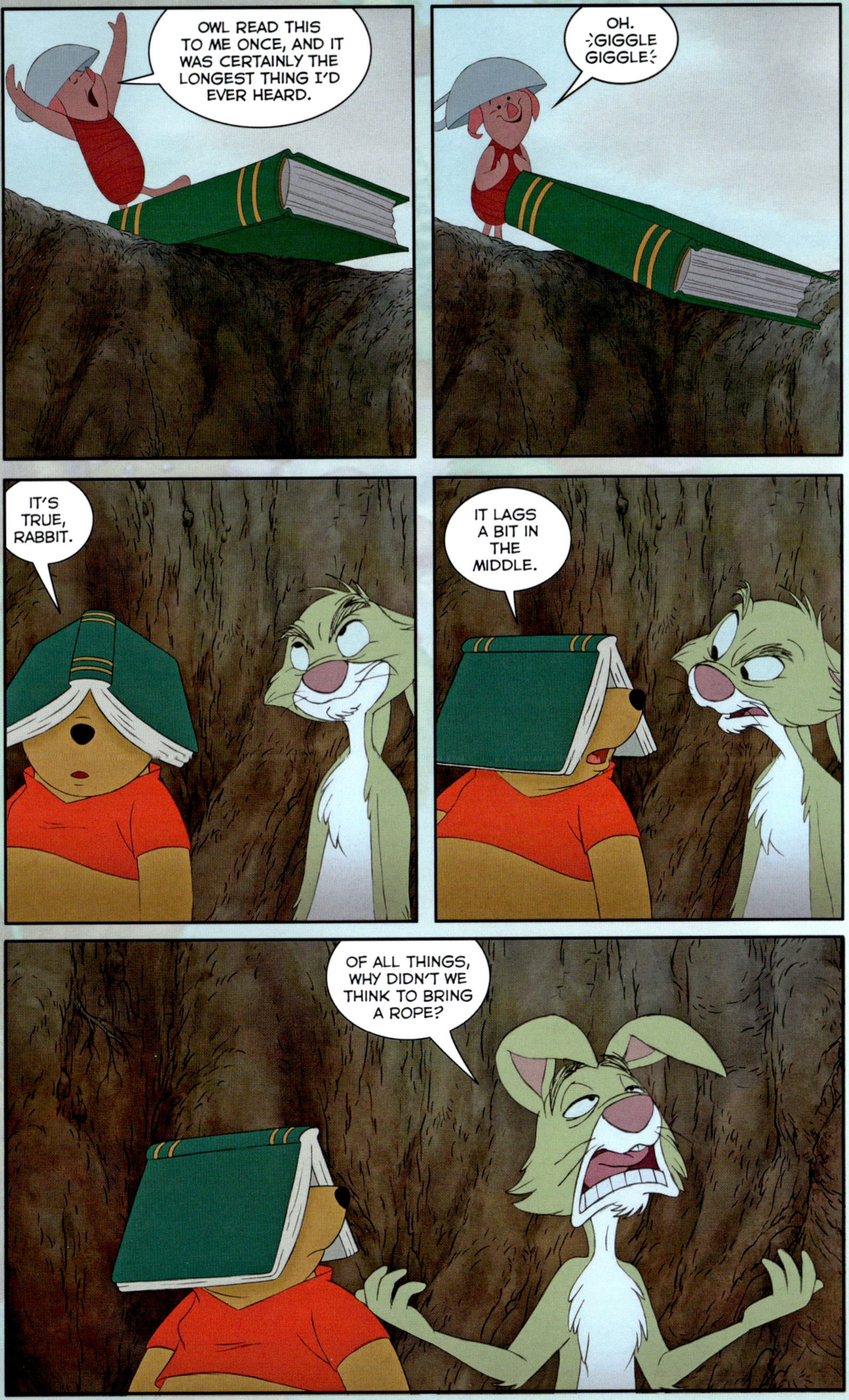
OWL READ THIS TO ME ONCE, AND IT WAS CERTAINLY THE LONGEST THING I'D EVER HEARD.
OH. GIGGLE GIGGLE
IT'S TRUE, RABBIT.
IT LAGS A BIT IN THE MIDDLE.
OF ALL THINGS, WHY DIDN'T WE THINK TO BRING A ROPE?

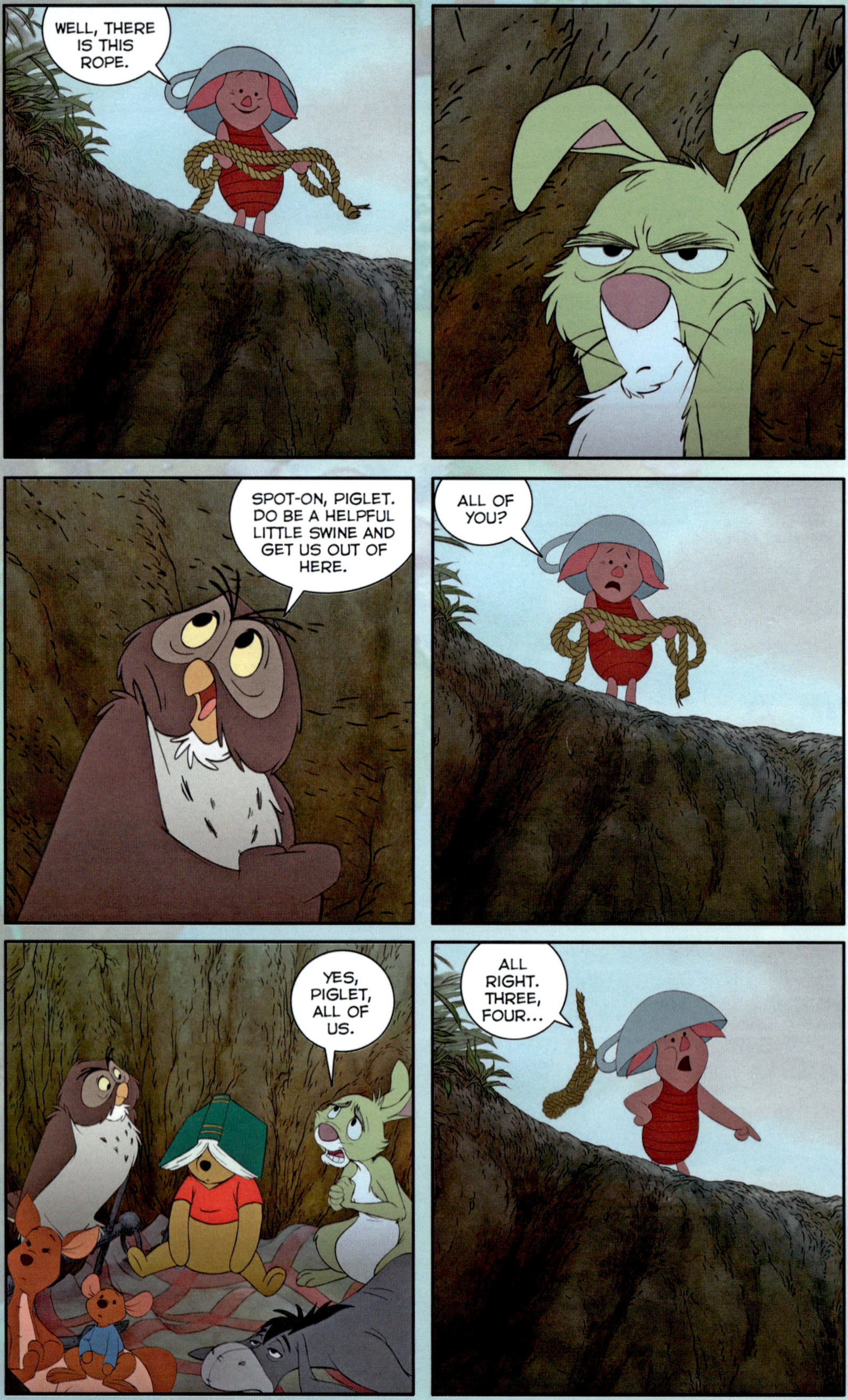
WELL, THERE IS THIS ROPE.
SPOT-ON, PIGLET. DO BE A HELPFUL LITTLE SWINE AND GET US OUT OF HERE.
ALL OF YOU?
YES, PIGLET, ALL OF US.
ALL RIGHT. THREE, FOUR...

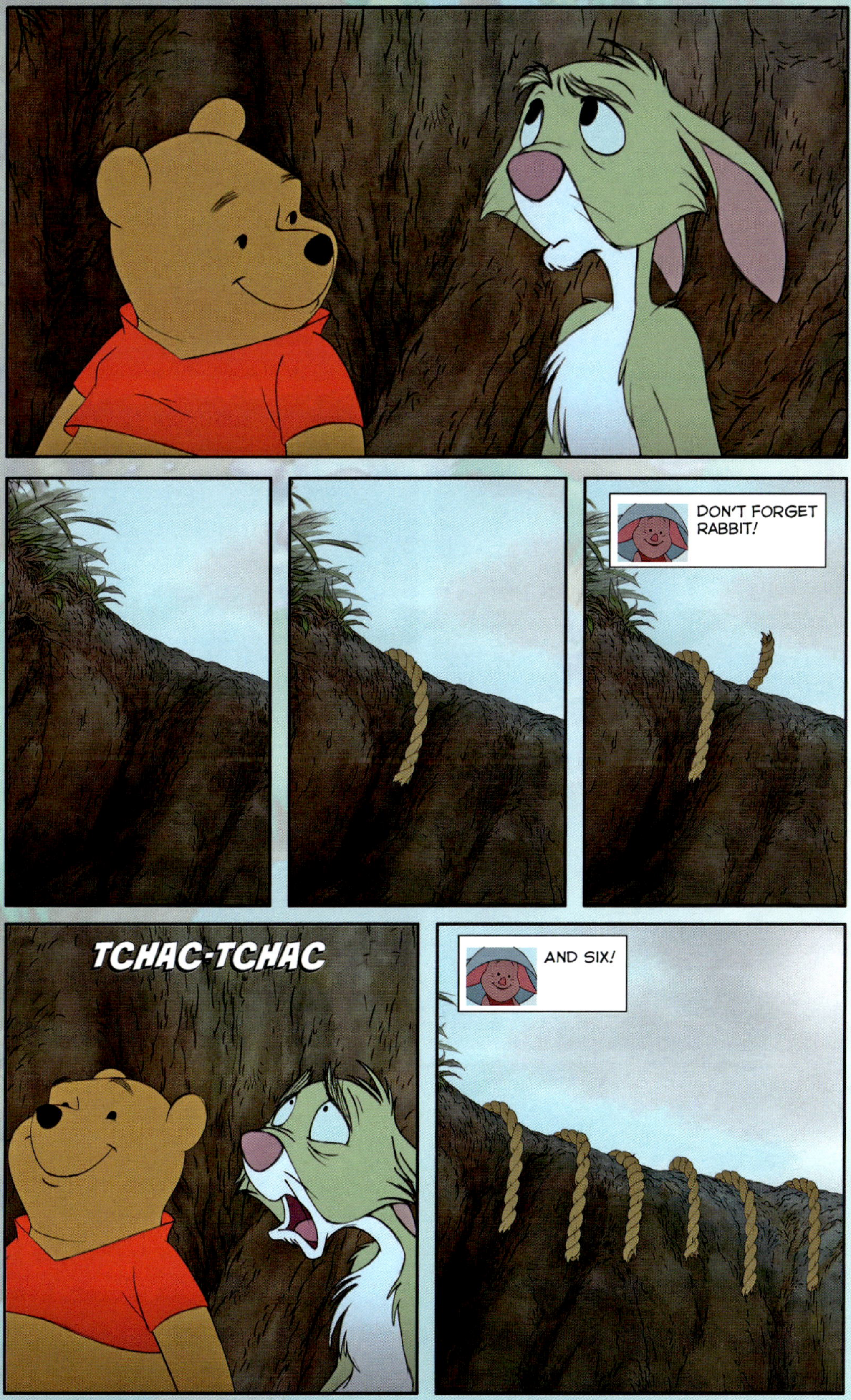
DON'T FORGET RABBIT!
TCHAC-TCHAC
AND SIX!

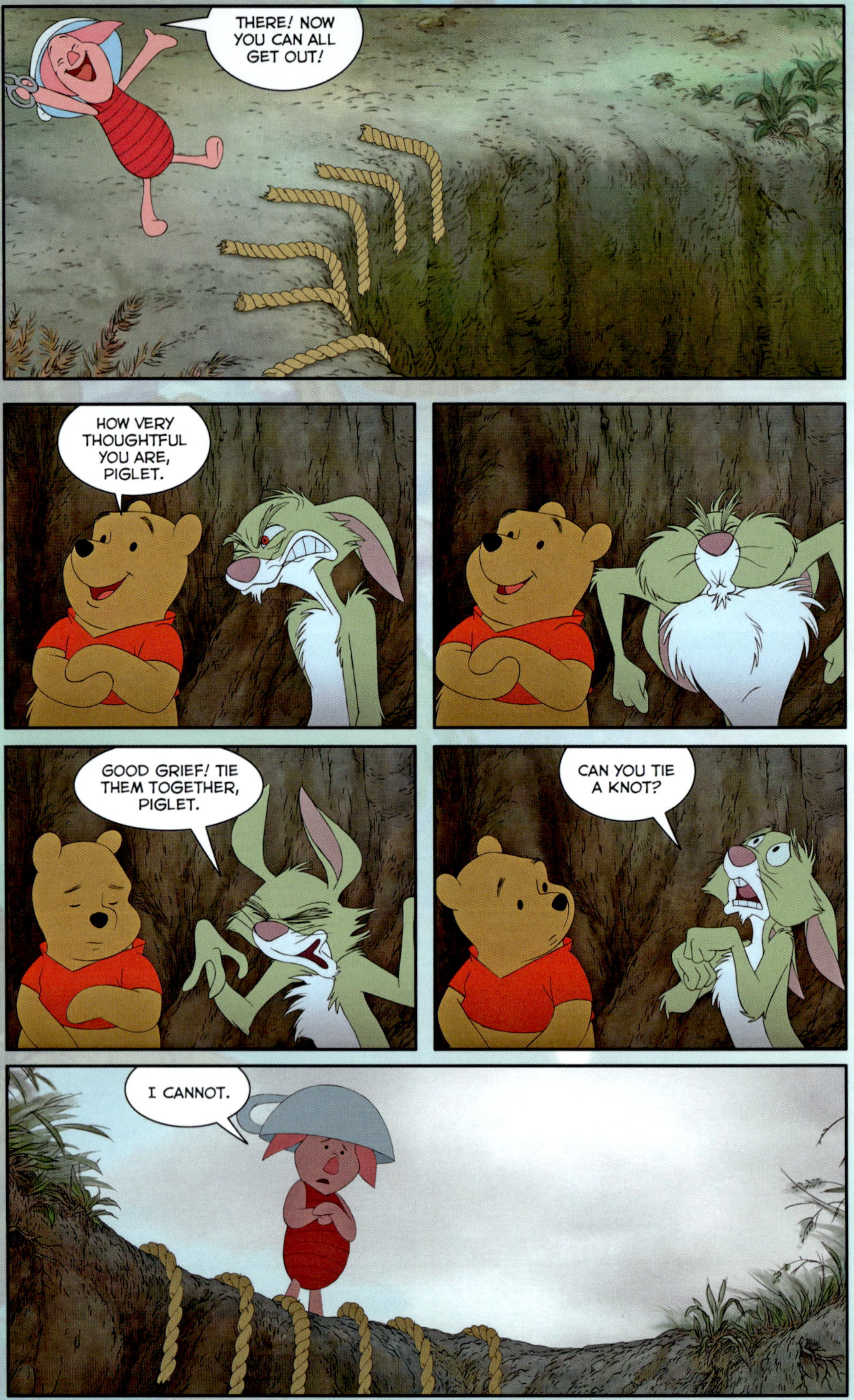
THERE! NOW YOU CAN ALL GET OUT!
HOW VERY THOUGHTFUL YOU ARE, PIGLET.
GOOD GRIEF! TIE THEM TOGETHER, PIGLET.
CAN YOU TIE A KNOT?
I CANNOT.

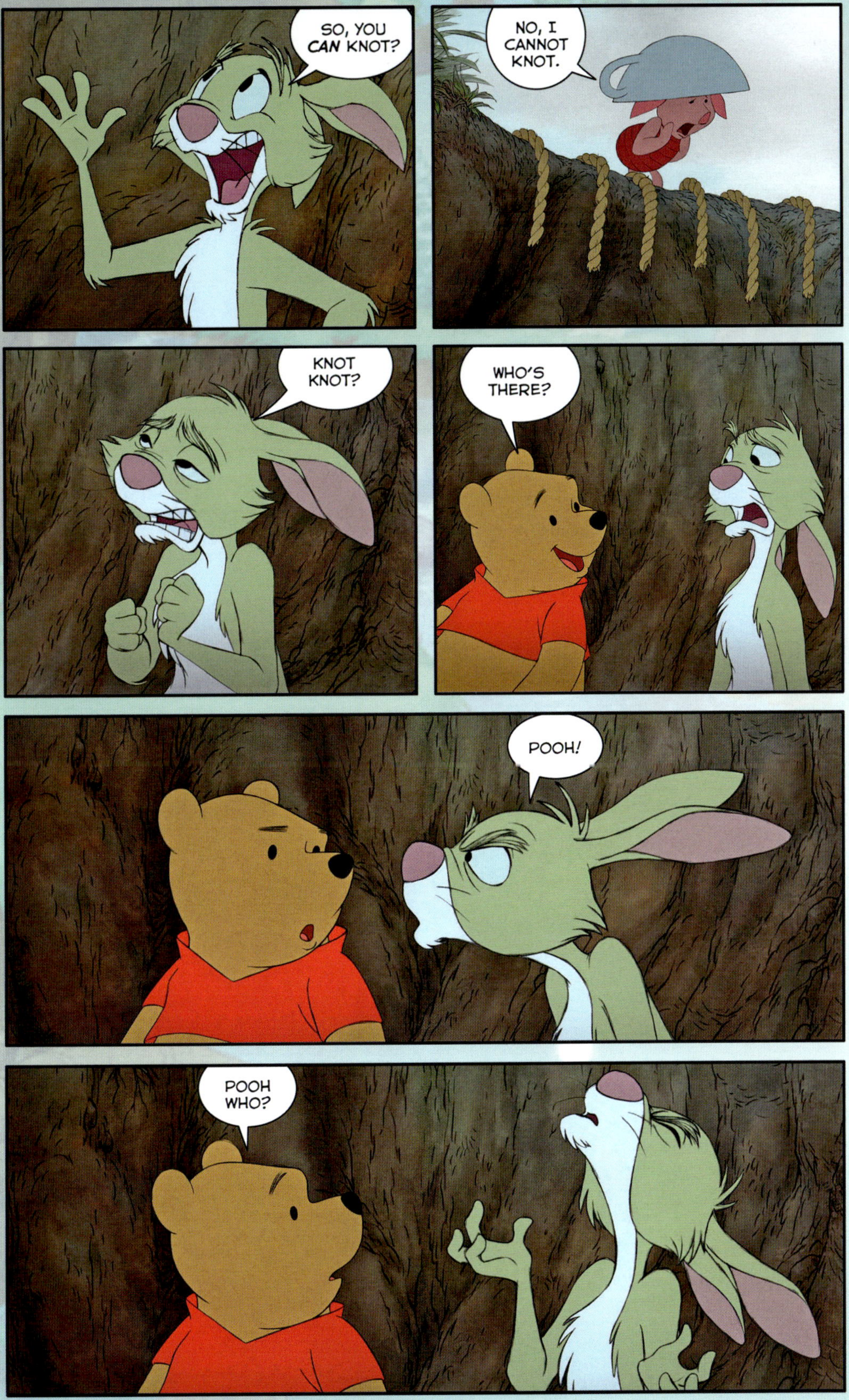
SO, YOU CAN KNOT?
NO, I CANNOT KNOT.
KNOT KNOT?
WHO'S THERE?
POOH!
POOH WHO?

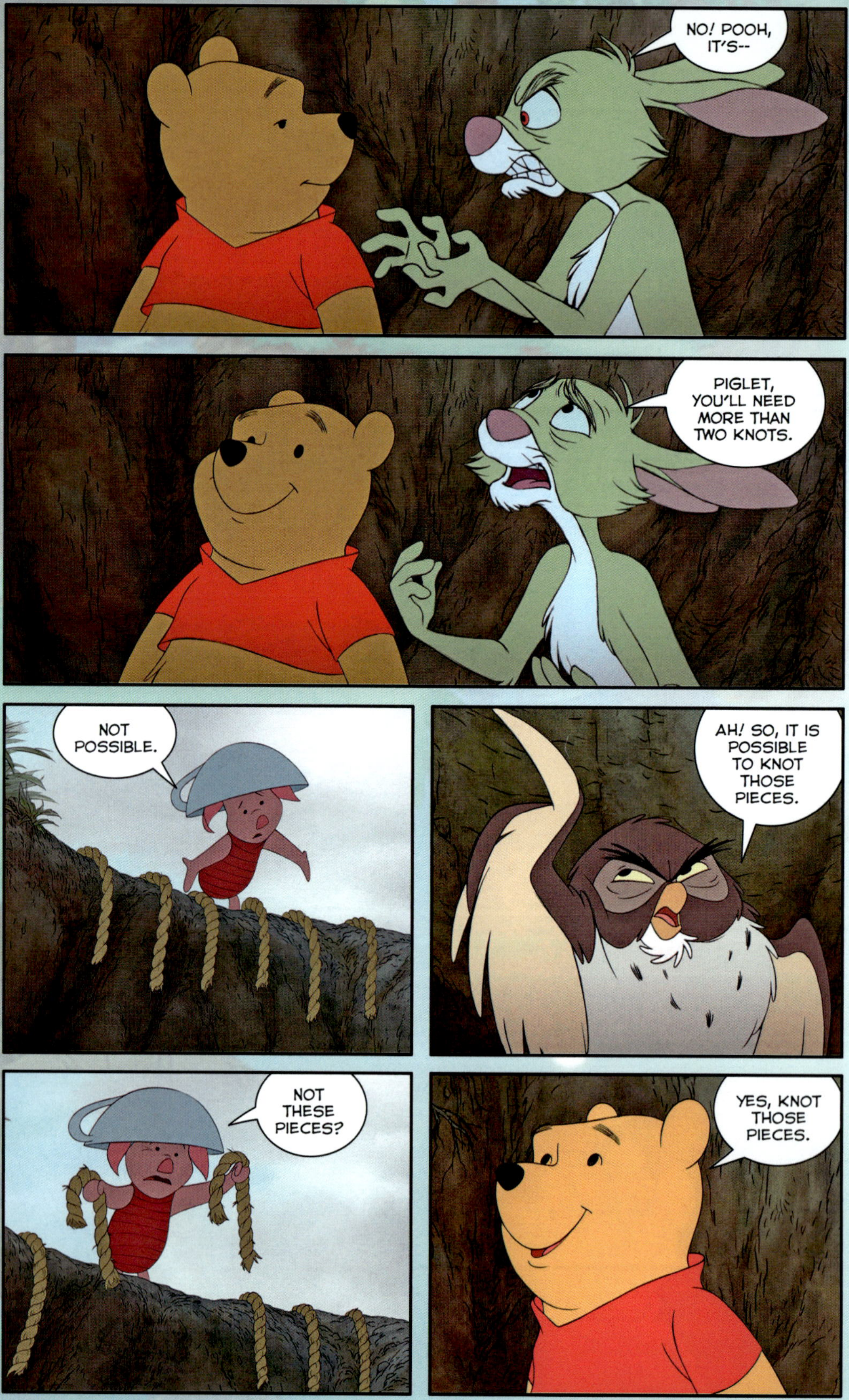
NO! POOH, IT'S--
PIGLET, YOU'LL NEED MORE THAN TWO KNOTS.
NOT POSSIBLE.
AH! SO, IT IS POSSIBLE TO KNOT THOSE PIECES.
NOT THESE PIECES?
YES, KNOT THOSE PIECES.

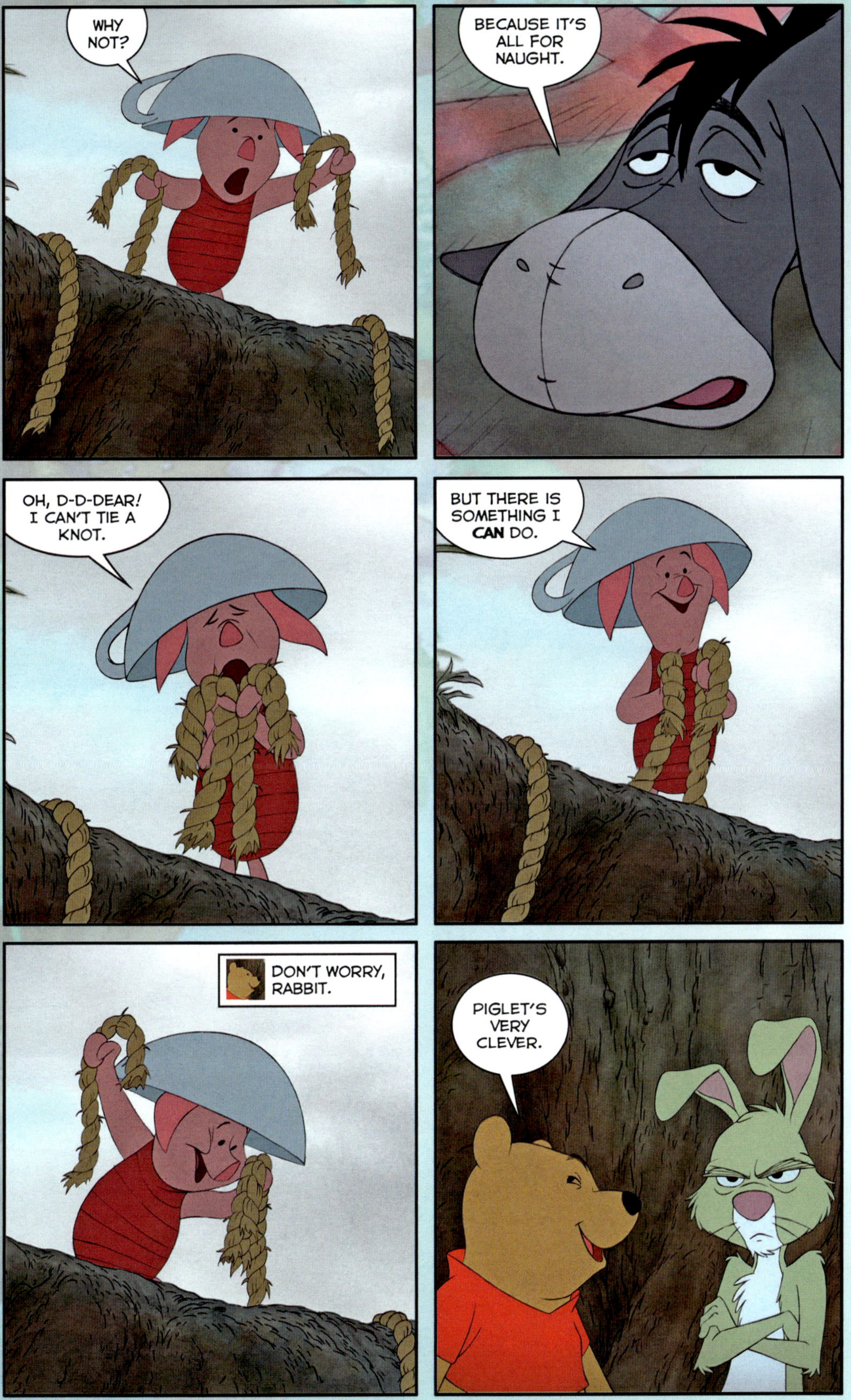

WHY NOT?
BECAUSE IT'S ALL FOR NAUGHT.
OH, D-D-DEAR! I CAN'T TIE A KNOT.
BUT THERE IS SOMETHING I **CAN** DO.
DON'T WORRY, RABBIT.
PIGLET'S VERY CLEVER.

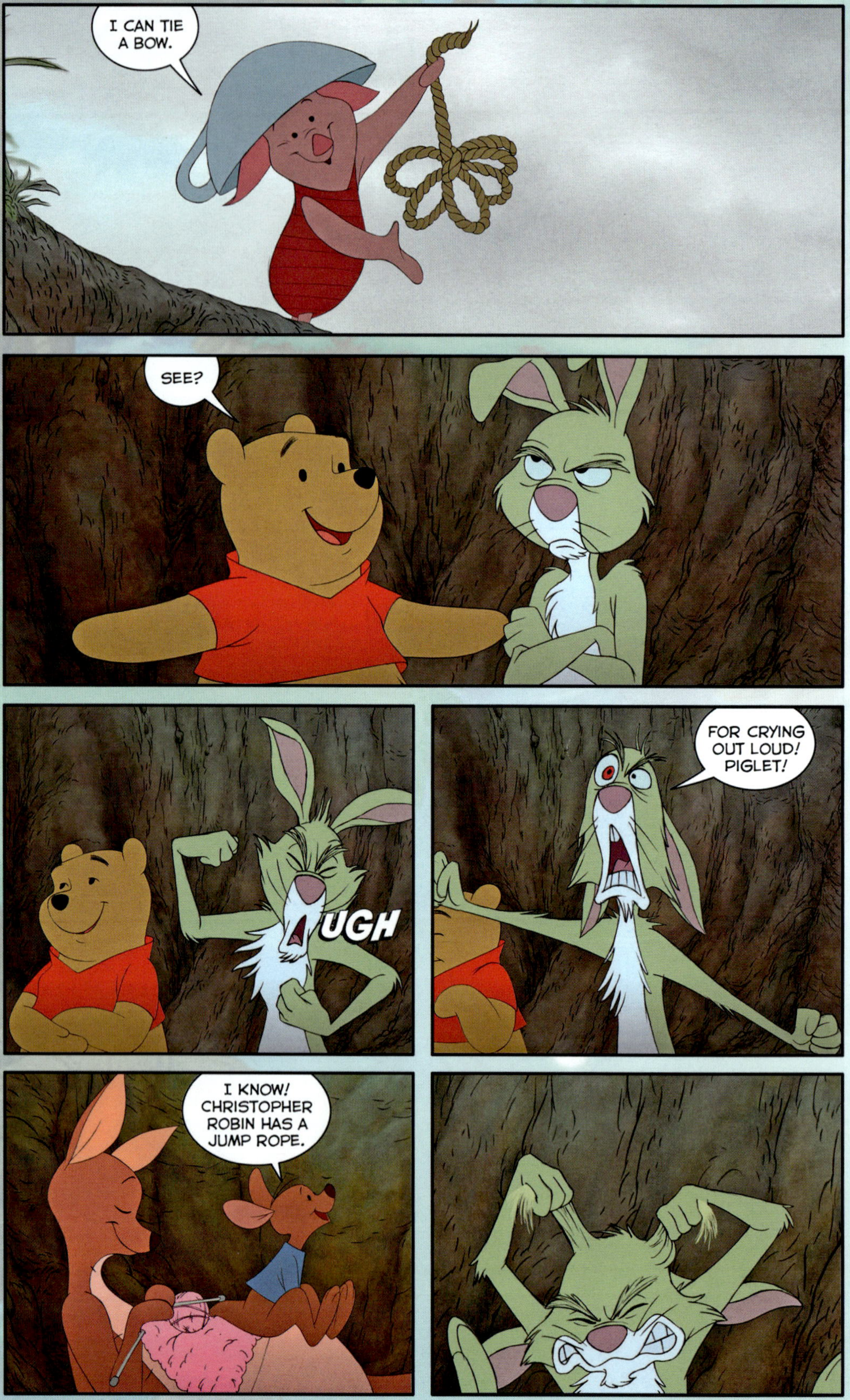
I CAN TIE A BOW.
SEE?
UGH
FOR CRYING OUT LOUD! PIGLET!
I KNOW! CHRISTOPHER ROBIN HAS A JUMP ROPE.

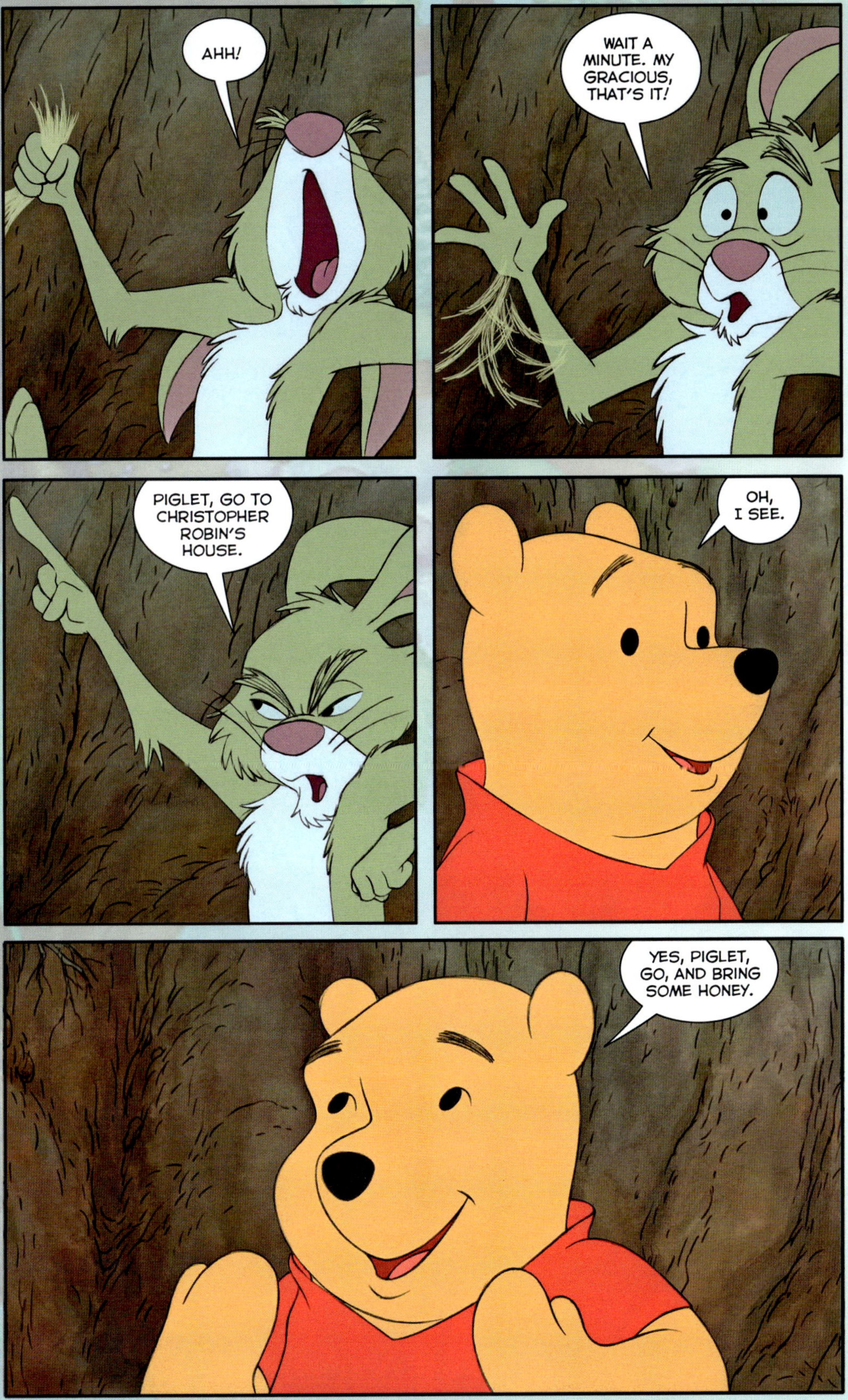
AHH!
WAIT A MINUTE. MY GRACIOUS, THAT'S IT!
PIGLET, GO TO CHRISTOPHER ROBIN'S HOUSE.
OH, I SEE.
YES, PIGLET, GO, AND BRING SOME HONEY.

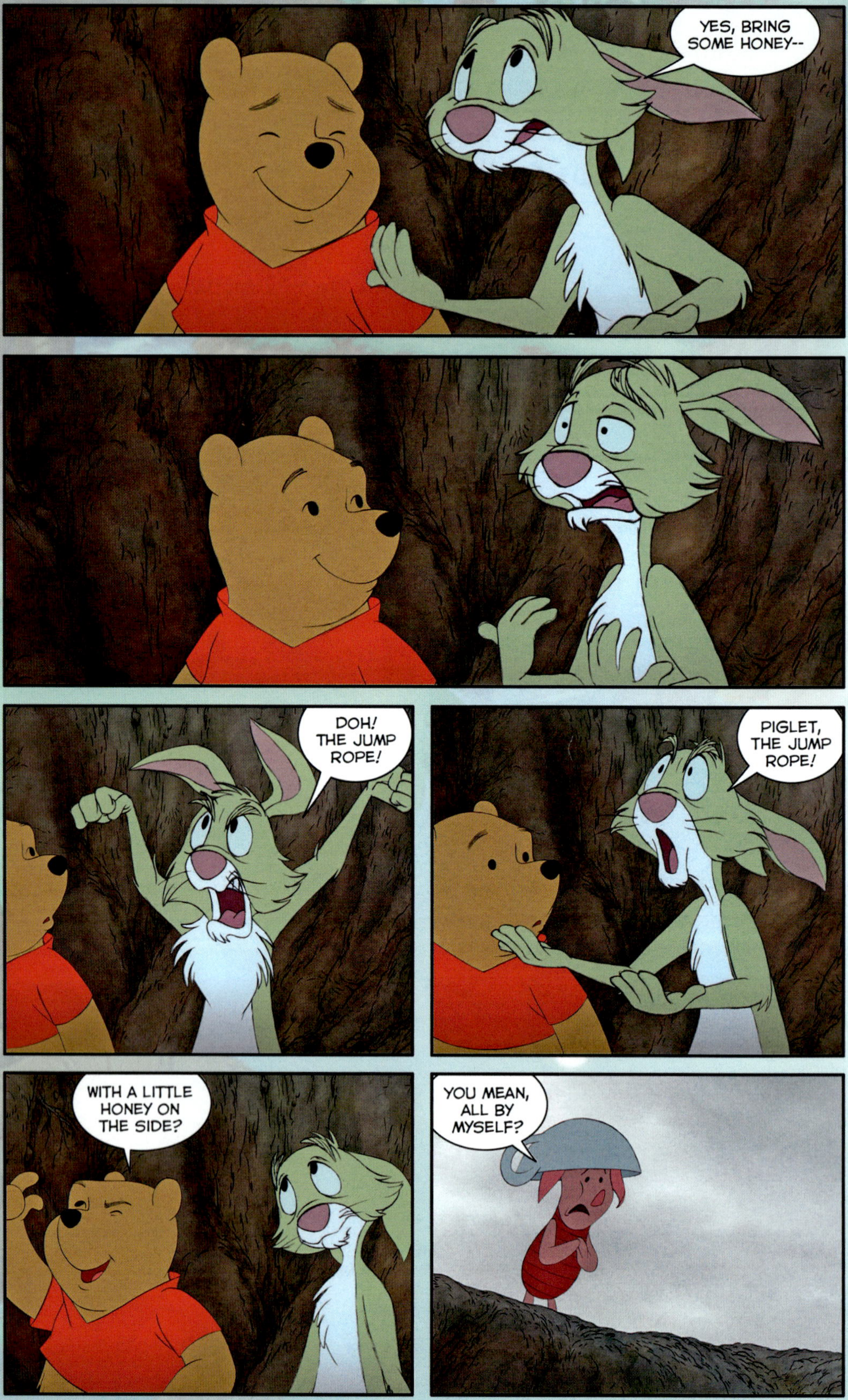
YES, BRING SOME HONEY--
DOH! THE JUMP ROPE!
PIGLET, THE JUMP ROPE!
WITH A LITTLE HONEY ON THE SIDE?
YOU MEAN, ALL BY MYSELF?

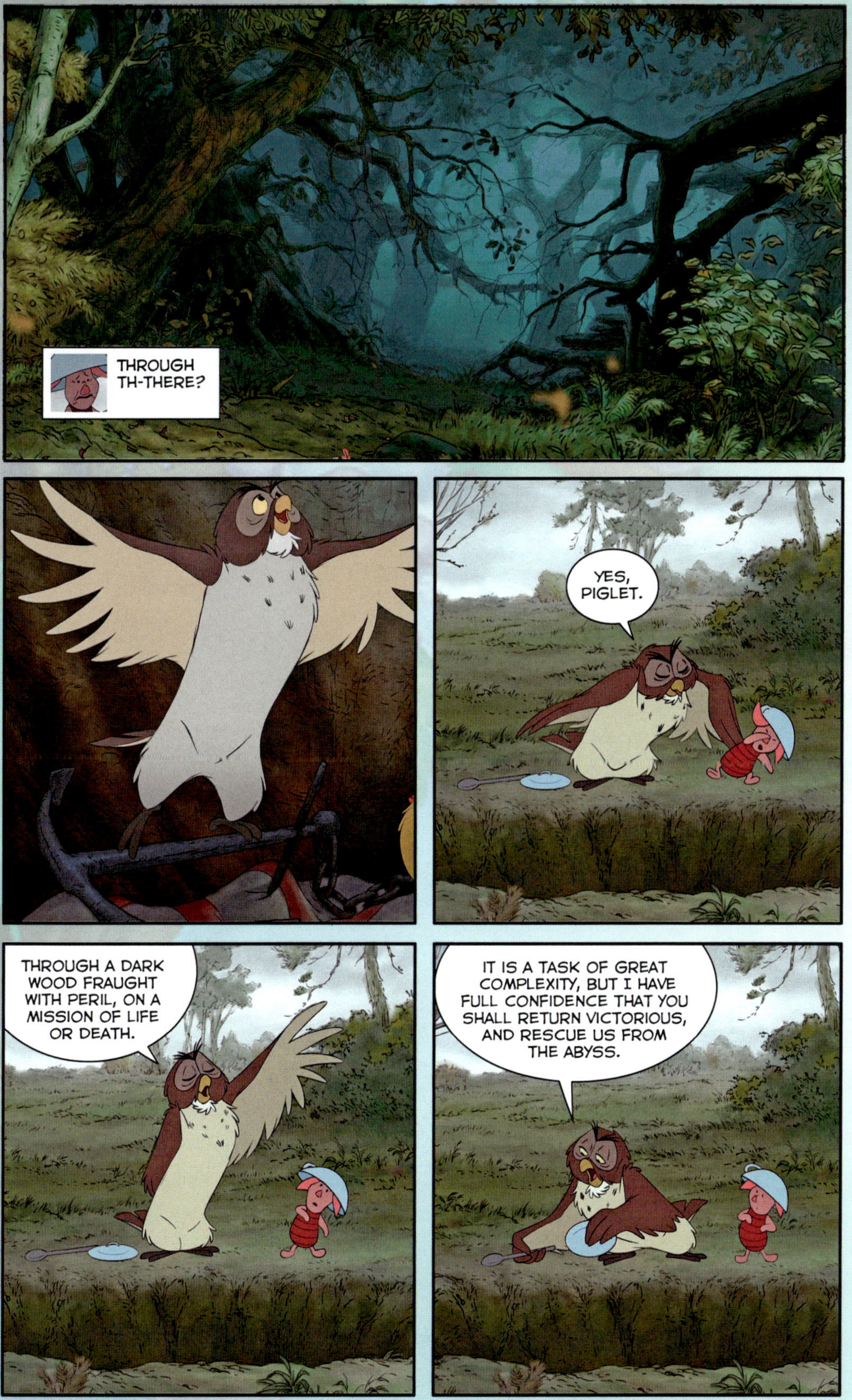
THROUGH TH-THERE?
YES, PIGLET.
THROUGH A DARK WOOD FRAUGHT WITH PERIL, ON A MISSION OF LIFE OR DEATH.
IT IS A TASK OF GREAT COMPLEXITY, BUT I HAVE FULL CONFIDENCE THAT YOU SHALL RETURN VICTORIOUS, AND RESCUE US FROM THE ABYSS.

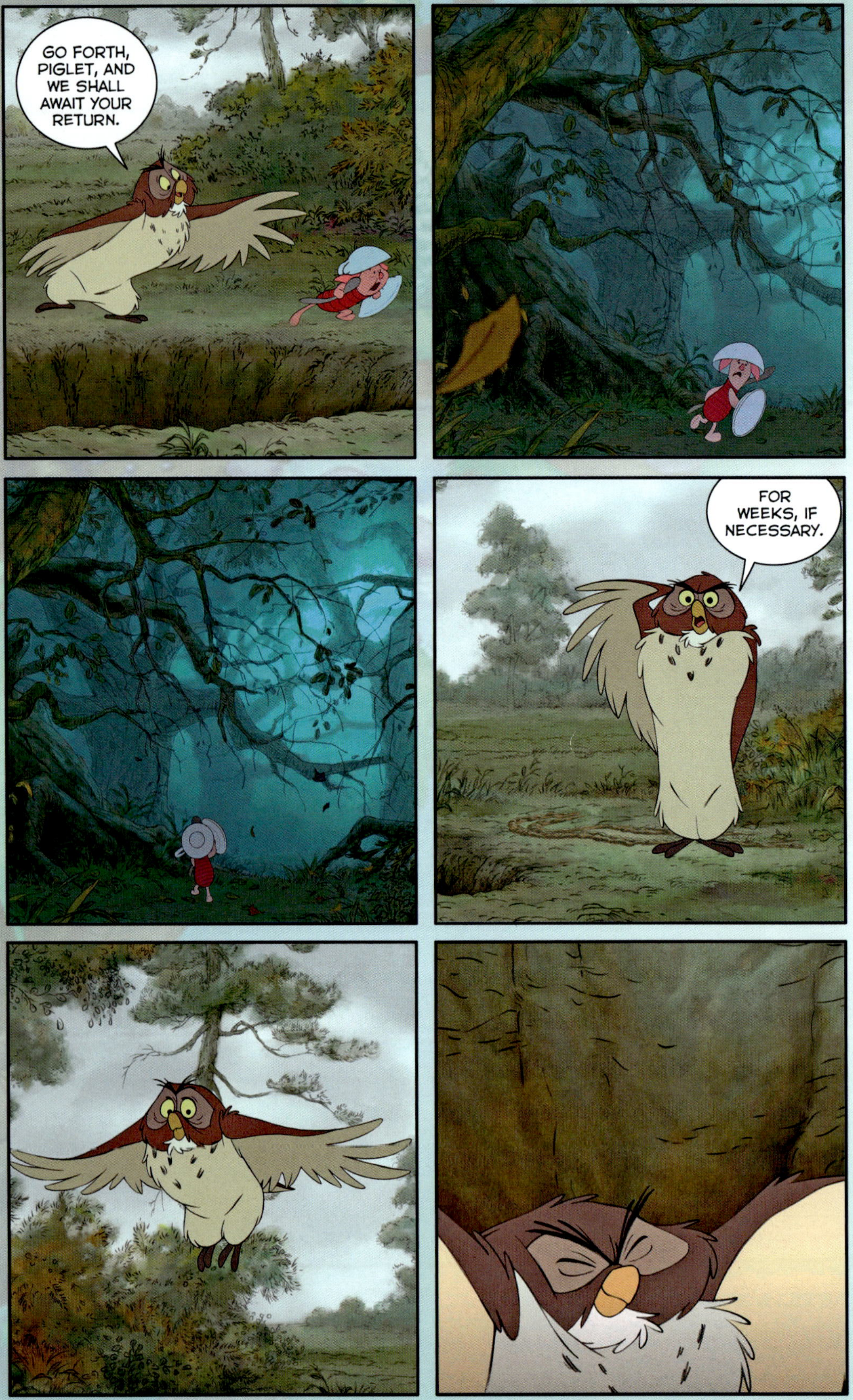
GO FORTH, PIGLET, AND WE SHALL AWAIT YOUR RETURN.
FOR WEEKS, IF NECESSARY.

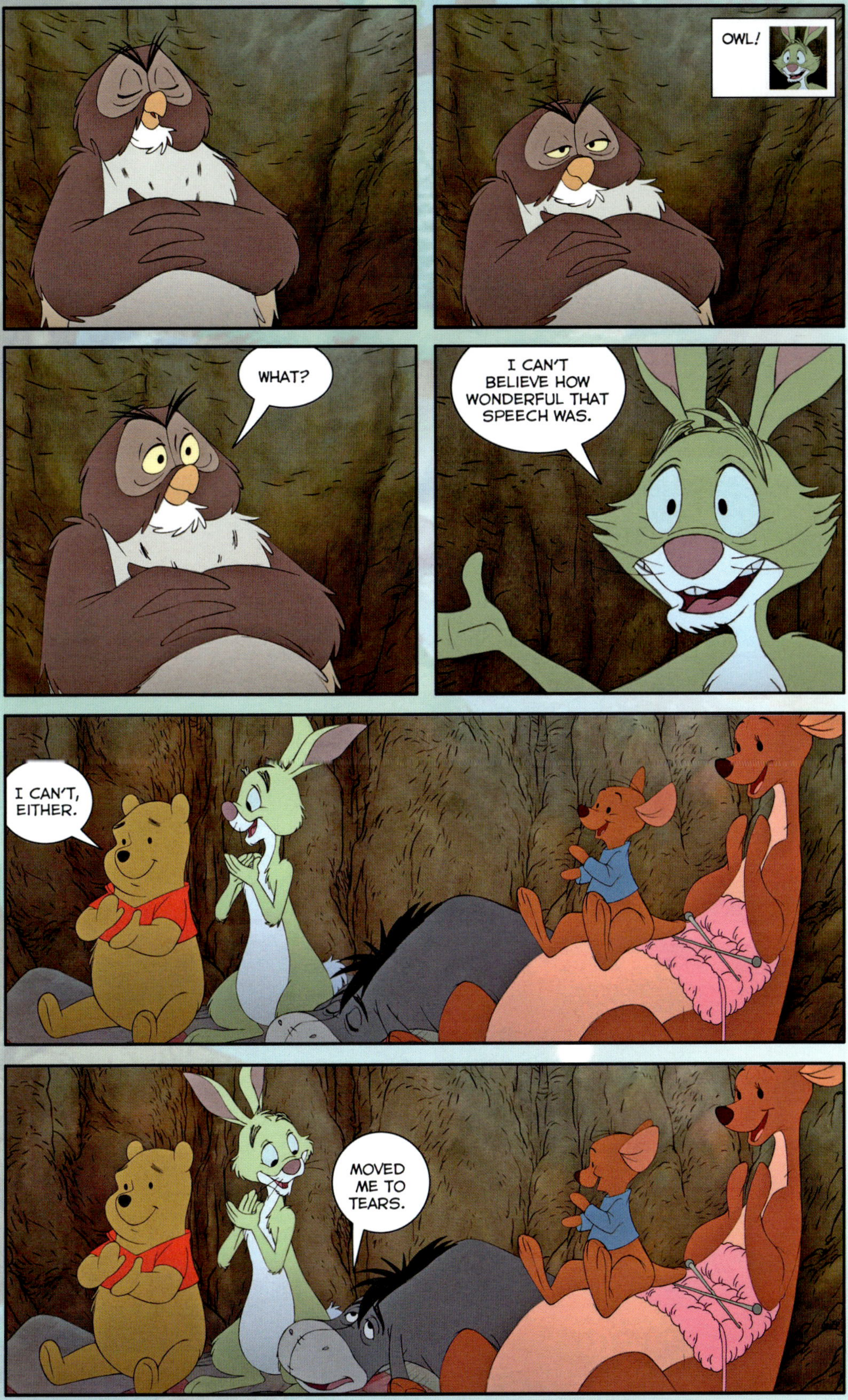
OWL!
WHAT?
I CAN'T BELIEVE HOW WONDERFUL THAT SPEECH WAS.
I CAN'T, EITHER.
MOVED ME TO TEARS.

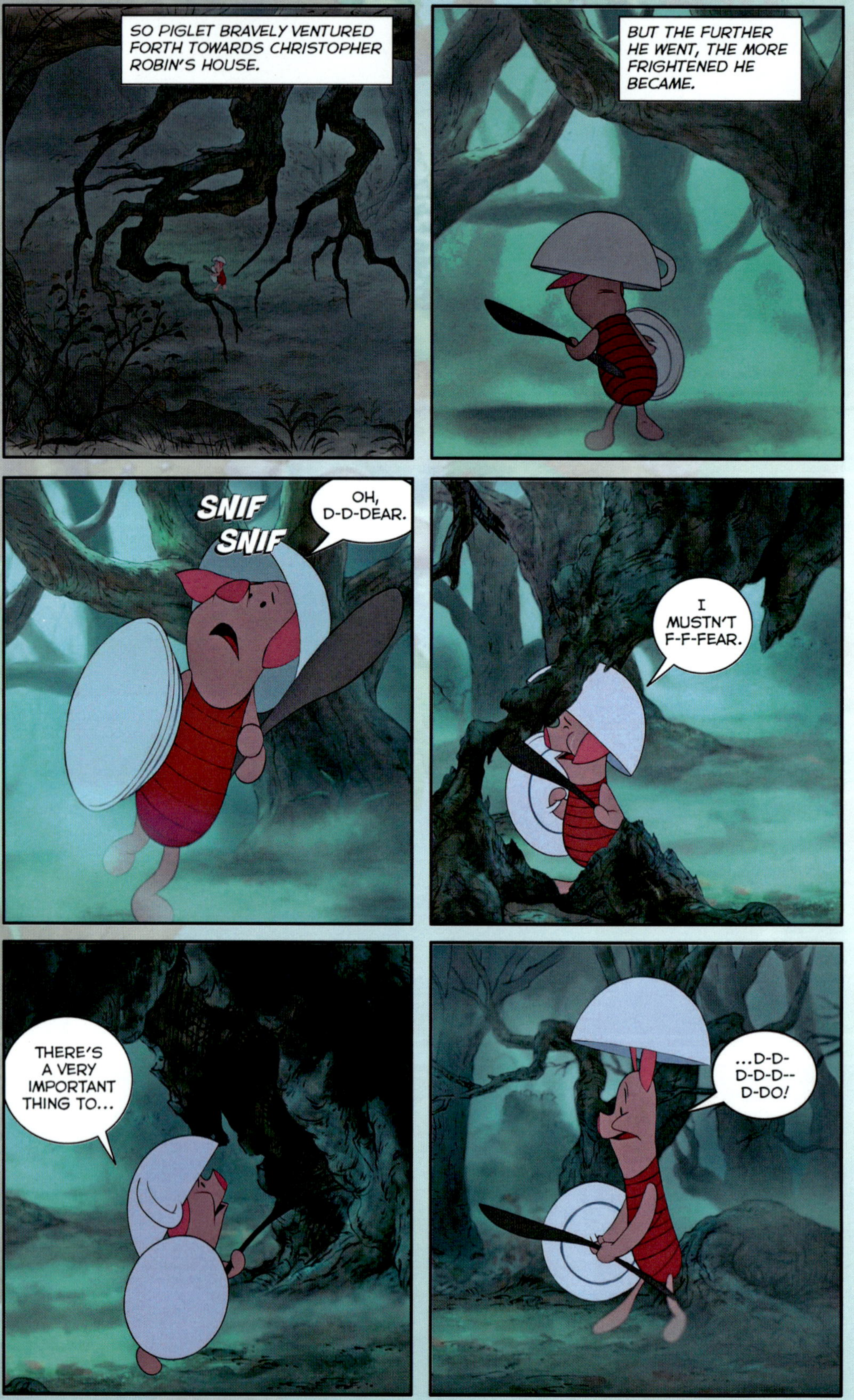
SO PIGLET BRAVELY VENTURED FORTH TOWARDS CHRISTOPHER ROBIN'S HOUSE.
BUT THE FURTHER HE WENT, THE MORE FRIGHTENED HE BECAME.
SNIF
SNIF
OH, D-D-DEAR.
I MUSTN'T F-F-FEAR.
THERE'S A VERY IMPORTANT THING TO...
...D-D-D-D-D--D-DO!

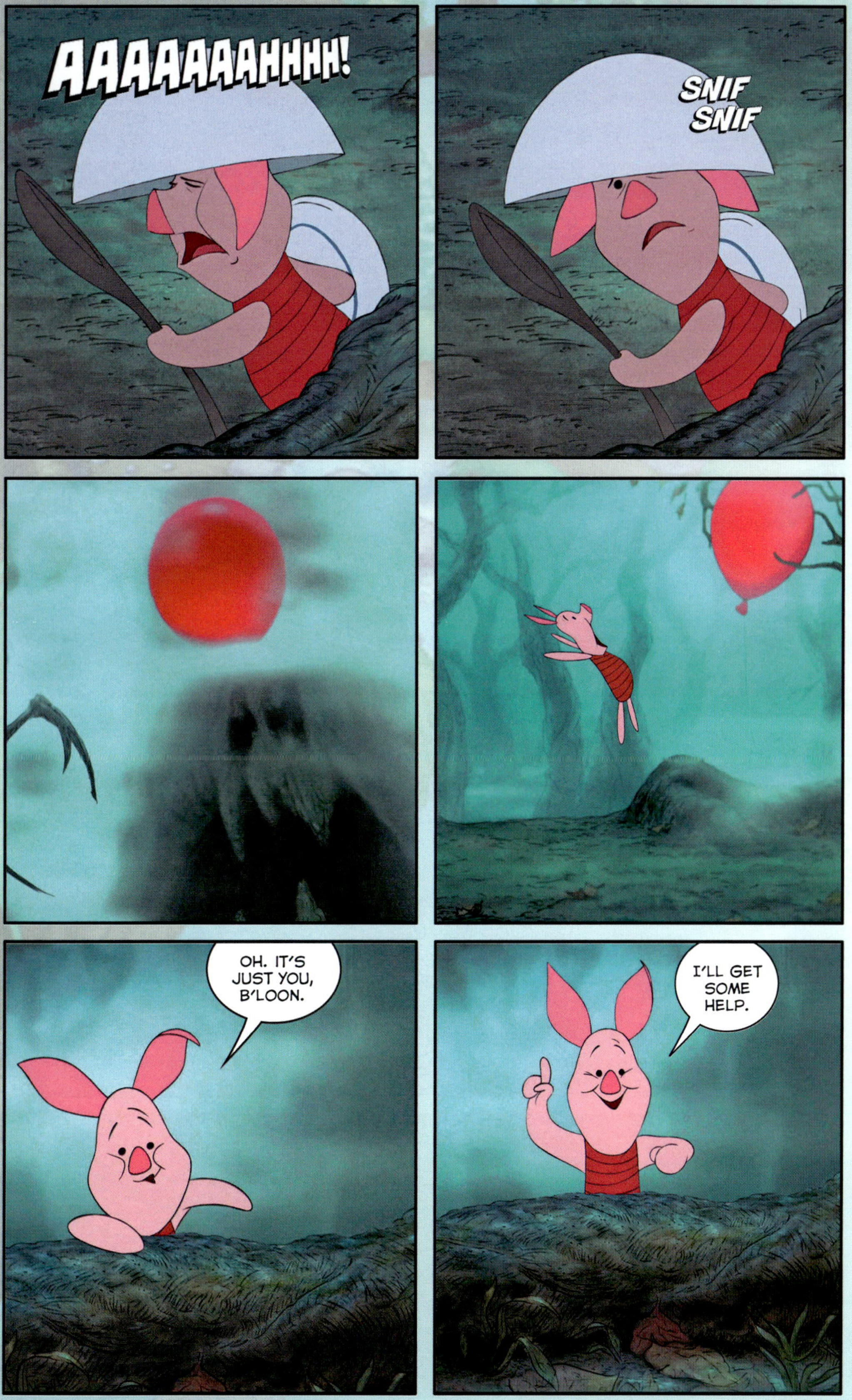
AAAAAAAHHHH!
SNIF SNIF
OH. IT'S JUST YOU, B'LOON.
I'LL GET SOME HELP.

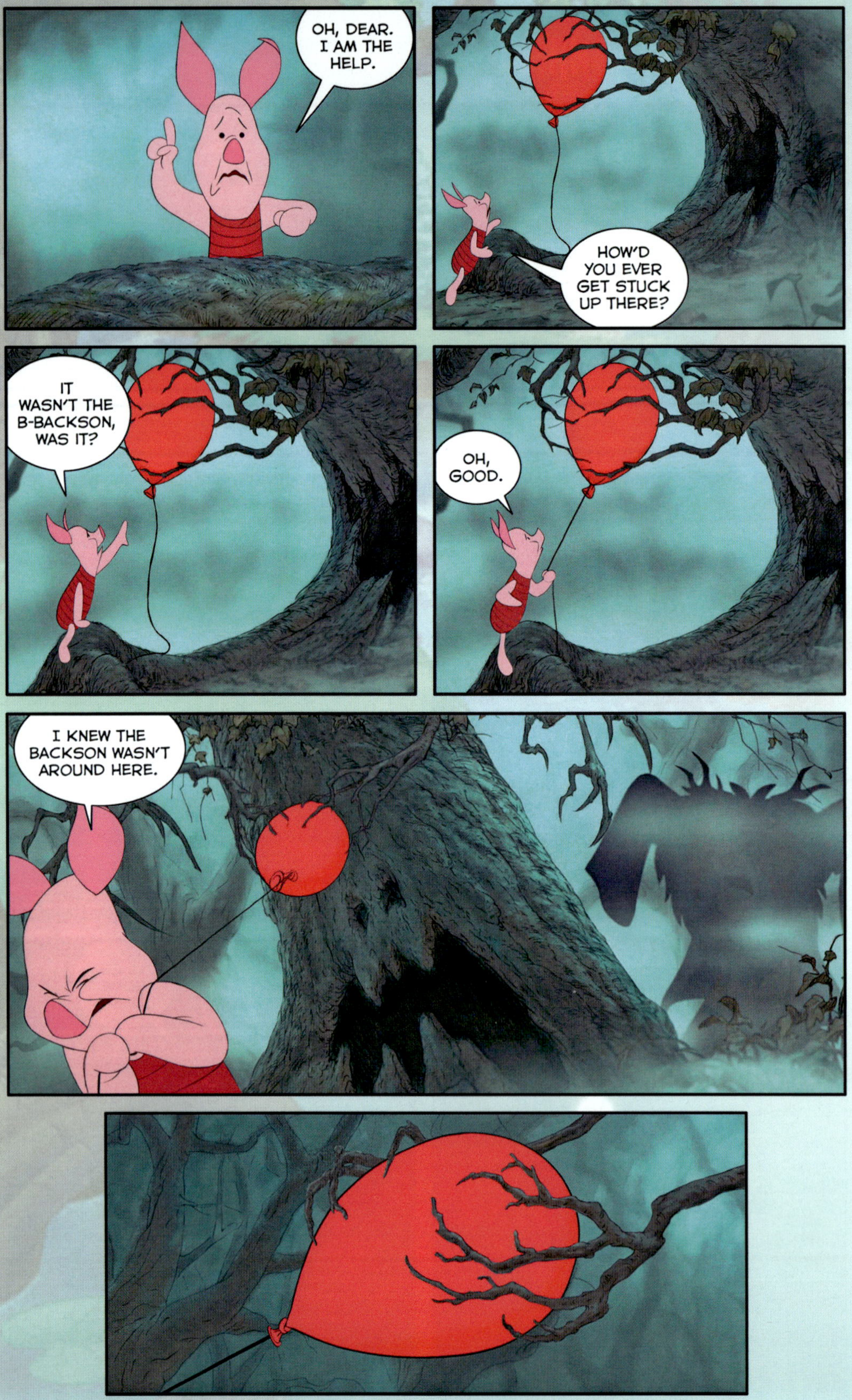
OH, DEAR. I AM THE HELP.
HOW'D YOU EVER GET STUCK UP THERE?
IT WASN'T THE B-BACKSON, WAS IT?
OH, GOOD.
I KNEW THE BACKSON WASN'T AROUND HERE.

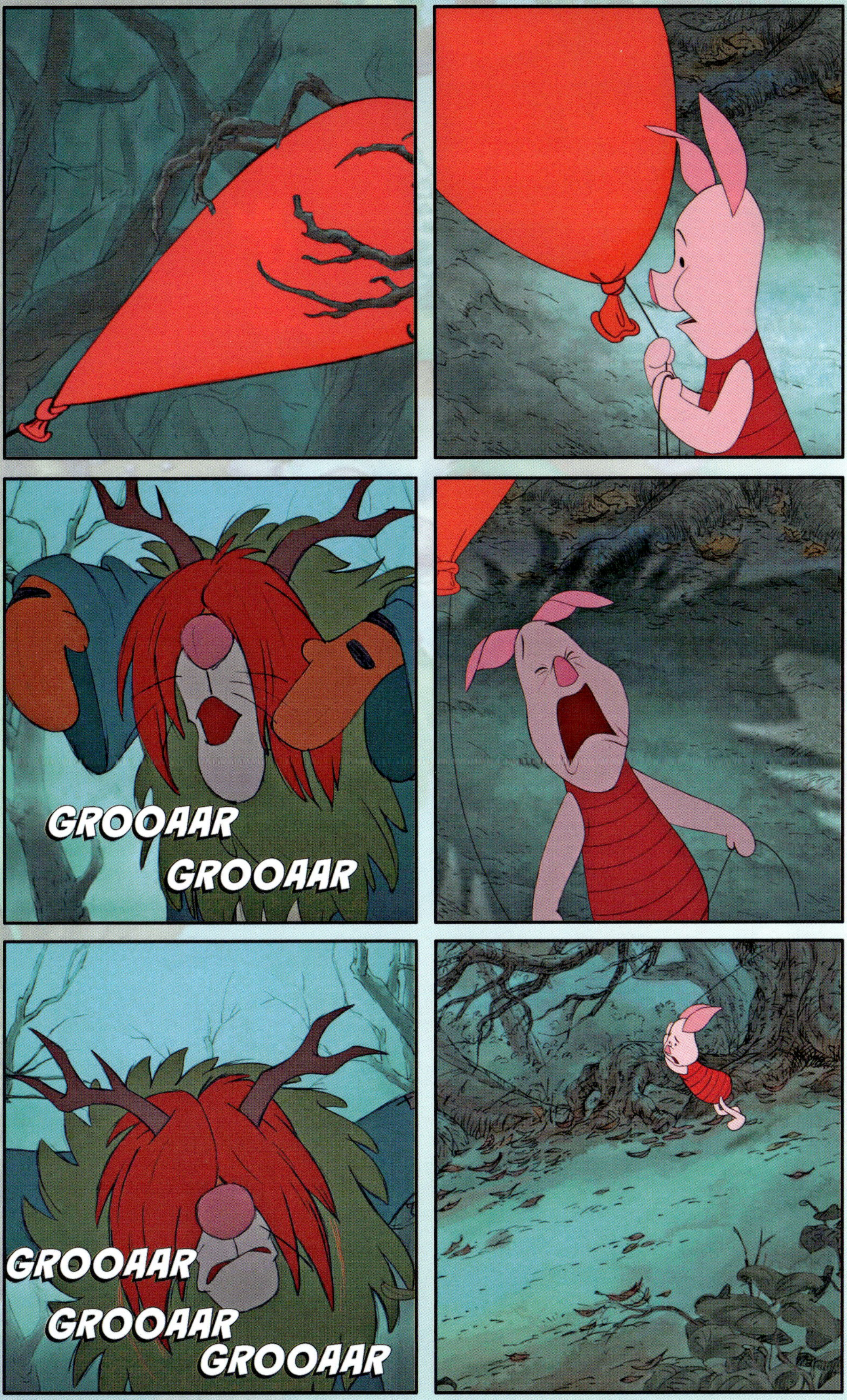
GROOAAR
GROOAAR
GROOAAR
GROOAAR
GROOAAR

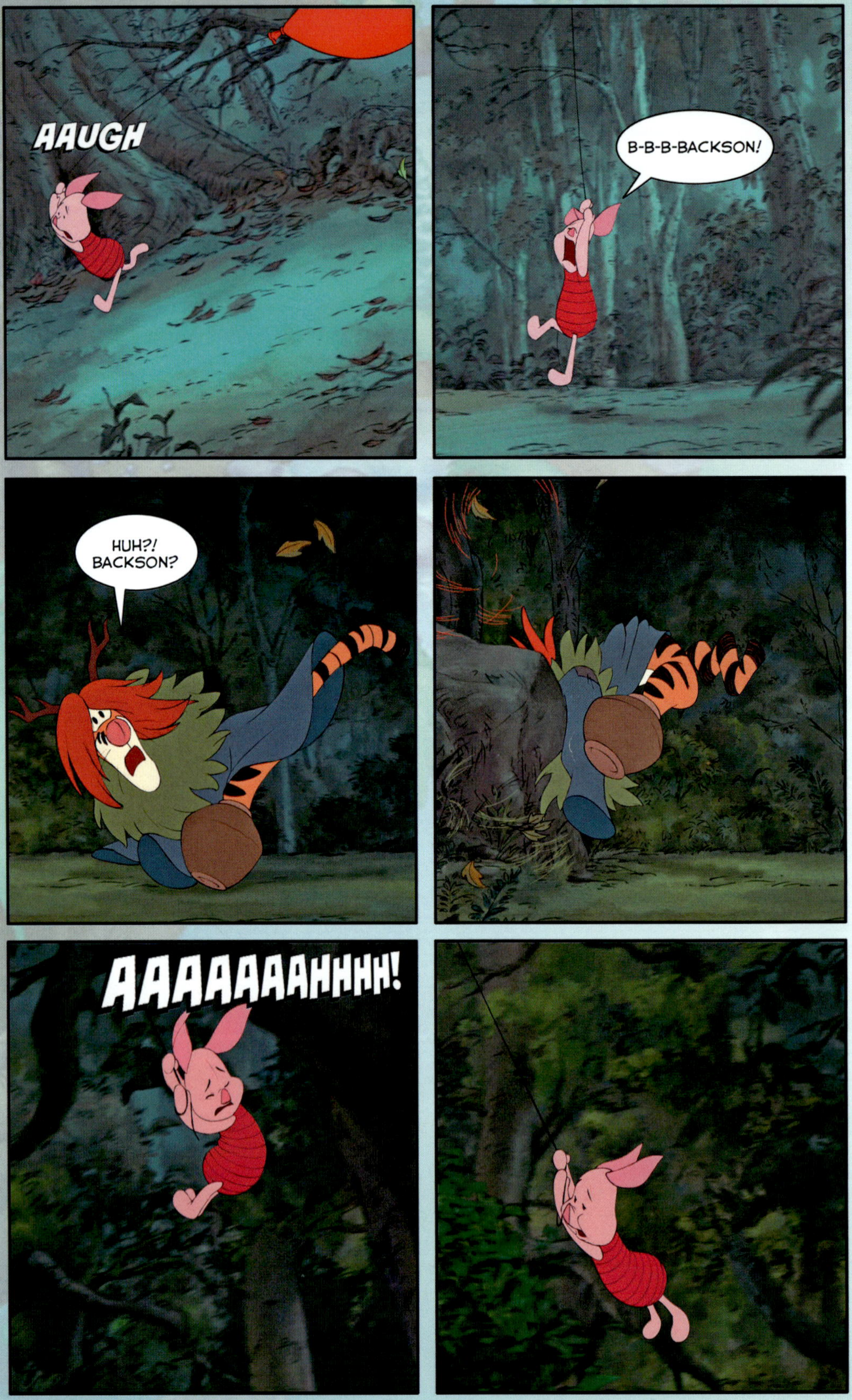
AAUGH
B-B-B-BACKSON!
HUH?! BACKSON?
AAAAAAAHHHH!

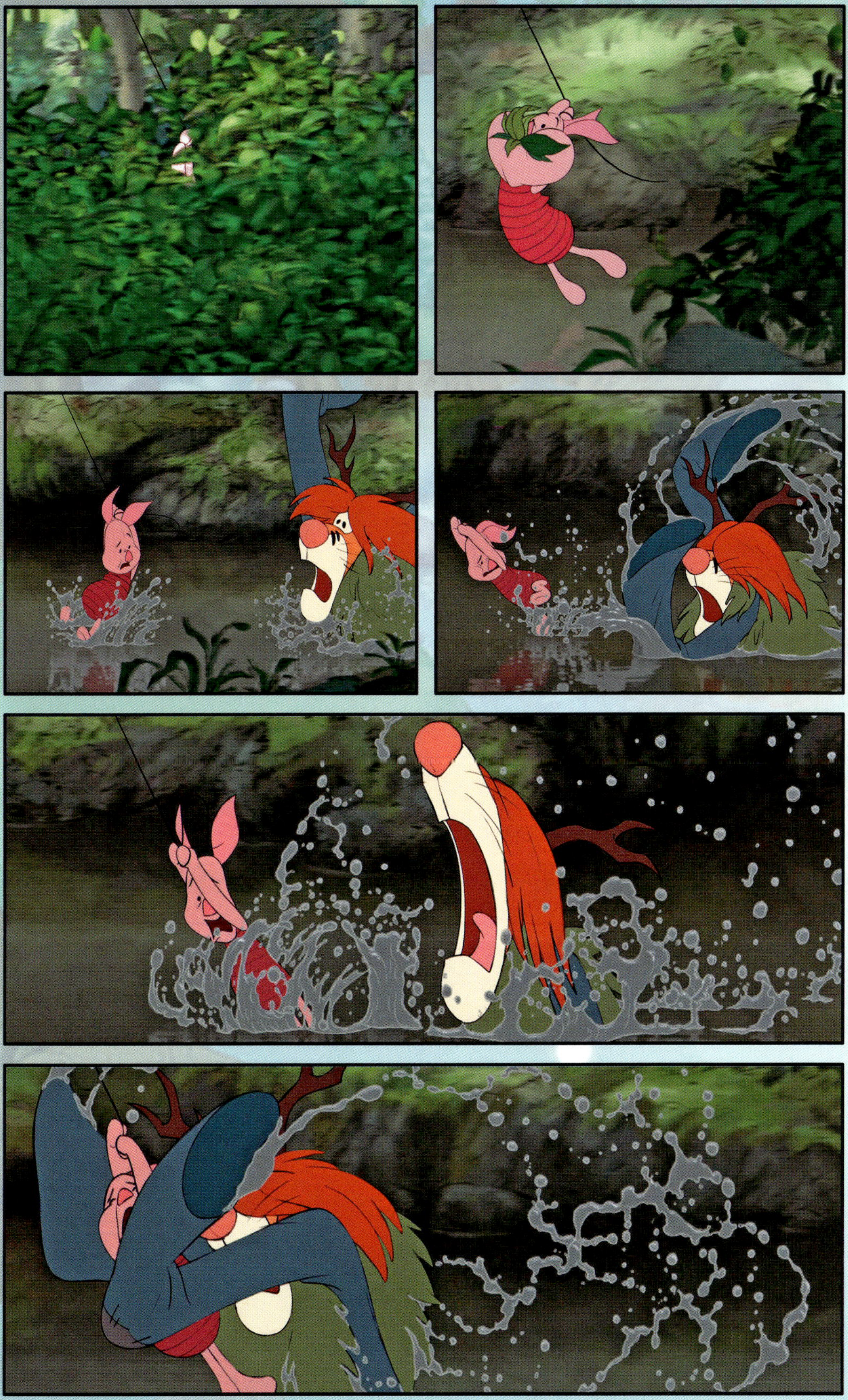

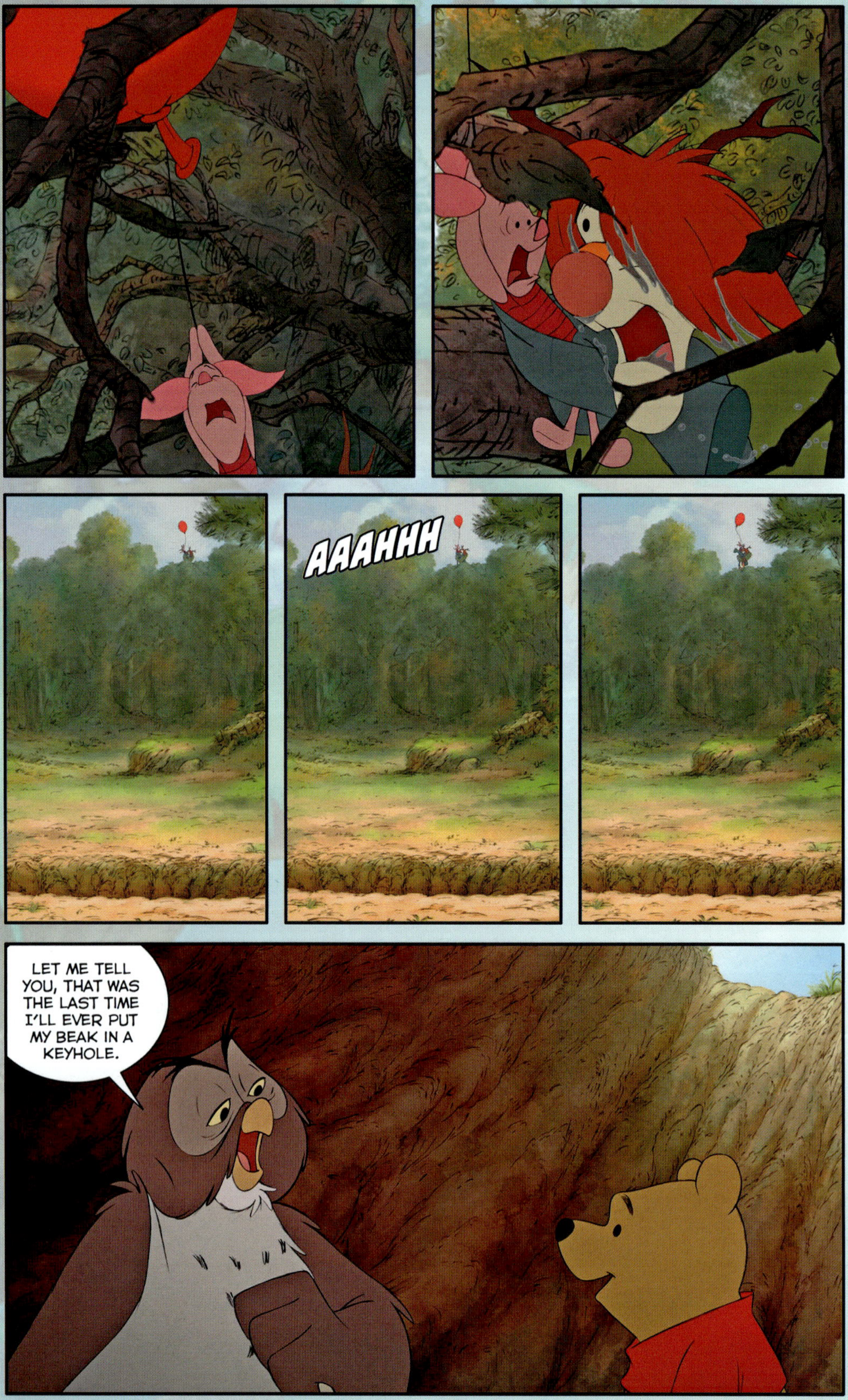
AAAHHH
LET ME TELL YOU, THAT WAS THE LAST TIME I'LL EVER PUT MY BEAK IN A KEYHOLE.

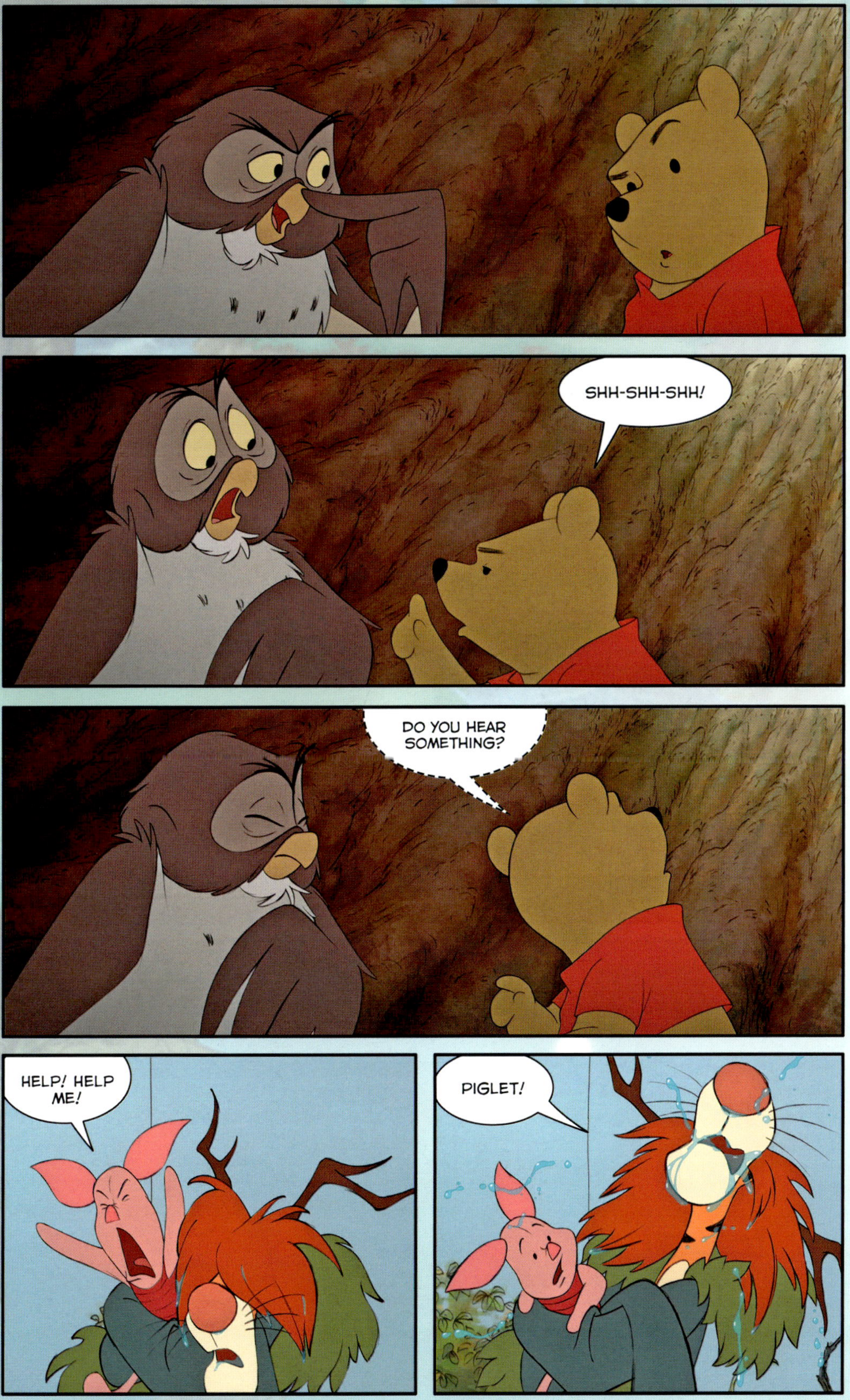
SHH-SHH-SHH!
DO YOU HEAR SOMETHING?
HELP! HELP ME!
PIGLET!

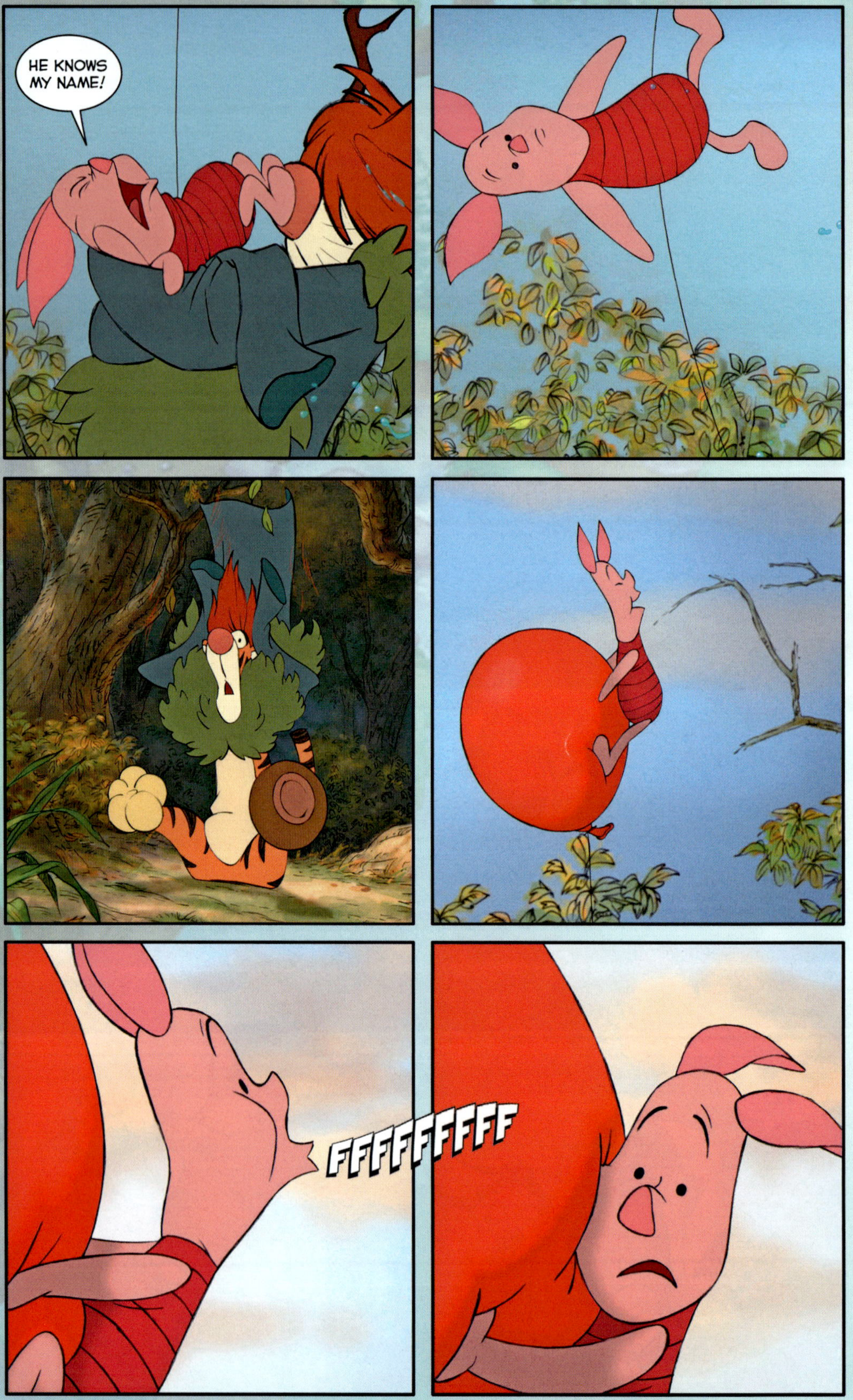
HE KNOWS MY NAME!
FFFFFFFFF

Piglet did the best he could to get to the others in the pit! He held tight to the string as B'loon carried him through the thick forest but the Backson was still close behind. This was too much to bear for poor Piglet!

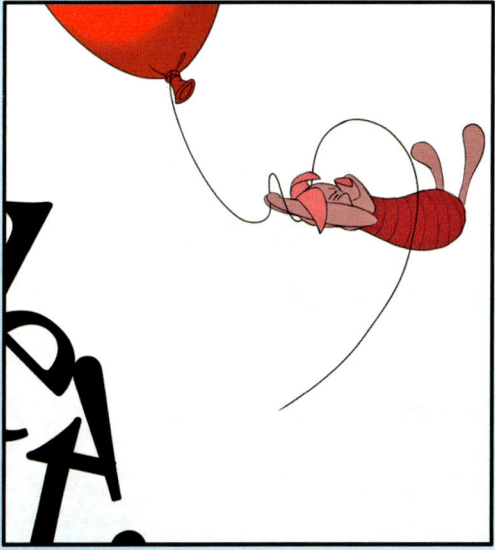

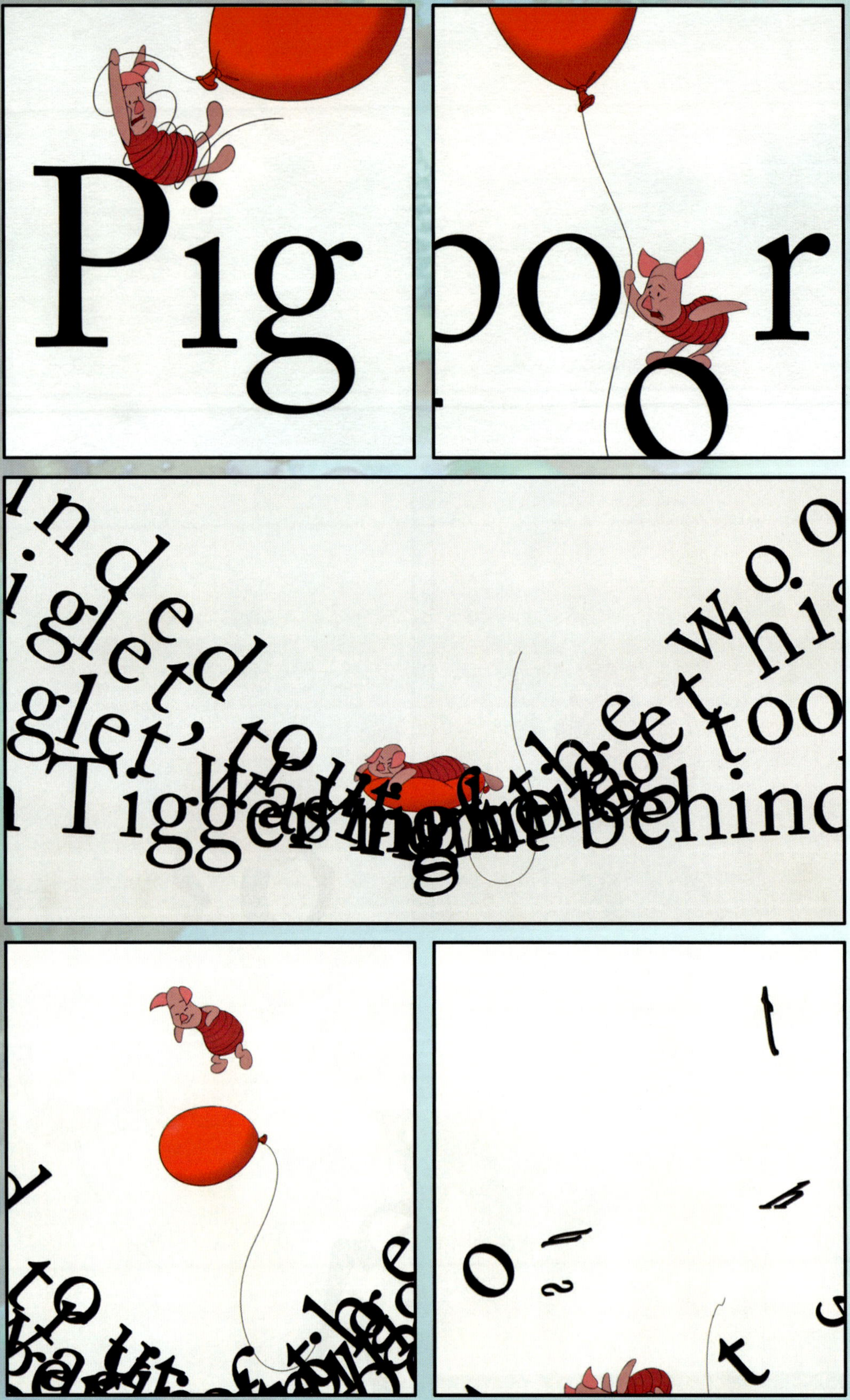
Pig
po r
Tigger
behind

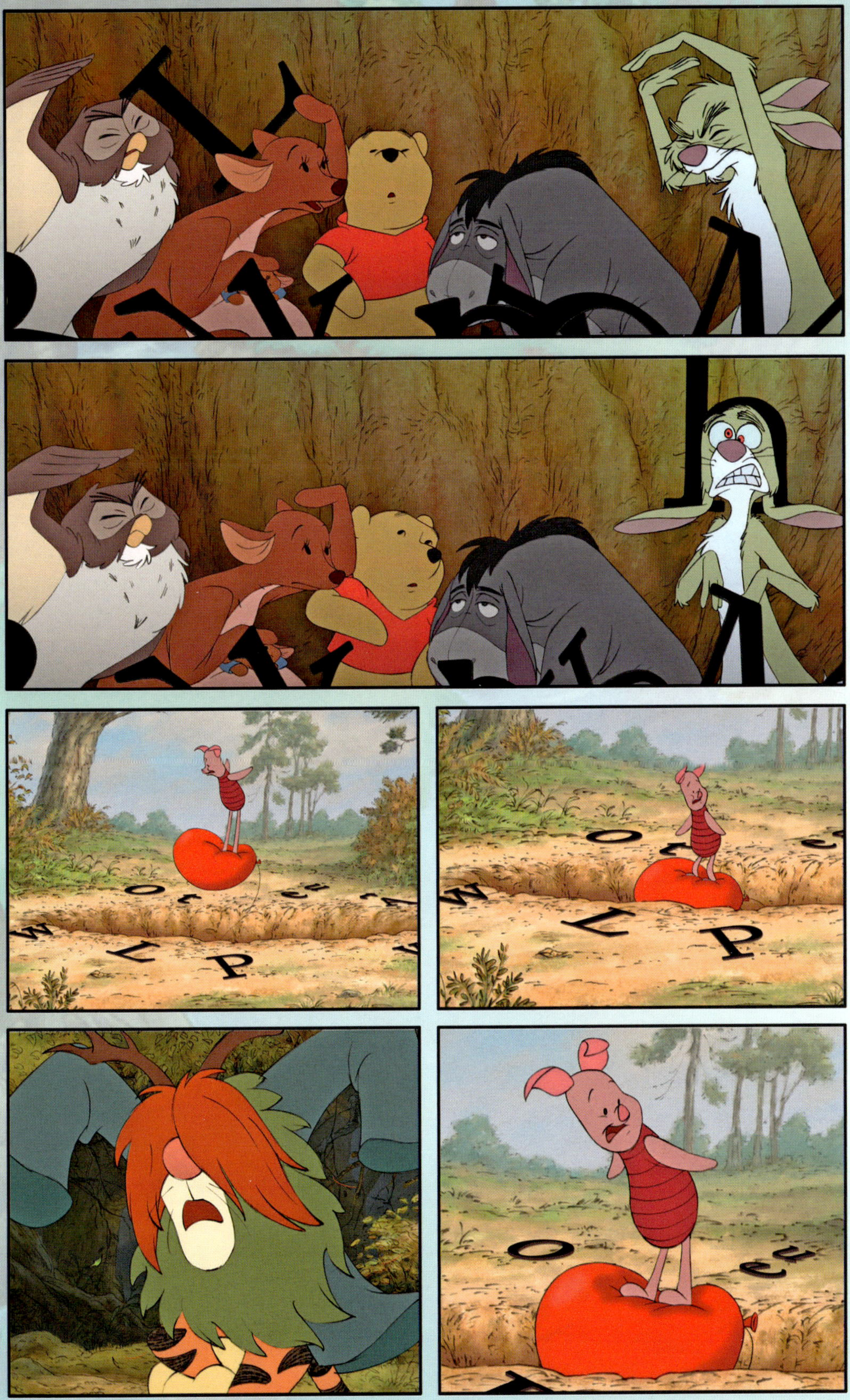

thick forest but the Backson was still close behind. This wa too much to bear for

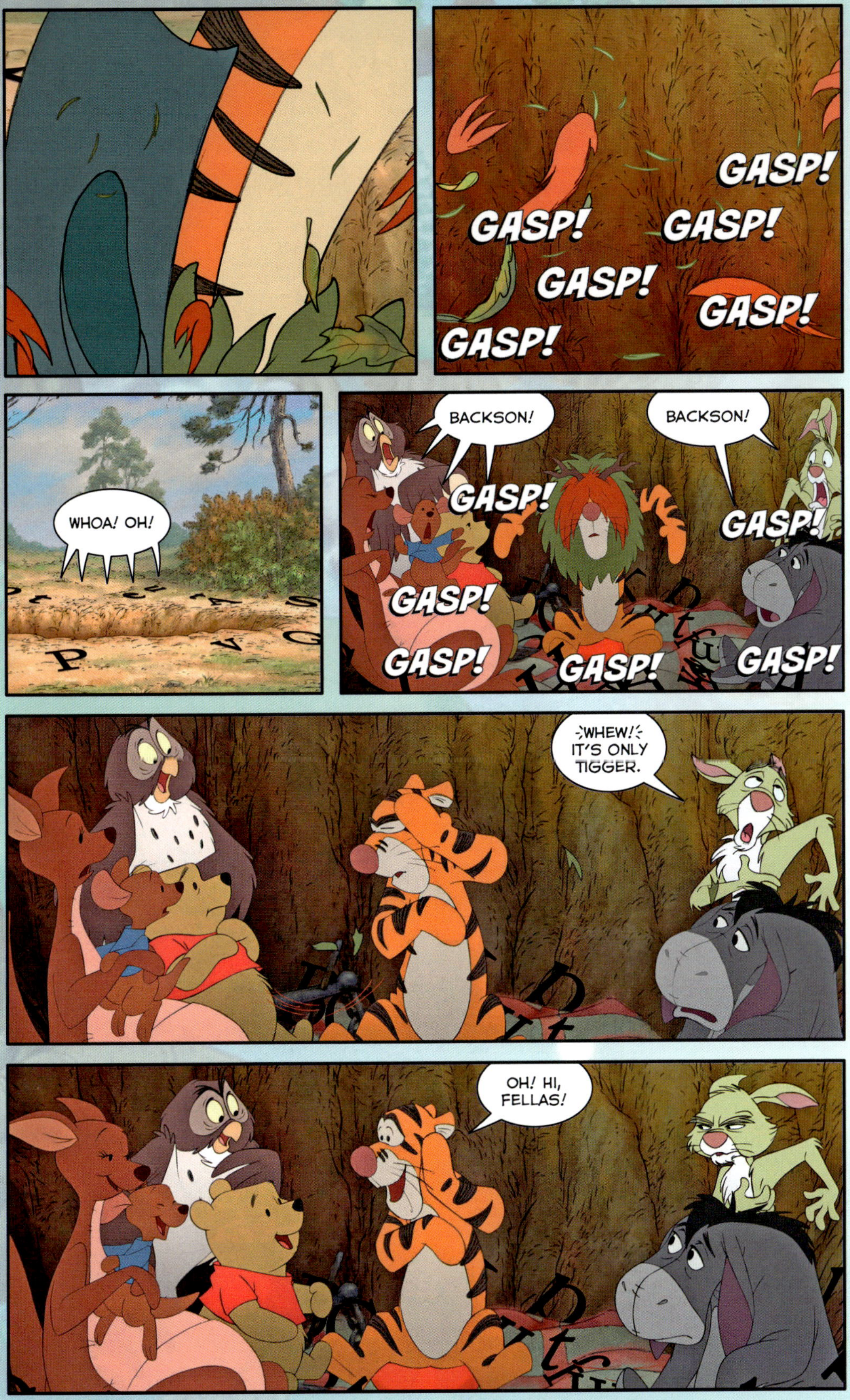
GASP!
GASP!
GASP!
GASP!
GASP!
GASP!
WHOA! OH!
BACKSON!
BACKSON!
GASP!
GASP!
GASP!
GASP!
GASP!
GASP!
WHEW! IT'S ONLY TIGGER.
OH! HI, FELLAS!

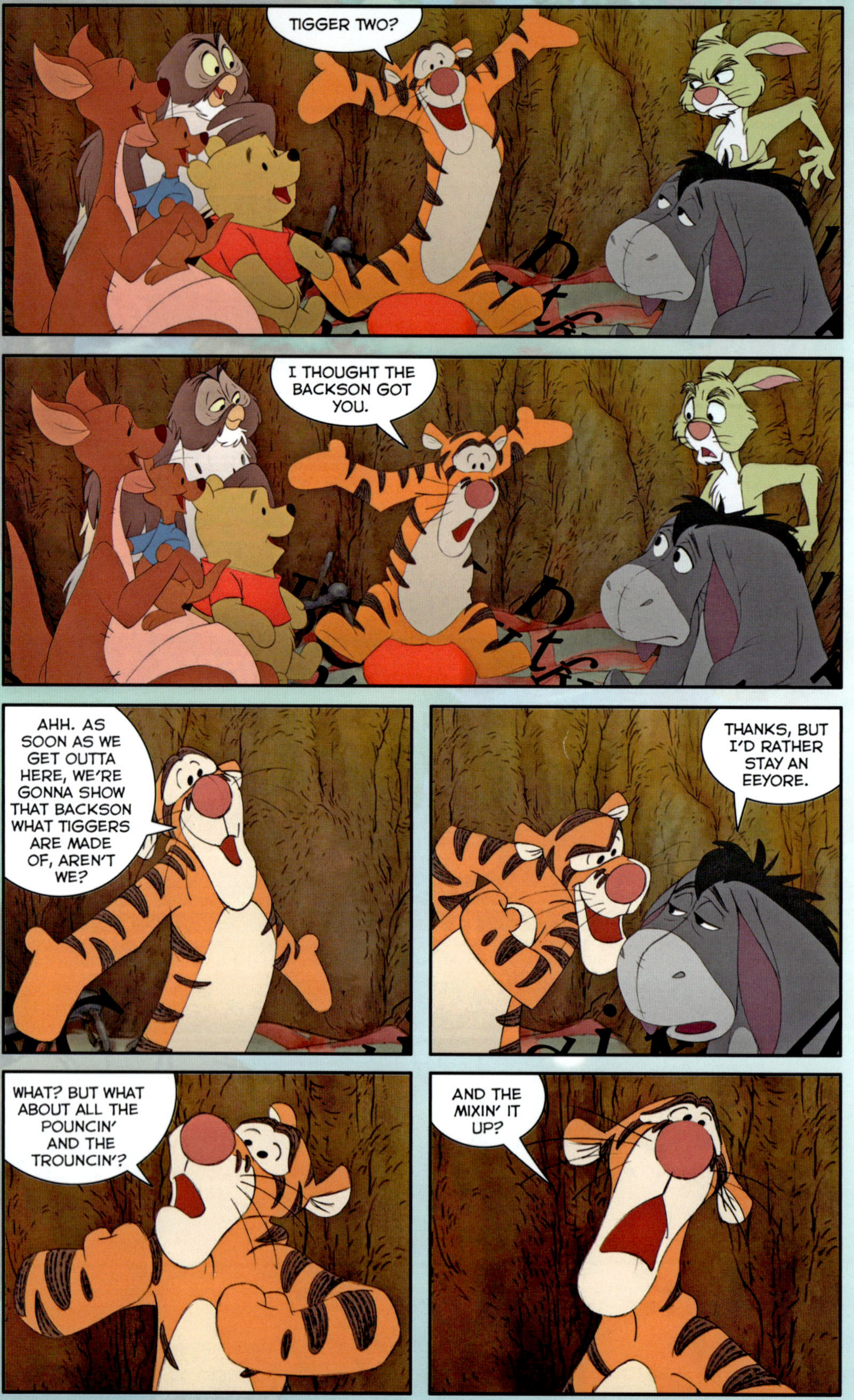
TIGGER TWO?
I THOUGHT THE BACKSON GOT YOU.
AHH. AS SOON AS WE GET OUTTA HERE, WE'RE GONNA SHOW THAT BACKSON WHAT TIGGERS ARE MADE OF, AREN'T WE?
THANKS, BUT I'D RATHER STAY AN EEYORE.
WHAT? BUT WHAT ABOUT ALL THE POUNCIN' AND THE TROUNCIN'?
AND THE MIXIN' IT UP?

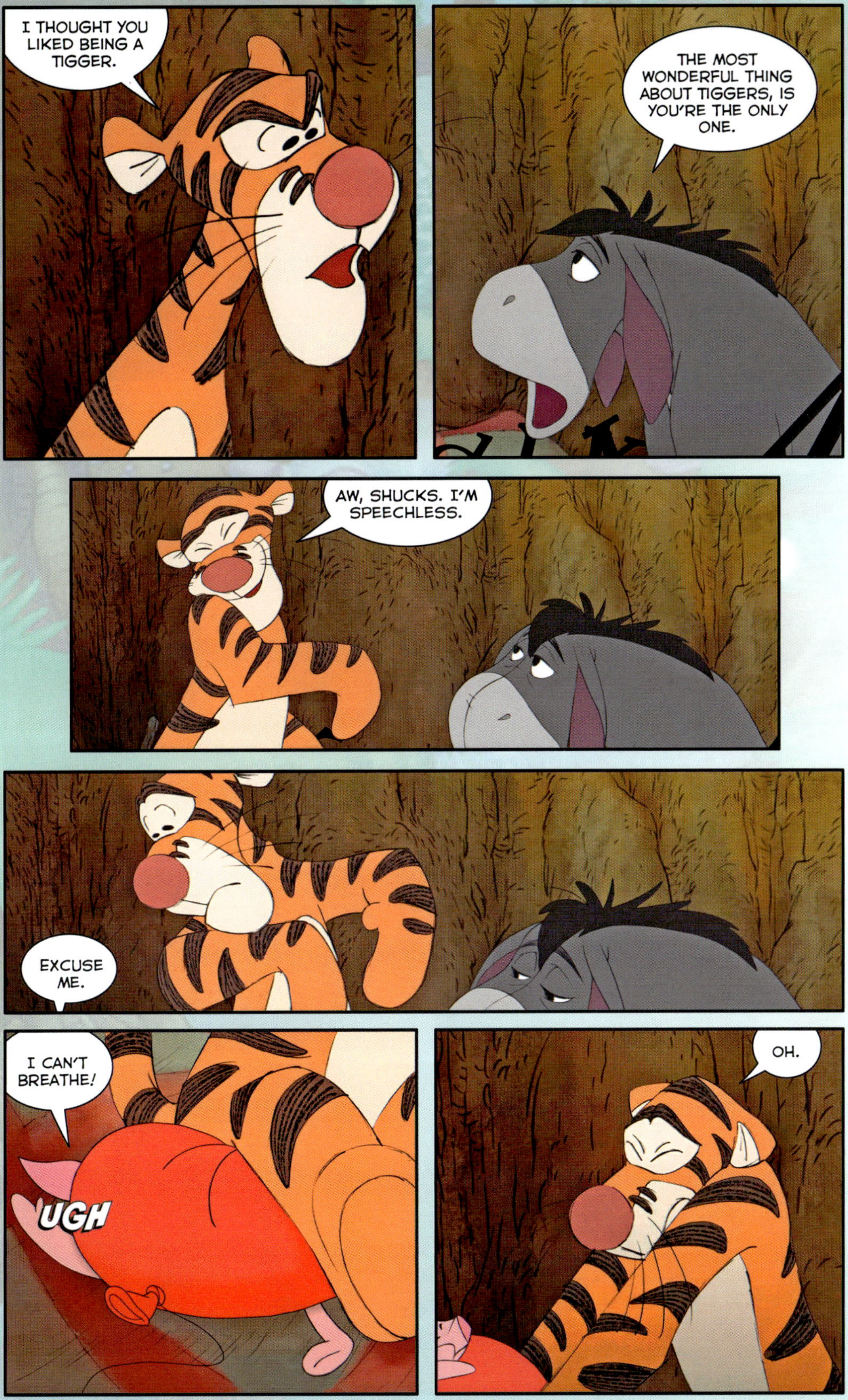
I THOUGHT YOU LIKED BEING A TIGGER.
THE MOST WONDERFUL THING ABOUT TIGGERS, IS YOU'RE THE ONLY ONE.
AW, SHUCKS. I'M SPEECHLESS.
EXCUSE ME.
I CAN'T BREATHE!
UGH
OH.

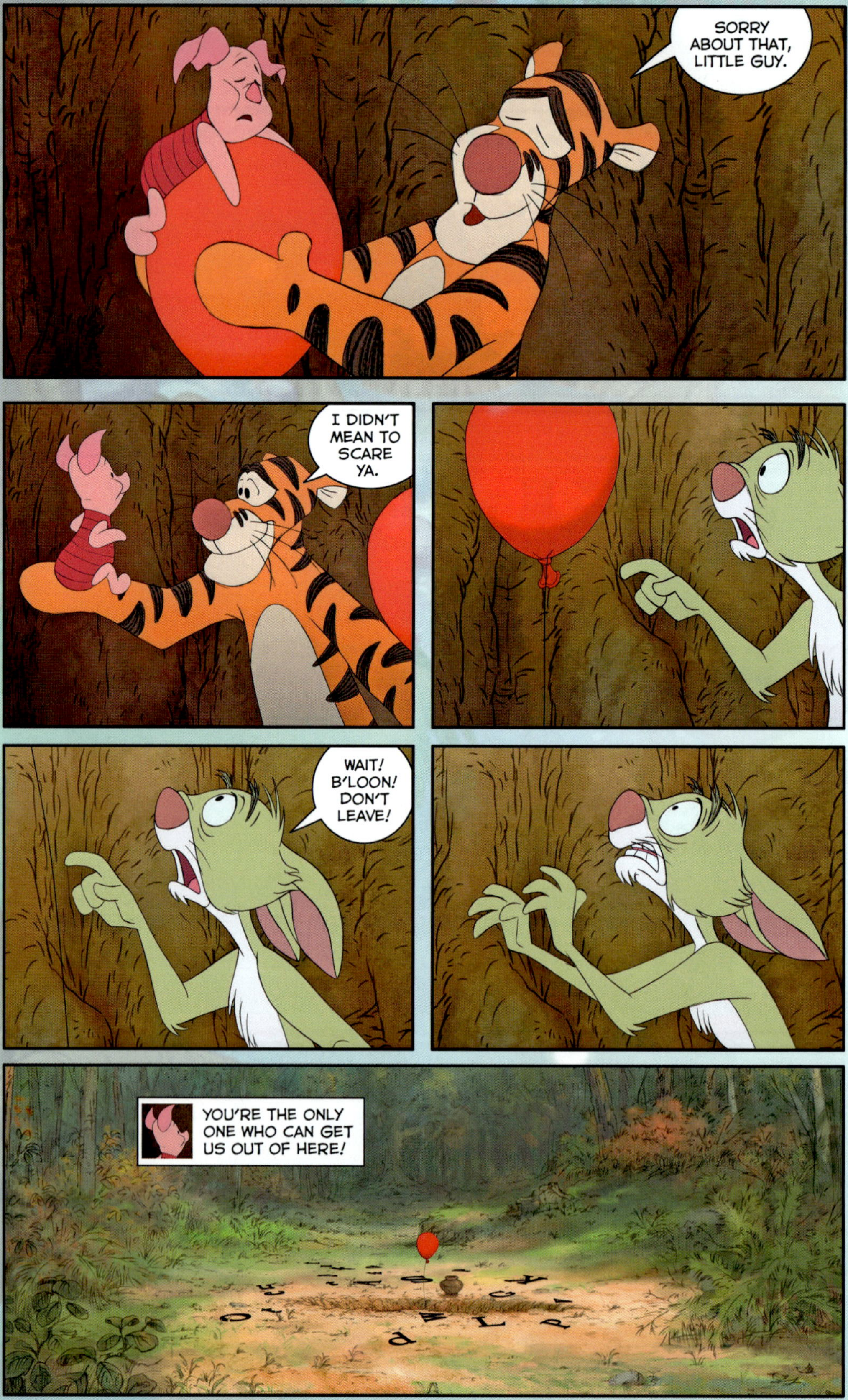
SORRY ABOUT THAT, LITTLE GUY.
I DIDN'T MEAN TO SCARE YA.
WAIT! B'LOON! DON'T LEAVE!
YOU'RE THE ONLY ONE WHO CAN GET US OUT OF HERE!

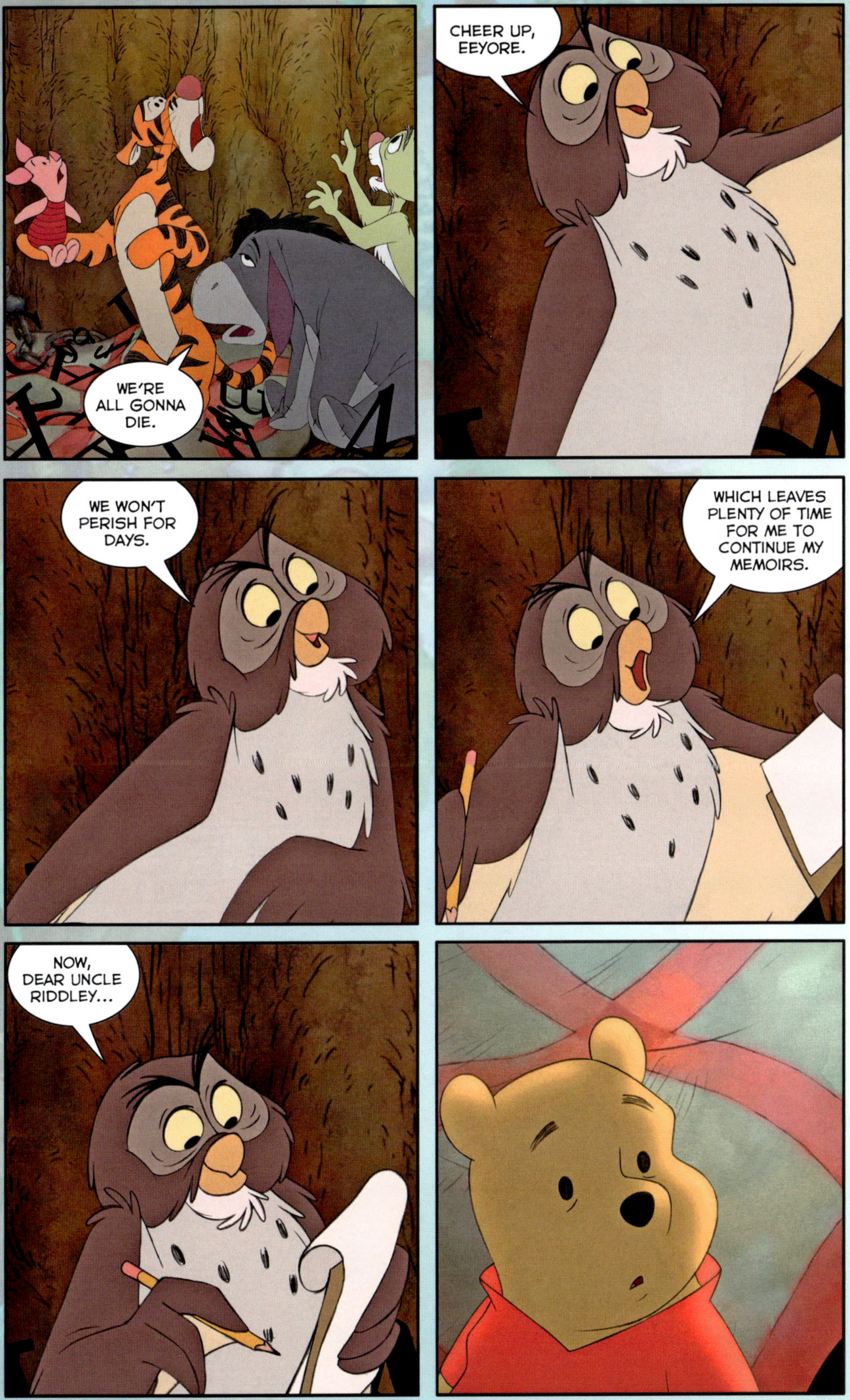
WE'RE ALL GONNA DIE.
CHEER UP, EEYORE.
WE WON'T PERISH FOR DAYS.
WHICH LEAVES PLENTY OF TIME FOR ME TO CONTINUE MY MEMOIRS.
NOW, DEAR UNCLE RIDDLEY...

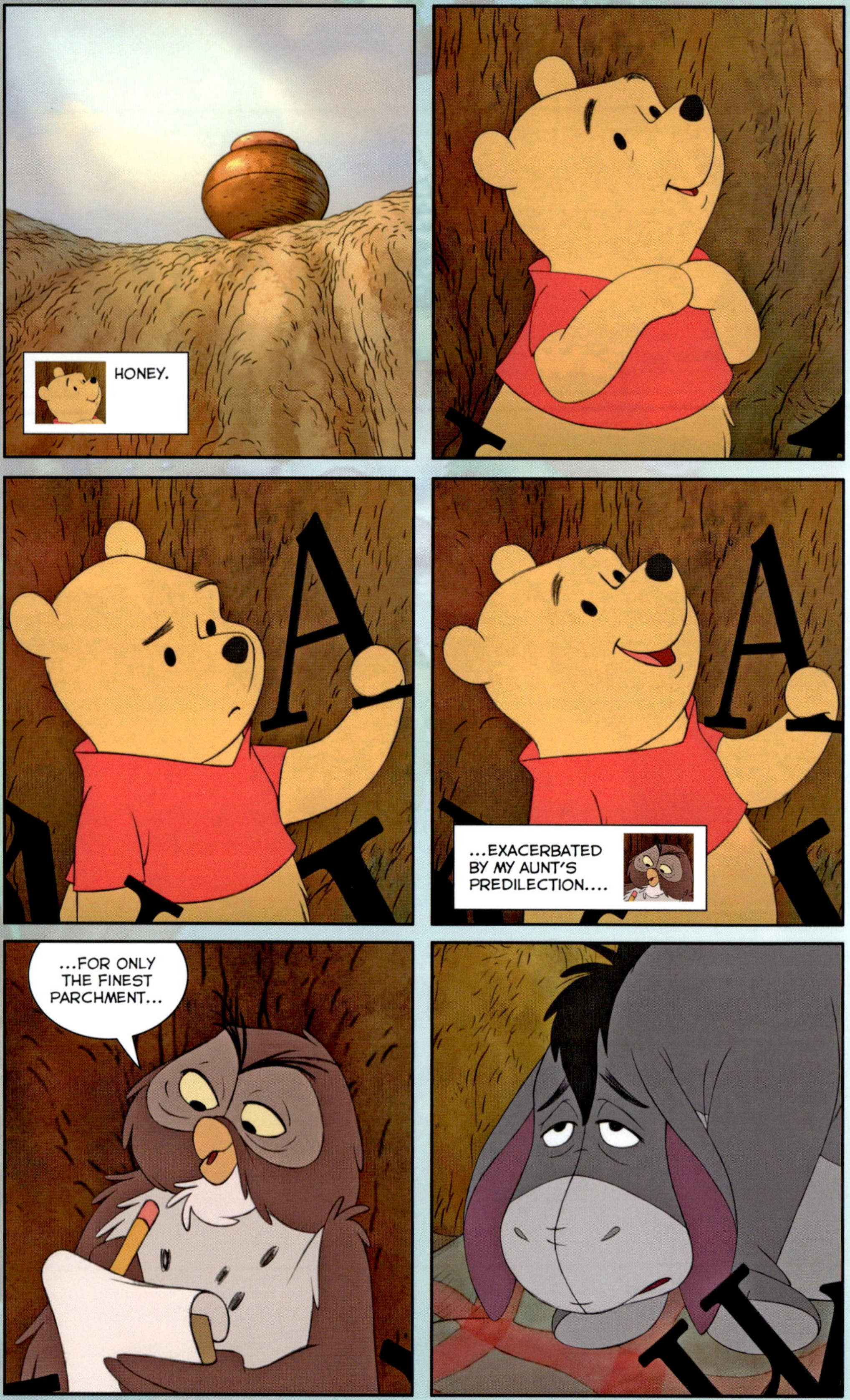
HONEY.
...EXACERBATED BY MY AUNT'S PREDILECTION....
...FOR ONLY THE FINEST PARCHMENT...

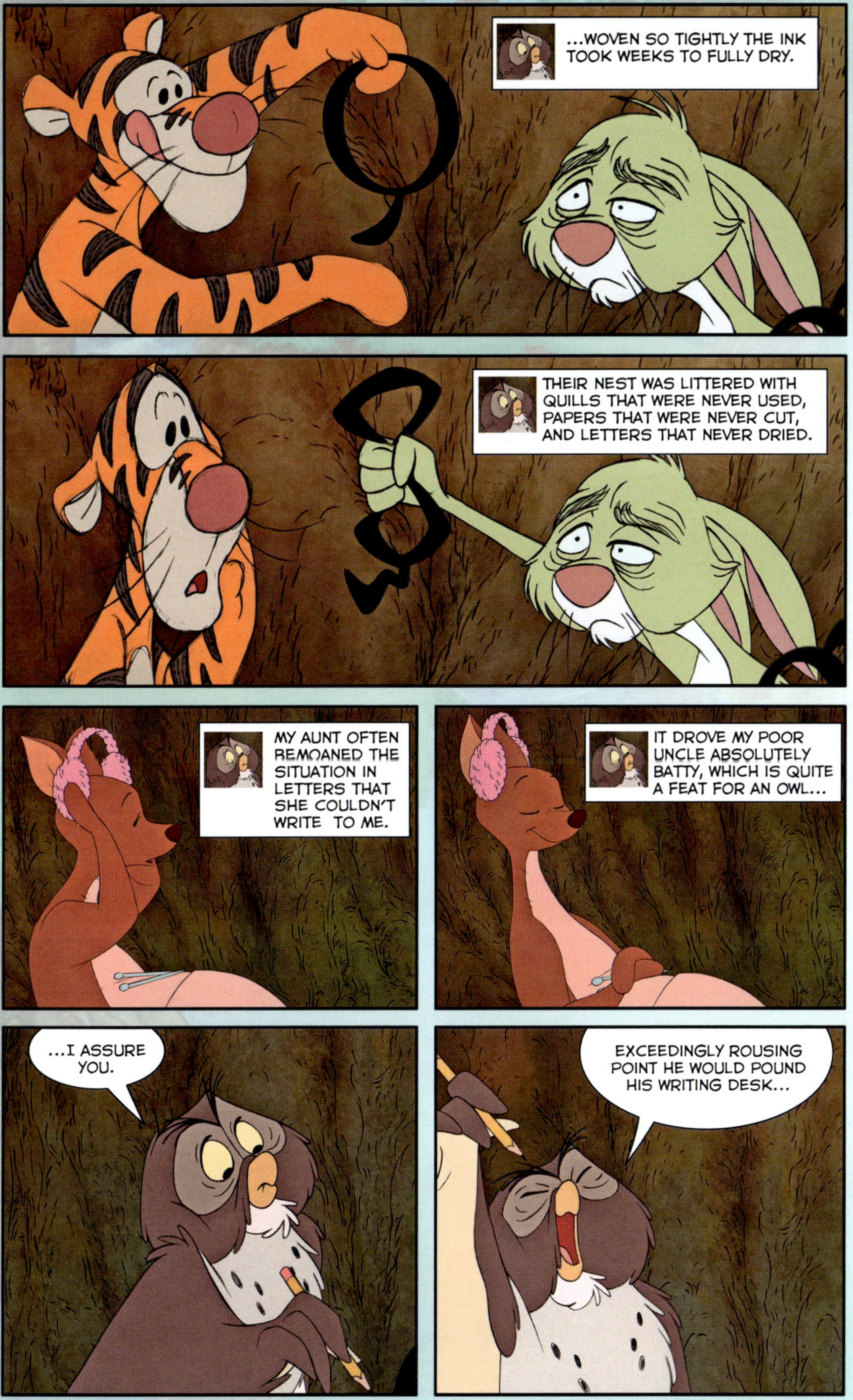

...WOVEN SO TIGHTLY THE INK TOOK WEEKS TO FULLY DRY.
THEIR NEST WAS LITTERED WITH QUILLS THAT WERE NEVER USED, PAPERS THAT WERE NEVER CUT, AND LETTERS THAT NEVER DRIED.
MY AUNT OFTEN BEMOANED THE SITUATION IN LETTERS THAT SHE COULDN'T WRITE TO ME.
IT DROVE MY POOR UNCLE ABSOLUTELY BATTY, WHICH IS QUITE A FEAT FOR AN OWL...
...I ASSURE YOU.
EXCEEDINGLY ROUSING POINT HE WOULD POUND HIS WRITING DESK...

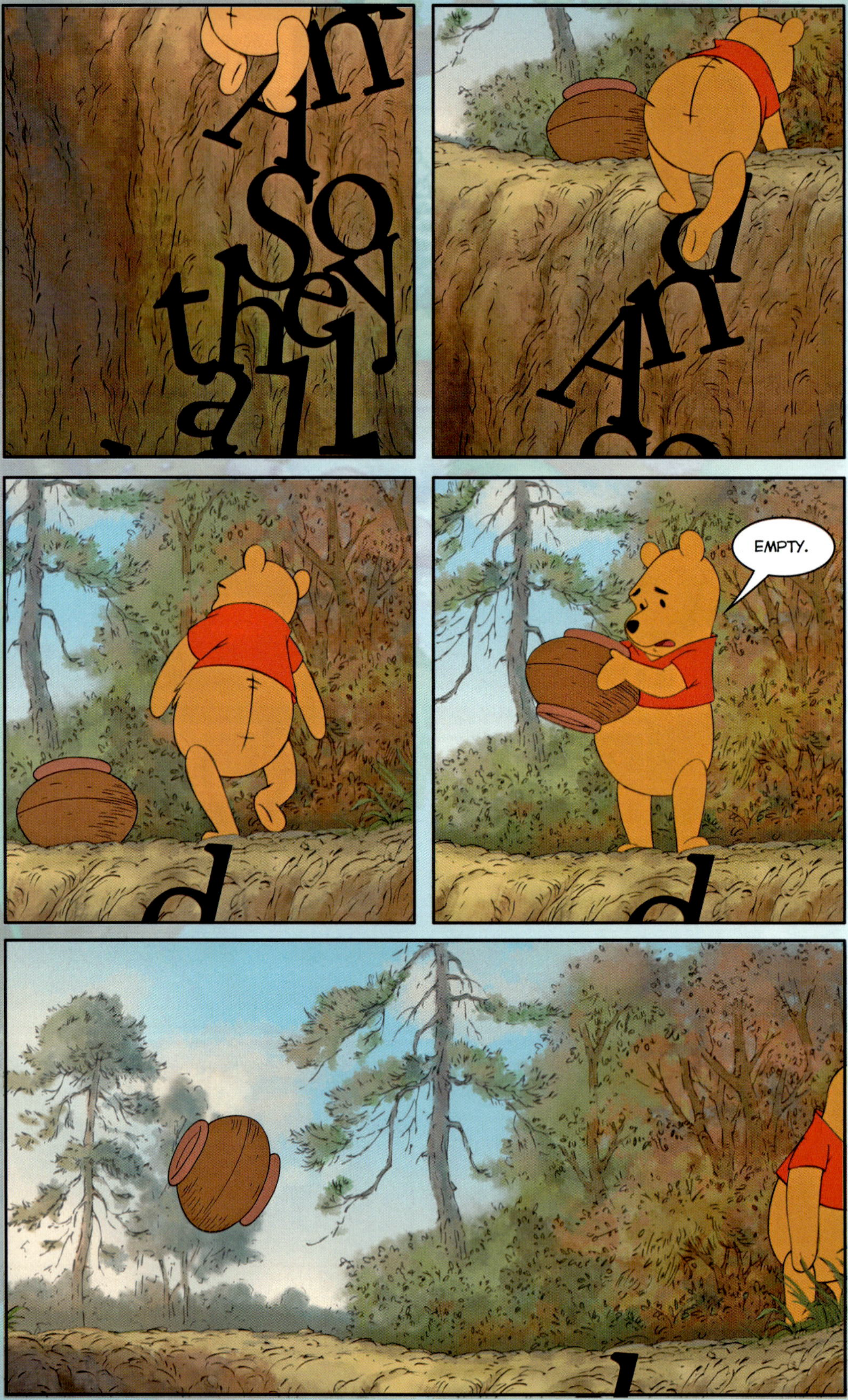
EMPTY.

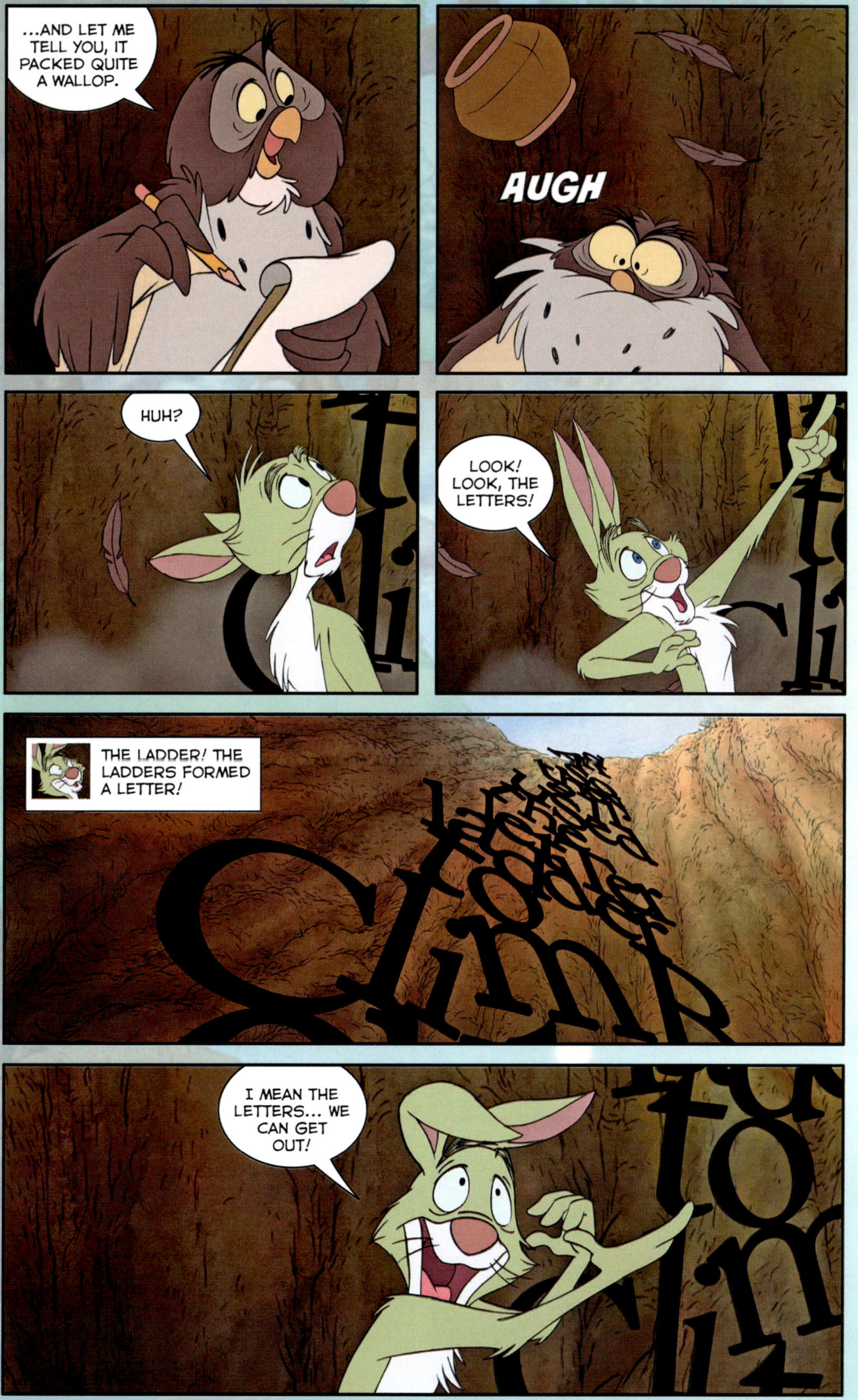

...AND LET ME TELL YOU, IT PACKED QUITE A WALLOP.
AUGH
HUH?
LOOK! LOOK, THE LETTERS!
THE LADDER! THE LADDERS FORMED A LETTER!
I MEAN THE LETTERS... WE CAN GET OUT!

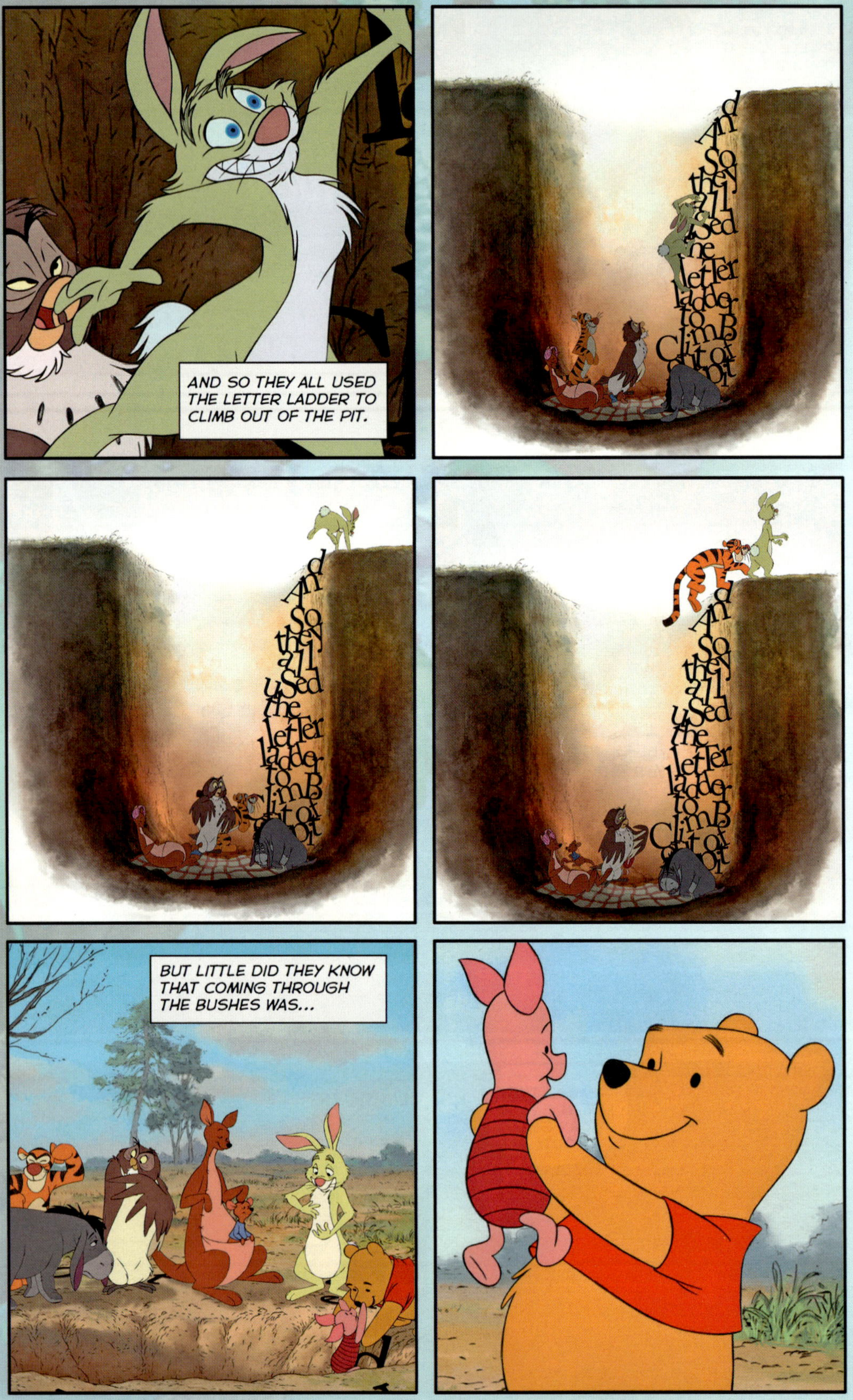
AND SO THEY ALL USED THE LETTER LADDER TO CLIMB OUT OF THE PIT.
BUT LITTLE DID THEY KNOW THAT COMING THROUGH THE BUSHES WAS...

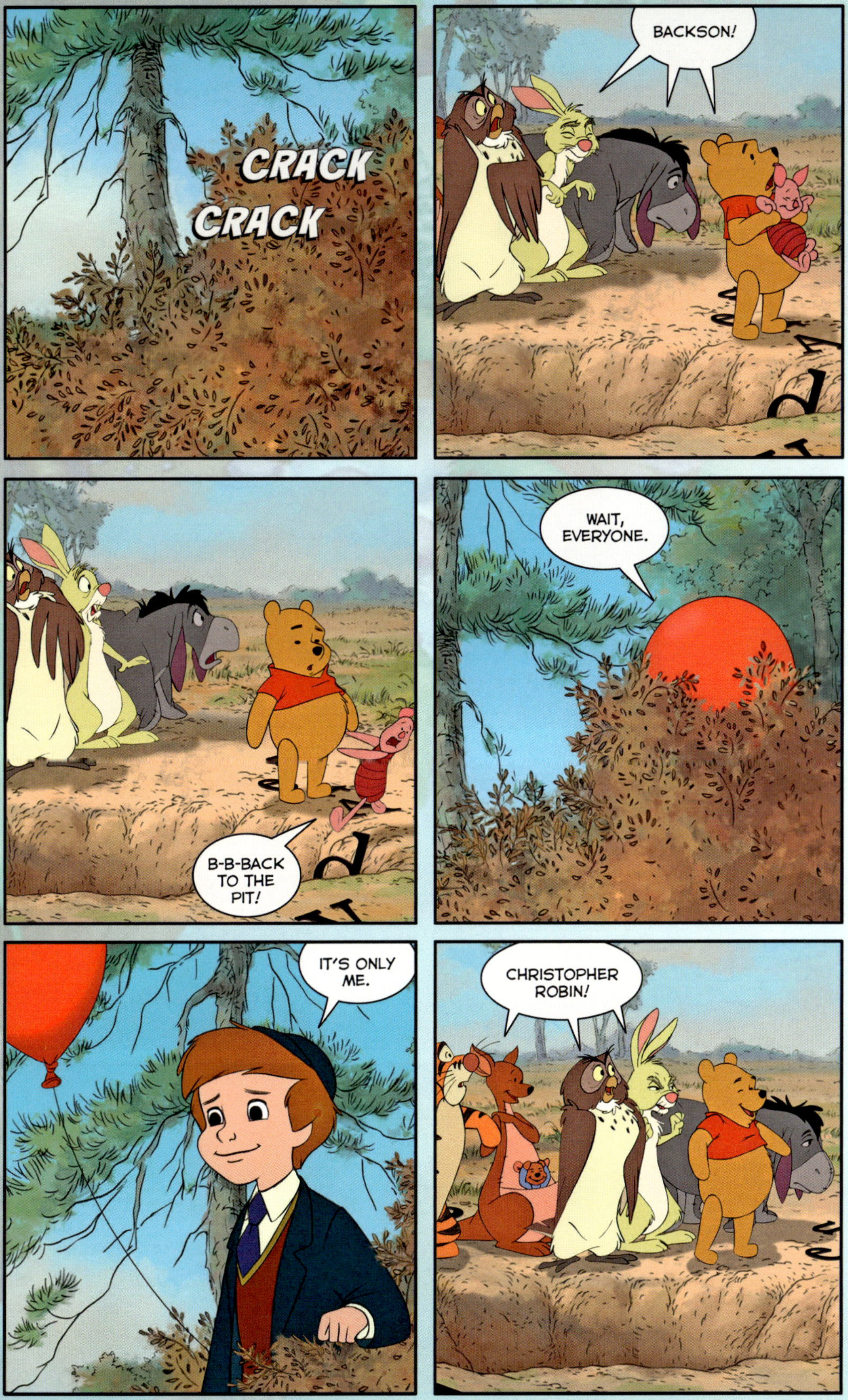
CRACK
CRACK
BACKSON!
B-B-BACK TO THE PIT!
WAIT, EVERYONE.
IT'S ONLY ME.
CHRISTOPHER ROBIN!

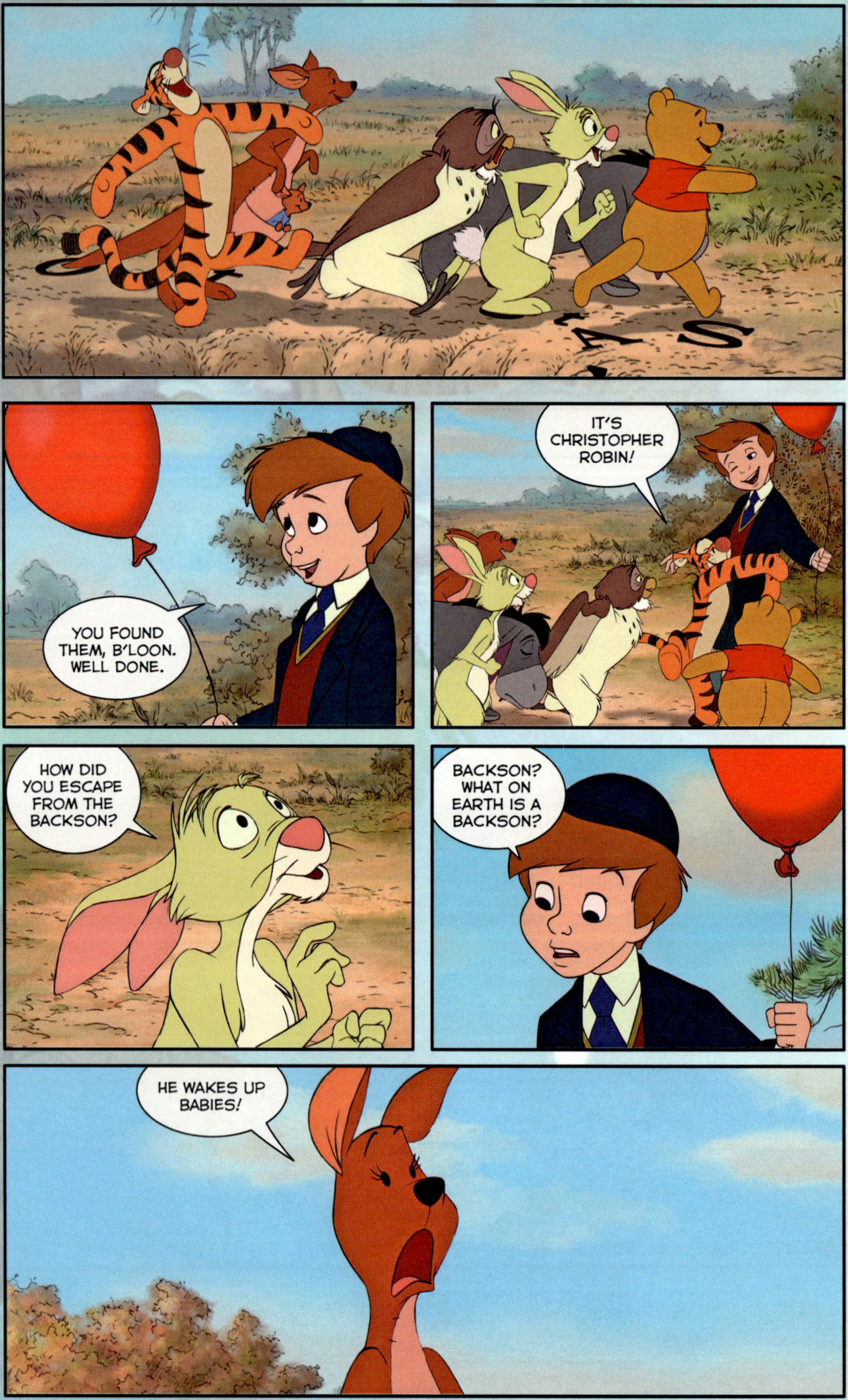
YOU FOUND THEM, B'LOON. WELL DONE.
IT'S CHRISTOPHER ROBIN!
HOW DID YOU ESCAPE FROM THE BACKSON?
BACKSON? WHAT ON EARTH IS A BACKSON?
HE WAKES UP BABIES!

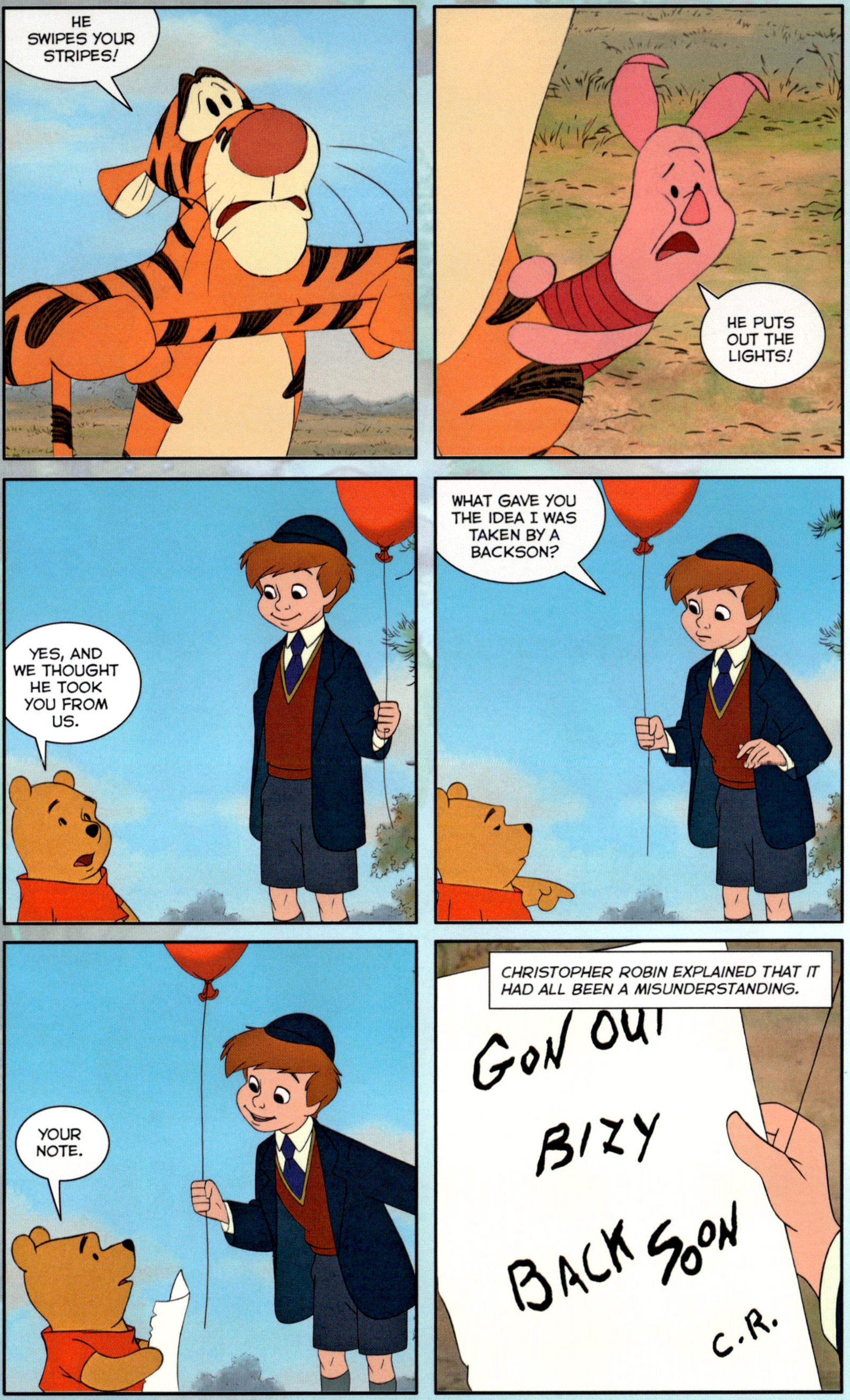
HE SWIPES YOUR STRIPES!
HE PUTS OUT THE LIGHTS!
YES, AND WE THOUGHT HE TOOK YOU FROM US.
WHAT GAVE YOU THE IDEA I WAS TAKEN BY A BACKSON?
YOUR NOTE.
CHRISTOPHER ROBIN EXPLAINED THAT IT HAD ALL BEEN A MISUNDERSTANDING.
GON OUT
BIZY
BACK SOON
C.R.

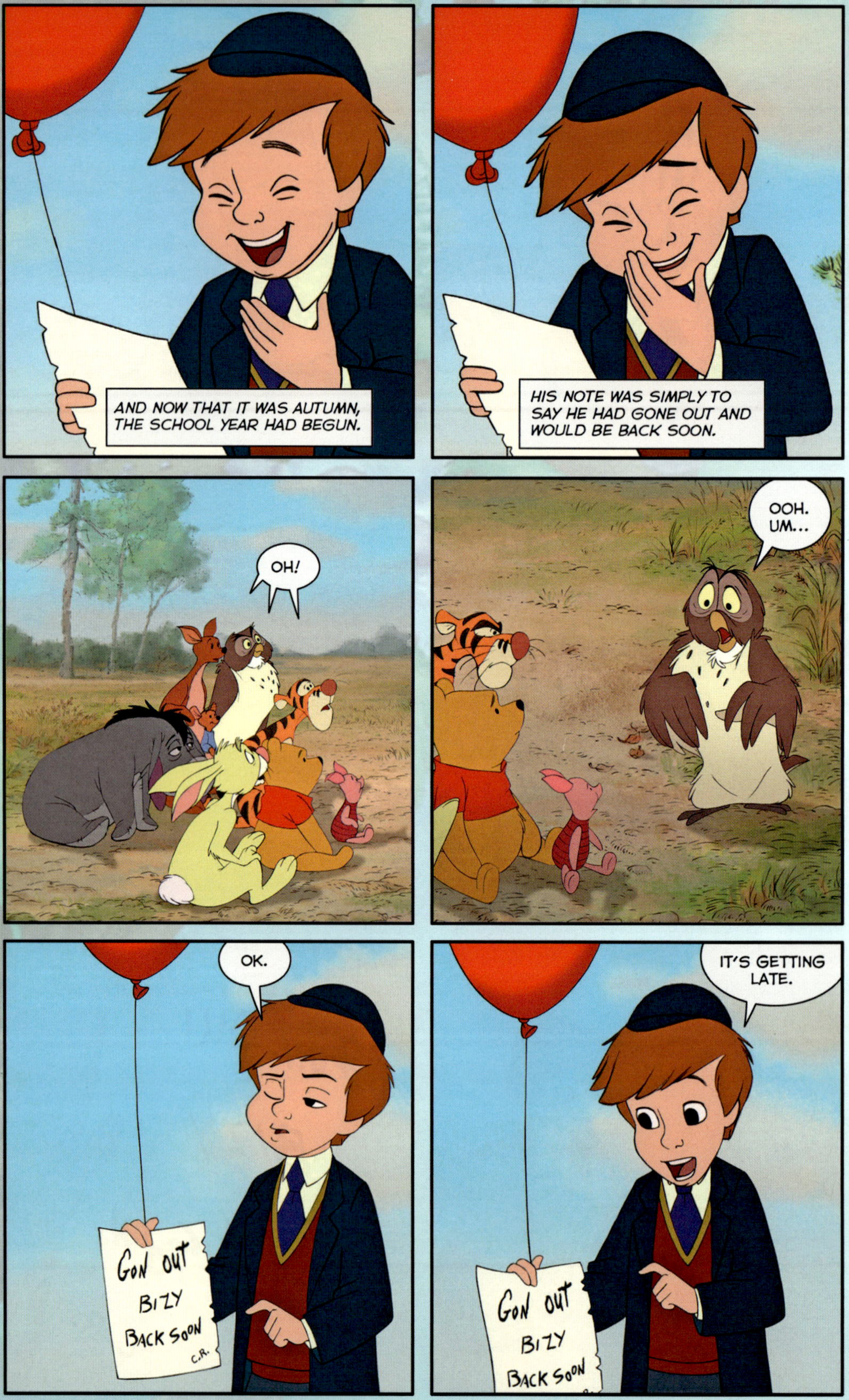
AND NOW THAT IT WAS AUTUMN, THE SCHOOL YEAR HAD BEGUN.
HIS NOTE WAS SIMPLY TO SAY HE HAD GONE OUT AND WOULD BE BACK SOON.
OH!
OOH. UM...
OK.
GON OUT
BIZY
BACK SOON
C.R.
IT'S GETTING LATE.
GON OUT
BIZY
BACK SOON

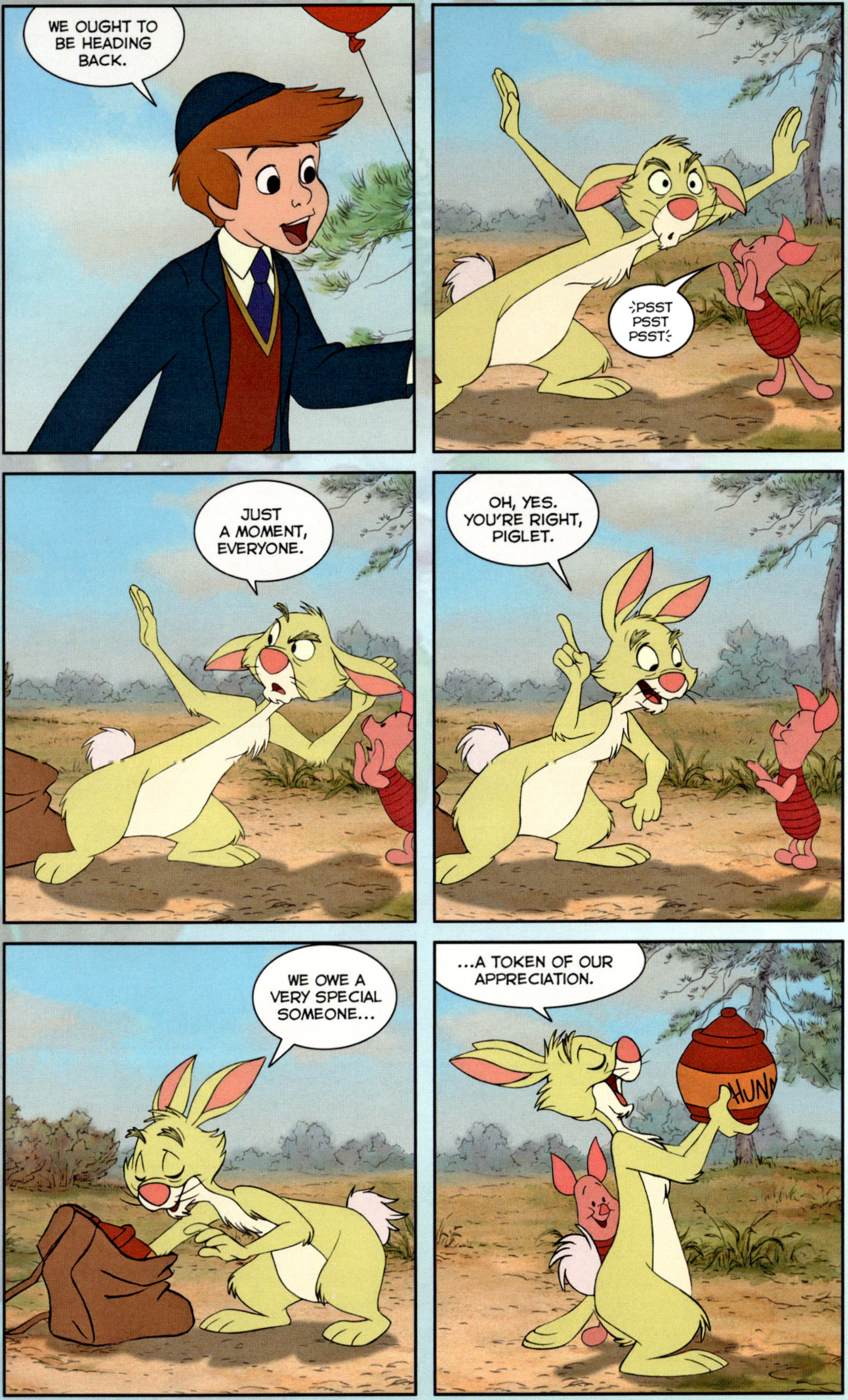
WE OUGHT TO BE HEADING BACK.
PSST PSST PSST
JUST A MOMENT, EVERYONE.
OH, YES. YOU'RE RIGHT, PIGLET.
WE OWE A VERY SPECIAL SOMEONE...
...A TOKEN OF OUR APPRECIATION.

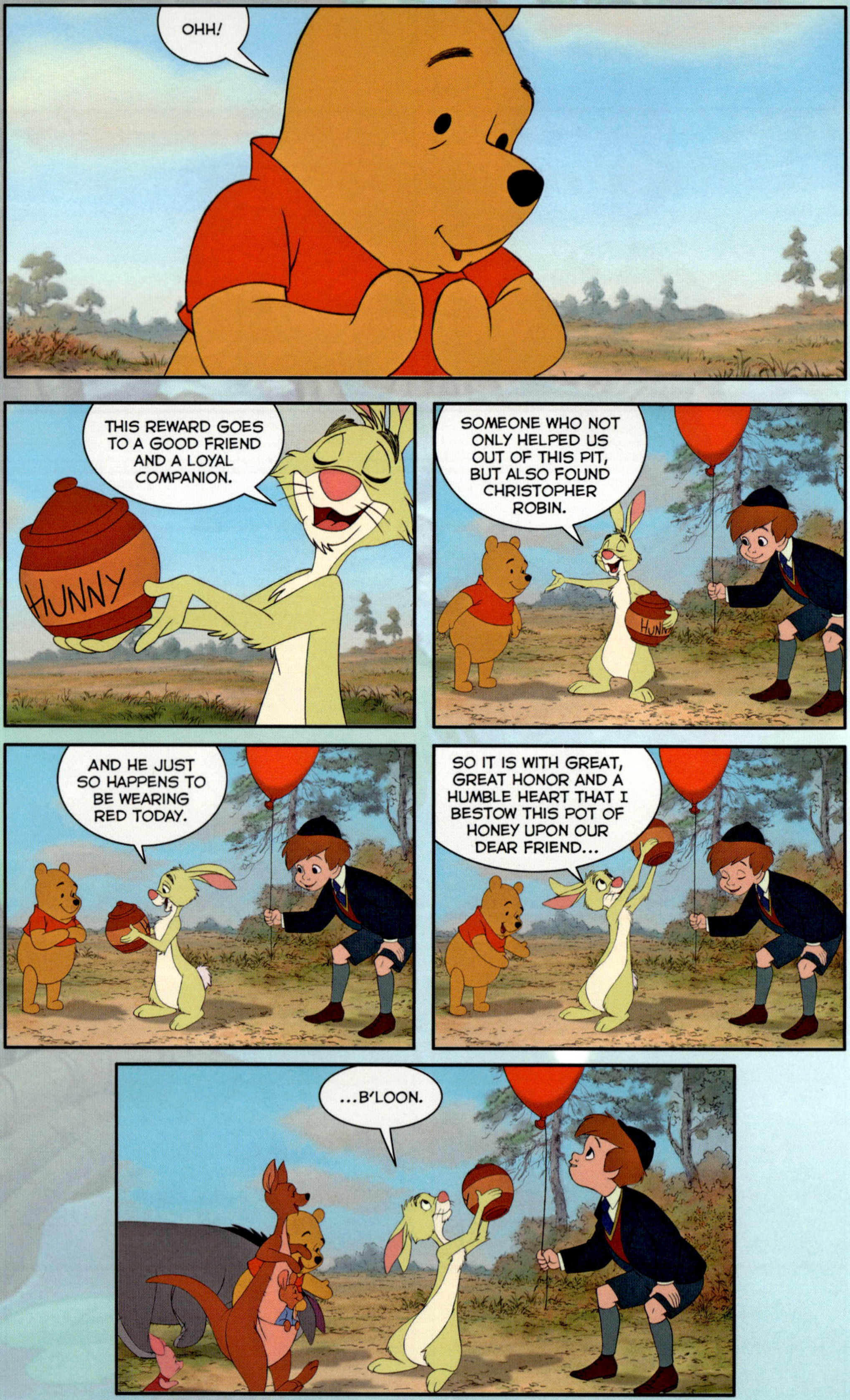
OHH!
THIS REWARD GOES TO A GOOD FRIEND AND A LOYAL COMPANION.
HUNNY
SOMEONE WHO NOT ONLY HELPED US OUT OF THIS PIT, BUT ALSO FOUND CHRISTOPHER ROBIN.
AND HE JUST SO HAPPENS TO BE WEARING RED TODAY.
SO IT IS WITH GREAT, GREAT HONOR AND A HUMBLE HEART THAT I BESTOW THIS POT OF HONEY UPON OUR DEAR FRIEND...
...B'LOON.

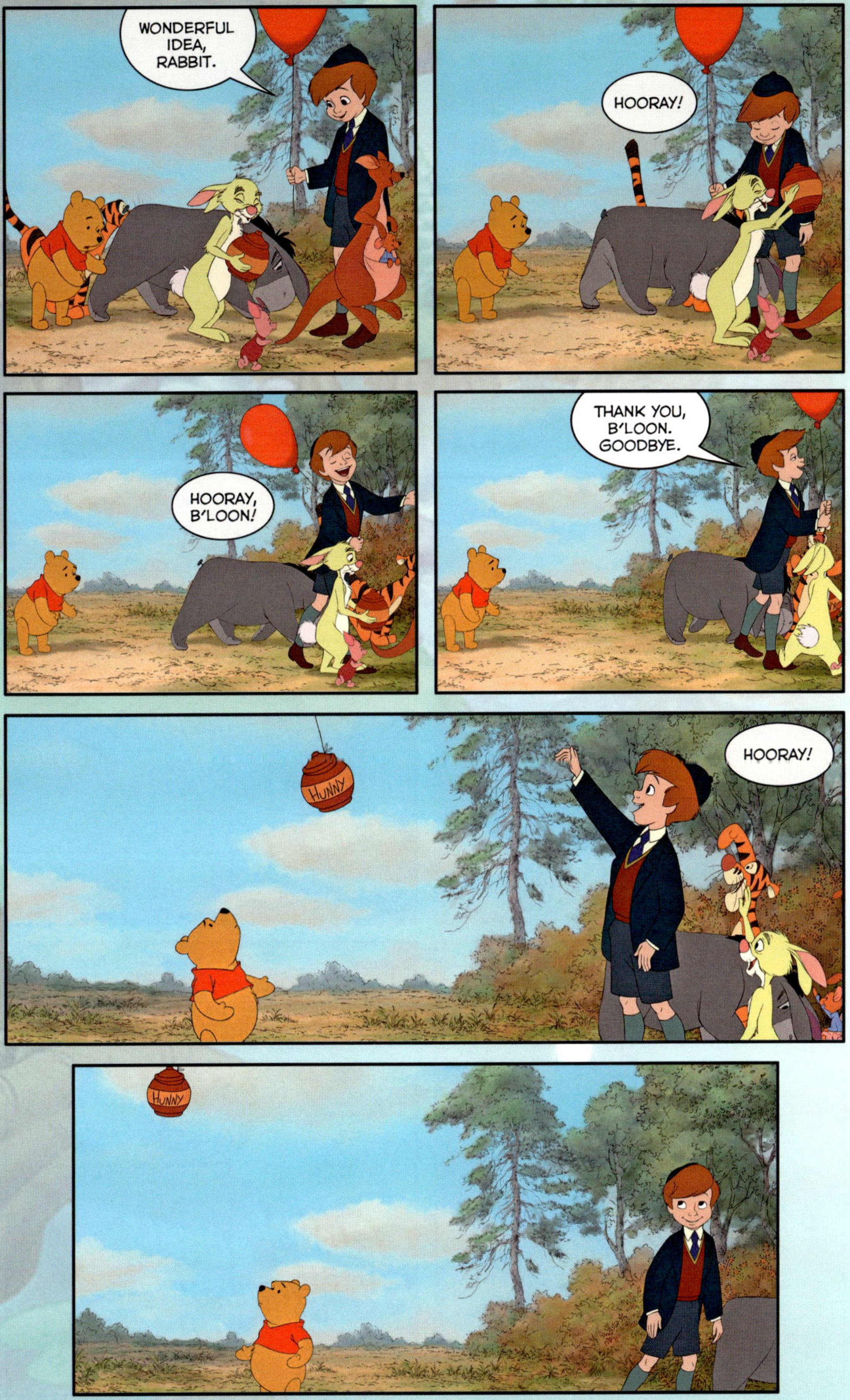
WONDERFUL IDEA, RABBIT.
HOORAY!
HOORAY, B'LOON!
THANK YOU, B'LOON. GOODBYE.
HUNNY
HOORAY!
HUNNY

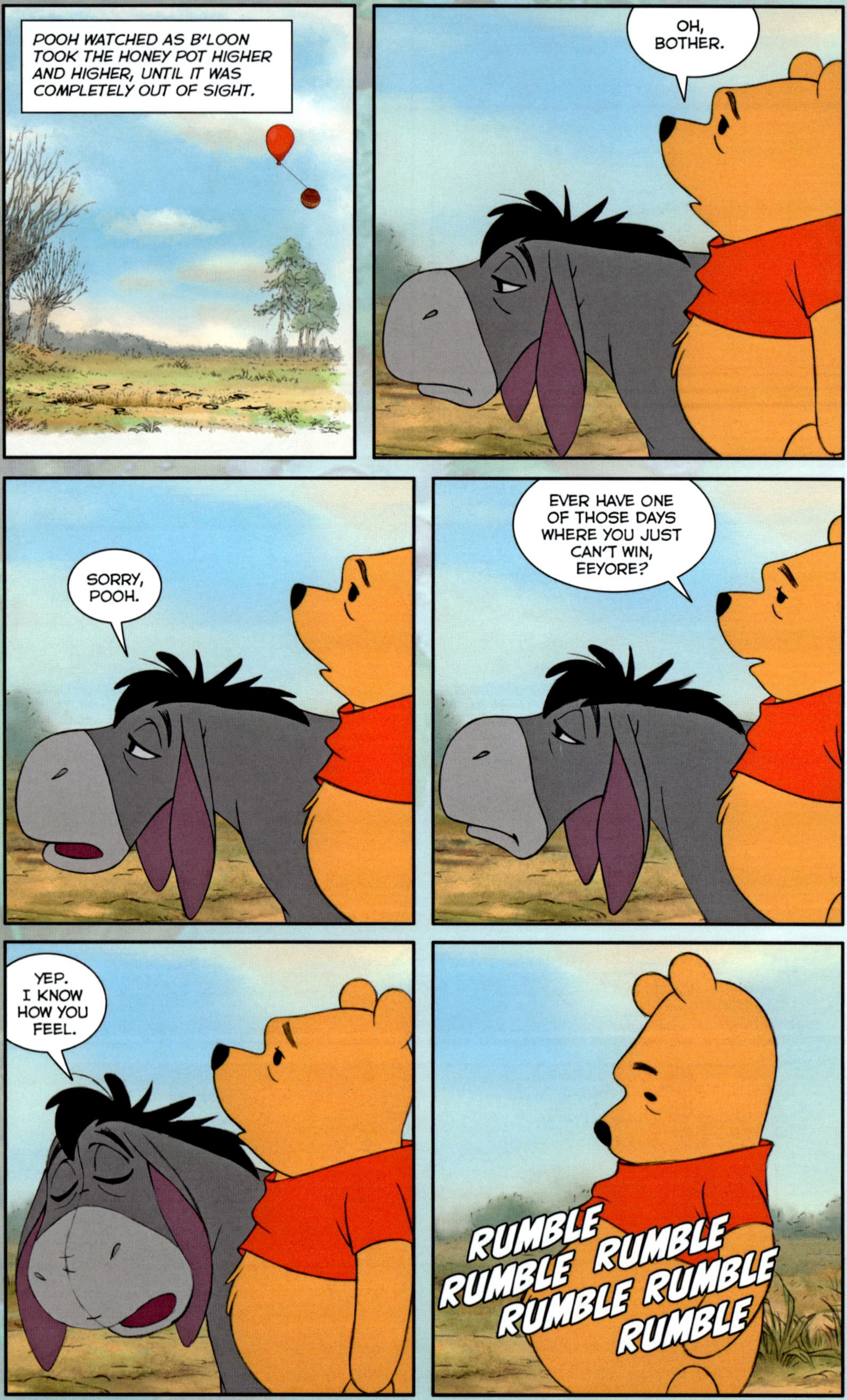
POOH WATCHED AS B'LOON TOOK THE HONEY POT HIGHER AND HIGHER, UNTIL IT WAS COMPLETELY OUT OF SIGHT.
OH, BOTHER.
SORRY, POOH.
EVER HAVE ONE OF THOSE DAYS WHERE YOU JUST CAN'T WIN, EEYORE?
YEP. I KNOW HOW YOU FEEL.
RUMBLE RUMBLE RUMBLE RUMBLE RUMBLE RUMBLE

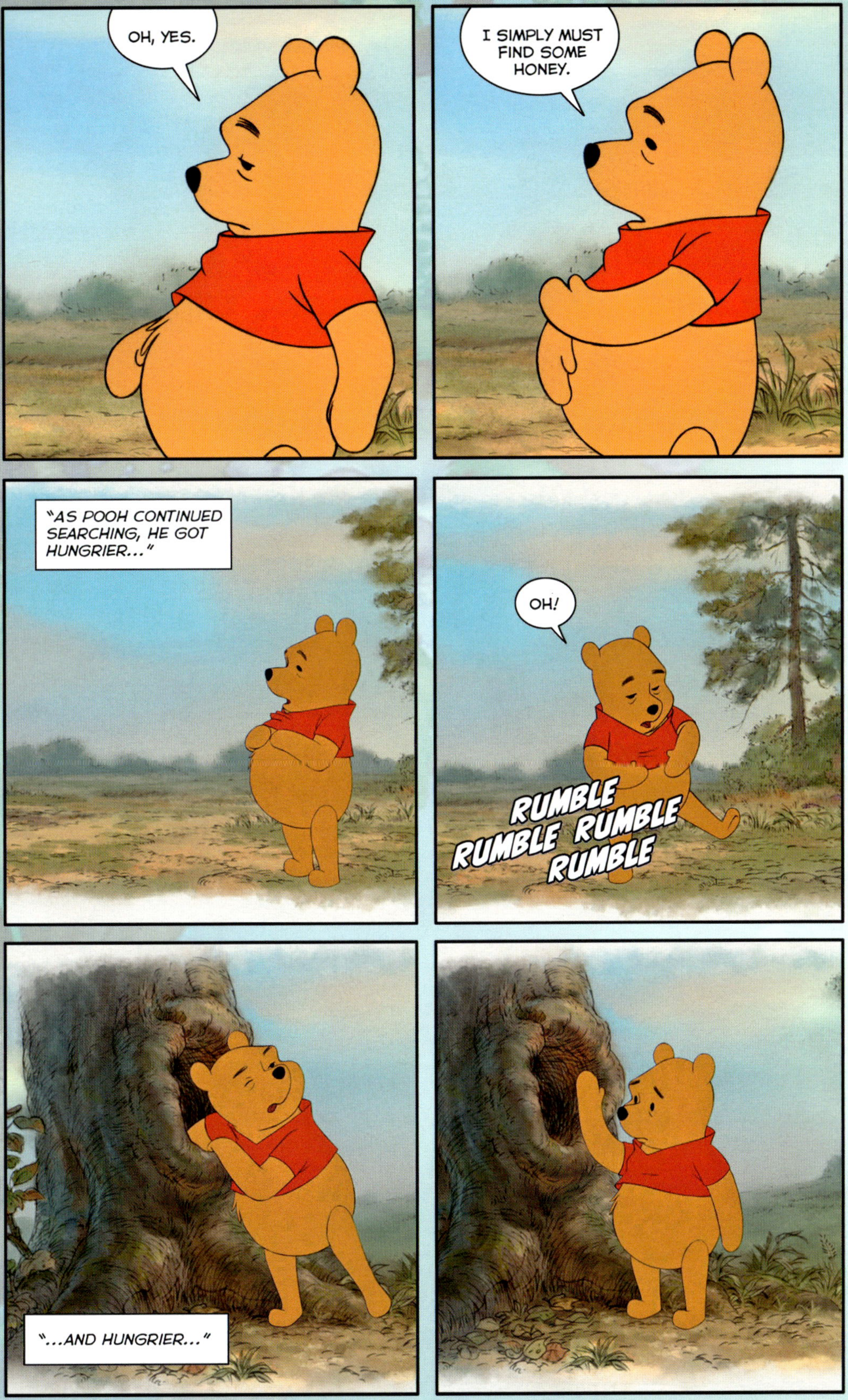
OH, YES.
I SIMPLY MUST FIND SOME HONEY.
"AS POOH CONTINUED SEARCHING, HE GOT HUNGRIER..."
OH!
RUMBLE RUMBLE RUMBLE RUMBLE
"...AND HUNGRIER..."

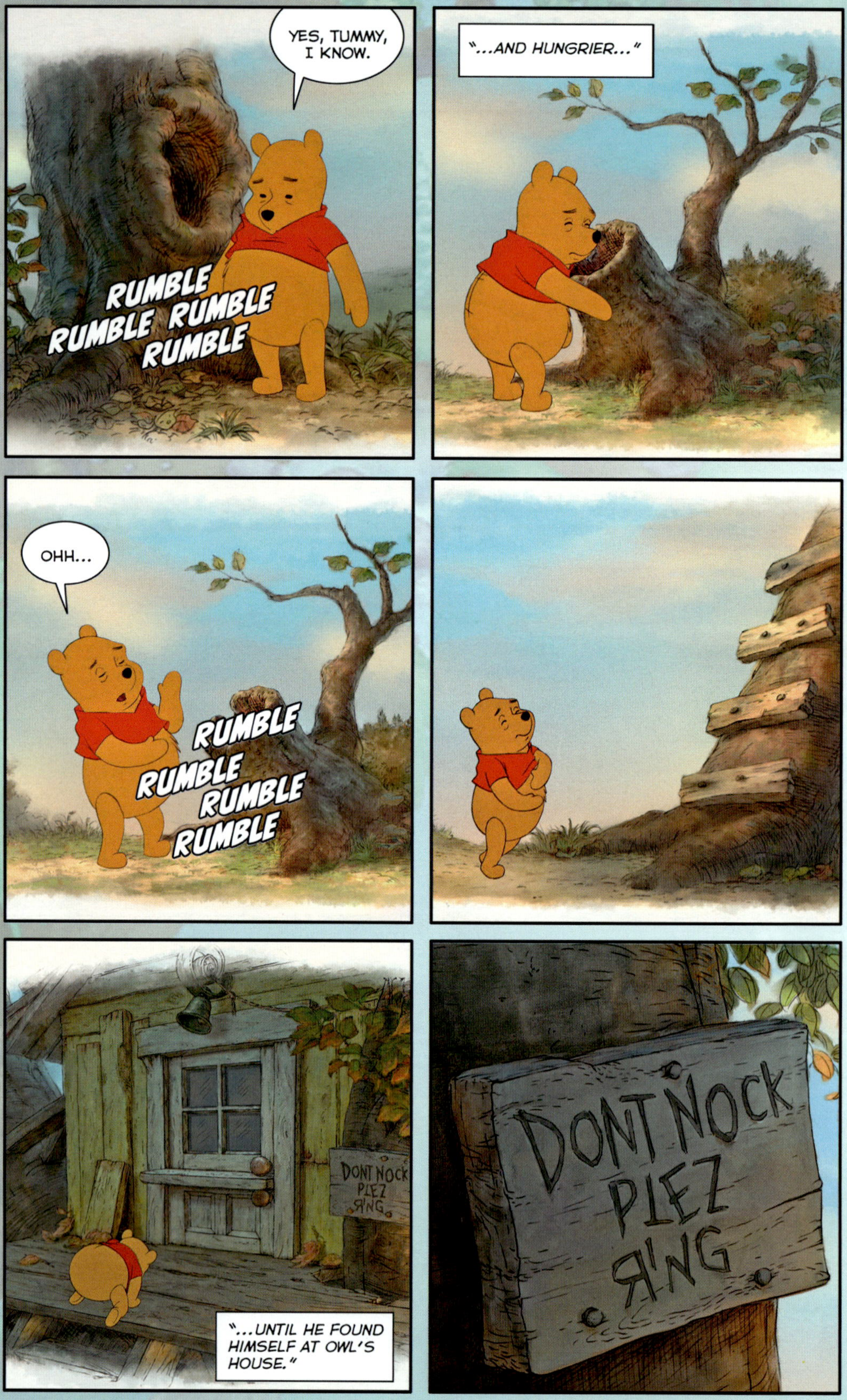
YES, TUMMY, I KNOW.
RUMBLE RUMBLE RUMBLE RUMBLE
"...AND HUNGRIER..."
OHH...
RUMBLE RUMBLE RUMBLE RUMBLE
DONT NOCK PLEZ RING
"...UNTIL HE FOUND HIMSELF AT OWL'S HOUSE."
DONT NOCK PLEZ RING

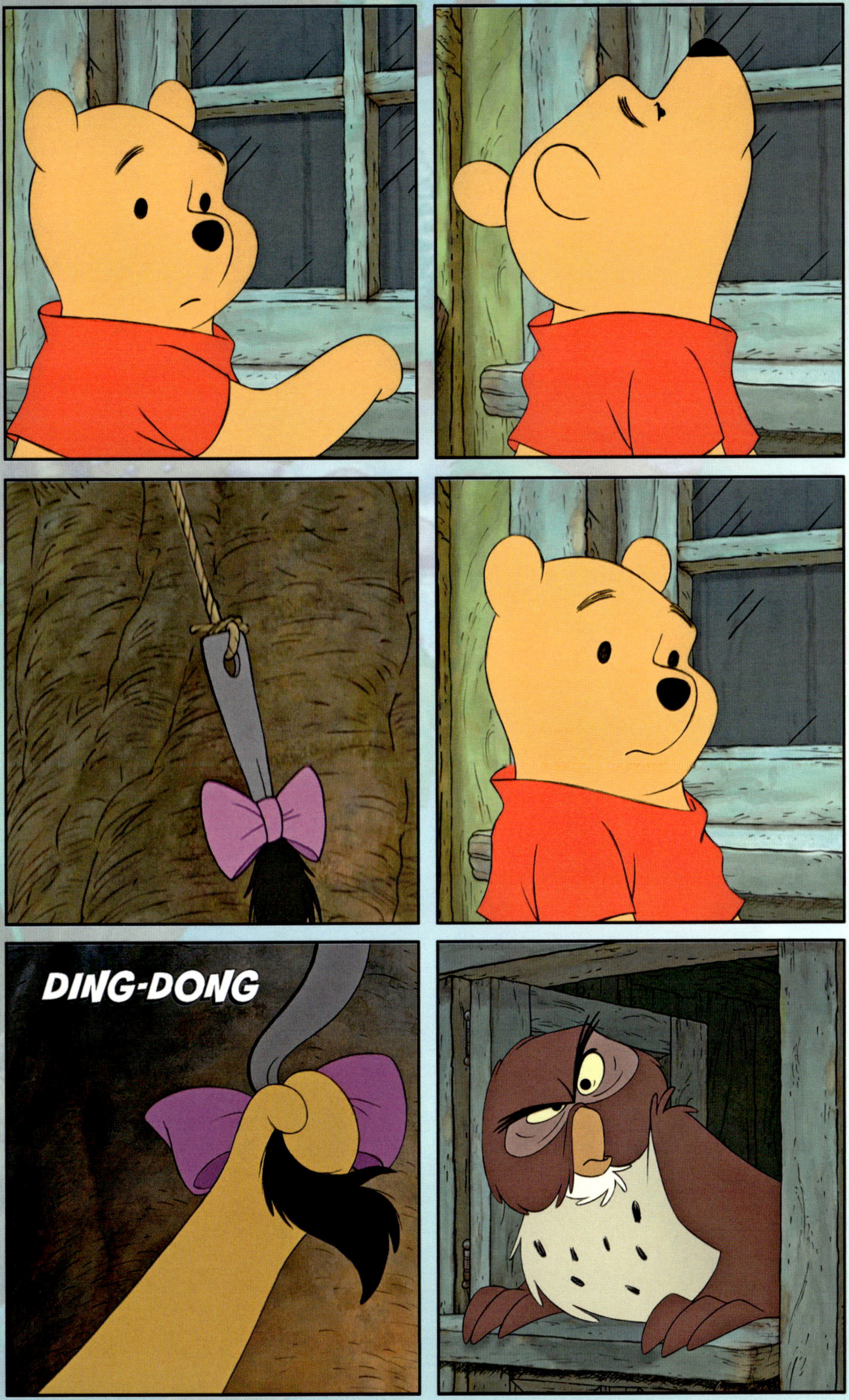
DING-DONG

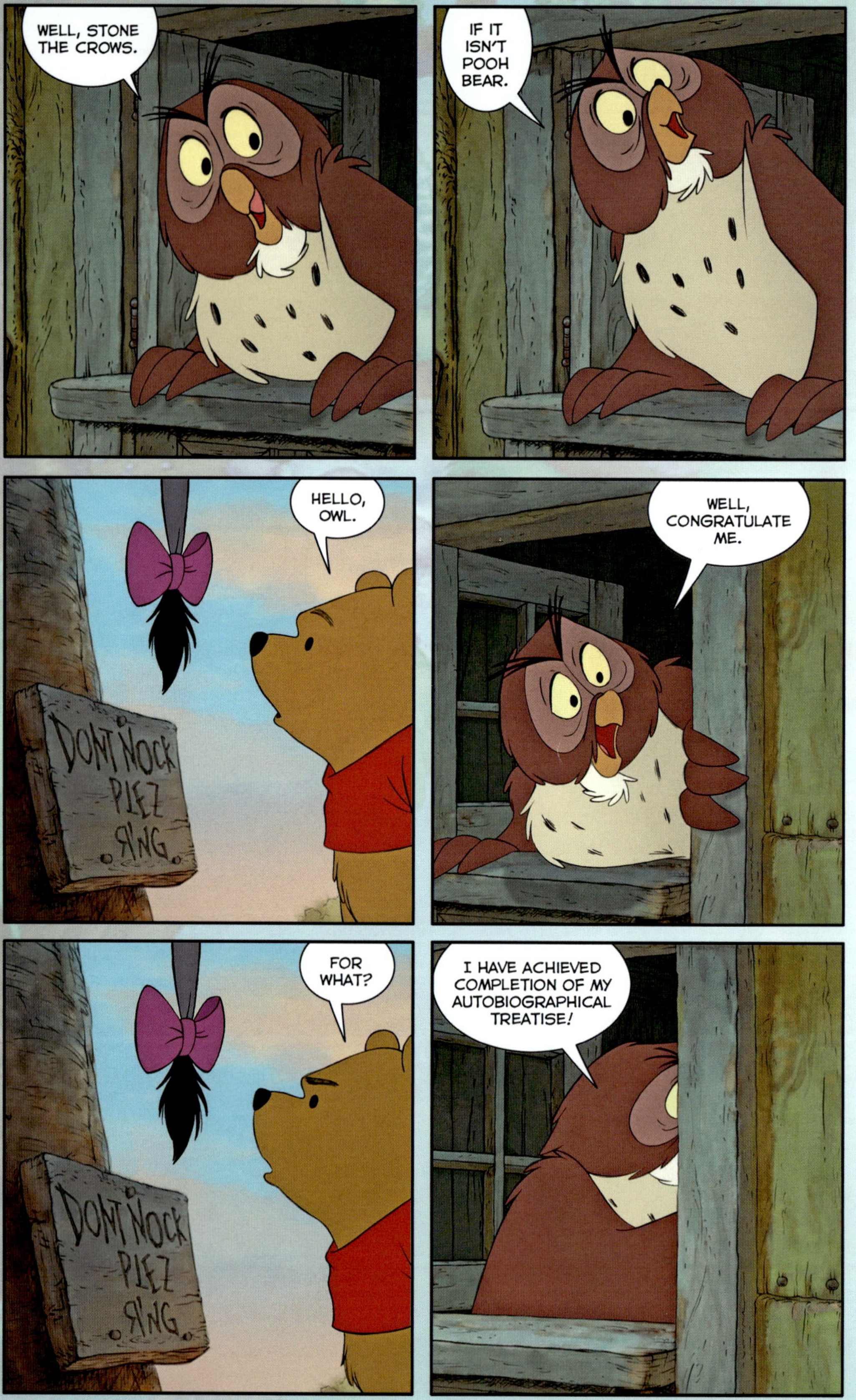
WELL, STONE THE CROWS.
IF IT ISN'T POOH BEAR.
HELLO, OWL.
DONT NOCK PLEZ RING
WELL, CONGRATULATE ME.
FOR WHAT?
DONT NOCK PLEZ RING
I HAVE ACHIEVED COMPLETION OF MY AUTOBIOGRAPHICAL TREATISE!

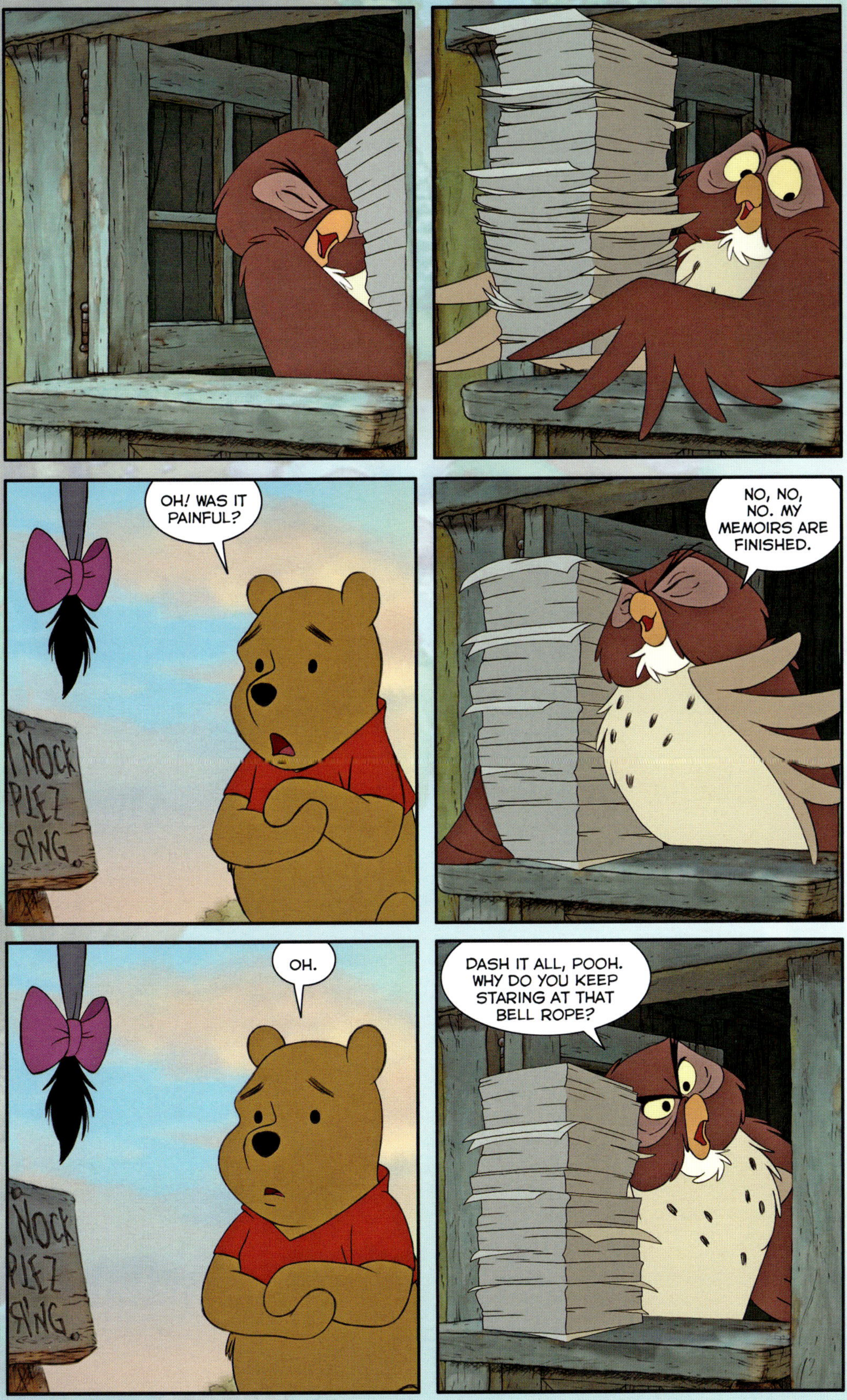
OH! WAS IT PAINFUL?
NO, NO, NO. MY MEMOIRS ARE FINISHED.
NOCK PLEZ RNG
OH.
DASH IT ALL, POOH. WHY DO YOU KEEP STARING AT THAT BELL ROPE?

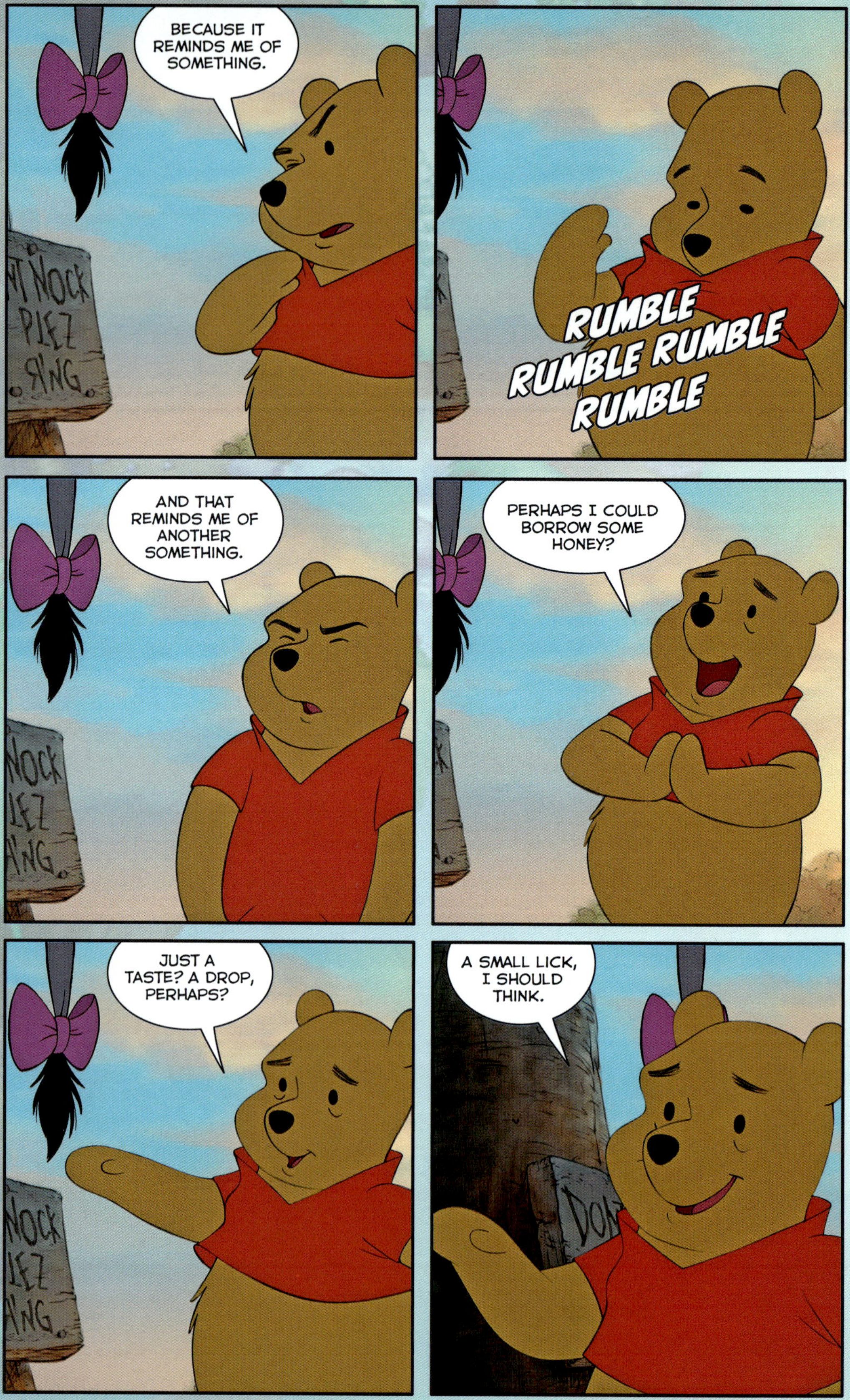
BECAUSE IT REMINDS ME OF SOMETHING.
RUMBLE RUMBLE RUMBLE RUMBLE
AND THAT REMINDS ME OF ANOTHER SOMETHING.
PERHAPS I COULD BORROW SOME HONEY?
JUST A TASTE? A DROP, PERHAPS?
A SMALL LICK, I SHOULD THINK.

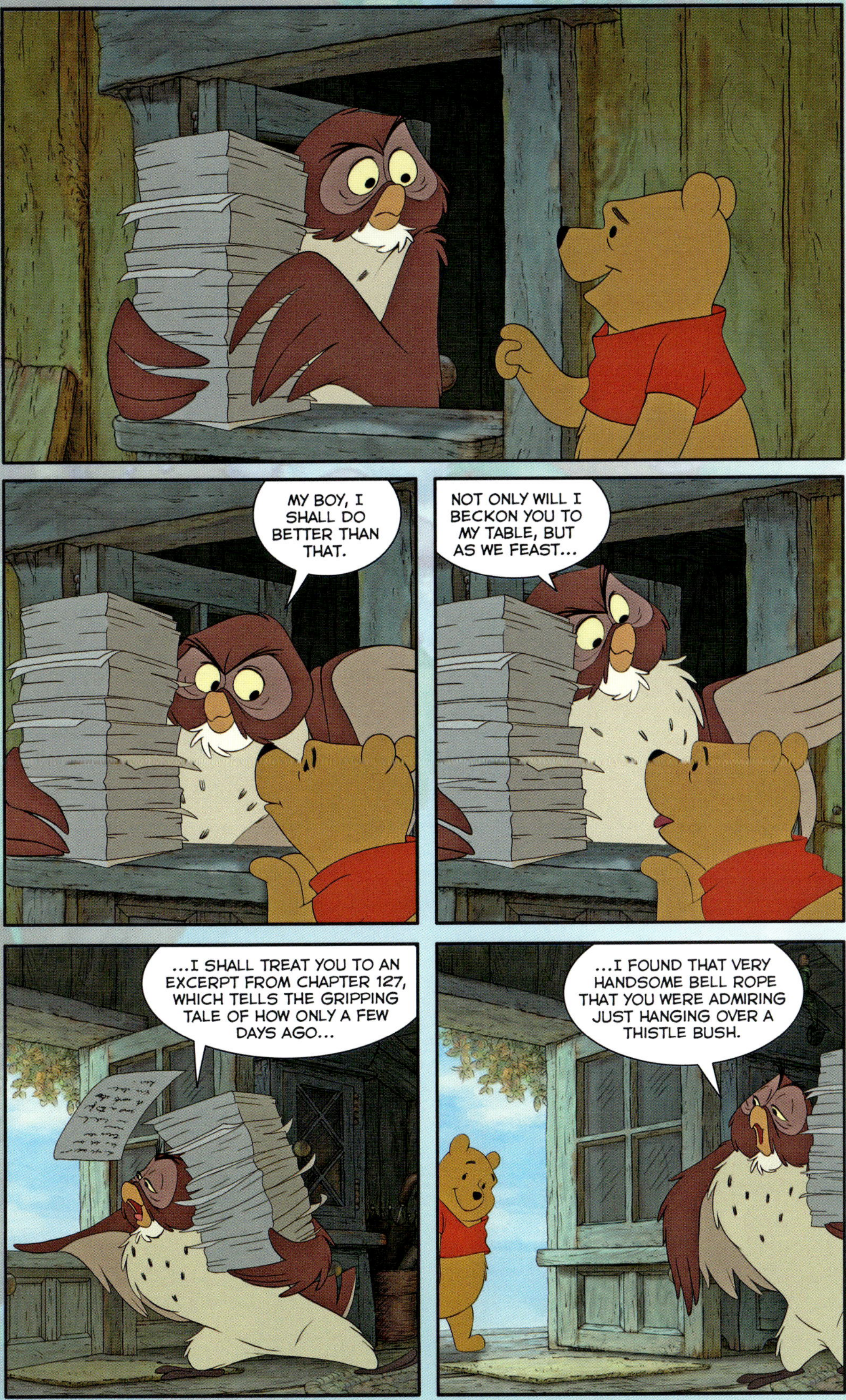
MY BOY, I SHALL DO BETTER THAN THAT.
NOT ONLY WILL I BECKON YOU TO MY TABLE, BUT AS WE FEAST...
...I SHALL TREAT YOU TO AN EXCERPT FROM CHAPTER 127, WHICH TELLS THE GRIPPING TALE OF HOW ONLY A FEW DAYS AGO...
...I FOUND THAT VERY HANDSOME BELL ROPE THAT YOU WERE ADMIRING JUST HANGING OVER A THISTLE BUSH.

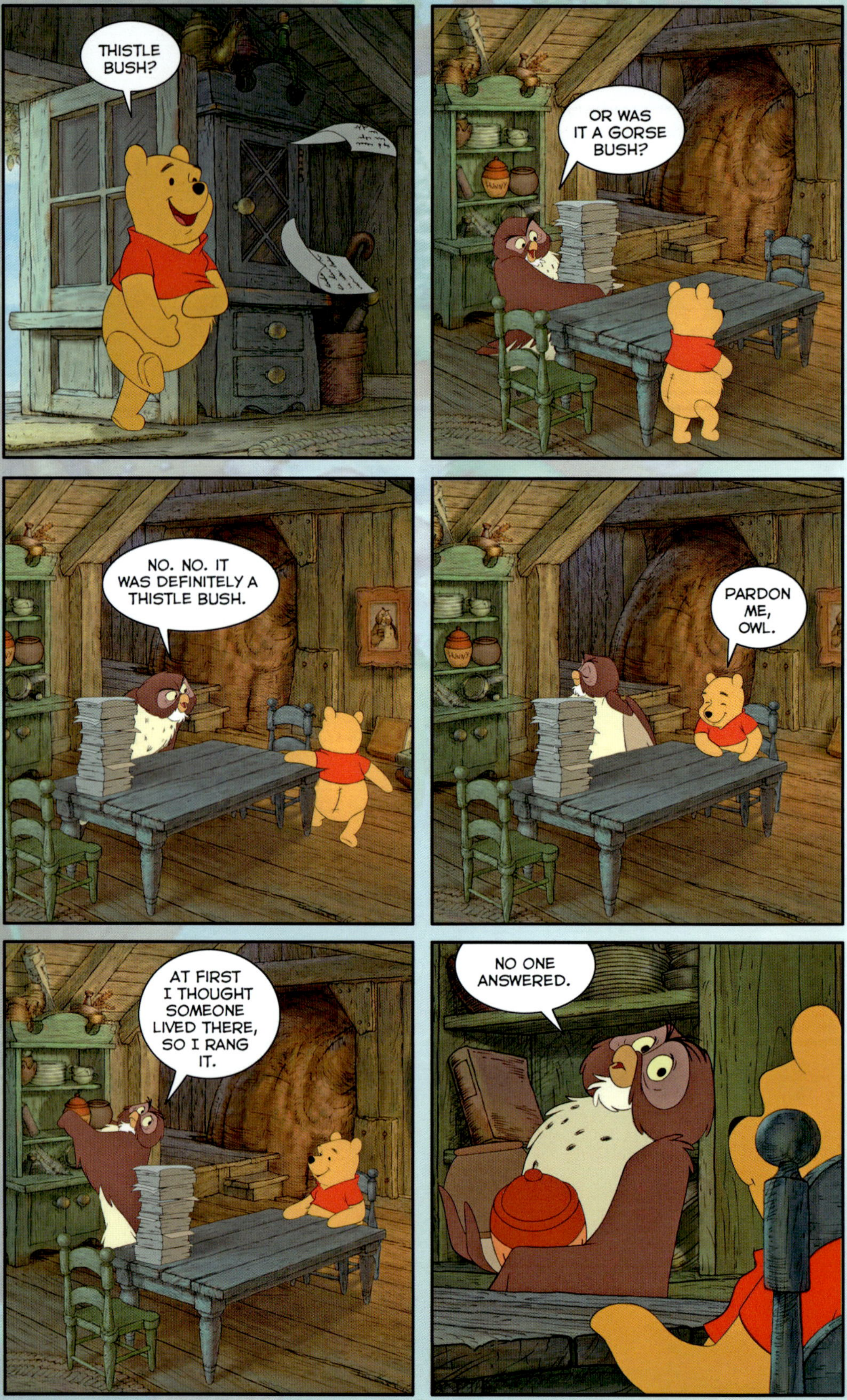
THISTLE BUSH?
OR WAS IT A GORSE BUSH?
NO. NO. IT WAS DEFINITELY A THISTLE BUSH.
PARDON ME, OWL.
AT FIRST I THOUGHT SOMEONE LIVED THERE, SO I RANG IT.
NO ONE ANSWERED.

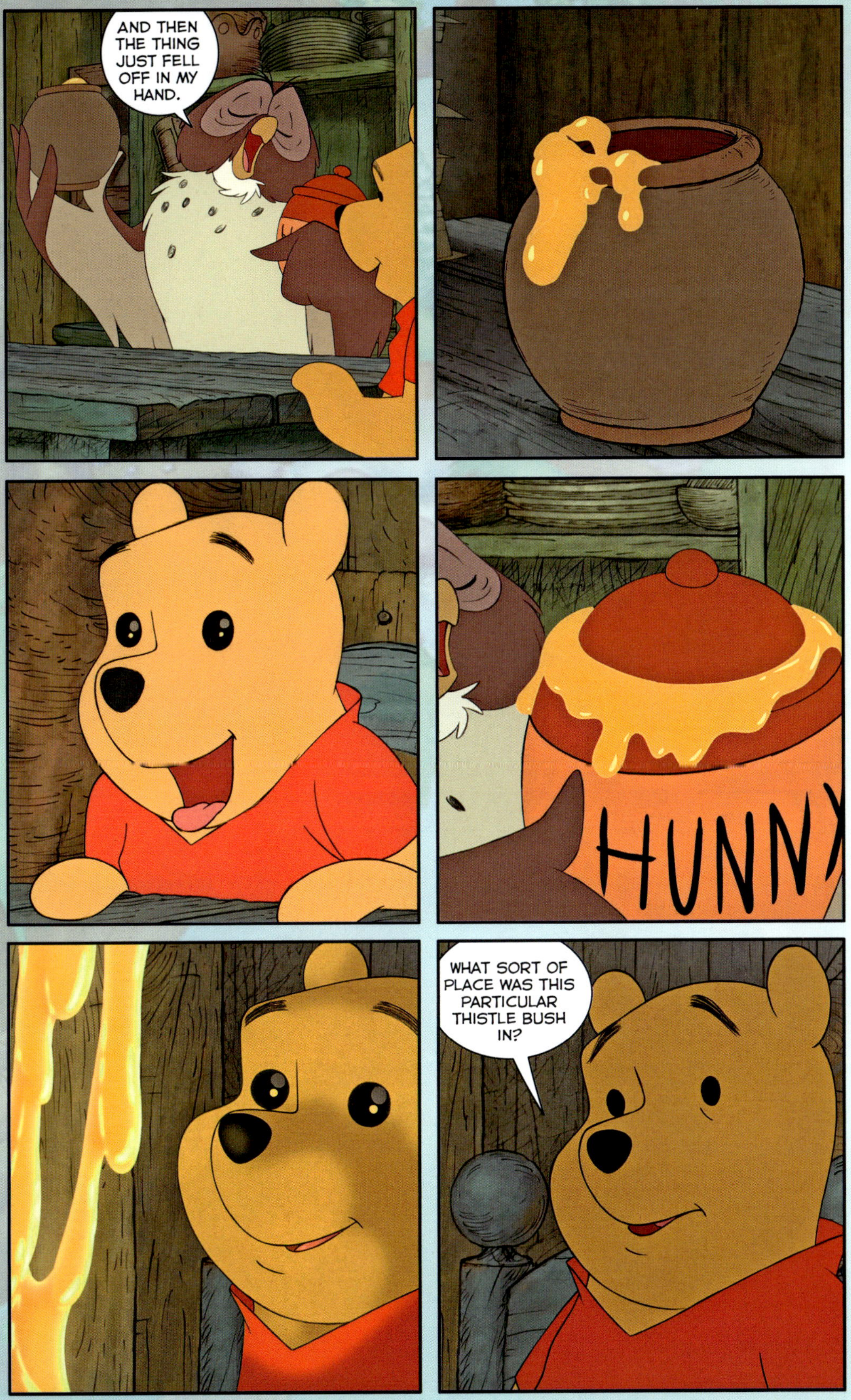
AND THEN THE THING JUST FELL OFF IN MY HAND.
HUNNY
WHAT SORT OF PLACE WAS THIS PARTICULAR THISTLE BUSH IN?

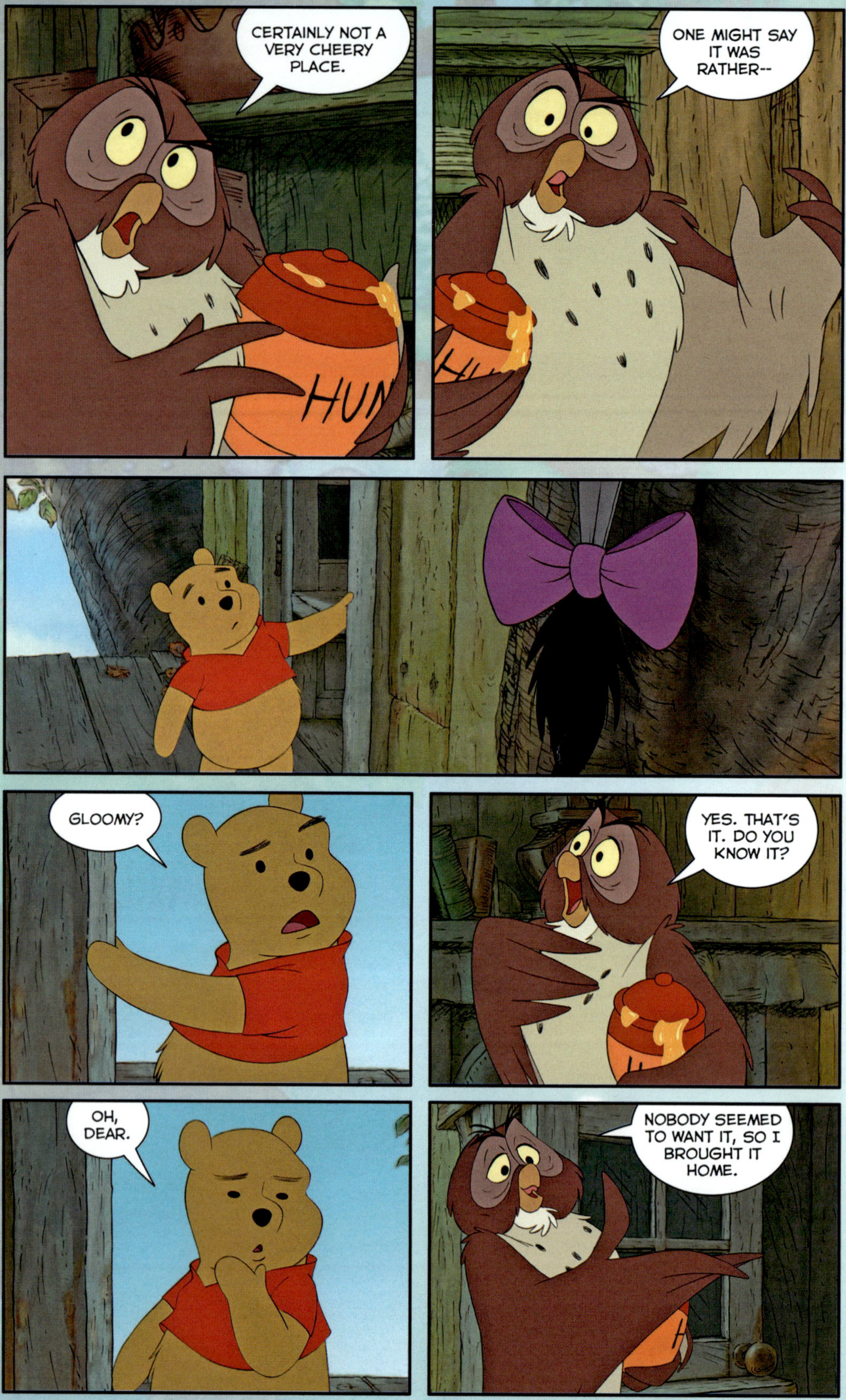
CERTAINLY NOT A VERY CHEERY PLACE.
HUN
ONE MIGHT SAY IT WAS RATHER--
GLOOMY?
YES. THAT'S IT. DO YOU KNOW IT?
OH, DEAR.
NOBODY SEEMED TO WANT IT, SO I BROUGHT IT HOME.

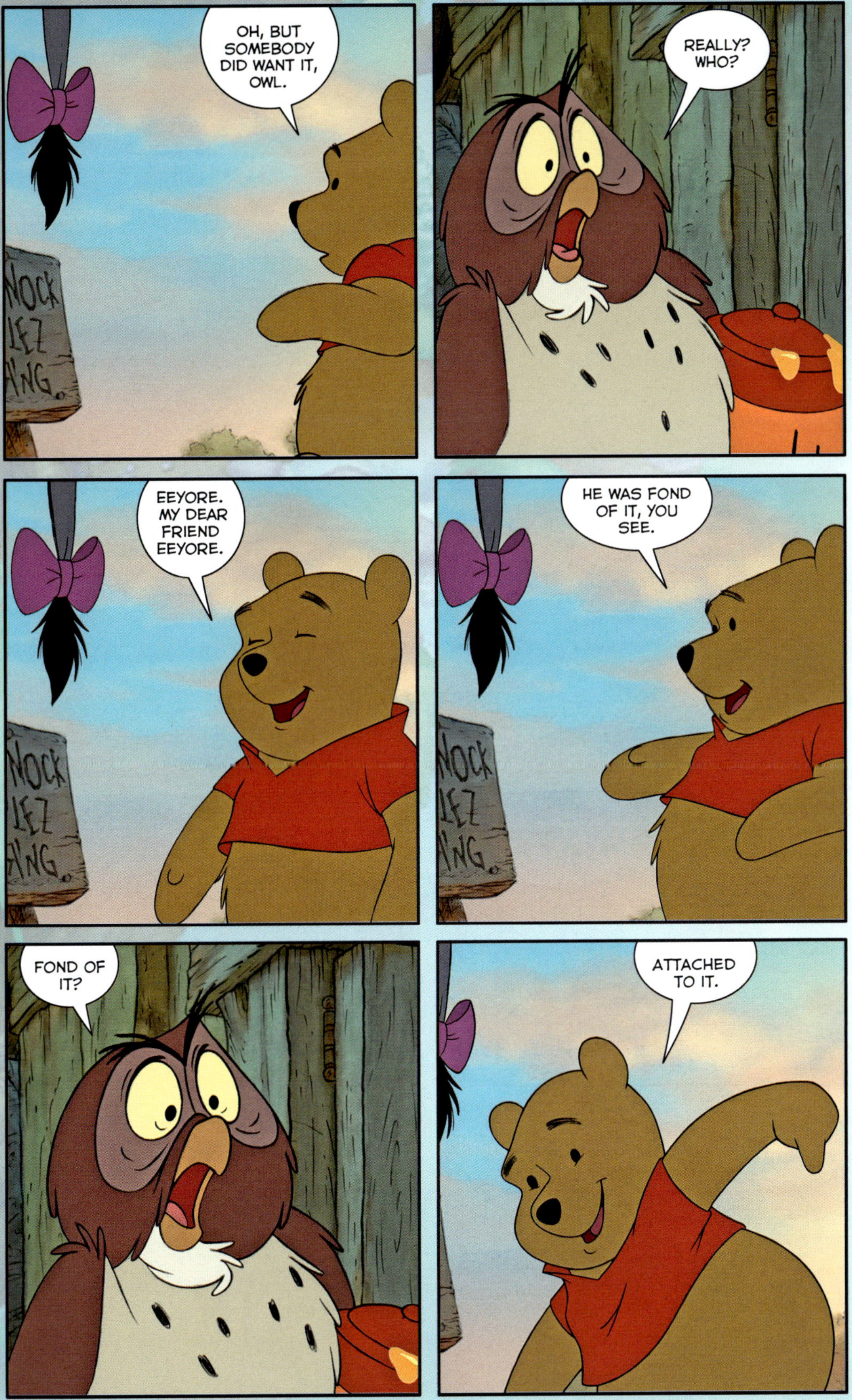
OH, BUT SOMEBODY DID WANT IT, OWL.
REALLY? WHO?
EEYORE. MY DEAR FRIEND EEYORE.
HE WAS FOND OF IT, YOU SEE.
FOND OF IT?
ATTACHED TO IT.

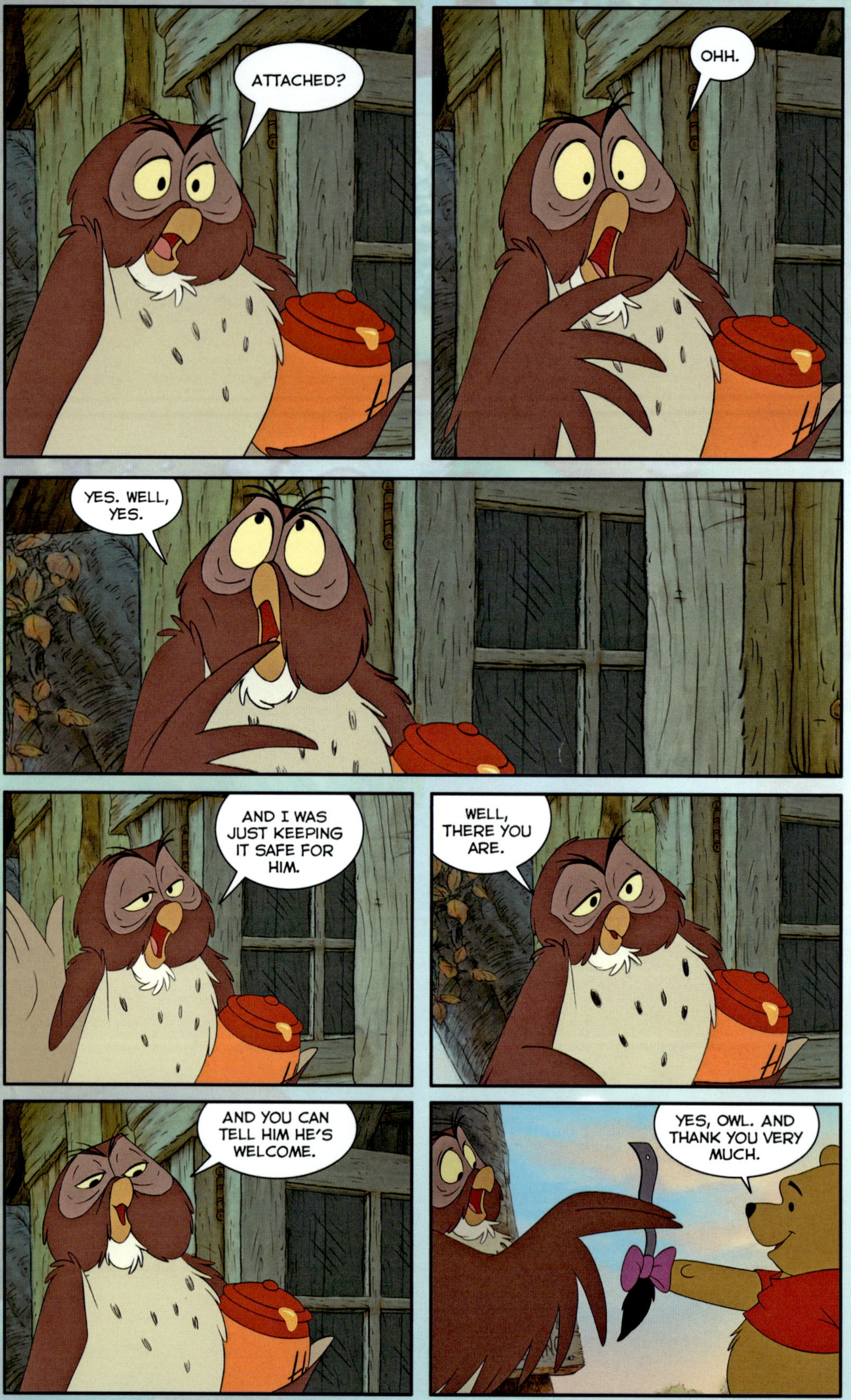
ATTACHED?
OHH.
YES. WELL, YES.
AND I WAS JUST KEEPING IT SAFE FOR HIM.
WELL, THERE YOU ARE.
AND YOU CAN TELL HIM HE'S WELCOME.
YES, OWL. AND THANK YOU VERY MUCH.

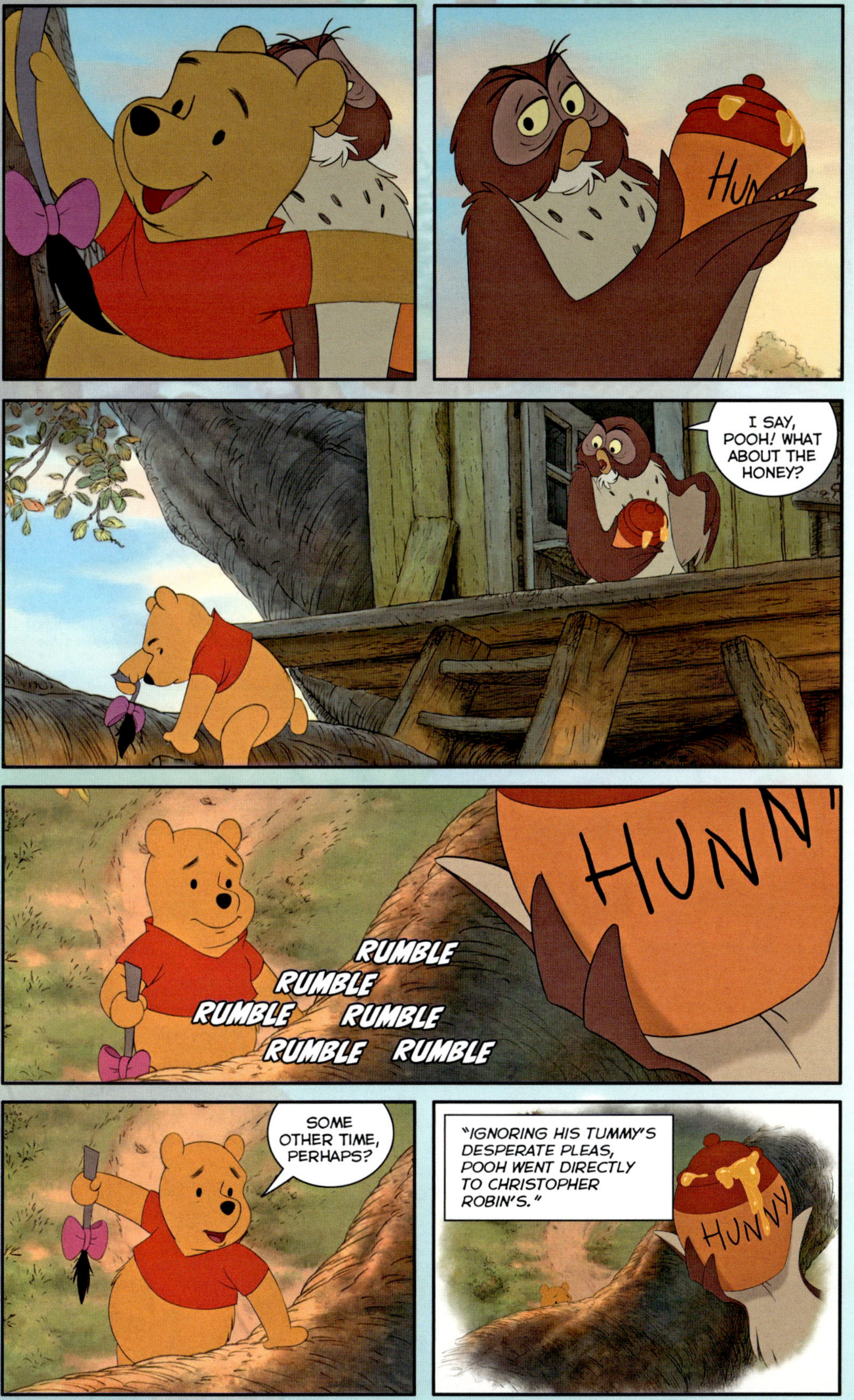
HUNNY
I SAY, POOH! WHAT ABOUT THE HONEY?
HUNNY
RUMBLE RUMBLE RUMBLE RUMBLE RUMBLE RUMBLE
SOME OTHER TIME, PERHAPS?
"IGNORING HIS TUMMY'S DESPERATE PLEAS, POOH WENT DIRECTLY TO CHRISTOPHER ROBIN'S."
HUNNY

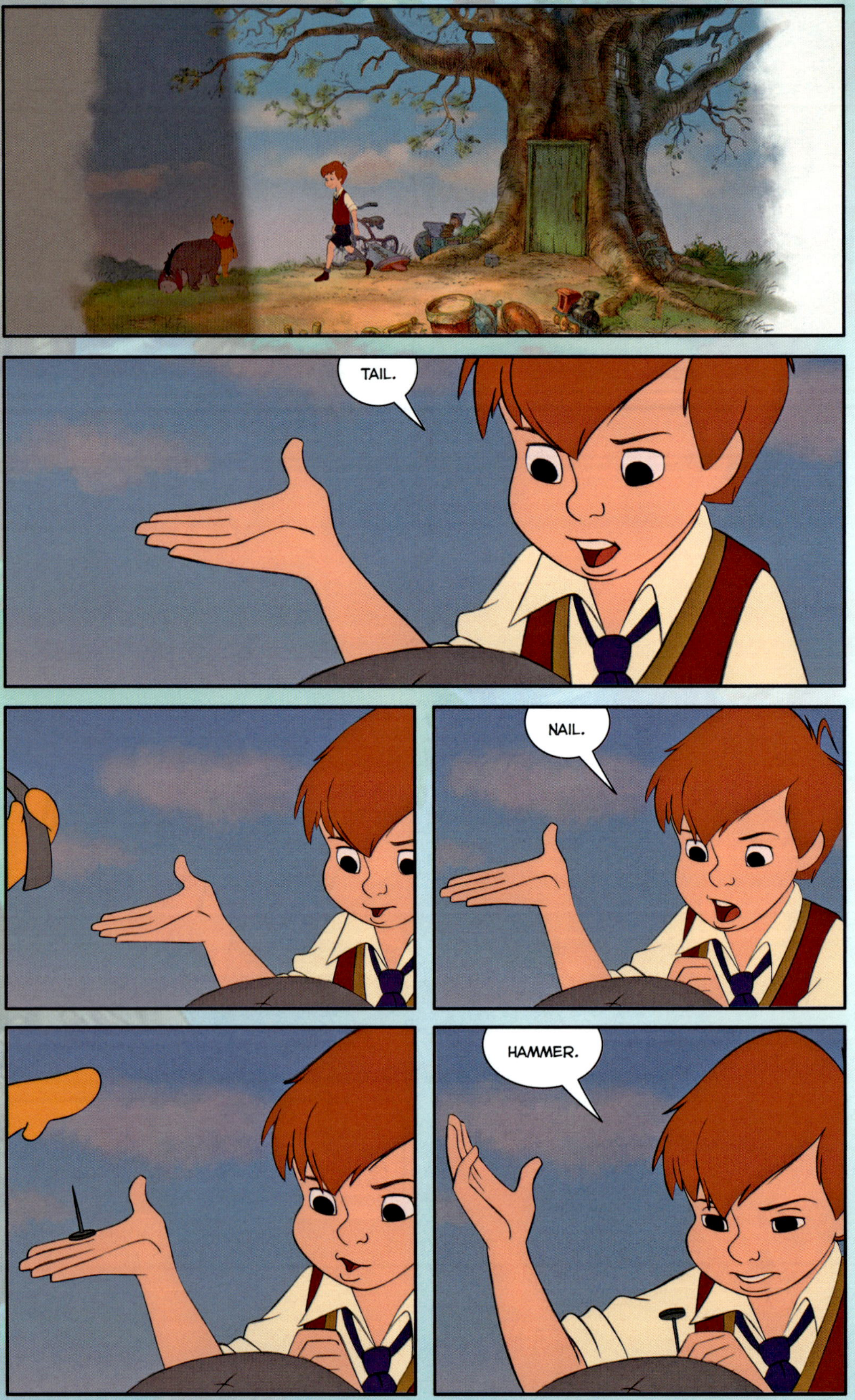
TAIL.
NAIL.
HAMMER.

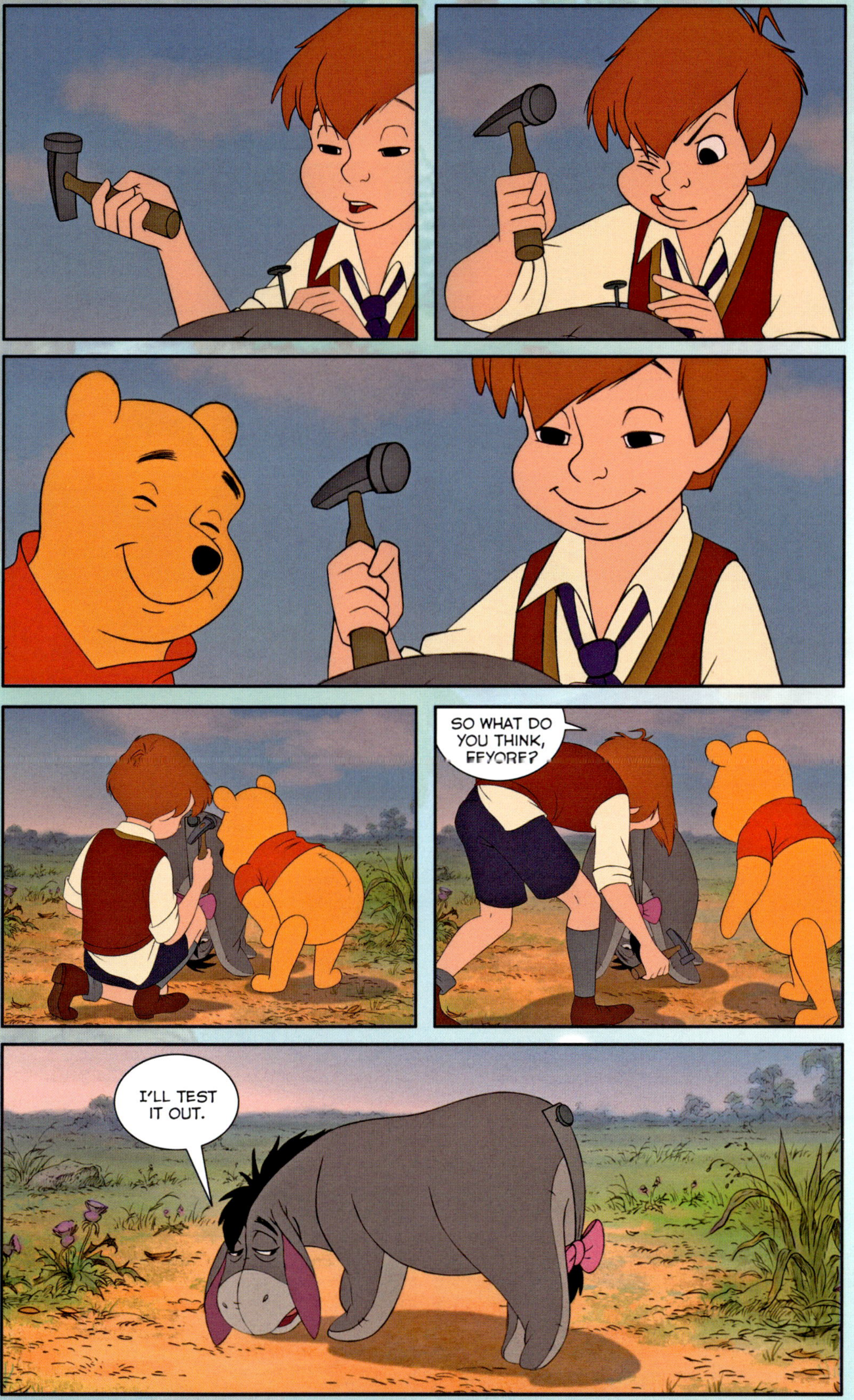
SO WHAT DO YOU THINK, EEYORE?
I'LL TEST IT OUT.

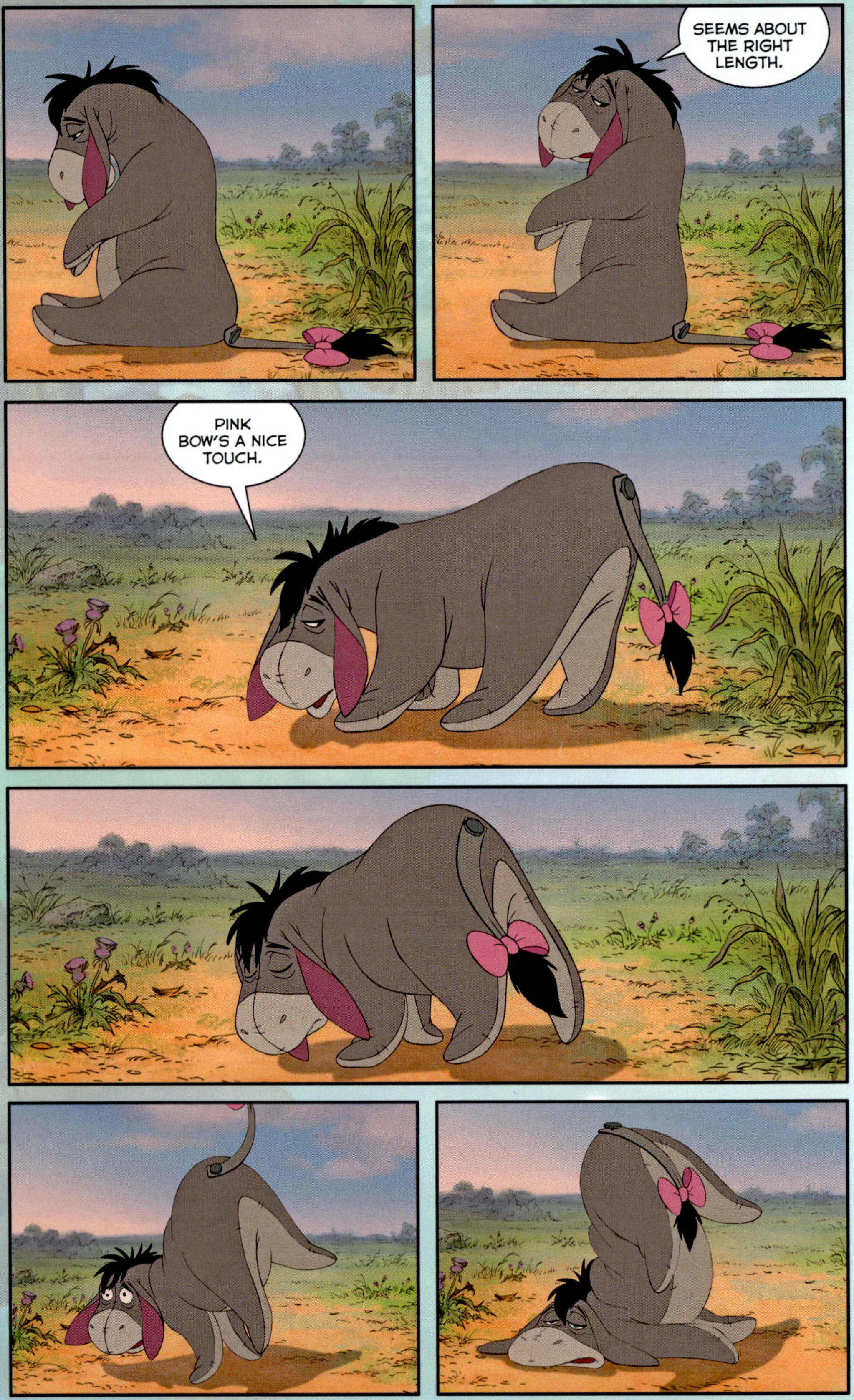
SEEMS ABOUT THE RIGHT LENGTH.
PINK BOW'S A NICE TOUCH.

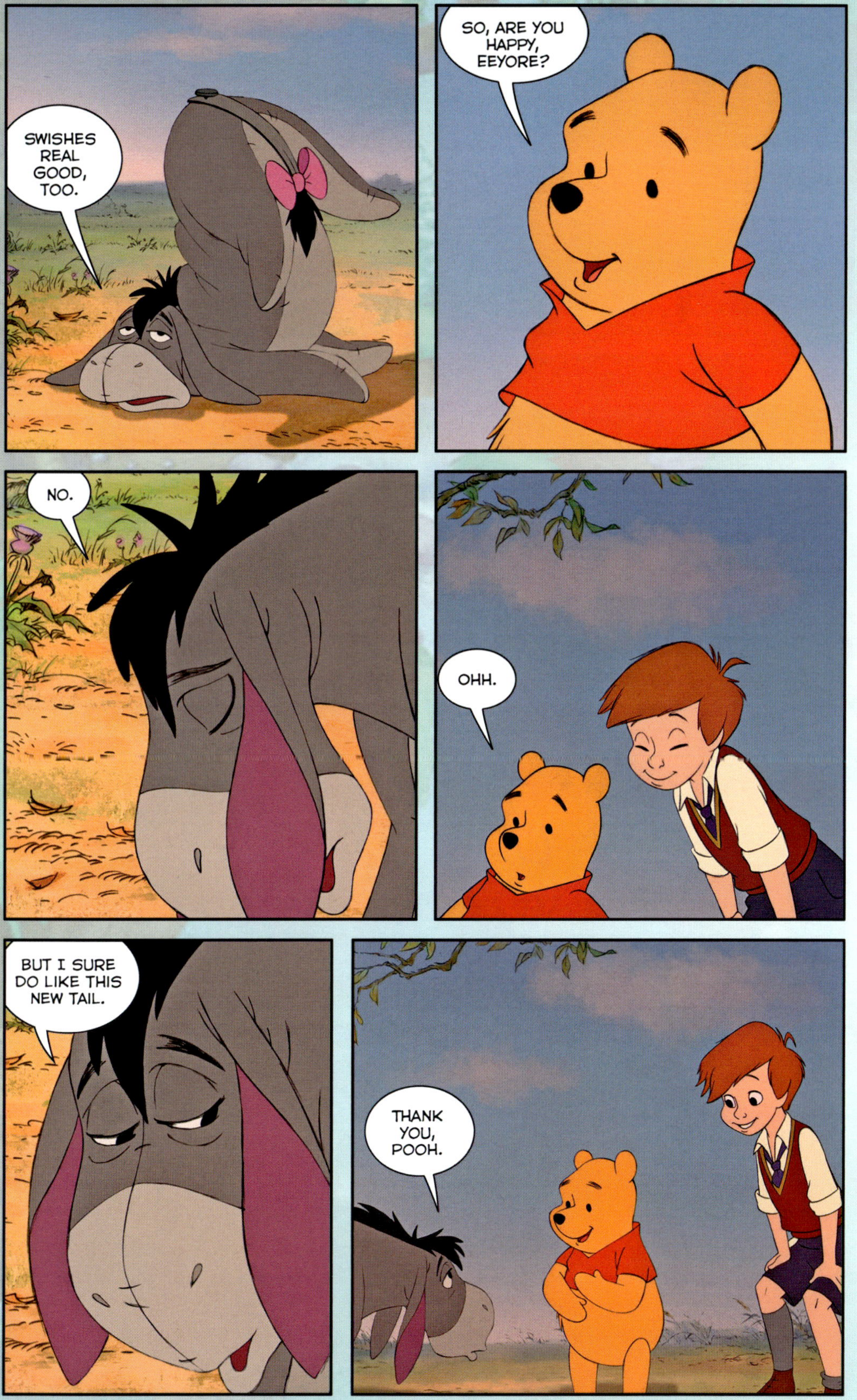
SWISHES REAL GOOD, TOO.
SO, ARE YOU HAPPY, EEYORE?
NO.
OHH.
BUT I SURE DO LIKE THIS NEW TAIL.
THANK YOU, POOH.

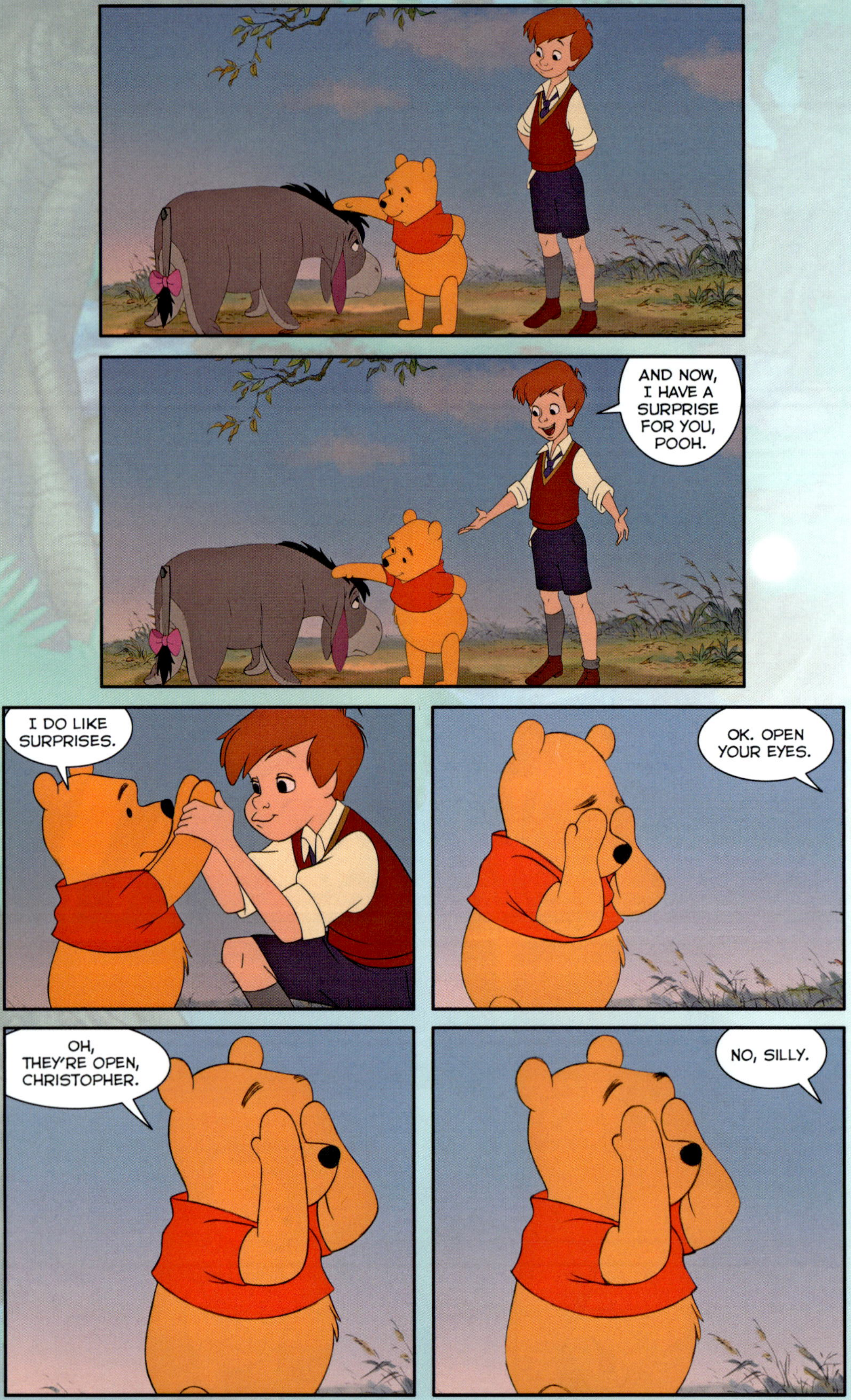
AND NOW, I HAVE A SURPRISE FOR YOU, POOH.
I DO LIKE SURPRISES.
OK. OPEN YOUR EYES.
OH, THEY'RE OPEN, CHRISTOPHER.
NO, SILLY.

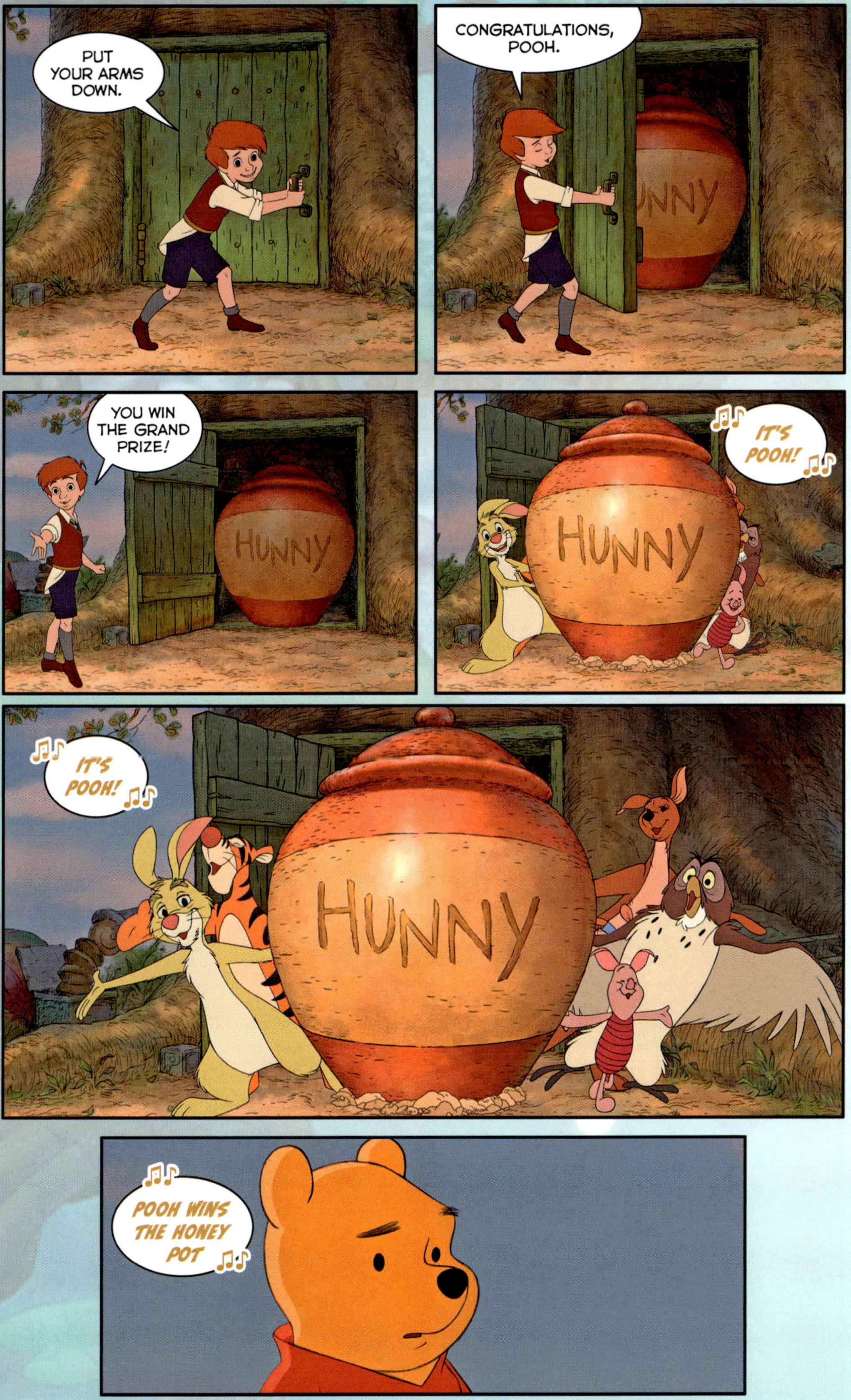
PUT YOUR ARMS DOWN.
CONGRATULATIONS, POOH.
HUNNY
YOU WIN THE GRAND PRIZE!
HUNNY
IT'S POOH!
HUNNY
IT'S POOH!
HUNNY
POOH WINS THE HONEY POT

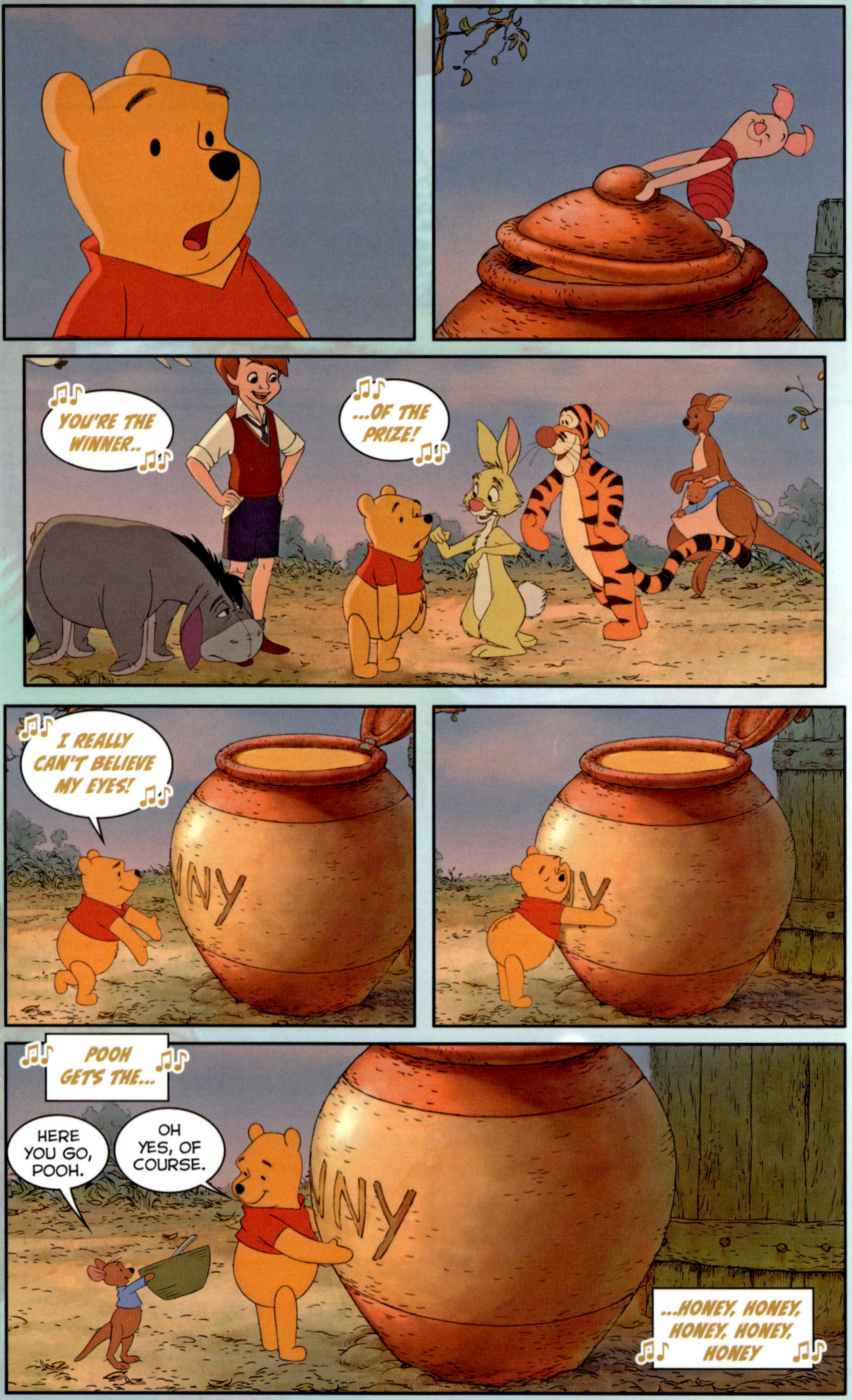
YOU'RE THE WINNER..
...OF THE PRIZE!
I REALLY CAN'T BELIEVE MY EYES!
POOH GETS THE...
HERE YOU GO, POOH.
OH YES, OF COURSE.
...HONEY, HONEY, HONEY, HONEY, HONEY

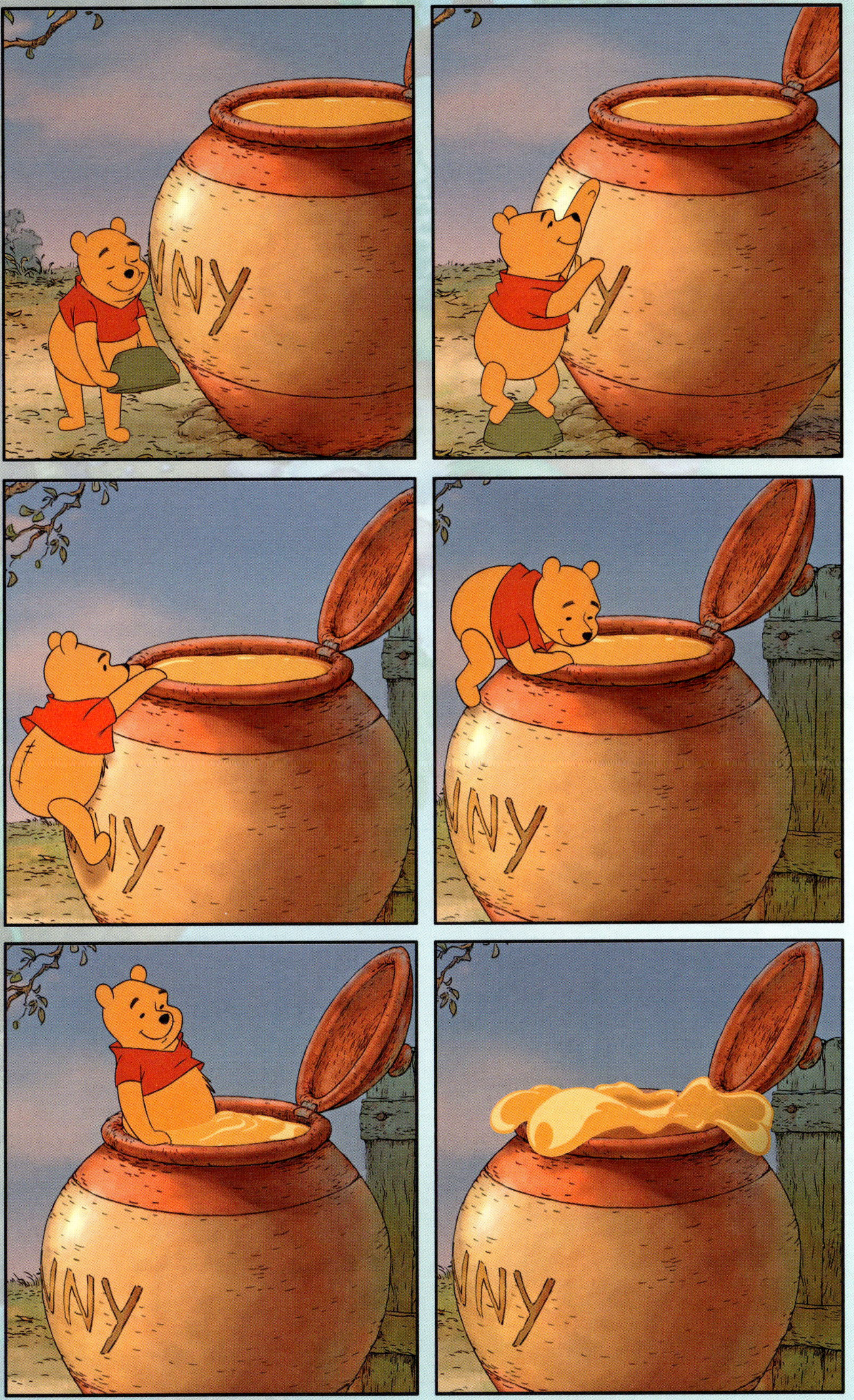

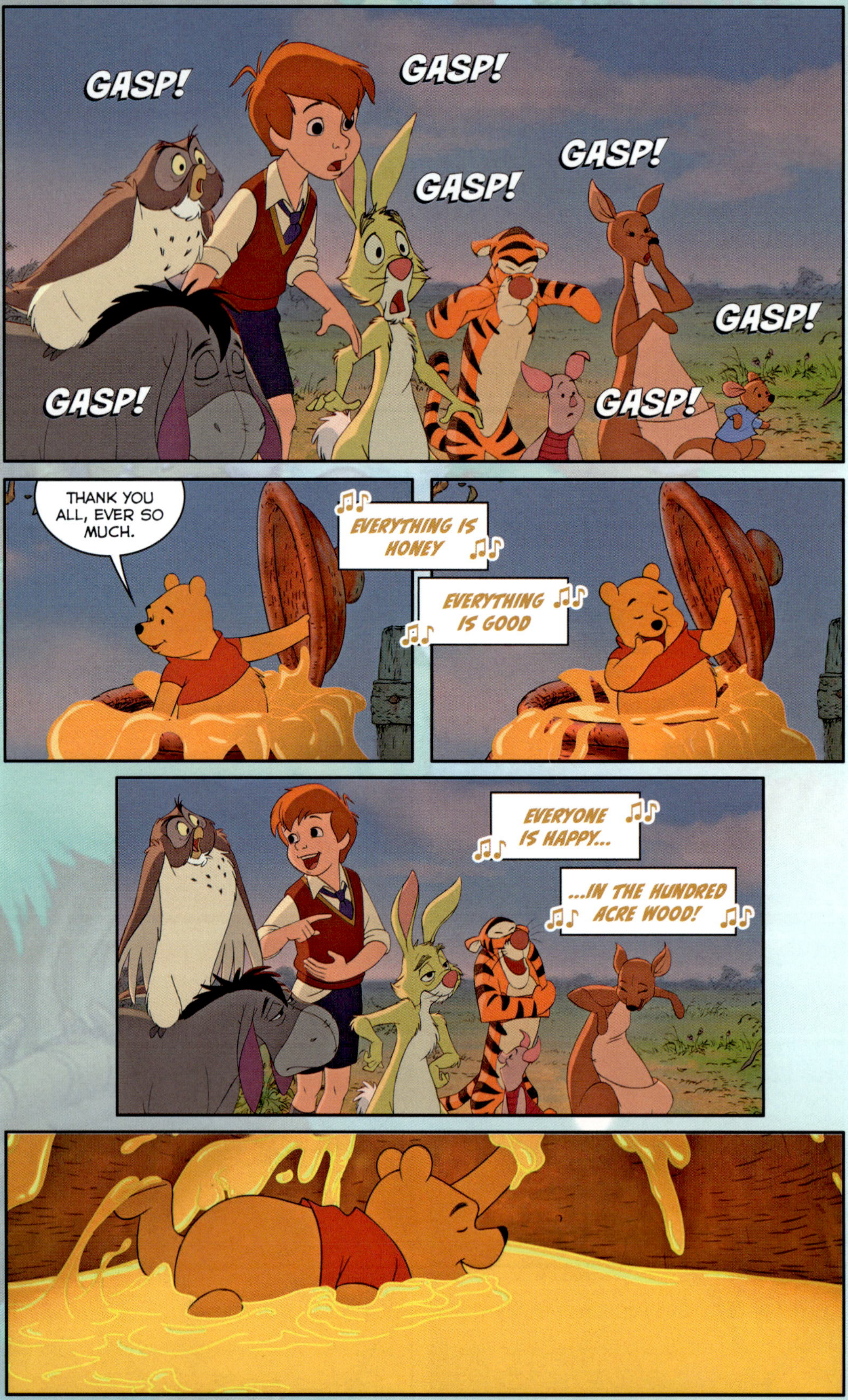
GASP!
GASP!
GASP!
GASP!
GASP!
GASP!
GASP!
THANK YOU ALL, EVER SO MUCH.
EVERYTHING IS HONEY
EVERYTHING IS GOOD
EVERYONE IS HAPPY...
...IN THE HUNDRED ACRE WOOD!

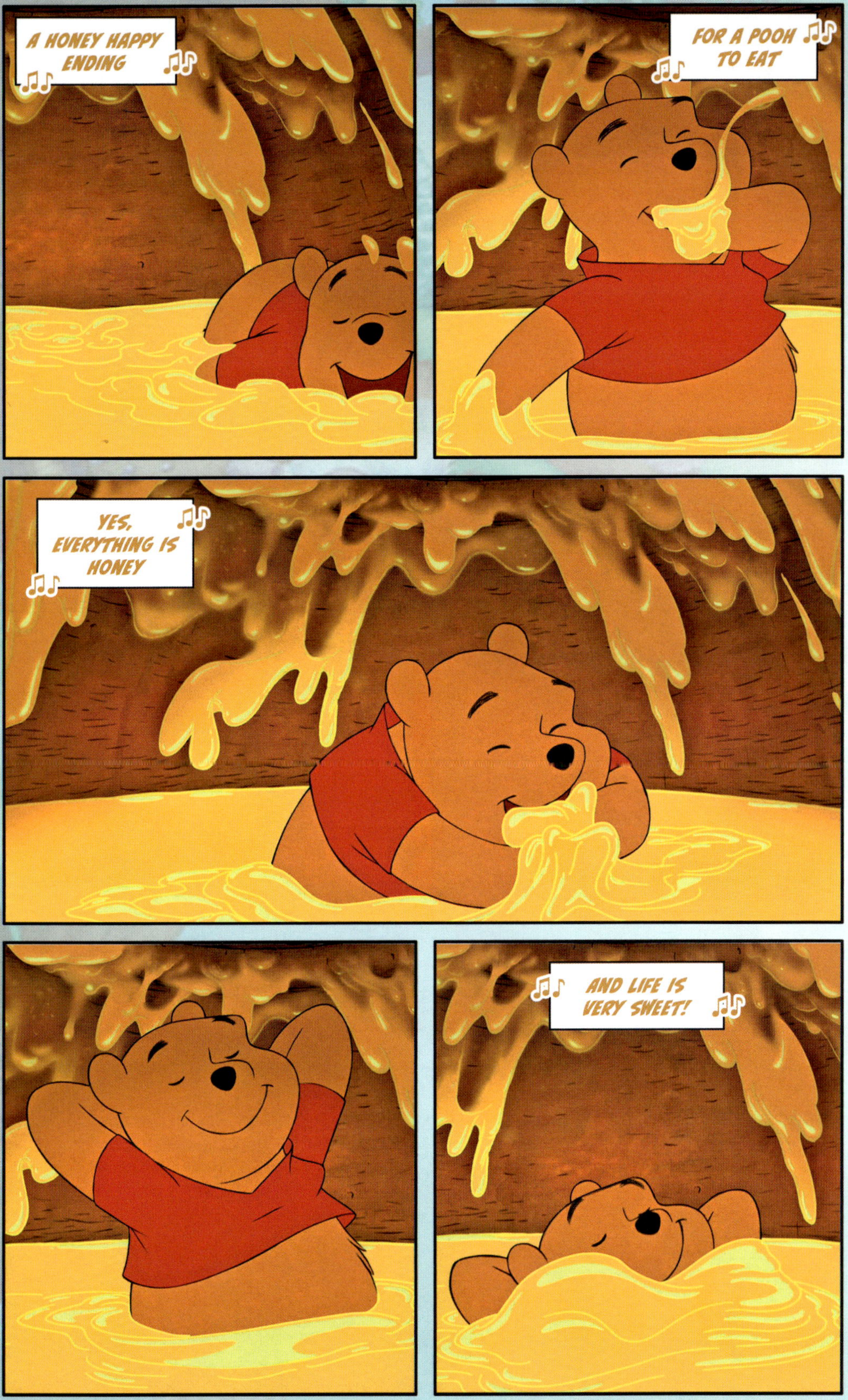
A HONEY HAPPY ENDING
FOR A POOH TO EAT
YES, EVERYTHING IS HONEY
AND LIFE IS VERY SWEET!

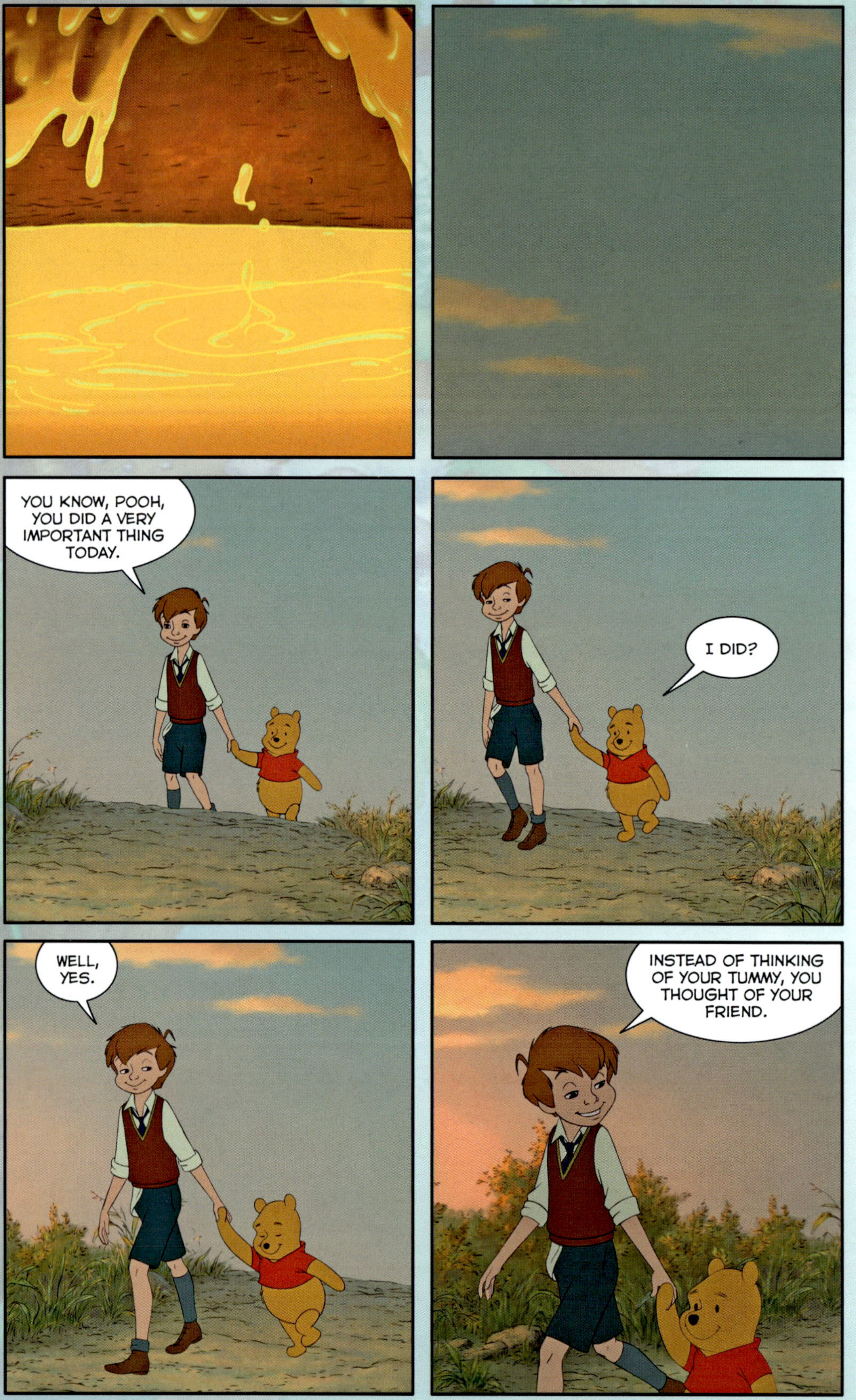

YOU KNOW, POOH, YOU DID A VERY IMPORTANT THING TODAY.
I DID?
WELL, YES.
INSTEAD OF THINKING OF YOUR TUMMY, YOU THOUGHT OF YOUR FRIEND.

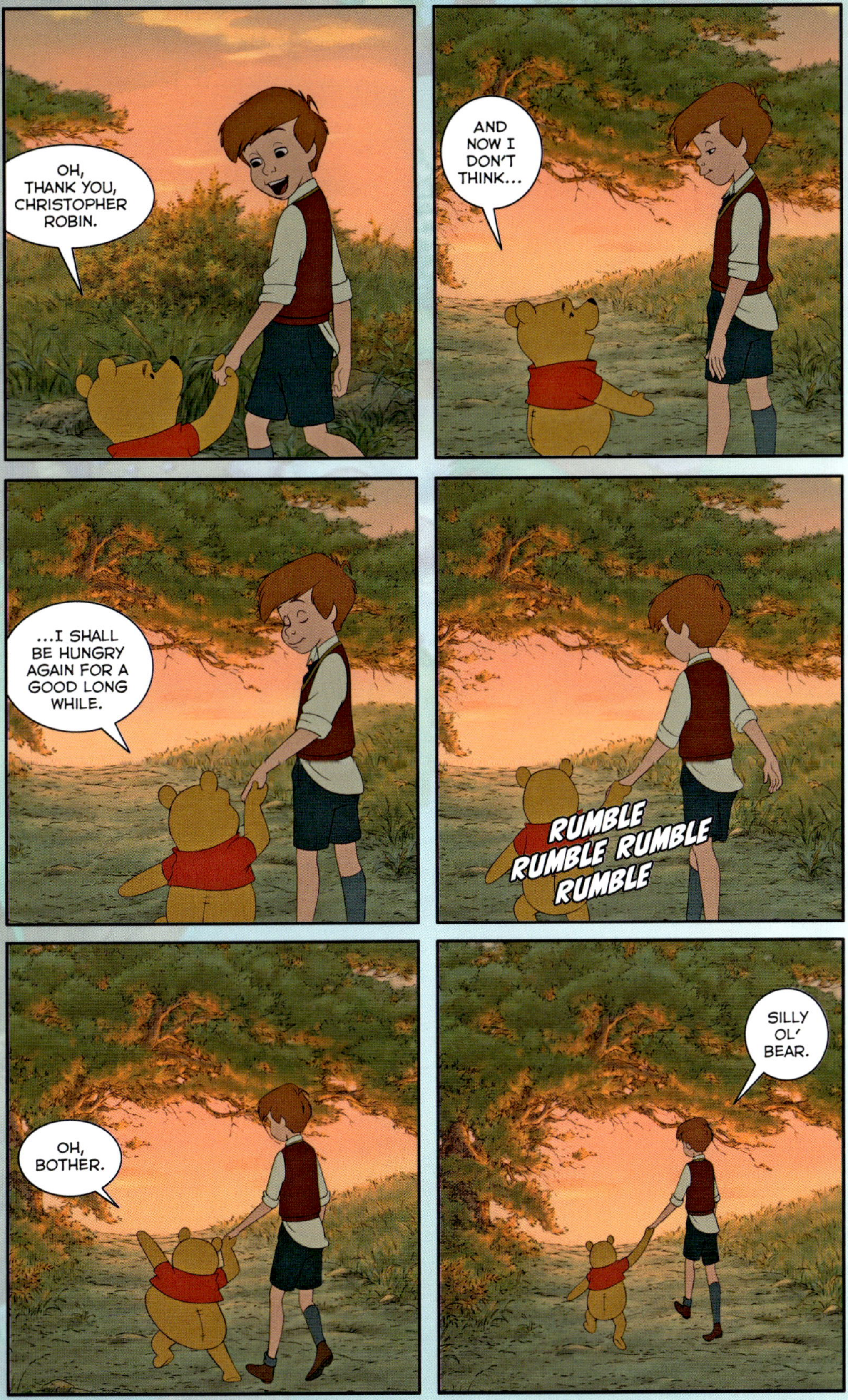
OH, THANK YOU, CHRISTOPHER ROBIN.
AND NOW I DON'T THINK...
...I SHALL BE HUNGRY AGAIN FOR A GOOD LONG WHILE.
RUMBLE RUMBLE RUMBLE RUMBLE
OH, BOTHER.
SILLY OL' BEAR.

"Oh, bother," whispered Pooh.
Christopher Robin laughed. "Silly old bear."
The End
"Oh thank you Christopher Robin. And now, I don't think I'll be hungry for a good long while."
Pooh's tummy started to grumble.
"Oh, bother," whispered Pooh.
Christopher Robin laughed. "Silly old bear."
The End
WINNIE
THE-POOH
A.A. Milne
WINNIE
THE-POOH
A.A. Milne

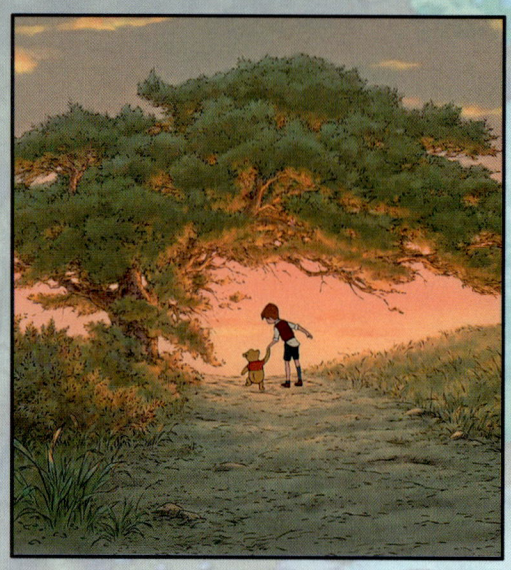

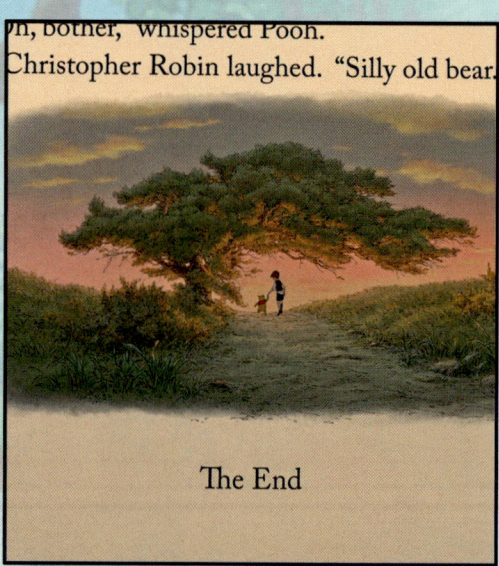

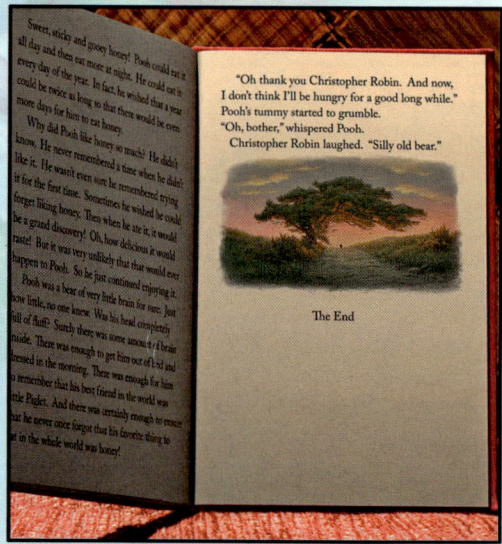

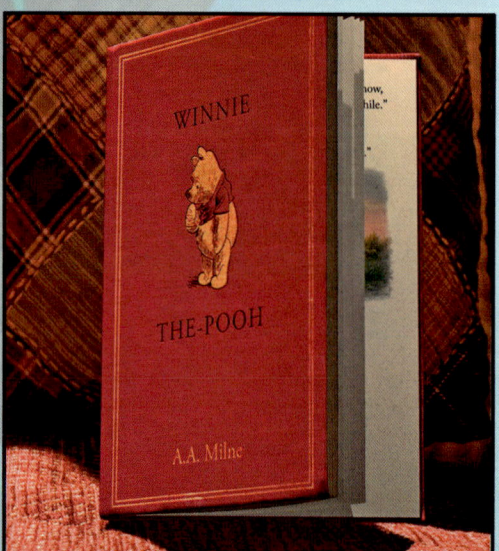

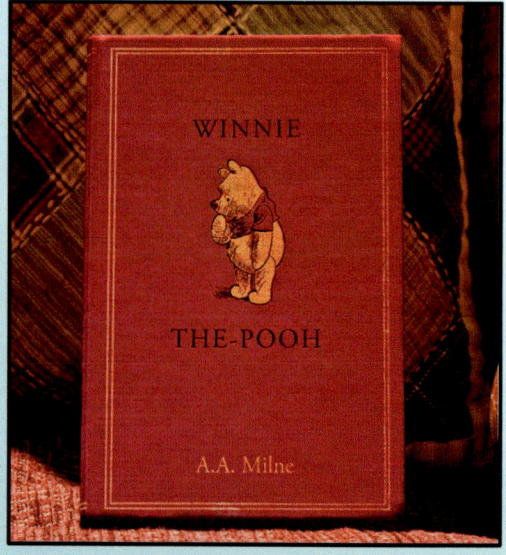

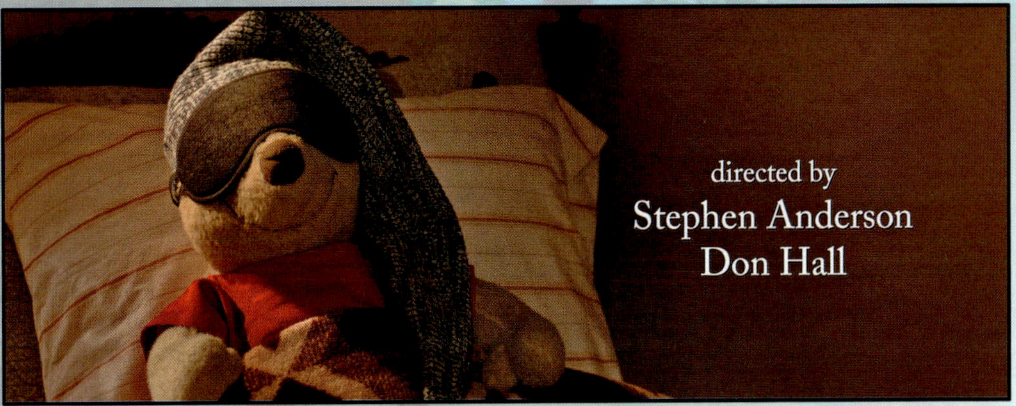
directed by
Stephen Anderson
Don Hall

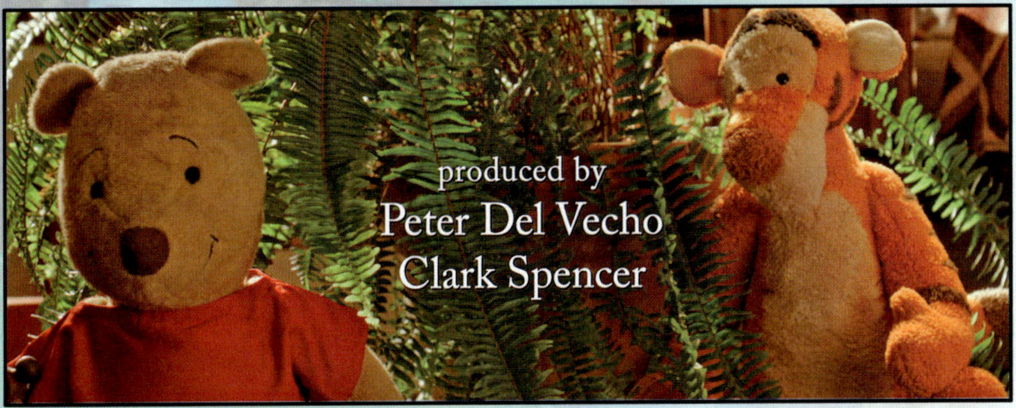
produced by
Peter Del Vecho
Clark Spencer

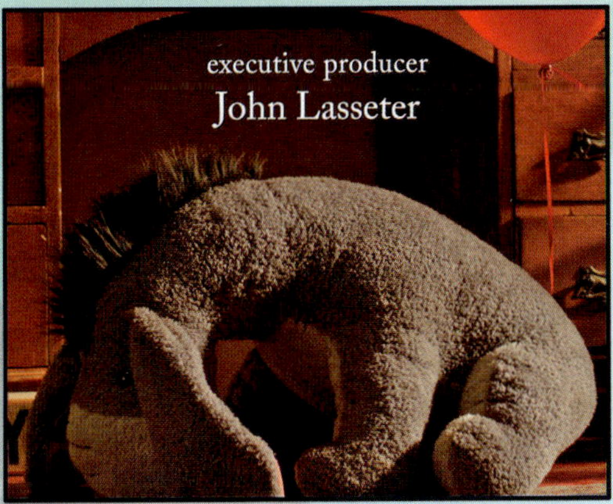
executive producer
John Lasseter

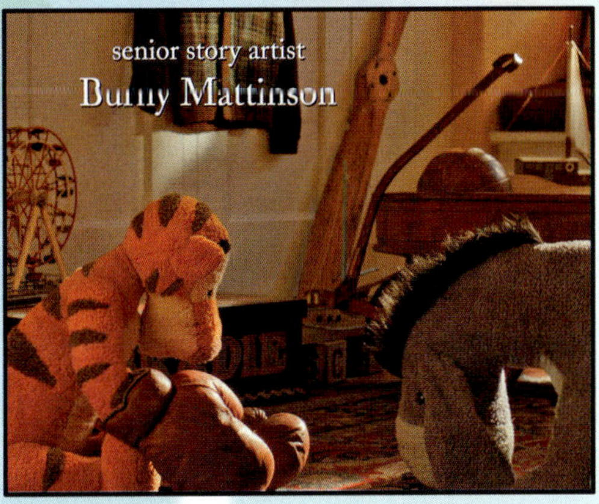
senior story artist
Burny Mattinson

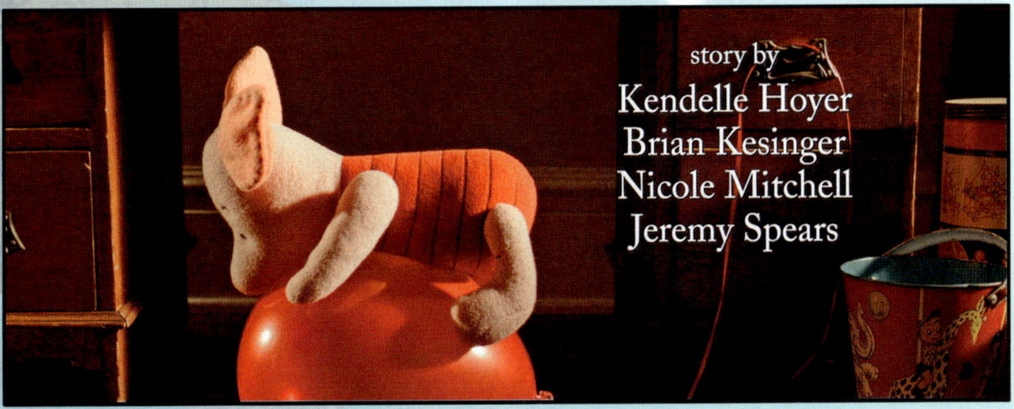
story by
Kendelle Hoyer
Brian Kesinger
Nicole Mitchell
Jeremy Spears

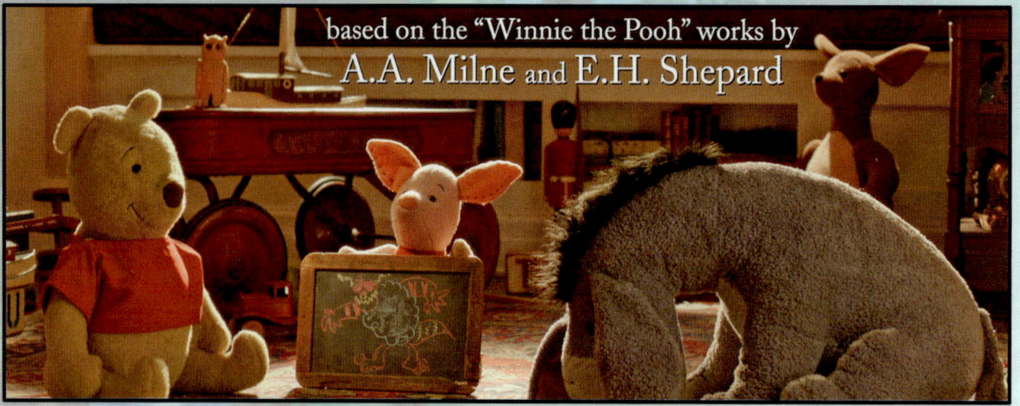
based on the "Winnie the Pooh" works by
A.A. Milne and E.H. Shepard

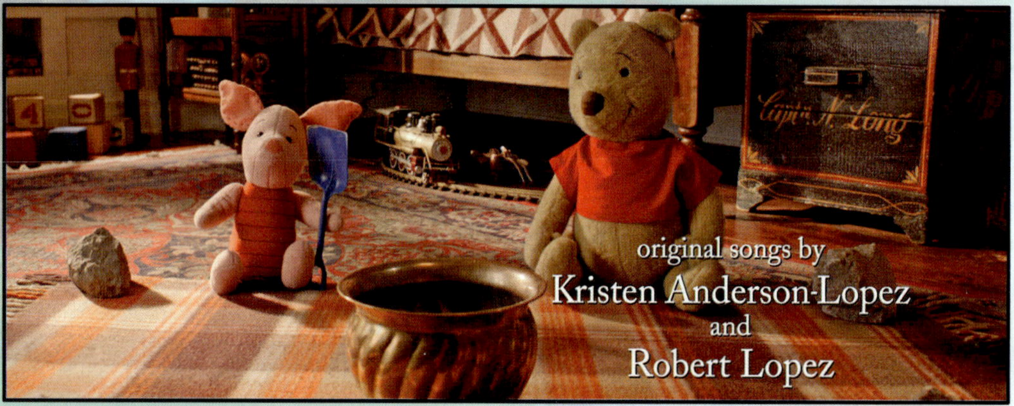
original songs by
Kristen Anderson-Lopez
and
Robert Lopez

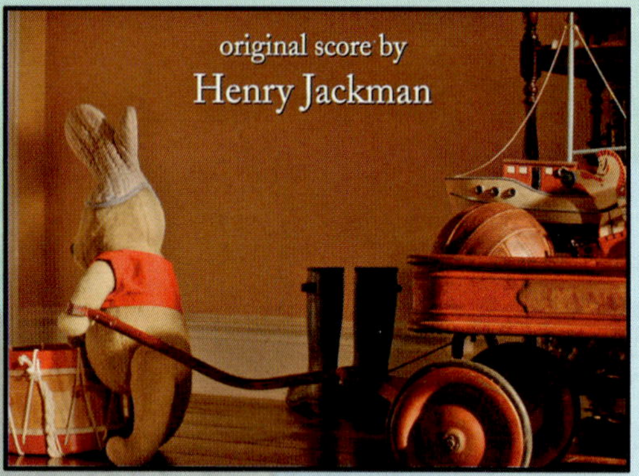
original score by
Henry Jackman

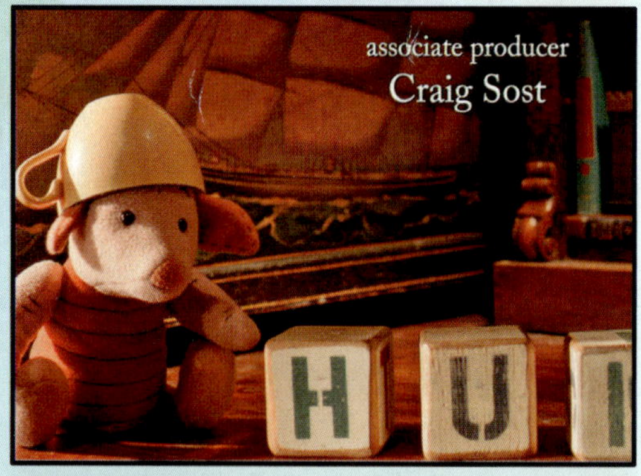
associate producer
Craig Sost

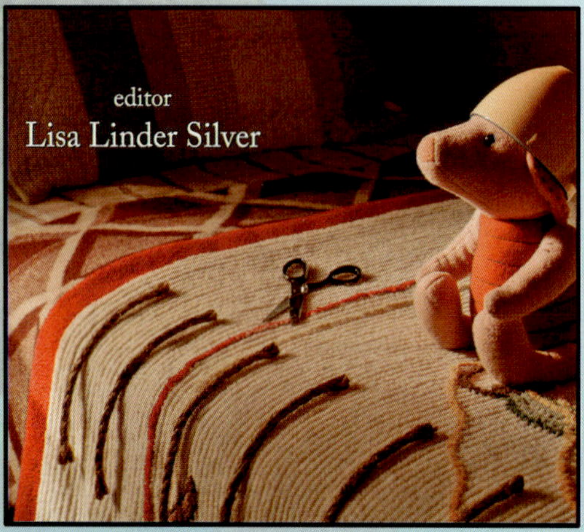
editor
Lisa Linder Silver

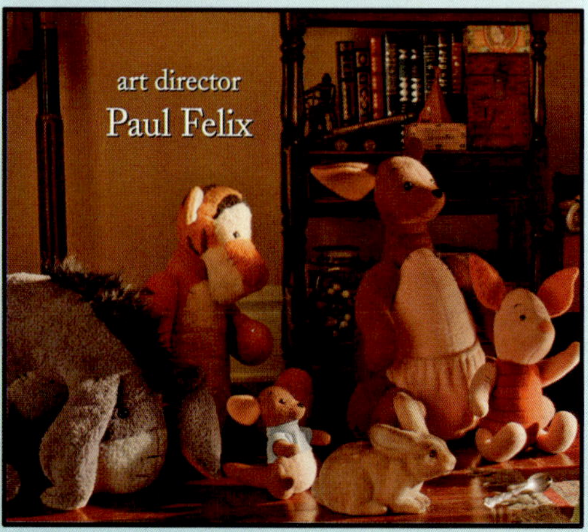
art director
Paul Felix

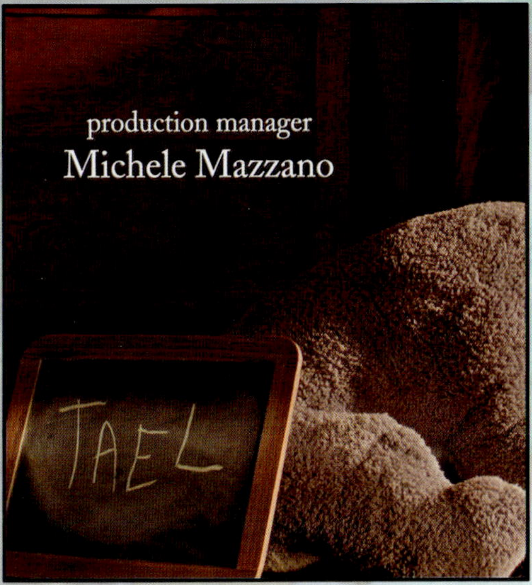
production manager
Michele Mazzano
TAEL

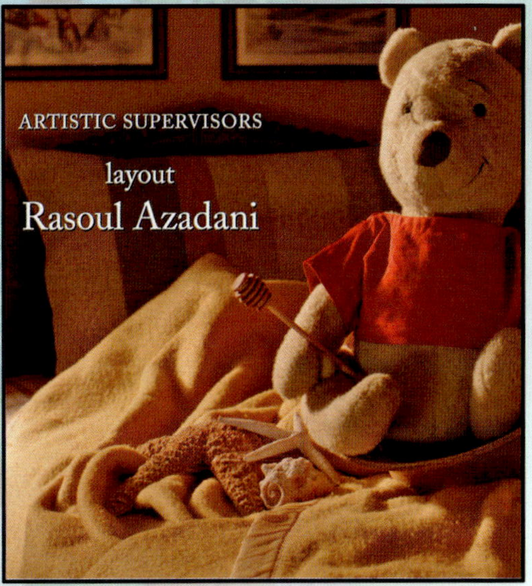
ARTISTIC SUPERVISORS
layout
Rasoul Azadani

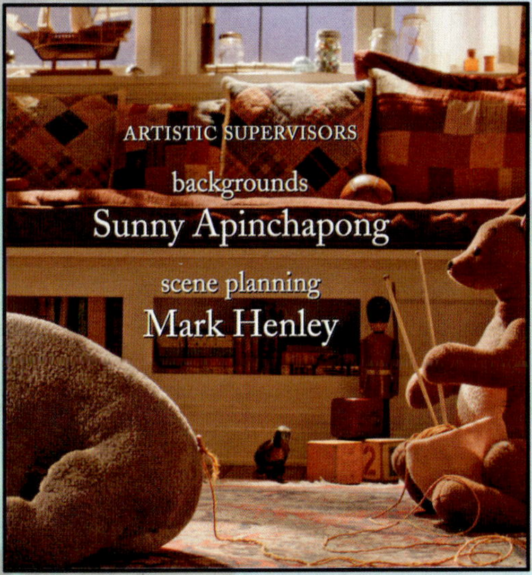
ARTISTIC SUPERVISORS
backgrounds
Sunny Apinchapong
scene planning
Mark Henley

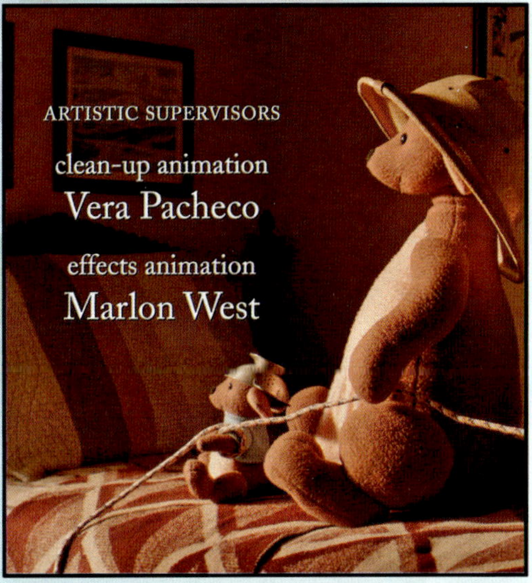
ARTISTIC SUPERVISORS
clean-up animation
Vera Pacheco
effects animation
Marlon West

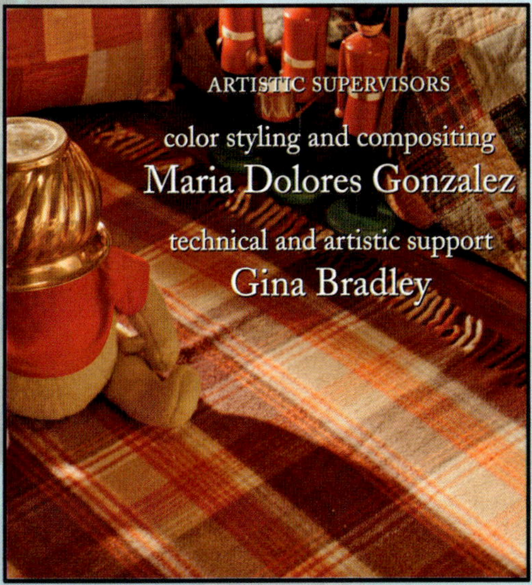
ARTISTIC SUPERVISORS
color styling and compositing
Maria Dolores Gonzalez
technical and artistic support
Gina Bradley

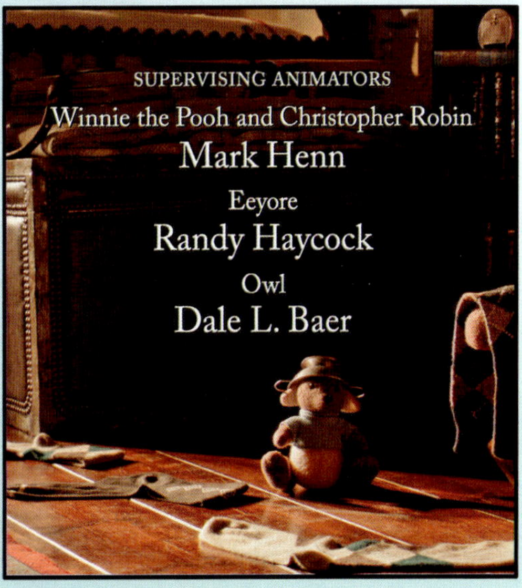
SUPERVISING ANIMATORS
Winnie the Pooh and Christopher Robin
Mark Henn
Eeyore
Randy Haycock
Owl
Dale L. Baer

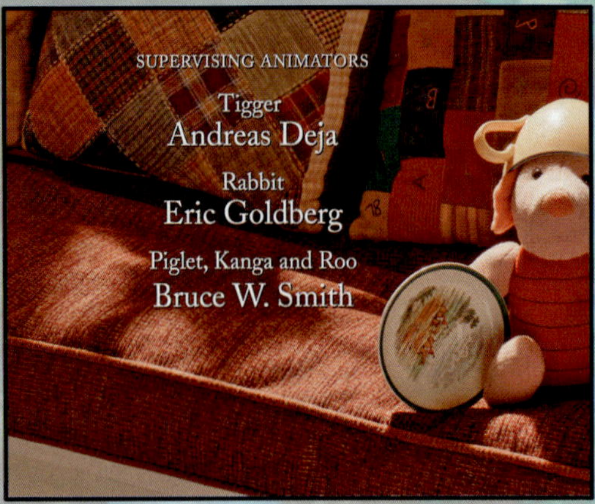
SUPERVISING ANIMATORS
Tigger
Andreas Deja
Rabbit
Eric Goldberg
Piglet, Kanga and Roo
Bruce W. Smith

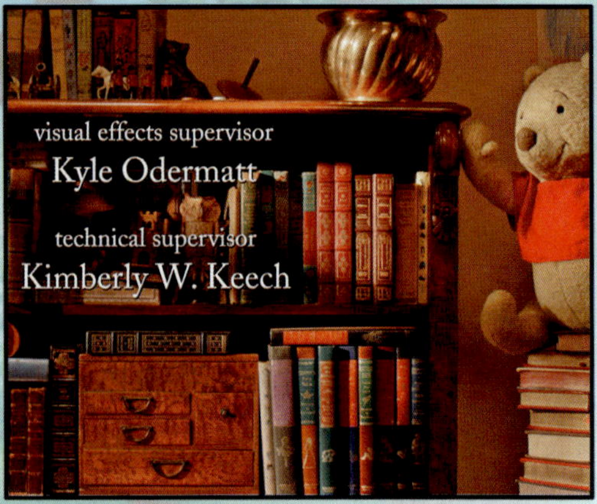
visual effects supervisor
Kyle Odermatt
technical supervisor
Kimberly W. Keech

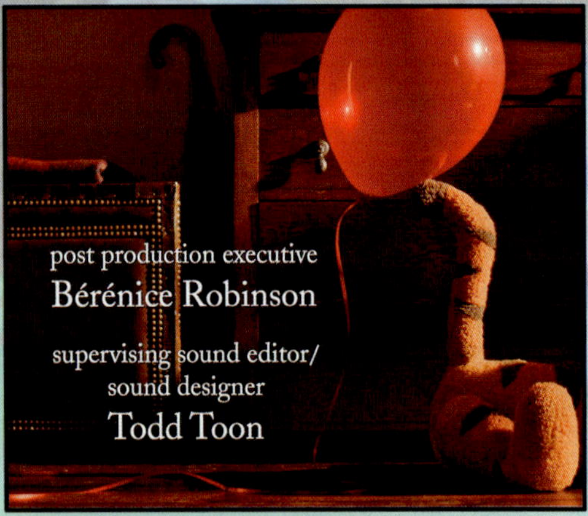
post production executive
Bérénice Robinson
supervising sound editor/
sound designer
Todd Toon

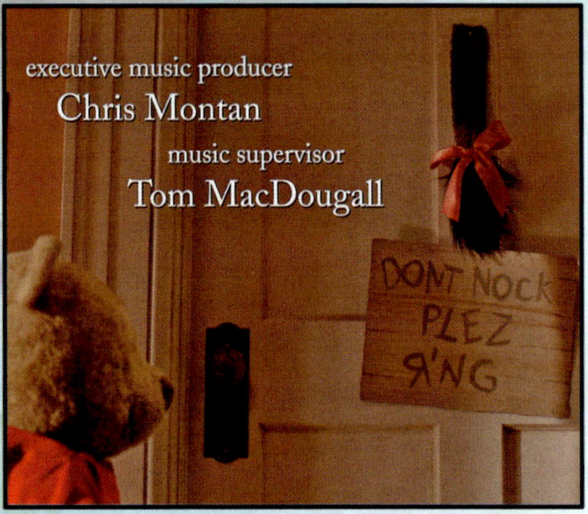
executive music producer
Chris Montan
music supervisor
Tom MacDougall
DONT NOCK
PLEZ

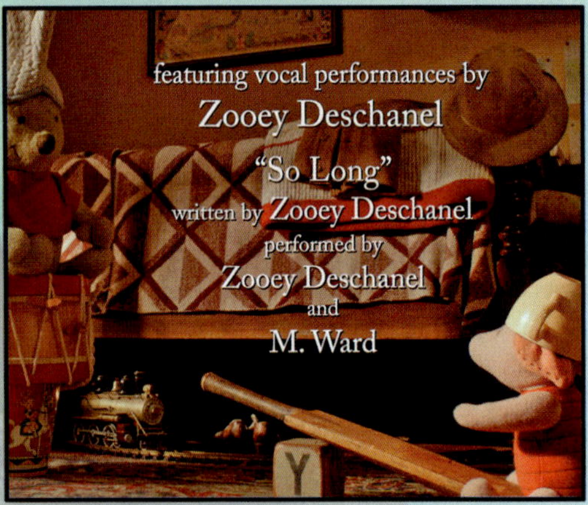
featuring vocal performances by
Zooey Deschanel
"So Long"
written by Zooey Deschanel
performed by
Zooey Deschanel
and
M. Ward

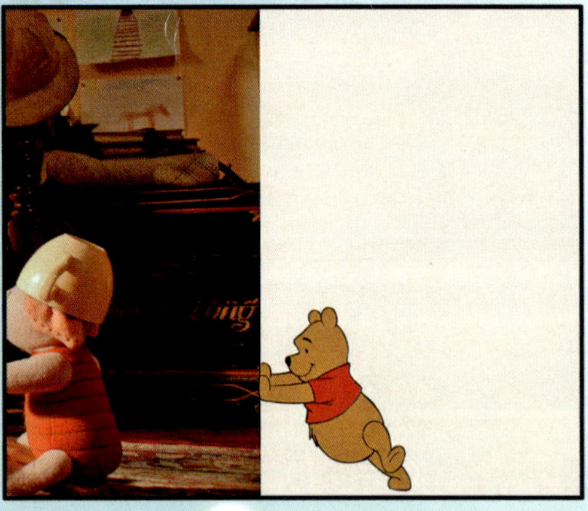

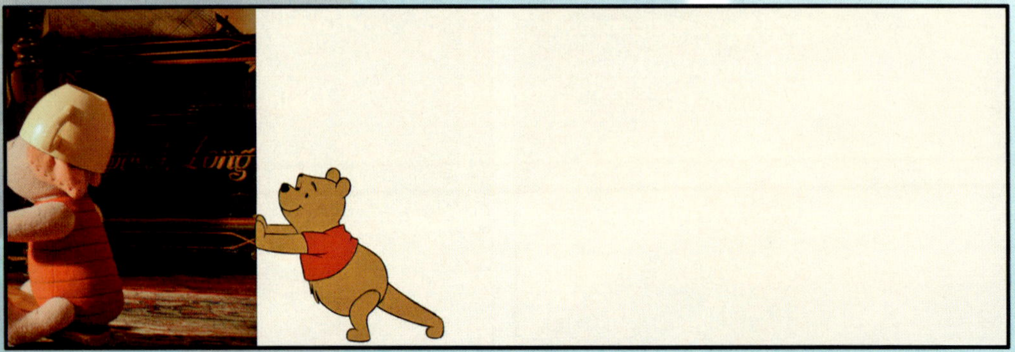

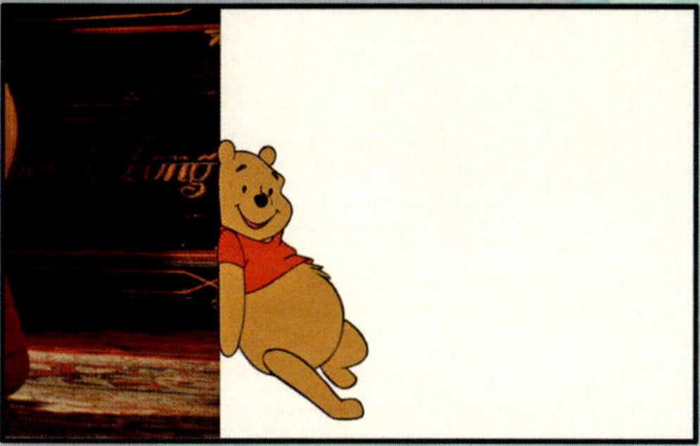

Casting by
Jamie Sparer Roberts, CSA

cast

Narrator — John Cleese
Winnie the Pooh — Jim Cummings
Eeyore — Bud Luckey
Owl — Craig Ferguson
Christopher Robin — Jack Boulter
Piglet — Travis Oates
Kanga — Kristen Anderson-Lopez
Roo — Wyatt Dean Hall
Rabbit — Tom Kenny
Tigger — Jim Cummings
Backson — Huell Howser

story

Production Department Managers — Nathan Massmann, Angela Frances D'Anna
Additional Story Material — Paul Briggs, Chris Ure
Production Assistant — Kyle Gabriel

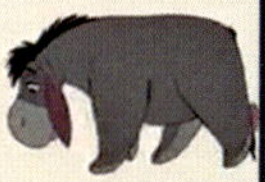

editorial

Production Department Manager — Nathan Massmann
Assistant Editor — Paul Chandler Carrera
Dialogue Reader — Hermann H. Schmidt
Production Assistants — Lauren Leffingwell, Steph Gortz

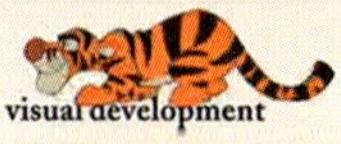

visual development

Production Department Manager — Jenny Bettis

Visual Development Artists
Lorelay Bove, Andreas Deja, Mike Gabriel
Shiyoon Kim, Bill Perkins, Joe Pitt
Doug Walker

Pre-Visualization — Matt Suzuki
Production Assistant — Dave Kohut

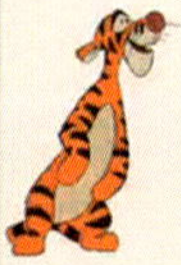

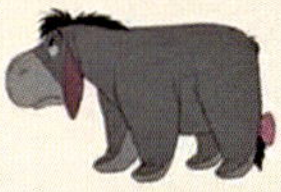

layout

Production Department Manager — James E. Hasman
Animatic Supervisors — Rasoul Azadani, Jean-Christophe Poulain

Layout Artists
James Alles, Nam Cho
Alfred "Tops" Cruz, Peter J. DeLuca
Jason Hand, Lam Hoang
Daniel Hu, Benoit Jean Claude Le Pennec
Jean-Christophe Poulain, Robert J. St. Pierre
Allen Tam, George P. Villaflor
Doug Walker, Jennifer Yuan

Production Assistants — Julie Baner, Brooke Randolph

backgrounds

Production Department Manager — Jenny Bettis

Background Artists
Doug Ball, Lisa Keene
Jang Lee, Dan Read
Leonard Robledo, Lucy Tanashian-Gentry

Production Assistant — Dave Kohut

scene planning

Production Department Manager — James E. Hasman

Scene Planners
Thomas Baker, George "Bingo" Ferguson
Dan C. Larsen, Richard Turner

Production Assistants — Julie Baner, Brooke Randolph

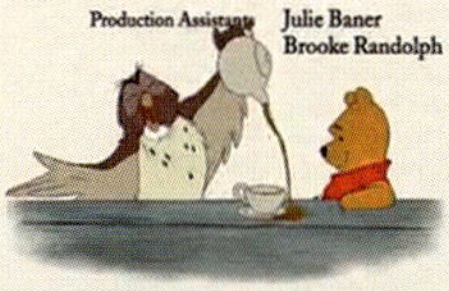

animation

Production Department Manager — Allison Norman
Animation Supervisor, Backson Song — Eric Goldberg

Animators
Ruben Azama Aquino, Anthony DeRosa
Russ Edmonds, Brian Ferguson
Bert Klein, Hyun-Min Lee
James Lopez, Frans Vischer

Additional Animators
Alex Kupershmidt, Nik Ranieri, Michael Surrey

Animating Assistants
Sarah Airriess, Erik Fountain
Mario Furmanczyk, Minkyu Lee

Trainees
Mael Gourmelen, Rory Madge, David Nam

Rough In-Betweener — Wes Sullivan
Production Assistant — Garrett Prince

clean-up animation

Production Department Manager — Lorry Ann Shea

Clean-Up Artist Lead Keys
Tigger — Kathleen M. Bailey
Winnie the Pooh and Christopher Robin — Rachel Renee Bibb
Rabbit — June M. Fujimoto
Piglet, Kanga and Roo — Tracy Mark Lee
Owl — Ginny Parmele, Lieve Miessen
Eeyore — Dan Tanaka

Clean-Up Keys
Nicola-jane Courtney, Millet Henson
Emily Jiuliano, Kellie D. Lewis
Brett Newton

Clean-Up Assistants — Patricia Ann Billings-Malone, Dietz Toshio Ichishita, Jan Naylor
Clean-Up Apprentice — Tapan Gandhi
Production Assistants — Kyle Gabriel, Alicia Lee Muller, Barbra Pushies

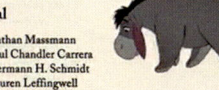

effects animation

Production Department Manager — Christopher Kracker

Effects Animators
Robert Bennett, Allen Blyth, Dan Lund
James DeV. Mansfield, David "Joey" Mildenberger

Effects Animating Assistants
Felipe Cerdán, Noé Garcia, Van Shirvanian

Additional Effects Animators — Brett Boggs, Eric Daniels
Production Assistants — Kelly Eisert, Lauren Leffingwell

color styling and compositing

Production Department Manager — Christopher Kracker
Color Stylists / Compositors — Brandon Bloch, Barbara Lynn Hamane, Ann Marie Sorensen
Final Check — Teri N. McDonald
Ink and Paint — David Karp, Teri N. McDonald
Production Assistant — Kelly Eisert

technical and artistic support

Production Department Manager — Jeremy Costello

Technical Directors
Ross Blocher, Darrin Drew
Todd LaPlante, David Scarpitti

Assistant Technical Directors — Dennis Matthew Johnson, Edwin S. Shorten
Animation Check — Susan Burke, Helen O'Flynn
Scanners — David Bonnell, Michael Alan McFerren
Production Software Development — John Robert Perry
Production Assistant — Melissa Genoshe

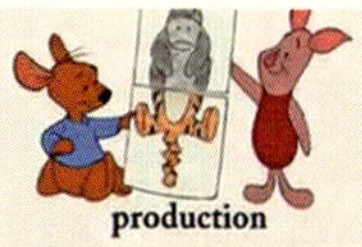

production

Production Supervisor — Bardo S. Ramirez
Production Finance Lead — Daniel Feiner
Production Finance Analyst — Nathan Curtis
Administrative Manager — Vicki Case
Ink and Paint Department Manager — Jeremy Costello
Publicity Department Manager — Jenny Bettis
Braintrust / Sweatbox Department Manager — Holly E. Bratton
Braintrust / Sweatbox Production Assistant — Melissa Genoshe
Assistant to the Producer — Erin Senge
Assistant to the Directors — Dustin Sterling
Secretarial Office Manager — Eileen Aguirre

live action production

Line Producer	Kathleen Courtney
Production Supervisor	Amanda J. Scarano
Art Director	Patrick M. Sullivan, Jr.
Director of Photography	Julio Macat, ASC
Set Decorator	Cheryl Carasik
Leadman	David Manhan
Buyer	Wendy Weaver
Camera Operator	Paul Sanchez
First Assistant Camera	Melvina Rapozo
Second Assistant Camera	Lisa Wolfion
DIT	Elhanan Matos
Chief Lighting Technician	Dwight D. Campbell
Best Boy Electric	Sebastien "Cbass" Amiri
Key Grip	Eric "Torch" Ward
Best Boy Grip	William McDevitt
Dolly Grip	Jamie Young
Construction Coordinator	William Gideon
Construction Foreman	Steven L. Scott
Labor Foreman	Javier Perez
Paint Foreman	Melanie Mahoney
Office Production Assistant	Wanjiru M. Njendu
Set Production Assistants	Ryan Willis
	Cherylin Lytle
Production Accountant	Justin Stirling
Assistant Accountant	Jonise Sullivan
Set Dressers	Charlie Montoya
	Kathleen Rosen
Ager / Dyer	Jill Tomomatsu
Standby Painter	Catherine Burns
Key Craft Service	Luis Ambriz
Video Playback	Gary P. Martinez
Set Lighting Technicians	Matthew Ardine
	David Kane
	Francisco Bulgarelli
Grips	Tony Porto
	Steve Jezewski
Special Effects	George C. Stevens
	Tim Gospodnetich

Original "Winnie the Pooh" Stuffed Bear by
Sylvia Mattinson

Other Stuffed Animals by
Disney Store

music

Original Songs by
Kristen Anderson-Lopez and Robert Lopez

"The Tummy Song"
Performed by
Jim Cummings and Robert Lopez

"A Very Important Thing To Do"
Performed by
Zooey Deschanel

"The Winner Song"
Performed by
Cast

"The Backson Song"
Performed by
Craig Ferguson and Cast

"It's Gonna Be Great"
Performed by
Jim Cummings and Bud Luckey

"Everything Is Honey" and "Finale"
Performed by
Jim Cummings
Zooey Deschanel
Robert Lopez
and Cast

"Winnie the Pooh"
Written by
Richard M. Sherman and Robert B. Sherman
Arranged and Performed by
Zooey Deschanel and M. Ward

"So Long"
Written by Zooey Deschanel
Performed by
Zooey Deschanel and M. Ward

"Winnie the Pooh" and "So Long"
Produced by M. Ward
Engineered by Al Schmitt
Mixed by Mike Mogis
Assisted by
Steve Genewick and Mike Coykendall

"The Wonderful Thing About Tiggers"
Written by
Richard M. Sherman and Robert B. Sherman

Original Songs Produced by	Kristen Anderson-Lopez
	Robert Lopez and
	Doug Besterman
Original Score Produced by	Henry Jackman
Songs Recorded by	Doc Kane
	Gabriel Guy and
	Frank Wolf

Score Recorded and Songs and Score Mixed by	Alan Meyerson
Songs Arranged, Orchestrated and Conducted by	Doug Besterman
Score Conducted by	Nick Glennie-Smith
Score Orchestrations by	John Thomas
Music Production Director	Andrew Page
Music Editor	Earl Ghaffari
Music Editor (Temp Score)	Tommy Holmes
Additional Music	Chris Willis
Music Business Affairs	Donna Cole-Brulé
Music Production Coordinator	Ashley Chafin
Executive Music Assistant	Jill Heffley
Score Technical Engineer	Jack Dolman
Technical Assistants	Edward Bainton
	Alex Belcher
Music Production Services	Steven Kofsky
Music Contracted by	Sandy De Crescent and
	Peter Rotter
Additional Music Contracting by	Reggie Wilson and
	Jasper Randall
Music Preparation by	Booker White -
	Walt Disney Music
	and
	Jo Ann Kane Music Service

Score Choir

Eric Bradley	Karen Hogle Brown
Reid Bruton	Elin Carlson
Randy Crenshaw	Tim Davis
Amy Fogerson	Abdiel Gonzalez
Scott Graff	Katie Hampton
Karen Harper	Angie Jaree
Bob Joyce	Michael Lichtenauer
Rick Logan	David Loucks
Chris Mann	Elyse Marchant
Donna Medine	Jasper Randall
Jessica Rotter	Nancy Sulahian
Kimberly Switzer	Suzanne Waters
	Gerald White

partner studio
yowza animation inc.

Studio Head	Claude Chiasson
Executive Producer	Pete Denomme
Production Manager	Pierre Chiasson
Clean-Up Assistants	James McCrimmon
	Mike Demur

Clean-Up Department

Kyung Hee Baker	Janine Cho
Yeon-Tae Choi	Rowena Cruz
Myung Hee Heo	Gloria Hsu
Brad Hughes	Weronika Kapelanska
Anne L'Ecuyer	Mi-Young Lee
Bev Lehman	Ron Migliore
Mike Milligan	Adriano Mondala
John Morgan	Paul Mota
Royston Robins	Cilbur Rocha
Nedenia Rocha	Dan Turner
Lynn Yamazaki	Seung-Gwan Yang
Head of Ink and Paint / Composite	Sonya Hassan-Carey
Ink and Paint Supervisor	Christine O'Connor
Continuity	Kemal Ally

Ink and Paint

Trudy Binder	Ian Chiasson
Keith Grachow	David Law
Lynda Lyons	Ken Ng
Andrew Smith	Maryla Straczynski
Devin Wagner	Michael Westman

Information Technology
Ceferino Asido	Andrew Klaassen

post production

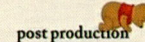

Post Production Supervisor	Brent W. Hall
Post Production Coordinator	Brian Millman
Post Production Assistant	Eduardo E. Sotelo
Original Dialogue Mixers	Gabriel Guy
	Doc Kane
Sound Services	424, Inc.
Re-Recording Mixers	David E. Fluhr, CAS
	Dean Zupancic
Sound Recordist	Kaspar Hugentobler
First Assistant Sound Editor	Pernell L. Salinas
Sound Editors	Charles W. Ritter
	Albert Gasser
	Don Malouf
	Odin Benitez
Dialogue & ADR Supervisor	G.W. Brown
Foley Artists	John Roesch
	Alyson Dee Moore
Foley Mixers	Mary Jo Lang
	Kyle Rochlin
Digital Imaging Specialist	Robert H. Bagley
Digital Intermediate Colorist	Paul R. Bronkar
Domestic Film Color Timer	Jim Passon
International Film Color Timer	Terry Claborn
End Title Designer	Mary Hogg
Transfer Room / Theater Operators	Lutzner Rodriguez
	Gabriel Stewart

additional production support

Christin Ciaccio-Briggs Kristen Kolada Caplan Terri Shevy

Casting Assistant Cymbre Walk

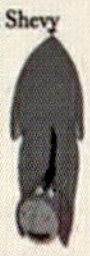

additional voices

Lisa Linder Silver Robert Lopez

film and digital services

Director Joe Jiuliano
Manager Suzy Zeffren-Rauch
Supervisor William Fadness
Technical Supervisor Christopher W. Gee
Digital Camera Operators Reza Kasravi
David Booth
Coordinator Patricia Adefolayan

software technology strike team

Project Manager Tamara Valdes
Principal Software Engineer David M. Adler

Dale Beck James P. Hurrell
Michael D. Kliewer Stefan Luka
Matthew Schnittker

technology

Technology Directors Dan Candela
Jonathan E. Geibel

animation technology

Technology Manager Evan Goldberg

Matt Chiang Catherine Lam
Gene S. Lee Chung-An Andy Lin
Dmitriy Pinskiy Alexandre D. Torija-Paris
Justin Walker

infrastructure

Technology Manager Kevin Gambrel

David Aguilar Mark R. Carlson
Dexter Cheng Paul Hildebrandt
Hide A. Hirase Christopher D. Mihaly
G. Kevin Morgan Uri Okrent
Wendy M. Tam Truong Vo

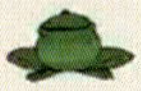

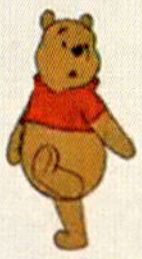

interaction design

Technology Manager Janet E. Berlin

Richard N. Kanno Matthew E. Levine
Krispin Leydon Brian Wherry

look/efx/dynamics

Technology Manager Rajesh Sharma
Principal Software Engineers Brent Burley
Mark A. McLaughlin

Lawrence Chai Dylan Lacewell
Ying Liu Andy Milne
Greg Nichols Andrew Selle
Maryann Simmons Shingo Jason Takagi
Daniel Teece Thomas V. Thompson II
Kelly Ward Brian Whited

media engineering

Technology Manager Ron Gillen

Jason L. Bergman Jeff Cornish
Glenn Dakake Norbert Faerstain
Taralyn R. Frasqueri-Molina Jeffrey L. Sickler
Kamaldeep Tumkur Srinath James A. Wargowski

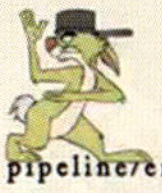

pipeline/engineering services

Technology Manager Darren Robinson
Principal Software Engineer Todd Scopio

Neil P. Barber William T. Carpenter
Yun-po Paul Fan Andrew Fisher
Thomas G. Kessler Eric Buus Larsen
Douglas E. Lesan John Longhini
Joseph W. Longson Eugene Stulyov
Roy Turner Lisa S. Young
Howard Wilczynski

systems engineering

Technology Manager Ronald L. Johnson
Principal Engineers Scott Burris
Marc Jordan
Doug White

James Colby Bette Richard Bomberger
Steven C. Carpenter Kevin C. Constantine
Tom Corrigan Carlos "Charlie" Estiandan
Eric N. Garcia Thomas Greer
Jay Hilliard James MacBurney
Michael A. McClure Stuart McDougal
Greg Neagle Kimberly M. Rios
Steven Seed Zachary Stokes
Paul Takahashi Matt Watson
Derek E. Wilson

technical support

Technology Manager Shannon R. Howard

Natalie Acosta Peter Lee Chun
Vince D'Amore Michael Dobson
Michael M. Fukumoto Danny Jewell
Navneil Kumar Josh Padilla
John Readick Michael Weissman

Technology Assistant Manager Dayna B. Meltzer

research

Vice President Joe Marks
Sr. Research Scientist Rasmus Tamstorf

Pooh Babies

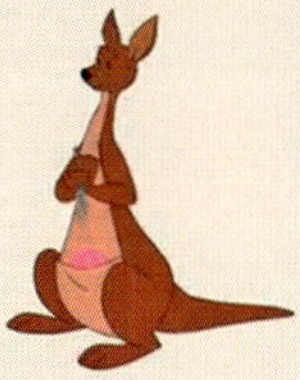

Alejandro
Alice
Amelia
Channing
Charles
Elijah
Francesca
Jack
Liam
Luke
Nicholas
Sebastian

The Staff of Walt Disney Animation Studios

studio leadership

John Lasseter Ed Catmull
Roy Conli Peter Del Vecho
Andy Hendrickson Ann Le Cam
John I. McGuire Dorothy McKim
Andrew Millstein Kristina Reed
Clark Spencer Cameron Walker

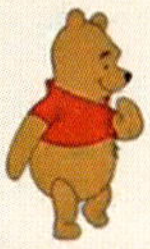

executive assistants

Dawn Halloran Charouhas Patti Conklin
John A. Danko III Heather Feng-Yanu
Tanya Oskanian Bonnie Popp
Wendy Dale Tanzillo

production resources

Jacquelyn Golomb-Perez Collin Larkins
Jason Hintz Llopis Gennie Rim
Melissa Roberts

development

Maggie Malone Karen Tenkhoff
Kathy Bond Bryan Davidson
Jessica Julius Katherine Ramos

global marketing and publicity

David Sameth David Bess Tony DeSimone
Joe Dunn Eric Elrod Mike Gortz
Emily Thompson Tia Mell Julia Orr

business and legal affairs

Edwin Khanbeigi Christine Chrisman
Gus Avila Jeri Howard
Rachelle Little

finance

Julianne Hale Rowena Barcelona-Nuqui
Christina Chen Bonnie Holmoe Hays
Frank William Knittel, Jr. Linda Y. Matsuoka-Narmore
Deborah L. Riley Branden L. Roberts
Jennifer Morgan Shoemaker

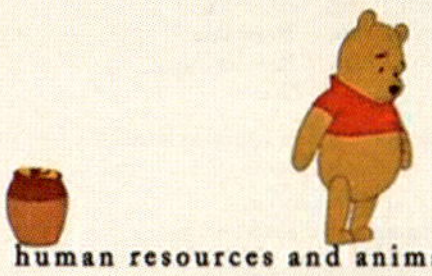

human resources and animation resources

Brandy Contreras Scott Campbell
Ginger Wei-Hsien Chen Alison Mann
Katherine Quintero Matt Roberts
Denise Irwin Stastny

talent development

Dawn Rivera-Ernster James Lavrakas
Lara McLaughlin Stephanie Morse
Deb Stone Kelsi Taglang

training

Tracy Bovasso Campbell Nancy Evans
Chris Chavez

environment and events

Tanja Knoblich Jenn Corrigan
Melissa Cole Fanfassian Kent Gordon
Tom Powell Marty Prager
Eduardo Ruiz Kevin Waldvogel-DeMonaco
Benny De Franco Barry N. Brysman
Rey Cervantes, Jr. Ken Lewis
Bruce Parker

caffeination

Carlos Benavides

animation research library

Lella F. Smith	Mary Walsh
Jill Breznican	Fox F. Carney
Tammy Crosson	Mark M. Dawson
Doug Engalla	Idris Erba
Mat Fretschel	Ann W. Hansen
Tamara N. Khalaf	Tracy Leach
Marisa Leonardi	Kristen McCormick
Heather McLaughlin	Jamie Panetta
Tom Pniewski	Mike Pucher
Amy Senstad	Jackie Vasquez
Meghan Veltri	Elda "Tita" Venegas
Patrick White	Mary Ann Williams

ink and paint

Rikki Chobanian	Jim Lusby
Peggy Murakami	Antonio Pelayo
	Sherri Vandoli

consumer products

Mary Beech	Jennifer Banzaca
Jennifer Kobashi	Renato Lattanzi
Olga Mosqueda	Pat Van Note
Henry Ong	Nancy Parent
	Emma Whittard

security

Michelle Howard	Forrest Iwaszewski
Terry La Raia	Alan Merchant
	Darryl Vontoure

in memoriam

Dan Read
an extraordinary artist whose talents, passion and courage
continue to inspire us all.

The filmmakers would like to thank the Disney Story Trust
for their invaluable contribution,
and the entire Disney Animation Studios
for their dedication, support, ingenuity, and good humor.

special thanks

Vincent Vedrenne
Abigail Akzin

Carlos Arevalo	Kate Dowd
Brendan Duncan	Roy Gilbrech
Dan Hassid	Rosendo Hernandez
Leon Ingram	Alastair Johns
Stéphane Kardos	Jeff King
Bhavesh Lad	Gary Levy
Gabriel Maldonado	John A. Mallet
Devin Martin	Elisa Muffelman
Ricardo R. Palma	John T. Quinn
Carlos M. Ramirez-Reyes	June Ridley
Mike Ridley	Lynwood Robinson
Arthur H. Shek	Jimmy Tsai
Tara Handy Turner	Angel Valles
Raffaello Vecchione	Nomi Vela
Jon Y. Wada	Rebecca Wong
	Aohan Zhao

Julia Beaumont-Jones and Christine Kurpiel
Tate London

Dr. Barbara Lasic
Victoria and Albert Museum

Jenny Ramkalawon
British Museum

The State of California
and the
California Film Commission

No stuffed animals were harmed in the making of this film.

© 2011 Disney Enterprises, Inc. All Rights Reserved.
For the purposes of copyright law in the United Kingdom, Disney Enterprises, Inc.
was the owner of copyright in this film immediately after it was made.

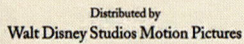

Distributed by
Walt Disney Studios Motion Pictures

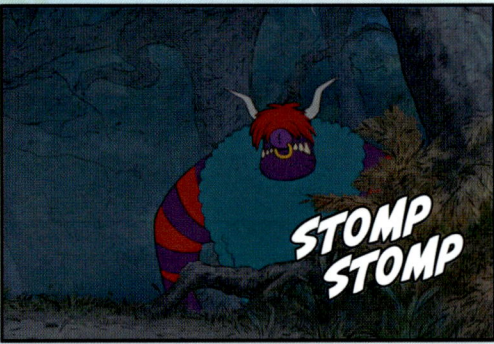

STOMP
STOMP

STOMP
STOMP

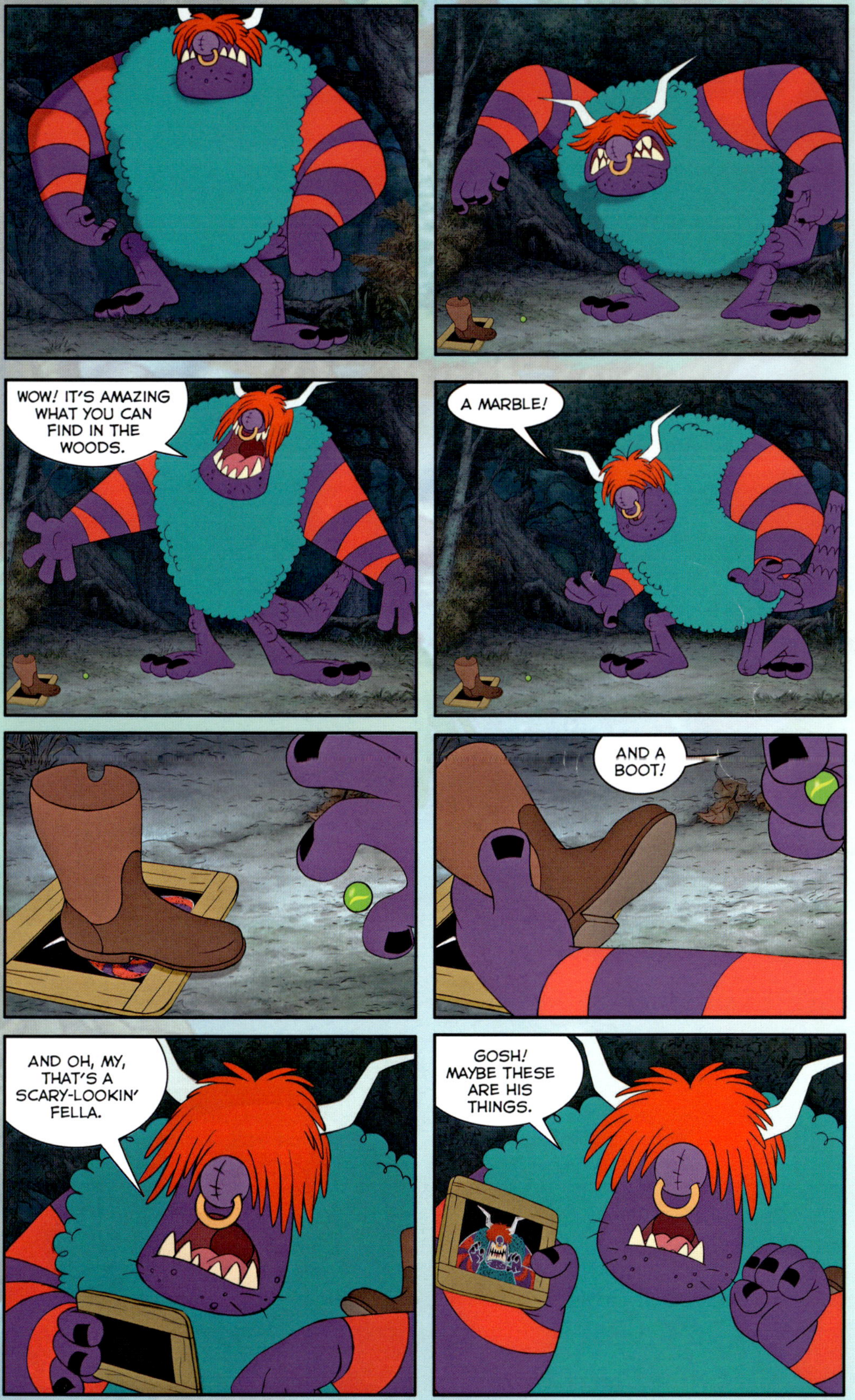
WOW! IT'S AMAZING WHAT YOU CAN FIND IN THE WOODS.
A MARBLE!
AND A BOOT!
AND OH, MY, THAT'S A SCARY-LOOKIN' FELLA.
GOSH! MAYBE THESE ARE HIS THINGS.

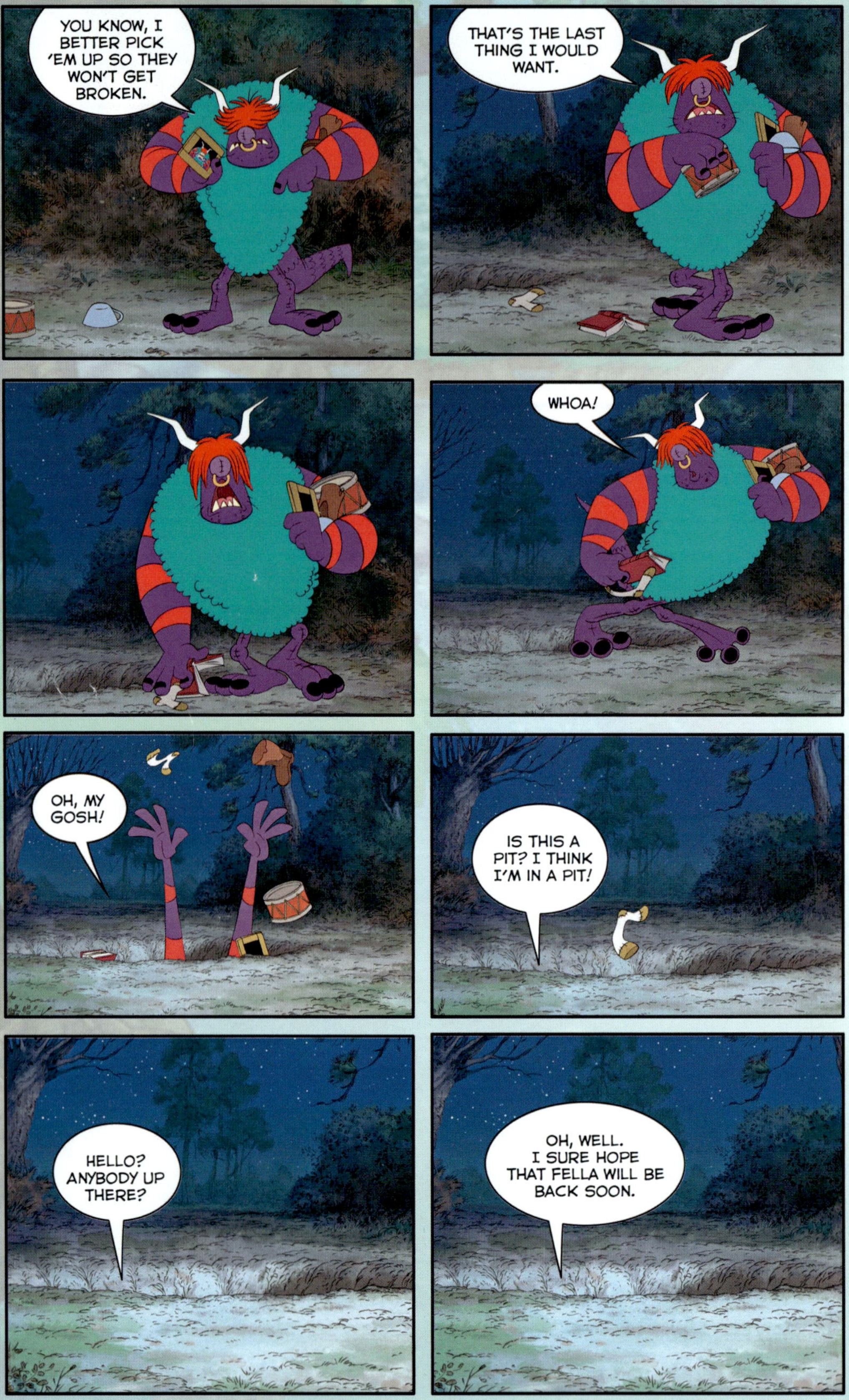
YOU KNOW, I BETTER PICK 'EM UP SO THEY WON'T GET BROKEN.
THAT'S THE LAST THING I WOULD WANT.
WHOA!
OH, MY GOSH!
IS THIS A PIT? I THINK I'M IN A PIT!
HELLO? ANYBODY UP THERE?
OH, WELL. I SURE HOPE THAT FELLA WILL BE BACK SOON.